Praise for Eric L. Harry's

Protect and Defend

The president is dead. The world is divided. The war is now.

"A frighteningly real scenario."

—Richard Steinberg, author of *Gemini Man*

Arc Light

Technology changed the rules of war. And nuclear destruction is only the beginning.

"Starts off with a nuclear war—then the action *really* starts . . . A scarier and more realistic picture of nuclear war than *The Day After* and a better combat war game than *Red Storm Rising*."

—*Flint Journal*

"Incredibly spellbinding . . . Altogether frightening."

—Clive Cussler

"Superb . . . You just know it could happen the way the author is telling it."

—*Houston Chronicle*

"Filled with intense and moving moments . . . Harry doesn't only excel in the novel's most extensive and vivid technical descriptions, he also includes many poignant moments."

—*San Francisco Chronicle*

"Terrifying and real. It's a page-burner and all-too-possible. Try putting it down."
—Richard J. Herman, author of *Dark Wing*

"Told through a series of rapid-fire climaxes, this novel, a political and military cautionary tale of considerable power and conviction, will keep readers riveted."
—*Publishers Weekly*

"Will thrill military-minded readers . . . whitening the knuckles of even hardened techno-junkies."
—*Booklist*

"A grim tale . . . Successfully evokes the bleakness and terror of an impending world war."
—*Kirkus Reviews*

INVASION

ERIC L. HARRY

JOVE BOOKS, NEW YORK

INVASION

A Jove Book / published by arrangement with
the author

PRINTING HISTORY
Jove edition / February 2000

The Penguin Putnam Inc. World Wide Web site address is
http://www.penguinputnam.com

ISBN: 0-515-12842-2

A JOVE BOOK®
Jove Books are published by The Berkley Publishing Group,
a division of Penguin Putnam Inc.,
375 Hudson Street, New York, New York 10014.
JOVE and the "J" design
are trademarks belonging to Penguin Putnam Inc.

PRINTED IN THE UNITED STATES OF AMERICA

10 9 8 7 6 5 4 3 2 1

INVASION

PROLOGUE

The North American continent is separated from Europe by 3,000 and from Asia by 4,000 miles of open sea. These expanses guarantee it a degree of immunity from external interference enjoyed by no other region of the world.... Two great oceans, a tranquil relationship with Canada, and a containable problem from the states to the south give the United States a sense of basic isolation and security. It is also a country which is almost completely self-reliant; faced with a loss of all external supply, the USA would "come through."... The oceanic factors retain, even in the nuclear age, the determining importance in the making of American strategy that they have had since the founding of the republic. The seas still protect America from invasion.

John Keegan and Andrew Wheatcroft,
Zones of Conflict: An Atlas of Future Wars (1986)

MONTGOMERY, ALABAMA
September 14 // 0720 Local Time

How did it ever come to this? thought eighteen-year-old Private Stephanie Roberts as she stared out at the dusty sandbagged roadblock that marked the new boundary carved into America.

Stephie, the youngest infantryman in the squad of nine and one of only two women, climbed aboard the truck. "I don't trust you," the hulking Animal said to her. At five-seven and 125 pounds, Stephie and her rifle were security for the lone machine gun attached to her squad. Attached to the machine gun was a 250-pound asshole who sank onto the bench seat beside Stephie. The white, former junior college football lineman was nineteen, but he had an emotional age of six. "I don't trust split tails," he whispered with breath that made Stephie wince, "so just stay the hell outa the way of my gun, or I might have to kill you to kill Chinese." Her squadmates ignored her clash.

"Suits me fine," Stephie replied. "And you stink."

It was a hot day. Throngs of refugees crowded the border of the Exclusion Zone two hundred miles north of the Alabama Gulf Coast. Two hundred miles north of her home. On the northern side, where all seemed normal. Laundry hung on clotheslines within a stone's throw of bunkered guard posts. Stores were open. Towns were busy. People went about their lives. Had it not been for the concealed machine guns, tanks, and missile batteries, the casual eye wouldn't have detected much change. Even the evacuee relocation center—tents pitched amid motor homes and barbeques—looked like a national park campground in summer.

The mixed team of MPs and state highway patrolmen raised the barrier and waved the dozen-vehicle convoy through. The diesels growled and belched noxious fumes, but Stephie was glad even for that breeze on the sweltering day. Their truck passed the sentries, and Stephie got the distinct impression that they were leaving America.

The sandbagged walls that rose up the road's shoulders parted, and the pavement began to flash by. They were in disputed territory. The no-man's-land between two great armies. Barren of life. Still and quiet and empty as if braced for the violence to come.

No maps had been redrawn to show the dashed lines that now defaced the southeastern United States, but the CO had shown everybody in their infantry company maps, stained with blood, that had been captured from Chinese reconnaissance teams. The American teenagers had passed them around in silence while seated on helmets and packs at the end of a week-long field training exercise. They were 110 brand-new infantrymen—only one month removed from the shocking rigors of boot camp, and four months from cocoons of middle-class comfort. All were grimy, sunburned, sweaty, mosquito-bitten, scraped, and bruised. They stank, and exhaustion was evident in their slumped reposes.

But as the maps were handed from soldier to soldier, anger crackled. It burned in squinted eyes. It swelled from rhythmically clenching jaws. It clawed at the swirling greens on the paper with talon-like, murderous grips. The maps had made the circuit by the time the trucks had arrived to return them to their makeshift barracks in a nearby Holiday Inn, but no one rose from the big circle in which they sat. The rides, to Stephie, meant back to a semiprivate room shared with nineteen-year-old Becky Marsh from Oregon, the other woman in Stephie's squad. It meant showers, air-conditioning, soft beds.

But the bone-weary teenagers refused to leave the field. Lieutenant Ackerman, their platoon leader, feigned annoyance while hiding a grin. Staff Sergeant Kurth, their platoon sergeant, and his noncoms never smiled.

That day, troops led their officers back into the woods. They spent another week digging holes, chopping brush, firing at trees, and assaulting a charred hump of dirt. For the names of the Alabama towns that were shown on the captured enemy maps were already printed in Chinese.

"Lock 'n load," Sergeant Collins, their squad leader, barked as the trucks picked up speed. The first deployment of their newly formed unit was a combat patrol of America's exposed Gulf Coast beaches. Metallic clacks of magazines and snaps of breech covers pierced the steady *whoosh* of the wind of the road. They had cinched up the truck's canvas sides to get a breeze, and Stephie began to point out the familiar landmarks of her native state. She knew the cracked two-lane highway like the back of her hand. They passed the Stuckeys where Stephie's stepfather had always stopped for peanut brittle on the way home from football games in Tuscaloosa. She recognized the service station where they had waited one long, hot day for their leaking radiator to be repaired. And there was the stand that her mom had always insisted carried the freshest watermelons of any place on earth. All were now boarded up. Abandoned. Forlorn.

Her squadmates, for their parts, pointed out the road's new attractions. A billboard with the image of a famous actress, who always played the high school slut in the slasher flicks, pressing her index finger to ruby red lips. The seductive image drew lewd comments and gestures from the boys, who overlooked entirely the point of the message. "Loose Lips Sink Ships," read the legend at the top. Stephie wondered at how bad the actresses's career must have turned to now be doing public service advertisements.

Concrete bunkers with periscopes and electronics mastheads—facing south—had been dug out of the banked earth of highway overpasses. Bridges had been marked with orange signs that read, "Warning! Wired for demolition!" In the distance, open farmland—potential landing zones if transport aircraft suicidally flew at their missile defenses—had been pitted with black craters by preregistered artillery. And along the side of the road, ubiquitous triangular markers warned not to stray from the pavement onto shoulders already dotted with land mines. The regularly spaced triangles—black skulls and crossbones on yellow signs—flashed by as the convoy drew ever nearer the dangerous sea.

Every so often, they passed small towns still being stripped by engineers. Tractor trailers were being loaded with everything militarily useful: portable generators, backhoes, transformers, propane tanks. What the engineers couldn't move, they destroyed. Columns of black smoke rose from all points of the compass. The convoy was stopped periodically by the demolition. Hoots and hollers rose from the parked convoy as charges toppled a metal water tower. Painted on the falling tank's side was a weathered, "Go Wildcats! Division II Basketball Champs 2001–02." After the great crash, the agitated male and female infantrymen reenacted the stupendous sight with hand gestures and special effects sounds. All were on their feet, agitated. Excited. *Scared out of their fucking skins,*

Stephie thought with a quiver as if cold on the hot, hot day.

Over the next half hour, the thunderous booms that rolled across the landscape from unseen engineers near and far eventually had the opposite effect of that big steel crash. The noticeable thumps of high explosives on their bodies soon quieted the anxious chatter in the truck. War hadn't yet come to America, but the thudding jolts that rattled their insides frayed their nerves with portents of death. The teenagers looked inward. Peer pressure demanded it. No one contemplated what loomed ahead out loud, except Becky. Stephie's roommate spent two weeks at the Holiday Inn imagining doom to all hours of the morning despite Stephie's pleas for sleep.

The convoy resumed their journey toward the Gulf and soon plunged into a thick, low-hanging haze. Some covered their mouths and noses with handkerchiefs against the choking smell. Stephie remembered. The Canadian Rocky Mountains, summer vacation, when she was eight. Her first smell of a forest fire.

The conflagration that consumed the Alabama woods was nowhere in sight, but the trees that lined the highway were now nothing more than charred hulks, brittle limbs, and pointed black fingers. The Chinese would find no wood for shelter or for campfires when the nights grew cold. There would be no brush to provide concealment from killing American fire. They would find nothing but death and devastation, Stephie thought with boiling hatred. A loud snapping sound—like she'd broken a tooth—came from her jaw. Her face twitched, and she fought back tears. Anger always made her cry.

Only PFC John Burns, seated beside her, noticed. He glanced her way, cracked a half smile from one side of his mouth, then closed his eyes to resume his slumber.

At first, he was the only one among the almost two dozen soldiers in the truck who seemed to be resting comfortably. The two squads and weapons teams were packed shoulder to shoulder. The warm breeze stifled conversation. Everyone other than Burns stared out in sullen silence at the cloud-shrouded, desolate scenery. They clutched their weapons as if for psychological comfort.

One by one, however, they began to drift off. Soon—miraculously, Stephie thought as she looked all around—every last one of her comrades had fallen sound asleep, including Animal, the beefeater next to her, who slumped her way.

Soon, Stephie felt the same pull toward slumber. The clicks from the tires as they crossed the regularly spaced seams in the aging concrete were almost hypnotic. The old truck's stiff suspension rocked steadily from side to side. But Stephie could never rest while on the road. She had never felt comfortable enough to relax in a moving vehicle.

John Burns flashed Stephie another encouraging smile before again closing his eyes and leaning his helmet back against the metal frame that held the canvas. Stephie had smiled back at the boy—the man, really, for the dark-haired Burns was a little older than the others in their platoon—out of a habit bred in high school. *High school,* she thought. *High school!* Four months earlier, she had walked across the stage and been handed her diploma. The night of the prom she and Conner Reilly, her boyfriend, on leave from his unit, had hopped until dawn from one party to the next in the rented limousine. *Four months ago.*

She felt depressed, on edge, dispirited, and suddenly totally unprepared. In the balmy silence of the late-summer morning, a single question dominated the eighteen-year-old's thoughts: *How did it ever come to this?*

Scenes of a distant war flickered across the television screen. Ten-year-old Stephie Roberts watched, though her mother ignored the grainy pictures of combat on the nightly news. "The addition of Thai army forces to the war in Vietnam has done little to slow the advancing Chinese." When the news moved on to some boring ceremony in Korea, Stephie returned to her journal. "Sally H. said today that we'll look really hot when we get our braces off, but that Gloria W. needs a nose job. I told Judy, who told the evil James Thurmond, who told Gloria, who got really, REALLY pissed at *me*," she underlined, "for some totally warped reason!" U.S. troops, the reporter explained, had been withdrawn as a condition to reunification of the North and South. On the eve of a nationwide free election, the North Korean government had collapsed as its leaders—fearing retribution—had fled the country. China and South Korea had both stepped into the void to quell the violence. Their armies had clashed, and China had occupied the entire Korean Peninsula: North and South. The Chinese-backed puppet government was now celebrating the long-awaited reunion. "Must destroy James Thurmond!" Stephie wrote as she muted the boring program. "Hey, hey!" her step-dad said, grabbing the remote. They listened to a report that affected the company where he worked. Despite falling defense appropriations, Congress was authorizing billions of dollars for an antimissile shield. Her stepdad was beaming. Her mother said, "Now, finally, maybe you'll get the guts to ask for a raise." Stephie went outside and took a walk down the beach barefoot in the fading Alabama sun, plotting the total social demise of The Evil One.

The blue water of the Gulf didn't look the same as it had in Stephie Roberts's youth. Nothing was the same as it had been before. "First Squad, *out*!" shouted Sergeant Collins. "Stay off the beach! It's mined! Look *alive*!" The six other men and two women of Stephie's squad climbed down from the green, canvas-covered truck with their weapons and combat loads. Tony Massera, a private from Philadelphia, stood on the pavement squinting into the midday sunshine before donning his army shades. "Is it *always* this fuckin' hot in Alabama, Roberts?"

"*Puh*-ssy," Animal coughed into his fist. His fit of faux hacking ended with, "Puh-, puh-, *pussy!*" and a smile at Massera to ensure that he'd heard it correctly. Had the insult come from anyone else, the wiry and tough Massera—Animal's assistant machine gunner—would clearly have faced the man down or pummeled him to the ground with a flurry of blows. But the hulking machine gunner they all called Animal—who was semipermanently attached to their squad—was a would-be offensive lineman for Ohio State. He dwarfed everyone else. Massera let it drop. Animal cleared his throat. "Sorry. *Shit!* Must be comin' down with somethin', Antonio."

"Tony," Massera corrected for about the hundredth time

since the crew-served weapons had been handed down to the platoons. No one else had anything to say.

By age twelve, Stephie was even less interested in world events. But she remembered the day her class was watching the big screen in the Internet Lab of her Mobile, Alabama, middle school. A grown man—India's prime minister—stood crying on a dock in Bombay. The sight riveted the darkened room filled with seventh graders. All were still young enough to take their cues from distraught adults, but not yet old enough to fully understand the reason for their shared distress. Indian civilians and soldiers were hastily boarding an overcrowded gray destroyer. "Does anyone know why the Indian prime minister didn't get on that ship?" the hyperstrict teacher asked the class. When no one answered, she said, "With Pakistani and Chinese troops just outside the city?" Again, no one ventured a guess. "Because the ship is *British*," the teacher explained with a sigh. It was a class for the gifted and talented. Stephie felt they were letting her down. "He was too proud to leave his country on a foreign ship." Everybody stared at the crying man. Stephie raised her hand and, when called upon, politely asked what had happened to him. "He was executed," came the teacher's reply. "Shot." All Stephie could think to say was, "Thanks."

"Shut up and shoulder yer loads!" snapped their squad leader despite the fact that no one standing at the back of the truck was talking. At twenty, Sergeant Collins was the oldest among them, and he was nervous. "This is the *coast*, in case you morons missed it!"

No one *had* missed the fact, of course. The nearer their convoy had come to the water, the flatter the terrain had grown. Over a month before, the Corps of Engineers had completed its work on the ghost towns outside Mobile. Peter Scott had commented that the blackened rubble of hospitals, schools, and courthouses already looked like the aftermath of heavy fighting. But Stephie had scrutinized the pictures of war's total devastation on the covers of newsmagazines. The selective demolition of public buildings paled when compared to the moonscapes left in Yokohama, Singapore, and Bombay. *And Tel Aviv,* she thought with a shiver.

Their first sight of the Gulf had come as a shock. The azure horizon visible in gaps between the tall pines had caused Stephie's stomach to turn flips. After they had taken the coast road, some of the soldiers had stared at the shore as if to confront their inner demons. Others had rested their helmets against the raised front sights of their army surplus M-16s, focusing instead on their boots.

At thirteen, Stephie's soccer team won the state championship. Stephie played all ninety minutes at midfield. Although she got no goals or assists in the one-nil victory, she ran her heart out from penalty area to penalty area, challenged every header, made crisp passes despite legs that ached from the week-long tournament. Her crowning achievement in life to that time came in the waning moments of the game when she cleanly slid-tackled the ball away from their opponent's greatest scoring threat. When the whistle blew, the entire team slid on their bellies into a pile on the rain-soaked pitch and hugged, cheered, and cried in equally shared, maximum celebration. At the beginning of the season, the coach had promised them that if they won state—and they had a chance— they would go as a team to soccer camp the following summer . . . in the south of France! They had practiced five days a week. Played regular season games, then driven to faraway tournaments and played again later the same day. Before the quarter finals in the statewide, all had agreed not to talk about the trip for fear of jinxing it. As they left the pitch after the semis, however, a muddy Sally Hampton shouted into Stephie's ear, "We're going to *France!*"

And she was right. They had won the state championship. Over the squeals of excitement, all heard their coach's voice. "Sorry, girls!" he shouted apologetically. They all looked up at him. "We're not going to be able to go." There were a couple of cries of *"What?"* but a half dozen cries of *"Why?"* He replied that because of the war in the Indian Ocean, the French had canceled the soccer camp. "Can't we just go *anyway*?" objected Gloria Wilson, their goalkeeper.

"Your parents don't think it's safe," replied their frowning coach. The girls, still lying prone rose to their cleats and descended upon the gathering parents, employing every conceivable argument. "We're not going by boat, we're *flying* over!" tried one. "The war is, like, a thousand miles away!" came another attempt. "You *promised*!" was the last, plaintive gasp. Their coach held out his hands to quell the uprising. "Everybody's really sorry, girls, but after the battle Europe lost to China in the Indian Ocean, it's just not safe to go overseas anymore. Nobody really knows what's gonna happen next." The girls were crushed. Some of the holdouts cried and argued all the way to the car. The only thing that prevented Stephie from doing the same was that she spotted her father—her *real* father—still sitting in the stands. Stephie's mother rolled her eyes on seeing him and seethed at his mere presence.

Stephie ran to him. He held out his arms and threw them around her, holding her tight. "I'm so proud of you!" he said into her hair as she grinned and pressed her face flat against his chest. "You ran so hard! You won so many headers! Your passes were all right on target! And that steal at the end from the other team's best player was what won the game!" Stephie raised her face to beam at him, but had to stifle the grin with lips that she curled over her teeth. "You can smile now, Stephie," her father said, gently grasping her chin and raising her face. "You're not wearing braces anymore. And you have always been, and are now, the most beautiful thing in heaven or on earth." She laughed and turned away. He tenderly cupped her mud-flaked cheeks in his hands. "I love you with all my heart," he said. At the team cookout, Stephie's angry mother had groused incessantly about her ex-husband ruining Stephie's wonderful day, and her sullen teammates had vented their ire on their parents about the canceled trip with a preagreed wall of silence. But behind her wall, Stephie had been euphoric. Absolutely euphoric. All was right with the world. Things were great.

Stephie backed up to her heavy field pack, which stood upright on the truck's tailgate. "You want me to carry some of your gear?" John Burns asked in a low voice. He was stooped forward under the weight of his own eighty-pound pack, and he wasn't even in Stephie's squad. Animal wagged his tongue obscenely up and down in the air. Her squadmates snickered at the machine gunner's crude mockery of John's offer. "I can handle it," Stephie said, hoisting the pack onto her back with a grunt. Her legs almost buckled but she clenched her teeth and tried to continue breathing while tightening the harness across her chest and stomach. She then grabbed her M-16, which came with an M-249. The 40 mm grenade launcher, mounted underneath the barrel, looked like a toy. The stubby, bullet-shaped projectiles bulged from sleeves on bandoliers crossed over her torso, making her look like some large-caliber *pistollero*.

Becky Marsh watched John join the ranks on the road without once offering her his assistance. She winced and grunted as she shouldered her own massive pack. "No, *I* don't need any help," she muttered sarcastically, "but thanks for fucking asking!" Becky glared at Stephie, who chose not to notice.

Third Platoon consisted of thirty-one soldiers. Lieutenant Ackerman and his commo and Platoon Sergeant Kurth stood in front of four, nine-man squads of infantry, which formed ranks for inspection. Of the twenty-seven infantrymen in the four numbered squads, nineteen were men and eight were women. Each squad had two fire teams, and the eight women were evenly distributed: one in each fire team. The squad leaders—three buck sergeants and a corporal—stood at the far right with their squads stretched at arm's length to their left. The soldiers in the formation raised their left arms for proper, parade ground spacing. The formation extended longer than normal because of the four soldiers added to the end of each squad's rank. A two-man machine gun crew and a two-man all-threat missile crew from the company's weapons platoon had been attached to each squad. With the four medics from the battalion medical detachment in the rear, Third Platoon today fielded fifty.

At fourteen, Stephie became obsessed with the opposite sex. And the latest in a series of the-cutest-boys-she'd-*ever*-seen was at an interdenominational prayer service for the victims of the Second Jewish Holocaust. He looked to be older—sixteen—and had shiny black hair, dark eyes, and smooth skin as white as paper. *He must have dermatologists for parents,* she marveled. Then, all of the sudden, Stephie realized that he must be Jewish. As the prayers wore on—some familiar, others in Hebrew—an imagined romance blossomed in Stephie's mind until her stepdad leaned over and whispered, "They brought it on *themselves,* you know. China *warned* Israel not to use nukes." Stephie's mom crushed her stepdad's toe in embarrassment. When he hissed in pain, Stephie's imaginary boyfriend looked back and shocked Stephie straight to the core. Tears flowed from "radiant pools," she wrote in her journal, down the mysterious boy's "porcelain skin." That night, Stephie got on the Internet and read news reports about Tel Aviv. It turned out that China *had* warned Israel against using nuclear weapons to try to stop their invasion. In retaliation to Israel's nuclear attacks on their massing armies, China had destroyed Tel Aviv with its population trapped inside. Stephie watched the video over and over. She couldn't read the Chinese characters in the lower right hand corner, but the countdown on the clock was universal. When the clock struck zero, half a dozen blinding flashes swallowed the city's skyline.

"First, Second, and Third Squads and attached crews," tall and angular Ackerman, the newly commissioned officer and platoon leader, announced, "will come with me and Platoon Sergeant Kurth for a patrol of the beach! Fourth Squad will guard the trucks!"

"Knock it off!" Staff Sergeant Kurth boomed, although Stephie had heard nothing from the troops. His stare menaced Fourth Squad in the rank behind Stephie. The squad that had drawn easy duty.

"Everybody patrolling the beach, keep your eyes open!" continued Ackerman. "West Point" is what most called him behind his back. "If you see any tracks, call 'em out! This is a free-fire zone! Watch for mines on both sides of the road. The mines underneath the pavement are under positive control and are currently safed. Weapons loaded. Rounds chambered. Safeties *on*." There was a steady clacking of metal as men and women pointed their weapons away from their buddies and checked their selector switches. Stephie ejected a curved, thirty-round magazine. The brass cartridges shone from atop their double stack. She reloaded the full mag into her assault rifle and loaded a 40 mm fragmentation grenade into the breach of her launcher. She slid the launcher shut with a snap like a pump shotgun and confirmed that the selector switches on both weapons were on "safe."

"Pursuant to the Coastal Defense Act," Lieutenant Ack Ack announced officiously, "this area is under martial law! We have orders to arrest any civilians we come across, and we are authorized to use deadly force! If we come into contact with any Chinese forces, we are to report in, engage, and destroy! Single file! Corporal Higgins, you're wired for the point! Take the lead! Let's *move* out!"

Fifteen was a time of questioning for Stephie. "Why'd those people in New Zealand throw garbage at our ship?" With his mouth still full, her stepfather said they were ungrateful 'cause we didn't defend 'em. Stephie's mom cleared her throat at her husband's table manners. "Why didn't we defend them?" Stephie asked. 'Cause it wasn't worth World War Three, 'specially right before the new, second-generation missile shield's in place. "Who's stronger—us or the Chinese?" Us. "Then how come we let 'em rape Manila?" Don't use that *word*, her mom said. Stephie's stepfather replied that the Chinese had used Korean shipyards that previously had built super*tankers* to build their new super*carriers*. They're five times bigger than our carriers and hold three times as many planes. Some are transport ships that can carry twenty thousand troops at a time. "How big is their army?" Stephie asked. Thirty, forty million, give or take. "How big is *ours*?" Dunno. A few hundred thousand. "Then how can you say *we're* stronger than *them*?" 'Cause of the missile shield his company was helping build. "But aren't *they* building one *too*? Isn't *every*body building one?" Her stepfather grew tired of Stephie's incessant questions.

• • •

One by one, the ranks headed down the highway parallel to the shore, straight toward Stephie's house. Her squad was third and last in line. With a ten-meter spread, the point man was over 300 meters ahead, but Stephie could see what Higgins saw from the point—an empty ribbon of road that swayed with the point man's every step—on a one-inch LCD screen suspended on a slender boom before her face. The old-style Kevlar helmets had been retrofitted with a strap-on electronics suite. It consisted of the screen and a microphone on the boom, headphones under the armored ear flaps, and a wire running to a battery and receiver on the shoulder of the webbing. To that ensemble, the point man added a tiny pen-sized camera and transmitter.

The electronics system of the newly-raised 41st Infantry Division was, however, basically just a hodgepodge. It wasn't nearly as advanced as the equipment of the lower-numbered divisions of America's regular, standing army. The system used by the professionals was fully integrated into their newer and lighter ceramic helmets.

Stephie scanned the dunes on the left and beaches on the right, but saw nothing save the litter common to any roadside. Candy wrappers. Coke cans. Yellowed newspapers half buried in sand.

"Lookie *here*!" Stephon Johnson said from ahead. His voice broke in and out on her balky left earphone. Johnson—a corporal—was a grenadier from Washington, DC, and the leader of Stephie's Fire Team Alpha. He kicked at a used condom with his combat boot. "Looks like you had yourself some good *times* down here on the Redneck Riviera, *Roberts*." Men laughed and commented in turn as they passed the wilted prophylactic.

"Cut the shit!" Sergeant Collins finally snapped. They marched on in silence, skirting a fresh crater in the cracked pavement that was half filled with brackish green water. It must have been from a practice bombing run, Stephie thought, or an air force attack on a Chinese probe.

Stephie's thighs and lungs began to burn. Her lower back and shoulders grew to ache from the heavy "existence load."

Sweat showed through the men's thick, woodlands-camouflage battle dress as they marched farther and farther from the trucks. Closer and closer to her house. The only contact they had with the outside world came in the form of an occasional crackle over the commo's audio/video gear, which carried on the ocean breeze from the middle of the formation where Ackerman and the commo were. Two other platoons in their company were on different stretches of the empty shoreline, and the company commander was with one of them. Although they weren't in range now, when they were within a four-mile radius of the transmitters, the CO could watch video from any of his four platoons.

Or so it was supposed to work. No one really had any idea what to expect. Their unit—the 41st Infantry Division—had first unfurled its colors at a ceremony at Fort Benning, Georgia, only one month earlier. The six hundred men and women of Stephie's 3rd of the 519th Infantry Regiment were in one of the division's fifteen infantry battalions. Charlie Company of the 3/519 had been given orders for this—their first mission—only the day before.

Stephie had wondered about the mission's real purpose ever since. During a semisleepless night, she had reasoned that they could reconnoiter the coast with airborne drones. But she knew they were sending units south every day. Maybe it was to give them tactical training on the theater's terrain. A chance to get a feel for the ground on which they would fight. Or maybe it was a purely symbolic act. Going down to the water's edge one last time to assert U.S. sovereignty over territory that would soon be the property of the Chinese. But even if symbolic, their combat patrol was dangerous. There were skirmishes practically every day. The coast was alive with Chinese scouts, pathfinders, patrols, and raiding parties. *But*, she decided, *we've gotta get blooded some time. Better now— against a recon team that we outnumber ten-to-one—than when we match up against the Chinese one-to-ten.*

Third Platoon's Caucasians, Hispanics, African Americans, and "Others" came from all parts of the country. There were practically no deferments from the draft, so they came from every socioeconomic class. But the representatives of their generation were more alike than any other soldiers that America had fielded in its history. In an interconnected world, they had melded into a uniform blend. And one attribute shared by the forty-odd teenagers was that none had ever killed a living thing. There was not a single hunter or outdoorsman among the teenage urban- and suburbanites.

Stephie had her first beer and smoked her first pot on her sixteenth birthday. On a walk down the beach, she ran into some juniors from her high school, who were drunk on the six-pack they'd bought at a nearby convenience store. Stephie stopped to cheer their game of beach football and stole sips of their beers until Conner Reilly, the coolest of the cool, finally gave her one. She was the only girl around. The sun shone off their chests and backs as they killed themselves to win a meaningless game. "Whoo-*hoo*!" Stephie shouted, pumping her fists in air as each team scored in the back-and-forth game. She somehow missed the end of the game and didn't know who had won, so she kept her mouth shut as they collapsed on the sand around her and the cooler, and lit and passed around a joint. She already had a buzz on from the beer, and when the thin, twisted joint reached her, she took a toke and coughed the smoke out. They laughed. The next time it came around, she held the smoke in despite growing red and almost choking.

"You know they're out there," said Conner Reilly, nodding at the Gulf, as soundless coughs still wracked Stephie's chest. Conner was tanned and tall—on the basketball team—but had green eyes and long eyelashes like a fashion model. He also dated the best-looking girl in school, Stephie reminded herself, who would crush Stephie, socially, if she perceived any threat, which she couldn't possibly. "Bullshit," replied Walter Ames. Walter's father was black, and his mother was white. Walter defined the word cool. Stephie felt cool just being around him, and she wondered if any of the boys would acknowledge her Monday when they went back to school. "They're too busy invadin' Japan," Walter insisted, but Conner was unswayed. "China's got bases," he said, rocking forward in the circle and drawing a map in the sand, "on those islands up and down the coast of Africa!" Conner's islands looked like freckles on his hand-drawn sea. With her finger, she completed the sea's smiley face. In very close proximity, Stephie studied the homemade leather bracelet that Conner wore on the hand that jabbed at the sand. *What if he decided to give me his bracelet,* she thought, *because . . .* She couldn't imagine why he would do such a thing, but she was content to fantasize about showing it to her friends. "*Je presente . . .* Conner Reilly's bracelet." Without realizing it, her eyes sank closed imagining the sweet life that would surely follow. "My dad says we'll be, like, at *war* some day," Conner insisted. Stephie looked at him, and the most amazing thing happened. He looked back. They all disagreed with him, including Stephie, who just wanted to fit in. "We're, like," she said, "total . . . *isholashunishts!*" The boys laughed at her because of the long word she'd used and because of the way she had slurred it.

They marched about a mile down the beach before they came upon a body. It had washed up on the shore and was covered in seaweed. You couldn't tell much more than that from the road. They took a break as the LT checked his map showing minefields, then sent two men out onto the beach. The soldiers recoiled in disgust and returned to report to the LT, who called a report in to the CO. Word quickly spread that it was a U.S. sailor who'd been in the water a long, long time. Men returned to the corpse, sunk a piece of driftwood into the sand, and tied a white towel to the upright marker.

"Must've been from the Straits of Havana," Animal said. He was sweating profusely and rested his heavy, vintage M-60 in his lap as he mopped his face with a towel. He and Massera were from weapons platoon—not a numbered platoon—thus they, like the missile team, were outsiders.

The ultimate *in*sider was Stephon Johnson, who knew everybody in every unit. He had advance word of just about everything important because of the network of contacts that he always touted. "I hear there was 30,000 squids 'n jarheads on those ships. That Chinese wolfpack had a hun'erd subs in it, just waitin'. Bodies been washin' up all the way over to Texas."

"And there are five million Chinese soldiers in Cuba," Stephie said in the low tones everyone else had assumed. Nobody said a word in reply.

By the end of Stephie's sixteenth year, her life had changed in two ways. Stephie had a steady boyfriend—Conner Reilly—and her stepfather had lost his job. "When is Dad's company gonna open up again?" Stephie asked as her mom straightened her hair before a date. Rachel Roberts feigned a smile. She always labored over Stephie before each date as if dating were Stephie's mission in life. "They can't get the parts that they need," her mother explained, "out of Japan, you know, because the factory was destroyed. And they can't ship anything to Europe because of the Chinese embargo." She wouldn't look Stephie in the eye. "But there are block*ade* runners," Stephie suggested, "that go back and forth to England." Rachel curled the corners of her pinched lips but shook her head. "So Dad's, like, unem*ployed*?" Stephie asked, trying not to let the fear show in her voice. Her mother nodded as she straightened the choker that Stephie wore, but ever more vigorously avoided eye contact in the mirror.

There was a long silence. "Why did you and my real father break up?" Stephie asked. With a shifty eyed, criminal look, her mother said for the thousandth time that her stepfather *was* her real father. Stephie sighed. "You know what I mean. You've never told me. Why did you break up?" Her mother replied that it was personal. "Well," Stephie laughed, frustrated, "I *know* it's *personal*!" She huffed. "Does it have anything to do with Aunt Cynthia?" Stephie asked, taking a stab. Her mother angered, as always, on mention of the aunt that Stephie had never seen, and abruptly headed for the door. "I mean she's your sister and you, like, never even *talk* to her!" Her mother wheeled on Stephie with surprising fury. "I said it's *personal*!" she snapped, then ran from the room.

We must be really *messed up!* Stephie fretted until Conner rang the doorbell. When Stephie headed downstairs, she heard her mother sobbing behind closed bedroom doors. *I did that*, Stephie thought guiltily.

"All right, let's form up," came their platoon leader's voice over their earphones. They headed in column further down the beach. High in the sky overhead were criss-crossing jet contrails. These weren't the lone white tracks made by commercial airliners. They came in the twos and fours made by flights of war planes heading out to sea. Stephie eyed them repeatedly—concerned that some might be Chinese—and Collins twice admonished her to keep her "fuckin' eyes on the fuckin' ground."

As they marched, there was too much chatter among the troops for the NCOs, and they barked and snapped and snarled. When the point man's hand went up and they halted, the platoon bunched up accordion-style. The platoon sergeant walked from soldier to soldier, down the column, cursing and slapping helmets in disgust. Ten-meter spreads were intended to prevent a single bomb or shell from killing more than five or six guys. Every half an hour or so, when the wary point man flattened his hand and went to ground, there was always far too much movement from a platoon that was supposed—on cue from the man's signal—to dive and freeze at the ready. The missile teams and machine gunners never had good fields of fire. Some soldiers correctly hit the quick release to drop their packs. Others didn't bother and lay beneath heavy loads to avoid the hassle of reattaching them. And the occasional maneuvering by a fire team to check the inland dunes seemed to Stephie both unprofessional and unprepared: four guys clawing their way up loose sand with swinging rifles threatening only the sky.

All Stephie could think as she lay prone with her rifle raised and seemingly ready atop the dropped pack was that the Chinese had won battle after battle in wars fought continuously over the last decade. They were veterans of a victorious army that knew exactly what the fuck they were doing, versus Stephie and Generation Z.

• • •

At seventeen, Stephie's childhood came to an end. In the middle of a school day in January, everyone was called into the high school's auditorium. It was a Wednesday, so all the senior boys like Conner wore their ROTC uniforms. Stephie, a junior, sat next to her now well broken-in boyfriend, whose hair was unfashionably short and whose khaki uniform was drab and lame. The principal quieted the large room and glanced down at a sheet of paper. His announcement was brief. "Chinese submarines have landed commandos on the islands of Barbados, Grenada, and St. Lucia in the Caribbean. The Mobile school board has decided to give the district a one-week special holiday." A cheer went up. Stephie squeezed Conner's hand, grinned, and said, "No school!" The principal had to raise his voice over the disturbance. "All students in the ROTC program are ordered to report to the gym in athletic gear!" Stephie cast a disappointed look at Conner, who sat pale, silent, and staring at the principal. For the first time she realized what the announcement meant. The smile drained from Stephie's face. *This wasn't a little thing,* she wrote in her journal that night. *A small fact in a tapestry of small facts.* This fact was different. This was one of those times that something new begins. The Chinese were coming this way. The war that everybody anticipated would not be in cut-off Europe. It would be right here. In America.

After two hours of road march, they passed a convenience store usually festooned with colorful floats. It was bare and boarded up as if in preparation for a hurricane, but Stephie thought that it was really a relic of an earlier era. The signs remained. Ice for a dollar. Lottery tickets for two. Live bait for five. As men checked out the store, Stephie extracted her canteen and took a swig of lukewarm, plastic-tasting water. Two years before, the cool high school juniors had used their fake IDs to buy the beer that was to be her very first.

It's been a good life, she wrote in her mental journal. *Just not as full as I'd thought it would be.* The fire team emerged with four thumbs up, and Stephie worked to reattach her load. *Imagine,* she thought. *That beer had been bought in that very same store. Life*, she thought, marveling at its richness. *I love life,* came a more personal inner voice. *I wanta live.*

The night before Conner's graduation, he took Stephie parking on a deserted stretch of beach. The bungee-jumping tower frequented by tourists was dark. "I'm leaving day after tomorrow," Conner whispered. *As if I don't know,* Stephie thought. She looked out at the water and rolled her eyes. He kissed and nibbled at her ear until she pulled away. The moon was jagged in the phosphorescent surf. "Maybe we shouldn't be down here," Stephie said as she scanned the dark dunes. Conner kissed her neck and murmured, "Who knows what's gonna happen?" Shadows from scrubby weeds held previously unimaginable fear. "Did you read about those Chinese they shot in Charleston?" she asked. "They say there're a half million Chinese 'advisers' in Cuba, but my stepdad says they're really soldiers." Conner obviously decided that now was the time to make his move. "This could be our last night together till I get my first leave." Stephie hung her head and mumbled, "My parents are thinking about moving to Canada." Conner was shocked and said, "But they cut off immigration from the U.S." She explained that they made exceptions, and her stepdad was an engineer. They were waiting to hear. "But what about *us*?" Conner asked. After drawing a deep breath, Stephie tossed her gum out the window, and they made love for the first time.

PART ONE

He that is master of the sea, may, in some sort, be said to be master of every country; at least such as are bordering on the sea. For he is at liberty to begin and end War, where, when, and on what terms he pleaseth.

Joseph Gander, *The Glory of Her Sacred Majesty Queen Anne in the Royal Navy* (1703)

1

"You recognize anything?" Peter Scott asked Stephie over the radio as they patrolled the beach. The voice of the boy from Michigan had quivered noticeably.

Stephie looked at the faded blue trash cans that dotted the saccharine sand. A fireworks stand was boarded with plywood. The rusting bungee-jumping tower was the dominant fixture on the beach. Stephie swallowed the lump in her throat, pressed the TALK buttom on the control stick, and said, "Yeah." Simmons snapped, "Off the fucking net!"

The breeze off the water carried the sounds of the surf as it had always had. The scent of lush salt air was, to Stephie, the smell of home. *Home,* she thought. Her house was only a short distance up the road, but her home seemed far away. It wasn't a town, but a time, and it seemed lost forever.

The next stop on the road was Stephie's street.

They halted on the highway by the entrance to the treeless, planned community. Stephie had never seen her neighborhood like this before. No cars, no people, no life. But the houses were familiar. Sally Hampton had been Stephie's closest friend as a child. The windows of Sally's house were grimy

and the grass in her yard a foot tall and brown like the weeds
in the dunes. Sally should just now be getting out of basic
training in the navy. And there was the Brubecks' house. They
hadn't taken the time to haul their boat off. It leaned on its
side against a peeling wall. Its white fiberglass hull had been
riddled with bullets, rendered useless, Stephie supposed, by
some previous passing patrol. Both of the two Brubeck
boys—jocks at Stephie's high school—were Marines. One
was stranded on Oahu; one was dead or a POW in Cuba.

And there was Stephie's house. Like the others, it sat atop
stilts. Only the carport and the storage room were on ground
level. Stephie could hardly bear to look at it, but at the same
time felt her gaze drawn to it, searching for sights both familiar and changed. "All right, First Squad," Collins said on
returning from a caucus with Lieutenant Ackerman. "We're
up. Let's do this right."

Kurth stepped to the fore. "This is my map of the minefields along this shore," he announced as he held the folded
map in the air. He placed it under the body armor of Sergeant
Collins, their young squad leader, and patted the Kevlar on
Simmons's chest. "Do not leave this behind."

"Yes, Staff Sergeant," were the unanimous replies from the
squad.

They dropped their heavy packs and proceeded into Stephie's neighborhood with only combat loads—rifles, grenades, ammo, canteens, and first aid kits—hanging from their
webbing. Stephie felt as if she were walking on the moon.

She considered informing Collins that they were approaching her childhood home. That she had lived every day of her
eighteen years in the stucco house on Sea Sprite Drive. That
she knew every nook, every cranny, every hiding place in the
cluster of twenty-year-old homes. But the words were stuck
in her throat. *We really don't own our house anymore,* she
reasoned. The bank had evicted them while Stephie was in
boot camp. After twenty years of paying the mortgage, her
unemployed stepfather had simply packed up and moved
north like everyone else along the coast after the naval debacle in the Straits of Havana. Like all the real estate in the
area, her mother had written her, the house was now worth-

less. "It never was worth as much as we paid for it" was her mother's throw-away comment, which had triggered a torrent of sobs as an angry Stephie lay in bunk after lights out. *That was my home!* she screamed, but only in her mind.

They proceeded single file down the street, which was still warm from the oven of the mid-afternoon sun. Four months ago, on Stephie's last trip home, it had been alive with kids beginning summer vacation. There had been boisterous play, music, and mothers calling their children to dinner. Everything had changed in the four months since the awful disaster at sea.

No one said a word as the soldiers nervously watched the mirrored windows for signs of movement. The street made a big U, with the base of the U resting on beachfront property. That's where Stephie's house was. At the bottom of the U, they made the turn. The breeze was stiff and heavy with humidity. Peter Scott was walking point. When he reached Stephie's driveway, he stopped at their shell-covered, concrete mailbox. Sergeant Collins made his way up to Scott, then pointed at Stephie and waved for her to join them.

Collins pointed at the plaque reading *The Roberts Family* as he scrutinized Kurth's minefield map. "This *your* house?" he asked. Stephie nodded. Scott said, "See? I *tol'* ya." Collins pointed at the houses—one, two, three, he counted from the turn in the U—and then did the same on the map. One, two, three. "Well, it's safe," Collins decided. "But stay *away* from that one," he said, pointing two doors further down at Dr. Rodriguez's.

Stephie couldn't help thinking that Collins should have looked at the map *before* marching down the street.

"You wanta . . . take a look around?" Collins offered. Stephie shrugged, then nodded. Collins tasked her fire team—Sanders, Johnson, and Scott—to accompany her, then radioed an explanation to the LT.

Stephie hurried into the cool shade of the carport before Ackerman could countermand the offer. "This is *yors?*" Johnson asked in disbelief. Stephie decided not to tell him about the foreclosure. "Man, I didn't know you was rich. I thought you was a *farmer* or somethin'. This changes the whole sit-

uation. What's yer stepdaddy do?" Stephie told him he was
an engineer—which was still true, even though he remained
unemployed—then turned to peer through the grimy glass of
the door. The darkened stairwell leading up to the kitchen
looked lifeless and distant, but when she closed her eyes, she
could smell the home-cooked meal that always greeted her
just inside. The door, she found, was locked.

"You mean you could just walk out to the motherfuckin'
beach?" Corporal Johnson yelled from the small backyard.
"You didn't even have to cross no highway? Man, on my
only trip to the beach when I was a kid, I burned the *shit* outa
my feet on that hot motherfuckin' highway." Stephie could
see in the window's reflection that he was staring at the blue
water.

"Let's get goin'!" Sergeant Collins shouted from the street,
not willing, if he didn't have to, to leak even the faint radio
signals of their short-range tac net for fear of some high altitude, loitering missile.

Stephie blinked to dry her eyes and compose herself, but
when she turned they all stared at her anyway. Scott said,
"Hey, I . . . I found this over there. You want it?" He dropped
a pink plastic ring with fake jewels into Stephie's hand. It
was part of a bucket of jewelry Stephie had gotten as a child.
One by one the colorful treasures had been swallowed up in
the sand. She and Sally Hampton had taken turns overacting
as they romantically asked for each other's hand in marriage.
The game was to draw "Ou-us" of disgust or excitement depending on which boy they revealed themselves to be in the
end. Stephie dropped the ring into the cargo pocket of her
camo trousers and bit her upper lip to rein in her fury and
her tears. Her buddies lent mostly clumsy words of support,
far missing the mark. Johnson put his arm around Stephie's
shoulder. "Hey, it's okay," he said over and over. "*Fuck* the
Chinese, man. We gonna *kick* they motherfuckin' asses!"

Grunts of "Yeah!" and curses of "Fuckin' A!" came from
Scott and Sanders. Stephie smiled.

"We gonna make the world *safe* again," Johnson said, "so
rich white folk like you can live in fine houses on the motherfuckin' *beach*!"

"Not on *this* beach," Scott commented on their way back to the street. "Did you see that map? They'll never find all them landmines in the sand."

Sanders asked, "So whatta ya think they got rigged up in *that* house?" He nodded at the Rodriguezes'.

Peter Scott, studying the structure, said, "I'd guess about a ton of C9 covered in half a ton or so of concrete and about a thousand of those real big nails."

Johnson drew his head back and said, "You're one of those fuckin' deranged white kids from the suburbs, I can tell. My momma warned me about people like you. How'd you get outa high school without shootin' the place up?"

They continued their loop around the U, crossing the street on passing the Rodriguezes'.

By the time Stephie's squad returned to the highway, the entire platoon had heard of Stephie's visit home. They all had words or looks of sympathy, even guys she hardly knew. Lieutenant Ackerman came up and asked if she were okay. Stephie shrugged and mumbled a noncommittal answer. Truth was, she ached to go back to her house, close the door to her room, and curl up in her bed. But the sun was low and noticeably redder. Darkness was fast approaching. The beach was a dangerous place at night.

The march back toward the trucks began uneventfully. They had already covered that stretch, and the sights had grown familiar. Plus there was the exhaustion. The feeling that your body—head to toe—was running on empty. Stephie's head grew light just as her legs grew heavy. The simple act of breathing seemed to take all her might. The blisters on her feet seemed to sprout new blisters, and her ankles hurt where she walked awkwardly to avoid the pain on her soles like a car with a flat tire running on the rims. She began to long for a halt to the steady, slow march. She watched Ackerman, expecting him to raise his hand at any moment. The sight of him calling for a break swam in and out of the swirl of images both real and imagined. She slung her rifle over her shoulder and pulled a canteen from its pouch to quench her parched mouth.

As she raised the plastic threads to her lips for her first sip of the tepid water, half a dozen automatic weapons opened fire at close range. She dashed to the side of the road in a crouch hitting her quick release and diving unencumbered by pack into the sand. The eruption of noise was stunning. She was totally unprepared. Guns were louder when fired straight at you.

The Chinese guns sprayed the road. The first shouts were not commands, but, *"Medic!"* Stephie rose and ran inland as bullets slaughtered the people who'd dropped onto the pavement.

Grenades exploded with searing flashes and whizzing shrapnel. Screams of agony and of *"Medic!"* filled the air. All Stephie could think was three more steps. Then two. Then one. Then she collapsed onto her belly. Then up again and run until one, then dive into the sand. Over and over. Over and over.

They never fired at her, which gave her the idea, maybe, to move a little closer to the enemy.

"Medic!" screamed the tortured casualties in the distance. The Chinese fire was focused on maximizing kills.

At the end of one dash, she dropped behind a thin spray of weeds just underneath a deadly sheet of fire. The fire slammed into the mound of sand collected among the weeds, which now gave her life. She lay on her stomach. Her helmet, face, and body pressed flat in the sand. The fire lessened, then moved on. Somehow she had lived.

When she raised her head, a splash of sand from a sliding soldier sent grit into her eyes. The guy drew Chinese fire. She cursed and spat and scraped painfully at the grains that stuck to her sweaty, sunburned face. Before she could open her eyes she heard the crack-crack-crack of an M-16. It was Burns, kneeling beside her, firing two aimed rounds per second.

She was glad for the reinforcements.

Her weapon was covered in sand, and she frantically brushed it. She flicked the selector to "semi" while Burns was reloading and slowly peered over her low cover. They would see her helmet, she knew, before she would see them.

Burns dove onto her under a roar of fire whistling through the wet air just above him. He moved. He wasn't dead. He rose and quickly resumed firing three-round bursts as fast as he could pull the trigger. She tried to rise again. He flattened her. "Cut that *out*!" she shouted, fending off his hand.

Animal's machine gun opened up from nearer the road.

Stephie rolled away and sprinted for the next dune further inland. The Chinese were heads down under Animal's fire. She slid to a stop.

The Chinese opened fire again on Burns. He was pinned where she had been behind a small exploding dune.

From Stephie's slightly higher elevation, she could see the boots of a prone Chinese soldier. She tore off again, rising higher up the dune and diving into the sand. The Chinese fire arrived with a vengence. She couldn't raise her head until they finally gave up firing at her, and then she waited an awful few seconds more.

She slowly lifted her right eye. Nothing but weeds, at first, then a thin topping of sand that wouldn't come close to stopping a bullet. Finally, she could see the lower torsos of two prone enemy soldiers.

To her left came her platoon's counterattack. A trail of five dead or writhing Americans led to four nearly equally luckless guys who were left to continue the direct frontal assault on the enemy. They dashed and dove and dug. One man rose and hurled a hand grenade thirty meters, but the enemy was fifty meters away. Fifty meters of open ground that the poor bastards had yet to traverse.

Stephie raised her rifle to her shoulder but wrapped her finger around the trigger to the grenade launcher slung underneath. Her right hand grasped the rifle's magazine guide like a pistol grip. Her eye was lowered to the sights. She had registered the highest score in her training platoon on the grenade range. Her left hand cradled the round launcher. She raised the elevation slightly. *Two hundred meters.* She applied a light touch to the trigger.

The grenade thumped out of the tube and sent the rifle solidly back into her shoulder. Stephie carefully maintained the tube's elevation and watched intently for her round to fall. She simultaneously loaded another thick grenade by feel. The explosion sent flame from a crater ten feet behind the Chinese. As she slapped the launcher's breech closed, the enemy soldiers scrambled to train their weapons on her. Rounds cut through the air all around. She lowered the elevation a hair. She was firing directly, not indirectly like a mortar.

Thump!

She dove to her side into the sand as the first bullets arrived. Her round went off. Its slap ended all enemy fire.

She lifted her head. Two Chinese soldiers lay in the open, rolled onto either side away from the burst, in which they had come apart. The Americans attacking their position rose on shouted command and dashed forward. Stephie, John Burns, and a dozen other riflemen riddled the wounded or dead with heavy fire.

The maneuver team hurled hand grenades through the air and dropped again to their bellies. This time, the pineapple-shaped devices lit the enemy redoubt with a half dozen explosions.

Everyone ceased fire on Ackerman's radio command as the three men and one woman reached the smoking dune and fired bursts straight at the ground beneath them.

The air was suddenly alive with helicopters. Gunships, medevacs, and scouts swarmed over the fallen, who littered the site of the disastrous firefight. They began putting down all around.

A chorus of cries of "Medic!" were clearly audible despite the noise of the engines.

Stephie and John rushed down to the road. Men and women writhed on the pavement untended. Some had managed to press half-opened bandage packs to gaping wounds that looked to have randomly opened their bodies. Others lay dead, never having succeeded in getting the packs open.

"Medic!" "I'm hit!" "Oh-God-Oh-God!" "Help! I need help!" "Medic!" "Medic!"

Stephie's head rocked back as she suddenly lost her equilibrium. She had to regain her balance before she fell. Burns and surviving medics rushed among the wounded as medevac helicopters belched flight-suited medical personnel. There was so much to do that Stephie was paralyzed staring at people who screamed for help or lay ominously quiet with wide glassy eyes in enormous pools of blood.

Stephie ran to and knelt beside the nearest wounded soldier.

She was an African-American woman from Third Squad. About Stephie's age. Trying unsuccessfully to raise her head to peer down at the shattered left forearm that she cradled. Each time, her helmetless head threatened to slam back down onto the pavement. She was disoriented from pain, blood loss, and shock.

Stephie raised the woman's head and lay it in her lap, remaining careful to ensure that her arm blocked the woman's sight of her wound. She got a bandage from the wounded woman's first aid kit and gently pulled the woman's right hand free of her left forearm.

Her wounded left arm moved unnaturally. Disconnected. A shouted moan suddenly erupted from the wounded woman. The pain or the psychological agony had awakened the poor woman. She now twisted and screamed and fought.

"Me-edi-i-ic!" Stephie screeched as she fought back. "It's gonna be okay! It's gonna be okay! It's gonna be okay!" she fought with words, but the woman thrashed her head from side to side.

Thankfully, paramedics wearing jumpsuits and flight helmets arrived. Stephie held the woman's head and mouthed soothing lies as the two medics gave the woman a shot of painkiller. Stephie wanted not to watch as they cut the sleeve away, but felt compelled to study how they took care of the woman. She felt wave after overwhelming wave of nausea, but she forced herself to do it.

When they lifted the wounded woman onto a stretcher, Stephie remained seated in the pool of the woman's blood. It had taken six or seven minutes until the evac was done. It had been an eternity spent with that woman and her arm.

Suddenly, as if waking from a slumber and finding herself soiled, Stephie felt revulsion and wanted desperately to wash the blood from her hands. She found that her canteen pouch was empty. She must have dropped her canteen when the ambush began. She rose and began to search the road for her canteen. Piles of equipment lay strewn all about. Blood dried black on the road's hot pavement. Both the unharmed and the lightly wounded sat slumped low to the ground like survivors of some great crash. The collision of two armies in war.

Stephie passed canteen after canteen amid the litter of gear until she found hers, which had emptied onto the pavement. When she replaced it in its pouch, she was surprised to find that she had two other canteens on her belt and wondered why she hadn't realized that before.

She washed her hands in a canteen's warm water. John Burns walked up. "Don't waste that water," he said. "You never know how long we'll be out here."

"But we're going straight back to our camp," she said.

He cocked his head and arched his eyebrows scoldingly. "You never assume that," he said, "if you're infantry." He stood so close that the pinkish water dripped from her hands onto his sandy trousers and dusty boots. His face was only inches from hers. "Don't be so stupid," he whispered angrily. "You almost got yourself killed."

With those words of reproach or of warning—Stephie didn't know which—he moved on and Stephie's mind again went blank.

Lieutenant Ackerman gave the order to form up. His voice sounded the same as it had before, but somehow everything struck Stephie as different. The sun was lower. It felt cooler, as though the seasons had turned. But it was more fundamental than that. Stephie felt as if she were moving through a world that had changed in some pervasive and indefinable way. The road. The beach. The sky. It was as if she had stepped out of reality and into some surreal alternate dimension. Or was it the other way around? Had she emerged from fantasy into stark reality?

When Stephie shouldered her heavy pack, ten thousand needles of pain shot down her spine and up her thighs. It was that pain that, on some visceral level, connected Stephie's present with her past. The dividing point between the two, however, seemed to remain fixed in time. There was the life she had lived before the first blood drenched her hands, and the existence into which she had descended that followed. She therefore clung tightly to the thread of her aching muscles, which were her only connection between the old world and the new.

On seeing Stephie stooped under the weight of her pack,

John Burns offered softly, "I can help." Stephie shook her
head no. Becky Marsh cleared her throat but was again ignored, so Becky sighed loudly and began to bitch. A second
thread: something else that hadn't changed. "That fucking
physical fitness test in boot camp!" Becky lamented for the
thousandth time. Lieutenant Ackerman was walking down the
line and talking quietly to each soldier. "They should've fucking *told* us what the test was for!" Becky had accidentally
tested into infantry in a boot camp fitness test. Stephie, by
contrast, had worked hard to get in. And now she was determined to carry her own weight.

Platoon Sergeant Kurth pulled Ackerman aside just before
he got to Stephie. They were whispering, but Stephie overheard them. Nine dead, Kurth reported. Sixteen wounded,
four bad. The news seemed to weigh heavily on Ackerman,
who repeated the numbers over the radio to the company
commander. It was a Chinese submarine raiding party, Ackerman reported. Heavily armed and with pouches nearly
empty of demolition charges that had been placed somewhere
inland. Four enemy killed in action. No survivors. He listened
for a moment, then had to repeat the figures. "We took *nine*
KIA and *sixteen* WIA! We have *four* confirmed enemy kills!
Repeat! *Four!*" The CO asked something else. Ackerman's
eyes rose to Stephie. "Negative," was his reply over the radio
as he turned away from the young private.

The CO signed off, and Kurth and the radioman left Ackerman alone. The tall, skinny lieutenant just stood there. Staring at the road with a look that Stephie couldn't fathom. When
he snapped to, he walked up to Stephie. "You okay, Roberts?"
the platoon leader asked. She nodded, not trusting her voice.
Four men, she kept thinking, *wiped out half our platoon.* "Ya
know," Ackerman said in a low tone that drew her scrutiny,
"one word and I could put you on one of those choppers."

"But . . ." Stephie began, but faltered, momentarily confused. "I'm not wounded, sir."

"That's not what I mean," he said quietly.

Stephie understood what he was saying and frowned. Her
squadmates—who had all miraculously escaped injury—
watched the encounter, Stephie saw, and waited for her reply.

Stephie shook her head, and Ackerman nodded. He moved on without comment, leaving in his wake only the stares of her comrades at Stephie. Some of them—like Becky—were incredulous.

But unlike Becky, Stephie had always demanded equal treatment. Or at least, she thought, treatment as equal as one could possibly expect to be accorded the daughter of the president of the United States of America.

WHITE HOUSE OVAL OFFICE
September 14 // 2030 Local Time

President Bill Baker stood alone at the window waiting. Outside, thousands of noisy pro-nuclear demonstrators—many refugees from the Exclusion Zone, which they claimed Bill had abandoned—called upon him to launch an immediate nuclear strike against Chinese forces. But the forty-three-year-old Republican was convinced that a nuclear war would spell the end of the country with whose survival he'd been entrusted.

Bill's personal secretary appeared at the door. Behind her stood almost a dozen Secret Service agents, who eyed all with stares that betrayed deadly serious intent. "The National Security Council has convened in the Situation Room," she reported. "And Mrs. Roberts is being ushered in."

President Baker nodded and turned back to the protest. People chanted and waved placards with obscure references to the Old Testament. One placard read, "Not one Chinese boot on American soil!" Another sign cried, "Do your job! Save America! Drop the bomb!"

But Bill saw clearly what only a handful of people in Washington and Beijing understood: the laws of Armageddon. Despite all the advances in antimissile technology, one fact hadn't changed since the earliest days of the atomic arts. The outcome of a nuclear war between two nearly equal nuclear adversaries will ultimately result in the destruction of both warring states. In a nuclear war, America and China would strike each other with staggering and repeated blows. Instead of being vaporized all at once, the early Twenty-First-Century combatants would die over weeks and months of hell on earth. The strategy of Mutual Assured Destruction had been replaced by Protracted Perimeter Engagement. Blow by blow, nuclear-tipped missiles would erode each country's defenses from the coastline, to the highlands, to the heartland. *When missiles penetrated the Great Plains states,* Bill Baker was convinced, *that would be the end.*

"You've got to get Stephie out of the army!" came Rachel's anguished voice. Bill turned to see his personal secretary close the door behind his ex-wife: the mother of Stephie, his only child. "She's only eighteen, and she's going to die. Your daughter's going to die, Bill, at age eigh*teen*! You're her father! It's time you started acting like one!"

Rachel's barb didn't sting Bill; it sickened him. *How dare she?* he thought—hating Rachel. "I *can't* exempt Stephie from service!" he explained, though he desperately wanted to do exactly that. "*I'm* the one who ordered women *into* combat! I can't exempt my own . . . !"

"I bet you haven't even *thought* about the risk of Stephie getting captured!" Rachel accused.

Bill didn't tell her, but she was wrong. The Joint Chiefs *had* warned of the risk in what Bill felt at the time was unnecessarily graphic detail. The Chinese had a certain history, it seemed, of using and abusing prisoners to gain leverage. Bill grew ill every time his thoughts strayed near the subject.

"You're only worried about *political* damage!" she accused. "You're going to kill your only child to avoid a black eye in the opinion polls! For a poignant story in the history books! *'Daughter of president dies defending his country!'* Well that's not what those books are gonna say, Bill! Not if the Chinese are the ones who write them! *You'll* have the distinction of *forever* being known as the *last* president of the United States!"

She had struck a nerve, and an awful tingle washed over Bill. He felt a sudden panicked need to flee.

"Where is the 41st Infantry Division?" Rachel demanded through teeth clenched in anger. Bill said nothing. "Where is my daughter's *unit*?" she built to a scream. The doors burst

open. Secret Service agents appeared with guns drawn. Bill
shook his head. They withdrew.

If I tell her, she would steamroll any junior army officer,
Bill thought to torment himself. *She would march right in and
yank Stephie out of harm's way.* God, how he wanted that to
be the outcome. But with all the life drained from his voice
Bill said, "It would be illegal for you to go see her." Rachel
opened her mouth to shout, but Bill tried to reason. "We can't
have parents dropping by units to visit! Plus, the location of
military units is a *secret*, Rachel."

"You're murdering your own *daughter*, you *bastard*!" she
shouted. "You know why she volunteered for the infantry,
don't you? Because of those B-grade stinkers you made before you got into this politician schtick! I found a box of
movie disks when we packed up her room. *Bill Baker—Space
Marine!* Maybe instead of keeping you two apart I should've
let her get to know what a *shit* you are! As it stands now, she
thinks you're a fucking *hero* because of those *god*-awful movies you made! Just what have you ever done in real life that's
truly heroic? Name one goddamn thing!" Bill headed past her
for the door. "You pig! You won't even do this for your own
child!" He stormed out of the Oval Office with Rachel shrieking, "Heartless *coward*!" at him from behind.

Bill fled through security checkpoints, with aides gathering
in trail, waiting for their turn to be recognized. At one metal
detector, Bill caught the eye of a burly, buzz-cut brute. The
bull-necked man looked out of place in a suit. His appointments secretary ran through the changes necessitated by his
five-minute confrontation with Rachel. "Who's that?" Bill
asked. He nodded at the watchful man, whose crossed arms
and oversized jacket concealed a large weapon underneath.

"He's Secret Service," his secretary replied.

"I don't want *any* new faces on my security detail," Baker
ordered. "You tell the special agent in charge. Okay? Nobody
that I don't recognize or *personally* approve." The elevator
door opened as the secretary scribbled a note. Bill felt his
heart race from the unpleasant rush of adrenaline. His panic
attacks were growing worse, and more and more frequent. He
turned away from the elevator and strode instead down the

corridor. He wasn't yet ready to play the role of commander in chief.

MOBILE, ALABAMA
September 14 // 2040 Local Time

Despite the hour, the night air was unpleasant. An afternoon thunderstorm had left behind sticky humidity. U.S. Army Special Forces Captain Jim Hart climbed up the ladder to the camouflaged metal deer blind. He held the rungs of the ladder with his left hand and his H&K machine pistol with his right. His combat boots' rubber soles made no sound. At the top, he scrutinized the darkness inside the small shelter. Rifles with long scopes leaned against the walls. Faint snoring fixed the two men's locations. They lay side by side and head to toe in two sleeping bags that were unzipped and flung back to catch the intermittent breeze on the sultry night.

Hart slung the H&K over his shoulder and soundlessly pulled his combat knife from its scabbard. The nine-inch blade was a dull black except along its cutting edges where the sharpened metal was silvery from honing with a stone stored on the scabbard.

Moving carefully, Hart climbed inside the tight enclosure between the two oblivious men. By their greasy, gray hair and the stubble on their double chins they looked to be in their late fifties or early sixties. The enclosed blind stank of their unwashed bodies. There was some uneaten bread and cheese on a small paper plate to go along with the six-pack of beer cans littering the forest floor fifteen feet below.

Hart held the knife's sharp edge to one man's unshaven neck.

The man's eyes opened wide. He looked up at Hart's grease-blackened face and opened his mouth. Hart pressed more firmly, and the words caught with a gurgle in his throat. Hart lessened the pressure of the blade, arched his eyebrows and nodded.

"B-B-Brad," the man whispered. "Brad!" he managed to squeak a little more loudly.

"Hm?" Brad asked from deep in his well of sleep. When

he opened his eyes, he saw the muzzle of Hart's H&K.

"Top of the morning, Brad," Hart said.

Brad let out a sigh of relief on realizing that Hart was American.

Hart removed his knife from the man's throat and stabbed a piece of cheese with it. The taste of the morsel was sharpened by its warmth. With his mouth full, Hart said, "You guys out here doing some hunting?"

"Well, sorta," Brad replied. He turned to his friend. "You was s'posed to keep a lookout!"

"You two know," Hart interrupted as he tore the loaf of French bread into mouth-sized bites and proceeded to devour it, "it's illegal to be in the Exclusion Zone." They said nothing. "I could arrest you, but unfortunately," he said, holding his hands out as proof, "I don't have any facil'ties to take pris'ners." He shrugged and made a show of being trapped by the circumstances while he tore and chewed his way through the long loaf. "So I could either kill you, or let you go on the promise that you clear outa here before you get yourselves in a whole world of hurt."

"You ain't from 'round here, are ya?" Brad asked almost as if in challenge.

"No. I'm from Michigan. But you're lucky I'm not from Harbin or Shanghai. There are Chinese pathfinders and long-range recon patrols out here," Hart said, looking at the tall, gently swaying pines just outside. "And the Chinese don't like partisans. Don't like 'em at all. It offends their sensibilities or something. I guess if you're the Chinese, you believe in playing by the rules when you field an army of sixty million regulars. So they wouldn't exactly extend you guys good old Christian charity, if you know what I mean. As a matter of fact, they've adopted an old trick from the New World to discourage partisan activity. You two good ole boys ever heard of a 'Venezuelan Necktie'?"

Both shook their heads.

Hart carved open a blade-width hole in a piece of the hard bread. "You cut into the neck, reach inside with your finger, and pull the tongue out through the hole." He ate the slice of bread in three bites. "Looks like a necktie. Get it?" He took a swig from his canteen. "It's, uhm, a slow way to go, shall we say."

Hart brushed his hands clean of the crumbs and grabbed a hunting rifle. He slid the bolt out, then did the same with the other three long guns.

"What're you doin'?" Brad asked.

Hart slipped the four bolts into his cargo pocket and climbed onto the ladder outside. "Saving your lives," he replied. "Now go home."

"This *is* our home," Brad said.

"Well, go take care of your families."

"Ain't got none," Brad replied. "My wife died near 'bout fourteen years ago. We didn't have no childern. Willy here, well, his wife wised up and left him awhile back, and his only boy . . . Well, he was in the Marines."

Willy's head hung. Hart looked back and forth between the two in increasing exasperation. "Look! If you guys wanta fight the fucking Chinese, at least join the militia."

"They won't have us," Willy answered. "Top age is sixty. We miss out by a coupla years."

Hart looked out at the surrounding terrain. They had a clear shot at Interstate 65 heading inland from the port of Mobile. It was, Hart knew from extensive prewar briefings, projected to be the main line of supply for the Chinese. At five hundred meters, it was within range of their hunting rifles.

The trees whose branches scraped on the metal siding of the blind with each gust might provide concealment from advance patrols, which probably wouldn't stray that far off the highway at first. Those same trees, however, would also provide concealment to Chinese troops who were maneuvering against the two old men. But the would-be snipers probably wouldn't last that long. A main tank gun on the road could fire a shell that would cover the distance in a fraction of a second.

"This is a bad idea, guys," Hart advised one last time. "You won't make it outa here."

"We know that," Brad replied. Willy nodded in confirmation. "We thought about strappin' bombs to ourselves like terrorists, but the first few we made just sorta burned real hot.

Finally, we figured we'd just do what we knew we could. We're both damn good shots." Willy nodded.

Hart frowned, took one last look around, and dropped the four rifle bolts on the metal floor of the hunting blind with a clacking sound. The two men stared at them, then at Hart. "What I said before," Hart warned, "about being taken prisoner, I wasn't bullshitting you. Don't let yourselves get captured. You two understand? If they close on you, you've gotta do the job yourselves. You've gotta take your own lives—quickly—before they do it . . . slowly. You two both understand that?"

Hart waited, and both men nodded again. Willy seemed to have trouble swallowing.

"We made our minds up," Brad said. "The two of us, we ain't never done nothin', you know, special. This'll be it, we figure. Even if nobody ever knows we done it, this'll be it."

Willy nodded.

The trees hissed as the breeze rose from the Gulf. A dull clanking sound again drew Brad and Willy's gaze to the deck of the blind. In the dim moonlight, their eyes took a moment to find the knobby, pineapple-shaped fragmentation grenade that Hart had dropped next to the rifle bolts. "Happy hunting," Hart said as he descended the ladder.

"Same to ya," came Brad's reply. Willy, Hart presumed, was nodding.

WHITE HOUSE MAP ROOM
September 14 // 2045 Local Time

Bill sought shelter from his emotional storm in the Map Room. For decades, it had been used for informal meetings—coffees, teas, receptions, televised chats—but Bill had ordered the room returned to its original use. As a consequence, Secret Service agents stood guard by the door. The tabletop electronic maps contained highly classified military information.

Bill stood at a flat-screen, high-definition display of the South, searching for Stephie's unit. He found the glowing blue unit marker on a map of northern Alabama. The 41st Infantry Division lay directly in harm's way, and for that he was responsible. He had put Stephie there when he had ordered all women drafted and put through batteries of tests. They were young, healthy, bright, and patriotic: the products of affluence, good nutrition, and athletic suburban lifestyles. Twenty percent would test into the infantry. After their country had afforded the young women every conceivable advantage and privilege—after it had cultivated and cherished its daughters—now it needed their lives in return.

Bill jammed his eyes shut at the horrible truth. It was a tragedy on an unimaginable scale. Yet that scale had a more measurable personal dimension.

Months earlier General Adam Cotler, chairman of the Joint Chiefs of Staff, had met with Bill behind closed doors in the Oval Office. He was the senior general in the army, and he had delivered the army's official report. "Your daughter, sir, is five-foot seven and weighs one twenty-eight. Her health is excellent. She begins eight weeks of basic training tomorrow."

Eight weeks later, Cotler had squeezed in a moment during Baker's last trip to the Hawaiian Islands. The president had just given a rousing speech to the 3rd Marine Division, which was dug into the sand and volcanic ash. "She has completed the first half—basic infantry training," Cotler had reported. "She was in the 82nd percentile overall." Bill had nodded and stifled a smile. As Stephie was entering womanhood, the world was only now finding out what Bill already knew: Stephanie Roberts was an exceptional girl. "That's the 82nd *percentile*, Mr. President," Cotler had explained, "of *all* recruits: women *and* men."

Cotler's report had continued. Bill couldn't stop it. "She's lost seven pounds in the Georgia summer heat and is down to one twenty-one. But that's a *strong* one twenty-one." The words had been spoken as softly as Cotler could manage. "She can carry a full load: rifle, ammo, pack, extra machine gun belts, grenades, all-threat missiles, and cluster mortars."

"Wait!" Bill had interrupted. "Are you . . . you're not *saying*, General, that . . . that Stephie is going to be in the *infantry*?"

Cotler had nodded with sincere compassion. "The young

women these days, sir, they're *very* athletic. You get an average eighteen-year-old soccer player, like your daughter, and put her up against a male Internet junkie, and you'd be amazed how favorably she compares." He had looked at Baker. "Fair tests sometimes give you the wrong answer, sir. The top twenty percent, Mr. President, of the most mentally and physically tough women go infantry. Your *daughter*, sir, is in the ninety-*eighth* percentile of female recruits. She lost two points on upper-body strength. But on *mental* toughness and leadership—which comes from evaluations by DIs after sixteen weeks of watching her—she totally maxed the test. Number *one* in her basic training battalion of three hundred men and three hundred women."

Bill had been helpless to avoid the slow-motion car wreck. Cotler had said in a low, guilty-sounding voice that they had offered Stephie her choice of assignments: communications, intelligence, military government, public affairs. She had requested—demanded, in fact—the infantry. Bill jammed his eyes shut again and rubbed his face.

"Do what you can," Bill had said, and in a subsequent briefing Cotler had reported that he'd put a good man in charge of Stephie's unit. "Secret Service?" Bill had asked. Cotler had shaken his head no. "His name is Ackerman. Formerly *Major* Ackerman, an instructor at Advanced Infantry School, now Lieutenant Ackerman, your daughter's new platoon leader. With all due respect, sir, he can do more to keep your daughter safe in combat than any Secret Service bodyguard."

Bill had suggested that the man must be pissed at being busted from major to lieutenant. Cotler had replied that, "He's just a lieutenant in the official records. He's a major for all other purposes. And, sir, he volunteered for the job." Bill arched his eyes in surprise. "It was his only way out of the training school," Cotler explained, "and into a combat unit. At least, it was the only way we offered him the transfer."

There was a knock on the door. Bill straightened his back and composed himself just as Admiral Thornton, Baker's new Chief of Naval Operations, stepped inside. The ranking naval officer reported in a deep, funereal tone that Guantanamo Bay,

Cuba, was finally falling. Bill felt drained. "How many of our people are still combat effective?" he asked.

After hesitating, the CNO replied, "Fifteen thousand sailors and about eight thousand Marines."

They're still useful, Bill thought as he took a deep breath and issued an order whose wording he had memorized from past use. It was phrased, he knew, in terms that would not need to be explained to the military. "They are to keep fighting, Admiral, so long as they have any reasonable means to resist."

There, he thought. *It's done. The order has been given.*

Thornton hesitated for a moment, clearly reluctant to relay the command. He stared fixedly at Bill. It took all of the willpower that Bill could muster not to look away in guilt. But it was the admiral who finally averted his gaze. He mumbled, "Yes, sir," and quietly exited the room.

The door's latch clicked shut, and Bill collapsed into a chair. He held his face in both hands and moaned, "Oh, God!" He shut his eyes and allowed his mind to go blank.

Bill was the commander in chief of the armed forces of the United States of America. The National Security Council was waiting for him to give the final orders for the defense of America against invasion by massed armies from China. He needed time to brace himself for the duties required of him. Time to torment himself with the most popular question of the day in America and the rest of the Free World: *How the hell did it ever come to this?*

Almost two years earlier, Bill Baker had been elected president for this very moment. As chairman of the Senate Armed Services Committee, he had been Cassandra to the American Troy—warning over and over of the growing Chinese threat to absolutely no avail. Early retiring baby boomers had bailed out Social Security at the expense of national defense. They hadn't been *about* to send their college-bound kids off to oppose Chinese territorial aggression in Asia! And no one wanted to risk nuclear war, for God's sake. Not even the Indians, who had used hand grenades to destroy their own

missiles while still in their silos to keep the Chinese from
seizing them intact.

But long before that came the first milestone along the road
to invasion of North America: the brief but bizarre Satellite
Crisis ten years earlier. It had been hailed as the first of a new
type of bloodless war, but in all probability it had been the
world's last bloodless war as well. Beijing had always
claimed that spy satellite overflights violated its territorial sovereignty, but no one had paid that claim much attention. Until,
that is, in a demonstration of its new antimissile system, China
had shot down all of the West's military satellites. The U.S.
and Europe had retaliated in kind until their telecommunications lobbies—which had hundreds of billions in orbiting capital at risk—had pressed for a treaty demilitarizing space.

Military reconnaissance had been set back forty years,
which constituted a huge gain to technology-poor China. Instead of receiving real-time satellite imagery, Western commanders had returned to the fog of war as seen through
periscopes and on radar screens. Western intelligence agencies had been reduced to reliance upon spies who, as it turned
out, had most often been Chinese double agents. Under the
shroud of total secrecy that descended over conquered Korea,
China had converted keels meant for supertankers into 300-
plane supercarriers. Rumors of China's secret shipbuilding
program had been secondary to world outrage over their land
war, which had simultaneously raged across South Asia. Even
after the ships began to put to sea in numbers, their significance was masked by the drama of China's push on the
ground ever closer to the Middle East. Inexorably the balance
of naval power had shifted, just as the era of strategic surprise
had returned. The significance of both changes was dramatically proven in China's victory over the combined fleets of
Western Europe's navies.

China had run headlong into the European Union at the
mouth of the Persian Gulf. It had been the first major test of
Europe's long-sought military self-sufficiency. Two fleets—
European and Chinese—had gone toe to toe in the Indian
Ocean until a previously unknown *third* fleet had arrived from
China. The only warnings European commanders had of the

impending naval debacle had been radar screens filled with three thousand Chinese aircraft. The Battle of Diego Garcia had been a replay of the Battle of Midway, only this time victory had gone to the ascendent Asiatic naval power.

America's incumbent Democratic administration—Baker's predecessor—had been torn between building more aircraft carriers or potentially revolutionary but longer-lead-time arsenal ships. While the former could hold their own against three or four Chinese supercarriers, the latter were totally untested weapons platforms. Some experts argued that relying upon the new arsenal ships was far too dangerous at such a perilous time. Better to go with the tried and true aircraft carriers, whose basic designs dated back fifty years. But others argued that massive arsenal ships—whose thousands of missiles ready for instant launch gave them ten times the punch of a carrier—would ensure America's mastery of the seas for generations. Studies were ordered and commissions organized to ensure the correct decision was made, given that decision's monumental cost and importance and the possibility that politics—which powerful congressman's district would build what vessels—might play a role. Valuable time was lost.

Meanwhile, Iran, Kuwait, Iraq, Saudi Arabia, and Jordan had all fallen—half through Chinese coercion, half by direct invasion. When China had at last occupied Syria and Lebanon, Israel had found itself surrounded. The Israeli David and the Chinese Goliath had each issued warnings, which tragically neither had heeded. Israeli tactical nukes had fallen on Chinese forces massing to the north in the Golan Heights, but the strikes had brought only temporary respite. Israel had been conquered by an attack-in-the-main from the south. The world had then watched live as troops cordoned off Tel Aviv. The population had not been allowed to leave the city as the Chinese staged a show of collective punishment. Chinese generals had condemned nuclear war on worldwide television while an on-screen clock counted down. At zero, engineers had detonated a half dozen nuclear "special demolition munitions" in and around the captive capital, killing and maiming hundreds of thousands. The demonstration had been a total success. No one thereafter would doubt China's will to retaliate in kind. It was "an eye for an eye" in the nuclear age.

Pro-defense Senator Baker had launched his bid for the presidency just as national defense had become America's sole political issue. By the end of the week before China seized Cape Verde and the Canary Islands off the northwest coast of Africa—the second milestone along their road to America—Bill's campaign had raised seventeen million dollars mainly from conservative political action committees and large defense contractors. By the end of the week that followed, his total campaign contributions had doubled, with the average size of the donations made that last week being $34.50. With Chinese bases in the Eastern Atlantic, Bill's political bandwagon had quickly filled.

Bill's mentor had, unusually, come from the other side of Capitol Hill. The venerable Tom Leffler, Republican Speaker of the House of Representatives from Georgia, had years before taken a liking to the freshman senator from California. Perhaps it was because Bill, a polished former Hollywood actor, was so unlike Tom, a crusty, old-style, joke-telling, rib-eating Southern politician. Perhaps it was because Tom's wife, Beth Leffler—who, Bill thought privately, was the key to Tom's success—had taken the measure of Bill early on and seen the same potential in him that she had seen in Tom forty years earlier. Regardless of the reason, Tom and Beth Leffler had taken social charge of the divorced Bill, frequently escorting him to the right lunches, dinner parties, golf outings, and party retreats and caucuses. With their nurturing, Bill's career had flourished. And in the fateful year of Bill's attempted leap from junior senator to the nation's highest office, events had broken just right for Bill, but just wrong for the beleaguered West.

All in Europe had watched the prodigious Chinese sealift surpass previous herculean American logistical records. Half-million-ton transports had deposited three million men on the islands that constituted China's strategically important Atlantic foothold. All awaited the seemingly inevitable Chinese invasion of Europe with equal measures of incredulity and dread.

By the time of the Iowa caucuses, Congress had sought political cover behind massive defense appropriations. The studies of the blue ribbon panels had all come in, and the largest single line item in the history of the budget had been one hundred billion dollars for construction of three awesome new arsenal ships. The flat-decked, 500,000–ton behemoths wouldn't cruelly hurl manned aircraft into the teeth of enemy air defenses. Instead, each arsenal ship could launch huge, long-range guided missiles at the rate of eight thousand every six minutes. Armored, flush-mounted vertical launch boxes would cover nearly every square meter of her decks. Auto-reloaders and robotic maintenance reduced the crew of the ship to only one hundred men and women—mostly officers. The commander would watch the battle from cameras mounted in the nose cones of missiles inbound for their targets in the air, on land, and on and below the surface of the sea. As a candidate, Bill had watched the impressive computer depictions of the attack from the full-size simulator used to train the captain and crew of a ship whose keel had just been laid. It would be an overwhelming barrage of ever-homing images. Even though, as a pro-defense senator, Baker had loudly championed the ships, his refrain in the debates had been, "Too little, too late!" A frightened electorate had turned out to vote in droves, and Bill had won primary after primary through the spring.

The EU had dispatched a million-man expeditionary army to their southern flank and shored up the wavering Turks. Without firing a shot on the ground, a united Europe had stopped war before it reached the Bosporus. That decisive and swift deployment had infused the continent with self-destructive pride. Their hubris had ultimately been their undoing. When three Chinese supercarriers had sailed north toward the Rock of Gibraltar, Europe's emboldened navies had sailed south and deployed into the western Mediterranean. They had denied China passage and immediately celebrated victory . . . until the arrival of another ten Chinese supercarriers.

In perhaps the greatest strategic blunder in modern military history, the surviving remnants of Europe's navies had been bottled up inside the Mediterranean. It was China's third mile-

stone on their decade-long route to America, although no one
saw it that way at the time. Analysts hadn't even known the
names of the Chinese warships that had appeared on the horizon without any warning. Western "human intelligence" on
the closed Korean peninsula had been reporting materials
shortages and labor unrest, but it had been classic Chinese
disinformation. The fanfare from Beijing upon commissioning
of each new warship had masked the three ships built in between.

Europe had promptly launched spy satellites in violation of
the international ban. All had been downed by Chinese missiles, but not before they had returned crisp photos of Korea's
bustling slave-labor shipyards. In real time, governments in
Berlin, Paris, and London had gotten their first glimpse of
another twenty supercarriers that were in various states of
construction. The *Sturm und Drang* that ensued had left Europe in complete disarray. China had downed Europe's civilian satellites in retaliation for their violation of the treaty
demilitarizing space. The resulting fragmentation of Europe's
telecommunications system had been an omen of the disunity
to follow.

The furious Britain—cut off from her fleet—had withdrawn
from the EU. Their army trains had been jeered all the way
from Turkey to the English Channel, but they had been
cheered at the cliffs of Dover. The remaining European expeditionary force had been forced to withdraw behind the
Bosporus, and Turkey had fallen south of Istanbul. The Ger-
mans had thought that the Chinese would now attack overland
from Turkey or the Caucasus. But the French had been certain
they would come from the sea into Iberia or directly into
France. So Paris had recalled its troops to build a Western
Wall along the Atlantic. The German army—left alone—had
dug in deep and held its bloody Balkan ground, hemorrhaging
daily in proxy wars with various Chinese-backed guerillas. In
the month before Baker's Republican presidential nomination,
the EU had acrimoniously dissolved.

For Baker, the general election had been a single-issue race
against a man whose Achilles' heel was that issue. The Democratic nominee—Phillip Peller—had been vice president in

the previous administration, which for eight years had chosen isolationism over containment. With withering overseas defense commitments, America's need for weapons and troops had waned. Naval construction had slowed to a crawl. The fleet had shrunk from eleven to only seven aging aircraft carriers. While each was still a match for two or three Chinese supercarriers, on Election Day they were outnumbered four to one.

Baker and Elizabeth Sobo, his vice presidential running mate, had won the general election in a record landslide. A special air of excitement had surrounded the inauguration at which Baker had given a Reaganesque morning-in-America speech. Washington once again led an embattled Free World. The Dow—which had crashed with the collapse of international trade—had rocketed skyward as capital fled Europe for bastion America. The gush of spending in Baker's doubled defense budget and the draft of the young had left Americans fully employed. Keels had hurriedly been laid for the three Reagan-class arsenal ships, and Atlantic blockade running was the talk of the day. Baker's first order as commander in chief had been to prepare to send three carriers escorting a military supply convoy on a daring voyage to Great Britain.

But in the middle of the night one month into Bill's presidency, he had been awakened to stunning news. China had attacked not north into Europe, but west into the Carribean. Chinese naval infantry had seized Barbados, Grenada, and St. Lucia. Bold plans for a rescue of Europe had given way to the grim task of defending America. An angry Congress had gutted the stunned CIA and vested intelligence-gathering in the FBI. After *all*, they had reasoned sarcastically, military intelligence would soon no longer be *foreign*!

The landings were just an audacious ploy to divert aid, some experts had argued, from the real target: Western Europe. But to Baker the landings were the final milestone for which he had long been waiting. The Chinese had finally arrived, and he had asked Congress for a declaration of war. For three days they had debated contentiously on worldwide television. *Surely* we weren't wed to this *Monroe* Doctrine thing! And the *casualties* . . . many had whispered. But a majority had voted with Speaker of the House Tom Leffler on whom Bill had relied to get America's formal, official commitment. With that vote—95 to 5 in the Senate, and 421 to 6 in Leffler's tightly run House—America had drawn the line in the Carribean, and not in the Gulf of Mexico.

Though the ink on the declaration of war was not yet dry—literally within minutes of the vote—Baker had sent two thousand warplanes into combat. A quarter had been lost but not before they had sunk four of eight Chinese supercarriers. The Battle of the Windward Islands had been proclaimed a victory, but China had retained its Carribean toehold, and in the spring it had begun an island-hopping campaign that inched ever northward. Martinique, Dominica, and Guadeloupe all had fallen. Baker had finally run out of pilots, and one new Chinese supercarrier had continued to arrive every two weeks.

With each landing, Beijing's peace terms had grown more and more onerous. Trade concessions had begun to resemble tribute. Arms reduction proposals had become demands that America disarm. Baker's final attempt to negotiate had been met by a proposal from China for the long-term lease of the Hawaiian Islands. When Baker had rejected the insult, China had attempted to blockade America's fiftieth state. That had siphoned off scarce American naval resources, the 3rd Marine Division and 1st Marine Expeditionary Brigade, and the entire U.S. Army IX Corps. Convoys had deposited troops and evacuated civilians until Hawaii had become an armed camp awaiting the inevitable invasion.

A combination of thinly veiled public hectoring by his old mentor Tom Leffler and explicit private urging by air force General Latham had forced Baker to contemplate nuclear war. During one long weekend at Camp David, he had met a procession of apocalyptic military wizards interspersed with economists, historians, and religious leaders. On Monday, Baker had gone on national television and announced his first major decision of the war. He had ordered total mobilization. He would fight a conventional World War III. A reluctant Tom Leffler had gotten Baker's conscription bill passed, drafting all able-bodied Americans—male *and* female—ages eighteen through twenty-four. But military pundits had pointed out the parallels between Baker's defensive strategy and that previously employed by Japan. Tokyo had mobilized during two years of blockade, but then had fallen island by island to the Chinese. In reality, Bill pinned his hopes not on the young troops, but instead on the three arsenal ships whose frames rose from keels like bare ribs in shipyards on the east and west coasts. And in so doing he had let the opportunity for a nuclear strike on the Chinese while still in the Carribean slowly pass. Many now viewed that to be a monumental mistake for which America would pay in territory and in the precious blood of its young.

The first year of Baker's presidency had been a blur. If he had been asked, as was the rage, "Where were you when . . . ?", he could have replied, with confidence, "In a briefing." As dogfights had raged in sunny Caribbean skies above abandoned luxury resorts, Baker had dwelled in deep bunkers watching wobbly pictures on high-definition TV.

Marines had made the first ground contact of the war. The 4th and 6th Expeditionary Brigades had dug deep into Antigua and St. Croix. But within hours of the Chinese landings, each of the brigades of 16,000 sailors and marines had been outnumbered four to one. Within days, they were outnumbered one hundred to one. After a week of fighting, the world had been treated to pictures of hollow-eyed Marines being marched off to prison camps. Their humiliation had galvanized the United States and extinguished incipient domestic peace movements, but Latin America had gravitated inexorably into the orbit of the world's new superpower. Panama had granted China unrestricted passage through the Canal until it had been destroyed by U.S. Army Special Forces personnel. The American attack had outraged South Americans and further driven their nations into the Chinese fold. The authorities in half a dozen capitals, anxious to please visiting delegations of Chinese, had made a show of cutting off the utilities and supplies of America's embassies, and had been cheered by throngs on the streets outside. Chinese diplomats had won great swaths of territory in the Americas as their military fought for yards of blood-soaked sand.

Finally, in the fall of Baker's first year in office, Chinese troop transports had been invited into Havana. Each transport had landed an entire army division with a full month of combat supplies. The buildup had quickly outflanked Puerto Rico. Most of the Puerto Rican population had been evacuated to Florida, leaving only the 10,000–man 92nd Infantry Brigade behind. The 6000 men and women who had survived three weeks of combat after the Chinese invaded now joined the swelling ranks of POWs.

It was then that Guantanamo Bay, Cuba, had begun repulsing round-the-clock attacks. The American base continued to support operations in the Caribbean until besieged by land, air, and sea. The 1st Marine Division and 25,000 sailors turned riflemen had then made one of the greatest defensive stands in history. But Chinese transports had continued landing in Cuba, and Baker had gotten a troop count every Friday morning. By Christmas they had numbered one million men. By the end of winter, they had doubled to two million. During the spring, three million Chinese soldiers had stood ready for orders. By summer, four million men were encamped on Cuba's northern beaches. The latest count Baker had received was up to five million troops with more arriving every day. They now completely dominated America's exposed southern flank.

Baker had developed an ulcer, and doctors had cautioned him about excessive levels of stress. *What a small price to pay* was Baker's only thought about the ailment, which nightly robbed him of hours of sleep.

The increasingly desperate plight of the Guantanamo Bay defenders had forced Baker into his second major strategic decision. He couldn't abandon the embattled patriots, who for his countrymen had become synonymous with the word *resolve*. So in the first heat of summer he had sent three carriers through the Straits of Havana escorting the entire 2nd Marine Division. It had been planned to be an unstoppable forced entry and evacuation, but it had turned into an unparalleled human disaster. For lying in wait on the sandy bottom of the shallow Gulf waters had been a hundred-boat Chinese submarine wolfpack. The primitive but silent diesel-electric vessels had sunk all three carriers and a dozen assault ships, and wave after wave of Chinese surface ships and aircraft had finished off the rest of the task force.

Proof of America's stunning defeat had for weeks washed ashore up and down Gulf Coast beaches. Many of the 30,000 dead sailors and Marines had been found by their comrades' parents, who combed the shore for the bodies of their sons and daughters. Every night, America's living rooms had been filled with heartrending scenes of intense grief, and it had triggered the panicked flight of forty million people from the South. Order had been lost completely from Fort Lauderdale to the Rio Grande, and advisers had beseeched the president to restore calm. But Baker had done nothing to reassure the frightened refugees or to stem the human tide. They were right to be panicked, he realized but never said. The reason for their fear had been real and not imagined. The defeat in the Straits of Havana had laid bare to Chinese invasion the soft underbelly of the United States of America.

Admiral Thornton—the new CNO—had appeared visibly shaken when he'd given Baker the navy's dismal news. America had been left with only four carriers split between the East and West Coasts. The Chinese had sixteen supercarriers in the Gulf. They could land anywhere along America's Third Coast that they wanted. Baker had turned to the chief of staff of the air force, but General Latham had informed him that China deployed 4800 carrier-based aircraft in the Gulf and another 4000 on runways in Cuba. Latham couldn't send his few thousand remaining combat pilots on suicidal attacks against the Chinese without robbing America's own air defenses of an integral and critical component. For while high-altitude Chinese missiles and aircraft were downed by ground-based American SAMs, most stealthy, low-and-slow, air-breathing cruise missiles were intercepted by pilots firing guns.

Baker hadn't bothered asking the marine commandant for help. The Corps had lost the 1st and 2nd Marine Divisions, and the 3rd was stranded in Hawaii. The 4th—a reserve unit—anchored fixed defenses around New Orleans. After the losses in the Carribean, all the marines had left were three 10,000-man Marine Expeditionary Brigades. Replacement 1st and 2nd Marine Divisions, plus the new marine divisions numbered 5th and 6th, had not yet been raised at Camps Pendleton and Lejeune. They would be ready to go to sea behind the firepower of the arsenal ships . . . if only America could hold on long enough to launch them.

Baker had turned then to the defender of last resort: the United States Army. It *is* possible, General Cotler had advised, that we could stop the Chinese on the beach. But repulsing their first attack won't stop their second, third, or fourth, and committing our reserves to do that may be *exactly* what they want. "It could shorten the war, Mr. President," Cotler had said, chilling Bill to the bone.

Baker had thus been forced into his third major decision. "I want *decisive* engagement," he had told the Joint Chiefs. "Since America can't take the war to the Chinese, the Chinese will have to come to us." Baker had known that the uniformed doubters who stared back at him had never once in their careers contemplated the loss of territory to invasion, and they promptly opened fire on Baker's plan. What if the Chinese land *ten* million troops? "Then we'll draft mothers of young children and old men," Bill had replied. What if the Cuban buildup is a strategic deception and they come ashore in New Jersey or California? "Then we'll fight in the Sierra Nevadas and Appalachians," Baker had answered, "and I want a contingency plan to do just that."

That night, after silencing the dissent in his NSC, Baker had lain awake half the night thinking, *What the hell do I know?* He had been a bit actor in male adventure movies whose name and face had won him a vacant senate seat. His political career had remained undistinguished until the China thing had caught fire. His marriage to Rachel Roberts, a starstruck co-ed nee Rachel Bachman, had been a total disaster. Because a second divorce would have made Bill virtually unelectable, he had shied away from any romantic entanglements since.

The result: Bill Baker now lived in his own private hell—alone under the crushing weight of the office. Just the night before, he had lain awake again till the early hours of the next day, wondering when the unthinkable had become the inevitable? Was it last spring when he had toured the South inspecting antimissile silos and heard the near constant thunder of sonic booms from Gulf-bound interceptors? Or was it on that clear, early summer night on the deserted beach in southern Florida watching the final sea battles from the Straits of Havana flash like lightning over the horizon? Or when announcing to the people at the port of Charleston that the navy would one day return, then later that night viewing the body of the first confirmed Chinese soldier in America—a commando who had been killed in a shoot-out with local police? No, he had decided as the dawn shown around thick curtains, he had long feared the vague menace of the Chinese resurgence. For the nation that Baker led was bounded by three thousand miles of undefended coastline. When America had lost control of the sea, the oceans surrounding her had gone from being her greatest asset to being her possibly fatal liability.

2

Clarissa Leffler waited outside the Situation Room before her first ever briefing of the National Security Council. At the relatively young age of thirty-five, she had just become the head of the State Department's now all-important China Desk. Most in her position would have been nervously rehearsing what she was going to say in front of the president of the United States. But Clarissa was an expert on her subject—Chinese politics—and was also at ease around powerful politicians. So instead she spent her time reflecting on the irony of having chosen treason in the name of patriotism.

The night before, her father—the Republican Speaker of the House—had hinted of a possible military coup. "Certain *stalwart* generals," he had said, "may seize *extra*-constitutional control and go nuclear in a truly *biblical* way!" In the last few years, American politics had taken a dramatic shift to the right, and her father, Tom Leffler, had ridden the conservative crest. Bill Baker's plan to defeat the Chinese using only the lives of draftees was not only heartless, it was doomed to failure.

She would *never* have dreamed that Baker would betray his country like that! In graduate school, Clarissa had cried futilely about China's threat to world peace to people who saw only fortunes to be made in trade. Then Baker had rocketed to office, trumpeting warnings of Chinese aggression. Clarissa had done low-level, back-office work on Baker's presidential campaign with her father's very willing permission. But now, how could the man she'd so ardently supported shrink from using nuclear arms when the survival of their *nation* was at stake?

Clarissa knew that historic roles lay ahead for certain, chosen people. A chance to make a real difference. The entire "extraconstitutional" undertaking was probably being planned with military precision, but in her imagination the presidential succession would unfold like an opera. The general story of the coup would be obvious to all, but the high drama of the actual event would be masked behind a language at whose precise meaning you could only guess. What part might *she* play in the patriotic overthrow of Bill Baker? Would she even see it coming? Would somebody tell her? Maybe ask her for help? And what about afterwards? Would counterplotters abound? Would loyalists refuse her father's commands? After all, though it had remained unspoken in their conversation, her father—third in line to become president—would be the plotters' obvious choice. And her father's new administration, she reasoned calmly, would need trustworthy officials after the coup.

After the coup . . . echoed the sobering thought. As happened every time that Clarissa imagined what would follow her father's oath of office, her stomach tightened as if it had been punched. Clarissa had always possessed a highly imaginative mind, but nuclear war on American soil to her still seemed completely and totally unimaginable. *Surely there's another way*, came her only solace every time that she contemplated such a dismal fate.

Each of the Joint Chiefs nodded in succession on recognizing Tom Leffler's daughter. As they entered the Situation Room, Clarissa wondered which of the straight-backed men would spring into action and save America from Baker's folly. The powerful FBI director—Hamilton Asher—raised an eyebrow on seeing Clarissa waiting beside the door. Richard Fielding—head of the neutered CIA—smiled and whispered, "Break a leg." She felt goose bumps, not from nerves, but from being a part of it all. Clarissa was in an exciting place, at an exciting moment, in an historic time.

The downcast president of the United States walked straight past Clarissa, oblivious to all around. But two men put their backs to the wall by the briefing room door and looked right at Clarissa. She turned away, unable to outstare the hawk-eyed agents, who were prepared to pull automatic weapons, she had heard, on a flinch.

Baker drew a deep breath in the silent room and let it out raggedly. "I would like to begin this meeting by making three points . . . for the record." Baker was playing the role of his life. He tried to make it sound presidential. "The United States of America will either *win* this war, or it will die as a nation of fifty united states. There will be no territorial concession. No negotiation. No capitulation. No compromise. No international mediation. No cease-fires or truces . . . and no surrender." He looked up and down the long table. Nobody coughed, blinked, or looked away. "From this moment forward, we're at total war . . . until *I* say it stops." He held up his index finger. "That's point one."

Almost all of the military men nodded.

"Point two. Our victory in the defense of America will come at sea. The Chinese may have sixty million men under arms, but it's their naval power that puts them at our shores, and it's their *naval* power that *I* intend to see destroyed. Therefore, every strategic decision that we make must *first* and *foremost* further *that* objective. If it means defending the ports of Charleston and Norfolk instead of Orlando or Atlanta, then that's what we do. If it means stripping air defenses from Chicago and Detroit to ensure *total* domination of the skies over the Philadelphia and San Diego shipyards, then so be it." He held up two fingers. "That's the second point."

No one shrank from Baker's gaze. The generals and admirals nodded again.

Baker held up a third finger. "Finally, I'm telling you to-day—*before* the opening battle on the American mainland—that this war will not end once we've swept China from the Western Hemisphere. It will end only when we've broken the blockade of Europe, liberated Japan and the Middle East, and rolled Chinese forces back across South and East Asia to their borders. And to accomplish that we will continue as a national priority total commitment to our longer-term weapons development programs contained within the black budget." There were nods this time only from the few who knew the contents of the U.S. government's secret expenditures. "That's point three."

The nods that Bill got from the two-thirds in the room who wore uniforms weren't, he knew, experts' assessments of his sketchy plan's military feasibility. They were, instead, a resolute acceptance of orders on the eve of momentous battle by men who had possibly ten years of war ahead of them. But the man issuing the orders—President Baker—had only six years, at most. *Assuming* reelection, he thought, no sure bet by any stretch of the imagination. Bill would be forty-nine and spent when he left the White House . . . unless he was earlier dragged out and shot by the Chinese. That recurrent scene played out in his head in the middle of the night more and more frequently. He had no family to speak of, and for the first time he thought that was good. It was fitting that he would be the one that the office would consume. It was also fitting that the president die in a chair. At a desk. In a suit. Surrounded not by guns, but by pens and paper—the implements of democracy. That was the image Baker had of how and where the last president of the United States should be found.

He turned first—as always—to the navy. "Where do things stand in the Gulf?"

Admiral Thornton had obviously been moved by Baker's performance. He cleared his throat and gathered his thoughts, "We've had screws turning the last eight hours or so, Mr. President. Hundreds of ships are under way. All our visuals so far have been of surface combatants—cruisers, destroyers, frigates—on antisubmarine and antiaircraft patrols. But they're sortieing in number, sir. The supercarriers and large transports are sure to be right behind them. We've got a screen of twenty attack subs north of Cuba ready to interdict and report, no matter which way the main force heads. We've blocked passage through the Bahamas to the East Coast with mines, a dozen attack subs, and seven cruiser-led task forces—twenty-eight surface warships in all—so I don't think they'll try to come that way."

Baker nodded and turned to General Latham—air force chief of staff. "Are we ready?"

"We've got nine hundred fighter-attack aircraft and two dozen B-1s and -2s armed with 2,500 SLAM-124s—Stand-off Land Attack Missiles—newly fitted with antiship packages. Their targeting control network is designed to overload one perimeter of Chinese antimissile defenses and will guide all the missiles into the singlemost efficient attack profile. They'll score hits on their pickets, Mr. President, but they won't punch through to the capital ships."

Baker returned to Admiral Thornton and said, in an accusatory tone, "I thought the whole *theory* behind the arsenal ships was to overload Chinese defenses with sheer numbers! Now, I hear the air force saying 2500 missiles can't punch through!"

The CNO was on the hot seat, but he betrayed no lack of confidence in the weapon that Bill counted upon to save America. "Mr. President, if I had two arsenal ships operational in the Gulf today, they'd sink every last ship in the Chinese fleet in half an hour. They'd volley-fire 16,000 missiles. About 500 of those missiles would have electronic countermeasures suites instead of warheads to confuse Chinese interceptors. Another 1500 would pack 12,000 antimissile missiles—eight each—that would strike out in an active defense. The remaining 14,000 missiles—which are supersonic, *highly* maneuverable, and guided by artificial intelligence programs that would undertake individual *and* coordinated evasive action—would each pack 2000-pound warheads, 600–700 of which would strike enemy ships. Six minutes later, another 16,000 missiles would be fired. Then another and another, and another, and another until all that steel is on the ocean bottom."

"Wouldn't you hold some missiles back to defend the arsenal ships?" Vice President Elizabeth Sobo interjected. "And what about the Chinese submarine threat?"

"Yes, ma'am, we would hold back some air defense missiles," Thornton responded. "That was just a theoretical scenario that I gave you. But we would also operate the two arsenal ships together, at first, and always in task forces that include one or two aircraft carrier battle groups with associated task forces of attack submarines. By integrating their battle management system, we should contain Chinese air, surface, and subsea threats."

"I don't understand," Hamilton Asher said. Baker felt his blood pressure rise at the interruption by the FBI director. "If it's just a matter of massing our fire, why didn't we do it with land-based missiles? We could've prevented the Chinese from landing!"

Secretary of Defense Moore replied, "General Cotler made a proposal for a system of mobile, land-based launchers like the Brits have deployed. But given the sheer numbers of missiles we would've had to build for the land-based or the sea-based systems, it was an 'either-or' choice: either arsenal ships or mobile ground launchers, but not both."

"So why not build the land-based launchers?" Asher asked. "We could've stopped the invasion!"

Moore looked at the president, then at Asher, before replying. "The launchers don't have any offensive capabilities."

"*Of*-fensive?" Asher asked, incredulous.

Bill said, "The arsenal ships can wipe the Chinese fleet from the sea. The land-based launchers can do nothing more than stand them back from our coastline."

"I think that a large majority of the American people," Asher said, grandstanding before the NSC, "would consider *that* outcome preferable to where we are today!"

"I ordered it," Baker said firmly and conclusively. He and Asher stared at each other until Baker turned to air force General Latham. "What about our antiaircraft defenses?"

Latham seemed reluctant to get the briefing back on track.

He had been an ardent supporter of the joint Army–Air Force mobile launcher system that Bill had rejected. Baker had heard that, in private, Latham had second-guessed the commander in chief's decision. "Well, sir," Latham finally began, "when the first navy sonar reports came in, we went to Air Defense Warning 'Red' nationwide—'attack by hostile aircraft imminent.' We grounded civilian traffic east of the Mississippi and south of Atlanta. Our air defense assets were dispersed to civilian airports that are defended by at least four air superiority fighters ready to scramble. And the NORAD antimissile grid is at a 98 percent generation level. If the Chinese try to go deep, we'll attrit them to hell."

Baker nodded. Half the heads turned to the army chief of staff before the president did. "Tell me where they're coming ashore," Baker asked the chairman of the Joint Chiefs.

General Cotler hesitated momentarily. It could have been nothing . . . or something. Cotler opened his briefing book as if the task were loathsome. "From Cuba, southern Florida is the closest . . . ," he began confidently—then faltered.

Cotler was from Chicago, Baker remembered, not the South. But even so, the army general could hardly bring himself to discuss the invasion of his country.

"Excuse me, sir," Cotler apologized. He squared his shoulders and spoke in a loud voice. "The army, Mr. President, is prepared to stop any advance—*any* advance—coming up the Florida peninsula." He ended his sentence with a period, not a qualification, caveat or qualifier. The army colonels behind him stood erect: all committing to do what no army on earth had done before—stop the Chinese anywhere. "We'll run a line from Tampa/St. Pete to Melbourne. The 3rd Infantry Division (Mech.) and 40th Infantry Division—also mechanized, but Army National Guard—together with the 53rd Infantry Brigade (Separate) are bunkered south of Orlando. That'll put the Everglades on the *Chinese* side—splitting their center. Their east and west flanks will be mutually nonsupporting. If they come ashore at Miami, sir, we'll stop them there."

"What if they try an amphibious leapfrog?" asked Elizabeth Sobo. "An 'Inchon-type' landing up the coast behind you?"

"The 278th ACR in Ocala will throw them back into the sea," Cotler replied.

"You mean *try* to throw them back?" Vice President Sobo challenged. She flipped pages in her briefing book. "That armored cavalry regiment has only . . . 3700 men, and they're all reservists. If they fail to smash the landing, the Chinese could cut off the *entire* Fourth Corps—one of only *twelve* corps that we've *got*—while defending the most exposed southern tip of one state?"

It was a fair question. Baker waited for Cotler's reply.

"We'll *try* to throw them back, ma'am," he clarified slowly. Honestly.

Sobo looked at Baker. She had done her job. Baker now knew of yet another scenario for total disaster. He took a deep breath and rubbed his face again. Through his hands he said, "If we know we can stop them in Florida, then they know it too. So where *will* they come ashore?"

Cotler had an answer. "Theoretically, sir, anywhere between Key West, Florida, and Brownsville, Texas. If they don't land in southern Florida, which would be their safest and quickest option to get men off those exposed transports and onto U.S. soil, they'll try to take one of the Gulf ports: Mobile, Biloxi, maybe New Orleans, possibly Galveston. The shorter transit times from Cuba make the ports *east* of the Mississippi, however, far more likely." An unseen technician changed the maps on the flat screens covering all four walls. An overlay depicting probabilities—like that for a hurricane's landfall—coated the Gulf Coast in bands of color. Low-risk yellow marked the beaches of Texas and Louisiana far to the west of Havana. Bloodred storm warnings bathed the Gulf sands of Mississippi, Alabama, and Florida. Nowhere was the red deeper in color—the invasion higher in probability—than in and around Mobile Bay. "Over a beach," Cotler explained, "they could put about fifty thousand men ashore every twenty-four hours. But a single functioning port could triple that. If they stay east of the Mississippi and grab a port, they could disembark five million troops in a month."

Secretary of Defense Robert Moore said, "Mobile is the most likely landing site. It's centrally located, has good anchorage, and lies at the southern tip of an extensive road/rail/canal net inland. Regardless of where they land, however, Mr. President, wargaming indicates that they should head toward the higher value objectives up the Eastern Seaboard. If they do that, we'll man a line along Interstate 16 from the Atlantic at Savannah inland to Atlanta, and along I-20 west from Atlanta through Birmingham and Jackson and on to the Mississippi River at Vicksburg. Actually, the line will follow the best defensive terrain a few miles south of the highways, which we can then use for quick lateral reactions and for supply. Anyway, when we drop the bridges across the Mississippi to the south of that line, the Chinese will be pocketed. The 218th Mechanized Infantry Brigade (Separate) will hold I-95 open up to Savannah from Florida to IV Corps's rear to prevent the Fourth from being cut off."

"We could still mine Mobile Bay," air force General Latham suggested. "I could do an airdrop with five or six hours' lead time."

Baker was shaking his head even before the general had finished. "Admiral Thornton said the Chinese could sweep the port and have it operational in days."

"We could destroy the docks," Latham persisted.

"Then they won't be able to land their army!" Baker snapped. He leaned back in his chair, cupped his hands over his head, and tried surreptitiously—as everyone watched—to massage the tension from the bundle of nerves under his scalp. His spine felt as tight as piano wire. His hands were freezing.

They had war gamed Baker's plan for six months, and the good guys had won more often than they had lost. Those war games had given everyone a feel for the theater: the limitations and broad contours of the battle to come as dictated by immutable factors such as distance, terrain and road network. But no one ever looked back at wargames after the battle had begun . . . except boards of inquiry, like after the debacle in the Straits of Havana. That operation had been wargamed too. Fight your way in with three carrier battle groups. Punch the 2nd Marines into the Chinese flank. Load up everybody at Guantanamo Bay under heavy air and naval artillery support, and sail home to bands and flag-waving crowds. Baker had met with the haunted former CNO after the board of inquiry had finished with him. The admiral had handed Baker his resignation, gone home, and shot himself in the head with his family in the next room. Baker wondered if he would ever see that look on a man's face again? A powerful, confident man hollowed out by self-blame.

"Okay," Baker said calmly, "what's our plan for winning this thing once the Chinese are fully committed?"

Cotler stood and straightened his green jacket. Rows of ribbons adorned his chest. Every soldier in Washington below the rank of colonel wore combat boots and battle dress. *Will the day come,* Baker wondered, *when even senior officers switch to camouflage?*

Three large pockets of green appeared on the map in Tennessee: secret staging areas for the Second, Third, and Fifth Corps. Baker had toured the depots the month before. Tremendous quantities of war stocks were piled high under camouflage netting that ran sometimes half a mile in length.

"Once the Chinese land six army groups," Cotler said, "about two million combat troops and a million service and support personnel, we'll counterattack with three armored corps straight at their port." On the map, three arrows stabbed at the Gulf like daggers. If the counterattack failed to stagger the Chinese—to "rock them back on their heels," as Cotler had once put it—the most promising hope that had been expressed to Baker was, "Maybe they'll get overextended." That hope had been shared by every country from Vietnam to Turkey before the last resistence had collapsed. Baker took a deep breath, forcing his chest to break the invisible bands that now seemed to bind it tightly.

"And in four months," Secretary Moore added in an optimistic tone—meant for Baker—"we've got three arsenal ships, and we go back to work at sea."

If we last that long, Baker thought as the briefing continued. Cold sweat beaded on his forehead in the chilly room. He fought the panic that threatened his composure, and his mind again wandered. *How did it ever* come *to this?* he raged . . . in silence and in vain.

•   •   •

"Excuse me, Mr. President," a paranoid aide said before closing Bill's black JCS briefing book. The glossy hardcovers
with vivid maps and photos were prepared for each NSC
meeting with only hours-old intelligence. It was information
warfare at Internet speeds. It multiplied the force of America's
manpower, but unfortunately not by enough. Bill noticed that
the wall-mounted screens now all glowed solid blue. Bill
clenched his jaw in anger when he saw that Hamilton Asher
was surrounded by a small cadre of military men. The director
of the FBI was not formally a member of the National Security Council, and Bill had no desire to hear his opinions.
The door opened, and as a civilian was led in, Bill turned to
his chief of staff, who immediately duckwalked to Bill's side
from his seat along the wall.

"Asher wasn't invited to this meeting," the keen-eyed
Frank Adams supplied his boss without even being prompted.
"He fuckin' thinks he's some kinda guardian of democracy
now that Tom Leffler's National Secrecy Act gives him carte
blanche police power."

Baker's secretary of state—Arthur Dodd—rose from his
place at the table and said, "I'd like to introduce the new head
of our China Desk, Dr. Clarissa Leffler."

Bill was shocked. He turned to see Tom Leffler's daughter
taking a seat at the table, nodding in acknowledgment of
greetings. Bill caught himself almost rising from his chair, an
aborted act of manners that drew several glances. Bill knew
Clarissa only socially, mainly from a distance. His chief of
staff squatted at his side. "I just found out about this," Adams
said, reflexively defensive. "But there's no way her getting
the China Desk is a coincidence. My bet is Dodd's tryin' to
take some of the heat off himself the next time he gets hauled
up to the Hill for testimony before Leffler's committee by
hiring the son of a bitch's daughter. The conservatives have
been on his ass ever since he paid that social call on the
Chinese minister of trade two years ago in Geneva." Bill
waved his chief of staff away like he was a waiter trying to
pour an unwanted cup of coffee.

Art Dodd was reviewing Clarissa's background, and Bill

listened with interest. From her credentials, it was clear that old Tom Leffler had a respect for the education that he never got growing up in rural Georgia. *But his daughter probably never even lived in Georgia,* Bill thought. *She only campaigned with him there.* Leffler had been in Congress for over forty years. Clarissa had been raised in DC by her mother. Bill knew little about the daughter, but he had known her mother well. Beth Leffler was the most gracious person he had ever met. She had lived life without a trace of guile or unkindness, which was unheard of in Washington society. Bill had cried when she had died just before his inauguration, and it was sad how her death had devastated old Tom.

Tom Leffler had long anchored the Republican party's right wing, which had swollen with popular support. The vast majority had turned hawkish years before the Chinese War as if they had sensed the predator's approach. The fiery Speaker of the House had ridden the conservative crest. Although both Bill and Tom were pro-defense Republicans, they had a history of political clashes. The most dramatic confrontation had been over the National Secrecy Act, which had been authored by the speaker but vetoed by Bill. It was a gross infringement on the right to privacy and violated the principle of the separation of powers among the three branches of federal government. But the opinion polls had backed Leffler, and Congress had overridden Bill's veto when conservative Republicans had outvoted the moderates in both parties.

Over the years, Bill had seen Clarissa from a distance at fund-raisers and once in a receiving line. At the latter function, Bill greeted an endless stream of dignitaries but had noticed Clarissa's approach from some distance. He had noticed, actually, her bare, slim shoulders, but as she drew nearer he realized that her voice rose and fell and glided in the distinctive patterns of fluent Chinese. She had been having a polite conversation with the ambassador from Beijing. Unfortunately, Bill hadn't stayed long enough to greet her. By prearrangement he was called away to be seated for dinner, snubbing the ambassador, who was next in line. After Bill took a parting glance back over his shoulder, the ever watchful Frank Adams had said, "Did you see his fucking face?"

Bill laughed, but in truth he had seen only Clarissa, who looked beautiful in the strapless velvet gown.

"Dr. Leffler has a doctorate in political science from Harvard," Secretary Dodd reported to the NSC. "She studied for years in Beijing and published several very interesting articles on Chinese politics that I sent to you, Mr. President." Bill nodded behind folded, church-spire hands, but he had no idea what articles Art was talking about. Only once before had he seen Clarissa with those academic-looking eyeglasses that she now wore. It was at her mother's funeral. He remembered because it was so rare to see people wearing glasses these days and because when he hugged her he had accidentally knocked her glasses askew.

When Secretary Dodd closed Clarissa's folder, everyone looked not at Clarissa, but at the President of the United States. Bill considered speaking words of welcome but took his cue from Clarissa, who stared back from behind an expressionless mask. She's probably fighting the battle of all children of important parents, Bill thought, and trying for a purely professional demeanor. He simply nodded for Clarissa to proceed.

"Good evening, Mr. President," she began. "The entire focus of my Desk, as I see it, is to monitor the single most important force at work in Chinese politics today: the worsening power struggle between the military and the civilians." She drily recited several reports received by chance. All indications from Beijing were of mounting tensions. Six months earlier, the civilian prime minister had publicly warned the war-weary Chinese of the "grave risks of military adventurism." All had interpreted that phrase to be a coded warning—for domestic political consumption—that nuclear war was a significant risk if the Chinese army invaded America. The civilians are now waiting in the wings, Clarissa explained, with an "I-told-you-so" should the American Campaign go poorly for the Chinese. "There is a chance," Clarissa said hopefully, "that we can take advantage of the political instability in Beijing."

She now had Bill's complete attention. He opened his mouth to ask, "How?"

"Is there any sign of friction in our hemisphere?" the chairman of the Joint Chiefs asked first.

"Not yet," Clarissa replied, "but Han Zhemin arrives in Cuba today, which could herald the start of the struggle." She cast Bill a look of hidden significance.

Most furtively looked at the president, who stared at Clarissa. "Are you suggesting that I meet with Han?" Bill asked Clarissa. Art Dodd rushed to "clarify" his subordinates' misunderstood position. "*No,*" Bill snapped, "it's a legitimate question! All of you have read *Time* and *Newsweek*. Han Zhemin is a spoiled-rotten son of a *bitch*," Bill said more loudly than he had meant, "but he was my roommate at Princeton and an acquaintance at graduate school and is, therefore, a legitimate personal contact that we might consider exploiting."

Bill turned back to Clarissa. "Would *you* meet with Han? Negotiate our way into an alliance of sorts with the Chinese civilians as a means of undercutting the Chinese military?" Complete silence descended upon the room. Like a judge in a court, a president who was comfortable with his power could ask anyone anything. "Would you give away southern Florida to strengthen the civilians' hand in the power struggle against the military? Or . . . or agree to some oppressive trade terms so that they can tout their prowess at diplomatic coercian? Or maybe disarm by treaty and live at the mercy of China's benevolence *forever*," Bill said, slamming his fist down and looking around the table, "if it would save eighty million Americans from incineration in nuclear war?"

Bill's gaze sank to the table. He had spoken aloud the questions he had imagined putting to Clarissa's father in a debate they would never have. He let Clarissa off the hook and took the step he knew he would have to take. He ordered the secretary of state to set up a meeting with Han Zhemin. Many were clearly stunned by his decision, but no one said a word. The president wagged his finger at everyone present and raised his voice. "I want this meeting kept so quiet that it never even happened!" He looked around the room, even at those who manned the walls. "I would consider it disloyalty to me personally—in the *extreme*—if anyone breathes a word of my planned meeting with Han outside this room."

Without intending it, his gaze ended on Clarissa, and he turned away. She looked far more attractive than he recalled.

THE STATE DEPARTMENT, WASHINGTON
September 14 // 2200 Local Time

Clarissa's people all worked late. She didn't tell them to, they just did. All were JFK School of Government types, who generated huge quantities of electronic paper through which Clarissa had to wade. But in the process of discarding their memos and notes, she absorbed countless details and opinions. That had always been her knack. She wasn't more educated than anyone else, necessarily, but she had the ability to synthesize patterns from information. Looking back over the last few years, Clarissa felt that she could've made decisions that would've changed the entire *course* of history for the better if only she had been in a position of power!

Support the Indians full-tilt. American air and seapower and Indian manpower. Stop China at the Himalayas. As it was, China seized India with fewer than a half million casualties. Spread across a 1.5–billion-person population, the Chinese families' grief was swamped by the outpouring of national pride.

But even after India, President Peller could've stopped the Chinese in the Indian Ocean. *Before* they seized the Persian Gulf and Caspian Sea! They wouldn't have had the fuel to power their non-nuclear fleets if Peller had only entered the fray! Clarissa's father had told her an incredible story that was absolutely Top Secret, although whispers had long hinted at something. In the Battle of Diego Garcia four years earlier, the war-winning *third* Chinese fleet on its way to the rout of Europe's navies had passed straight over American fourteen attack submarines, which lay in perfect ambush position. Peller had issued *iron*clad orders to the navy not to risk any confrontation with the Chinese. As a result, the American submarine commander had remained submerged, deep and quiet. Thirty minutes later, the skies above the European fleet had been black with Chinese warplanes.

Clarissa banged the keyboard suspended above her knees

with her fist as she reclined in her chair. *If only Peller had ordered those submarines to radio a warning and then attack!* Clarissa raged. The man was a gutless fool!

Her flat screen *binged*. The computer thought she ought to look at three more memos before going home. A red "Paging" icon also appeared in the upper right-hand corner. She did nothing as the computer defaulted to "Answer." A picture of a gold key indicated the video call was from a secure outside line.

A full-screen picture of her confused father appeared. "It *beeped!*" he yelled out to his secretary as he tapped to no effect on his keyboard.

"It's *me*, Dad!" Clarissa said. She closed her office door in the faces of two curious passersby.

"That's all right!" Tom Leffler shouted. "It's Clarissa!" He looked so old as he peered straight into the camera. He could never find a mouse, but could always find a lens. "Thank *God* it's you, Clarissa. I called you earlier."

"I *know*, Dad. I was replying." He was baffled. Clarissa more chastised than explained. "When you sat down at your desk, *your* intelligent agent told *mine*, and they jointly decided that this would be a good time for us to talk! I've explained the system to you before!"

"Does this have anything to do with that new key chain I have to carry?"

"You don't have any keys anymore, do you Dad? It's called a *'remote,'* Dad! It's an intelligent agent. It's what unlocks your *car*. Takes care of your charges at restaurants, assuming you ever pay."

"This is not what I called to talk to you about, Clarissa. But let me get *my* intelligent agent. Ms. *Stewart*! Could you close my door?" When it was done, he leaned toward the lens for a close-up. His face spread wide in the fish-eye lens. "Is your office secure?" She told him that it was swept every day. "I ask because," Tom Leffler whispered, "they bugged my house."

"Who?" Clarissa replied.

Her father shook his head and shrugged. "I don't know.

Capitol Hill Police found these little things all over the place! High-tech, state-of-the-art stuff, they said. They said they'd never seen anything so sophisticated."

Clarissa sat back and cupped her hands behind her head. *The FBI,* she thought. *Baker's fucking K-G-B!* The president was abusing the very National Secrecy Act that he had assailed as a violation of rights to privacy, that hypocritical *bastard*! Baker and Hamilton Asher were warping a good law written by her father—the single most decent man in Washington and Bill Baker's former political guardian angel—and using it against him! She was incensed.

"I have to tell you something," Clarissa said. "Baker is meeting with Han Zhemin!"

"I guess he knows what he's doing," Tom Leffler muttered.

Clarissa rolled her eyes and huffed theatrically. "You don't *get* it! It's *treason*!" She decided to embellish the story a bit. "At the NSC meeting, he talked about, Jesus, outrageous things. Like ceding southern Florida to China! It was unbelievable!"

Instead of focusing, her father drifted off, which he now did more and more frequently. He hissed not in anger, but with lips moving in some half-spoken interior monologue. His jowels shook, and he blinked as if he had lost his train of thought. Clarissa almost cringed as he began to mumble— mouthing something just under his breath. "Are you saying something, Dad?"

"What? No. Nothing."

"Because it looked like you said something like, 'Now is the time for all good men to . . .'"

"Sh-h-h-h!" he erupted, leaning right up to the lens until his eyes and the bridge of his nose filled Clarissa's screen. "Where did you *hear* that?"

She laughed at the absurdity of his behavior. "From *you*, Dad! You *just . . .* !" She stopped herself. *Now is the time for all good men to come to the aid of their party,* she thought. It was a patriotic call to arms. A motto, at the least, or perhaps even a coda before the launching of some daring undertaking. It was brilliant! She felt goose bumps.

"Don't ever say those words again," Tom warned sternly.

"Where did that come from?" she asked.

"Sh-h-h-h-h-h!"

"Jeeze, don't strain yourself, Dad! I meant, was that some great line or phrase from a famous patriot or something?"

Her father was now slumped and holding his face with spotted hands. "It was a typing exercise," he answered. "Something to type when you learned keyboard skills as practice."

"Oh," Clarissa said, slightly deflated. "But still." The feeling of inspiration lingered. "Listen, Dad, I can help. I *want* to help. With the, you know." Before he could *shush* her, she said, "I'm an adult now, Dad. I'm in a position to help."

Tom refocused and shook his head. "Too dangerous, Clarissa. Don't do anything till we talk. I'll be in touch." He searched for a mouse or button then remembered and said, "Computer, hang up now."

Clarissa huffed in frustration when the screen abruptly went blank.

HAVANA, CUBA
September 15 // 0830 Local Time

Forty-two-year-old Han Zhemin deplaned to a blaring military band on the steaming tarmac of Havana's airport. A military band played strident martial music. Han wore a dark wool business suit despite the unbearable heat. Pausing at the top of the stairs, he saw no platform or podium awaiting him. There were throngs of press but no General Sheng, the army commander.

Waiting instead, to Han's great surprise, was Han's son. The eighteen-year-old Lieutenant Wu—fresh out of military school—saluted his father crisply. Han put an end to the military greeting by shaking Wu's hand. "Why are you here?" Han shouted over the noise from the army band.

"I just arrived! I'm on General Sheng's staff! General Sheng sends his apologies, sir!"

"Who said you could come to Cuba?" Han asked. "I want the name of the person who authorized your deployment."

"It was Defense Minister General Liu Changxing, sir!" Wu replied somewhat sheepishly.

The answer rocked Han. Its implications were numerous. "I see," was all he said. Han turned and walked through a gauntlet of bright television-camera lights. Wu followed. A colonel marched by Han's side with his sword unsheathed but never said a word to Han or seemed authorized even to make eye contact. The band was intensely loud, and Han winced and rushed for the terminal, pausing only for the requisite minimum number of poses. Wu, in particular, was the photographers' favorite because of his half-Caucasian, foreign mix of features. The cameras lingered on the boy, and Han waited.

It was his son's debut. His first exposure to the voracious international press corps. *File photos,* Han thought with amusement, watching the blinking, uncomfortable boy. But he replaced the smile creeping onto his face with the more appropriate look of gravity. Despite almost twenty hours advance notice of Han's flight from Caracas, Sheng hadn't met him at the airport. It was an intentional insult, and Han had to be furious. That was the only correct response.

Han strode briskly to the terminal building. Wu again followed. The moment the doors closed, Han asked his son, "What is your deal with Liu?"

Wu looked all around to ensure they were alone. *Good,* Han thought. He is careful. "I asked General Liu if I could serve at the front like all my classmates. *Every*body's here! Tsui has command of a platoon!"

"I don't know who Tsui is, and I don't care," Han replied icily.

"He was my roommate at school," a deflated Wu explained, "for the past six years."

"When did you meet with Liu?" Han demanded to know.

"It was at my graduation," Wu answered. "General Liu said that I could serve on General Sheng's staff."

Han had also talked to Liu at his son's military academy graduation. For thirty tense minutes in the school's plush senior officers' lounge, they had agreed upon the ground rules for the coming American campaign and the governance of occupied territory. "No surprises," had been Liu's personal pledge to Han. It had been the only commitment that Han had been charged with obtaining from the man who commanded all of China's armed forces.

"Where is Sheng?" Han asked his son.

"General Sheng is at the port, sir."

"Then let's go see him."

"Right now?" Wu questioned. "He's probably very busy, sir."

Han was weary from the whirlwind diplomatic mission that he had just completed. Ten Latin American capitals in seven days. Ten small countries jockeying for position via the fine nuances of agreements made with China in Spanish and Portugese. It was exhausting, vital work.

"Do you know why I'm here, Wu?" Han asked simply and in a conversational tone. Wu shook his head. Two Chinese film crews shot the scene from a distance of thirty feet. One crew wore civilian clothes and had longish hair. The other— standing side by side with them—wore combat fatigues and had no hair at all. Han raised his voice loud enough to be overheard by both. "I have been appointed the Administrator of Occupied American Territory! I have full 'gubinatorial authority'!" he said, using the two words in English employed in Beijing to define the very highest level of colonial administrative power. "General Sheng and all units of the Chinese military in the Americas report to me!"

Wu stared at his father in silence before finally turning to the stoic colonel with the chin strap, who had sheathed his sword but stared straight ahead, as before. "Organize a motorcade," the teenage lieutenant commanded the middle-aged colonel, who immediately set off to comply.

Han and Wu rode in silence in Han's limousine until Han, looking out the window, said, "Desolate country. It's not Bali."

"I've never been to Bali," Wu commented in a soft voice.

"You've never been anywhere outside of China!" Han

chastised. What he was really saying, both understood, was, "What have you gotten yourself into?" With the rebuke delivered, Han smiled and said, "You will go to Bali when you get back. I will send a girl with you. It's the only way to see Bali, Wu. With a beautiful girl. Trust me."

Wu looked out the window at fields full of American POWs digging trench lines around missile batteries. The men were shirtless, dark, and dirty, and they were bent by the labors. Stooped. Defeated. The realization strangely made Wu's heart no lighter. "The fighting here was bad," Wu said as he looked out into the thick vegetation. "I spoke to Tsui. He fought here." Wu turned to stare at his father, who stared back with arched brow. After a moment, Wu sighed and returned to the window. His breath fogged the glass. "Tsui said that the Americans could be three feet away in the cane fields and you couldn't see them. Sometimes, Tsui said, you smelled them first."

"Poor bastards," Han commented.

"Which?" Wu asked. "The Americans or the Chinese?"

"Both," Han replied. His gaze remained fixed on his son, who returned the hard stare without flinching. "You will never be in combat, Wu," Han said in a tone more informational than sympathetic. "Learn to deal with it. It has been agreed at the highest levels. It is not your best use."

Wu turned away, and they fell quiet for a long time, with Wu occasionally glancing at his father. Wu was Han's only child from a casual affair. Initially, the boy had been unacknowledged and had been given the common name "Wu." On orders from their family, Han had just attended the military school graduation of the boy, whom he hadn't seen for years before that. Han had informed the cadet that he would, henceforth, assume the Han family name, also on orders of their family. Thus had his son officially become "Han Wushi," although everyone still used his old surname "Wu."

Wu was half-Caucasian, half-Chinese, and he'd boarded at Beijing military schools from ages four to eighteen. As happened with the top graduates at their nation's elite military prep schools, Wu had opted to receive his commission at age

eighteen. Han thought that the boy had appeared proud to
have graduated commander of each military school's corps of
cadets as if it had been his accomplishment, and his alone.
He hadn't yet realized that it was all about power. Their family's power, to be exact. For Han's uncle—Wu's great-
uncle—was prime minister of China.

"You issued orders well back at the airport," Han commended his son.

"I'm an officer now, not a cadet," Wu grumbled.

Han laughed. Wu seemed surprised by his father's open
display of amusement. "But you're a *lieutenant*," Han said,
"and you issued an order to a colonel! Why is that? Would
your friend Lieutenant Tsui command such deference?" When
Wu pondered the question, Han laughed and looked back out
the window. Han could feel Wu watching him closely. It was
rare extended time with his father. *Let him watch,* Han
thought. *Let him learn.*

Out of the blue, Wu asked, "Why did the family switch
from publicly *warning* of nuclear war with America, to privately supporting the invasion of the mainland?"

Han was stunned. He held up a hand to quiet the boy and
pulled out his sweeper to check for bugs. The sophisticated
new Chinese army devices had been miniaturized to near microscopic. Wu watched Han wave the device around the limousine . . . and directly over Wu's army tunic. When father's
and son's eyes met, the father returned the sweeper to his
pocket and answered his son's question. "America's human
capital is the most productive in the world, Wu. I have been
sent there to harness it."

"Is that why the prime minister . . . ?"

"You *shouldn't* worry about politics," Han interrupted.
"You shouldn't worry about *anything* because everybody
knows exactly who you are. The family gives you a shield
and a sword, and you fight for the family's grasp on power.
Whether we *lose* that grasp, Wu, depends on what I do in
America over the next precious few months."

Neither said another word on the drive. *"Liu Changxing,
what are you up to?"* Han thought in English to better frame

the question, trying to discern the plot being hatched by the defense minister.

The ocean appeared out of the car windows. Han looked wistfully across the blue water as the motorcade took the coast road. He had fond memories of his college and graduate school years in America. Wu, Han noticed, also stared across the sea. This was the homeland of the mother he had never known.

General Sheng walked along the docks watching troops board transports as Han's motorcade arrived in the distance. He was worried about the American Campaign far more than any before it. Sullen troops filed up gangplanks showing none of the enthusiasm of earlier armies who had boarded assault ships bound for Japan, India, or Saudi Arabia. Sheng nervously eyed the sky overhead. While at anchor, the invasion fleet was dangerously exposed. Their antimissile defenses—like the Americans'—could stop almost all inbound airborne threats. But if the one that got through was tipped with a nuclear warhead, the damage would be immense.

Sheng's aide-de-camp, Colonel Li, arrived at his side. "I have part of the information you requested, sir," he reported. "It's called 'Operation Olympic'." Sheng nodded. "I'll inform Defense Minister Liu," Li said.

"No," Sheng ordered. "There are too many leaks in Beijing. Too many uncertain loyalties."

Han Zhemin and Wu got out of Han's limousine and walked down a dirt road to the docks. Han organized his thoughts in silence before the opening moves in the key political battle of the twenty-first century. Han felt rested from the car trip and up to the fight. He'd been groomed for it, in fact, his entire, privileged life.

As a young boy, Han hadn't appreciated the immensity of his family's fortune. He had lived a cloistered existence in palatial Hong Kong with an English tutor, an English nanny, a house full of servants, and a nurse, who was in charge of Han's household.

But a lot had changed when Hong Kong had been handed

back to mainland China. In the uncertain times, Han was sent to Princeton and then Harvard. "Do whatever you want in America," his father had said, "but study political science carefully." He had then told Han that his family's plan for him was not to follow his father into business. It was to follow his uncle, instead, into politics, where the true fortunes were to be made in the next century.

Han's father had turned hundreds of millions of dollars in wealth earned through trading goods in East Asia into trillions of yuan in investments in Communist China. But Han's *uncle* had been appointed the governor of Hong Kong by the aging Communists in Beijing. The city had unexpectedly flourished. That success had catapulted Han's uncle to Beijing during Han's graduate school years, spent at Harvard.

Those years of Han's life had been his most carefree. Never having gone to school of any kind, he had immersed himself in local culture and had met many beautiful women, including Wu's mother, at parties. But marriage to an American could never be. Han had been led to expect that a superb match would be made very soon by his family back in Beijing.

Colonel Li introduced himself and led them the last stretch of the way to the commanding general, Han's extremely dangerous and principal foe. The civilian government led by his uncle had everything at stake in Han's coming conflict in America. Publicly, they had opposed the invasion out of fear that it might trigger a nuclear war. Privately, they had argued that the U.S. was "a country too far." Behind closed doors and in back rooms, Han had insisted that America was too large of a conquest even for China. At cocktail parties, private dinners, during rounds of golf or between sets of tennis Han and other civilian emissaries had warned of a quagmire draining blood and resources. But the real reason that the family opposed invasion was out of fear that it would succeed.

After the spectacular string of military victories, Defense Minister Liu was riding high in the opinion polls that mattered among millions of faceless Chinese bureaucrats, who had been handed new territories to govern, new economies to exploit, new opportunities for the greater profit of all. If it weren't for those bureaucrats' fears of unchecked military rule, the uniformed conquerors would long ago have been handed the reins.

The yin to the military yang was the civilian leadership. The new, non-Communist, non-anything mandarins in government and business wanted a stable system of checks and balances, but stability was not to be. Defeating America would so raise the esteem in which China's "electorate" held the military that the civilian government would literally be handed their heads. America would be the climactic battleground of both the international military and domestic political struggles.

Han and General Sheng walked along the dock side by side. Han looked out of place on the busy wharfs in his dark business suit.

"I've gotten agreements," Han reported, "to supply your army with petroleum, oil, and lubricants from Venezuela and Mexico. Beef from Argentina. *Et cetera, et cetera.* We've done our part. You must do yours. Ruling America will not be like ruling India."

Sheng's garrison hat came up only to Han's padded shoulder, but Sheng's slight stature didn't diminish his commanding presence. Soldiers and sailors stiffened to attention as the seventy-year-old general passed their ships. Sheng was commander of Eleventh Army Group (North), which was now the most powerful army on earth.

"I understand," General Sheng responded—choosing his words with care—"that your special *sensitivities* to America were why you were chosen to be governor."

" 'Administrator,' " Han corrected.

"I merely meant . . . ," Sheng said pleasantly.

"I studied in America," Han interrupted.

The two stopped and faced each other. Vessels were everywhere being filled with palettes of supplies. Han had met Sheng only once before, when Sheng had commanded the army that took Tel Aviv. The army in the line of march ahead of his had been decimated by twenty-three tactical nuclear warheads. Sheng had been given the honor of retaliating on express instructions of Defense Minister Liu. The genocide in

Tel Aviv was on Sheng's and Liu's hands. Han had been sent from Beijing to Israel after the genocide.

"I merely meant," Sheng continued, "that it makes sense for an *expert* on America to *govern* America." Han smiled, and they continued walking in silence. Transports and supply ships were moored all across the harbor.

Through the gaps, Han could see blue water. "General Sheng," Han said, "you have been briefed about China's broader goals in this war. Imagine incorporating the intellectual capital of America into our sphere of economic cooperation. You *must* educate your officers and men about this paramount objective. I view it to be your prime task. I cannot win Americans' hearts and minds if our troops commit crimes. There absolutely *cannot* be a repeat of the problems we had in Israel."

"I have received my orders from Beijing," General Sheng said. "But, for the record, I did have valid authority to release those special munitions."

"They were for engineers to demolish dams and dig canals," Han replied to the overt verbal check. He was alert to danger. He picked up sounds from the dock. Smells carried on the ocean breeze. It had been the same in Tel Aviv. Han was the civilian sent to take command of Sheng's nuclear weapons. He had first viewed the blackened remains of Tel Aviv on a flyover to steel himself for the task.

"It must have been very difficult for you," Sheng said— looking up at the sun—"the executions, I mean. Thirty-seven officers. My entire staff."

"It wasn't difficult in the least," Han replied. "They were guilty of their crimes." *And so were you*, Han thought, *but you were too senior.* Sheng now held the most sought-after command in the army. If anything, Tel Aviv had given Sheng's military career a boost.

Sheng was smiling faintly when they stopped at the end of the wharf. "But still," the general said, "a *pistol*? Thirty-*seven* pistol shots to the head. You had to get so close to such an ugly task, Administrator Han. You really should have used a rifle."

Han nodded as if in appreciation of the advice. "Next time," Han replied, "I will."

BIRMINGHAM, ALABAMA
September 15 // 1630 Local Time

A thick white cloud—not a gray rain cloud, Stephie thought with relief—floated past, covering and uncovering the sun. The brief respite from the heat ended with the return of the intense rays. Stephie's trousers, bra, and T-shirt were soaked with sweat. The only thing that prevented perspiration from dripping off her was the dust and dirt that stuck to her skin and absorbed the moisture, forming a gritty crust on her arms, neck, and face.

She was putting the finishing touches on her fighting hole's roof: a third layer of sandbags piled atop rough-hewn timber. A few soldiers had used chain saws to clear young pines from their killing zone. Most had taken turns holding sandbags open and shoveling dirt into them. There was very little chatter among the traumatized teenagers after the mauling they had taken on the coast.

Stephie was late in getting started on her hole. She had thrown a fit when she and Becky Marsh had been assigned to guard the communications gear. The male commo specialist had been put to work chaining logs onto the backs of tractors. Becky had tried on the ultralight, electronics-laden helmet. "Look at this video," she had said, watching four screens that extended on slender wands from the ceramic helmet. "Hey, and there's, like, *air*-conditioning in this helmet! It's *heaven*!" She had crossed her arms over her chest. Her eyes had flitted from screen to screen. She had pulled one wand up to her eye for a closer look. "Here's a picture of somebody walkin' point. There are leaves slappin' against his helmet."

"You *know* they put us here so we won't have to fight!" Stephie had boiled over. "We're not digging, Becky! Night's gonna fall, and we won't have a fighting hole! Without a hole, we'd get sent to the rear."

"And?" Becky had shouted with arched eyebrows, incredulous. "What the hell is your problem with that? Hey, you

wanta fight, you go, girl!" Her eye had returned to the screen. "Looks like they're checkin' out a McDonalds. Or a Burger King. It's a Burger King."

Stephie had struck out to find Ackerman and pull rank on him. " 'No special treatment,' " she reminded her platoon leader, repeating the brigade commander's orders. Lieutenant Ackerman had relented. Stephie had gotten a fighting hole to dig. Becky had gotten a job as platoon commo.

The only collateral benefit to that last assignment had been the commo gear's E-mail capability. During a rest break, Stephie had taken the helmet and vest full of electronics and sat at the base of a broad tree for privacy. She had sent a cheery video mail to her mother and stepdad. She had then sent another to the army post office addresses of Conner Reilly, Sally Hampton, and Gloria Wilson. As an afterthought, almost, she had recorded one to her real father, and sent it to "www.whitehouse.gov."

Stephie's back ached as she heaved another sandbag onto the roof. Animal returned with an armful of leafy branches bowed under the weight of his machine gun and a belt of ammo. They carried their personal weapons at all times.

"Here!" he said as he dumped the branches and his weapon and ammo beside Stephie's roof as if finished for the day.

"You're not done!" Stephie snapped.

He was breathing heavily. His face was beet red. "Yeah, I am."

Stephie rubbed her back and said, "You're taking a break from gathering goddamn *camouflage*?"

He swayed like a tree in the wind. "Simm's sent me half-f-fuckin' mile away so w-wouldn't strip foliage here!"

"Hey, man. Sit down!" Stephie said. "You might have heat exhaustion."

"Fuck you," Animal said, but he sat next to Stephie's hole. He nodded at her roofed fighting hole. "Your little fort ain't gonna do shit. One hit, and it's DNA testing to identify you, Roberts."

"Yeah, well . . . I'll live longer than you will. At least this would stop a mortar."

Stephie's head ached just as much as her back. She had

never been able to sleep on hard ground. She was sweaty and
eaten up by mosquitos and bugs. She had cuts, bruises, and
blisters. It had rained on them the night before, and she was
getting a rash from going too long in damp, dirty clothes. She
spread Animal's green branches over the bare dirt that threatened to betray their position, then crawled down into her dark
fighting hole. The air was stale. No breeze penetrated the
single entrance, which was barely large enough to squeeze
through. You had to stick your face to the firing slit to draw
a fresh breath. Stephie wondered how stifling it would be to
sleep there at night. She wondered what it would be like when
smoke from her M-16 fouled the still, dank air.

Someone squeezed in beside Stephie, trampling her.
"Sorry!" John Burns apologized. They were jammed alone together. "There's a big shake-up with Becky getting commo,"
John explained. "Sanders has gone to Second Squad. I've been
transferred to your fire team."

"They're splitting teams up *now*?" she asked. "Why would
they bust up Fire Team Alpha? Becky's in *Bravo*! We've
trained together for, like, a *month*!" John just shrugged.

It was just like the shrug when he'd been asked why he
was a PFC. John Burns had joined their platoon late—after
the unit was already formed. He was older than most of the
teenagers who filled out the ranks. There had also always been
a certain aloofness about him except where Stephie was concerned. Stephie's First Squad had been full so he had gone to
Second. But now, he lay next to her like the blind wheel of
fate had just happened to land him there. She snorted. He had
gravitated toward her from day one. He must be as happy as
a clam now. *He really thinks he can get laid,* Stephie marveled, *playing this strong, silent, protector-type.*

"You know," Stephie said, "this is really a one-person
hole."

"I didn't get a chance to dig one," John replied. Stephie
smirked. He ignored the unspoken skepticism and said, "Oh,
you and I are s'posed to go on a chow run."

"Oh-h, *shit*!" Stephie groaned. "I'm dead tired." She looked
out through the slit. It was growing dark.

"I'll go by myself," he began, but she cut him off with a shake of her head.

When they climbed out, Animal sat outside grinning at them. He stuck his tongue out far enough to touch his nose. "U-o-oh, *Jesus!*" Stephie moaned in disgust both at the John situation and at Animal's mischaracterization of it.

They emptied their field packs and trudged up and over the hill. They walked down a short, newly bulldozed road. "How old are you?" Stephie asked.

"Twenty-three," he replied.

"You seem older," Stephie commented. "Did ya go to college?" He nodded. "Then why aren't you an officer? I mean ROTC was mandatory, right? There's nothing medically wrong with you, or you wouldn't even be a PFC!" John smiled but didn't answer. *Okay,* she thought all of a sudden, *I know who you are.*

At every mailbox on the road to the grocery store flew a small American flag. As was the custom, Stephie and John saluted each one they passed. The occasional car and truck that roared by honked their horns at the two soldiers. Kids protruding from windows cheered. They came to the store, which was crowded with civilian shoppers. An old security guard waved them around the metal detector. People had grown used to soldiers in uniform with weapons. Stephie's rifle and John's squad automatic weapon took up most of the cart, so they slung them over their shoulders, and down the aisles they rolled.

"Say, John," Stephie said, "whadda ya think the kids want for dinner? Maybe some broccoli? Spinach?"

John laughed. "How about hot dogs and beer?" He began heaping packages of wieners into the basket.

"Shouldn't it be more *nutritious*?" she questioned.

"They'd kick my ass!" John replied, cursing for the first time Stephie could remember.

"What about *my* ass?" she asked.

"That they wouldn't kick."

Stephie laughed. "Why not?" She looked around at her backside as if to see what was wrong with it.

"I wouldn't let them," John replied.

Stephie stopped the game. "Look, John, this is kinda getting silly." She stood there in full battle dress with a rifle, and yet he was assuming the role of protector in chief.

An old woman wheeled her cart up unexpectedly and grabbed Stephie's hand in hers. Her white hair was done up as if for the occasion of going to the store. She was wrinkled and bowed with age. "I just wanted to come up here and say something to you two." She reached out and grasped John's hand also. "I have been passing soldiers on the side of the road for months now, and I've never taken the time to stop and say what I have been thinking. But what I have wanted to say to you and to all the other young soldiers I've seen is . . . *God bless you*! God *bless* you both, and *a-all* the other soldiers. I think about you every hour of every day, and I'm *so*, so proud of you! All the talk about your generation not being as patriotic as past Americans is just bunk. Your parents did right by you. All of you. You're saviors and heros. Thank you. Thank you. Thank you."

She left without Stephie or John knowing how to reply. Her words affected them deeply. They finished shopping in silence, then checked out and stuffed their field packs with their platoon's all-important meal. John insisted on carrying *both* packs, and Stephie let him, a grin creeping onto her face. When he was laden with as much weight as he could possibly bear, Stephie handed John his weapon and—suddenly, without any warning—kissed him on the lips. She laughed right into his mouth. Her teeth *clicked* off his so she laughed even harder. But when she stepped back from him, John wasn't smiling. *That was wrong,* she knew instantly.

Distant gunfire erupted from over their hill. She grabbed her pack, and they ran out of the parking lot and down the short road with their rations rattling loudly. They cached their packs at the bottom of the hill and ascended the rear slope with weapons in hand. It sounded as if the entire company was engaged in the fight. At the crest of the ridge, the noise was stupendous. A hundred and fifty automatic weapons blazed.

Television cameras, generals and reporters all stood in a semicircle around Stephie's fighting hole. Animal's grinning face and smoking machine gun were bathed in camera lights. When they saw Stephie, someone said, "There she is!" and cameramen came running. John fended them off, and they parted to reveal a major general. "Private Roberts!" he boomed. "It's a pleasure!" They shook hands instead of exchanging salutes.

WHITE HOUSE OVAL OFFICE
September 15 // 2115 Local Time

Bill clicked the mouse and hit play for the third time. The picture of his daughter—sitting somewhere in the Alabama woods—came to life in the V-mail on his desktop screen.

"Hi, Dad," she said, waving and grinning. She looked as beautiful as he'd ever seen her. Her white teeth shone from a tanned and dirty face. But her smile, which before had seemed so effortless, now looked unnatural. Forced. "Hope you're doing well. We're, well, I can't say where we are, I guess, but you probably already know. Anyway, I'm fine. We're all fine. And I'm *well* taken care of, thank you." She laughed. Bill wasn't sure what she was saying. "The weather's been okay. A little hot, actually. We get three meals a day. A lot of our food comes from local stores, and we cook it near our positions. It's really kind of like a camp out, only with weapons," she said, giggling at her joke. "We're all just, you know, waiting," she said with her inflection rising on the last word. She chuckled and shrugged, maintaining an artificially cheerful demeanor. "Nobody knows, you know, exactly, when they're going to come, except maybe *you*, I guess." She shrugged again and made an uncertain face. "So, that's about it from Camp Stephie. If you receive this, just reply, and I'll get the platoon commo to pass it on. Love you," she said more seriously. Her eyes dropped to the ground, then rose again to the camera. "I love you very much, Dad, and I miss you." She blew him a kiss.

She reached down. The picture shook. The video came to an end.

Bill reached for the mouse and clicked play again.

THE STATE DEPARTMENT, WASHINGTON
September 16 // 1000 Local Time

Clarissa leaned back from her desk, propped her feet up, and began thumbing the cursor through her accumulated E-mails. "What time is it?" asked one sender, who declined to identify himself. Frowning, she traced it. A slender finger—a tiny sleuth of a program—scurried across the network, and came back to report that the E-mail came from a "Secure Government Server." A solid wall. You could go no further.

Everybody in national security used the same anonymous router. It guaranteed destruction of all traces of the data that passes through the Internet courtesy of the Department of Defense. *You don't want the Chinese being alerted,* Clarissa had been told, *to an unusual surge in late-night pizza orders at the Department of the Navy or the Air Force when something big is up.*

"What time is it?" asked the empty dialogue box. She typed several entries, but to no avail.

She moved on. Memo, memo, invoice, memo, memo, confirmation, memo, memo, memo. *What time is it?* She concentrated, trying to force the answer from her brain through sheer mental effort. *What kind of answer do they want? Is it some kind of inside joke about time?*

Suddenly, she remembered. *"Now is the time,"* she thought, and nodded. She typed the four words as she mumbled them in the subvocal range reserved for monologues. When she hit "Enter" and nothing happened, she hissed, "shi-," which was sufficient when communicating with herself. She tried again. " 'Now is the time for all good men to come to the aid of their party.' "

Before she could hit "Enter," the document unscrambled before her eyes. Her mouth hung open in surprise. *Letter,* she mentally catalogued the E-mail.

She smiled. It must be Dad with a newfound penchant for cloak and dagger.

A clock counted down from ninety seconds in the upper right-hand corner as she read. *What's that for?* she wondered.

We both want to save America. You by assisting us in
what I dare say is a noble cause. Your father by being
the right man at the right time to lead this country.

The clock was down to one minute and counting.

We are leaders at the very highest levels of the American government establishment. I am a high-ranking official whose identity will, for the time being, remain
undisclosed. But I was in the Situation Room with you
today.

Was it her boss the secretary of state? Or perhaps the secretary of defense? Or the national security advisor? Or a military officer? Or who?

Would you give away Southern Florida? Or would you
fight? Every way that you can? With all your might and
resources? We choose the latter. We choose the way
which is, dare I say, the way of the immortal greats.
We need your help. Your country needs you, Clissa.

"Clissa?" she read and reread, then wondered. Only her
father called her that! He had for as long as she could remember. The clock was down to forty seconds.

Any agreement Baker makes with Han Zhemin could
lead to the ruin of our beleaguered nation. We must
know what Baker's intentions are with respect to his
deal before he betrays America. If you do not wish to
join us, do nothing. This message erases itself ninety
seconds after you open it. But if you want to save
America, click on the button below immediately. Regardless, I must warn you, never, ever discuss this E-
mail. I feel that I must be quite clear on this point. We
patriots are at great risk in this endeavor. There can be
no exceptions made for anyone.

What? she thought in alarm. The clock read fifteen seconds. Her cursor hovered over the lone button on which were printed the words "I Accept." *I can always change my mind later,* she reasoned. Almost reluctantly, as if giving in to curiosity, she clicked. A new window popped open.

> Installing anonymous router. Done. Reply to our E-mails by typing the password on the address line. ERASING ALL MEDIA.

The computer *binged.* Her E-mail reader appeared as before. The treasonous invitation that she had accepted was gone.

I'm in, she thought, and then she grinned in excitement. *Jesus. I'm really in!*

RITZ CARLTON HOTEL, THE BAHAMAS
September 17 // 0800 Local Time

A grim-faced President Baker waited alone while Han Zhemin—also alone—crossed the large, carpeted, high-ceilinged room. Baker didn't rise or otherwise greet Han, and he wore what Han took for a surly expression. Before sitting, Han extracted a small black device. He waved it around the room, then returned it—satisfied—to his jacket pocket.

Han sat on a sofa directly across from Bill's chair, separated by a well-appointed coffee table. Han poured himself coffee and held the urn up to Bill, who didn't bat an eye. Han shrugged and said, "It would have been better to meet again after all these years under more pleasant circumstances."

Bill's right eyelid fluttered, Han noted. A nervous tick. *That's new.*

"I want to be absolutely clear about this," Bill said without any preliminaries. "I want to know, with absolute clarity, if there is *any* way that the invasion can be averted?"

Han shrugged and arched his brow. "There might, dare I say, be one way," Han replied before pausing to study his old friend. In the end, Han just smiled. "But you would *never* agree to conditions!" Han waited. Bill's eye twitched, as did his pinched lips a moment after. "Certainly not with me across the table!" Han finally continued. "How *preposterous*!" Han loosed a good-natured laugh at the thought.

Bill couldn't force his lips into a smile. He wore his hatred on his sleeve.

You're really new at this, Han thought, studying Bill's pale face. Han took a sip of coffee and sweetened it by stirring a tiny pastry in the warm liquid. He popped the soggy, saccharine dough into his mouth and mumbled, "Now I have a question for you." Han wiped his mouth with a napkin. "*If we invade America, will you resort to nuclear weapons?*"

One corner of Bill's lips turned up as if to leave implicit some vague and sinister threat.

Clint Eastwood, Han thought, almost laughing out loud. He shook his head. "You see, don't you, Bill, that your answer is 'No.' "

"I have not given you an answer," Bill stonily objected.

Han shook his head. "But you *have*! You have! Don't you see? This is not the time for an ambiguous reply unless your answer is no."

"If we use tactical nuclear weapons," Bill changed the subject, "will you retaliate with strategic weapons?"

Han frowned and shook his head again, hinting that this was not a productive use of their meeting. "Do you remember the old skit on the television show we used to watch? The night that Rachel's friend brought the marijuana over to our apartment?" He sat up and held his hands out to his sides as if ready to draw his six-shooters. "The imbecilic gunfighter, you remember, whose practical joke it is to pretend to draw his weapon in the gunfight, but in fact he doesn't really draw." Han quick-drew his fake gun in the shape of a finger and a thumb. "Don't you remember? How many times did we reenact that skit? It was so humorous, of course," Han said in a flat and humorless tone, "because the joke was on the jokester, who got shot and killed by his opponent."

"This is different," Bill said.

Han nodded and smiled, wistfully recalling those days when he and Bill were inseparable friends. "Yes, it is," Han admitted. "Everything is different." He popped another micro-pastry into his mouth and laughed. "But I always thought that skit was hilarious. It was such a stupid mistake for the gun-fighter to pretend to draw when both sides were so tense and ready to kill each other." Han paused to ensure that Bill understood his warning. There was no evidence on Bill's face that he did understand, so Han frowned and said, "If you intend to launch nuclear weapons at China if we invade your shores, Bill, it would be imbecilic not to say so clearly and without qualification or hesitation."

"If we use tactical nuclear weapons," Bill asked in exactly the same words as before, "will you retaliate with strategic weapons?"

"Of *course* not!" Han replied firmly and unequivocally. Bill's eye twitched again. *At least he saw through that*, Han thought. *He's totally transparent*! "If, Bill, we are ever, say, allied against Europe, let me do all the negotiating, *okay*?" Han laughed, but he never took his eyes off Bill, searching for a glimmer of comprehension of what Han was proposing.

"I will never be your ally," Bill replied in an acid tone.

At least he picked up on the offer, Han thought.

"Is the prime minister now firmly in command of China's nuclear arsenal?" Bill asked.

Han smiled to mask his anger at Bill's question. "Firmly," Han replied clearly in case the Americans had bugged the room. His sweeper was only certain of detecting Chinese military listening devices.

"How firmly?" Bill prodded, annoying Han further, widening his smile. For it had, after all, been Han's job to wrest complete control of the weapons from the military. The minor exception to which he had agreed, for engineers' nuclear de-molition munitions, had been Han's mistake and Tel Aviv's tragedy. It was to cover up for that mistake that thirty-seven of Sheng's officers had been executed. It was to vent Han's intense anger at the potential career setback—narrowly avoided—that Han had done the killing himself. "Does the prime minister have sole possession of the launch codes?" Bill persisted, finally cracking what looked like a smile.

"Launch codes!" Han blurted out before reining in his anger and smiling pleasantly. "What do they matter? Codes can be changed. The prime minister has much more effective 'people' controls."

"You mean that he holds military families hostage to the secret police," Bill interpreted.

"Yes," Han confirmed simply, directly, and this time truthfully. "And as you know, the prime minister has publicly warned of the dangers of nuclear escalation and is committed to avoiding any such *terrible* outcome."

Baker looked Han straight in the eye and said, "Bullshit! You don't give one shit about the lives of your troops or my people! All you care about is power! And your power would be enhanced by a nuclear war, wouldn't it, Han? The people of China would turn against the military, and they have nowhere to turn but to you!"

Han smiled, took a deep breath, and sighed. "Let me put this simply so that you will understand—with no games— what I'm saying. You must very soon make your choice whether to use all weapons at your disposal, or to rely on your army," Han laughed, "against ours."

Bill Baker sat there eyeing him for a moment, then stood. "Fuck you," he said, and headed for the door.

MONTGOMERY, ALABAMA
September 18 // 2045 Local Time

Rain, Stephie thought as she gazed up at the starless sky. *There's a storm coming.*

Their platoon was on its first patrol since the mauling on the beach. Their second patrol—for real, not in training— ever. At night. One hundred and twenty miles north of the Gulf Coast. Seventy-five miles south of friendly lines. Through a neighborhood filled with dark windows and a hundred hiding places.

Stephie was petrified. They had replenished their platoon with replacements for the casualties they'd taken, but Stephie had no confidence anymore that their unit could do the job, that they could survive again the kind of fire they had received on the beach. Plus, the invasion could come anytime and anywhere, and yet they sent them into abandoned Montgomery at night! *What were they thinking?*

The only light visible in the Alabama state capital was the brilliant sparkling of an engineer's torch as she cut down a street sign and her comrade tossed it into the back of their truck. A dog barked here and there. Occasionally, tires squealed and engines revved in the distance. The city wasn't totally empty. There were still tens of thousands of civilians holed up in the two hundred-mile Exclusion Zone. Some— stubborn and old—just stayed put. Others were unofficial defenders of America. They would be out on a night like this carrying M-16s just like Stephie. Stephie's unit had been warned to take no chances. It was a free-fire zone. They were to shoot anyone they saw on sight.

Stephie lay in the overgrown front lawn of a modest home, swatting at the occasional mosquito. Her squad was set up in a protective screen to refuse contact from all sides with the street corner where the two engineers worked in the middle. The woman with the torch made short work of a metal sign-post. The other combat engineer tossed it into their truck. The female engineer wheeled her bottle off toward the next inter-section, leaving one less directional aid to guide the Chinese.

"Up!" Sergeant Collins barked. First Squad's two fire teams—weapons raised and at the ready—advanced across front lawns on opposite sides of the street. Fire Team Alpha— Stephie, Burns, Scott, and Corporal Johnson—took the left side. Fire Team Bravo took right. Collins and the weapons team—Animal and Massera on the -60, and the two men with the all-threat missile launcher—advanced tree to tree down the sidewalks. The thirteen-man protective screen moved in formation around the exposed engineers and driver, but the going was tough for the infantry through the two-foot-tall grass.

At the next street corner, Stephie found cover behind a stone-walled flower bed. She had good fields of fire down the intersecting streets. She could fight from there. She liked her position. *You just gotta look ahead for cover as you advance,* she lectured herself. Her rifle barrel crackled through withered flowers as it traversed the junction they defended. John Burns plopped down beside her. "Hey," Stephie whispered, "spread out!" But Burns ignored her and remained at her side.

There was movement to the left. John rushed that way, putting his body in Stephie's line of fire, absolutely infuriating her. "Friendly!" Corporal Johnson called from the side street at the far left. "Friendly," John repeated to Stephie.

"I *know*," she replied, annoyed.

"I mean pass it down," John said.

"Oh," she said, nodding. "Friendly!" she called out in a loud whisper to Scott, the next person to her right. The warnings continued into the distance.

The arriving Second Squad joined up with them from the left. Stephie heard other calls of "Friendly!" from the right. Their entire platoon was gathering at their intersection.

"All right," came Collins's voice over the squad's net—its Minimal Emission System—in Stephie's right ear, "we're pullin' out. Secure your weapons. Safeties *on*!" There was a hint of urgency in his voice. They all rose, muscles aching, got in formation, and dressed right with Simmons at the far end of their rank.

"Squad leaders?" Staff Sergeant Kurth inquired.

He got one, "All-presn't-an'-'counted-for, Staff Sergeant!" and three, "All present!" replies.

To be doubly sure, Kurth counted helmets with his trigger finger.

Stephie watched him closely. *Don't leave people behind*, was her mental note.

The trucks, filled with street signs, pulled up from side streets. It was just like the dozens of field exercises that had filled Stephie's four months in the army: playing soldier then waiting around for the trucks to arrive. The end to training was always waiting around. This exit, however, was hurried and quick.

There was a stirring among the twenty men and women as they climbed onto the trucks' tailgates. Their attention was drawn to the dark street behind them. "What *is* that?" someone asked. Stephie heard nothing, but her skin began to crawl. "Mount up!" Kurth bellowed. Soldiers on the ground shoved the butts in front of them up into the trucks. A woman's curse drew laughter. Packs were lobbed into the trucks' rears. A fight almost broke out in Third Squad, and then Kurth—fists balled but remaining at his sides—almost pounded the two pissed-off guys. Adrenaline pumped through Stephie's veins.

Light flashed in the treetops that formed their horizon like the headlamps of a turning vehicle. "Shit," Peter Scott said in disgust. "Rain again."

Stephie shook her head, "No," absolutely terrified. Deep down, she had thought that they would never come. That something—some secret weapon—would stop them.

A low rumbling rose from the ground all around them. "Earthquake!" someone shouted. John Burns appeared at Stephie's elbow.

The sonorous roar, emanating from a great distance, ascended in ten seconds to unbroken thunder. The southern horizon—the Gulf Coast—was on fire.

3

Lieutenant Wu stood in the darkened combat command center next to the fleet commander. On the screens, they watched thousands of inbound American missiles approach the first of a half dozen layers of fleet air defenses arrayed around the command ship. The sailors on the ship were nervous. All feared a secret American superweapon. Lasers and particle beam weapons were their favorite fears.

"Don't worry," the ship's captain had said. The naval officer now stood on the bridge as they plied deep water a few hundred miles off the coast of southern Alabama surrounded by two hundred missile-firing surface combatants. Wu had descended into the bowels of the ship to the combat information center. "We're not at risk from the enemy's missiles," the captain had pledged. "We can withstand anything that the Americans throw at us."

But not so the exposed periphery of the fleet, which even now was entering the mouth of Mobile Bay.

The missiles approached slowly on the large, rectangular plasma display. But Wu knew that they streaked through the night sky at the large shapes of Chinese warships at supersonic speed.

"First missiles away," the air defense coordinator announced.

New blips—these emanating from the rearmost ships in the fleet—appeared on the screen. The tiny specks of light flew northward to meet the American missiles. As the formation of Chinese missiles overflew the next ships to the north, more missiles were fired, adding dozens, and then hundreds to the wave. They numbered over a thousand by the time they reached the center of the screen. The center of the fleet. Wu felt the decks of the supercarrier shudder at a gut-shaking pitch. He grabbed onto the console but found the vibrations through his hands disturbing.

Television screens lit up with fiery rocket thrust from flat decks at the stern as the command ship added its fire to the fleet's defense. Choppy reflected light danced off the black sea. On the screen, the wave of antimissile missiles, heading north, extended from one side of the fleet's roughly circular formation to the other. One hundred miles from east to west.

"Where are our aircraft?" the fleet commander asked.

The radar technician punched a few buttons, and the screen was suddenly filled with a totally confusing clutter. Thousands upon thousands of new symbols—combat and electronic warfare aircraft and helicopters flushed from decks of ships now under attack—rendered the scene incomprehensible.

"Show only our air defense aircraft," the old admiral—a contemporary of General Sheng's—instructed. With a few more taps on the console, the technician removed hundreds of symbols.

The pattern was now much clearer. The navy's combat aircraft flew in dozens of hundred-plane formations from the southeast and southwest. Although there were murmurs into microphones from dozens of stations all around the dimly lit nerve center, the large compartment seemed to Wu strangely quiet and surreal. It wasn't like the war Wu had spent his childhood imagining. All the field training exercises he'd been through in military school had been cacophonous, noisy affairs. War was loud and messy: a furious tapestry woven of swirling bravery and violence.

"Thirty seconds to intercept," the air defense coordinator announced calmly from his console next to the radar screen. Banks of television monitors toward which everyone turned showed huge missiles dropping from open bays of sleek fighter-bombers. There suddenly appeared several thousand additional Chinese missiles from the larger blips representing combat aircraft. "Naval air wing commander reports missiles away," came the matter-of-fact voice. "Repeat. Missiles away. Timed on target. Joint strike combined time to intercept: twenty seconds. Long live the glory of China."

The missiles' engines ignited one after another just beneath the fuselage of the aircraft, which flew less than a dozen meters off the wingtip of the plane carrying the camera. The pictures shook, and light washed them out momentarily as the aircraft with the cameras loosed their own ordnance in similar fashion. But there was no noise in this disconcerting, soundless battle.

The two lines of missiles inched toward each other. A constantly changing readout in a data window reported their closure rate at four thousand kilometers per hour.

Suddenly, as if they were piloted, the American missiles broke formation all at once and began to turn singly or in small groups of half a dozen or more. Their colors—which represented altitude and previously had been a uniform amber—became a low-altitude red or a high-altitude yellow as they evaded their Chinese interceptors. The Chinese missiles quickly changed colors in shades of blue. In the computer-controlled melée, it was possible to make out individual duels as purple, corkscrewing American missiles were stalked by similarly turning Chinese missiles in darkening blue.

A small white "x" appeared at the points of intercept as the attackers and defenders came together. The "x" lingered until it changed to green for "killed" and faded from the screen, or to red and began to flash after a miss. Wu had to convince himself that this battle was really taking place. He forced himself to imagine the embers that surely must be falling from the sky.

All was soundless.

The voices were calm. *This is war,* Wu thought, *in the Twenty-First Century.* It seemed wrong. False. Unreal. *Somewhere else there is reality*, he thought. *On the troop ships.*

Not all of the American missiles were intercepted. Flashing red "x"'s closed on the large shapes of Chinese ships. At crimson, they merged with the frigates, destroyers, and cruisers—the fleet's pickets—in Mobile Bay.

The white ships that they struck—one by one—took on the crimson hue of their executioner.

When the last small blip of a missile disappeared from the screen, joy and celebration erupted from the staid command center. What had been calm and professional combat management turned into a release of tension Wu hadn't even known existed. He understood why when the air defense coordinator quietly reported over his shoulder to the fleet commander, "All warheads were conventional, sir. No EMP. Bridge reports several bright flashes, but the detonations were clearly in the subnuclear range. Probably ships' magazines."

The admiral nodded.

The command center returned to its normal quiet. *That's it?* Wu thought. He looked at the fleet commander, then followed the old man's eyes to the radar screen. Nearly a dozen ships glowed crimson. Wu trailed the admiral, who headed to the communications bay. Monitors bore ships' names. Some showed pictures of serene bridges where all seemed normal. A few were ominously static-filled. There were long shots on a few of a flaming ship in the distance taken by a nearby vessel. The reflections of the shipboard fires lit the water in between, sometimes broken by the dark shape of a passing, speeding ship.

"What's our worst loss?" the admiral asked quietly.

The communications officer replied, "The supertransport *Hefei*, sir. They are carrying the 351st Infantry Division and the 1107th Motorized Transport Brigade."

"Can you raise her?" the old man queried.

The younger officer answered, "Audio only, sir."

In the silence that followed, Wu found the *Hefei* on the small video screen. The picture was snowy white. They waited. The communications officer pressed a button, and a speaker came alive.

Blaring klaxons filled the cathedral-like combat command center. Wu winced on hearing an explosion followed by screams from several men. Howling jets of flame, groaning steel, loud pops like machine gun rounds cooking off randomly in a fire, shattering glass, and the shouts of a terrified man. "Listing thirty-eight to starboard! Thirty-eight, still! Thirty-nine! *Now thirty-nine!* Forty! Listing forty degrees to starboard! Forty-one! Accelerating! Accelerating! Forty-three! We're going over!"

A rending, crashing sound like the collapse of a building cut the audio from the half-million-ton ship to total silence.

When Wu looked up, he found the admiral staring at him with glassy, tired eyes. Using the handrails, the old man looked decrepit as he slowly retired to his cabin.

Wu went to his cabin also. In his private dining room, a deep dish of crème brûlée and a shot of cognac sat atop a white linen tablecloth. He picked at the dessert and thought about the captain's revelation earlier that evening.

Wu had met the captain alone in his large, comfortable wardroom. As they departed to meet the admiral for dinner, the captain had reached for the doorknob but not opened the door. Standing there, awkwardly stooped, not looking Wu in the eye, but determined, the man had said, "There's one more thing that you should know about the military situation, Lieutenant Wu." His white-gloved hand held Wu prisoner. "We do not know what weapons the Americans are working on in secret, but they do not matter. What matters, Lieutenant Wu, is their arsenal ships. It is the considered opinion," he continued formally, "of the majority of my fellow line officers in this invasion fleet that if we ever go into battle against even a single American arsenal ship, our fleet will be devastated. We hope, Lieutenant Wu, that you will make that view known to the appropriate people."

The civilian leadership, Wu thought. *My relatives.* He had found the captain looking him in the eye, and Wu had nodded. He had committed to do what the man had requested. Another intrigue in what Wu had thought would be the relatively simple process of going to war.

Wu downed the cognac in one gulp. Five minutes later, as he was undressing for bed, he forced himself to think about the nearly 30,000 troops and crew aboard the capsized *Hefei,* who were now, most likely, sucking oily water into their gasping lungs.

Wu made a dash for the head, where he vomited everything that he'd eaten into the immaculate, stainless steel toilet.

MOBILE, ALABAMA
September 18 // 2045 Local Time

Captain Jim Hart lay rolled in a fetal curl within a hundred yards of a curtain of fiery geysers. *Too close!* he knew. *Too close!* The cacophony of violence and tumult allowed no other thought. The ground thudded against him. Clumps of smoldering earth and burning embers from shards of trees plummeted from the sky, pelting him. The choking smell of high explosives fouled the air. Jim Hart waited for the slight adjustment in the enemy's fire that would be all that it would take to kill him instantly, leaving no identifiable remains.

An even more stunning silence descended. He still heard the fury of hell in ears that rang, but he felt the silence with every cell of his still living body. Jim waited. And waited. And waited. The Chinese rolled their fire, they didn't lift and move it. Other stretches of the shoreline were being pounded, but they were through with this beachhead. That was it. He had lived.

The thirty-one-year-old Special Forces officer rose and brushed the dust and blasted debris from his camouflage-covered suit. Major Andrew Richards, an observer from the Royal Marines, did likewise. Hart gave Richards a thumbs-up. The Brit responded in kind. They lowered built-in night vision goggles from their helmets without need of spoken command. They picked up their equipment and trotted up the slight rise through shattered trees whose upper branches had burned themselves out. The crest of a low ridge—which they had avoided knowing the Chinese would pound it—offered a multitude of holes. They chose a crater whose main attraction was the wooden breastwork of a large, fallen tree. Unlike the other blackened pines and elms, this tree was white. Stripped bare of bark by the explosive force of a near miss. The trunk, Hart discovered, was silky smooth to the touch. The two men settled into the crater behind their cover. The singed earth of the crater wall was still warm.

About a quarter of a mile away, landing craft left white, luminescent wakes through Mobile Bay. Major Richards whispered, "Pathfinders meeting a boat." The British marine didn't point. He had fallen in love with the American integrated display system. His thumb rolled a small track ball mounted atop the right index finger of his glove. Crosshairs on the screen in Hart's goggles aimed at a dark stretch of beach. You couldn't quite tell where the water ended and the land began until the phosphorescent surf lapped against the shoreline. Richards—who was well-trained at recon—was directing Hart's attention to Chinese troops already on shore that they hadn't seen before. They had come out of hiding just like Hart and Richards immediately after the barrage had lifted and were greeting a landing craft. With the new system, Richards could just as easily be designating the landing craft as a target for an aircraft, missile, or shell. That was what was so hard for Hart to swallow about their mission. It didn't allow for engagement.

Hart left Richards and headed off toward a rare surviving outgrowth of weeds and bushes. He had to keep his movements slow and not cast any shadows from the stars that might be visible to light-amplified binoculars, so he crawled on all fours. His entire body was covered by a chemical protective suit that served dual purposes. It also reflected heat inward. If he hadn't worn it, his body would glow on infrared. Dehumidifiers in the toe-to-hood gear kept him cool so long as he frequently drained the bags of sweat at his shins, which were now filling rapidly.

He slithered into the bushes and extracted a pointed black stalk, which he sank into the churned and blackened soil. He then mounted the camera to the stalk and plugged his goggles' umbilical into the camera. Instantly, the view through the camera appeared on his goggles' screens. When he moved his head from left to right, the camera traversed Mobile Bay. The camera was "slaved" to the movements of Hart's helmet.

Just like a fucking target designator, he thought. He centered the picture shown by the camera on one open landing boat. In the background—out in the bay—water splashed white off the bows of dark ships.

Hart angrily continued with his routine. The camera was functioning properly. He removed the umbilical, and his regular view reappeared. He covered the camera with netting, ensuring with care that the lens was not obscured.

Captain Hart was a Green Beret—a member of the 5th Special Forces Group—and was used to working with dangerous implements. But the final step on the checklist was the one he liked the least. Without looking up at his partner, who was forty meters away installing British state-of-the-art surveillance equipment, Hart whispered into the intercom, "Self-destruct system's armed. Fire in the hole."

"I'm right behind you," Richards replied. The sound of his voice came from the right over the directional earphones in Hart's helmet. Hart had less than sixty seconds. *Plenty of time,* he reassured himself. He plugged a different jack into the camera's output. From it protruded a tiny filament. He began unreeling the nearly invisible wire behind him as he crawled up the slight rise of the cleared forest. By the time he was six feet away, he was safe. The motion detectors would blow the eight-pound charge mounted at the base of the camera the next time anyone came close.

At the first standing tree on the top of the ridge, about twenty meters away, Hart activated the microwave transmitter and raised its single telescoping leg to about twice his head height. At the top, the hollow black cylinder was already buzzing with an electric motor that searched the horizon for a carrier signal. There was a *beep* of success in his headphones, and he stapled the slender metal leg to the tree on the side opposite the bench.

A radio signal arrived through a swirl of attempted Chinese jamming. Hart heard, not from Richards, but from much farther away, "Angel Six, Angel Six, this is Sentry One. We read you five by five. Execute Romeo Alpha. Repeat, Romeo Alpha. Acknowledge. Over." Hart's eyes narrowed behind the electronic lenses. "Acknowledge, Angel Six."

"This is Angel Six. I acknowledge. Execute Romeo Alpha. Repeat. Romeo Alpha. Angel Six, out."

Richards joined him at the tree. "What *is* Romeo Alpha, if you don't mind my asking?"

"For you, it's evac. Let's go catch a ride."

They returned to their crater of first choice. At least a dozen boats were disgorging troops. The first warships—expendable frigates and corvettes—now patrolled the deeper water with radar domes, missiles, and guns. The Chinese had gotten amphibious landings down to a fine art. It was an art that particularly impressed the marine, Richards, who whispered bits of praise and admiration. "I can't tell you," he finally said enthusiastically, "how *thankful* I am that you agreed to me coming along. It's a *wonderful* opportunity. My report to London is already half written in my head." Richards stopped talking when he looked at the only part of Hart's face he could see—his unsmiling mouth—and then said, "I'm . . . I'm so sorry. I apologize."

Hart concentrated on the enemy that was invading his country. He grimly designated inbound assault formations with his track ball, all the while gritting his teeth in anger. If only there were orbiting missiles ready to navigate to the precise coordinates that Hart's targeting system computed or to ride Hart's laser beam down to the Chinese. It would take them an hour to kill him. In the meantime, eight-hundred-pound warheads would rain down onto their heads.

Why that wasn't his mission, Hart didn't know.

Several platoons formed up and headed left. Only one went right. That's the one Hart designated with a press of his trackball. Richards nodded in silent agreement.

The Chinese were crack assault troops, but Hart was Special Forces, and Richards was Royal Marine recon. They followed the Chinese from a distance of about two hundred meters without being observed, skirting minefields that twice bloodied the Chinese. The platoon periodically stopped for artillery prep, which devastated the path ahead. That was why Hart and Richards trailed.

The American and Brit peeled off after three miles. Three

miles of Hart itching to open fire on troops left behind to ambush anyone like Hart and Richards. Three miles of Hart silently praying the Chinese would make a wrong turn into the minefields whose location only he knew. Three miles of Hart daydreaming of slitting the throat of a wounded straggler who so brazenly defiled his country.

They uncovered their two three-wheeled ATVs. Their engines were acoustically silenced and made almost no noise. "You know the route?" Hart asked.

"You're not coming?" Major Richards asked. Hart—goggles still covering his upper face—shook his head. Richards asked, "Just what is 'Romeo Alpha'? That plan wasn't part of our briefing."

"Like I said, for you it's evacuation. Head north on this highway. Stay off the shoulders. The mines are already active there. You've got about two hours before the mines under the center of the roadbed are activated."

"And what are you going to do?" Richards asked. Hart didn't answer except by his silence. Richards understood. "All right, then," he said sadly. There was an awkward pause before Richards said, "Captain Hart, I bid you farewell. Good luck." He held out his hand, which Hart shook. Richards settled behind his motorcycles' handles, but then turned back to his American ally. "Captain Hart . . . win this war. Stop the Chinese. And let's have a beer—on me—to celebrate when this whole thing is over." Major Richards soundlessly drove off.

Though now all alone, Hart answered the Brit's question about the orders he'd received. *Romeo Alpha,* he thought. *Seek targets of opportunity while awaiting further orders.* "And by targets of opportunity," the colonel commanding the 5th had said, "we mean kill as many Chinese soldiers as you possibly can."

A cheer had risen in the crowded Birmingham auditorium from the 5,000 men assigned to South Alabama.

Hart revved his silenced engine and took off down the road into the black night.

Bill Baker watched Chinese troops disgorge into Mobile Bay on a large, ultra-high-definition screen. Roll-on/roll-off landing craft were beached twenty across. Ten thousand men marched up the slight rise. "How'd we get these pictures?" Bill asked.

"Special Forces," General Cotler replied.

"But who?" Bill asked again. "Was it five men, or ten, or a hundred who went and put it there, or was it only one?"

Cotler took a deep breath and said, "We'll find that out, sir." He made eye contact with a colonel, who nodded and rushed out.

The water was gray. The burned-out environs of the camera were gray. The predawn sky matched the gunmetal gray of the missile-laden Chinese cruiser and several destroyers. An occasional gray helicopter made furtive flights from ship to shore, not risking an altitude of even 200 feet for fear of being detected by loitering, infrared-seeking, probably gray American missiles.

The mood in the room was somber. The conversations were muted. Bill was the focus of everyone, but he was all alone. Each of the Joint Chiefs and the secretary of defense had whispered to him about this concern or that. It was now Air Force General Latham's turn.

"Sir, we've got a firm fix on them in Mobile Bay. There are at least three hundred thousand troops packed into those transports, and they haven't deployed their ground-based missile defenses yet. They're still not on U.S. soil. The radioactive contamination would be *minimal*."

Baker was tired. "They'll retaliate," he replied.

"We could still employ the 'Heartland Defense,' " Latham quietly suggested.

"I will *not* see America's coasts destroyed!" Baker shouted and slammed his fist onto the table. Latham didn't look around self-consciously at the suddenly stilled NSC. He stared Baker straight in the eyes. "Fifty percent of our population,'' Baker explained, ''our culture, and our industry lie within 100 miles of our three coasts. You said yourself that they would penetrate and destroy targets up to 100 miles inland if the nuclear war lasted thirty days. What's to stop the war from going sixty days? Ninety? What's to stop both sides from launching weapon after weapon as fast as they can manufacture them for *years*? How deep would their warheads reach by then, General Latham? Two hundred miles inland? Three? Five?''

Baker turned his attention to the dozen or so men and women standing and sitting around the room, who stared silently at the president. ''We will defeat this invasion at *sea*! We have to regain mastery of the *sea*! To *do* that, we have to remain a *sea*going *nation!* That means we need *ports*, and *ship*yards, and *navies*! There will be no 'Heartland Defense'! I will *not* authorize the use of nuclear arms because I will not destroy this nation to save it! Don't come to me with targets of opportunity! This is a *strategic* decision, and I—and I alone—have *made* it!''

The long seconds of tension that followed was broken by the opening of the door. An army colonel entered and whispered into General Cotler's ear. Baker turned to Cotler, spread his hands in air, and asked testily, ''*What?*''

''That picture, sir,'' Cotler replied. He nodded at the now brilliant blue water of Mobile Bay. The sun had risen. White shores and lush green pine forests rimmed a sparkling sea. White radar domes festooned the upper decks of ships.

On the screen beside it, the smiling photo of an athletic-looking young twenty-eight-year-old soldier appeared. Data on the man flashed in a window. Cotler said, ''The camera was planted by one man, Captain Jim Hart, who had along with him a major in the Royal Marines observing the Chinese landing in order to report to London.''

Bill stared at the American captain. In the several-years-old picture, he looked too young even to be in the army. Tanned after obviously just getting his green beret, he seemed carefree and proud. ''What's this man going to do next?'' Baker asked. ''What are his orders?''

Cotler's aide fumbled when handing the general an old-fashioned paper folder. Cotler read the downloaded file. "We've got three Special Forces Groups—the 5th, the 7th, and the 20th Alabama National Guard, about 15,000 Green Berets in total—positioned in South Alabama, South Mississippi, and North Alabama, respectively. Captain Hart has the same orders as the vast majority. 'Mission Romeo Alpha': sabotage, assassination, espionage, training and arming of resistance, and special missions, as ordered by controllers," he put the folder down, "and otherwise targets of opportunity."

Baker stared at the boy as he had been in his mid-twenties and wondered whether he would live to his mid-thirties? *If he does*, Bill thought, *he'll be different. They'll all be different.* We'll *all be different*, he knew, and it sickened him.

THE STATE DEPARTMENT, WASHINGTON
September 19 // 0800 Local Time

When Clarissa arrived at work, she went to get coffee. A secretary with dark bags under her eyes stood by the machine, complaining to a co-worker. "Whenever my boss says 'Anvilhead,' I'm supposed to cancel doctors' appointments, vacations, *dates*!"

Clarissa asked, "What's 'Anvilhead'?"

The two women looked at each other. The exhausted secretary who had been voicing her workplace grievances replied awkwardly that she couldn't really talk about it. Her friend waved her off and said, "She's the head of the *China* Desk, for Christ's sake! The speaker of the house's *daughter*! She's got Top Secret clearance."

The secretary proceeded to whisper Baker's plan to counterattack the Chinese invasion forces.

In the still and quiet of her office, Clarissa loaded the anonymous router, replied with the password, "Now is the time . . ." *et cetera, et cetera*, and began to type an E-mail. "Baker is letting Chinese forces land virtually unopposed so that he can counterattack them later on!" It was lunacy! Madness! She was livid. When she was done, she dispatched the report and quickly "shredded" the file with the standard Department of Defense–provided utility.

SOUTH OF TUSCALOOSA, ALABAMA
September 19 // 0900 Local Time

Two distant *pops*, and the long burp of aircraft cannon high in the sky overhead woke Captain Jim Hart from a fitful sleep. High above the clouds came the whining engines of a rare dogfight. Both pilots were taking a terrible risk in the missile-rich environment.

The grunt of U.S. Air Force Captain Nick Waters became a continuous growl as he held his F-26 in a 6-G turn. His prey—a Chinese fighter—dove down into the cloud cover, but the head-up display projected his position onto Nick's windshield. Blood rushed to his head as he sticked over into a 9-G outside roll. He spun the aircraft upside down to turn the maneuver into an inside roll, but still he had trouble maintaining his focus, and he blinked his eyes repeatedly. With his face set firmly in a grimace, he dove into the clouds. His vision tunneled, but at the center of the tunnel was the wildly turning image of the Chinese fighter at which he'd already fired his last air-to-air missile.

Waters had been in his cockpit for almost nine hours. That included two landings to rearm and refuel during which he had kept his engines running in preparation for a hasty take-off. Even on the ground, Waters's defensive suite blared threat tones into his ears. But that beat the hell out of the brief screams over the radio in the past six months of air war that had accompanied the deaths of a dozen of his squadron's original twenty-two pilots. The Americans gave more than they got, but each time they swept the southern sky clear of Chinese aircraft, huge numbers of hypersonic Chinese missiles lit up their radar screens as they hurtled toward them from over the horizon.

But for a day—maybe two—it would be different. The Chinese hadn't yet disembarked their ground-based missiles, so both pilots were out of range of Chinese fleet-based missiles to the south and American land-based missiles to the north. The result was that pilots did battle in old-fashioned dogfights. It was for just this moment that Waters had joined the air force. This wouldn't be his first kill of the war. He had six over the Gulf, and three more that morning alone. But every kill was personal to Waters. Every kill was different. "Die, you motherfucker, die!" he shouted as he lined up the cross-hairs and gripped the stick's trigger ever tighter. This would be his first kill with guns.

"*Damn!*" he shouted as the Chinese jet rolled sharply and got away. Waters panted for breath as he pulled straight up in an 8-G inside loop. Cuffs in his G-suit painfully squeezed every inch of his body below his neck to force the blood back to his head. He swam through a sea of dizziness, nausea, and sweat. He breathed in great pants like a weight lifter. Biomed sensors strapped to his chest and scalp triggered a blaring, "Black out!" warning.

He leveled, and it took him several pounding heartbeats to realize that he was head-to-head. Waters squeezed the trigger. His F-26 shuddered from the recoil of the .30-mm buzz saw directly beneath his rudder pedals.

A flick of the stick raked 300 rounds over his enemy's nose.

The Chinese fighter veered into an out-of-control roll.

The computer coolly announced, "Auto-eject. Auto-eject. Auto-eject."

As the three words were spoken, an automated sequence jerked traps around Waters's helmet, arms and legs, pulling him painfully to the chair. The canopy slipped away from the aircraft, and wind assaulted the cockpit.

Bam-BAM! came two explosions. Waters shot out of a fire-ball. The high-thrust rocket on the armored bottom of his seat jettisoned him through the explosion that consumed his cock-pit and then his entire F-26. The computer, knowing of humans' slow reaction times, hadn't bothered alerting Waters to the exact nature of the threat. It had simply punched him out.

His body slammed into a howling 500-mph wind before the rocket motor rotated the seat and doubled its thrust. His body weighed a ton during two seconds at 13 Gs. The seat steadied in an upright position—Waters sitting atop a rocket shooting skyward—for its seven-hundred-foot ascent. The motor abruptly shut off. The straps released Waters. Despite his deep sink into the form-fitting cushions, the seat fell away.

He was in free fall. Down, up, down, up. *Gotta . . .*

A loud snap and violent jerk ended his plummet. His chin smacked into his chest, and his teeth cracked together. Pains warned of major damage to his body. He took a deep gulp of air. His head flopped backwards.

His parachute above him was deployed in a perfect, open blossom. He took another breath. That was up. He filled his lungs, but his head still spun. From two miles below came the *crump* of the enemy jet hitting the ground. That was down—toward the ground—he decided.

Waters fumbled with his helmet and finally raised his dark visor and checked his risers, which weren't tangled.

He was descending through the altitude of his aerial battle-field. Two puffs of black smoke—one the Chinese he'd killed, the other the scene of his aircraft's destruction—were separated by a gently curving white trail. It was the contrail of the Chinese missile fired at point-blank range. He could smell the smoke as he descended between the nearly simultaneous mutual kills. He wiggled and wormed in the harness to take a last look at the ghostly history of his battle, then to get comfortable, then to see if he was hurt. The effort brought grunts and groans of pain. He was battered and bruised by his collision with a brick wall of thin air. He finally settled—limp—and got on the radio to report his ejection. He got no reply. He had no idea if anyone heard him.

Waters drifted down into a solid cloud, and his mind went blank. It was misty, gray, cool—then the ground reappeared.

Flames rose from the brown farm field eight hundred feet beneath him. It was the wreckage of the Chinese jet. Waters instantly grew angry. Pain burst from a hundred places when he shouted at the top of his lungs, "*F-fuck* you, you son of a bitch!" He dangled underneath his nylon parachute and stared at the flames with grinding teeth.

That makes ten, he thought, keeping score.

All of the sudden, he saw the green plume of another parachute draped over the few trees that provided shade around a farmer's house. The bastard who'd shot him down *hadn't even died*! Waters raged. He kicked and cursed and twisted in air. He ground his teeth until a stab of pain shot into both jaws. He didn't have *ten* kills, yet, even though the air force only counted planes. His fight wasn't over.

He was so focused on the sight of the offending parachute that he was caught by surprise at the ground rush. He went from looking down at the earth to around at it. His survival kit landed like an anchor on a tether twenty feet beneath his feet. His ground speed was too great to try to stick it standing. At the last instant he firmed and angled his shock-absorber legs and plowed into the straight rows of brown dirt. The dozen deep bruises he'd gotten from ejection were punched all at once. He crashed into the dirt on his side and he had time to moan just once before a gust of wind tightened the risers.

With a snap, his harness yanked him face-first into the dirt and began dragging him across the dry furrows at ten knots. His mouth filled with dry dirt, but the thing that pissed him off the most when he finally succeeded in hitting the harness release was that he'd been dragged farther away from the farm house.

He rose to his knees with his head swimming, braced his hands on his thighs, and spit over and over, all the while staring at the distant copse of trees, looking for movement. His survival kit lay at the end of its tether. Waters rose unsteadily and in pain and stumbled over the plowed ridges to the tight pack. He unzipped pockets till he found the canteen. He swished and gargled then drank half of its contents. Still no movement at the house. When he returned the canteen to his kit he grabbed the butt of his automatic and pulled it from its green nylon holster.

Waters chambered a round, zipped the kit up, and slung it by a strap over an aching shoulder. All was silent save the steady whistling of the wind past his green flight helmet. It was so unlike the electronic squall of aerial combat. He removed his helmet and let it drop to the dirt as he began his march—at first slow—across the field. "Fuckin' bastard," he mouthed under his breath. "Fucking *bastard*!" he shouted, not content to wait for his feet carry him to the green parachute. He half expected the Chinese pilot to emerge from the trees firing like a gunfighter. Like they had just done in the air. "You think you can come in *my* country!" Waters shouted despite the pain from his ribs. "Can out-*fly*—out-fight *me*?" The effort of rising onto his tiptoes to scream hurt, but his pace grew more determined. "Can you hear me yet, you son of a bitch?" he shouted. "*Can you hear me, mother-fucker?*" he screamed.

No reply came.

He had no idea how many men in his squadron had died that morning—maybe all—but he knew for a fact that one who'd died had been his wing man. They'd returned to the fight—rearmed and refueled—and entered the melee just after dawn. Their first scrape, while carrying a full load of missiles, had gone well. Three times Nick and his wingman had volley-fired eight missiles each. According to the electronic monitoring system, each pilot had made three kills. But they had strayed too close to the coast and barely outrun enemy fleet surface-to-air missiles by burning two-thirds of their remaining fuel on afterburners. As the fast-approaching Chinese missiles had run out of fuel, they had detonated. They had been close enough to buffet his aircraft's control surfaces, which was fed back to Waters through the artificially generated vibration of his control stick.

His wingman had called out that he had yellow lights in his cockpit, so Waters had maneuvered closer for an inspection. He saw clearly the fine mist trailing his partner's left wing. The self-sealing tanks should take care of it quickly. As Waters had opened his mouth to inform his buddy of the fuel leak, the F-26 had disappeared in a blinding ball of flame. Waters had flown past the fireball and shaken his head before he believed what his eyes had told him.

Waters dropped his survival kit at the edge of the trees and entered the wooded stand with both hands on his raised pistol. The house showed no signs of forced entry. Waters followed the parachute, still visible in the treetops. Beneath it, the Chinese pilot lay in his harness, on the ground, crumpled, tangled in a web of risers. In his hand he held not a gun, but a green emergency locator transmitter. The beacon would be radioing beeps that would lead combat search and rescue straight to the grievously wounded man.

A single shot from Waters's 9 mm scattered circuit boards across the grass, destroying the transmitter. The Chinese pilot raised his head halfway, but couldn't seem to make his contorted body respond. Waters walked right up to him and stood over him looking down through the sights of his pistol. The Chinese pilot's glassy eyes stared back blankly. Their whites were crimson from burst blood vessels.

"You think you can come into my fucking country?" Waters asked. "You think you've got that right? Huh? *Huh*?" His enemy lowered his helmeted head and said nothing, which infuriated Waters. "Fuck you! *Fuck* you! I fuckin' *win*!"

His trigger finger pulled as fast as it could, and fourteen rounds lit the shaded side yard of the decrepit Alabama farmhouse.

Waters was tackled with a stunning blow. He hit the ground so hard the wind was knocked out of him. He began to struggle, but the man who sat on top of him held his hand over his mouth. It was an American soldier, Waters realized. The grease-painted white man raised his finger to his lips. He could just as easily have slit Waters's airpipe with the huge black combat knife sheathed on the shoulder of his body armor just above Waters's face. Ragged breath slowly returned to Waters, and he sat up.

The snake-eater had another huge fucking knife strapped onto his boot.

The flyboy grew more defensive about what he had done the more he calmed down. But Jim Hart was anything but calm. Not only would the sound of all those rounds—almost all wasted—bring any nearby Chinese patrols, but the transmitter beeps, sending location information, might bring heavily-armed heliborne troops from afar. The two Americans hurried across open fields in broad daylight. If they were sighted, they were dead. At least Jim was. He knew every minefield in the area. There would be no Chinese interrogators in his future. That decision, made long before, had been easy.

"That son of a bitch . . ." the air force guy began, shaking his head and not even paying attention to the treeline. Or the road. Or the horizon. "I lost my wingman this morning," he explained to an uninterested Hart. "He just . . . They . . ."

"I don't give a shit, okay?" Hart replied. "You shouldn't have used your pistol."

"I know," Waters said. "Shit! I don't know what the hell I was thinking. I shouldn't have . . . He probably was going to die anyway."

"I mean you shoulda had the sense to use a goddamned knife!" Hart chastised. "Now shut up!" They sprinted the last few dozen yards to the safety of the deep Alabama woods. The guy was almost crying.

Hart just looked at him and said, "Reload, Goddammit."

MOBILE, ALABAMA
September 19 // 0900 Local Time

To the consternation of the naval officers, who had so far flawlessly handled Wu's shipboard stay, Wu declined the power launch that had been arranged to take him ashore. Wu arrived instead at the crowded well deck wearing full combat gear and carrying an assault rifle. The bright morning sun lit the open end of the supercarrier. Wu looked behind him. He still couldn't shake his escorts. Soldiers made way and eyed Wu and the senior naval officers in their white summer uniforms that trailed him as they wove their way through the masses.

Wu's naval escort whispered to an army colonel, whose eyes widened. The colonel shook Wu's hand and greeted him respectfully, then ushered him to a place in the enclosed, armored landing craft. Wu waited for other troops to join him, but the rear doors closed with only him in the craft. He cursed to himself. The crew—whose legs were visible to Wu as they stood at their controls in the front of the amphibious vehicle—kept ducking from their open hatches to steal glances at him before they closed their hatches, fired up their engine, and drove off the ship's rear ramp into Mobile Bay.

•   •   •

When the double doors at the rear of the armored craft opened, a camera awaited Wu. The cameraman wore army fatigues. Wu emerged into the sunlight and onto a gravel-covered parking lot. It served a grassy, thinly wooded park with picnic tables, wooden shelters, and barbeque grills that were being bulldozed out of the way. Its sandy beach was now being used as a small beachhead. Amphibious vehicles like Wu's rose out of the bay with water cascading from their armored hulls. Their steel tracks ground up the sand and sod as jets of black diesel smoke shot straight up from their huge engines. Wu turned. The camera's eye—from two meters—filmed Wu against the backdrop of the powerful, surging equipment.

A major saluted Wu and escorted him to a waiting limousine. Wu looked at the trees, at the curb markings in English, at the houses across the highway, at the commercial buildings down the road in the distance. He soaked up the sights and sounds of America, the home of the mother he'd never known. He was conducting an experiment on himself.

Wu arrived at the old office building near the port of Mobile that was, for now, army headquarters. It was one of the few useful structures the Americans hadn't destroyed, booby-trapped or bugged. The massive explosive charges at the port had failed to fire, which was a monumental stroke of good luck. So far, the mission had been yet another extraordinary success. Another something with which Wu had nothing to do.

Upon Wu's arrival at General Sheng's office, a very pretty secretary—General Sheng's apparently—buzzed her boss's office. "Just a moment," she told Wu, smiling. The walls of the old American, 1990s-style office building were cracked and grimy beneath the wainscoting. It was unair-conditioned, poorly ventilated, and hot.

Wu could hear murmurs through the open transom above General Sheng's door.

"Would you like coffee while you wait, Lieutenant Han Wushi?" asked the girl. She was standing, beaming and solicitous. She faced Wu full on from across the room, looking slender with her arms clasped behind her back. She wore what was probably a strikingly expensive business suit, though her jacket was hung on a hanger on the wall. Her satin blouse was tight and revealed without showing. Her only accommodation to the war effort was that her civilian attire was a rich shade of green. But what Wu noticed most was that she had gleaming hair and sparkling eyes and a perfectly symmetrical, powdered white face and black lips.

Wu nodded.

The secretary lowered her eyes demurely and left Wu alone in the outer office.

He stepped close to the door. The transom above it was open to allow the air to circulate. Wu could see a slowly turning ceiling fan inside.

Sheng asked, "Are we *absolutely* sure Olympic is not a double agent? What are the chances there would be someone so highly placed in Washington?"

Colonel Li replied. "It's always a possibility that Olympic is passing American disinformation. You have to be highly suspicious of such things."

Sheng's secretary returned with a mug of coffee to find Wu standing by the door. Her smile flickered, and her eyes darted up to the transom just above him.

The door burst open, and General Sheng said, "Ah, Lieutenant Wu! I see you've found where we've cached our supply of beautiful Chinese ladies!" Sheng and Colonel Li laughed heartily and in unison. His secretary returned to her desk with Wu's coffee, counting cracks in the floor and trying to suppress a smile. "Are you ready to go meet your father at the airport?" Sheng asked. "I wouldn't want to make the mistake twice, now would I?"

The shy young secretary avoided Wu's gaze as he passed her desk. "I'm sorry," Wu said, "about the coffee."

"Some other time," she said. Wu smiled, but his eyes didn't quite rise to hers so he didn't know how she meant it.

As soon as Lieutenant Wu left General Sheng's outer office, the smile drained from her face. She looked Sheng in the eye and nodded once.

•   •   •

Han Zhemin emerged from his personal jet into the bright sunlight and descended to the shimmering tarmac of the Mobile Airport. The runway wasn't cratered. The terminal wasn't gutted. The facilities looked entirely unscathed. Something was wrong. Bill Baker would fight for every square inch of American soil, and yet the landings had gone virtually unopposed.

A military band played its strident, martial tune, and an honor guard with glistening bayonets lined a long red carpet. Chinese television cameras—civilian and military—recorded the pomp surrounding Han's arrival. At the foot of the stairs waited General Sheng, Colonel Li, and Wu. Han shook each of their hands. The military men pivoted and walked ceremoniously along the red carpet to Han's left, in step with the senior civilian. They passed a military honor guard wearing crisp uniforms and peaked hats, and carrying rifles with polished white slings. Behind them stood a liveried conductor, who stabbed his baton in the air leading a symphony of exaggerated brass and drums through movements of soaring patriotic music. They finally came to a raised platform filled with senior military officers before a crowd of steadily applauding soldiers. Everyone in attendance was Chinese military . . . except for the bulging international press corps.

I'm being set up, Han thought.

Instead of ascending the platform to speak into the cluster of microphones that festooned the podium, Han kept on walking toward the terminal building. His unanticipated deviation from the highly choreographed arrival ceremony threw Sheng and his aide, who had to grab the gleaming swords they wore and rush to catch up in a few jogging steps. Wu, however, had anticipated the move and remained at Han's side. In a glance, Han saw that Wu wore an expression that could be either amusement or satisfaction. The general and colonel eventually fell back into step with the lieutenant and the civilian for the long walk to the terminal.

It had been a deft trap by the usually ham-handed military, Han thought. The public announcement of Han's appointment as civilian administrator against the backdrop of conquered America would have guaranteed wide television coverage

back in China and across the Territories. But Han was bred
to play the game in which Sheng only dabbled. The point of
the photo op was to show the world that the military—not
the civilians—had presented China with the great victory. Han
would have been handed his power by Sheng in a respectful
but overt way. And watching that display of the military's
superiority would have been a hundred million bureaucrats,
whose sense of the symbolic was finely tuned. They were
readers of tea leaves who, merely from the place where you
stood in a photograph, could discern the ebb and flow of
political tides. Men and women whose only vote was cast by
the secret ballot of loyalty either to Han's civilians or Sheng's
military.

Once inside the deserted building, Sheng said, "We had
actually planned a small ceremony, Administrator Han. I
thought your staff had been informed."

"I wasn't satisfied with the security situation," Han replied
coolly.

"We have total control here," came Sheng's response in
his first ever openly menacing tone. By his fixed gaze on Han,
Sheng made clear the broader import of his comment.

"I prefer to deal with assessments based on fact, not opinion," Han said as his next move. "We lost two supercarrier
transports and over a dozen surface combatants to American
submarine and cruise missile attacks, and over one thousand
warplanes were shot down."

"Those were well within the parameters for a successful
landing operation of this size," Sheng quickly rebutted.

"But how many killed, General? Fifteen, twenty, thirty
thousand?"

"We planned for one hundred thousand ground casualties
by now, but we have had practically none."

And that's what is wrong, Han thought. *It's a trick.* He
smiled at the strangely unconcerned Sheng. "Perhaps," Han
said, "victory is indeed at hand."

A group of Chinese, South and East Asian, and South
American reporters had collected at a respectful distance from
the two most powerful men in the New World. Without looking their way, Han raised his voice and said, "*Now*, General

Sheng, I will inspect the men's positions and deployments.''

Han took off at a brisk stride down the concourse. He had no idea which way to head, but the act forced Sheng and his aide to follow, not lead.

Han swept his armored limousine for bugs then looked out at the American countryside that streaked by. Wu sat quietly at his side. Han spent the time stewing because there was too much that he didn't know. Finally, he turned to his son.

"I understand Bill Baker perfectly," Han said. "He thinks America is unique in history. That no power on Earth can defeat it. And he would do almost anything to prove that belief true."

"What if Baker used nuclear weapons to buy time to launch the arsenal ships?" Wu asked.

"He might use nuclear arms," Han noted. "Now that's an interesting question. But forget about those arsenal ships. We have been assured that they're either a massive disinformation effort, or Bill Baker's desperate and delusional dream of some superweapon. Perhaps they're some of both."

"But what if they weren't just a delusional dream?" Wu asked. "What if they *could* defeat our fleet? What if they could gain total supremacy of the sea?"

"What are you telling me, Wu?" Han asked in almost a whisper.

Wu looked around nervously, then related to his father his meeting with a senior naval officer without revealing who it was.

Han listened attentively. "If this is true, Wu," Han said slowly, "then the Americans mustn't launch those ships. We must, at all costs, seize or destroy those shipyards, because if we don't, we lose everything. We lose China. Our job, Wu, is to turn this supposed fact of yours to the advantage of our own family. If what this 'naval officer' said is correct, then surely Sheng must intend to destroy those shipyards at all costs. At all costs, Wu. Now how do you think those costs will be paid? They will be paid by classmates of yours like this Tsui, and they will be paid in numbers and at a rate that we have not seen in ten long years of war. Those casualties,

Wu, will be highly unpopular at home—highly, highly un-popular—and so would the military. Think of it. All those families losing their one and only male child. Their 'little emperors.' ''

Wu was quiet as he contemplated Han's analysis. Wu's jaws ground against each other. "Would President Baker use nuclear weapons?" Wu finally asked again.

"Perhaps," Han replied, "if he had no other choice. For he, too, will pay all costs. Look at his commitment of women to ground combat."

"His own daughter is a soldier," Wu eagerly pointed out.

"But if he went nuclear," Han said, "we would destroy his ships, shipyards, and ports with nuclear counterattacks. So the point is, Wu, that if we play this right, the ships will be destroyed, the military will be weakened and highly unpop-ular, and we will have America to govern." Han smiled at the simplicity of it all. "But we have to manage things just right. To do that, information is key. If you want to take part in all this, which you obviously do or you wouldn't be here, then you must continue giving me information. I know Sheng. He would never dissipate his advantage in combat strength by ceding the initiative to the Americans. He's not the reactive sort. He's hiding something—some plan—and it's your job, Wu, to find out what that plan is."

As Han again turned to the rural landscape, he felt Wu studying him. After a mile or so of silence, Wu said, "Maybe you shouldn't *worry* about military operations." Han's head snapped around to Wu after the insolent remark, but Wu quickly continued. "*Maybe*, for instance, Sheng has a," he shrugged, "special intelligence source in Washington. Some-one at the very highest level."

Just before Han's anger peaked at the boy's arrogant lec-turing, he realized what Wu was saying, and smiled. "Tell me what you know, Wu, and tell me now."

"There is a spy," Wu explained, "in Washington, code-named 'Olympic.' ''

Han's eyebrows rose, and he waited for more, but Wu fell silent. "I see. Well? What else do you know about this 'Olympic'?"

"Nothing," Wu answered. "He's an army spy, that's all I know."

Han's mouth hung open for a moment, then he arched his brow and said, "Interesting."

Wu doesn't know everything, Han thought, *but Sheng must.* He said, "Good job, Wu. Now what I want you to do is to find out everything you can about this 'Olympic'—every detail, every development—and report them to me immediately. But most importantly, I want you to find out who Olympic is."

Wu nodded, but his distracted gaze sunk to his lap.

"What is it, Wu?"

The boy's reply seeped from him, bubbling straight from some deep well of thought. "What if the American army stops our forces from seizing the shipyards without resort to nuclear arms?"

Han laughed. Wu looked at him with knitted brow. "Their army is filled with pampered schoolchildren. We have a veteran army that in a few months will outnumber them fifteen-to-one. Do you really think they can stop us?"

Wu slowly shook his head. "No. But what if they do?"

Han shrugged and sighed. "Then we lose," he said in a matter-of-fact tone.

General Sheng's aide, Colonel Li, opened Han's limousine door. He and Wu fell in behind Han and General Sheng as they walked along the edge of Mobile Bay. Chinese ships filled the harbor. Eight of the huge supercarriers were berthed at the wharves, each debarking troops at the rate of ten thousand per day. Eight more were anchored in the bay behind them. Troops lined the rails to look out at America.

They walked past a battery of large missile launchers: eighteen sealed canisters atop tracked vehicles. With a total of thirty such batteries ringing Mobile Bay plus fleet air defenses, Sheng informed Han that they had total air supremacy for sixty kilometers inland.

"I noticed as we were driving here," Han said, "the lines of trucks and armored vehicles parked on the shoulder of the road. Why weren't those troops moving?"

"They probably need fuel," Sheng replied. "The Americans were very thorough. They removed or destroyed all petroleum, oil, and lubricants. They appear to have destroyed practically everything of value."

"Not the port," Han said, looking out across the water. "Not the airport." He waited, but Sheng did not reply. "It still seems, however, that you should have anticipated that the Americans would not leave fuel waiting for us on the beach. Why didn't we bring enough fuel with us to keep those units moving?"

Sheng was finally baited into reply. "Those men were in our assault wave. They were to be expended in establishing the beachhead. Their idleness is the result of our success. We did not supply them with any more fuel than was necessary for them to reach objectives a few kilometers inland from the coast."

"In other words, you expected them all to be dead," Han translated. "And yet they appear to be very much alive and well . . . and of no current utility."

Sheng let the barb pass. But from behind, Colonel Li said, "We are working on new operational orders for the assault troops. We will supply them with fuel from our theater reserves. But follow-on forces have integral fuel stocks, so they are already pressing north to try to establish contact with the Americans."

General Sheng cut his aide-de-camp off. "I'm sure," he ventured loudly, "that our civilian guest is bored by all the details of our operations."

Han was thrown into a flurry of calculations. He considered shoving the word "guest" back into Sheng's face with appropriate—but not excessive—force. But Han decided on a different tack. Instead of reminding Sheng who it was that governed the territory on which they now strolled, Han picked up the more important thread left dangling by Sheng's comment.

"You're correct, General Sheng. I am, in fact, less concerned with *our* operations, and more interested in the Americans' plans, dispositions, and capabilities. I don't need to convey, I'm sure, the trepidation felt by our countrymen over the outcome of the American Campaign. The eyes of China are on your performance here, General Sheng.''

The septuagenarian general stopped in front of a Southern colonial-style home with broad verandas that faced the breeze from the bay. Han allowed himself a smile, but was slightly unnerved when Sheng smiled back.

Han and Sheng sat in padded chairs at a table covered by a linen tablecloth in the backyard of an antebellum home. Tall magnolia trees provided ample shade. Wu and Colonel Li sat nearby in silence. All were served iced tea—a local drink, as was the custom after first landing in conquered territory—by white-jacketed Chinese waiters. The grass on the lawn was too tall. The paint on the gazebo was peeling. The swimming pool was dark green and nearly overflowing. But the breeze and the shade made the hot day pleasant. Han craned his neck to look back at the dark, abandoned house that overlooked Mobile Bay. The door had been kicked off its hinges, presumably by Sheng's advance security team.

''I have never been to America before,'' Sheng said pleasantly. He peered across the bay seeming totally at ease.

Far too at ease, it seemed to Han. ''But this isn't America,'' Han replied. When Sheng looked at him, Han reached down and pulled a fistful of tall grass from the lawn and held it up to Sheng. ''*This* isn't anything. The resource that we're after—that we *need* to continue our economic expansion—is America's people. Their productivity. Their ingenuity. Their skills at innovation and the application of technology to new products. By fully integrating the American economy and workforce into our system of commerce, the world can finally rebuild after a decade of war and ascend to new records of profitability and efficiency at all levels of enterprise.''

Sheng seemed demoralized. No trace of good humor remained. He spoke in a strangely unguarded and distant tone. ''Is that why we're here?''

Han didn't even know whether or how to reply. It wasn't a challenge, or a lunge to be verbally parried. It seemed almost like the disillusioned comment of a tired old soldier.

They sat in silence, sipping the foul iced tea, watching the ships slowly maneuver in the harbor.

"We will win this war, Administrator Han," Sheng said with the formality of a pledge. "We will seize their two shipyards at San Diego and Philadelphia before they launch their arsenal ships. When that happens, America will have only two choices: continue fighting a bloody ground war until we exhaust their supply of manpower, or go nuclear." Han realized that Sheng was looking at him.

"I fear," Han said, "that many have underestimated the resolve of the American fighting man. The Defense Ministry concluded that American soldiers are over-reliant on high-tech weaponry and have no stomach for infantry warfare."

"The eleventh Army Group (North) has made no such miscalculation," Sheng said icily.

"My point is simply that they are now fighting for their homeland, and one cannot know what to expect from them under those circumstances."

"I expect that they will fight bravely and to the last man," Sheng answered, "and when that last man is dead, we will win."

"Let's just hope that you do seize their shipyards before they launch those arsenal ships. As I understand it, the navy stands no chance of countering their prodigious firepower. And I needn't remind you that 100 percent of your army's supplies and replacements arrive by sea. Plus, there are rumors, I'm sure you have heard, of other, more advanced weapons systems under development."

"They will not launch those ships," Sheng promised.

"I merely make the point," Han replied, "because San Diego lies on the opposite side of a large continent with the easily defended Mississippi River in between."

Sheng said nothing about the military's plan.

SOUTH OF TUSCALOOSA, ALABAMA
September 20 // 2200 Local Time

"Why don't you come with me?" air force Captain Waters suggested to army Captain Hart. "I mean, we can get across friendly lines tomorrow morning. You and me. Together.''

"I can't," Hart answered from the darkness. "I'm supposed to stay behind Chinese lines."

"For how long?" Waters asked.

"It's up to me," Hart replied.

"Then come *with* me! I'm five million dollars worth of government equipment. You're my *escort*!"

"You won't have any problems from here," Hart mumbled. "Besides," he said, finally blurting it out. "I haven't gotten into the fight yet."

"Oh," Waters said, accepting the explanation. "So go. Go on. Do your Green Beret thing." Waters rose and held his hand out to Hart. "Hope to see ya again," the pilot said. Jim nodded and shook his hand. Waters hoisted his kit and Hart his load. They headed in opposite directions.

Hart saved his night vision goggles, whose batteries were low, and relied only on his eyes and ears. He had to take a circuitous route around a minefield, which was sown across a road. On the map that Hart had committed to memory the field was designated, "Delay Fuse/First Contact." The first unit up the road would pass mine after mine, all of which would go active on the passing of the second.

Jim Hart was on the side of a ridge opposite the road when the first mine exploded. Three, four, five mines exploded in quick succession thereafter. A wounded man began to wail long and hard in total agony. The shouts of officers and NCOs obviously got the soldiers to remain still. They were shouting at them in Chinese. Explaining. *You're in a minefield!* Hart imagined. *Don't move!*

Hart flicked the safety of his M-16 off and donned his goggles. Night turned to day, and his path became clear. He trotted up the reverse slope of the hill that overlooked the road and minefield. The last few meters, Hart crawled. When he crested the ridge, he saw them spread out—lying on their bellies—on the open road below. He counted forty men. A platoon out on patrol. Obviously, the second unit to pass.

He raised the M-16 to his shoulder, but he didn't seize the pistol grip. He grabbed instead the trigger for the 40 mm grenade launcher mounted under the rifle's barrel. Loaded in the breech was HE frag: a high-explosive fragmentation grenade. The shot was easy. Pulling the trigger, however, was hard. He squeezed harder, and the rifle bucked. The *thump* was followed a half-second later by an explosion that split a man in two. Hart was already reloading. Soldiers were shouting to each other in Chinese. Hart felt confident they couldn't see him. He lined up another man in the sights, fired, and watched him roll over twice, landing on a mine. Pieces of him were sprayed to treetop level. His remains rained onto his comrades' lowered heads.

Hart froze in terror as, on a command, the entire platoon opened fire. He pressed low as weapons raged below. For ten or fifteen seconds all hell broke loose. Then, on command, the weapons fell silent. In the sudden quiet, Hart could hear new magazines being fed into hungry, empty receivers. None of the rounds had come anywhere near him.

Hart's third grenade killed the platoon leader or sergeant, who had been taking careful steps and shouting commands. When Hart killed the only other man trying to take charge, desperate soldiers began to shout pleas in broken and pitiful English. "Plees!" came a cry, which was repeated by others. "No shoot!" begged the more accomplished linguists. Hart fired grenades number four, five and six, and a dozen soldiers broke and ran. Six or seven mines exploded as men made headlong rushes through the field. Hart picked off the only target remaining upright with a single three-round burst.

But someone on the road below didn't panic. A machine gun opened fire, and bullets whizzed by Hart. He slammed his head to the ground as adrenaline shot through his body and urged him to flee. Some alert veteran of earlier wars had seen flashes from Hart's rifle despite the bulky flash suppressor on its muzzle. Hart couldn't bring himself to rise into the cutting death and fire. He lay with his face in the dirt. A round glanced off his body armor at the shoulder like a sledgehammer. Hart groaned at the searing pain. From the angry buzz of passing heavy-caliber rounds, he knew that he was very soon to be dead.

An explosion ended the near fatal rain. Hart looked up. A soldier—oblivious to the machine gun's checkmate—had panicked and sprinted by. A frightened recruit had set off a mine that had killed the wily veteran behind the gun and saved Jim Hart's life.

No one moved down below. At least, almost no one. A muffled groan and thrash drew Hart's attention. One soldier playing dead held his hand over his legless comrade's mouth. The maimed man's pain was too great, however, to be held in by his friend. They struggled for a moment, then Hart saw the friend make a cutting stroke across his wounded comrade's throat. The moaning and thrashing ended. Hart had found yet another Chinese combat veteran.

He switched his M-16 to "Semi" and aimed at the man's pelvis. Dead men are easy to care for. It's the permanently crippled that tax enemy resources. *Pow!* Hart's rifle boomed. A sound—like a siren winding up to full volume—told Hart unmistakably that he had a hit. The man's screams with every breath that he took added to the backdrop of the scene's noise.

When Hart occasionally drew fire from a rifleman, he would launch a grenade. When a man broke and ran, a three-round burst brought him down if Hart was fast enough to beat the mine that would quickly trip. The number of survivors dwindled.

More out of fear of a gunship than either mercy or the lack of targets, Hart disengaged and scampered down the reverse slope of the ridge listening to the wails of the hopelessly wounded. For after that first man, all of his shots had been aimed at the helpless, prone men's pelvises.

The only sentiment that Hart could muster in reply to the chorus of rising and falling screams was "Fuck you!"

BIRMINGHAM, ALABAMA
September 21 // 0110 Local Time

Despite the confined space of the fighting hole and the contortions necessary to fit her body into it, Stephie drifted ever closer to sleep.

"Wanta send your father a V-mail?" Becky Marsh asked Stephie.

"I'm *trying* to *sleep*," Stephie snarled, lying on her side and facing away. She wore her helmet and kept her eyes closed the entire time. The blanks began appearing in her mind again.

"Did you have a boyfriend?" Becky Marsh asked.

"Shut the fuck up, Becky, *Christ!* Why are you here?"

"Ack told me to bed down in your hole," Becky replied.

"Why?" Stephie lamented aloud.

"He said it was to keep you from getting raped," Becky answered.

"*You?* Keep *me* from getting raped? Hah!"

"Why are you so mean?" Becky asked, sounding hurt. "So now you're saying that you're better *looking* than me, *too*?"

"What?" Stephie whined, raising her hands and rubbing her temples. "*What* are you *talking* about?" she said.

"Knock it off!" they both heard demanded in a whisper from a nearby hole.

Stephie's head ached right behind her eyes from lack of sleep. She rubbed her eyelids too.

Becky whispered, but with a combination of anger and tears in her voice, "You come in here from this, like, *totally* great life, and you're smarter, and you can keep up with the men. You're just *better*! But, but, but," she faltered, "but so *now* you're saying you're better *looking* than me, *too*? *Jeeze!*"

"I am not saying that! Are you *ripped*? Where'd you get that from?"

"I said Ack put me here so they'd rape *me* first, but you're just so positive they'd rape you instead! Well, let me just tell you something! They look at me, too!"

"They look at *every* woman! They're *guys*! Now would you *please* just shut up!"

Becky began whimpering annoyingly. Stephie rose onto her forearms. Becky's well-lit face was fixed in a pout. The tiny video displays flickered off tears in the corners of her eyes. "You're out of your fucking mind," Stephie said, collapsing in a heap. For an instant she thought Becky might just fall silent. Stephie's anger faded the closer she drew to sleep.

"So *do* you have a boyfriend?" a wide-awake Becky Marsh asked.

Stephie said nothing. After a while, she heard a rustle of fabric. Becky, Stephie registered, raising her hands to return the tiny speakers to her ears.

Stephie had lived her high school years wearing earbuds like the ones dangling from Becky's commo gear. She'd worn them, too much for some, apparently, she remembered with shame and horror. She'd been lampooned at a senior party when her friends didn't know she was listening. Something about her always saying, "Huh?" and removing the buds in her ears whenever anybody said anything to her. The memory of the ridicule woke her up and pissed her off. Like everything else, however, her ire quickly sank into the swamp of fatigue.

Her stepdad was a good engineer, she now realized. Their house's A/V system was zoned room by room, and Stephie ruled the bandwidth within the four walls of her bedroom.

She'd once been listening to music—at sixteen, two years ago—when Conner had opened her bedroom door unexpectedly. He must have knocked, and she hadn't heard it. She hadn't even known he was coming over. When their eyes met, he had nodded, and ringlets of hair—each tight bundle of strands tied at the end—had bounced in a *very* cool way. He'd been seventeen and tanned. He had been at that moment—with that look—exactly the person to whom she'd been first and most attracted.

In that moment, everything had been perfect. She'd been in her house. In her room. Her favorite song was playing right at that very moment. Life was good. With practiced expertise she slung her silver-plated, Cartier-imitation control stick—from where it dangled on a bracelet on her wrist—straight into the palm of her hand. She thumbed the volume on her preprogrammed play list lower, and rose to her knees on the bed to kiss Conner on the lips. They both grinned, their teeth clanked, and Stephie drew away laughing.

"So? How was Dork*stadt*?" she asked

"It was *basket*ball camp," he whined. "Can't you just call it that? I mean Jeeze! You've been to every *soccer* camp in the south!"

"Yeah, but soccer's cool."

"Oh, yeah?" came Conner's retort. He arched his brow and morphed from being pissed, to reaching into his pocket, to trying to hide his smile. "You wanta see cool?" he asked, retrieving his garish purple control stick from his pocket. But Stephie hit hers first. "Oh, Steph, Jesus! *Just* let me just *play* it for you!" he whined again. "You're such a control freak!"

"I *am* not!" she replied sternly, offended by the comment. "You'll purge my *video* cache!"

"I *told* you I could fix it so it didn't do that."

"So could *I*, jock-boy," Stephie replied with razor wit that beamed straight over his head. "System," she said, not to Conner but to the round plastic node that protruded from her room's multimedia outlet, "transfer video cache to personal drive."

"Personal drive is full," replied the control system in a voice that Stephie had personally trained.

Conner chuckled. "That sounds just like you," Conner remarked as he plopped down on the bed and bounced her into the air.

She flashed him a growling expression. "System," Stephie commanded, "store the video cache on Dad's disk array, only please don't tell him."

"Acknowledged," replied the pleasant voice.

Stephie smiled and batted her eyelashes at Conner. She uttered a fluttering, Southern Belle laugh. "Oh-h-h! These new video servers are just so *complicated*! And I'm just a *girl*!"

Conner's response was both unexpected and totally in keeping. He tried to kiss her.

She pushed him away. "Dream about it," she said in a worldly tone.

He smirked and tapped a thumb on his control stick's membrane, lighting a succession of glowing color buttons and crisp white text on the purple stick.

"Video source from Conner Reilly 5468?" questioned the perfect girl's voice.

"Not just 'Conner'?" he asked. "It calls me 'Conner Reilly 5468'?"

"She doesn't know you that well yet," Stephie replied.

"System," Stephie commanded, "accept and play Conner Reilly video source, and create shortcut: 'Conner Reilly 5468' equals 'Conner.' "

"Done," the computer replied.

Conner smiled. Stephie kissed him.

The video appeared on her off-white, wall-mounted plasma screen, which blended into the off-white walls. He pulled away even though she didn't want him to. On the screen, a bunch of sweaty boys sat on a shiny basketball court in a semicircle in front of empty tables. "The final trophy," shouted a man in long, baggy gym shorts, "will be presented by Coach Fortner."

"The man!" shouted all the boys in unison on hearing Coach Fortner's name.

Stephie rolled her eyes and leaned her head on his shoulder, her lips upturned to his.

"Watch," he said, eyes fixed on the screen.

She sighed, aggravated by his clumsiness. The gym-shorts guy held out his hand to another man in shorts, and said, "Coach Fortner?"

"The man!" shouted all once again on hearing the man's name.

"Oh, *God*," Stephie commented. "This is so diseased."

The Man said, "Thank you, Coach Wilson."

"The Almost Man!" chanted the budding young basketball players.

Stephie laughed. "What total Dorkdom yonder lies!"

"And now," The Man announced, whistle dangling from his neck and touchpanel in hand, "the award we've all been waiting for. This camp's highest honor: the Charlie Hustle Award."

"The 'Charlie *Hustle* Award'?" Stephie ridiculed, feigning a coughing fit that ended with heaves as if she were vomiting from the nausea of it all.

The Man glanced at his touchpanel. "I'd like you all to give a Warrior Basketball Camp round of applause to the one guy who busted his ass up and down the court all week long, every day! Conner Reilly, would you come up here!"

As Conner rose on the screen and began to step over seated boys, The Almost Man shouted, ''One-two-three!'' Fifty boys—as one—clapped thunderously. ''One-two-three!'' *Clap!* ''One-two-three!'' *Clap!* ''One-two-three!'' *Clap!*

Stephie looked at Conner out of the corners of her eyes but he was too busy watching himself. She returned her eyes to the screen and held her withering sarcasm. With schizoid humility, Conner looked everywhere but at The Man, whose hand was outstretched for a firm shake. Conner grabbed for the small trophy and belatedly saw the proffered hand, and tried to slap it just as The Man took it back.

Conner stabbed at his control stick and stopped the video. Stephie couldn't help dissolving into laughter. ''Charlie *Hustle*?'' she cried, flopping onto her back.

Conner appeared on top of her and kissed her open-mouthed on the lips, but roughly. She regained control by kissing him back with even more abandon. Soon she could hear him breathing heavily through his nose, his mouth becaming more urgent, more demanding. She pushed his hands away from her and stood up. ''Time to go home, Conner,'' she said, but she continued to feel the excitement of his touch on her body.

Stephie lay wide-awake in her fighting hole, roused by the strangely vivid memory.

Stephie was awakened by John Burns. She emerged from the roofed shelter to find men in dark business suits and wingtips. Although she was armed and in full combat gear, the men surrounded her like bodyguards. She was so groggy, and the agents were so efficient, that she was over the hill and on a helicopter before she had cleared the cobwebs from her head. But once she was alert, she didn't need to shout questions over the engine noise to ask what was going on. It was obvious. The men had earphones and American-flag lapel pins. She was being taken to meet her father.

She leaned her head against the small window. The pilots flew on night vision. The only indication Stephie had that they were only a hundred feet above the ground was the shimmering lake that flashed by in the moonlight.

Every time Stephie tried to ask her mother about her brief marriage to Bill Baker, Rachel Roberts had instantly angered. As he had rocketed to national prominence, Stephie's mother had grown even more vindictive. Her hatred more naked. Some of her diatribes against her ex-husband had even sparked bitter fights with Hank Roberts—her new husband and Stephie's stepfather—especially after Hank had lost his job. "You're just pissed off," Stephie had heard him say through their closed bedroom doors, "because you're not the goddamn First Lady!" Hank had shouted.

"And *you're* just pissed off because my *first* husband still has a *job*!" Stephie's mother had screamed. Without ever acknowledging that she'd heard it, Stephie never forgave the awful remark.

Rachel Roberts had kept Bill and Stephie apart out of spite. Stephie had been four years old when Bill Baker first ran for the Senate. A *Washington Post* reporter had discovered that Bill had a child by his ex-wife. Stephie had been conceived a couple of months before their divorce and had been born just weeks after Rachel's marriage to Hank Roberts. Something had broken up her parents' marriage, and in Stephie's confident days before high school she'd asked her mom, "Was it Hank?"

Her mother had laughed derisively. "Hank?" she had dismissed as ridiculous. Hank Roberts had been obsessed with Rachel since school days, her mother informed Stephie, to ensure that her daughter understood the way things were. But Rachel Roberts—who with her sister had cornered the beauty queen circuit in their early teens—had never given the poor bastard the time of day . . . until Rachel married him eight months pregnant with Stephie. On questioning, Stephie's mother had firmly resisted discussing the subject further. Stephie had come to realize that something was hidden in the seven months between Rachel's divorce and her eventual remarriage on the eve of Stephie's birth. Some crucial piece of the story was missing.

Bill Baker had appeared at their door to visit the confused and excited little girl just days after the newspaper article had run and photographers had begun stalking the four-year-old. Stephie had gladly given them photos of her big grin. Apparently, Stephie's mother hadn't told her father that she was pregnant or that Stephie was his daughter. "Don't get your hopes up," she had dully warned Stephie. It had taken her new father an hour of heated fighting with her mother just to get to see Stephie, who had been ordered to remain in her room. There, she had tried to peer through the crack between the door and the carpet, and had listened to her shouting mother curse.

Her real father had finally entered Stephie's room, almost banging the bottom of the door into her forehead. His white teeth had shone, and his eyes had sparkled in a grin that disappeared the instant he saw that she was crying. "It's okay," Stephie kept repeating. "I'm okay. You can smile again." Her tears had dried up as his had begun to flow while he sat beside her. She remembered his tone—soft, sweet—and definitely remembered the tear that she watched form in his eye and then roll down his cheek. But the first words of his that she could recall still tore at her heart. "I shouldn't have come," he had said. She had instantly hugged him. When he had hugged back—holding her so lovingly—Stephie had known, for sure, that he really was her father.

Thereafter, he hadn't come. Her mother had sworn she would ruin him if he had fought for visitation rights, Stephie learned later, so instead her father had only sent cards and letters. By the time Stephie was a teenager, she had demanded that her mother quit opening the correspondence from her father. There was never anything in the letters of any substance, but each birthday card or letter handwritten on Senate stationery had gone into Stephie's treasure trove. The same place she had hidden each movie disk that she had clandestinely ordered on the Internet and had shipped to Sally Hampton's address. She and Sally had watched her father's old movies. He was gorgeous. And in the movies Bill Baker had always played the hero.

Stephie and Sally had gotten into an embarrassing fight when, despite Sally's denials, it had become obvious that

Sally had developed a crush on Stephie's father. "He's just playing a part!" Stephie had said with all the fake conviction she could muster. "He's not *really* like that in real life." Sally had not asked Stephie how she would know what he was like in real life, and their friendship had survived.

The only other times Stephie had seen her father was when he made surprise appearances at her championship soccer game and then on her sixteenth birthday. A huge fight had ensued in front of Stephie's friends, and her mother had later blamed her father for ruining the party. But in truth Stephie blamed her mother for the humiliating spectacle. And she was thrilled that her father—in the middle of what would be a successful presidential campaign—had taken the time to visit Stephie on her sixteenth birthday. She meant something to him.

He had told her how beautiful she had looked even though her hair was pinned up and she had been wearing faded jeans and Conner's dishwater-gray basketball camp T-shirt at the all-girl sleepover.

She sat strapped into her jump seat across from the expressionless Secret Service agent and looked down at her filthy camo trousers, and caked and muddy boots. She smelled of the outdoors.

The helicopter landed amid the headlights of a half-dozen black sports utility vehicles on the broad lawn of a large, private home. The vehicles' lights were immediately extinguished. Three other helicopters were parked nearby, as were dozens of cars, trucks, armored fighting vehicles, and tanks. Stephie was ushered into the house past a lit swimming pool and three all-threat missile crews scanning the dark sky.

Bill Baker waited for her in the entry. Stephie leaned her rifle against the wall and thought about saluting, but wiped her hand on her hip and held it out for a shake instead. He wrapped both arms around her. Their hug was awkward through her body armor, grenades, and ammo pouches. Plus Stephie resisted feeling much intimacy because she had gone several days without bathing. She practically cringed when he perused her from her hair matted by her helmet to her mud-caked boots. He misunderstood her desire to maintain a distance and seemed saddened.

"I love you," she said to correct his impression, but his spirits seemed not to rise.

They headed into a cozy study. He asked how the men were treating her.

"Oh, okay," Stephie replied. "One boy in particular." She couldn't help what her mother disapprovingly called her junior-high giggle.

A broad smile spread across his face, but his eyes remained unhappy. He seemed to her melancholy and disturbed, so unlike his always self-assured public persona. His mood also didn't match Stephie's. Her face was streaked with day-old grease paint. Her camouflage fatigues were caked with dirt. She was the picture of a soldier, and she was suddenly filled with pride that her father had gotten to see her this way. Before . . . whatever.

"Stephie . . ." he began, but he seemed to lose the words. She waited on the edge of her seat. "Would you like a transfer to the rear?" he asked without looking her in the eye.

Instead of expressing pride, he had offered her a coward's pass. "You don't know me at *all*!" she burst out in anger. The words seemed to hit him with more force than she had intended. He forced his guilty gaze up to her and swallowed hard several times. His eyes misted.

"I guess I do now," he practically whispered in a crestfallen tone.

There was a loud rapping on the door. Both looked up. A military aide entered and waited for an invitation to speak. Bill finally nodded. The aide, a naval officer in khakis, proceeded to update her father about some minor naval engagement in the Pacific on which he had been briefed. It had—in the intervening hours, apparently—turned into a catastrophic rout. Ten Chinese supercarriers had pounced upon a U.S. Navy convoy heading from San Francisco to besieged troops in Hawaii. They had sunk one American carrier, and were chasing the other damaged carrier north toward Aleutian anchorage.

The naval officer's eyes darted back and forth between Stephie and her father. He looked as if he were falling ill right before their eyes. "I'm sorry, sir," he said as if it were all his fault. "But . . . China has just invaded southern California."

Stephie turned immediately to her father. His head wobbled visibly as if the world had shifted beneath him. Goose bumps of fear rippled across Stephie's body in complex patterns. "The landings are currently under way in force," the downcast aide reported as quickly as he could get the words out, "both north and south of San Diego. The commander of the 5th Marine Expeditionary Brigade reports that at least three divisions of amphibious assault troops—probably directly out of Japan—are coming ashore and maneuvering against the San Diego naval shipyard. Several thousand landing craft are visible. His men are engaged, but he reports, sir, that he won't be able to hold much longer. Not very long at all."

The aide, in khakis, went on and on, but Stephie's father didn't seem to be listening. A convoy on the way to supply Hawaii was being routed by ten Chinese supercarriers. One American carrier had been sunk. Another was damaged and being chased toward Aleutian anchorage.

Her father looked stunned. "Is there any . . . ?" he began. "Can the . . . ?" The military aide waited for a question. Stephie looked at him, joining him as if grieving over his purely personal loss. But it was more than that. China, she understood, was now on the verge of seizing one of the three arsenal ships that America had under construction. "Does the navy," her father managed to say in a hoarse, croaking voice that drew her instant scrutiny, "report anything happening off Delaware Bay?" She had never heard of Delaware Bay. The naval officer shook his head, then realized the import of the commander-in-chief's question—of his terrifying fear—and shook his head again more vigorously.

Stephie watched her father. He had grown pale. The lips around his open mouth quivered as he tried to form the words. "Destroy . . . the ship," he managed. His military aide hesitated, forcing the president to repeat his order with absolute clarity. He took a deep breath and spoke slowly. "I am ordering the commander of the 5th Marine Expeditionary Brigade to destroy the arsenal ship, the dies, the designs, the warehouses and stores, and the dock facilities," he said in a raspy, lifeless voice, "and to fight to the last Marine."

The aide hesitated, swallowed, and cleared his throat. "Do you want me to get the secretary of defense on the line, sir?"

Stephie's father shook his head. "No. I want you to relay my command."

The khaki-clad aide nodded reluctantly. "And, uhm, sir, what about Operation Anvilhead, sir?" he asked. "The West Coast is screaming for troops. Los Angeles is . . . is at risk."

The dazed commander-in-chief was already nodding. Stephie couldn't tell whether the nods signified understanding of their need for reinforcements, or internal confirmation that the worst had just happened. "Abort Operation Anvilhead," he replied, wincing at his own words. With his eyes closed, he said, "Send the troops west."

"Sir," the naval officer said, "I'm sure I can get the SecDef on the . . ."

"You give the order. I'm sure I'll hear from the Secretary soon enough."

The aide departed quietly. Stephie rose and said, "I'd better get back to my unit."

She expected him to try again to prevail upon her to accept a transfer to the rear, but he instead held his head in both hands and stared at the floor. She had never heard of "Operation Anvilhead" and didn't then appreciate what its cancellation would mean for her and the other undermanned defenders of the South, but the second invasion and the loss of one of America's three arsenal ships was terrible news for America, she understood. At that moment, however, what absolutely perplexed and terrified her was her father's obvious fear. He seemed frozen by it. He didn't move. Didn't talk. Didn't look up. He was totally catatonic.

"Hey," she said in a quiet, high-pitched tone, taking a step closer to him, "it'll be okay. We're ready." His head rose slowly. He looked at her through bloodshot, exhausted eyes.

"You can trust us, Dad. You can count on us. It's our turn to fight, and we're gonna stop them," she said. "We'll win."

Tears of anger clouded her vision and ran down her cheeks. Her father wrapped his arms around her to comfort her. He didn't understand her at all.

PART TWO

Victory at all costs, victory in spite of terror, victory however long and hard the road may be; for without victory there is no survival.

Winston S. Churchill,
First Statement as Prime Minister
to the House of Commons (1940)

4

Lieutenant Wu had been awakened to news that he would attend the prime minister's teleconference in one hour. Han had told his son that he would face the three most powerful men in the world: the civilian leaders of China. He had instructed Wu to wear a suit, not a uniform. "And who's the girl who answered the phone?" his father had asked in a conspiratorial, confidential tone although Wu felt sure that Han already knew.

"What's going on?" asked Shen Shen, General Sheng's secretary. When Wu had replied that it was nothing, she had let the sheet slip from her breasts as she motioned for him to kiss her good-bye.

Wu's hair, though short and bristly, had still felt wet when he had arrived at his father's office complex. Outside, mammoth portable air-conditioning systems pumped frigid air through orange ducts into the buildings. Wu sat in a two-seat video conference center and tried not to shiver. Han Zhemin sat opposite his son and stared daggers at Wu's camouflaged battle dress. His smirking gaze ended on skin that had tanned beneath Wu's close-cropped, military-style haircut.

Three images appeared on the semi-circular array of screens before each of the two padded leather chairs of the room's conference center. Camera lights integrated into the consoles illuminated Han and Wu, who stared across real space at each other. The prime minister in the center screen—Han's uncle and Wu's great-uncle—was the most powerful of the three old men. Han's father—Wu's grandfather—on the right screen was second in command and China's minister of trade. The third man, on the left screen, was unrelated to Wu and Han. He was the head of China's state security agency and the reason the powerful Han family—the security chief's longtime political allies—survived from day to day.

The prime minister convened the meeting of the executive committee of the Chinese council of ministers. "Lieutenant Wu," he began in a grave tone, "were you, or were you not aware of the Chinese army's plans to invade California?"

Wu looked across at his father. There was no nod or shake of Han's head—however slight—to hint at which way he should answer. Instead, Han cocked his head and awaited Wu's reply.

Wu stared at his father, girding himself for the effort of enduring the ordeal alone. There was no one there to help him.

Wu looked straight into the camera. "As a part of my job on the general staff of Eleventh Army Group (North), I am privy to certain classified military secrets. While I am committed to the belief that the civilian leadership of this country should have all relevant national security information," he said—looking at each of the three men—"I do not believe that it is *I* who should be disclosing that information to you."

Wu's great-uncle looked at Wu's grandfather, who was across the same room back in Beijing. The even older security chief watched from a remote location. They were never all together in the same location at once for obvious security reasons.

Wu took a deep breath. He had been awakened so early and thrust into this meeting with so little preparation that he was speaking unrehearsed. "But perhaps," he suggested, "entrée might be had at the office of Defense Minister Liu

Changxing?" Han Zhemin rocked back in his reclining chair. The camera and lights automatically followed him. He was surprised—for all to see—at Wu's audacity. He made a show of it, Wu noted. The executive committee of the council of ministers—on which the defense minister naturally sat—had been constituted specifically to keep the military from wielding civilian governmental power. General Liu was these men's mortal enemy.

"What do you know?" the prime minister pointedly asked Wu.

The boy looked up at Han, who seemed surprised by the question. Confused. Wu stifled a smile. "I know what's coming," Wu said. Han now rocked forward to the edge of his seat. Everyone else was stilled by Wu's words. "I've studied every battle," Wu said, "of every campaign, of every war over the last decade. We have gotten used to a five-to-one kill ratio over our enemies, but that statistic was skewed by our enemies' enormous losses in Southeast Asia and India. What if, in the American Campaign, that ratio is reversed, or worse? What if *ten* Chinese soldiers die for every American? Twenty? *Fifty*-to-one, one classified defense ministry paper projected."

All four men's attention was riveted on young Wu until the security head looked off-screen and smiled at his co-workers. That was a significant datum of intelligence for the old cloak-and-dagger warrior.

"I *think*," Han said—this time surprising Wu—"that what *Lieutenant* Wu means is that China's casualties in America might grow intolerable." Wu ground his teeth at his father's opportunism. Han had sensed that Wu's idea had traction, and he was making it his own. "Perhaps we might approach Liu when popular support for the military has eroded due to a costly, grinding, exquisitely *bloody* campaign. And in that weakened political condition," Han proposed as he sat back in satisfaction, "we might restore the country's political balance to the center."

"I *mean*," Wu interjected, "that Defense Minister Liu may already be troubled by the casualty projections, and the time to approach him is not *after* we lose ten million dead, but *before!*"

They ignored Wu's point, and by the end of the teleconference they had adopted Han's plan. They were to monitor closely the results of the military campaign and assess the evolving political consequences. Wu noted, to his disgust, how worried all four men were by the success of their country's two invasions.

Wu went back to his suite, stripped naked, and crawled into bed. Shen Shen conformed herself to his back, skin to skin. "Does it bother you?" she asked softly. "Being in America? Being half American?"

He pulled free and rose with such force that he took the satin sheet with him and almost spilled Shen Shen onto the floor. "I am *not* half American!"

"Oh, *no-I-didn't-mean-that!*" she shrieked. She was panicked and horrified at her misstep. She held her hand out to him then brought it back to her mouth to cover her sobs.

"I am Chinese!" Wu said. "I am . . . Chinese!"

INTERSTATE 5, SAN DIEGO, CALIFORNIA
September 23 // 1030 Local Time

". . . many armored vehicles!" shouted the forward air force's air observer over his radio.

Sergeant Conner Reilly monitored the radio nets as he sighted his shoulder-fired, all-threat missile on the lead main battle tank. "Heading north on I-5 past Mission Bay!" the air force lieutenant croaked through a parched throat. "Main battle tanks! Armored fighting vehicles! Armored missile carriers! Armored rocket launchers! Amphibious assault craft! Self-propelled artillery! Self-deploying bridging equipment!" The FO had to pause to swallow. To breathe. Conner's heart pounded, and his own throat felt as if it were pinched between his finger and thumb. "Estimated at least regimental size! Say again. At least regimental size!"

Conner commanded the FO's small security team. One squad of armored cavalry scouts. Nine men. One woman.

They were dismounted because they had flown in on requisitioned civilian airliners from Tennessee, where they had been poised and waiting for a long-planned and well-rehearsed counterattack against Chinese-held Gulf Coast ports. Their armored fighting vehicles were being loaded aboard much slower rail transport.

The ten armored cavalrymen and women—seat fillers on an aircraft filled with a company of combat engineers—had landed at Miramar Naval Air Station the day before, two days after the first Chinese landings in California. When Conner stepped through the plane's door, the sound of distant fighting had hit him. A continuous rumble over the horizon toward the beach and city to the southwest. Sitting on the tarmac and waiting for orders or transport had been thousands upon thousands of troops with nowhere to go and nothing to do. The army's typical disorganization had angered Conner. It was obvious which way the enemy was.

He had led his nine soldiers in search of a mission. They had found the air force lieutenant wandering among clusters of harried army officers trying to bring order to the chaos. "Just give me somebody!" the guy had demanded. "I've got my equipment! We've got the ordnance airborne! I just need a security team so I can get up to the fucking line and call it *in*!"

Conner had pulled the man aside, and they had a mission ten minutes after landing. Five minutes later, a smiling, eager Hispanic house painter had offered to give them a ride in his pickup. Conner and the air force officer had ridden in the unairconditioned cab. Conner's cavalrymen had climbed into the back with the painter's teenage son. "I talked to my cousin," the grinning man reported, clearly happy to be of help. "They're coming up I-5."

"Then let's go to I-5," the air force guy had said, looking at Conner. Conner shrugged and nodded.

Off they had driven. Traffic jams had forced detours through the front yards of homes whose owners were frantically packing. Military policemen at checkpoints brandishing loaded M-16s had at first leveled their weapons on the wildly weaving, paint-flecked pick-up. But when the driver had lain on his horn and the MPs had seen his load of combat-bound troops they had waved them through the barricades toward the coast without stopping them.

As they neared I-5, the traffic had come to a complete stop. It was a parking lot filled with angry drivers standing beside their open doors and craning their necks to see what the holdup was. Conner had ordered his men to dismount and had thanked the always smiling painter. His son had climbed into the cab.

"Vayan con dios, amigos!" the man had shouted to Conner and his men as they began to climb a dry hill.

"Give 'em hell!" his son had called out before saying to his father, "Let's go back and get some more!" The truck had made a U-turn and headed back in the direction of the Naval Air Station.

At the top of the hill, they had seen blue water, but they had no idea where they were. Conner and the air force lieutenant had returned to the road and gone from car to car until he'd found a family with a map. The air force guy had pulled out a portable scanner and swiped the image of the map into his palmtop. He printed out eleven copies, and they were in business.

For the first few hours, they had seen nothing but panicked refugees. They had set up on the hillside overlooking Mission Bay and watched as both north- and southbound lanes of Interstate 5 had filled with hundreds of thousands of people fleeing San Diego toward Los Angeles in bumper-to-bumper traffic. But the sound of the fighting carried. The *crumps* and *bangs* were near constant.

By late afternoon, they had begun playing a game of cat-and-mouse with pilotless Chinese reconnaissance drones. When a drone had finally clearly spotted them—flying in lazy circles overhead like a vulture—Conner had fired a shoulder-launched missile from the hilltop. An explosive burst of gasses had belted the slender missile from its disposable tube and rocked him backward a step. At a safe distance of about thirty feet in the air, the weapon's rocket motor had ignited. The drone hadn't even bothered to take evasive action, but had instead continued its tight circle above their position beaming images back to some Chinese command post of a lone American soldier standing out in the open. Just before the drone had disappeared in a ball of flame to the exultant cheers of his well hidden troops, Conner had vigorously thrust his middle finger skyward to give the camera and its remote operators one last, defiant pose.

The smoking debris from the drone had dented rooftops and smashed windshields of family cars clogging the highway, further panicking drivers. Conner decided that they had to relocate because their position was in the Chinese databanks. As they climbed through the hills, they lost sight of the Interstate. But horns that had begun blowing upon the downing of the drone continued to sound for an hour. By the time they set up in their current position, the traffic flowing out of San Diego was flowing again and growing ever lighter.

By midnight, only the occasional speeding car roared up I-5 from San Diego. The forward observer had established good, continuous contact with airborne flight controllers operating over Escondido a safe distance to the north. Just after midnight, Conner had made fleeting radio contact with Green Berets operating to the south of their position. The Special Forces team had reported that Chinese troops had bridged the San Diego River at I-5 and that lead elements were at such-and-such a grid coordinates. Conner had explained that they had no army maps with grid squares.

"They're just now passing Sea World!" had come the Green Berets' shout.

By daylight, the Chinese still hadn't arrived. Conner's team were deployed along a fifty-meter line in gouges dug out of the hard-baked north shoulder of a state highway, which intersected I-5 at a road junction 200 meters to the west. Sandy flats offered them good sight lines toward the junction and the bay beyond it, but once the Chinese vanguard passed under the state highway's overpass, they would lose sight of them completely. The scrubby hills to their backs obscured their view of I-5 North, but the hills' steep cuts also offered their only means of withdrawal. There were no thick pine forests like the ones in Conner's hometown of Mobile:

the terrain on which they had trained to fight for the last three months.

The air force lieutenant in the next hole to the west continued screaming out his sightings to the airborne controllers. Conner checked again on his squad's lone woman, Private Deborah Stuart, whose hole was just to the east of Conner's. He had promised her father, when the man had illegally visited their unit, that he would watch after his daughter.

The lead elements of the Chinese army were now drawing even with the road junction to the west.

The air force FO turned to Conner and said, "We've got a fire mission!"

Conner nodded and returned to his missile sight. The green crosshairs turned red when the lead tank disappeared under the overpass and he lost his lock. He picked another of the plentiful armored vehicles and instantly got a green *Target Designated* and a faint tone in his headphones.

"Missiles away!" came the FO's shout.

"Incoming!" Conner warned over his squad's Minimal Emission System radio net. "Heads down! Heads down!"

The only warning emitted by the inbound, heavy missiles fired from orbiting attack aircraft miles inland were their high-pitched shrieks—like noisy fireworks that didn't explode—as their rockets powered them straight into the earth. These fireworks, however, did explode.

The ground bucked underneath Conner, and the air pounded his body and ears with a gripping, disconcerting shake. His eyes were forced closed by the flash and searing heat, and he found himself tumbling into disorientation as the slamming blows washed over him. The smooth pavement of the state highway cracked and buckled like in an earthquake as it rose into the now listing highway's overpass.

He forced his eyes open and his head up. The long, level pavement behind which they took cover offered Conner a stable horizon, and his senses finally steadied. He could see no Chinese column on the Interstate beneath the twisted bridge through the heavy black smoke. He switched his missile's sight to thermal, but all it displayed were the plumes of heat from that rose like fiery towers from a dozen belching vehicles.

"Target destroyed!" the FO reported ecstatically. "Target destroyed! Target destroyed! Great shooting!"

"Contact! Contact! Contact!" came frantic screams from several sources over Conner's MES. His helmet's audio system placed the panicked calls of Conner's men to his left—inland, to the east—*away* from Interstate 5! Conner, however, searched the clouds of smoke rising from the highway to his right, thinking the directional steering of the audio to be in error.

"Tanks! Tanks!" shouted Hickson, the man on his squad's left.

Conner turned to see Hickson come apart in time to the jarring crack of a main tank gun and its shell's simultaneous explosion beside Hickson's shallow hole. Hickson's arms, legs, and head were flung in different directions. His torso simply disappeared.

Behind the ghastly scene Conner saw a column of armored vehicles bearing down the state highway toward the junction with I-5 at Mission Bay. Straight toward their position.

"Pull back! Pull back!" Conner shouted, although his men were already running for the hills. Two were blown to bits by a single round fired into the dirt at their feet from a tank gun. Heat from the explosion licked at Conner's face, and debris stung his neck and hand. Heavy machine guns rattled from atop the armored turrets of a long column of tanks that crested the inland hill to their left. Blistering rounds knifed through air, and men fell amid geysers of dry earth and smoke. Conner sprinted for the hills like the rest. It was every man for himself.

The air force lieutenant, a dozen yards in front of Conner and at the base of the first hill, let loose a shout and sank to his knees beside his severed right arm. Before Conner made it to him, the left hemisphere of his head exploded with an exiting, large-caliber machine gun round, and he toppled to that side.

Everywhere, rounds sung through the air and explosions rocked the earth.

Conner found Debbie Stuart curled up at the bottom of a narrow gully where the occasional rainwater channeled toward a small pipe under the road. Tears streamed down her face, which was pressed onto the ground. He dropped beside her in the same instant that explosions and machine gun fire erupted from a new direction. From the direction of I-5.

They were caught in a crossfire of lethal projectiles, which buzzed over their heads. Pelted the dirt. Skipped along the ground. Skimmed great sheaths of earth from the hillside all around.

"Whatta-we-do?" Debbie shouted.

Conner looked back and forth—left and right—at the armored pincers closing on their position. The Chinese tanks' main guns were now silent for fear of striking their comrades in the closing jaws of their vise. Their heavy machine guns reduced their fire to aimed bursts. The crackle of rifle fire rose and fell as Conner's men's lives were snuffed out singly and in pairs.

"What do we *do*?" Debbie again yelled.

Conner could see dismounted Chinese soldiers bobbing and weaving through the fingers of hills that ran to the road. On the Interstate to the west, he could hear the sounds of engines. The northbound traffic was no longer concerned with the minor firefight on their flank. Debbie Stuart was watching him. Conner took a deep breath, filling his lungs. When he exhaled, it sounded like a sigh.

Debbie read something into his sigh. She lowered her cheek to her rifle's stock and aimed at the onrushing Chinese infantry. Conner, slow to appreciate the decision that she thought he had made, raised his own rifle from where he lay prone beside her.

Debbie fired two three-round bursts before Conner could take aim. The Chinese that at first had filled Conner's sights dropped into depressions in the earth and behind wisps of trashy brush. When Debbie fired again, Conner squeezed his trigger and fired into a clump of desert greenery behind which he had seen one man dive.

The air around them turned instantly lethal. Metal projectiles cut close by Conner's head and shoulders as a dozen brown hiding places erupted with orange fire. Conner ducked just in time. A bullet slammed into his helmet.

A rifle grenade whizzed in at far slower speed and exploded. Debbie screamed in terror. Both American rifles had fallen quiet, but still the Chinese poured on the fire. Another grenade—far closer than the last—slammed into the earth, and Debbie's wails ended abruptly. Conner raised his unsteady head.

A third grenade erupted without warning in the narrow space between Conner and Debbie, rocking Conner and wrenching his gear to one side. Lashing nerve endings up and down his right side, leaving them numb—insensate—like after a splash of frigid water. His world spun once, and then again, and his head dipped as if he were beginning to doze on a long car trip. Then he was wide awake.

Conner caught his head and focused on Debbie. She was horribly wounded. Her left side was chewed up and bloody. It was impossible to tell where her gear ended and the pulp of her body began. Her dull eyes stared his way unmoving. Unfocused. He reached for her.

Nothing happened. His head spun again, and he blacked out for an instant. He reached for her again. Nothing. He looked down. His severed arm lay beside him, but that made no sense. His dizziness was worsening. He was hallucinating. His gaze was orbiting its intended focus as his head swung in broad circles until it collapsed.

"It doesn' ma se'se," Conner mumbled, now looking up at the bright morning sky. "It doesn' . . ." A ring of helmets appeared around him, staring down at him. Chinese soldiers. They clutched their weapons but didn't fire. They didn't move to frisk or disarm him. They did nothing but stare down at him wide-eyed. Horrified.

"Go-to-'ell!" Conner cursed with his last breath.

SUBURBAN ATLANTA, GEORGIA
September 25 // 1940 Local Time

"Dig the slit trenches deep!" Sergeant Collins ordered. Stephie dropped her crushing pack onto the front lawn of a suburban Atlanta home. *"Fire in the hole!"* yelled an engineer down the street. Everyone dropped where they were and lay flat on the ground. Suddenly, the busy street was still. Stephie waved the kids, who were waiting on the front steps, back inside their house. A stunning boom rattled Stephie's nerves and broke several windows. Two pines fell across Mason Street, barring traffic to the west.

They rose and resumed their labor. "This is it," Animal said as he dug a pit. Stephie, John Burns, Stephon Johnson, and Peter Scott were digging a slit trench through the well maintained grass that connected Animal's machine gun nest to the side yard and the shelter of a retaining wall. The blades of their short-handled, metal shovels were locked at ninety-degree angles. They picked at the sod with rapid blows. The narrow, shoulder-height crease through the earth would be the machine gun crew's only means of escape.

The kids in the last family to flee Mason Street again waited on the front steps as their mother and father fought loudly inside. The enemy was only three hours away, but since neither side could effectively project air power, there was little chance of a surprise air raid. Three hours meant three hours.

Stephie grunted in excruciating pain with each pick and lever motion. She had dug two dozen holes in the week since the invasion, falling back without fighting every time.

"Ya know," Animal growled, "I can't believe we gave up four *hunderd* miles without a fuckin' fight!" Stephie looked at Animal but kept up her pace. Men paused to shed heavy webbing and hot body armor. Animal shook the bushes and ornamental tree behind which he dug as he punished the earth with a long-handled shovel. Heaps of angry dirt flew into branches overhead. His M-60 rested on a bipod pointed down Mason Street toward the enemy. The killing ground fell away into a gently curving, tree-lined street. *"One* fuckin' week they been," Animal chopped the ground and grunted, *"pourin'* outa them ships, and we ain't fired a *single* fuckin' shot!"

Stephie stretched her back to ward off a cramp and stared at the vocal machine gunner. He shouldn't be talking. He shouldn't be saying what he was saying. "We were *da-a-amned* lucky," Animal bellowed, "we weren't *pock*eted on that highway! *Twice*! We could be Chinese PO-*Ws* right now. The *Fightin'* 41st captured sittin' in a fuckin' traffic jam with our all our weapons safed so we don't accidentally fuckin' *shoot* anybody!"

"There are kids on the porch!" John admonished.

"Oh," Animal paused to snap, "and *so* fuckin' *what*, prick? You realize the Chinese destroyed the 3rd Armored and 6th Infantry Divisions in two days! *Two* days!" His meaning was clear. The lower-numbered, regular-army divisions were America's top of the line. Animal pointed across the chimneys, now useless satellite dishes, and verdant treetops. "You hear any *guns* out there between us and them?" There was silence. Always before, a solid wall of fire had separated their lines from the onrushing Chinese. "We're *it*, compadres! The new front line!" Animal had stopped digging, and so had the men and women of first squad. "Now, me and Mass*era*, here," Animal said, casting a thumb at his assistant machine gunner, "we'll go all the way with you fuckers. *All* the way! But if you run like scared rabbits, I'm gonna *turn* this-60 on yer *motherfuckin'* asses and mow you down!"

"No-obody's running!" tore out of Stephie's throat, cutting Animal short. Her shout echoed off houses. Other squads stopped digging, and Staff Sergeant Kurth —at the bottom of the street—turned. "We're not gonna fold!" Stephie shouted with equal parts conviction and hope. "If we're gonna die, we die together! Fighting! With honor!"

The street was silent for what seemed like forever.

"Remember Guantanamo Bay!" someone cried from down the street.

Men and women by the dozen rallied to the cry by repeating the three words. It helped steel Stephie's nerves and shut Animal up.

Kurth marched up the painted white line down the center of Mason Street, but he did nothing to stop the full-throated shouts of the forty teenagers. By the time Kurth paced up the sidewalk past Stephie, all had returned to digging and planting landmines without Kurth uttering a word. "Kids," he said to the children at the front of the house with one foot resting on the steps, "git yer par'nts and git goin'." Kurth scared the children—and everything else—without meaning to. The kids disappeared, then quickly reappeared with their father, who checked the tightness of bungee cords on his lamp-covered SUV. The well-heeled, cyber-yuppie survivalists were prepared, Stephie thought, for the escape.

Peter Scott chopped into a sprinkler line, which instantly sprayed the reeling trench diggers. Animal's escape route began to fill with water. "Shit! You fuckin' *moron*!" Animal bitched. The rapidly soaked soldiers—John, Stephon, Peter, and Stephie—whose nerves were jagged and on edge, began to laugh their asses off. The homeowner returned to the utility keypad outside the house and turned off the house's water main.

Staff Sergeant Kurth stood with his fists planted on his hips. Within seconds, magically, the front door flew open. The man of the house headed for the SUV. The oven-mitt-clad woman of the house emerged with a tray and handed Kurth a freshly baked cookie. With the same pissed-off expression that he always wore, Kurth accepted the cookie and, to the surprise of everyone, seemed to savor every bite. The woman went from soldier to soldier handing out freshly baked cookies. Stephie chuckled safely from a distance. But when the kind-looking woman held the tray out to Stephie, the woman said, "I don't do too many things well, but chocolate chips are the very tastiest thing I make. I wanted you and the boys to have it."

Stephie slowly took a cookie into her dirty hand. A bite made it into her mouth before her lips quivered. The woman handed the waiting Animal her tray and wrapped her ample arms around Stephie, who bit her lips and jammed her eyes shut.

The woman's husband began backing down the driveway. "Quick, Mom, *quick*!" came the high-pitched voices of her children. She grabbed Stephie's wrists and said, "Don't worry. It'll be . . ." She faltered and fell silent. *It'll be what?* Stephie wondered. *It'll be what?* The woman never again made eye contact. The last family on Mason Street left to the sound of squealing tires.

Lieutenant Ackerman took center stage. Staff Sergeant

Kurth lent him Kurth's street. The slender but tall lieutenant was a graduate of The Citadel, which oddly enough had given Third Platoon the nickname "West Point." The name really derived from Ack's military-school bearing. During the early days of training, everybody in Charlie Company had longed to be not in Ackerman's Third Platoon, but in the much more laid back First Platoon called "Malibu," which was digging in on the next street over. But now, Stephie thought on the eve of their first major battle, "West Point" would do just fine.

"Listen up!" Ackerman ordered loudly. All forty men and women looked his way. Ackerman rarely gave speeches. "The civilians are clear!" Ack announced. "B'talion scouts are five miles out and pullin' back fast! Since none of 'em are crossin' the lines anywhere near here," he said, pointing down Mason Street, "the next folks who come up that street I want you to kill."

Just after Ackerman's little pep talk, he had taken a look at the positions being dug in the front lawn by Stephie's First Squad and had ordered them to fight from inside the newly abandoned house. Kurth had eyed the lieutenant for a moment before relaying the order. Other squads were dug in on lawns, and Animal and Massera had to stay where they were to have a good field of fire. But First Squad was set up to fight from inside the brick house at 3134 Mason Street. *Where it's safer,* Stephie thought with irritation.

Stephie had a hard time believing that they actually would. Every time before, the order to retreat had come from on high, where fears of flanking or encircling moves had dictated retreat. But this time, they peered through empty windows with weapons at the ready and no such order came.

Animal and Massera lay hunched behind their machine gun in the water-filled pit just outside. The carpet in the previously immaculate house was tracked from the trench diggers' muddy boots. The furniture was moved and overturned. Becky Marsh's face glowed faintly in the light from her multiple, miniaturized screens. Her webbing sprouted black batteries, transceivers, and processors. The screens that bracketed her high-tech helmet went dark as Becky switched to her night reticles. The two tiny, see-through screens an inch from her eyes gave her stereoscopic Panavision.

Stephie left the front window and went to Becky, who lay behind an interior wall and wore a three-quarters suit of Kevlar that draped like a wool greatcoat to her shins. "Where'd you get that body armor?" Stephie asked in disgust.

"I met this guy in aviation. These are for V-STOL pilots. Close air support guys are very particular. They won't go up, apparently, unless their balls are covered."

"You mean you screwed this pilot for his body armor," Stephie translated. "Where's your fucking fighting load, Becky?" Becky replied that a guy over in transport was "transporting" it for her. "So," Stephie snapped, "you're just gonna fuck your way into light duty, live off *our* rations, and ride the war out inside your little video/Kelvar cocoon! Thanks at least for bringing your rifle!"

"Chill out, Roberts," Sergeant Collins ordered. "And get back to the window."

Stephie looked around the room. Her squadmates stared at her from their darkened hollows. No one raised above window level. Stephie looked at Becky and said, "I'm sorry."

Becky didn't hear her. She was holding both sides of her helmet and staring into the two reticles. "Here they come," was all she said.

Stephie got back to the window just in time for a comm check. A thumb switch was aftermounted to her M-16's pistol grip. Up meant she would talk to Sergeant Collins, the squad leader. Down would radio the words she spoke into her helmet's mike to the other members of her fire team: Burns, Scott, and Corporal Johnson. "Can you hear me?" John Burns asked over their fire team's radio net. Stephie looked past Scott to the far side of the window and nodded. "*Yes*, dear," Animal replied, mockingly imitating Stephie's voice over the radio from where he lay in the bushes outside. "I can hear you just fine, sweetie." A squeaking kiss brought laughter from the others. John changed places with Peter Scott, who started to bitch but ended up just shifting positions. Stephie didn't complain about John moving closer. He sat on the floor and raised a pencil-thin flexible tube like an aerial. Its end was bent like a periscope. A picture of the street appeared on the four-inch screen at the long tube's base. "What's that?" Stephie asked, sitting beside him.

"I got it at Sharper Image," John mumbled as he scanned the street. The device offered a perfect view of Mason Street without exposing the viewer.

"Oh look," she said, pointing at a button. "It's got *night* vision. How much did this thing cost?" John shrugged. "You don't know?" she probed. He said nothing in reply. She searched the hard green plastic monitor. It bore no brand name or other marking of any kind.

John abruptly said, "I gotta go to the bathroom."

Sergeant Collins told him to make it quick. John didn't go down the hallway, however. He left out the back door. "I've gotta go, too," Stephie said.

But Collins replied, "*No* way! Get back to your post. She-esus!"

Stephie waited by the window, listening. They all heard a loud *crack* of wood breaking from the backyard.

"I'll go check it out," Stephie said and hurriedly took off with her rifle while Collins was checking positions in the study. Johnson grabbed Stephie's leg from where he lay in the darkness. "Don't be long," was all he said. On the radio, Animal was complaining about the noise from the rear of the house.

Stephie found John prying boards out of the rotting wood fence at the very back of the property, widening a hole. He had already cut through cyclone fencing on the other side. "What are you *doing*?" she asked.

"Always make sure there's a way out," John replied. "This leads to a storm ditch. Go left. It's got branches in different directions and some good-sized pipes running under roads. Keep bearing east . . ."

"Nobody's *running*," Stephie said, indignantly shaking her head. "And where'd you get wire cutters?" she asked.

"Roberts! Burns! Get back in here!" snarled Collins over the squad's net.

• • •

"Any second, now," Becky counted down. Stephie powered up her night vision goggles and peered over the broken-out windowsill at Mason Street. Black shadows were now lit to brilliant day. A stunning burp of small arms fire erupted from several blocks to their left. The noise rose to a crescendo when the Chinese returned fire. Concussions from tank cannon, missile warheads, mortars, and soon artillery rattled the air. The night sky alit with orange barrages of ten and fifteen rounds at a time, bracketing their position on Mason Street. Stephie's mouth was so dry she couldn't swallow. *How could anyone survive that?* she worried.

"Contact," came Sergeant Collins's whispered voice over Stephie's earphone. "Hold your fire."

John hunched lower over his black automatic weapon, tapping the box magazine to ensure that it was seated. Stephie raised her M-16. Tiny phosphorescent dots on the front and rear sights gave her an aim line lit to brilliance by her light amplification goggles.

Two six-wheeled amphibious scout vehicles crawled down the center of Mason Street, stopping well short of the two fallen trees. The first vehicle continued on alone. Mechanical lifts in the second smoothly and swiftly raised two box-shaped missile launchers, which pivoted to point up the street. When the lead vehicle reached the first tree, it traversed the trunk at an angle with one huge tire independently climbing over before its opposite did the same. A slender black barrel protruded from a small turret atop the vehicle, swivelling left and right as its last tire descended the second and last tree.

Stephie was shivering. Freezing. Her teeth were chattering. A second angry firefight broke out, this one to their right and close. Probably Second Platoon. The trailing Chinese scout revved its engine up and followed. When it was halfway across its second obstacle, Stephie heard *whooshing* sounds. Streaks of brilliant exhaust were followed by *thumps* as sparks flew from both vehicles. Their turrets and wheels were stilled. A crew hatch flew open, and a glow of white fire inside lit Stephie's goggles. A burning Chinese soldier swatted at his radiant clothes as he stumbled and rolled and finally lay burning on the street.

"Get down!" John Burns shouted as he dove, reaching out for Stephie. In the next instant, a dozen shrill, whistling artillery shells shattered Mason Street. Shrapnel peppered the living room. Screams came from terror or from pain. Debris shot through dust and smoke as sheets of plaster were shorn from walls and ceiling. In the distance—somewhere through the open window—a man screamed shrill but in a dying voice. John raised his fiber optic periscope. Rapidly moving vehicles filled his screen and Mason Street.

American missiles hissed through the air past their house. *Thump! Thump! Thump!* went half the Chinese vehicles. But from the others rose multiple rocket launchers.

"Take cove-e-r-r!" John shouted.

He dove on top of Stephie. Thudding missiles hit the bricks just outside. The floor bounced underneath Stephie and John. Hellish screams echoed through the house. The living room and dining room behind them exploded. The flames that shot through air quickly dissipated, but not before maiming and burning. Stephie couldn't breathe. She was dead. She was alive. She couldn't tell.

She pushed John Burns off of her. He didn't look to be wounded, but he couldn't seem to focus his eyes.

Sergeant Collins and Peter Scott lay beside Stephie and John, cleaved into large pieces.

Animal's M-60 blazed. Friendly missiles streaked down the street. In the study, Fire Team Bravo fired furiously. John slid the rest of the way to the floor moaning as Stephie grabbed her rifle and rose to her knees. Through the smoldering window frame, she had a perfect view of hell. She shouldered her M-16 and fired a fragmentation grenade. It exploded at the base of a tree and felled three men who were firing from the kneeling position sixty yards away. One struggled—stunned—up onto his knees. Stephie squeezed off a three-round burst and killed him. She had nine more three-round bursts left in the full, 30-round magazine. She grew more expert at killing with each pull of the trigger. She had survived the first, worst tidal wave. In the ebb and flow of small unit warfare, she now joined the surviving Americans in the extraction of the price that the Chinese would pay in taking Mason Street.

No vehicles could make it through the flaming traffic jam. No Chinese aircraft survived even a single overflight. Helicopters from both sides crashed into unlucky houses like meteors on an alien landscape. Missiles flew from the ground like shooting stars in reverse. Artillery batteries began their devastating, war-winning barrages but were blown to oblivion fifteen seconds later by pin-point, massed counterbattery fire. Using a radio to communicate meant risking that enemy computer screens as far away as Beijing would nearly instantly show exactly where you are. That block. That house. That room. Commence firing. The weapons systems of the two armies clashed and canceled each other out. War returned to square one and tested its most primitive fighting system.

Chinese infantry appeared. Not a squad, or a platoon, or a company, but several infantry companies. Easily a battalion. Hundreds of men, bobbing and weaving behind abundant cover, advanced up Mason Street past bonfires from vehicles that consumed their comrades.

Stephie aimed and fired. When her ten pulls of the trigger emptied her first magazine, Stephie grabbed John's squad automatic weapon and went full auto with six hundred rounds. Animal yanked the M-60 off the ground under Stephie's covering fire and slogged through the muddy slit trench toward the retaining wall, the side yard, and ultimately escape to the rear. Limbs and branches fell onto his rounded back as bullets shot from over a hundred bobbing and weaving fireflies clipped through trees. Over a hundred Chinese automatic weapons flickered orange and roared at Stephie's ears from 300 meters, and 200 meters, and 150 meters. Rifle range distances.

Stephie stood nearly oblivious to the gale of bullets that *buzzed* through the window and clapped into the sheet-rock walls behind her head as she emptied the 600–round box.

She hunched over the ripping weapon, which vibrated nearly uncontrollably atop the window sill. She misused the weapon, firing it in continuous full auto, cutting great swaths, she felt sure, though she could see almost nothing save the winking fireflies. The weapon's lubricants began sizzling on the white-hot receiver, rising in a smoking stench above the rocking gun. The pistol grip in her itching hand was almost too hot to touch, but she gripped it with all her might.

When the magazine finally ran dry forty seconds later and the gun ticked and hissed like a teakettle, Stephie saw Massera, Animal's abandoned assistant machine gunner. Massera didn't rise from the machine gun pit. He could barely raise his head.

All of the sudden Stephie saw pinned Chinese infantrymen launch two dozen grenades into the air. She dove like a goalkeeper to the floor. The walls, roof, and lawn were struck by half a dozen 40 mm grenades. The study from which Fire Team Bravo fought fiercely—weapons blazing—burst into flames. When the smoke cleared, the study was still.

"Let's go!" John yelled. He snatched up Stephie's M-16 and pulled her toward the rear. Stephon Johnson hobbled along with them, ducking low under a flaming kitchen ceiling. Just behind them, the living room erupted. The overpressure blew the rear windows out and sent them tumbling into the back yard. The barrel of the SAW that she was dragging one-handed, muzzle down, landed against Stephie's left leg and scorched her trousers. She yelped and rolled away. John took the weapon from her, burning his hand and cursing. Stephie grabbed her M-16.

"Over here!" Becky shouted from the hole John had made in the fencing at the rear. The backyard was becoming dangerously well lit by the home's blaze. After a sustained burst along the side of the house, Animal—who had been firing over the retaining wall at the side of the house—joined them in flight with his big-60 at port arms and 100-round brass belts flapping and glinting in the light from the fire. From the house you could hear confidant commands being given in Chinese.

The American survivors descended into the refuse-filled drainage ditch and ran—splashing—as far away and as fast as they could. They had no plan other than to escape. Suddenly, the air above Atlanta became the battleground. At the eruption of repeated, low-altitude explosions, Becky shrieked

"Jesus!" and ducked her head. Missiles streaked up from American launchers all around the city. Chinese jets, missiles, and helicopters exploded in stunning bursts.

Their ditch blazed with each *pop* of an intercepting missile, *boom* of an exploding fuel tank, and *roar* of a vehicle crashing to earth with tanks filled with jet fuel and pylons festooned with explosives. They tried to continue their desperate flight, but the air battle rose steadily in intensity for several minutes. Stephie looked over her shoulder to see that Becky, who appeared unwounded, had collapsed in a fetal curl on a small sandbar at the concrete edge of their escape route.

John stooped and said something softly, soothingly into Becky's ear that Stephie couldn't hear. Stephie—with her shoulders hunched against the raining fireworks—slung her rifle, squatted beside Becky, and loosed a growl as she used her legs to lift the surprised girl to her feet. Stephie pointed down the ditch toward the others, who waited. Stephie also put her lips close to Becky's ear.

"Get-going-down-that-goddamn-ditch-right-fucking-now-or-I'll-kill-you!" Stephie shouted.

Becky took off running.

Stephie's chin quivered just short of tears. John was staring at her. "What's wrong with you?" Stephie snapped angrily, and took off.

Only twenty-six of the fifty-nine men and women fielded by Third Platoon that morning were present for muster that night. By sunup, Lieutenant Ackerman had collected a few more stragglers. As if more people would miraculously appear if he counted one more time, Ackerman had another roll call. The human inventory was taken in a small park amid colorful preschool swing sets against the steady crackle of a still raging battle. Stephie sat with her back to a tree getting treated by a medic for the burn on her calf and scraped knees.

When finished with those present—now thirty-one in number—Ackerman read the roll of the missing in a croaking voice.

"Aguillar?" he called out. "Dead," came the reply. "You sure about that?" Ackerman challenged. The hollow-eyed soldier from third squad replied in anger, "*Po*-sitive." And so it went. "Sergeant Collins?" Ackerman asked in the "Cs." "Dead," Stephie replied. By then, Ackerman had quit asking for confirmatory details. He only wrote "Missing" if no one replied to a name, like "Higgins," whose entire Second Squad was lost to a man.

Animal answered for Massera. "Dead," he said simply.

Stephie said, "He was still alive when we had to pull back."

A bitter Animal replied, "He took shrapnel in the small of his back under his vest. I stuck my fingers up inside the hole in his back. His backbone was in two pieces, and his guts were spilling out into that muddy water. He couldn't move his legs, and . . ."

"All right!" Ackerman interrupted. He made his official notation.

When Ackerman got to Private Sanders, Stephie's former fire-teammate, the answer was more complex. "Well . . . ," she began. Everyone waited on her to continue. Stephie thought back to the shower of Chinese grenades. Sanders had lost an arm at the shoulder and a leg at the knee, but still crawled through the rapidly burning house. The explosions and conflagration had completely consumed the structure. "Dead," she finally replied in a voice similarly devoid of life. "Peter Scott?" was the next man up. "He's dead, too," Stephie answered with absolute certainty.

Somebody finally asked about Staff Sergeant Kurth. "He's dead," Ackerman answered. "Damn," somebody else said. "I didn't think they could kill that motherfucker."

Stephie's original squad of nine men and women was now down to three—Stephie, John, and Corporal Johnson, the new squad leader—to whom Animal and a griping Becky were attached. "I'm platoon *commo*!" Becky argued. Ackerman didn't even reply. Stephie raised her knees and rested her face, covered by her hands, atop them. John Burns settled onto the ground next to her, his body warm against her side. With her face still covered, Stephie leaned against John until her head was on his shoulder. No one other than John noticed Stephie's bucking chest or ragged gasps for breath from behind her hands. Half the survivors cried like Stephie. The other half—

like John and their platoon leader—stared insensate into space.

"Are you all right?" John whispered.

"I'm fine!" came Stephie's reply, muffled by the clasp of her two hands. "I'm just fine! Can't you tell?" Sobbing racked her chest.

John tried to pull her hands away from her face, but she wouldn't let him. "It's okay," he said, "to grieve for your friends, Stephie. It's okay to feel sad."

She dropped her hands and shouted, "I'm not sad! I'm angry! I cry when I'm angry, okay?"

The shaken company commander arrived—strangely helmetless—and announced, "Gather your gear. We're pulling back."

Atlanta was falling to the Chinese.

BESSEMER, ALABAMA
September 29 // 2130 Local Time

The first touch of chill made the night air pleasant. Breathable. The hills weren't high, but they were high enough for Jim Hart's .50 caliber sniper rifle. He was a kilometer from his target, but he had a perfect view of the lounging Chinese soldiers through a 120-power, motion-stabilized digital scope. When the monstrous weapon was fired on full auto, the scope gave a usable, steady image atop the rocking and rolling receiver group. At twenty-two pounds, including its sturdy bipod, the automatic rifle was called "light-weight." But that was only relative to the fifty-round box of five-inch-long, thumb-thick rounds slung beneath the hellish weapon.

Hart had stashed his M-16 at his personal arms cache, which could have supplied a platoon for a month of intense combat. But how long would the war last for Hart? How long could he possibly expect to survive?

Not that he'd done too much fighting. Standing prewar orders were to go to ground for a week and let the initial wave of combat troops pass, which he had done. Security had lessened, as expected, but Hart had spent the last two frustrating days under his infrared reflecting shelter waiting for a rat to come along and take the cheese. He checked the rats again. They were smoking cigarettes at the only service station in the county left with tanks completely full of gasoline.

"Now why wouldn't they wonder why those tanks were full?" Hart mumbled to himself. His whispered monologues were a luxury he dared allow himself. Even so, he used his vocal cords only a few times a day. The noise discipline—and remaining still and quiet for days on end—were the hard part. He was ready to do the easy part.

But it was, at least, simple operating completely out of contact with higher command. Three years earlier, Hart had deployed into the Sinai Desert. Six times a day—every four hours—he had reported into Washington. He would tape and encrypt a message, "burp" it up to a commercial satellite, and then go back to sleep. The exercise was a royal pain in the ass. For two weeks, he had observed the same highway but had seen absolutely nothing to report.

He might as well have saved his batteries for his last message. "Tanks. Total number unknown. In excess of sixty. Probably Chinese armored division. Heading north." His orders to exfiltrate had arrived live via satellite. Four hours later, he had sped across the Gulf of Suez in a high-speed, rubber boat. He had traveled light. He wasn't there to fight. Instead of heavy weapons, he had humped satellite gear and a video camera with a telephoto lens. Its digital pictures had been beamed real-time right to the top. When Hart had returned home he had been told that President Peller, himself, had watched video recordings.

Home, Hart thought. He was now in his own country but couldn't even talk to Washington. There were a few buried fiber optic cables, but Hart didn't trust them. They were shared with other men operating around him. Hart instinctively didn't trust anything shared. A man would do anything—say anything—if captured alive by the Chinese.

But before the war on a field training exercise he had tested the line. It was covered by rocks in a hollow not far from there. The Pentagon operator had asked for the access code issued especially for the test, and then had said, "How may I direct your call?" Hart had laughed, unprepared for the question. He gave the woman the only number that came to mind. After a few clicks he was connected to his hometown: Lansing, Michigan. His ex-wife had sleepily answered the phone. Hart had hung up without saying a word.

A wave of sadness washed over Hart at the recollection. "I'm a total fucking idiot!" he said softly to himself. He then repeated the words with a studied southern drawl. Hart had spent the last three months honing his accent. He was better at crude Arabic than at the intonations and dipthongs of southern American English. But he was certain that no Chinese soldier would think him out of place for any reason other than the obvious: Hart was a male of combat age.

"Barely of combat age," he said to himself. He had joined the army late in life. At twenty-four, his wife had left him for another man. Lansing had seemed too small after that. She had kept going to the same places they had gone when they were together, only now with her new husband, Hart's former boss. Hart had a college degree and a job he didn't like. He had joined the army, whose ranks were just beginning to swell. "Figur' I saw it comin'," he drawled, satisfied.

Hart had kicked much ass in Officer Candidate School. The few years spent working after college had given him the edge in discipline over his early-twenties classmates. He had gone on to eat airborne and Ranger schools for lunch. By age twenty-seven, Hart had gotten his coveted green beret. Although the physical hardships had been grueling, the mental rigors had been therapeutic. He had killed his ex-wife and her new husband over and over again on the rifle range. Twice, in the sawdust-filled close-in combat pits, he had been warned about going too far. "Save something for the Chinese," the instructors had said to him quietly on the side.

And now, here he was: a baby-faced thirty-one-year-old trained killer sent out to kill.

The rifle seemed heavier when Hart again raised its butt and checked the scope.

"Sh-*shit!*" he said in a hiss. Chinese army trucks were arriving at the gas station. The few soldiers posted to guard the fuel cache that they had finally discovered first waved and then saluted dismounting officers. Hart traversed the rifle a few degrees. Truck after truck pulled to a stop. *Five, six, seven!* he counted silently, finally stopping at fifteen.

He raised his lower-power, wider-angle field binoculars. A convoy bunched up along the road. Rows of men's backs could be seen under the trucks' canvas. Hart's scalp began to crawl as the magnitude of the target sunk in. Twenty or thirty men per truck. Twenty or thirty trucks in all. Maybe five or six hundred men. *An entire fucking infantry battalion*, he realized. It screamed for an airstrike, but airstrikes weren't an option. Nothing less than hundreds of aircraft or missiles could penetrate this deep into Chinese airspace. Plus he was out of contact and couldn't even call it in. This wasn't the kind of war for which he had initially trained.

Hart pulled his three spare boxes of .50 caliber rounds from his pack as goose bumps tickled his skin. He looked closely in surprise at his quivering hand, then laid the ammo boxes beside his full-auto sniper rifle. That was it. He was ready. He had two hundred of the most potent rounds in America's small-arms arsenal, but even more potent had been the advance planning that had taken place several months earlier. He tried now to wait the last few minutes for the shot.

The growing crowd of soldiers soundlessly hooted on the two-inch-diagonal screen before his eye. He dialed the scope's power down to take in a wider field. Soldiers jostled for position in line. Special Forces Command had had months to dream up dirty tricks. They had stocked the soft drink machine and left the power running. While drivers began refueling trucks, thirsty infantrymen pooled their American coins and began to greedily guzzle frigid Coca Colas.

There had to be sixty or seventy of soldiers in the cluster.

Hart powered up his detonator panel. The "ready" light initially glowed amber, but the LED switched to steady green before Hart had time to worry about his batteries. He flicked open the switch's cover but hesitated. With the naked eye he could barely make out the line of trucks beyond the ridge that rose between Hart and the road. But he knew there were some guys at a dusty gas station drinking cokes. Others stretched or pissed beside their rides. It could have been any number of convoys in which Hart himself had ridden. He could even imagine the substance of their banter.

He didn't doubt the justness of his cause or question his right to take the act. He just took a moment to overcome thousands of years of socialization. To override the ancient dictate against murder.

He pressed the button firmly with his thumb and held it for a full second.

A boiling mushroom cloud of orange flames—soundless for an instant—shot two hundred feet into the sky. The shock wave clapped his face and ears. He quickly raised the rifle and braced his boots against the half-buried rock at which he had camped. On full auto, the long rifle kicked like none other he had fired. But the recoil was straight back, which was where Hart came in. His heavily padded shoulder would absorb the pounding blows. His feet would hold him in place.

Through the scope he saw nothing but flames where the buildings and pumps had been. Dozens of smoldering bodies littered the hill and roadside like ants. Hart moved the weapon's aim down the line of vehicles. The first half dozen were blackened and burning. A flaming river of gasoline flowed straight down the road beneath the convoy—yet another of Special Forces Command's deadly tricks—but no Chinese moved until Hart got to the tenth vehicle in line. Those men were thrashing and flailing, on fire. Hart traversed the rifle all the way to the last truck visible before another hill obscured his view. As luck would have it, that truck was trying with difficulty to turn around on the narrow, two-lane road.

Hart dialed the scope back to 120. The crosshairs steadied on the engine block.

The .50 caliber roared, battering its human shock absorber and threatening to wrench itself from his grip. The half-second burst put only five rounds on target, but in the calm that followed Hart saw flames and steam shooting from the truck's buckled hood through the thin smoke that rose from his muzzle. The windshield was completely gone. So was the driver behind it. As he watched, the truck rolled off the side of the hill and into freefall. Troops dove out the rear, a few successfully, most to their death as the truck flipped in air and tumbled down the steep drop.

"Shit!" Hart cursed. He had wanted to use the truck as a roadblock. He raked the next truck in line broadsides flattening both tires. Men poured out of trucks as their drivers tried to maneuver. Hart winced as three men were crushed between the fenders of two trucks. One driver stuck his head out to look back as they screamed. Hart took aim and blew his head off his shoulders. His truck remained in reverse, dooming the three crushed men. Hart's .50 caliber doomed the rest.

Puffs of smoke began erupting from the road. *Popping* sounds arrived moments later. But apart from the occasional clipping of tree branches or slap against a rock, Hart got no sense that he was receiving fire. He scanned the road and killed the few missile and machine gun crews who were setting up on the road. He then began firing single, deadly shots at the officers and NCOs who gave their lives trying to bring order to the chaos. Finally, Hart switched to auto and mowed down the men who sprinted along the road in flight from the river of burning gasoline.

The Chinese soldiers ran headlong into sheets of huge slugs that dramatically upended them and sometimes killed their comrades directly behind them. Some got away, but enough died of such horrifying wounds that most of the rest of the soldiers just took cover.

They must be young, Hart thought. *Green.*

The realization bothered him, but not enough to stop his killing. He switched his aim to those who chose to climb slowly up or down the hill. It was a turkey shoot. Each round killed a helpless man. Every so often, Hart just couldn't fire. The crosshairs rested steady and true on the broad back of some poor guy who clung precariously to the crumbling hillside, but he couldn't pull the trigger and he moved on. The inhibition defied explanation. He would kill four or five men without a care in the world, then the trigger would seem to stiffen, and he would skip one. On occasion, he would find the same man in his scope again and he would blow his head off without the least hesitation. The randomness of Hart's killing disturbed him.

He interrupted his single-round sniping only to load another box magazine and to let his gun cool. A large mass of men cowered in a shallow ditch behind the high-slung chassis of their trucks, but not for long. Hart had only their helmets and the tops of their backs as targets, but the slowly flowing, burning gasoline poured into their ditch and flushed them. Truck by truck, they were forced to make a run. Hart switched to full auto.

He held on tight to the pistol grip and strafed their path as nearly horizontal to the road as he could. The running men were cut to pieces.

He went through an entire box of ammo. When the river of gasoline finally burned itself out, he shifted his fire to the men who had chosen to remain pinned in ones and twos to the road. More efficient, more intentional single shots sufficed for them, but he didn't waste any time in between. The bullets' trajectories were so true that the moment his sight crossed a form he squeezed, and the man died a half second later. Hart finished off his third box and ate into the fifty rounds of his last box at a practiced rate of one round every second-and-a-half. In a little over a minute he was done.

Flames still raged at the blackened foundation of what had been the roadside service station. Dozens of vehicles up and down the column had inch-and-a-half-wide holes in their side quarter panels behind which lay engine blocks that were similarly holed. Hart was out of ammo, but few Chinese soldiers risked moving, even though hundreds had survived unharmed. They must have thought Hart was pausing to load fresh rounds that would soon resume popping eyeballs out of sockets with the huge bullets' kinetic energy. They had lived, they just didn't know it yet.

Hissing sounds from the hill above alerted Hart to the danger. His head jerked left and right as he checked the sky. Three small missiles streaked off down the valley. Three treetop-scraping Chinese helicopters met the missiles with their windshields. The gunships crashed to the valley floor in nearly balletic, fiery unison that produced magnificent pyrotechnic displays. The pre-positioned automatic launcher had only three missiles left in its tubes.

Chinese gunships would shortly arrive in even greater numbers. Hart began to stow his equipment in his pack haphazardly. Speed was what he needed now. The pinned commander of the infantry battalion would be on the radio.

Hart left his thin, infra-red absorbing Mylar enclosure behind. He had a dozen more back at his primary cache. At the crest of the ridge behind him, Hart knelt and looked at his watch. The entire engagement had lasted less than ten minutes. His silent mental count put Chinese dead at over two hundred. It was a stunning, one-man victory that left Hart strangely depressed.

WHITE HOUSE SITUATION ROOM
October 3 // 0700 Local Time

The conversations fell quiet when President Baker entered the darkened Situation Room located in a bunker a hundred feet beneath the White House. He settled into his familiar place at the head of the table, feeling a lack of confidence so extreme it reminded him of stage fright. He was nervous, agitated, and hyper-alert for no particular reason. He interpreted casual greetings as signs of loyalty or betrayal. Eye contact was a signal that they would stick with him to the bitter end. An averted gaze that they would turn on the failed leader who had led the nation to the brink of destruction.

"Good morning, Mr. President," General Cotler said, staring Bill straight in the eye. The bags under the general's puffy eyes were so dark that he looked like a boxer after a fight. Baker felt the prickly rush of panic slither up his arms and torso as all eyes—friend and foe—measured their president. "The last units have been withdrawn from Atlanta, sir," Cotler said in a funereal voice. "The 218th Infantry Brigade held I-95 open long enough for Fourth Corps to withdraw to Charleston and Columbia, South Carolina, in good order. But the Two-One-Eight is now surrounded in Savannah. They've taken about 33 percent casualties: 3700 killed or wounded. They and the local Savannah militia have entrenched around the city. The brigade commander is awaiting your orders, sir."

Baker opened his mouth but had to close it again to swallow. He cleared his throat. Some unseen but attentive technician—taking his cue from the general's briefing—put shaky pictures on the screens behind Cotler's head. Bright yellow backhoes and bulldozers dug tank traps around the southern city. Periodically, the camera shook as self-propelled artillery in the background pounded out rounds, adding to the black wall of distant smoke that marked the approach of the enemy.

Baker issued his orders in a drained, wooden voice. "They should continue to fight so long as they have any reasonable means to resist." The orders were becoming Bill's mantra. Cotler nodded. The men and women in Savannah would be measured against the standard set by the Marines and sailors at Guantanamo Bay. It was better known in the public as "fight to the death."

Baker was suddenly seized by a need to breath. He inhaled, but the wind caught in his chest, and he inhaled a second and then a third time until his lungs were full. More eyes were averted after the effort than before.

"So the Fourth Corps," the vice president said, consulting her briefing book, "minus the 218th, which is a separate, free-standing brigade, made it out of Florida intact." She made a note, keeping her own private ledger whose entries were accounted for in lives. *Or are they in deaths?* Baker wondered. Elizabeth Sobo then asked, "What about Seventh Corps?"

All heads swivelled from the VP to General Cotler. Seventh Corps had borne the brunt of the first week of fighting. The media had taken to calling them "human traffic cones"—supposedly named after the orange warning markers placed across highways, which was the closest the media was allowed to the fighting and therefore the standard reporting vantage for dashing news anchormen. But Baker's blood boiled in anger at the double meaning—the bitterly sarcastic mental image of impotent *thumps* heard on the undercarriages of speeding Chinese tanks.

Cotler didn't look up as he read. "The 3rd Armored Division retired from the field with sixty-two serviceable tanks and about five thousand effective troops. The 6th Infantry with about twenty tanks and seven thousand men and women. But both are totally disorganized and disrupted. It'll take months for them to re-form."

"We don't have months," came a voice from down the table. It was Hamilton Asher, Director of the FBI.

"Excuse *me*?" Baker responded indignantly. "This is a meeting of my National Security Council! If I have any questions about domestic counterintelligence, I'll call on you." Asher held his tongue. Baker turned to Cotler and said, "What about the rest of Seventh Corps?"

"I'm afraid it's not very good, sir," Cotler responded. Bill felt a chill wash over him. "The 29th Infantry Division— which is Army National Guard—was stretched out as a screening force along I-16. In the past few days their line was breeched by the Chinese and then closed back up again by some tough, *tough* counterattacks."

By the word "tough" Bill understood Cotler to mean high casualty.

"The Chinese finally threw about six divisions of fresh troops against the line last night, and," Cotler cleared his throat, "I'm sorry to report, Madam Vice President, Mr. President, that the 29th couldn't hold. It was breeched in about half a dozen places and . . ."

Bill waited, but Cotler didn't finish. Bill asked, "How much of the 29th will make it back to the Savannah River?" He waited. And he waited. The chairman of the Joint Chiefs shuffled some papers even though he obviously would find no answer there. Bill even waited some more until finally Admiral Thornton put a hand on Cotler's forearm. "General?" Bill said. "Are you all right?"

Cotler cleared his throat and said, "I'm sorry, Mr. President, but I have a very dear . . . I . . . My grandson, my only grandson, is a scout platoon leader in the 29th, sir. I apologize again." He kept on going before Bill could even open his mouth. "Nothing larger than a battalion-strength unit from the 29th will make it back to the Savannah. Some companies and platoons. Mostly squads down to individual soldiers."

"General Cotler," Bill finally said, "I didn't know that you had a grandson." He quickly added, "In the military. In the

29th. I hope that he's okay. Have you . . . ?" Something finally made him stop.

"He's dead, sir," Cotler reported.

"Oh, God," Bill muttered in an unguarded tone. "General Cotler—Adam—you have my very, very deepest sympathies."

"Thank you, Mr. President," the man was forced to reply.

"Do you need," Bill asked, "you know, any time off? To be with your family?"

Although no trace of any expression was betrayed on Cotler's face, to Bill the man pled for him to drop the subject.

Others obviously read the same thing in the man. Bob Moore—Baker's secretary of defense—tossed Cotler an easy question. In a businesslike but low voice, he asked, "Are we going to declare Seventh Corps combat ineffective?"

Cotler said, "Yes, sir." Secretary Moore took over the briefing. "Bill, with three intact ports—Mobile, and now Gulfport and Biloxi—the Chinese have already landed two point five *million* troops. Half of those are on roads in northern Georgia heading up the Eastern Seaboard. When they hit the Savannah River, they'll outnumber our troops there ten or more to one. For that reason, we've cut roads running from the Savannah River straight back north to the next line of defense at the Santee and Saluda Rivers about sixty miles to the rear."

"So," Bill said, "we're already planning for defeat at the Savannah River?" He was immediately disappointed with his tone. It was cheap sniping instead of a statesmanlike poise.

Moore ignored the remark, only making Baker feel worse.

"Current estimates," General Cotler said, rejoining the briefing, "put the Chinese at the Santee and Saluda Rivers along I-26 in six to ten days, depending on how long we *try* to hold the Savannah River. The longer we hang on at the very end of the engagement, sir, when the line is about to break, the less orderly the withdrawal will be and the more units we'll lose in the process. The same thing happened to the 29th along the Savannah-to-Macon line. If the Chinese cross the Savannah River before we've begun the process of pulling back, unit cohesion will be difficult to impossible to maintain. Units will be overtaken and captured whole. The roads that we are building will help get those units back safely, then we'll destroy them as best we can."

Baker nodded his agreement with the plans.

"Eighth Corps," Cotler continued in a monotone that reminded all of the great loss he'd just suffered, "is manning the Savannah River. At the northwest end—around Hartwell Lake and sitting astride I-85—is the 40th Infantry Division, which is Army National Guard. To their left—around Columbia and blocking I-20—is the 37th Infantry Division, also a Guard unit. Then, to *their* left, is the 41st Infantry Division, which is, of course, regular army."

Baker noted that Cotler used the words "of course." Everyone in the room knew that the otherwise undistinguished, newly formed 41st Infantry Division was home to the president's daughter.

"Finally," Cotler said, "we committed Eight Corps' reserves—the 31st Armored Brigade (Separate)—to plug the gap between the left flank of the 41st Infantry and the Chinese siege troops around Charleston and to block I-95."

Baker nodded, clenching his jaw to silence the questions he wanted to ask about Stephie's unit.

But Vice President Sobo asked. "Wasn't Eight Corps hit pretty hard at Atlanta?"

"Yes, ma'am," Cotler answered. "Some battalions in the 37th and 41st took heavy casualties. But others withdrew unscathed. We're rounding out the units that suffered the worst losses with replacements."

The units with the worst losses, Bill thought, *like Stephie's.* Cotler had reported the details of Stephie's one and only bloody firefight in suburban Atlanta. The "engagement," he had said, had lasted fewer than five minutes, but her platoon had suffered almost 50 percent casualties. Bill had called Stephie's mother afterwards. He had been ready for the worst, but Rachel had been calm and drained of her previous vigor. "Please, Bill," she had beseeched in a whisper at the end. She didn't need to complete her plea. He was tempted to tell her that he had tried to talk Stephie into accepting a transfer to the rear, but that wouldn't really have been true. He had merely given her the option, and even doing that had been a mistake.

". . . have made contact with the 73rd Infantry Brigade (Separate) at Chattanooga, Tennessee," Cotler continued. Bill tried to refocus. "Two and Three Corps are now both engaged in California, having completed transit of their lead combat elements directly from staging areas in Tennessee. Five Corps is blocking the Chinese from heading north between the Appalachians and the Mississippi and is getting significant pressure." Those words, Bill knew—"significant pressure"—were not as bad as "tough" fighting in Cotler's vernacular. "The Fifth is also covering the redeployment to the east and the west of the war stocks that we had amassed for Operation Anvilhead."

As the briefing wore on, Baker grew more and more desperate. All of Florida and all but the northernmost slivers of Mississippi and Georgia had been abandoned. Southern politicians were already crying for Baker's impeachment. Admiral Thornton warned that while the Chinese forces in Cuba were still blocked at the Bahamas from moving by sea directly up the East Coast, they could make a huge sweeping move out to sea from the Gulf or stage from long-distance as they had for the invasion of California. Over the weekend, the Chinese had seized the Azores in the Atlantic, which put them less than half as far from Philadelphia as the Japanese ports from which they had launched the invasion of the West Coast. The risk was that China could leapfrog American defensive lines with an amphibious landing to the army's rear.

Bill questioned their rear area defenses. Cotler reported that the 157th Mechanized Infantry Brigade had dug in deep around the Philadelphia naval shipyard. Bill ordered the Twelfth Corps to guard the Atlantic wall from Boston to Philadelphia, and the Eleventh Corps to defend the coast from Washington, DC, to the rear of the front lines. Unlike the Gulf, the Atlantic beaches would be defended.

Bill listened to the briefing with only half an ear as he searched desperately for a solution "outside the box." All that came to mind was forging an alliance with the Chinese civilians against the Chinese military . . . and Clarissa Leffler, who had first suggested the ploy.

Baker motioned for his secretary of state to come to the head of the table. The briefing continued even when the president swivelled his chair around. "Art," Bill whispered, "I'd like to keep open the possibility that we somehow exploit the split between the Chinese military and civilian leadership." Dodd gave Bill an exaggerated nod, encouraged that his people might help with a possible diplomatic initiative. "I'd like to get regular briefings on Chinese politics from the head of your China Desk," Bill said nonchalantly. *Clarissa What's-Her-Name,* Bill thought, *is what that sounds like.*

Art Dodd cast Bill a quizzical look. "Clarissa *Leffler*?"

Bill was embarrassed by his sophomoric attempt to avoid revealing that he had taken more than just a passing interest in Clarissa. But the fact was that he couldn't get her out of his mind. "I'd like for her to give us an update," Bill instructed Clarissa Leffler's boss. Art nodded and returned to his seat without comment.

At the far end of the long table, an aide handed the FBI director a thick sheaf of papers. Bill interrupted the NSC meeting. "May I ask what those are?" he snapped.

Asher paused. "I would like to discuss the matter in private."

"This is my National Security Council," Bill caustically pointed out. "It doesn't get more private than this."

The director's gaze hardened. He rose, rounded the table, and laid the papers on the table in front of Bill. "It's a search warrant and a subpoena," Asher explained. "We have credible evidence that there may be ongoing violations of the National Secrecy Act by a member of your staff. The violations might involve contact with the Chinese."

Baker read the papers with grinding teeth and rising anger until he finally exploded. "You want to *wiretap* White House *phones*? Get unlimited security clearance into the White House for your agents at any time day or night?"

Baker pressed a button that quickly dialed the Justice Department on the videophone. The camera showed an empty chair just before the attorney general, Gerald Pritchard, sat.

"I want you and the solicitor general to petition the supreme court to declare the goddamned National Secrecy Act unconstitutional," Bill ordered, "so get people working on it! In the interim, you are to advise every agency in the executive branch that compliance with that illegal act is a crime!" Before Pritchard could respond, Bill punched the button for his secretary of the treasury, who was donning his jacket when the camera focused on him. "Effective immediately, no FBI agents are allowed into the White House! No exceptions! Order the Secret Service to compile a list of all current and former FBI personnel and exclude them from the grounds! Both uniformed and protective detail personnel are authorized to use force to enforce the exclusion." The secretary's jaw hung open. "Deadly force," Bill amended, then hung up.

Hamilton Asher fixed a stony glare at Baker, who turned to scan the room. From the uncomfortable expressions on the faces of his NSC, Baker knew that they believed him to be overreacting. *Fuck all of you!* Bill thought before turning back to Asher. "Now, you . . . get the hell out of my house."

The NSC briefing had split in two. One group—chaired unofficially by Elizabeth Sobo—faced an army general on a video screen reporting the relatively good news from the West Coast. I Corps—pronounced "Eye" Corps among the cognoscenti—had pocketed the Chinese invaders in San Diego. General Cotler credited the navy with that success. Admiral Thornton explained that the lengthy Chinese supply lines were being interdicted by three dozen hunter-killer submarines out of Pearl Harbor, sinking 1.2 million tons of Chinese shipping per day. "The sub pens at Pearl are being hit with round-the-clock missile attacks," Baker heard with half an ear, "but so far they're relatively undamaged." The Marine commandant, whose 60,000-man III Marine Expeditionary Force—including the 1st Marine Expeditionary Brigade and the 3rd Marine Division—was dug in deep around Pearl Harbor, said, "They're gonna have to come in and try to take it."

Bill had met the commander of the 3rd Marines on his inspection tour of Hawaii. The general had defined success by saying, "If we're all dead and the Chinese hold the beach, I'd give my Marines a 'Good.' If we're all dead and the Chinese *don't* hold the beach—now *that* rates an 'Outstanding.' "

At the end of the table opposite Bill Baker, the vice president and the other half of the NSC discussed war of a different kind. "Fire Asher," Attorney General Pritchard advised. "No!" Frank Adams jumped in too loudly. "Firing Asher would be political *suicide*! He's got strong backing on the Hill! There would be bipartisan support to investigate us if the grounds were providing safe harbor to Chinese *spies*, for Christ's sake!"

The maps adorning wall screens all turned to solid blue. The door opened, and Clarissa Leffler entered. She was ushered to an empty chair by a military aide with close-cropped hair. Clarissa sat and extracted files as the conversations around her turned to whispers. She hurriedly read before being called upon to give the impromptu report to the president.

The lawyers debated whether to file Baker's challenge to the National Security Act in the DC district court or to petition the supreme court directly. "You work it out," Bill ordered.

He turned to Clarissa's briefing. A single wisp of hair refused to be bound to her head by some sort of clamp that Bill studied every time she turned to answer the vice president's questions. Her neck was long and, like her shoulders at the state dinner, slender.

"I would call the coincidence extraordinary, yes," Clarissa confirmed. "But there's no way of knowing if the minister of trade actually met with the defense minister. All we know is that Minister Han and General Liu Changxing were both on Bali for one day and that their visits appear to have been on the *same* day. Drawing the inference that they met is just that, an inference."

"What would it mean if they met?" the president asked. Conversations in low tones all around the room quieted. Clarissa's briefing had assumed greater importance when the president joined in.

"To the best of our knowledge," Clarissa replied, "there have been no private meetings between any of the civilian troika—the prime minister, the minister of trade, and the head of state security—and Defense Minister Liu since just after

Tel Aviv, when the civilians reasserted complete control over all nuclear weapons. They've been on a political collision course ever since."

Baker's national security advisor asked if she thought the civilians opposed the Chinese policy of aggression.

"No. They just oppose the military. In the earlier years, the civilians coerced and intimidated countries into alliances that accounted for nearly half of China's territorial gains. The minister of trade and his son, Han Zhemin," she said, looking Bill in the eye, "negotiated alliances with Laos, Malaysia, Indonesia, Pakistan, Iraq, and Kazakhstan. China's military victories would have been impossible without those key diplomatic coups. After Tel Aviv, however, the military has gone it alone—without diplomatic support from the civilians— and has stalled at the Bosporus Straits."

"They've succeeded in invading *us*," Elizabeth Sobo pointed out sarcastically.

"But they haven't *beaten* us," Clarissa replied.

Baker couldn't help but smile at the comeback. "No," he said. "They haven't. But you're saying the Chinese military would be a helluva lot more formidable acting in concert with and not in opposition to the civilians. I agree. It should become our policy," Baker announced—looking at Art Dodd, Clarissa's boss—"to ensure that the schism in the Chinese leadership is never resolved and is, preferably, widened."

Secretary of State Dodd nodded. After a moment, he lowered the tip of his pen to his notepad, but he seemed not to know what to write.

How could we possibly influence Chinese politics? Bill realized after his grandiose foreign policy pronouncement. In making a foreign policy pronouncement that he was impotent to effect he was beginning to move imaginary armies on the maps in his bunker. Nearly everyone obviously had the same thought and avoided eye contact with Baker. The only person who didn't turn away just then was Clarissa Leffler. She studied him.

5

Young Lieutenant Wu stood staring at the concrete, shell-covered mailbox at the end of the driveway. A squad of troops nervously eyed the empty houses all along Sea Sprite Drive, none of which had been checked. Hot wind poured off the glistening blue Gulf waters. Tall reeds that obscured most of the white beach bent and bobbed in the breeze.

The house was nothing special. In fact, it was rather odd. Like all the other weather-beaten dwellings in the area, it was built on stilts. The dark windows were streaked with dirt.

Under the cover from the machine gun mounted atop the armored command car, Wu headed for the front door, which of course was locked. The squad, sensing his intentions, secured all four corners of the property. Wu rounded the house and stood in the shade of the open carport. The door there was locked also. He nodded at the sergeant. A quarter of the man's face bore an unsightly scar from a bad burn. He was a combat veteran despite being, at most, twenty years old.

The sergeant shot the locks off the door. The roar of his weapon jarred Wu's nerves in the semi-enclosed space. In all of his time around weapons on military school ranges, he had worn ear protection. His virgin ears now rang.

The splintered door was easily pried open, and Wu entered.

"Sir!" the sergeant said. There wasn't room for his men to squeeze by Wu up the stairs and sweep the home in advance. Wu didn't want them to. He wasn't a civilian, like his father. He drew his pistol, chambered a round, and proceeded up the stairs.

Besides, he thought, *the house is empty.*

The kitchen lay at the top of the stairs. It was bare of any traces of life, as was the family room. Wu drew the slatted, folding shades back, revealing a wall of windows overlooking the snowy beach and deep blue Gulf.

The soldiers held their rifles raised, but their faces grinned as they looked back and forth among each other. Silently commenting on the beautiful scene. The beautiful home.

The sergeant barked an order, and they dispersed to secure the remainder of the home.

Wu searched. Master bedroom. Master bath. A small sitting room or study. A smallish bedroom with tape marks on the walls where posters had been hung. *This is it,* he thought. In the bathroom there was a vanity with a round mirror inside an oval of bright lights.

He looked through each of the drawers in the bathroom. There was nothing there but a few strands of hair, some Q-Tips, and a Band-Aid. The soldiers watched in curiosity as Wu got on his knees and looked inside cabinets. He retrieved from the carpet a plastic comb that goes in a girl's hair and slipped it into his pocket. He looked in the closet.

"Come here and give me a boost," he said to the men at the door.

One flexed his knees and cupped his hands. Wu stepped into his hands as another soldier steadied him. He was boosted up to the top shelves inside the closet, almost slamming his head onto the door frame. The straining soldiers argued over the near miss in whispers beneath him.

Wu reached for the flat disk that lay under a coat of dust on the shelf.

When he was lowered to the floor, he blew the dust from

the DVD. The label read, *Space Marines No. 3: Alien Invasion.* In small print, it read, "Starring Bill Baker."

Wu chuckled, and the soldiers smiled without knowing why.

Wu took the disk with him and left.

WHITE SANDS MISSILE RANGE, NEVADA
October 4 // 1620 Local Time

The small military helicopter landed with a thud amid swirling sand. Bill Baker could see nothing through the window but clouds of dust. Crew members stirred and helped the president unbuckle as the rotors spun to a stop. The door opened to admit the sounds of wind and of the voices of command.

"There!" someone barked. "Chock it!"

Bill emerged into brilliant sunlight and still swirling grit. He winced as the tiny pellets pelted his eyes. He ducked and averted his face. Men crawled under the helicopter, placing rubber chocks in front of and behind its tires. Hands seized Bill and ushered him across the hard ground.

At his feet opened a dark mouth whose teeth were rows of concrete steps.

Sand ground under the soles of Bill's shoes as he descended into the quieter hollows of the earth. The breeze died amid the hard walls. Then the sound. Then the light. A hatch was held open by a man in an air force jumpsuit, who saluted with his free hand. Bill nodded and entered the cavernous facility.

Thunderous applause filled the underground factory. Workers wearing hard hats and color-coded overalls clapped and cheered below the railing at which Bill stood. There was no microphone, but there was no need for one. When the hatch shut behind Bill, the thud and squeak echoed off the hard walls, floor, and ceiling.

Bill had no prepared speech. The applause died down to a stir common to roused crowds. Bill felt at home despite the unusual surroundings.

"I *appreciate*," Bill boomed out over the heads of his audience as he held his hands out to the surroundings, "such a

warm welcome in your little home away from home, here."
There was laughter. Everywhere that Bill looked in the
bunker-like chamber he saw strictly utilitarian decor. Painted
lines—color-coordinated with workers' overalls—branched
out through round bore holes through the earth. Railings criss-
crossed the ceilings in what looked like a train terminal hung
upside down in the bizarre, subterranean land. It was all concrete and steel with one exception that captured Bill's rapt
focus. A large American flag hung from one lone, bare wall.

"You are engaged," Bill continued as many heads turned
to follow his to stare at the flag, "in a great endeavor that
may soon save our beleaguered nation. While no one yet
knows of your great, secret mission, one day all will praise
the work that you have done." The applause erupted again.
Bill thought it was particularly fervent. These people—scientists, engineers, programmers, accountants, workers—had
left their families over a year ago as if departing on a long
voyage. The secrecy, he realized—the separation—must
weigh heavily on their hearts and minds. "Now, I can't wait
to see what you've done."

Bill headed for the metal staircase and descended into the
boisterous throng. He shook hands as he made his way across
the broad floor.

The craft into which Bill peered was smaller than he'd expected, but the cockpit was larger than a normal fighter aircraft's. "This joystick," the pilot sitting in the ejection seat
below Bill lectured, "automatically switches from controlling
your ailervators to the attitudinal thrusters based on air pressure and speed."

"How does it fly?" Bill asked the chief test pilot.

"Well, sir," replied the African-American colonel with a
good-natured smile, "in the atmosphere I'd clearly rather be
in an F-26. Of course, all we've had to date were unpowered
dead drops from pretty low altitude. I'd say it glides a little
better than the shuttle."

"Did you know the pilot we lost on the drop last month?"
Bill asked, then quickly amended his question. "I mean, of
course you knew him."

Without looking Bill in the eye, the pilot gave the answer with which he was comfortable. "Weather was minimum when the flight took off. Winds gusting thirty to forty-five. They flew around for about four hours before deciding to scrub. It was a key test, though, of the wing deployment system. Whether the hydraulics could deploy the wing from its stowed to its deployed position after reentry." He glanced surreptitiously at Bill. "Best we could tell was that Doug accidentally hit the emergency drop lever."

That wasn't what Bill had heard in the official report. General Latham's investigators had concluded that Major Douglas Crenshaw had violated range safety orders and gone ahead with the test flight. Latham had recommended that Crenshaw be court-martialed posthumously. Bill had instead awarded his young widow a medal.

"Have we fixed the hydraulic system?" Bill asked the colonel.

"I guess I'll find out firsthand," the smiling pilot answered, "next week."

"Did the wind have anything to do with the crash?" Bill asked.

"Not with the hydraulics failing to deploy the wing, sir," the colonel replied. "But there were stiff, gusting crosswinds at about twenty thousand when Doug tried to deploy the parasail."

"I thought that parasail was supposed to be deployable at high speeds in case of battle damage to the spacecraft," Bill noted.

"Yes sir, it is deployable at high speeds, but not at low altitude in the thicker atmosphere." He looked up at Bill. "Besides, sir, I think I can speak for the test pilot corps in saying that none of us likes the parasail. We'd rather try to fly the Falcon in—battle damage and all—than pop that parasail. Doug's ejection seat got fouled in the goddamn *risers*!" the man said before apologizing. "It's just extra weight, sir. I'd rather have more fuel, oxygen, and ammo."

Bill turned to the chief designer of the XF-36 Fighting Falcon, who immediately became defensive. "The parasail is just like every other system on the vehicle, sir. We're working out the bugs, but we feel that the chute is a vital safety feature, Mr. President."

"Don't you think you ought to listen to the men and women who'll be flying the aircraft?" Bill suggested. "They're the ones who're going to be heading into combat strapped into this thing."

The engineer frowned, averted his gaze, and said, "We do have a team looking into the possibility of eliminating the parasail rescue system, sir."

Bill nodded and stood upright. Gathered around the aircraft were the heads of the various departments working night and day on the crash program. The stubby left wing beneath Bill was deployed into the traditional "locked" or "aircraft" mode. The wing on the opposite side was upright and swept forward to the nose of the XF-36 in the "stowed" or "spacecraft" position. The titanium reactive armor on its underside would shield the craft as it streaked through shrapnel from Chinese antisatellite weapons.

But the craft's principal defensive system was its maneuverability. Its unpainted, pewter-colored fuselage bristled with nozzles from its control jets. And from beneath the twin vertical stabilizers at the rear protruded two enormous hybrid engine exhausts. In space, the engines were liquid-fueled rocket motors. In the atmosphere, they were jets that breathed air through a giant intake that was slung under the fuselage. The air intake doubled as a reentry heat shield and gave the XF-36 its name—the Falcon—because of its vague similarity to the old F-16, which last bore that name. But any similarities of the new spacecraft to prior combat aircraft ended with that lone intake. The ambitious vehicle was not intended to be a test platform for its half-dozen bleeding-edge technologies. It was intended to fly into combat, and soon.

"How long," Bill asked to the gathering of men and women about the room, "until the Falcon will be operational?"

The engineer beside Bill—the head designer—cleared his throat, adjusted his glasses, and looked around to ensure that no one else intended to answer. "Three years, sir." Bill's head shot to the man. "Uhm, maybe, two, if we cut some corners."

Bill was incensed. Two or three *years*! They didn't *have*

that long! It was the same estimate that the same man had given him when he'd asked the same question six months before when they'd had only a metal cage in the rough shape of the magnificent machine beneath him.

The chief test pilot loosed a sigh as he looked not at the engineer but at the brightly lit controls that ringed his cockpit. The sound that he'd made—evincing the same frustration that Bill felt—had been amplified by the total silence in the underground hangar.

"Do I hear any other estimates of when this vehicle will be certified airworthy?" Bill asked, staring down at the colonel. The man—jaw bulging—glared up at his commander in chief. Bill felt a sudden easing of his own aggravation on seeing the pilot's even hotter anger. "Yes?" Bill asked the still silent colonel.

"This is a war, sir," the man replied. "I'm ready to fly." There was an eruption of objections from a dozen lab-coated experts, who were silenced by the pilot's shouts. "We've got *propulsion*, *guidance*, and *weapons*!"

"Mr. President," the chief designer said in a plaintive voice, "the XF-36 project *dwarfs* the arsenal ship construction program, not in size of budget, but in complexity. The only comparable program in man's history was the Manhattan Project. Now, when you authorized us to get started, we identified over 10 million discrete milestones of research, design, construction, testing, and debugging. On your orders, we reduced that list by cutting corners everywhere that we possibly could to 2 million line items that are clearly set out along a critical path that is currently being followed by 250 subcontractors and over 100,000 engineers, scientists, and workers all across the country. For your information, we've passed a little under *half* those milestones!"

The man was growing red-faced and increasingly certain of his response.

"If we launch now," he continued, "we'll lose vehicles, pilots, and the element of surprise. The Chinese will begin working on counterweapons before our vehicle has even become useful!"

Bill wanted so badly to order one of the fighters to overfly

China. To soar thousands of miles above the maximum range
of their current antisatellite weapons, flaunting America's
technological superiority. It would be a morale boost to America and its embattled army, and there were those among the
few who knew about the program who thought that morale
was all it was for.

But Bill was not among that group. He had far higher
hopes. Those hopes, however, would apparently be realized
only years down the road in a later phase of the war. *If*, he
thought, *we last that long.* "Get it ready to go as quickly as
you can," he instructed, giving the victory to the chief engineer, who beamed.

On the helicopter ride back to Air Force One, Bill felt optimistic. The arsenal ships would give America control of the
seas, and the Fighting Falcons would eventually dominate
space and the skies beneath it. They would escort a manned
weapons platform currently being built in Colorado into high,
geosynchronous orbit. The space station bristled with weapons, but those weapons' principal purpose was defensive. The
main utility of the platform was intelligence. Once again, they
would be able to see over the horizon, and by seizing space
they would deny the Chinese the same vantage.

An aide handed Bill a palmtop computer. Stephie's grimy
face appeared in a V-mail player. Bill inserted an earbud and
hit play without taking the time to prepare for the emotional
storm to follow.

"I'm alive," Stephie said simply and without much enthusiasm. "But I guess you know that already. We, ah, we took
a lot of casualties," she said with a sudden quiver in her voice
as if the bulwark she'd erected against the trauma shuddered.
"I guess you—I'm sure you must have—heard that too."

Bill's world was bounded by the tiny five-by-three picture,
whose edges he caressed with his thumbs. The camera shook
in Stephie's grasp as her face loomed above and filled most
of the screen. Bill could see bright sky and waving tree
branches above her head, but she appeared to be in the shade.

"I love you, Dad," Stephie said straight into the camera, as
if she'd come to the point of her V-mail. Bill's skin tingled,

and his head spun as he felt lost and adrift in the powerful current. "I just wish—I *really* wish—we'd been able to spend more time together, that's all." Bill's eyes dropped closed, and he just listened. She talked about the food, the weather, and their daily routine, but said nothing about the fighting or her comrades. "Well, I know you're busy. I won't take up any more of your time. But I just wanted to say, 'I love you.' Bye, Dad. I'll talk to you soon. Love you," Stephie said before the camera shook and the picture spun as she fumbled with the controls.

The last picture that Bill saw was of a shirtless man in the near distance who stood chest deep in a hole. He wore gloves with which he gripped a long-handled shovel and a paper surgeon's mask over his nose and mouth. Dirt flew out of the hole from the blade. Black rubber body bags lay beside the hole. The picture faded to black.

RITZ CARLTON, ATLANTA, GEORGIA
October 4 // 2330 Local Time

Wu and Shen Shen made love twice. The first time was hurried, she gratifying him. The second time was slow, for her, and from her pleasure his desire arose anew.

Afterwards, as always, she ordered room service. Totally naked, giggling on the phone, she said, "All right then, how about the 'pe-can pie'? What is that?" Another giggle. It didn't bother Wu. He rose and went to his camouflage trousers, which hung over the back of a chair.

"You've gotta *great* body!" Shen Shen said while still on the phone.

Wu did not reply.

"Yes, with *ice* cream!" she said, slamming the phone down. "This hotel doesn't have shit. Can we find another one?"

"This is the only one with electricity," he noted.

She was already snorting another line of coke when he looked back at her. Some spilled from the end of her small glass tube, and she tried to snort it from her flat stomach just above her pubic hair. When she failed, she lay back, looking at him.

"You?" she said, nodding at the small dusting of white powder.

"No thanks," he said, fishing the DVD from his trouser pocket.

"Oo! A *movie!*" Shen Shen said, popping up onto her knees and bouncing.

"It's old," Wu said.

"How old?" Shen Shen asked warily. "Like, a year or two?"

"No. Real old. Like, from the 1990s."

"A-a-aw," she said, disappointed.

Wu put the DVD in the player and settled in beside Shen Shen, lying on their stomachs with their heads at the foot of the bed. Looking at the main menu, he said that it was in English and asked if she wanted Chinese subtitles, but she said she didn't. He hit play. She nestled beside him through the rousing but ridiculous opening scene. The hero who saved the day flew a small space fighter plane, which by current technological standards seemed utterly implausible. The actor looked familiar to Shen Shen. "Oh, that's Bill Baker!" she finally said. "He looks younger."

The doorbell rang. "*Ice* cream!" Shen Shen said. She ran to the door wearing nothing.

"Put some clothes on!" Wu admonished.

"No," she said over her shoulder, padding into the living room. "If they look at me, I'll have you put their eyes out!"

She opened the door, and he heard her giggles.

When she returned, Wu asked lazily, "Did he look?"

"He saw *every*thing," she replied. "But don't be jealous. He was an American." She settled in for another snort. "Can't have ice cream without another line," she said, realizing that Wu was watching her.

"Hurry up," Wu said, not hiding his annoyance, holding the remote control.

The two snorts were loud but quick. Expert. When she bounded onto the bed, rocking him, melted ice cream sloshed onto her left breast. She made Wu lick it off.

"*Now* can we watch?" he asked.

Shen Shen's eyes were bloodshot, and she held the bowl of ice cream to her mouth and shoveled like a hungry peasant with rice. With cream on her chin, she asked, "Do you think she's pretty?"

"Is who pretty?" Wu replied.

Shen Shen shrugged and put the bowl on the nightstand. "Never mind. Let's watch," she responded, settling in beside Wu and kissing his back with freezing cold lips.

He rolled away, laughing. "Who? Do I think *who* is pretty?"

Shen Shen avoided his gaze. She was caught, Wu realized. She was high and had misspoken.

"The American president's *daughter*, of course!" she said aggressively, covering.

Wu scrutinized Shen Shen's face. She stared at the paused picture on the television, but her eyes darted hyperactively about the frozen frame. "What makes you ask about her?"

Shen Shen sighed. "Because you're thinking about her. I know."

Wu expelled air, derisively, in a response not yet fully formed in words. "What in the hell makes you say that?"

She sat up abruptly. Her exaggerated gestures were coke-induced, Wu knew. But her reaction now was more than just that. Frustration, perhaps. Misplaced jealousy, maybe. "It's obvious!" she blurted out.

"Based on what?" Wu pressed.

She slapped her tight thighs in exasperation. "Going to her school and spending half an hour there, even though it was just a pile of rubble!" Shen Shen wasn't a very good actress. She was angry. "And that request you put in to Intell to see any changes to her file! Look, I know you went to her house today, okay? I know that's where you got that disk! I mean, I *am* General Sheng's personal *secretary*, you know!"

"And is that all you are?" Wu asked in almost a whisper.

She grew outraged, her reaction accentuated by a nervous system wired to the max with Colombian cocaine. "And what's *that* supposed to mean? Do you mean do I *fuck* that wrinkled old sack of bones?"

"No," Wu replied. He felt sad. Depressed. "That's not what I meant." His forehead sank to the bed.

Shen Shen blew warmly on her hand and lay it softly on

Wu's back. She nuzzled close to his ear and kissed him. Her hand roamed. Wu rolled on his side to face her, already becoming erect. She kissed him openmouthed as he tried to put his lips to her ear. When he broke free, he kissed her neck under her thick, fragrant hair. "Who do you work for?" he whispered.

She flashed him a pained expression in reply. He turned away. Her face found his and wore an even more insistent expression of apology. "Please," her lips said soundlessly before they found his again.

She made love to him. He never moved. It took him a long while. As she labored frantically, Wu decided that she probably doesn't work for Sheng, who had been in the field for over a decade. Shen Shen had Beijing written all over her.

When Wu came, they watched the movie.

Wu enjoyed it, laughing at the humorous parts and feeling moved by the tragedies suffered by the story's hero. The one thing that moved Wu most, however, was the dogged determination of the young officer portrayed by Bill Baker. His character was pure Hollywood contrivance, of course, but that meant that it possessed in distilled form all the attributes Wu had been raised to admire. Bravery, of course, but bravery explained by the character's sense of duty. Risk taking guided by purpose. Leadership in the true sense of the word, never asking your troops to do what you had not done first.

But there was also another attribute of Bill Baker's film character that had not been instilled in Wu by instructors, but that had lain inherent in Wu from birth. Innate. Hard-wired into his nature. That attribute was compassion felt both for comrades-in-arms and for the enemy. Death and suffering weren't depicted cavalierly. They had lasting consequences, measured by the emotional scars they left on the soul. The most intriguing thing Wu found about the movie was how the hero reconciled compassion and empathy with duty. Fighting and killing were shown not to be inconsistent with feeling and caring. It gave Wu hope.

"So," Shen Shen mumbled, "do you think she's pretty?"

"Who?" Wu asked.

"The president's daughter!" Shen Shen replied, bounding

up onto her knees and sighing as if impatient with his dodging of her long forgotten query.

"I don't know!" he replied, dodging.

"You've seen her picture," Shen Shen said accusingly. "You've watched news footage of her in army training camp. There are school pictures of her in her file." Shen Shen shrugged, holding her hands to her sides. She then sank onto her stomach, nearer his ear. "It's a simple question," she whispered. "Is she pretty, or isn't she?"

Wu rolled over onto his back, twisting the sheets tight around him. He stared at the mirror on the ceiling. Shen Shen had picked the Honeymoon Suite. "But what's *not* so simple," he said, "is why you keep asking me that question?" He looked at the reflection of his chest. It had more hair than was common for Chinese, a fact that had led many of his classmates to tease him. He looked at Shen Shen's back. Each vertebra and rib stood out sharply beneath perfect skin.

She was chewing on the satin sheets. "Well, let's see," she said with a quaver in her voice. "Why would I be interested in that question?" She laughed, but her red eyes were moist, and her mouth hung open in a totally unguarded, unposed expression. "Who do you find prettier, Wu," she asked in a whisper, "Chinese girls? Or American girls?"

So that's *it*, Wu finally realized. He shook his head at her ridiculous insecurity, but then turned back to his reflection in the mirror. He looked Chinese, but his features were muted. Rounded. Pale. He saw what she saw, and he understood her question. To her, to every Chinese, he appeared to be straddling some line of loyalty. Torn between his two halves. But in truth he wasn't torn at all. Or, at least, he hadn't been.

When he looked back at Shen Shen, all he saw was her luxuriant hair. She had laid her cheek on her hands, facing away from him. Small quivers shook her smooth back. Wu rolled against her and held her. He hadn't answered the question because it strayed too close to the conflict that had lain dormant for all his days. The conflict that now, however, he could no longer avoid. But in his silence she thought he had answered.

So she doesn't know everything, the calculating part of his

brain deduced. She knew about his current comings and go-
ings, but not his history. Wu's family had kept that a secret
so closely guarded that her handlers hadn't included it in her
briefing.

For if they had, she never would've had to ask why he was
interested in Stephanie Roberts.

SAVANNAH RIVER, SOUTH CAROLINA
October 5 // 0500 Local Time

The air was damp and cool. Words came with faint wisps
of smoke. "Dawn's comin'!" Stephon Johnson shouted from
outside the bunker. His words echoed off the bare walls of
concrete. "Burns! Roberts! Get out here."

Stephie ached deep down to her bones. For ten days, they
had been preparing a defensive line along the river: digging
trenches, filling sandbags, burying cable, putting thick timber
and earthen roofs over machine gun nests, building nine-foot-
high walls of sandbags around mortar pits. Everything was
designed to weather an unimaginable storm of high explosives
and high-velocity lead. *What in God's name is coming?* came
the recurring thought as Stephie and her comrades burrowed
underground. All Stephie had decided was that whatever came
their way didn't come in the name of God.

"Get the fuck out here!" Johnson barked in a hoarse voice.
Stephie pushed herself up from her sleeping bag against the
leaden force of gravity. Her face was molded into the rough
texture of two dirty towels she had used as her pillow. The
flat taste and smell of fresh concrete filled her mouth, nostrils,
and hair. Stephie and John hoisted their weapons and headed
for the lone exit.

Animal snored uninterrupted from the corner of the bunker's single large chamber. Becky had cotton balls plugged
in her ears. The five of them—including Johnson—were all
that was left of the thirteen soldiers who had made their brief
stand in and around the house on Mason Street. Stephie and
John entered the passage into and out of the bunker, which
always reminded Stephie of some mysterious corridor in an
Egyptian tomb. The simple maze wound its way first right,

then left, forming a reinforced-concrete "U." The design prevented direct fire and shrapnel outside from entering the bunker through its opening into the trench, but it also created a sense that danger lay in wait just around the passageway's next bend.

Before exiting into the fresh morning air, Stephie touched the wall for luck. The concrete had been wet when they had been assigned bunker 9G. In search of immortality, the five survivors of the reconstituted First Squad had written their names on the curing, three-foot-thick walls. As in life, "John Burns" was right next to "Stephanie Roberts."

Stephie, John, and Johnson stood like hunchbacks beneath the lip of the forward, fighting trench. The forward slope beneath their bunker's single, narrow firing slit led down to the Savannah River. The riverbank and cleared hillside were a killing field laced with mines and criss-crossed with preplanned fields of fire. Every night—from somewhere within earshot along the line—something or someone had come to a noisy, explosive end. Becky thought it was wandering deer, who unknowingly roamed their old, now lethal haunts. Animal bet it was luckless Chinese probes, which would explain the mortar-fired flares and thirty-second bursts of American machinegun-fire that usually followed each mine's detonation. Regardless, all kept their heads low in or near the main fighting trench. No one knew what lay across the river. All the patrolling the Americans did was to their rear.

"Roberts," Johnson said, "I'm putting you in the lead of Fire Team Alpha."

The words cleared Stephie's head of the morning's grogginess. "What?" she shot back. "What kind of . . . ? *Me?* What about John? He's a PFC."

"No," Johnson corrected, "he's a corporal, and he takes over Fire Team Bravo. I just made sergeant and got First Squad. And by the way, Roberts, *you're* a private first class. Congratu-fuckin'-lations."

"What kind of bureaucratic army bullshit is this? They've decided it takes *three* people to lead—what—one person? Becky Marsh?"

"We got replacements," Johnson explained before heading

off down the trench. John and Stephie followed. The main fighting line ran along the crest of a ridge that overlooked the river 150 meters below. The walls consisted of packed brown earth shored up here and there with wooden timbers that had been yanked from a rail bed and countless numbers of sand-bags. The crude drains on the trench floor were quickly being clogged with run-off. Stephie walked along the higher and drier edges, not down the sloppy center where mosquito-infested pools of water stood.

Overhanging the trench, in stark contrast to the squalid slop in which they dwelled, swayed verdant South Carolina pines. Every so often their scent wafted down to the soldiers' depths, replacing the stench of human filth. Stephie breathed deeply of those cherished few breezes, which transported her far away from that awful place.

They turned off the main defensive line into a narrow communications trench that dropped away steeply as they descended the hill. Railroad ties had been laid across the floor every so often, but they failed in both their purposes. They neither stemmed the mud slides washed loose by the rain nor—slick with mud—allowed for sure footing.

At the bottom of the hill, they scaled a rough-hewn ladder made of discarded packing crates and rose to ground level. There, they were careful to remain within the twisting path marked by twin lines of stakes topped by tiny strips of dangling cloth. The mines to either side of the clear pathway were supposedly inert until activated by an engineer's signal, but no one was willing to risk their life on a supposition.

As the small group approached a newly carved but already rutted dirt road, they heard terse commands being issued in low voices. A mass of helmeted soldiers stood in dark ranks. The groaning brakes and grinding gears of the last of the trucks that had brought them there betrayed the driver's desire to get the hell away in a hurry. Headlights flashed briefly through narrow slits in black tape across ranks of several hundred infantrymen.

Johnson got in a line that led to a laptop computer, which, like its owner, sat atop an empty ammo box. The squeaky clean replacements—"cherries"—had long been the objects of derision by Stephie and her hardworking comrades. The embittered survivors of the bloody clash in Atlanta had felt that they needed rest to recover from the shock. It should have been the *cherries,* fresh from boot camp, who did the digging. Those same cherries who now stood in loose ranks and clean uniforms. Stephie's cheek twitched as she frowned at their nervous laughter, which was quieted by an NCO's surly growl. The fuckers had been sleeping in beds, taking showers, using bathrooms with toilets, Stephie thought, while they had been living in the muck like animals.

"I need seven," the newly minted Sergeant Stephon Johnson reported.

"*Seven?* For one squad? You can have *five,*" the staff sergeant with the laptop said. In the dim starlight and glow from the computer's screen, he held his hand up toward the road with five fingers spread. Five privates, fresh from training platoons, were cut from the herd. The three men and two women gave their serial numbers. The staff sergeant tapped on the keyboard. "Okay," he said, "you five are in First Squad, Third Platoon, Company C, Third Battalion, 519th Infantry."

The five cherries grinned at each other on hearing the official-sounding news, which obviously seemed to them to hold great import. One even muttered the important data repeatedly under his breath in an effort to commit it to memory.

"My name's Sarge' Johnson," their fearless leader slurred. "This is Corporal Burns and PFC Roberts. Safe your weapons. Keep your mouths shut. Keep your heads down. Don't touch anything. Stay in line. Le's go."

Stephie and John followed Johnson, the sergeant/father-figure in the cherries' new world. The five replacements followed the two fire team leaders. "Stay inside the flags," Stephie cautioned as they marched single file through the minefield. The clear path through the flags was well-worn and would be obvious to any Chinese who attacked from the rear. But the safe lane wouldn't do them much good. The barrels of machine guns protruded from two sandbag-roofed nests on either side of the ladder down into the slit trench. Their interlocked fields of fire would lay waste to any Chinese who circled back to envelope their stretch of the line after a break-through.

The eight soldiers descended one by one into the brown gash in the earth and made their way up the rear slope of the ridge to the main defensive line. The going was slow, as the cherries labored up the hill under heavy packs, which occasionally got caught in the narrow confines of the slit trench. Each time the hapless cherries slowed the procession down, they drew curses from Johnson and Stephie. That was especially true when the fucking idiots stopped to take in the novel sights of an aid bunker, a command bunker, an ammo bunker. The cherries whispered remarks to each other like tourists in a cathedral.

"Shut the fuck *up!*" Stephie snapped. Their chatter came to an abrupt halt.

The higher up the ridge they progressed, the lower the three veterans stooped. The replacements marched, by contrast, parade-ground erect. "Keep your fucking heads down!" Stephie warned in an incredulous, shrill tone. They bent low, but raised their weapons to port arms as if Chinese might drop from the trees. Stephie shook her head and rolled her eyes at their cluelessness.

When they reached the main trench, they passed an observation post. The gaggle of cherries stopped to gawk at the several flat-paneled displays, which glowed brightly from the dark sandbagged enclosure. On the screens, the cold black river beneath their line snaked through glowing white terrain. A lounging soldier with a joystick panned a camera across the front and stopped on any mysterious, bright-hot shapes. The camera sat atop a motorized mast raised above the trench a few meters away. Its actuator emitted a faint electric whine.

"Would you keep *up!*" Stephie whispered. "Je-esus *Christ!*"

When they reached their squad's bunker, Sergeant Johnson knelt at the thick walls of the entrance. The others joined him on the floor of the trench. The cherries—careful to avoid muddying their uniforms or gear—squatted. Stephie sat on the driest spot she could find. Johnson said, "Roberts, you get Marsh and two 'o the cherries."

"I can't deal with Becky!" Stephie objected. "No way!"

"I'll take her," John volunteered, then looked the five replacements over: three men—two with squad automatic weapons—and two women. "You and you," he said, picking one man with an SAW and one woman, and leading them into the dark bunker. One cherry collided noisily with the concrete bend in the passageway and cursed.

"I gotta go report to fuckin' Ackerman," Johnson said. He trundled away and left Stephie alone with her fire team.

The two men and one woman were all about Stephie's age. They stared at their fire team leader expectantly. From inside the bunker Animal shouted, "Shut the fuck up!" as John had a chat with his new people. Stephie realized she probably should say something important. Impart some life-saving wisdom learned in the trials of combat. "Keep your heads down," she said as she rose. Without being instructed, they followed her down the trench line to an empty ballistic shelter, which was carved out of the wall and covered with logs and sandbags. Stephie plopped onto the dirt inside the enclosure. It was intended for people caught under a barrage in the open trench in between the concrete bunkers that dotted the ridge every forty to fifty meters. One cherry almost knocked down the lone wooden support that braced the sagging roof above Stephie's head. "Watch out!" she snapped as the private tried to straighten the support but only made it worse.

The cherries stood outside and began to shed gear without being ordered. "Can I go to the bathroom?" one asked. "No," Stephie replied. "And keep your fucking *heads* down, I said!" With their knees bent and helmets ducked, they found it awkward to drop packs and remove bandoliers filled with extra ammo. "Names!" Stephie ordered.

"Dawson, Rick, Private," blurted the guy with the squad automatic weapon. He had the complexion of a redhead, but when he accidentally knocked his helmet off his head Stephie couldn't see any hair on his tightly shorn scalp. He was tall and seemed solid enough.

"Tate, Patricia, Private," came the high-pitched voice of a rifleman/grenadier. *Scared shitless,* Stephie thought as Dawson helped the girl drop her pack. Stephie worried whether the slightly built Tate could carry her own load.

"Shelton Trulock," said a slightly-built, bespectacled soldier, who stood with his knees pressed together like a child who needed to go to the bathroom. "You're the president's daughter, aren't you?" he asked.

"Go take your piss," Stephie replied. Trulock asked where the latrines were. "Fuck the latrines," Stephie replied. "Piss anywhere. The latrines are for taking a shit." Trulock arched his eyebrows at her foul language, then headed off. "Just keep your head down!" she hissed after him.

Dawson and Tate turned their full attention to Stephie. "Can I . . ." Patricia Tate began hesitantly, "Can I ask a question?" she finally said. Stephie nodded. "What's . . . what's it like? Combat, I mean?"

Stephie lowered her gaze to her lap. Ever since Atlanta, she and the other survivors had lived only in the present. No one had asked "What was it like?" because all had been witness. They all had their own memories and perspectives, which by tacit agreement had been locked up tight. In the week since their first bloody shock, no one had even mentioned Mason Street. *What had it been like?* she asked herself, but her mind refused to answer. She had the key to unlock the memory but chose not to use it. She looked up into the two anxious faces but said nothing.

Animal emerged from the bunker, stretched and yawned loudly, then urinated into the trench for what seemed like far longer than humanly possible.

"That's Animal," Stephie introduced.

"Gross," Tate remarked.

"He's our machine gunner. They're different," Stephie explained.

A scraping sound preceded Trulock's fall from the trench wall onto the ground. The cherries ducked in unison as a distant *boom* rolled across the hills. The report from a large-caliber rifle echoed through the trees with a crackle. Stephie scrambled to the unmoving body of the replacement on the trench floor. It took a moment in the darkness for her eyes to gather enough data to form a picture of what had just happened. There was no point of reference for Stephie to begin assessing Trulock's medical condition. There was no head attached to Trulock's neck.

"You okay, Shelton?" Patricia Tate asked before hurling herself backwards and exclaiming, "Oh-my-God!" and subsequent unintelligible utterings. That set off sobs and jagged, panting breaths. Dawson clutched Tate to his chest as Animal knelt beside Stephie.

"Who the hell was that?" Animal asked.

"Some replacement," Stephie replied from the bottom of a well of total shock. "Trulock," she said. "Shelton Trulock."

"That's not much of a name," was the extent of Animal's eulogy. "I'll get his body if you try to find his head."

"There's not enough left," John Burns said upon arrival.

Stephie's eyes sunk closed at the thought of all the boots what would trod across poor Shelton Trulock's most precious remains. His head had become just so much refuse. Part of the litter and waste left behind.

"Shit!" Stephon Johnson cursed when he saw what had happened. "I'll go try to get another one before they run out." The exhausted man sighed at the inconvenience.

When Animal grabbed Trulock's boots to drag him to graves registration, John stopped him and said he would help. The two lifted the body, and Stephie rose in a daze, almost fainting from light-headedness. Stephie stumbled toward the bunker, fighting tunnel vision, but stopped dry mouthed and in a cold sweat beside Tate and Dawson. Tate's face was buried in Dawson's flak jacket. "Keep your heads down," Stephie warned yet again.

The upper branches along the ridge top across the river were touched by the first rays of dawn. As in ancient days, time moved by sundials instead of second hands. Gray half-tones were slowly replaced with vivid green pines. The sky was probably cloudless and blue, but Stephie couldn't see it through the three-foot-thick firing slit that was angled down toward the river. There was barely enough room to insert into the slit the raised front sights and barrels of her M-16 and underlying grenade launcher.

Johnson, Burns, and Stephie stared across the foggy river

bottom from behind concrete and rebar. Their bunker's single
chamber was thirty feet wide and fifteen feet deep, but its
low, six-and-one-half-foot ceiling made it feel cramped and
claustrophobic. Lying prone on the floor were nine soldiers:
the rest of First Squad, plus the attached, two-man machine
gun crew, a platoon medic, and Becky. Stephie's two shaken,
surviving fire team members cowered close to John's two
cherries. Johnson had been unsuccessful in getting a replacement for Trulock. Animal and his new assistant machine gunner lay on the hard floor around their weapon, which Animal
lovingly caressed with an oiled cloth patch. Specialist Fourth
Class Melinda Crane—their exhausted medic—slept at their
feet directly beneath the firing slit. Becky sat alone by the
wall next to the exit.

The river's stillness was appropriate to the early hour, but
it seemed to Stephie eerily quiet. Their bunker was roughly
in the middle of their battalion's position. The six hundred
men and women manned a line along the half mile of river
front that brigade planners had judged most easily forded. But
the sandbars' gentle banks and the wide beaches below their
bunker had been laced with thousands of landmines. Huge
antitank mines were built to fire straight up into the lightly
armored undercarriages of Chinese fighting vehicles. Anti-
personnel mines had been scattered about to protect them. The
latter were modern-day Bouncing Bettys meant to maim but
not necessarily kill minesweeping crews. When slender wires
were tripped, the disks popped three feet into the air and
sprayed eight hundred flesh-ripping darts in every direction.

John Burns kept looking at Stephie past Johnson, whose
eyes were glued to binoculars. John tilted his head toward the
bunker's lone exit. Stephie followed him, stepping over the
prone replacements and Becky. John and Stephie emerged
into the sandbag-lined trench, alone under pine branches on
the cool, damp morning. Stephie leaned against the wall and
tilted her helmet off her forehead.

"Johnson says . . ." John began.

"I know," Stephie interrupted. "He heard they were going
to try to push across here. He said he heard it from a major

on brigade staff. Now how many majors does Johnson know?"

"Yeah, but it makes sense," John reasoned. "They'll probably try to cross the river in half a dozen places, and this looks like one to me."

"But it would be *suicide*!" Stephie whispered as if it were a military secret. "I mean . . ." she began, slapping her hand on the cold concrete of the bunker wall. John frowned and shook his head condescendingly as if at Stephie's naïveté. "Oh," she responded, "and just *how* the hell do you know what the Chinese are gonna do, von Clausewitz?"

"We've got to have a plan," John said.

Stephie stared at him uncomprehending. "A plan? A *plan*! My *plan* is to fight from this fucking *bunker* with my *squad*! My *plan* is to kill as many Chinese as I *can*!"

"Stephie, if they overrun us, every second counts. The first wave to crest the ridge will keep going to disrupt our rear. The second will put a machine gun on this bunker exit and bring in flamethrowers. Okay? We've got to be out of the bunker, down the ridge, and into the thick woods on the other side of the dirt road in the chaos before the Chinese get organized. That means you, me, Johnson, and our people, because if we don't we'll be POWs, or dead."

Stephie nodded.

"Don't go up to ground level," John continued. "That's suicide. Fight your way through the communications trenches back to the rear. Got it?" The chill of the morning air kept Stephie from trusting that her voice wouldn't break. "Do you understand, Stephie?"

She nodded again.

"Stephie," John began, with his eyes downcast, "there's something I've been wanting to tell you."

"No," Stephie said, quieting him with her fingertips on his lips. Her skin there was sensitive enough to tell when his lips pressed, and when the kiss parted from her outstretched hand.

The rumbling sound of a freight train descending from the sky rattled the air overhead. John shoved Stephie into the bunker's entrance just ahead of a series of thunderous eruptions. Stephie bounded off walls until she fell flat on her face.

They crawled on their bellies around the bend in the passageway as smoking debris smashed high off the walls. The concrete floor thudded beneath Stephie, and ice picks stabbed at her ears. She quickly grew sick to her stomach as clouds of dust and smoke poured into the main chamber. Flame shot through the firing slit. Her ears chimed with every blast. She lost her bearings completely, tumbling end over end even while lying on concrete.

The next sound she remembered hearing was coughing. Then, outside, men shouted. Mines exploded like firecrackers. Mortars, cannon shells, and missiles crashed onto the face of their bunker and sprayed fire and dirt through the slit. One soldier—a replacement—lay at the rear of the bunker. The crimson smear along the wall marked his descent from sitting position to crumpled death. Another replacement screeched at the top of his lungs as the medic used scissors to cut his smoking uniform. Melinda Crane kept her knee on her patient's chest to contain his insensate thrashings and cut nearly indistinguishable sheets of skin and cloth to expose the smoking wound.

The remainder of First Squad lay curled on the bunker floor, not yet having entered the fight. Stephie rose to her knees—fighting dizziness and nausea—and shouted, "Get up!" John got onto all fours beside her. Sparks flew into the firing slit and burst off the ceiling, spattering soldiers with flecks of concrete. Spec Four Crane scrambled to a newly wounded cherry with the burned replacement clutching wildly after her screaming for more painkiller.

John sat on his heels but doubled over and vomited. Animal gained his footing and lifted his M-60 to the slit. Johnson echoed Stephie's orders in a croaking voice. Stephie climbed up the wall with both hands to the slender horizontal opening, which was now filled with debris.

Fires dotted the hillside and burned even from the middle of the river. Hulks of Chinese vehicles littered both banks and dirty brown sandbars. One amphibious scout car floated downstream shooting fireworks high into the sky as the vehicle turned slow circles in the stream. Missiles streaked from American lines and killed Chinese vehicles with unerring ac-

curacy. Chinese guns and missile launchers from across the
Savannah River tried to thread the needle of bunkers' firing
slits in return.

Survivors spilled out of flaming troop carriers on the near
side of the river at the foot of their killing ground. Against
what seemed insurmountable odds, the Chinese infantrymen
formed into teams in the shelter of deep craters and blazing
armor. Soon, Stephie realized, they would rally into squads
and platoons, then companies, battalions, and regiments unless somebody did something about it.

She raised her M-16 to her shoulder and rested it on the
stable ledge of the firing slit. She paid little attention to the
insignificant, air-bursting mortars, even though their shrapnel
hailed down on their bunker and randomly ricocheted through
the slit. She lined up a Chinese soldier who duck-walked from
one clump of men to another, pointing and issuing orders.
Her first shot kicked up a splash of white water behind him.
Her second sent red spray onto the sand. The stunned Chinese
soldier sat on his butt and patted his shoulder and chest, mind-
lessly searching for his wound. Stephie fired again and blasted
his helmet into the stream.

The huddled clusters of soldiers were now leaderless. Stephie picked them off one at a time. There wasn't much to
shoot at—a helmet, an ass, a pair of legs—but she sent rounds
down the hill with cool precision. She blew the exposed heel
off of one man's boot after firing three aimed shots at his
legs. When he spun wildly to clutch at his wound, she killed
him with a devastating shot through the back of his neck.
Another of Stephie's rounds clipped off a piece of a man's
crooked elbow. What was left of his arm flopped sickeningly.
A dozen soldiers rose in unison to rush up the ridge. She fired
five shots—downing two—before Animal opened up with his
-60 and killed the rest with belt-fed, 7.62 mm rounds.

A missile sparked in the trees across the river. Its smoking
trail wiggled before steadying, and Stephie ducked. Flames
shot into the firing slit just above her. The heat was searing
but winked out in a flash. Even so her exposed skin felt sunburned.

John tried to coax a quivering replacement—Animal's new

assistant machine gunner—to allow him to look at the wound to his eye, but the man adamantly refused. Tate and Dawson, who appeared unscathed, huddled together on the floor. *"Get the fuck up and . . . !"* Stephie began before being knocked to her knees with a stupendous blow.

What happened? she thought, trying to make sense of it all.

A cold chill spread down her body like the onset of fever. Prickly fingers of pain began to cast a web outward from her neck. Her mouth hung open—halted mid-sentence—as the pain rose, and rose, and rose. On all fours, she stared down at the single drop of blood that spattered the dusty concrete floor. A second droplet, then a third was soon a steady rain. The blood, Stephie realized, was hers.

John took her helmet off and rolled her onto her back. The pain—now excruciating—grew worse with every breath, which was now exhaled in panted, moaning cries. Stephie couldn't force herself to think straight. She lay her left cheek on the concrete and focused on the spent cartridges that rained from Animal's M-60 and grew into piles on the floor. John probed the base of her neck, which erupted into flames of agony. *"A-a-ah!"* she screamed. "Oh-God! God! *Sto-o-op!"*

"You're gonna be okay," John said as he poured water from his canteen onto her neck.

"Stop! Stop it!" she demanded, swatting at him and slapping at his face. But when she saw the blood that dripped from his bare hand, she clenched her teeth, jammed her eyes shut, and puffed through pursed lips as if enduring the rigors of childbirth. The pain grew even greater when Crane began to sew up her ripped flesh. Stephie grunted, rolled her head along the concrete to lift her shoulders from the floor. Moaned to blot out everything. Then saw Dawson and Tate staring at her in horror. "Get the f-fuck up there and f-fight!" she spat, and they rose.

"You've got a two-inch long gash across the base of your neck," John said calmly over the roar of weapons. Melinda Crane coated Stephie's neck with freezing antibacterial spray. Stephie stifled her screams by clenching her aching jaw. Sweat gushed from every pore. A sharp sting in her arm preceded an almost instantaneous feeling of contentment, which loosened her clenched jaw and relaxed her cramping muscles. She sighed deeply as John dried and bandaged the nape of her neck and Crane scrambled off to other patients.

Rifles and machine guns roared. Grenades, mortars, and exploding 20 and 30 mm cannon shells popped just outside Stephie's secure nest of pleasant feelings. Only the *booms* of 120 mm main tank guns against the front wall of the bunker managed to rouse any vague sense of fear in Stephie. She lay on her back watching cartridges rattle around on the floor next to Stephon Johnson's combat boots. She followed news of the war writ in flashes through the slit onto the ceiling far, far above.

She was surprised when John helped her sit up with her back to the wall just beneath the firing slit. She had so much she wanted to say, but brass rifle casings clattered off her helmet and she lost her train of thought. A thick bandage covered the back of her neck just under her helmet. Every time Stephie turned her head, the dull ache lit up like fireworks, so she stiffly turned her entire torso to peruse the bunker. John now stood at the firing slit firing round after aimed round. Crane had moved on to Animal's screaming assistant machine gunner, whose hands she still couldn't pry off his face. The hand of the man who'd been burned was outstretched toward the chamber in general, but his fingers formed a still, dead claw.

Stephie's rifle lay by her side. It seemed heavier than she remembered when she tried to stand beside John.

"Get down!" John shouted. His hand on her shoulder shoved her roughly to one knee, which landed on a shell casing. Pain burst from both her knee and the wound on her neck. The next time, she was ready for John's hand, which she slapped away and stuck her rifle into the firing slit. The sight before her was surreal. There were fires and muzzle flashes everywhere. Bullets picked at the bunker's facade. One in every few dozen ricocheted into the chamber through the slit. But what drew Stephie's attention was the awesome sight of a regiment of fifty tracked and wheeled Chinese vehicles rushing down the opposite hill in line. They weaved amid the flaming wreckage of earlier waves: first, second, third, she had lost track. At the water's edge, the row of vehicles disappeared almost in unison behind huge splashes from their boat-shaped amphibious bows.

In the water, all slowed to a crawl. The swimming vehicles—sitting ducks for American missile crews—exploded by the dozen in mid-river. They gained traction and rose onto sandbars—gaining speed with water cascading off their hulls—but still they exploded. They exploded on the near bank. They exploded as they rose up the hill. Stephie stood at the firing slit watching.

Grenades launched by infantrymen arced through air toward their bunker. Everyone but the dazed Stephie ducked. She felt their hot bursts on her exposed face and hands. Shrapnel rattled harmlessly through the firing slit. Stephie raised her rifle and took patient aim, striking a grenadier squarely in the chest. He wore body armor and the round simply knocked him onto his back, but still exposed.

"Stephie . . ." John said, grabbing her shoulder. Her second round flew harmlessly into the river.

She pulled herself free and snapped, "You made me miss!" The grenadier was crawling down the hill to retrieve his helmet. Stephie fired a round straight into his right butt cheek, which must have fractured some major bone. He rolled over and looked around in confusion. She fired once more and bounced his bare head off a tree stump.

From the burning hulks that had made it halfway up the hill poured more and more Chinese infantrymen. More and more targets for Stephie's bucking M-16.

The *thwop* of beating helicopter rotors rose suddenly above the battle. The slope just outside erupted in flame. Stephie ducked below the slit just as a Chinese gunship raked their bunker with its 30 mm automatic cannon. Melinda Crane yelped and grabbed at her left calf before an even louder explosion ended the aircraft's cannon fire. Stephie and the others immediately rose up to the slit. The helicopter had rolled over once from its collapsed skids onto its Plexiglas canopy, which had settled into a crater on the hillside. The pilot and co-pilot hung upside down in their seats. They flailed at their harnesses not forty meters beneath the bunker.

Animal stitched the wreckage with M-60 rounds, which did nothing more than put a string of stars across the bullet-proof canopy. "I got it!" Stephie shouted and laid her M-16 on its side, ensuring that the under-barrel grenade launcher had a clear path to the target. John said be careful, and Stephie snapped, "I've *got* it!"

The pilot sat on the roof of the upside-down aircraft and worked to open an escape hatch. When Stephie's aim was true, she checked one last time to ensure the grenade wouldn't make contact with the concrete. Satisfied, she pulled the launcher's trigger. The *thump* sounded nearly simultaneously with the bursting grenade. The co-pilot's blood splattered the inside of the canopy, but the pilot kicked the hatch open. The fire was rapidly consuming the cockpit from the outside, but the pilot succeeded in squeezing out through the flames and raced away from the growing conflagration. *Pow*, came a single shot from John's rifle. The unlucky pilot tumbled down the hill already dead.

The helicopter's missiles, tracers and shells shrieked off in all directions until its under-pylon fuel tanks exploded. The heat from the petroleum flames washed across the front of their bunker, forcing all to duck behind the concrete shield. Stephie looked around the bunker's chamber. The guy along the blood-streaked wall and the burned guy—both replacements—were dead. Animal's assistant machine gunner sat against a side wall with bloody bandages covering his face, methodically pounding his clenched fist against the floor. Only seven were left: Stephie, John, Stephon Johnson, Animal, Dawson, Tate, and John's lone surviving replacement, whatever his name was.

A burst of static preceded Ackerman's shouts into everyone's earphones. "Clear the trenches! The Chinese are *in*! Clear the trenches! Clear the trenches!"

John motioned for Animal to follow. He grabbed his lone man and Stephie's cherry, Dawson. The sound of blistering fire from automatic weapons entered the bunker through the opening at its rear. Becky scooted back into the main chamber from where she had weathered the storm just inside the passageway.

"Get up here, Marsh!" Johnson shouted as he blazed away with his M-16. Stephie's fire joined his, but she couldn't rid herself of the crawling skin that warned of danger to the rear. The few targets who cowered on the hillside below were mere victims at a massacre.

Stephie turned and headed for the exit. "I'm gonna check the trench!"

Johnson shouted at Marsh to get the hell up to the firing slit. Stephie stepped over Becky's legs wearing a look of utter disdain. Becky returned the glare defiantly.

Outside, the main fighting line was in complete disarray. Craters enlarged or collapsed the trench walls. Thick smoke obscured the muddy floor. Animal lay hunched over his machine gun amid toppled sandbags defending the bunker's lone exit with the squad's most awesome weapon. He held it aloft prepared to swing his fire left or right, as needed.

"Which way did they go?" Stephie yelled over the rattle and pop of gunfire in both directions.

"The two cherries went that way," Animal pointed to the right, "and Burns went that-a-way."

Stephie followed Animal's finger—and John Burns—to the left and keyed her helmet's boom mike. "Dawson, you read me? Over?" A panting, whispered acknowledgment confirmed they hadn't made contact on the right. "John?" Stephie next asked expectantly, staring down the smokey trench after him. She got no reply. "John, do you read me, over?"

Pop! Pop! Pop-po-po-pop! erupted the reports of vicious, close-in combat from the direction in which she was headed. Stephie cautiously advanced toward the sound of the firefight over fallen timbers and landslides. Her rifle was planted firmly in the hollow of her shoulder. Her eye was glued to her sights. Her finger was within a hair's breadth of releasing the sear. Ghosts formed and dissipated in the drifting smoke. Stephie stifled coughs that might draw blind fire by clamping her lips tightly shut. The imaginary aimpoint beyond the raised front sight of her rifle was her sole focus.

The smoke swirled from a draft in the wake of a warily approaching Chinese soldier.

Crack! Stephie's rifle recoiled.

The Chinese soldier's face exploded ten feet in front of Stephie.

She dove behind a pile of sandbags as the trench erupted in full-auto fire. The top layer of sandbags above her disintegrated in rips and sprays from thirty or forty rounds. *Covering fire*, she thought as she fumbled with a hand grenade. She pulled the pin, let the handle pop, and tossed the frag no more than five feet over the fallen trench wall.

The explosion thumped into her back and sent loose earth cascading from the walls. A severed arm landed at Stephie's feet. She flicked the M-16's selector switch to "burst" and rolled into the smoke pulling the trigger repeatedly. Her three-round bursts stabbed randomly into the drifting haze. Under her own covering fire, Stephie rose and dashed across the trench past three dismembered Chinese and a small, smoking hole. Black objects arced past her in the opposite direction. She dove into a sagging ballistic shelter as half a dozen grenades erupted at her former position.

The shelter's single support—a misaligned wooden brace—barely held aloft the drooping roof of logs, earth, and sandbags. Stephie lay on her side with her rifle raised. From out of the clouds of heavier-than-air smoke around a zig in the trench line came a parade of rifles followed by men. *One*, she counted to herself on the appearance of each new, oblivious Chinese soldier. *Two. Three. Four.* None had seen her behind a jumbled pile of sandbags that had fallen from the shelter's roof. Each Chinese soldier carried large, square satchel charges: thirteen-pound blocks of bunker-busting plastic explosives. *Five,* she counted. *Six. Seven. Eight.*

Animal's machine gun opened fire. The first three men never made it back to the wall over which Stephie had flipped her grenade. The five others cowered behind it on Stephie's side amid their dismembered comrades' entrails. Still others arrived from around the next bend in the main trench to join the forwardmost troops. One worked to fuse his satchel charge. They were preparing to hurl the charge onto Animal's position. Once the machine gunner was dead, everyone else in the bunker would die too.

On the left—from the direction John had gone—a grenade burst in the trench. Chinese were shredded by the fragments. A lone M-16 fired three-round bursts.

Four Chinese soldiers on Stephie's right pressed themselves low to the ground as the fifth fused his smoking satchel charge. The man arched way back to hurl the canvas square toward the bunker.

Stephie killed him with a burst from her rifle. The satchel charge fell into the middle of the man's four comrades a dozen feet from where Stephie lay.

She kicked at the shelter's lone support and the roof collapsed on top of her. But that was nothing compared to the next staggering blow.

Stephie awoke inside a dark, smothering coffin. Her head was spinning, and she passed in and out of consciousness. Several times through the night, she awoke to the sound of gunfire, but each time she drifted out again. When her head next cleared, she saw light through the cracks. It was daytime, but which day? Over loud ringing in her ears Stephie heard grunts and cracking wood and gripes muttered in English.

". . . fuckin' ridiculous when we could be gettin' some sleep."

The words grew louder just ahead of the blaze of sunlight and rush of fresh air. Dirt drifted into Stephie's eyes as someone yanked at the logs covering her.

"Hey. Hey-hey-hey! *Here she is!*" Private Dawson shouted. *"She's over here!"*

As the remnants of the bombardment shelter's roof were pulled off Stephie, dirt rained onto her face. Someone dabbed at Stephie's face with a cold, wet cloth. She opened her eyes to see a face half covered with a bloody, red bandage. The one nostril that was visible was plugged with bloody gauze. The chinstrap of the man's helmet dangled beneath him as he worked patiently to wash her face.

"I thought . . . you were dead," Stephie croaked.

John Burns unearthed her as if she were an archeological

artifact: slowly, painstakingly, expecting to find her broken into pieces. She was dazed and stunned but surprisingly unharmed. A single tear plowed a furrow down John's dirtcaked cheek as he lifted Stephie into his arms.

JACKSON, MISSISSIPPI
October 10 // 2000 Local Time

"They look good," Han said to the event coordinator as they looked at the monitor. The two men stood backstage at the buzzing studio where the American audience had been gathered for Han's televised town hall meeting. "They look like they just came from church," Han commented.

"That's where we got them," the civilian media professional from Beijing said. "Say, are you going to be here for the editing?"

Han shook his head and replied, "No, I've got a photo op in Atlanta."

"Hospitals and refugee centers?" the publicity man asked.

Han nodded. "So I'll leave you in complete charge of the editing. I'd like the theme to be upbeat: people happy because they're industrious. We've got to get them to go back to work quickly or the net present value of their lost productivity screws up the rate of return on the whole campaign."

"I've got some stock footage of American industry," the coordinator suggested. "But I'm not sure about the . . . the tone."

"Don't worry about inciting American patriotism. In fact, I want you to expressly *appeal* to it. If the military censors give you any trouble, call my cell phone. What I want is for you to make them feel *good* about themselves and what they produce. But stay away from any heavy-handed, Maoistlooking crap. No tractors or assembly lines or steel mills. Give it a Twenty-First Century feel."

The audience fell quiet as a smarmy American stepped up onto the stage. He was the mayor of some town unknown to Han. The coordinator explained that the mayor of the state capital had evacuated with most of the population. "We needed an audience warm-up and someone to do your intro. He was the best we could do."

"Now I *know*," the pudgy man said to the captive studio audience, "that all of you are wonderin' why we're here. Now I don't really know, myself, but if we all just keep calm . . ."

"That guy is wrong," Han said. "No energy. I'm going on now."

The coordinator ushered Han over to the curtain. A make-up artist touched up Han's face and brushed his hair. Han was handed a wireless microphone. A well-dressed civilian assistant politely removed the local politician, whose only comment into the mike was, "Oh, okay." The event coordinator held five fingers up and counted down to his fist. The music began, and the "Applause" sign lit up.

A smiling Han took the stage to the clapping of four hundred pairs of hands. The grim-faced locals had been briefed by a flier with bold-faced warnings against behavior viewed "inappropriate or anti-Chinese."

"Thank you! Thank you!" Han said. The applause died down a beat too quickly as if it had been coerced, which of course it had. "Welcome to this town hall meeting! I'd like to thank the people of Jackson for turning out in such numbers." He walked down the steps to the central aisle. "I know that these are uncertain times for all of you, but it's that uncertainty that I'd like to address here tonight. I'd like to put you at ease about the change in administration."

Han walked up to a dumpy woman who was somewhere between her late twenties and early fifties. "Ma'am, do you live here in Jackson?" The woman swallowed and nodded. "And before the war, did you or your husband work?"

She nodded. "Yes." She wasn't finished, and Han dipped the mike again. "I mean, we both worked." She had a deep Southern accent.

Han checked the pinch-lipped faces of the crowd to make sure that everyone understood the answer. "And what did *you* do when you worked?"

"I was a bookkeeper," she replied, "at . . . at an auto body shop."

Han thought she seemed perfectly suited to such a job. "And do you work now?" he asked.

She shook her head. "No, sir. The owners, they're gone. They left before . . ."

Han nodded sympathetically. He didn't shrink uncomfortably from the subject. He felt her pain. "But . . . tell me something. Their establishment still stands, doesn't it? There's still a building." She agreed that was true. "And inside there are tools, and parts, and books to keep?" She shrugged. "And so the only thing preventing you from returning to your job is that these owners have fled, leaving their property behind."

"And . . . And they locked up."

There was a murmur of anxious laughter. Han beamed as if she'd told the most marvelous joke, and he decided to tell a joke of his own. "Oh, that's okay. *We* can take care of that."

The Chinese studio directors, stagehands, and even the young soldiers in dress uniform all spoke English and thought Han's remark amusing. But the Americans sat deathly still, wearing masks of fear or hatred or both.

Han had decided to do a town hall meeting for several reasons. The format was American. It would show people hiding in houses that they weren't alone. It would exhibit interaction between Americans and the benign Administrator. And, finally, the audience would also serve as a test market. Han's joke had not gone over well and would be edited from the broadcast.

Han rewound that tape in his mind and picked up as if he'd never attempted humor. "Well, I'm here to tell you that you can go back to your jobs. If you don't have work, we will provide you with it. It's your inalienable right to have a job, and we'll see that you have one and are paid for the work that you do. I have commissioned census takers who will be visiting your homes to take account of your needs and skills. Once everybody is again gainfully employed, your economy can continue as before."

Han now turned to a camera they had designated for close-ups. He paused thoughtfully for a few seconds. "If truth be told—and I speak for all the Chinese here in America, civilian and military—we have always been in awe of you Americans." There were vigorous nods from the civilian crew, but a military camera crew filmed close-ups of stern-faced guards at the door, who with judicious editing of their own would appear to roundly disagree. "War is always, *always*," Han emphasized, in one of his principal, scripted sound bites, "a terrible thing that every nation should strive to avoid. But no matter how hard all we men and women of good intentions strive, it sometimes cannot be averted. My personal view is that you've got to make the best of every situation, and the opportunity we Chinese and you Americans now have before us is to create a new and lasting partnership that will endure long after we Chinese have gone home."

Now, Han had everyone's attention—Chinese and Americans, soldier and civilian—equally. The end of war and the return of the Chinese to China was a desire shared by everyone below the rank of general . . . and below the rank of Administrator.

"We can teach you, and you can teach us. And together, we can show the world what true . . ."

A middle-aged man—seated sixth row center—bolted to his feet. Han's heart skipped a beat, but the fool wasn't armed. He shouted, "Death to the Chinese! Everybody take arms and fight!" Han's mike sagged to his thigh, and he sighed as the yelling continued. His emotion metamorphosed from momentary fear into pity. "Kill every one of 'em you see! Long live America!"

Security troops seized the man, and Han shook his head. "We can beat them if we . . . !" Handsome soldiers in dress uniforms, moving efficiently but not hurriedly, put the man in an arm lock and covered his mouth with white gloves concealing ether-soaked gauze. He went limp, and men on either side easily hauled him from the studio. A replacement American civilian was brought from the back of the studio to fill the man's empty seat. The event coordinator joined Han on the stage. "You wanta start over from the entrance?" he asked.

"No," Han replied, "let's take it from here. Just give me a second to talk to them." Han raised the microphone and held it close to his lips so that his voice was louder than before. "That's exactly what we didn't want," he boomed. The audience fell deathly silent and still. Han pointed at the dozen high-def studio cameras that ringed the captive crowd like machine guns. "This town hall meeting will be shown on television . . . *tomorrow* night. It is, of course, not a live broadcast."

A single gunshot from outside was clearly audible. Han frowned and shook his head slowly at the waste. But it was really a perfect punctuation mark. He didn't need to say anything more. He turned to the event coordinator and said over the studio speakers, "Let's try this one more time."

SAVANNAH RIVER, SOUTH CAROLINA
October 12 // 1730 Local Time

It was cold outside, and colder still in the concrete bunker. Stephie, John, Animal, Becky, Dawson, and Crane sat in the caked blood that had accumulated on the floor. Stephie and John both cradled in their laps squad automatic weapons with 600-round box magazines. Stephie's neck was still heavily bandaged, stiff and sore. Her right arm and ribs were discolored from bruises that over the last week had turned six different colors. Her right arm rested in a self-made sling when, as then, she wasn't fighting. Her ears still rang, and her head pounded dully against the the painkillers she took six times a day. Everyone in the bunker popped pills that left them in a stupor. Everyone, that is, but John Burns.

John sat beside her with his forehead creased by a bullet and closed with stitches, both ears plugged with cotton turned yellow by drainage, and his left cheek peeling and scabbed from flash burns. Both wounds had been received on the same day as Stephie's—one week earlier—when the Chinese had made it into the main trench. John had played dead when he'd encountered overwhelming numbers of Chinese, who had advanced past him toward Stephie. John had then attacked the Chinese from the rear. The distraction and death of the Chinese troops had saved Stephie's life, just as Stephie had saved the lives of the rest of First Squad. And while the satchel charge had given Stephie—who was shielded by the collapsed roof of the ballistic shelter—a mild concussion and numerous contusions, it had blown John six feet through the air and punctured both of his eardrums.

Stephie kept a close eye on Animal, who sat along the far wall with a dirty M-60. His original, beloved weapon had been destroyed when it—and Animal's heavily bandaged left hand—had been shot clean through. He now carried a new M-60 they had scavenged from a machine gun pit. Animal hadn't even bothered to clean the blood of the dead gunner from the stock. Stephie was worried about Animal's emotional detachment because they needed his big gun to survive.

Becky was the only one in the bunker with recharged batteries. She got a ration of them from Ackerman every evening. She was their sole source of big-picture intelligence. Despite the fact that she hadn't once fired her weapon, she had saved their lives several times. Once, when a Chinese flamethrower crew had approached their bunker, she had spotted them on her helmet's one-inch screens. Her frantic, screamed warnings had sent everyone but Stephon Johnson fleeing from the bunker just in time. Johnson had kept shouting, "I got 'em! I got 'em!" as he fired through the slit at an extreme angle.

The wave of superheated air had rushed from the exit as the bunker had filled with flaming, jellied petroleum. The burst had lasted less than a second. Johnson's screams had lasted much longer. Stephie jammed her eyes shut at the memory.

"Are you hurting again?" John asked. "You need a painkiller?" She shook her head.

They were now all proficient at the medical arts. Melinda Crane, their medic, had used each of the infantrymen as assistants in every manner of emergency surgery. They had probed massive, open thoracic wounds with their hands and reported the devastation to Crane, who was busy saving another life. They had performed desperate tracheotomies only to find that there were two sources of the awful sucking sounds: the one in the neck that they had seen and the other, unseen, in the chest. They had learned to administer anesthesia into veins that flowed back through the heart and not through open wounds onto the concrete. Almost all of their efforts had been spectacular but unsuccessful attempts to save the lives of their teenage friends.

Spec Four Crane lay curled in the corner facing away from everyone else. Following each tragedy, her flame had burned less brightly. Dark eyes that had once sparkled with life had dimmed. She didn't want to talk, to get to know you, to accept any kindness or favor from people whose bleeding holes she might soon fail to patch in time. She had withdrawn into a shell to forestall the emotional agony of yet another failed lifesaving attempt.

Dawson was the only one who seemed to have adjusted to this new life, which for the first five days had been near constant combat. He cleaned his M-16 of accumulated grime after each firefight. After sweeps of the trench, he promptly refilled his webbing with grenades in well-ordered fashion. "Any word on replacements?" he asked Becky Marsh.

Becky lay flat on her back with her head propped on a pack watching the army's version of local TV. "They all got diverted north up to Clark's Hill Lake. The Chinese broke clean through twice but were so spent they couldn't follow through and exploit. All our replacements and reserves were committed to fill the gaps."

"Now how the hell do you know that?" Stephie challenged from across the bunker. "You didn't hear any of that over the company, or even the battalion video net." Becky glared back at Stephie. Stephie said, "Are you fucking Ackerman now?"

"Eat shit, you stuck-up cunt," Becky shot back.

Stephie's fingers inched closer to the pistol grip of her SAW. Everyone in the bunker noticed. John's eyes darted between Stephie's face and her hand with his brow knit in reproach. Sergeant Burns was the squad leader. Stephie—now a corporal—was his lone fire team leader. It was their job to tamp dissension among their thoroughly dispirited troops.

First Lieutenant Ackerman appeared in the bunker's entrance. "Pack it up," he said, "We're pullin' back."

"We're bein' relieved?" Dawson asked.

"No. We're pullin' back," their platoon leader repeated.

"You mean we're abandoning this *line*?" Stephie almost shouted. She rose to look through the blackened firing slit down the hill toward the river. There were over two hundred destroyed hulks of Chinese assault vehicles frozen in every imaginable repose of death. And there were thousands upon thousands of contorted and bloating bodies. When the wind shifted and blew up the hill, everyone tied kerchiefs scented with shaving lotion to their faces. "It's totally quiet! There's no pressure at all! *Why the hell are we giving ground*!"

"Stephie . . ." John began in a voice that sounded designed to soothe the demented.

"*No!*" she snapped. "This isn't right! We fought our asses off for this goddamn line! We can still hold it! They've thrown everything they've got at us and we . . . !"

"The line broke," Ackerman interrupted with a hoarse shout, "up at Clark's Hill Lake. We're bein' flanked. We got trucks meeting us on the road down in fifteen minutes. Get your gear and be there waiting in ten." He turned and left.

Everyone rose to stuff their packs with gear. "Those National Guard bastards in the 40th!" Stephie groused, wincing with pain at almost every movement of her neck. "Pro'bly cut 'n ran when it got too tough."

"They took a hell of a beating," John commented in a low voice. "And if they did run, they're all dead now."

"You can stay here if you want, Roberts," Becky suggested sarcastically.

Stephie turned and shouted, "Yeah! I *do* wanta stay here!" John restrained her as she screamed as loud as she could. "*We've gotta stop them somewhere! Why not here?*" Her voice was painfully loud inside the bunker.

"Because they're flanking us," John reasoned. "They'll surround us, pound us, then kill us."

Suddenly, Stephie didn't care anymore. She pulled herself free of John's grip and haphazardly crammed gear in her pack, oblivious to the pains from her wounds. Oblivious to everyone and everything. Her mind a blank. John knelt beside her. She looked up at him, and she whispered to him, "No more painkillers. I don't want any more." He looked piercingly at her, then nodded in agreement. She was too close to the edge, and the drugs made it worse.

As they exited the bunker, all touched the names inscribed

in concrete, even Dawson and Crane whose names weren't included. Stephie lingered—her fingertips brushing across the names of the men and women who had died in bunker 9G—but she felt nothing for them. *No more painkillers,* she told herself again.

The main trench was little more than a collection of interconnecting, rainwater-filled craters. The only hints of where the original earthworks had been were burst sandbags, broken wood bracing, and dozens of strands of field telephone wire that had been run, cut by shelling, and run again and again.

The entire crest of the ridge was now a moonscape. The once forested hill provided no shade. The shattered trunks of pine trees were stripped bare of bark. Midway up their trunks, fingers of wood spiked skyward, attesting to the fury of heavy artillery.

The six soldiers marched single file down the hill toward the rear through the slit trench. Their heavy loads made climbing over collapsed walls and crawling under fallen trees far more difficult than it had been a week before. No one said a word. All was quiet. Stephie began to wonder whether they were all alone. Maybe everyone else had deserted.

The ladder lay in pieces, but it wasn't needed. A large shell crater presented a gentle, smooth slope. The sickly-sweet stench of death hung thick in the air. They covered their faces with their scented kerchiefs and wound their way carefully down the well-trod path through the mines. Flies buzzed thickly around the blackened and bloated bodies of the Chinese soldiers who had fallen in the minefield, some just a few feet from the safe pathway. No one had risked policing them up.

Suddenly, they all dropped to the dirt on hearing shells rattle through the air overhead. But these were "friendly," and even more important they were on target. American artillery began to pummel the far side of the Savannah River to cover their withdrawal. They rose, didn't bother to dust themselves off, and continued on toward the road. Every so often low-flying Cruise missiles shrieked overhead causing everyone to duck. But these were American missiles sent against Chinese artillery batteries, Stephie guessed, who were forced to displace but might otherwise have shelled their retreat.

At the road they finally saw other soldiers. Their battalion formed into companies to board waiting trucks. Fewer than two hundred of the six hundred with which they had begun the fight stood in the loose ranks for a final head count. Some companies, which with attached weapons crews had numbered 180 men and women, now had only a dozen or so bedraggled, bandaged survivors. Almost everyone, Stephie noted, was wounded in some way. Some officers and senior NCOs issued orders from stretchers.

Ackerman was the last surviving officer in their company of fifty slumping soldiers. Their platoon was down from thirty-one to eighteen, and that was after being reinforced with replacements. Twice. Third Squad had been wiped out to a man. No one said a word, but everyone's head was on a swivel. People in the surrounding platoons stared straight into each other's blank eyes. Stephie didn't know what everyone else was thinking, but she had only one thought. *How the hell did I survive?*

John Burns helped Stephie climb aboard the back of the truck, but she halted halfway up. A single white cross had been planted on the opposite side of the road. Beyond it lay a long mound of freshly turned earth. Everyone in First Squad noticed. Stephie had no trouble imagining that she now lay in the mass grave in which her comrades were buried. So little seemed to separate the living from the dead.

She sat in the mostly empty truck amid her taciturn and morose comrades. Their heads drooped and their eyes were downcast. They had won their battles and yet they were retreating. The canvas-covered truck began to roll.

"We're gonna win this war!" Stephie said to her surprised squadmates. What began as a blurted bolt out of the blue rose in energy and conviction until it became an impassioned plea. "I can *feel* it. They hit us with *everything* they've got, and we didn't break. We *held*! They hurt us bad, but we hurt them worse! There's no way *any* army can keep taking casualties like the Chinese took here! *No* way!" They all looked at her now. "We *won* this battle! And we're gonna win the *next*! And the *next*! And the *next*! We're gonna *win* this war! I can feel it in my bones! This is *our* country, and *no*body takes it from us! *Nobody!*"

"Fuckin' A!" Animal replied, roused as if by an inspiring speech before a big game. He smiled, looked around, and pulled an oily cloth from his pocket and began to clean his filthy machine gun.

"We're gonna kick their fuckin' asses!" Dawson chimed in, slapping his forward rifle grip with a *pop*.

Melinda Crane looked back and forth from face to face, a faint spark returning to her dark eyes.

Becky furtively—sheepishly—glanced up at Stephie.

John eyed Stephie with what looked to be surprise.

The South Carolina woods streaked by as the truck rumbled in retreat ever northward, toward Washington, DC. Stephie vowed secretly to make herself believe the inspiring prediction she had just made, but found herself consumed by doubt.

BESSEMER, ALABAMA
October 14 // 2100 Local Time

A stiff wind carried the approaching cold front. The frigid air curled under Captain Jim Hart's collar, forcing him to take his helmet off and don wool headgear that left only his face exposed. When he reseated his helmet on his head, he returned to his watch of the modest house. He'd had it under surveillance off and on for a week.

There were plenty of abandoned houses, but signs of life in them would instantly be noticeable to Chinese military police. He couldn't risk holing up in an abandoned house.

The family below lived far off the beaten path down a private drive road so overgrown with foliage as to be nearly invisible. The driveway's gate at the seldom used county road was kept chained, and there was no mailbox or other sign that a residence was nestled in the hills a few hundred yards distant.

The family that lived in the out-of-the-way place kept their heads low. Hart had observed at various times the father, mother, and teenage boy and girl shuttle stocks of food and supplies from the storm shelter to the roomy, two-story house.

They had a greenhouse and a generator, which they had used when the power was off, like now. Hart had felled the high-tension power lines two nights ago.

He had chosen this house for a simple reason: he hadn't seen a Chinese soldier within miles. He shivered from the chill, which was gripping the hills every morning. He was hungry, tired, and filthy, but more than anything else, Hart was extremely lonely. In the last three weeks, Hart had either hidden from the only people he had seen, or he had sent them to their graves.

He took one last check of the road, then struggled to his one good foot. Using a branch for a crutch, he hobbled down the hill for the front door with his broken or severely sprained left ankle. He had, days before, lain in wait along a road with monitors in place, mines laid, and field of fire planned. But no convoy had rumbled past in two days.

Finally, he had given up. On his way back to his nearest cache of supplies he had stumbled upon a line of vehicles. He had hastily set up and fired at the target of opportunity—a convoy in the darkness—without the preparation that his training dictated. He was motivated to act, he realized, out of frustration, and it had been a huge mistake.

Hart had thought the vehicles were all soft trucks, but two tanks had begun firing back at point-blank range. They had forced him to make a life-or-death decision. He had clung to the shuddering earth while explosions erupted all around. Heavy machine guns had raked the rocks and trees surely as covering fire for maneuvering infantry. If he had stayed there, he would've died, so he had risen and run blindly leaving much of his equipment behind. He had survived, but in the darkness he had hurt his ankle in the rocks.

Over the next twenty-four hours, he had narrowly escaped Chinese patrols several times. Once, in broad daylight, they had passed within ten feet of the pile of leaves under which he had lain totally still. Scent deadeners had kept their dogs from pinpointing him, although his tracks kept the Chinese searching for him in the vicinity. All the while, his aching ankle had swollen and swollen. Finally, he had given up on trying to reach his cache, which was thirteen miles away.

Hart knocked on the front door of the ramshackle house. Through the grimy glass panes and thin curtains he saw that the foyer was dark. He gave the door another, louder rap. The curtain moved, and he heard feet thumping away. After a few moments Hart could see a much larger form approaching—the father—carrying a long, black shotgun in both hands.

"What the hell do you want?" the man asked through the door.

"I need help," Hart said simply.

There was a long pause before the locks began to rattle. The muzzle of the double-barreled gun was the first thing he saw.

The man behind the shotgun surveyed Hart's camouflage battle dress. "*Jee*-zus!" he exclaimed before jerking Hart inside and closing the door behind him. "You're a *soldier*?"

"Captain James R. Hart, United States Army."

"Who is it?" came his wife's nervous voice from a dark doorway.

"Stay put!" the man ordered. He turned to Hart and asked with a thick Southern accent, "You an escaped POW or some-thin'?"

"No. I'm in the Special Forces. The Green Berets."

"My-y-y lord! You're one o' them that's been blowin' everything up. The Chinese gotta be lookin' for you all over! You cain't stay here!"

The woman of the house must have heard everything. She appeared from out of the darkness with their two kids just behind. "Jo-o-*oe*!" she said. "He's *hurt*!"

"Well, he cain't stay here! It's too dangerous!"

But she was already issuing orders to her kids, who ran off for medical supplies. "You come with me," she said, putting her shoulder under his arm in lieu of his crude crutch. Hart hopped into the kitchen and sat at the breakfast room table. He had walked for miles through the hills on the busted ankle, but when she began to unlace his combat boot the pain brought tears to his eyes.

The two children—the boy in his early teens and the girl a little older—were both clean. Hart was filthy, unshaven, and reeked. Both kids winced when they saw his purple, swollen ankle, but the woman gingerly laid his foot in her lap. She cleaned it with rubbing alcohol and a towel. The towel ended up black with accumulated grit. Hart was embarrassed by the poor state of his hygiene.

"You cain't stay here," repeated the agitated, forty-something father as he poured himself three inches of bourbon in a water glass. He downed the drink and exhaled noisily. "You cain't put that kinda risk on me and my fam'ly."

The mother didn't look up or voice a word of objection, but her teenage son did. "We cain't just put him outa the *house*!"

"*Jimmy,*" the woman chastised, but the boy was undaunted.

"No, ma'am!" he said to her, shaking his head. He turned to his father. "No, sir." To Hart's surprise, the father backed down. He poured himself another drink and took it and the shotgun into the darkened living room.

"The Chinese got the power goin' again, but it's been knocked out twice," the mother said as she bent Hart's ankle to and fro. "Was that your doin'?" He nodded once, and then gasped as she probed his swollen foot with her fingertips. "We need our electricity to last the winter. Cain't raise these children like animals."

"Why are you still here?" Hart asked.

"We *live* here!" the father shouted from the next room. "It's our home!"

Hart searched the tight-lipped woman for her version, but he got nothing more from her expression than general disdain for her husband, Hart sensed, not Hart. He looked at the two kids.

"Dad got in trouble with . . ." the boy began.

"Jimmy!" his sister snapped.

In the silence that followed, the father returned still carrying his shotgun. "I ain't got nothin' against the Chinese," he said. The two kids and their mother averted their gaze from Hart.

Hart lay in the bathtub immersed in water that had been hot but now was cool. He had dozed off several times, but his head had struck the tiled wall, waking him. He kept his ankle elevated as Mrs. Lipscomb had instructed.

He finally forced himself to rise. The pain was excruciating. Several times, he almost slipped and fell as he hopped on one foot. It took twenty minutes to dry himself and get dressed.

The hallway outside the bathroom was dark. Hart could hear the man arguing with his wife, and he hobbled toward the sound, but he came first to the boy's open bedroom door.

"Hi," the kid said from a desk where he drew pictures on a notepad.

"What're you up to?" Hart asked.

"Working on my Chinese," the boy replied.

Hart took a hop closer. Shiny poster paper contained blanks being filled in pencil with inexpert Chinese characters. The boy had made numerous erasures. "That's homework?" Hart asked.

"Kinda," the now defensive boy replied. "Soldiers handed these out at school. We're s'posed to turn them in tomorrow."

"It's okay," Hart reassured him as he put his green beret on his head, which had grown hair for the first time in years. "You gotta know your enemy and be smarter than him."

The boy brightened. "Yeah!" He now wore a broad smile.

Hart moved on toward the raging argument in the family room, but along the way was another doorway from which peered the boy's sister. The family seemed almost as lonely as Hart had been. She disappeared then returned with aluminum crutches. "You can have these," she said. "I hurt my knee last year in PE."

The crutches were far too short, but were adjustable and would be a great improvement over the tree limb. "I'm not gonna do 'em," the girl said with a sneer.

"Do what?" Hart asked.

"My characters. My teacher says I'm gonna get an F, but I don't care. There's no chance I'll even go to any college anyway." Hart started to object—to insist that she could make it—till he realized that he was being naive. The Chinese would provide nothing more than technical schools for all but the very best and brightest.

"Don't quit studying," Hart said finally, succumbing to distant parental instincts.

"Why not?"

"Because we're going to win this war," Hart replied.

"Don't be fillin' the girl's head with nonsense," her father called down the hallway. "You can sleep in the storm cellar, but just for one night. You gotta leave tomorrow."

Hart hobbled past the man's wife for the rear door. "We'll see," she whispered to Hart.

COLUMBIA, SOUTH CAROLINA
October 16 // 0920 Local Time

The sun was hot despite the early hour. Its rays beat down onto the dusty roadside. One last gasp of heat from the blistering summer. *Boot camp,* Stephie thought. *Fort Benning. God that had been hot.* She had graduated from advanced infantry training only two months earlier. *Two months ago!* And high school. *High school! Five months ago I was in high school!* She railed at the lunacy of it all.

Stephie's squad worked along a roadside to build a blocking position that would be manned by someone else. But the quiet combat veterans didn't complain about their transformation into manual laborers. The distant rumble that arrived periodically on the shifting winds reminded all how good this job was.

You gotta pace yourself, she told herself as she stepped onto the blade of her short folding shovel. She didn't mean pace yourself at the hard digging, but in the fighting—in the dying—that the war periodically demanded. The blade slipped into the loose fill that a backhoe had gouged from the road's shoulder. The rivulets of sweat on Stephie's neck changed course as she dumped the shovel's load, filling a sandbag. Their squad's medic—Melinda Crane—closed the bag with a plastic tie. Both were stripped down to their olive drab T-shirts despite the furtive stares of their male squadmates. It was hot, and they were all tired. And if anyone did anything more than look, the two women also had rifles.

A continuous line of pain ran from one end of Stephie's

spine to the other, but its character changed along the way. Stabs between her shoulder blades brought sudden winces and loud hisses. They contrasted sharply, however, with the dull ache in her lower back, whose tendrils rose like a vine to wrap around her chest. Stephie straightened her back, arched her shoulders, and rolled her neck. But no matter which way Stephie stretched, she couldn't loosen the vise that seemed to grip her lungs and rob her of breath.

An ordinary civilian car approached from the southwest, the direction of the front lines. The road was to be mined later that day, but for now it remained open like a causeway, Stephie thought, down which people escaped from an approaching storm.

Stephie's squadmates took the opportunity to stop and stare at the sight. They had seen no traffic since just before daylight when the trucks had left them there. The car wound its way purposefully toward the north.

"Refugees," Melinda said. Still, everyone watched with what Stephie thought was a vague sense of foreboding. They didn't fear the car's occupants, but the news that they might bear. *They've broken through!* Stephie imagined. *They're right behind us!* The clarity of the panicked words in Stephie's head startled her.

Just as in Stephie's imagination, the car slowed to a stop and cracked the window. The lone occupant—a woman in large sunglasses—leaned onto the passenger seat. "Can anyone tell me . . . ?" she began, but was interrupted by Stephie.

"Mom?" Stephie asked with an incredulous, high-pitched tone.

"Oh! *There* you are! Finally," Rachel Roberts said with a discordant note of irritation. She parked the car and emerged with an old pink and green school backpack that bulged with hidden contents. Stephie met her at the car door.

"You should wear a bra," her mother whispered.

"What are you *doing* here?" Stephie belted out before lowering her voice and saying, "It's illegal for you to be here."

Rachel snorted. "Another of that jerk's stupid laws, and one that doesn't seem to apply to him, I'll have you note."

"They're not the president's laws," Stephie icily replied. "They're passed by Congress."

Her mother rolled her eyes as if Stephie didn't understand, then kissed her cheek and squeezed her arms. "You're filthy!" she proclaimed on inspecting her daughter closely. With flicks of her tongue on her fingers as if to turn the pages of a book, she wiped smears of dirt from Stephie's face. She then tried to arrange hair that had been pressed flat under the webbing of Stephie's helmet. Stephie recoiled with each insult.

"Mother! *Stop* it! People are *watching*! Stop!" Finally, she pulled away with a, *"Grrr!"*

"When I visited you in boot camp," her mother said disapprovingly, "it seemed like the army was obsessed with hygiene. It looks like you haven't had a shower since."

"Why are you here?" Stephie asked again.

This time, the question seemed to throw Rachel. She started to say something but stopped several times before words escaped her. "Here," she finally said, handing over the school backpack. "I brought you some things. Extra toothbrush. Some nightclothes. A couple of trashy paperbacks."

Stephie stared in horror at the bright girlish colors on the pack that she had discarded as too juvenile even for junior high. She looked over her shoulder at the others. The snickers and whispered jibes were already spreading. Across the road behind her mother, she saw John and his team carefully descending the hill stringing wire for explosives meant to topple an avalanche of rocks across the road.

"I don't want that stuff!" Stephie insisted through gritting teeth.

Her mother frowned. "Fine," she said, tossing the pack through the window into the passengers seat in a fit of pique.

"Where did you come from?" Stephie asked, turning to the again empty road to the south.

"I was given bad directions by some halfwit," Rachel griped. A shiver rippled up her spine to her shoulders. "It was awful down there," she said, turning toward the distant sound of thunder drifting gently through the hills. "People were running everywhere. Nobody knew what was going on. And the poor wounded boys," she said, shaking her head. "You're much better off up here working on road construction, let me tell you." Stephie's mouth opened wide to object, but her mother said, "I know it's hard work, Stephie, but really it's better than fighting."

"Mom," Stephie said, trying to keep a lid on her temper, "you don't understand. We're a *combat* unit! I'm in the *infantry*!"

"Of course you are," Rachel responded, smiling and patting Stephie's cheek. Stephie slung her head away from the patronizing, offensive touch. "But you don't have quite the same kind of job as Conner Reilly," she said.

"He's armored cavalry," Stephie blurted out. "I'm infantry. *They* find the enemy. *We* fight them."

"He's dead," Rachel informed her.

The news seemed to still the breeze and bring to a close a chapter of Stephie's life. Induction into the army and boot camp had not spelled the end of her teenage years. Even after the shock of combat, she had felt much the same age as before. Now, however, although still eighteen, she was no longer young.

"How?" Stephie asked, before swallowing to wet her throat. "How did he die?"

"Fighting," Rachel replied. "Somewhere in California."

"But *how* did he die?" Stephie insisted on knowing. "Was he shot? Killed in a barrage? By a mine? Friendly fire? Enemy fire? How?"

"He was just killed, Stephie," her mother said gently. "I don't know how." After a few moments, Rachel said, "It's all right to cry, Stephie. It's okay. Go ahead."

Stephie focused. "I'm not crying," she said simply. After all these years her mother still didn't know her. Stephie felt not even the faintest tremor of tears.

Her reaction seemed to distress her mother, and like all ambiguous emotions Rachel Roberts experienced, it slowly turned to annoyance. "So," she said, "you see, I understand that this is, in name, a combat organization that you're with. But Conner was with the regular army, not one of these new groups that they've thrown together at the last second." She shook her head. "Those poor boys. It's terrible for them up there, Stephie. I've seen it with my own eyes. Consider your-self lucky that you've got the job that you've got," Rachel said. She inspected with an approving cast of her eye the half-built machine gun nests and the rocks piled on the shoulder of the road to be used as a barricade to prevent traffic from straying into the mines. "At least you'll never have to know the horrors of combat like poor Conner did, God rest his soul."

Stephie considered the many alternative replies, some of which screamed out to her. *"Have you ever heard of the Battle of Atlanta, Mother? Or the Savannah River?"* But in the end, she said only, "I guess you're right."

John Burns crossed the street from behind Rachel Roberts wiping his face and then his hands with a small towel and tucking his helmet under his arm. When he stepped up to their side—standing in the no-man's-land in between—Rachel's face assumed its vivacious public front. She grinned broadly at the tall, clean-shaven and tanned boy.

"Mrs. Roberts?" John said, extending his hand. "John Burns."

"Oh, yes!" she replied. "Of course!" As they shook hands, Stephie scrutinized her mother. She acted as if she knew about John. But Stephie had never once mentioned John to her. "I hope you're taking good care of my daughter."

John's gaze shot to Stephie, who bristled and replied to her mother's remark. "I can take care of myself."

A tense standoff ensued. During the quiet, the sound of fighting seemed noticeably louder. All eyes, however, turned to the sound of a convoy of trucks arriving from the north. Stephie said, "Looks like our ride's come back early."

"Change of plans," John said, turning to their squad. "Gather your gear!" he barked.

"What about this roadblock?" Stephie objected.

"Whoever's gonna man it can finish it up," John replied, replacing his helmet on his head.

"What's the hurry?" Stephie asked.

John shrugged. "The Chinese are coming," he guessed.

"Then by all means," Rachel commented, "get going. Stephie, collect your things."

Stephie donned her camo blouse, buttoned it up, and then zipped closed the camouflaged body armor. Over that she draped her webbing from which hung magazines, hand grenades, and first aid kit. Her mother tried to help by adjusting the lie of the shoulder straps, which were already in the right place. Stephie broke free by stooping to snatch her assault rifle from the knee-high sandbag wall against which it leaned.

When Stephie turned, her mother looked pale. Men climbed aboard the old diesel trucks as Rachel Roberts checked out Stephie's fighting load. The mother eyed in alarm the daughter's familiarity with the weapon, which Stephie checked to ensure was safed. Despite the scrutiny, Stephie's mother missed entirely the twin chevrons—the corporal's insignia—that adorned Stephie's collar.

"Mount up!" Stephie ordered the three milling soldiers of her fire team.

Rachel Roberts jumped slightly at the loud command.

"You'd better get going, Mom," Stephie said.

Her mother's lower lip quivered, and she threw her arms around Stephie. All of Stephie's irritation melted as she hugged her mother for perhaps the last time.

PHILADELPHIA NAVAL SHIPYARD
October 17 // 2145 Local Time

President Baker wore a hard hat as he stood on the deck of the enormous arsenal ship. Somewhere up above it was nighttime. But down in the dry dock, stadium lights lit the expansive flat deck of the vessel in artificial day. With no satellite overflights to fear, thousands upon thousands of men and women worked under the open night sky along the ship's four-football-field length. Sparks flew from dozens of welding torches working at open, armored hatches that would, in a few months, house long-range missiles currently undergoing final tests in New Mexico. All of it—the two massive ships with their complex systems and brand-new missiles—would take to sea in record time: just two and one-half years after being given the "Go."

At least, Baker prayed that they would.

The admiral in charge of the yard escorted Bill below
decks. The president's entourage of aides and communications technicians followed, all surrounded by watchful Secret
Service agents. They descended several flights down a metal
ladder and emerged onto a service catwalk. The noise and
sights were stunning. Tens of thousands of men welded,
drilled, riveted, and wired in a beehive of hectic activity. Arrayed eighty across and hundreds deep were flat-sided metal
boxes: launch tubes for the arsenal ship's arsenal. Beneath
them men tested robotic conveyers. They moved independently of each other in fits and starts along the ceiling. Their
curved fittings would grasp missiles then raise them into upright positions for automatic reloading into the launch boxes
once every six minutes.

Bill shook hands with passing workers, who paused only
briefly before hurrying off on their appointed task. "We're of
course running round-the-clock shifts!" the civilian contractor
shouted over the commotion. "The reactor core should be
loaded next month, and we'll start generating at higher and
higher power levels, with propulsion last!"

"Are we ahead of schedule?" Bill asked.

The civilian shrugged. "We can't possibly know, sir, until
we test and debug her systems! We've made a lot of progress
since your visit last month, but this is a half-million-ton ship
with eight thousand missile launchers! The systems are massively complex and totally innovative! We have over five million automated subsystems, all networked together! All the
hardware and software will be in place by January, but
whether it works together . . . ?" he ended, shrugging.

Bill stopped on the catwalk and turned to the contractor
and the fidgeting admiral. "What he's trying to say, sir . . . !"
said commander of the shipyard, playing diplomat.

But Bill held up his hand like a traffic cop. "Everything,"
he yelled to the contractor, "*everything* depends on *this* ship
and its sister ship across the harbor! They will be launched
in January, go into all-out combat on their shakedown cruise,
and run the Chinese fleet out of the western Atlantic!"

The admiral looked back and forth between Baker and the

contractor. Finally, the civilian nodded. "All right, Mr. President! All right!"

The White House military aide tapped Baker's shoulder and leaned close to Bill's ear. "We've got the final results of the withdrawal from the Savannah River, sir." Bill immediately terminated his tour. They led him to a quiet conference room. Wires dangled from bare walls where high-definition screens would hang. Cables awaited installation of computer workstations. Fast-food trash and cigarette butts lay crumped in the corner. Bill and the military aide—a navy lieutenant commander—sat on metal chairs at a table made from two sawhorses and a piece of plywood. Large, crumpled electrical diagrams lay atop the table. Coffee mugs and scraps of metal plate kept them from curling. The naval officer read the report from the screen on his palmtop.

" 'The 40th Infantry Division, which was dug in around Clark's Hill Lake along the Georgia-South Carolina border, has been rendered combat ineffective due to near eighty-eight percent losses in the week of fighting at the Savannah River. In their last battle, they were hit by seven Chinese armored and mechanized infantry divisions.' "

There was a long silence before Bill asked, "How about the rest of the line?"

The commander was struggling with his report. "Uhm, the 37th Infantry Division, sir, which is also Army National Guard, disengaged cleanly along its center and left. But the better part of a brigade was fixed by heavy contact on the right—on the flank where the 40th was overrun—and was enveloped. They're at—uh, with replacements—they're back up to eighty percent. All but their two, right-most battalions, which couldn't disengage, passed the Santee and Saluda River line at Columbia, South Carolina."

Bill nodded, and waited.

"The 31st Armored Brigade withdrew up I-95 in good order to the junction with I-26. They held that junction open until the evacuation of Charleston was complete, then withdrew into position to block I-95 North along the Santee." Bill nodded again. It was all according to plan. The commander returned to reading the report on his palmtop word for word.

" 'The 41st Infantry Division disengaged from its positions along the Savannah River in good order and withdrew to Sumter, South Carolina, to regroup. Casualties during the disengagement were light.' " Bill's military aide looked up. "I'm sorry, sir, but that's all it says. 'Casualties were light.' "

Bill nodded. He was relieved, but not yet totally at ease. He would contain his powerful urge to know how Stephie had fared until he got back to Washington and talked to Cotler. *Or maybe I'll call from the plane, or from the car on the way to the plane,* he thought.

The lieutenant commander continued reading. Bill wished he hadn't. " 'From heavy casualties taken during intense combat earlier in the week, the 41st is now rated at only forty-five percent combat effectiveness. Approximately thirty percent of its surviving personnel suffer from wounds or illness that render them unfit for duty and may require medical rehabilitation.' "

Bill headed for the car. " 'Grazing flesh wound on the nape of the neck,' " General Cotler briefed him over the phone. " 'Mild concussion from the nearby explosion of Chinese satchel charge.' Word is, Mr. President, that your daughter saved the lives of her buddies at great risk to her own," Cotler said, stopping himself short. He aborted his praise and returned to his dry litany of near-death experiences by Bill's only child. " 'Major contusions and possible hairline fractures of the rib cage along her right upper torso.' No indication of how she sustained that injury, Mr. President. She's pretty banged up, sir." He spoke slowly. "We *could* have her declared unfit for duty and medevac her."

The president had not responded. It had taken every ounce of his strength to remain quiet.

6

Han Zhemin's limousine finally ended its bumpy ride in a billowing cloud of dust. His coughing aide waited outside until the dust subsided, then opened the administrator's door. The smell of death filled the cool forest air. Under the mumbled pretense that he was allergic to dust, Han extracted a handkerchief and held it to his nose.

Wu wore combat gear like all the rest of the soldiers, but unlike the others Wu was clean. He saluted and then shook his father's hand. "Let's get into my car where we can talk," Han suggested. Wu replied that he first wanted to show Han something. Frowning, Han followed his son toward the ridge line.

Han had summoned Wu for a talk, but Wu had asked that his father come meet him at the still fresh field of battle. The eerie quiet of the blasted and charred landscape was still new to Wu, but Han had seen it all before. The smell that he tried to mask with his handkerchief had been the same in Asia and the Middle East.

Wu turned to warn his father to stay inside the flag-topped

markers. Han rolled his eyes at his overly solicitous son. Han had been visiting battlefields since before the boy had reached puberty. He knew better than to stray into a minefield. Wu descended into the narrow trench that led up the hill, but Han stood atop the crater and glared at his son. "It's just right up here," the eager boy insisted. With a sigh Han climbed down. His highly polished, Italian leather shoes didn't provide him quite the traction of Wu's combat boots, so the going was slow for Han.

They proceeded up the hill through the nearly collapsed trench. Han repeatedly brushed dirt from his dark, immaculate suit. Near the top of the ridge, he had broken a sweat. "Wu, I came here to . . ."

"We're really close!" Wu insisted.

He was a child playing soldier, Han thought. Despite the enormity of their army's casualties in futilely attacking this American position, Wu still found the place fascinating. At the top of the ridge, they entered the main trench, which was dotted with huge, water-filled craters. Wu scampered over the shattered fortifications pointing at bits and pieces of abandoned American equipment. The tight turns in the zigzagging line were filled with hundreds of spent shell casings, some American, Wu stopped to show Han; others Chinese.

"Wu . . ." Han began, intending to inform him that he wasn't interested.

"It's right here," Wu interrupted, heading for the entrance of a bunker half buried in collapsed and split sandbags. "9G" was stenciled above the dark opening. Wu led his father into the low-ceilinged concrete enclosure. Wu's virgin nose probably missed the smell entirely, but Han's more refined palate detected the odor immediately. Someone had been burned in that bunker. It smelled of human flesh. In confirmation, Han looked down at his shoes, which crunched through black ash on the floor.

Wu, however, directed Han's attention higher. The young lieutenant lit the wall with his flashlight. A series of names—written in English—were crudely inscribed in the concrete. Wu waited until Han saw "Stephanie Roberts." Wu's excited, beaming face glowed in the reflected light.

Han nodded, looked at Wu, then led his son into the bunker's main chamber. In addition to the residue from the conflagration that had burned floor, ceiling, and walls, there were thousands of shell casings large and small. Wu inspected the spent cartridges from rifles and grenade launchers. Han wandered among pools of caked blood, whose dark color was lost against the charred concrete to all but the discerning eye.

"Look at this," Wu said, holding a small, plastic ring—like a girl's toy—out to Han. Its cheap plastic band and fake stone seemed incongruous amid the carnage of the charnel house. Han abruptly turned and departed the bunker for the fresh air outside. Wu inspected the ring closely, then slipped it into his pocket.

Outside, Wu joined his father, whose mood had soured. Wu said, "I read an intell report tracking the whereabouts of President Baker's daughter. They're monitoring American news media to determine whether she survived the battle here." His father said nothing. "I thought you'd want to know." Han looked impatiently at his son. "So," Wu ventured tentatively, "President Baker's daughter is really in the thick of it."

"No," Han replied coldly.

Wu's brow furrowed. "What do you mean 'no'?"

"I mean no, you can't go into combat."

Wu was exasperated. "But . . . !" He held up his hands as if the blasted trench line was somehow an argument in his favor. Han grabbed Wu's arm roughly and dragged him up the side of a crater to the forward lip of the trench. Wu pulled himself free and looked down the slope toward the river. There was nothing but blackness and death beneath them. Not a single sprig of life sprouted from the devastated hillside or riverbank. Here and there, small teams of engineers with mine detectors cleared lanes through the American killing field. They would eventually reach and bury the thousands of stinking, bloated corpses, but they concentrated first on recovering the vehicles. Some of them could be repaired.

Han scrutinized Wu, to whom he spoke in quiet, urgent tones. "You predicted this in the videoconference with Beijing last month! Your talk about our army's rates of loss have the old men back in Beijing asking me for statistics every *day*!

Well, do you want to hear some figures? Along this line we killed, wounded, or captured somewhere between twenty-five and thirty-five thousand American soldiers. But *we* lost one hundred and forty-five thousand *dead* and three times that number wounded! Seven hundred thousand casualties! And this was just a *temporary* line! The next one will be built stronger. And the one after that even stronger!"

"That's why I should go into combat," Wu replied defiantly. "Our nation needs its best and brightest in the lead."

"And that, of course, means you!" Han snapped, barely managing to contain his anger. "You're a . . . !" Han began, but he bit off the words and forced his mouth closed. He turned to take in the views of Hell beneath them. "What did they teach you in military school, Wu?" The father's and son's eyes now both roamed the battlefield. "Have you been initiated into the cult of death like the others? Is this the glorious '*victory*' to which you aspire?"

"You're being defeatist," Wu mumbled, casting a dangerous criminal charge at his father in a halfhearted tone.

The two glared at each other in open hostility until they were interrupted. Wu's civilian aide clawed his way on all fours over the mounds of freshly churned earth then brushed the dirt from his manicured hands. "Excuse me, Administrator Han—Lieutenant Han Wushi—but there is a delegation of American civilians from a nearby town that would like to speak to you." He nodded down the reverse slope toward the dirt road on which Han's motorcade was parked. Three Americans stood amid twice as many armed soldiers.

Han, still seething at his son's arrogant accusation, retraced their route down the hill without saying a word. Wu and Han's aide followed. Han shook hands with the three Americans, who stood amid the half-dozen muzzles. Han waved the soldiers away.

"I'm the mayor of Augusta," an elderly woman said. Han smiled and said he was pleased to make her acquaintance and that he looked forward to working with . . . "Your army is massacring my people," she interrupted. "Innocent civilians. They're being rounded up and sent to a concentration camp."

Han's mood changed abruptly from gracious to angry.

"Where?" was all he asked. They gave directions, but Han had them point out the place on his aide's map. The man nodded to Han when he had what he needed, and Han ordered his entourage to board their two armored scout cars, which sandwiched Han's limousine and communications van. Han's aide held the limo's door open, and Han got inside. Wu stood on the road wearing a defiant expression. "Get in," Han ordered his son.

After an hour's ride in total silence, Han and Wu passed through a barbed-wire enclosure. To both sides of the asphalt road, American POWs sat or lay in open pens. Many, if not most, were grievously wounded. Pitiful soldiers held their arms out and shouted pleas for food, water, medicine. Wu seemed struck by their sight. In his short life, he had seen war only in censored newsreels.

The camp commandant greeted Han at the steps of his air-conditioned trailer. Wu saluted the colonel, who didn't bother to return the martial salutation but instead shook the young lieutenant's hand. He had obviously been forewarned of their arrival and knew exactly who Wu was. He ushered Han and Wu inside and seated them on a comfortable sofa. Soldiers served them hot tea, sweets, and salted meats. Han ate mainly to rid his mouth of the taste of death from the Savannah River. Wu picked at the food and glanced repeatedly at his watch.

"We've heard reports," Han said to the camp commandant, "of civilian disappearances from the town of Augusta, Georgia."

The colonel seemed surprised. "That's in my district, but I've heard nothing about any disappearances. I can't imagine, really, that anyone would know because our census hasn't even begun. It's probably just people who've ignored our orders and left their homes in search of a way across the lines."

Han smiled and nodded as if satisfied by the answer.

Wu looked back and forth between the two men. "Well, that's not what we just heard," he said in an insolent tone. "They had very specific reports of people who had been taken from their homes by our troops."

"Who is 'they'?" the colonel asked pleasantly, reaching for a pad and pen.

Wu's eyes narrowed and he kept his mouth shut.

Good, Han noted as he took a last sip of his tea and rose. "Thank you, Colonel. I'm sorry to have troubled you." They shook hands again. "It looks like you've got quite a few POWs to contend with."

"What a wonderful victory, wasn't it?" the commandant said. He turned to Wu. "Maybe one day you can return to your alma mater and teach a course on how we won the great Battle of the Savannah River!" The colonel laughed and raised his hand to shake Wu's.

Wu stared at the man, ignoring the proffered hand.

Han took it all in and then thanked the colonel again. They left the cool trailer for the increasingly hot morning sun. Han could detect the faint smell of death in the air, and he checked to ensure that Wu smelled it too. He did, the boy's glance told his father. Several hundred yards away, a gathering of American soldiers was pleading for something. Stoic camp guards on the opposite side of thin wire made no reply but held their weapons up and at the ready.

Han and Wu got into Han's limousine and followed the pointed directions of a guard who trotted ahead of the lead vehicle. His hand signals directed them to go to the next intersection and turn right. Han picked up the phone and ordered the motorcade commander to turn left, instead. The four-vehicle procession thus began wandering seemingly randomly among the POW enclosures and makeshift barracks, but Han directed each turn. Wu split his time between looking out the windows and watching his father. American POWs gently slid a body wrapped in bloody bandages under the wire. Chinese guards wearing paper masks tossed the corpse into the back of a truck.

A short while later, Han said, "Stop the car," on an empty stretch of road. American POWs surrounded by soldiers wearing cotton masks dug with shovels in an empty field. Han got out and beckoned the sullen Wu to follow. A dozen trucks were parked bumper to bumper along the side of the field.

Their drivers tossed cigarettes onto the ground and wandered off, fleeing the civilians in expensive suits.

Wu winced and covered his mouth and nose. Han's aide—who had been with Han through a decade of similar visits—turned up the corners of his lips in amusement. Wu noticed and forced his hand to his side, and he followed his father to the back of an army truck. Its green fenders and canvas looked brown under the thick coat of dust. At the tailgate, Han threw back the canvas.

Wu recoiled in utter disgust. Flies boiled above stacks of half-clothed bodies, which lay pale and bullet-riddled. They were mostly men, but some were women. They were mostly adults, but some were children.

They were all, clearly, civilians.

Wu vomited, emptying his belly of the undigested sweets and tea. His father closed the canvas and escorted Wu down the road. A cordon of army guards—Han's ever-present escort—kept a respectful distance from their charge.

"Why?" was all the pale boy could ask while half doubled over his still uncertain stomach.

"*This* is war, Wu!" Han said. "You've been *lied* to! *Brainwashed!*"

Wu spat, stood erect, and forced a hard stare at the mass grave. "Why is our army doing this?" he asked.

"Because my job is to convince the Americans to return to work," Han explained. "They're not working because they're frightened. Your General Sheng is trying to keep it that way."

"But the whole *point* of the war is to harness American productivity!"

Han faced his son. "You're bright, Wu. Think. Can't you see for yourself what's happening?"

The boy stared back, but didn't reply at first. His eyes flitted aimlessly about Han's face as he pondered his father's question. "General Sheng," Wu finally replied, stating the obvious, "is trying to sabotage your efforts to coax Americans back to work so that you—and the civilian leadership—can be discredited as failures."

Han smiled and clapped his hand on his son's shoulder. "In stark contrast," Han added sarcastically, "to the army, which proceeds from victory to victory like the great Battle of the Savannah River."

Wu didn't nod or, by his expression, endorse in any way his father's conclusion, but he asked, "What are you going to do?"

With his hand still rested lightly on Wu's shoulder, Han smiled and answered with a question of his own. "What have you learned about the army's spy in Washington? This 'Olympic'?"

When Wu avoided his father's gaze, Han squeezed Wu's shoulder tightly in his grip. The boy winced and looked straight into Han's eyes. With his jaw set, Wu said, "Olympic is a woman. I heard Sheng refer to her as 'she.' "

"That's all?" Han asked. Wu nodded. After a moment's reflection, Han grinned and clapped his hand again on Wu's shoulder. "Good work, Wu! Good work. But now I need a name." Han then turned and headed back toward the car. Wu looked after him for a moment and then caught the gaze of the soldiers who provided their security. They were younger, even, than Wu. They had been watching—and listening to— the two men's conversation with more than just idle curiosity. For Wu and Han were, Wu realized, the gods who held the fates of those soldiers in their hands.

COLUMBIA, SOUTH CAROLINA
October 20 // 1740 Local Time

The crisp, cool, still afternoon was perhaps the finest Stephie had ever experienced. The sun felt warm on her skin but not hot. The air refreshed her lungs but didn't chill her limbs.

The only thing that spoiled the glorious weather was the artillery barrage just over the horizon. Stephie dozed to the sound. It was always there, though never discussed among the battleweary veterans. But on her closed eyelids danced visions of the hellish fire that went on and on, hour after hour. The barrages along the Savannah River had never lasted more than a few minutes. These went on all day long.

Although the front lines were over a dozen miles away, you had to raise your voice to talk over the fury of the Chinese bombardment. Not that anyone in First Squad had much to say. The senior commanders had left their battered, depleted unit alone. The soldiers had responded by sleeping ten, twelve, fourteen hours per day. The more time spent asleep, the less the time to contemplate what had just happened and what lay ahead. *But it's a helluva thing to do,* the thought nagged at Stephie, *to waste your last days on earth sleeping.*

"Hey," came the annoying voice of Becky Marsh. Stephie pretended to be asleep. "You got a V-mail from your dad."

Stephie sat up. "What? Lemme see." Becky handed Stephie her commo helmet and sat down beside her. "Do you mind?" Stephie asked.

Becky snorted. "I've already watched it," she said to Stephie with a sneer. Nevertheless, she rose and stomped away.

Stephie lowered two small screens and adjusted them until the stereoscopic image came into focus. The images were so close to her eyes that they created the impression of a large-screen TV. On them was a frozen picture of her father sitting at his desk in the Oval Office. If it weren't for the relatively poor image quality and the fact that he'd removed his suit jacket, the pose and setting reminded her of an address to the nation.

Stephie found the control stick and hit play.

"This is the president of the United States, and I'm sending this V-mail to my daughter, Stephanie Roberts. I would appreciate it if whoever receives this locates her and allows her to view it." He paused and took a sip of Diet Coke from a can. He was presumably giving Becky the time to pause the V-mail so that she could find Stephie, but Becky, of course, hadn't taken the opportunity. That pissed Stephie off.

"Stephie," her father began, "I've gotten your two V-mails, and I wanted to reply. I don't really know what to say. My life seems so," he struggled to find the word, "*uneventful* compared to yours." Stephie screwed up her face and hissed out a laugh. He was the *president*, for God's sake! She was just an ordinary soldier. "I think about you all the time. I have to admit," he said, growing wistful, "that sometimes during briefings about the progress of the war I sit there listening not as commander in chief, but as, well, your father." His eyes sank to his hands, which were spread—palms down—flat atop his desk. "Stephie, I have to say this," he resumed, still not looking at the camera. "And you've got to forgive me for saying it. There are lots of jobs in the army. Lots of important jobs other than in the combat arms."

"Shit!" Stephie cursed, both because her father was again urging her to quit, and because Becky Marsh had seen it all.

"I'm not saying that I would pull any strings. According to General Cotler I wouldn't have to." Stephie laughed at the mention of the chairman of the Joint Chiefs of Staff. He was the seniormost general in the U.S. army, but to her father he was a military aide to be asked questions about his daughter. "A lot of soldiers are being rotated to different jobs after serving for a time at the front."

Stephie growled in anger and extreme frustration. Several soldiers in her battalion had been "rotated" back, but nobody from her company. That fact was a point of pride for Charlie Company survivors, and the word "rotation" was scorned and reviled.

"General Cotler tells me," her father continued, still looking down at his splayed fingers, "that they *particularly* need combat veterans as instructors. That you could be doing a helluva lot more for your country—and save a lot of young lives— imparting what you've learned to new recruits." He sighed and finally looked up. "Just E-mail or V-mail your reply, and I'll—and General Cotler—will see to it."

Stephie was crushed, disappointed, and thoroughly dispirited. *How* could *he be doing this?* she wondered, wallowing in the pain.

"I love you, Stephie, with all my heart," her father said with a quivering voice. The V-mail went black, and Stephie realized that Becky Marsh had returned. Out of the corner of her eye, she saw Becky's boots. The woman had a keen sense of timing. Stephie removed the helmet from her head but kept her gaze on the far wall of her fighting hole. Becky took the helmet from her, then sat.

"So?" Becky asked, almost whispering. Stephie could barely here her over the distant rumbling. "What're you gonna do?"

"What do you *think* I'm gonna do?" Stephie snapped.

"I dunno," came the woman's thoughtful reply. Stephie looked up. Becky scrutinized her with brows knit. *What the hell does it matter to you?* Stephie thought. Becky said, as if that were news, "He really sounds like he loves you."

"I'm not going to *rotate back*!" Stephie angrily replied. "*Jesus!*"

Becky seemed to relax. "No," she said, smiling slightly and looking away to hide it. "I didn't think so." Stephie glanced sideways at Becky, wondering at the curious behavior. "But still," Becky said, "that was really sweet of him. You know. To ask and all."

Stephie started to say that anybody's dad would've done the same thing. That Becky's parents would've, too. She realized then, however, that she knew nothing about Becky's family. She instead considered inquiring about them, but she looked at Becky and thought better of it. The woman seemed too pleased by her glimpse at Stephie's warm family life. *Or is she just happy that I'm not going anywhere?* Stephie wondered.

Becky left. Stephie donned her helmet and curled up on the grass beside her hole.

Stephie was roused from deep sleep by the sound of an old Humvee, which approached on the empty street. She lifted her head from her pack. Third Platoon's well-spaced holes were dug in half-assed fashion around a tennis court turned emergency helipad that they supposedly guarded. The Humvee's big tires rode over the curb, crossed concrete walks, and stopped between the pebbled water fountain and a soft, rubberized bench. Two trucks followed the Humvee but parked on the street. Burns and Ackerman got out of the Humvee and headed for Stephie and Animal's positions, which they had dug on either side of the preschool swing sets. The two soldiers lay on the thick grass beside their fighting holes and rose only to their elbows. Ackerman barked hoarsely for the others to join them. Becky and Dawson came over from their holes by the grills. Stephie rolled her eyes and sighed. The two had screwed twice the night before.

That was all of First Squad. Melinda Crane was pulling duty with the battalion's aid station up at the defenses along the River.

Lieutenant Ackerman walked up wearing black captain's bars pinned on the collar of his camo blouse. Stephie did a double take when she saw John Burns's collar. On it was pinned the single black bar of a second lieutenant. The brakes of four trucks groaned loudly from the street behind them.

"Congratulations, Cap'n Ackerman," Animal said sarcastically from the ground where he lay. He turned to John. "Whose dick did you suck, Burns?" Ackerman's hand reflexively shot out to John's chest as John took a step toward Animal. "Oh!" Animal said. "Hold-him-back! Hold-him-back!" The huge lineman never rose from his back in protest of John's promotion. "What the hell gives makin' a goddamned buck sergeant a fuckin' lieutenant?"

"Burns got a field commission," Ackerman replied. "He's your new platoon leader."

"Oh!" Animal persisted. "*I'n't* that just fine and fuckin' dandy! Glad to know this is a pro-*fessional* army! Why the hell didn't you make *me* a fuckin' officer?"

" 'Cause you're too stupid," Ackerman replied drily.

"And ugly," Stephie added.

"And you smell like roadkill," Dawson said, topping it off.

Animal flashed a "fuck-all-of-you" frown and said, "I s'pose *that's* our new platoon?" Replacements climbed down from the tailgates of trucks and stretched their backs and legs before shouldering heavy packs and accepting proffered weapons.

Ackerman said, "They're the best and the brightest the Selective Service System has to offer." He knelt on one knee and took off his helmet to massage and scratch the stubble covering his scalp.

John reached into his blouse pocket and tossed Animal a small, black plastic insignia. "Hand off your -60 to one of the new guys," John ordered. Animal tilted his head one way then the other as he looked at the three tiny stripes. "You got First Squad."

Stephie was incensed. *Animal!* John was platoon leader and Animal squad leader!

John tossed another set of sergeant's stripes to Dawson. *Dawson!* He was only two weeks out of boot camp! "You got Second Squad, Dawson. Chambers over in Third'll get her stripes and keep that squad. Shepherd'll keep his fourth."

Stephie was so angry that she couldn't even look at Burns or Ackerman. She could feel the burning flush of her cheeks. Burns knelt at her side and removed the corporal's double stripes.

"What the fuck are you doing?" Stephie snapped and swatted at his hand.

John held up the three stripes with two rockers underneath—the insignia of a staff sergeant, then pinned it on her collar. It seemed to take forever. The rest of the platoon arrived from the other side of the helipad. Everyone watched. "You're platoon sergeant, Third Platoon," John said somewhere in the process. The image of Staff Sergeant Kurth consumed Stephie's thoughts. *How the hell can I be him?* she panicked, overwhelmed by the daunting assignment.

When she looked up she saw thirty odd subdued privates—half women, half men—gathering one by one around the edge of her fighting hole. She sat up. Many of the cherries held their weapons at the ready. About half were staring through the trees at the ominous crackle scorching the horizon. The other half eyed the ground.

Ackerman rose and greeted the cherries in a raised voice. "Welcome to Third Platoon, Charlie Company, 3rd Battalion, 519th Infantry Regiment!" He swept his arm past the grimy veterans. "These seventeen soldiers here have taken everything the Chinese threw at them—not once but dozens of times—and they didn't break! They kept their cool, stood their ground, followed orders, and gave better than they took. That's exactly what's expected of you!" he said to the wide-eyed replacements. "They call this platoon 'West Point'! This was *my* platoon! And it *is*, in point of fuckin' fact, the best goddamned platoon in the battalion! Maybe the best platoon in the whole goddamned U.S. Army! Don't fuck it up!"

When he finished, Stephie and Animal rose to their feet.

The cherries stared back, their attention riveted on the suddenly inspiring Captain Ackerman.

"All right, give me two groups!" John shouted and pointed. "Machine gunners and missile crewmen over there! The rest stay put!"

No one moved. That really, really pissed Stephie off.

"Get the fuck over there!" she shouted and lunged at them. Almost all of the soldiers began to move toward the place John had directed the weapons crews to gather. "Not *you*, you moron!" she chastised a cherry. "What the hell're you carryin'?" He had to look down. *"Is it a machine gun or a missile tube?"* she screamed.

"*No*, Staff Sergeant!"

"Then stand fast!" The others got the idea and quickly formed two groups.

Ackerman departed trying to stifle a grin. John and Stephie doled out replacements to the squad leaders and attached crews that technically belonged to the weapons platoon, but which were now permanently assigned to the numbered platoons. When Staff Sergeant Roberts saw Animal's First Squad get a female medic, she said, "Put her back! You got Crane."

"No," John countermanded before looking at the veterans and lowering his voice. "I put the new medic there." Stephie caught John's eye. He shook his head. Animal, Dawson and Becky saw it too. All understood. Stephie looked off toward the sound of the crackle on the horizon. Melinda Crane was dead.

"Get back over there!" Stephie ordered the uncertain female medic. "You heard the LT!"

RITZ CARLTON, ATLANTA, GEORGIA
October 21 // 2315 Local Time

"Don't get me in any trouble, Wu," whispered his former classmate as he shook Wu's hand on departing the hotel bar, which was crowded with army officers. "This is top secret. The source is highly sensitive. I could get shot for doing this, you know." Wu nodded.

The boy was Wu's age, but he'd graduated a year early

than everyone else. The army was even more desperate for computer programmers than for infantry platoon leaders.

Wu took the memory stick concealed in his friend's palm and slipped it into his pocket.

"Gotta go," Shen Shen said into the phone as Wu entered their suite. She punched a button on her cellular phone, and then punched several more.

Erasing her call log, Wu thought as he pretended to ignore the insistent beeping.

Shen Shen slipped the phone into her purse and then looked up at Wu as if on first seeing him at the door. She bounded across the marble entryway wearing a short satin robe that opened to reveal no panties or bra. She kissed him open-mouthed, then drew away. "Are you having an affair?" she asked with knitted brow.

"Yes," Wu replied. Shen Shen retained her grip around the back of his neck. Her hair hung loose. Her face was still made up from the day. She was obviously preparing to bathe. "With you," Wu explained, and she grinned. "Why'd you ask?" He pried her hands from his neck, unbuckled his pistol belt, and laid the weapon and holster on a writing desk.

"I smell alcohol on your breath," Shen Shen explained, embedding a question in her reply.

"I met a friend for a drink downstairs," Wu said.

"A *guy* friend?" Shen Shen asked. Wu tilted his head and smirked as he sat at the small writing table. "Well," she said in a little girl's voice as she straddled his thighs with her bare bottom and sat, with her robe casually opening further, "those American prostitutes downstairs are so *pretty*." She rocked, and rubbed, and crept ever closer to Wu. Her smiling mouth hung half open, and her robe slipped down her slender arms.

"He was a friend from school," Wu explained as Shen Shen breathed hotly into his ear and kissed his neck.

"I'll take a shower," she whispered with her lips brushing against his ear. With a flick of her tongue against his lips and a smile promising more, she rose and headed for the bathroom letting her robe fall onto the floor in her trail.

"I wanta surf the Net while you get ready!" Wu called after

her. He pressed the power button on Shen Shen's laptop, which sat on the writing desk. "What's your password?" he asked.

Shen Shen returned slowly to his side. "My password?" she asked. On the flat screen of the small portable computer, the cursor blinked in its dialog box. She laughed. "Here," she said, grabbing the computer from the desk. "I'll get you onto the Internet." She walked over to the sofa and sat facing him with the screen facing away from Wu. Her expressions alternated between intense concentration on the screen, and brief smiles and blown kisses at Wu. The muted beeps of the computer belied her hurried work.

She was naked. Her body was smooth and thin. Her breasts were full. But Wu felt the desire drain from him. "*Here* you go," Shen Shen said on rising from the sofa, sounding winded as if from frenzied exertion. She handed Wu the laptop. The browser was open onto a page of news headlines from Beijing. "VICTORY AT THE SAVANNAH RIVER" read a banner headline.

Wu drew away from the casual brush of Shen Shen's nipple against his face. She laughed playfully—hyperactively—and bounded for the shower. Wu found that her E-mail reader required yet another password that he didn't know.

He fished the memory stick from his pocket and inserted it into the computer's slot. There were three files—Microsoft V-mails—on the stick. A player launched with a simple click of Wu's fingertip on the touchscreen. A smiling Stephanie Roberts appeared on the screen.

One after the other, Wu watched the three V-mails. Two from Stephanie Roberts to her father. One from the president to his daughter. The last, particularly, upset Wu. Would she take the easy way out that he offered? Had she seen enough fighting and was done? But that wasn't what upset Wu, he realized.

"I love you, Stephie, with all my heart," said the president, sounding like he was on the verge of tears.

When the water in the shower turned off Wu deleted the files and turned off the computer. He tossed the memory stick into the fireplace and headed for the bedroom. "Do you want me wet, or do you want me to dry off?" asked Shen Shen from the bathroom.

"Dry off," was Wu's reply. It gave him a few more minutes to think while lying on his back and listening to the whine of the hair dryer.

WHITE HOUSE OVAL OFFICE
October 22 // 2330 Local Time

Clarissa slipped just inside the crowded Oval Office. But standing beside the busy doorway, she kept having to apologize as aides bumped into her, so she edged her way along the wall until she found a quiet eddy amid the frenzy and sat. Her narrow chair was as far out of the way as it could be, almost hidden behind an antique secretary. She searched for but couldn't find Secretary of State Dodd, who had summoned her to the White House with instructions "to bring good news. Anything will do."

Clarissa couldn't see President Baker's desk through the crowds awaiting their ten-second audience.

"No, no, no, Admiral!" President Baker interrupted with a shout. "I *clearly* remember that *you* said that the Chinese navy could *not* force its way through our blocking positions in the Bahamas!" Admiral Thornton began his unacceptable reply. "If holding fucking Florida was so goddamned critical to your defense of the East Coast," the president shouted, "then why didn't you *mention* it? You just waltz in here with sightings of Chinese surface warships in the Atlantic as far north as Wilmington, North Carolina, and tell me there's nothing you can *do*? For the love of *God*, Admiral! For the love of God."

The chatter in the room had waned. Some now whispered. Most just looked at the focus of everyone present: the leader of the shrinking Free World. A quieter voice advised that they need to redeploy at least one corps of reserves to defend the Atlantic coast south of Washington.

"General Cotler," Baker said in obvious distress, "you just told me that the line along the Savannah River just broke! We're running out of *corps*, general! And divisions, and brigades, and battalions, and . . . and troops. One month into this war and we've lost 160,000 killed or captured! One *month*! And 300,000 wounded, 50,000 so bad they'll either be a *year* in rehab or they're *permanently* disabled!"

The room was quiet. Heads were trained on the president. Some faces showed concern. Others were inscrutable masks. Anything could lie inside those men's and women's hearts, but one thing was certain. All of the coup plotters' faces would fall into the latter category of expression. Clarissa caught the White House chief of staff eyeing her. Frank Adams didn't look away when their eyes met. Instead, Clarissa did.

She then heard tinny sounds of explosions on a speakerphone. There were rattling machine guns. Booming artillery. Background shouts whose volume was overridden by the thunder of high explosives.

". . . most of our observation posts!" screamed a man at the top of his lungs. His shouts were alternately either far too loud, or totally drowned out by a nearby explosion. "There are Chinese landing craft at beaches Saipan, Tarawa . . ." an explosion scratched at maximum volume, "Okinawa, and Guam! Beaches Saipan and Tarawa appear fully consolidated already!" He kept shouting even through another shattering blast, hurrying to get his report off. ". . . out of the sixty tanks have been destroyed! We're attacking the beachhead on Okinawa with unsupported Marine riflemen even though Chinese naval artillery has sealed off the approaches! They're heading dismounted through a wall of fire, Mr. President! A solid, solid curtain! And if they don't retake that beach in an hour, sir, we'll never see blue water again! Not at the rate they're . . . !"

There was a burst of static. Silence followed. Clarissa heard someone say, "No, that was the only command we could raise on shortwave. The subsea line to Oahu was cut. We can't raise 3rd Marine Expeditionary Force headquarters at Pearl."

Admiral Thornton informed the president that, "We are redeploying our submarines to Bremerton, Washington. I'm afraid Hawaii is going to fall, sir."

A few moments later, Clarissa noticed that the room was beginning to clear. In ones and twos, the Oval Office was emptying. She searched for Art Dodd, but found Frank Adams, Baker's chief of staff, who caught her eye again on passing, smiled, and winked. *What the hell does that mean?* she wondered. The president stood behind his desk, his back turned, staring out the window into the darkness.

Clarissa hesitated and looked at the lonely man, then turned to leave, but Frank Adams shut the door behind him. She had been left alone with the president of the United States, who didn't seem to know that anyone was there. He just stared out the window unmoving. Clarissa tried to clear her dry throat but it didn't need clearing, and the effort didn't produce the desired noise. She opened her mouth but couldn't speak. She couldn't imagine what she should say.

"Mist-Mister President . . ."

Baker turned, and Clarissa was stunned. He was crying. He quickly returned to his watch at the window.

It was an epiphany for Clarissa. Everything she had thought changed in that moment . . . or had it? She sailed into a dense fog of uncertainty. She laid the files she had brought on his desk and tried desperately to think of something to say. To sort her scattering thoughts and her even more disorderly feelings, which sprung powerfully from out of nowhere. The raw, unsorted feelings all around as she edged her way along the desk to the president's chair. "I . . ." she began, but she had nothing to say.

He turned. Drying streams ran down his now composed face over which he ran the back of his hand. His eyes never rose from the floor. "I'm sorry," he said. "Forgive me." Her head began a jerky shake too late to object that no apology was owed her. "Sometimes," he tried to explain from the depths of an agony Clarissa had never seen, "I can't help thinking that this is the end. That it all stops here. That everything . . . everything I love, I always lose. And that soon—in the end—I'm going to lose this country."

"Oh-h . . ." she moaned, aching to her joints from the pain he radiated. She reached out and rested her hand lightly on his shoulder. His warm cheek descended to her hand. With his eyes closed, he nuzzled her skin at once innocently and in a desperate display of need. His lips grazing her fingertips.

She had been wrong about him, so wrong . . . or had she?

Her choices were now clear. A half step away from him and she could sail into open water, find her bearings, and set a course for return to the world of black and white answers. But a half step toward him led to a tumultuous sea of churning gray conflicts where waves were topped with white caps and troughs parted to expose black rock.

In the end, she made no choice at all. She merely drifted . . . closer. So close that she stood under Bill Baker's chin. So close that the lengths of their bodies touched. She could feel his breath. She lay her cheek softly against his chest. Her eyes closed to better be absorbed in the moment. For the sea, she found, was electric. The air freshened. The sting of spray sent ripples along her skin. And when his arms enveloped her, the storms no longer mattered. He breathed her hair and savored her neck as if it were a delicacy.

Clarissa was in free fall. No effort was required, and none could alter her trajectory. She tumbled into the unknown.

CONGRESSIONAL DINING ROOM
October 24 // 1230 Local Time

"Nothing is ever black and white," Clarissa said to her father. "You know?"

Tom Leffler was devouring his food and looked up only to acknowledge greetings from passing Congressmen. He was more animated than he had seemed since . . . since her mom died, actually. "You're telling *me*!" he replied with a full mouth. "You can't trust anybody. Everybody has an angle. An agenda. They may not be doing what even *they* think is right, but somebody's gotten to them, and they think they have no choice."

"Well, that's not exactly what I meant." She looked down at her lunch, which she hadn't touched. Her stomach fluttered. She wasn't really hungry. A committee chairman dropped by to exchange inane pleasantries at which Clarissa smiled and the speaker of the house loosed howls of laughter. As soon as they were alone again in the room filled with Congressmen and lobbyists, she leaned over and whispered, "I mean . . .

sometimes life takes funny turns. You end up in situations—doing things you never thought . . ."

Her father stopped eating—knife and fork in hand—and looked up at her. She had struck a chord. He was nodding. "That's true," he said, lost deep in thought. He resumed his meal at a more deliberate pace, his mind draining the resources he had previously devoted to eating. "But let's say," he continued, "at some critical juncture, you know what's right. And only you are in position to take an action that would at less critical times violate every principle by which you've lived." He was now so consumed by the mental effort that all other activity came to a halt. "But at that moment—in the context of that time—the act you know you have to take is right. Just. It's not moral relativism or hypocrisy, it's your duty. What would you do?"

"What?" Clarissa asked in exasperation. She was angered by her father's confusion. "What are you *talking* about?" One possible answer presented itself. She leaned forward and whispered, "Does this have to do with the coup?"

His knife had been sawing a piece of chicken breast, but when she uttered the word "coup" it fell idle. His fork remained planted to the plate where it stabbed the uneaten morsel. He didn't look up with his face, but with his eyes, and not all the way. His gaze stopped at Clarissa's blazer and flitted about. Clarissa found herself checking her attire. "What?" she asked defensively.

He continued his sawing, but with slow, deliberate motions and carefully lifted the next bite to his mouth. His chewing seemed to buy time for him to ponder her remark. After he had swallowed, he looked straight at Clarissa. "I have no idea what you're talking about," he replied.

REFUGEE CENTER, GREENVILLE, SOUTH CAROLINA
October 27 // 0745 Local Time

The television cameras followed Han's every move. These pictures weren't for broadcast in occupied America. They were being made for the Chinese television audience that now spanned three quarters of the globe.

"How are conditions here?" Han asked, kneeling before a typical American family. The vacant mother clutched an attentive, thumb-sucking girl. The overweight father sat stoically braced with hands on knees and arms stiff. The pimple-faced boy showed braces in what would've been a defiant sneer were it not so comic.

The mother glanced up at the slender boom mike over her head. Its tiny, foam-covered tip hovered above the scene just out of the cameras' fields of view. "Well . . . I dunno," she opined.

Han grabbed his chin and nodded as if pondering her insights. He snapped his finger and pointed at her. "I have an idea! *Your* home was destroyed, so you're living in a high school gymnasium. But there are *empty* houses all around this city of Greenville, South Carolina—right?"

She shrugged.

"So why don't *you* to move into the *empty* houses?" He marveled at the simplicity of his spur-of-the-moment plan, which had been worked out months earlier. "And in return for free housing, say, maybe, you go back to your jobs! That would be a fair trade don't you think?"

Her furrowed brow showed not thought, but concern. "You mean we'd be takin' other peoples homes?" she asked.

Han looked up—over his shoulder—at the news program's director. She shook her head and frowned. Even if the meaning conveyed by the American woman's tone was lost in translation, the expression on her face had been too obvious. Taking someone else's home was clearly the most disgusting thing Han could have proposed.

Han rose with a slight groan, straightened his jacket, and thanked the family. The entourage moved on in search of another typical American family to try the script one more time. Han would try coming at the proposal from a different angle. Maybe ensure the next family that the solution was temporary, and that prewar property rights would be honored after Chinese victory. He winced at the thought of how that would be received, and rethought the approach he would take.

One of Han's advance men intercepted Han before he began the next interview. "It's the prime minister," he said breathlessly, handing Han a tiny cellular phone.

"It's late!" an exuberant Han remarked in Chinese.

"I want you to go to the Orlando, Florida, airport," the prime minister said without greeting his nephew. "There's someone there that I would like you to meet. Her plane arrives in two hours. I'd like you to treat her very, very well."

ORLANDO, FLORIDA
October 27 // 1000 Local Time

Han Zhemin and General Sheng waited at the bottom of a carpeted staircase on the breezy airport tarmac. A slender Chinese woman of twenty descended the stairs of a sleek, supersonic long-haul jet. She was fashionably dressed and wore movie-star sunglasses. She didn't bother holding her skirt, which revealed shapely legs with each gust, but she did make certain she didn't tumble off high heels to the concrete by taking her time with each carefully placed step.

Liu Yi presented Han her smooth cheeks for a kiss. Her skin was powdered white, and her lips were red, not blackened by the glittering lipstick that was the choice of her generation. Han kissed both cheeks and said in Chinese, "The last time I saw you, you were crawling on the floor of your grandfather's foyer."

"That must've been a long time ago," Liu Yi replied in perfect English. A bright smile lit a beautiful face. "I haven't crawled on the floor in a long time."

General Sheng stiffly shook the girl's hand.

She promptly took Han's proffered arm and headed for the limousine with General Sheng three steps behind. Liu Yi's hair shone brilliantly in the sun of a crystal clear morning. As they walked, her hip swayed against Han's. "Where have you been these last few years?" Han asked. Their conversation had switched to English. With the change of language, their culture changed. English allowed for less time-consuming rituals of behavior and was, therefore, for most of the educated young, the more comfortable language of greeting.

"Studying," she answered, cheerily affecting a coquettish display. *But who is she really?* Han wondered. Was Liu Yi—

at age twenty—a sophisticated citizen of the world, or was she playing the role of her life? "I graduate from Beijing University next spring," she informed Han.

Han laughed. He had thought she was at least out of university. Yi checked his face uncertainly. Her smile had given way to concern. "And what," Han continued airily, "Ms. University Co-ed, are you studying at Beijing University?"

"English literature," she tentatively replied.

Han laughed, stopped, and turned to her at the car door. He took both of her hands in his and beamed. Yi's smile again lit her face, although she was clearly uncertain why they were smiling. Han slowly reached up and removed her sunglasses. Her eyes didn't sink in feigned modesty. They bravely burned back at Han.

"Have you ever been to America?" Han asked. She shook her head. *Of course not,* Han thought. The wars began when she was ten. "Then where would you like to go today, university student Liu Yi?"

"Disney World," she replied confidently and without hesitation.

Han laughed again and so did Yi. She had perfectly straight, white teeth. Han turned to the commander of Eleventh Army Group (North) and said, "We're going to Disney World, General Sheng!"

Han was absolutely ebullient for one simple reason. Yi's visit augured Han's ascent into the top tier of Chinese power. Han had been chosen, he now realized, and he felt buoyant and full of energy. All of which infected and clearly elated Liu Yi. No telling how long the poor girl had worried that she would embarrass herself and her family. That she would botch her enormously important first adult undertaking. But she was gracious, proper, and strikingly good-looking.

Han and Yi got into the lead limousine. Sheng boarded the trailing one. The morose old general obviously understood that the point of the visit was for Han to get to know the defense minister's favorite granddaughter.

One of the few things that the Americans hadn't destroyed in their retreat was Disney World. But only a few local residents had been trapped by the Chinese army and forced by census takers to return to their jobs at the amusement park. In fact, the huge place seemed eerily quiet. If it hadn't been for the Chinese troops—who boisterously laughed as they lay on the grass—there would have been no life in the park at all. Yi and Han strolled side by side, her arm in his.

Yi said in English over her shoulder, "I see, General Sheng, that you allow our troops a trip to Disney World for relaxation." Colonel Li whispered the Chinese translation into the old general's ear. "I think that's admirable. They deserve it!"

A group of soldiers that they were approaching were quickly gathering their combat gear and walking or running across the grass in the opposite direction. A now fetid artificial lake separated the entourage of VIPs from the rapidly retreating gaggle of men.

As they neared the artificial hillock, it became apparent why the troops had taken flight. On the wind wafted the pungent smell of marijuana smoke. Yi giggled and glanced at Han, sharing their secret discovery of the deserving troops' harmless lawbreaking.

But Sheng had smelled it too. "Seize those men," he ordered Colonel Li in Chinese. He used the word "seize," not "arrest," and there was a difference. The former didn't connote much in the way of due process before punishment.

Yi spun with surprising energy to face Sheng. "No, you *won't!*" she shouted. It sounded terribly rude when delivered in Chinese. Orders could be given to an elder, but not in that way. Yi had made the mistake of switching languages but not switching cultures, which was a problem increasingly common among the young. And she appeared not to care in the least. *So that's who she really is,* Han thought in amusement. *At least she won't be dull.* "Those poor boys risk their lives for our country!" she chastised. "What's wrong with a little infraction of the rules if it takes their minds off the war for a day?"

"Drug abuse is not a 'little infraction,' " Sheng replied, steadily but not forcefully.

Colonel Li hesitated, not relaying Sheng's orders in the face of Liu Yi's adamant tone. *She commands well,* Han noted with satisfaction. She had probably led the life of Defense Minister Liu Changxing's little princess.

"I heard my grandfather," Yi said icily, "discussing your casualty figures over dinner." General Sheng's face grew even stonier. "Perhaps your worrying about how your troops spend their leisure time isn't the best use of *your* time."

Han watched the confrontation as if he were at a sporting match, but there also was information in what Yi said. Criticism of the American campaign's casualties was obviously growing. The astute university student knew which button to push.

General Sheng didn't need to countermand his earlier order. Yi had already done it for him.

Back at the airport, Yi didn't bother to say goodbye to General Sheng. But to Han, she said in English again, "I had a really good time, even though there was only that one ride." They had ridden a stomach-wrenching roller coaster. She had squealed at a frequency Han had thought reserved for dolphins. General Sheng, unsteady on his feet after climbing out of the small car, had declined her mocking offer to go for a second ride. Despite his growing nausea, Han had gone around twice more.

"I hope," Han responded, "that the next time you visit America we can see more sights. And I certainly hope we'll have more time to spend with each other."

"I would like that," Yi replied, smiling. "Maybe we'll have more privacy too."

Han arched his brow, and kissed her hand and then both of her cheeks. After his second peck, she pressed her warm, open mouth against his.

ALONG INTERSTATE 20, SOUTH CAROLINA
October 28 // 0945 Local Time

It was cool and overcast. Stephie eyed the gray sky. There would be rain soon. She could smell it on the fresh breezes that occasionally cleansed the air of the stench of rifle fire. She walked along the line of prone riflemen. Her men and women. "Squeeze 'em off!" she shouted hoarsely as they aimed at paper targets mounted on a wooden fence that traversed a hill two hundred meters away. The Interstate at their backs was empty. Dirt rose in splashes from the hillside backstop at the other end of their makeshift rifle range. The fire from her platoon was a steady crackle of single, aimed shots. They had been at it for more than an hour. Smudged brass shell casings were piled inches high beside smoking rifles to be collected, turned in, and reloaded. Each soldier had been given fifteen 30-round magazines. They were nearing the end of their 450 rounds of target practice. "Make 'em count!" Staff Sergeant Roberts croaked.

She kicked the boots of one woman. "Spread your feet! You need a stable platform for that weapon!" The girl nodded. Her helmet flopped on her head. The next cherry in line—a boy just out of boot camp like most of the others—aimed and aimed. Stephie stopped and waited, but he never fired. His pile of spent shell casings wasn't nearly as high as the others, and he had five full magazines stacked beside him. Stephie walked up to him, and his eyes left his sights momentarily to take in the scuffed toes of her dusty boots. Even then he aimed, and aimed, and aimed.

Stephie boiled at the sight of the son of a bitch. It took only a few of them in a platoon to get them all killed on first contact with the enemy. She leaned over, bent at the waist, and filled her lungs with the noxious air. *"Fire that goddamned weapon you motherfucking shithead!"* she shouted at the top of her lungs.

He jerked the trigger. The rifle bucked.

"Again!" He complied. "Again!" A casing spun out of the chamber. "Again!" she shouted, raising her binoculars. A puff of dirt flew from the hill five feet from the guy's target. "Again!" She heard the report, but the round landed somewhere outside her binocular's field of view.

With her teeth set painfully together, she glared down at the bastard. He was fucking crying like a baby! She hauled off and kicked him in the kidney, and he grunted and doubled over. She dropped to one knee and grabbed him by his collar, twisting it and pulling until the button on the front of his blouse choked him.

"You're gonna kill somebody," she said in a low voice as he stared bug-eyed up at her and gasped for breath. "You're gonna put a round right through somebody's fuckin' face, and you're gonna watch his brains fly out the back of his head. Or you're gonna drill him square in the chest so his eyeballs pop outa their sockets. Or you're gonna dismember him—cut his arms and legs off—round by fuckin' round until he's dead, you understand me!" The guy nodded jerkily.

"Sergeant Roberts," Stephie heard. It was John Burns. *Lieutenant* John Burns. He stood behind her, staring at her. So was everybody else nearby in the line.

Stephie released the coward, rose, and raised the binoculars that hung from her neck. The guy's target—stapled to a decrepit wooden post—was unscathed by one hour's fire. She looked back down at the fucker, whose face was planted in the dirt beneath him. "You've got 150 rounds, motherfucker," she said. "I want that fence post your target's mounted on hangin' loose on barbed wire before you leave here. You understand me, private?"

"Yes . . . ! Yes, Staff Sergeant!" he managed before coughing.

The firing up and down the line resumed. Stephie brushed past John, who had expected her to stop. He grabbed her arm and yanked. She pulled free. "Lighten up," he said in almost a whisper.

"No," she replied in just as low a tone.

John cocked his head. "Lighten up," he repeated, "*Staff Sergeant* Roberts."

She turned to face him square. "No, *sir*." She resumed her walk down the line, ripping new assholes with redoubled anger.

By early afternoon, a steady cold drizzle fell from the sky. Their training, however, continued. On the shoulder of the highway beside a low-slung armored fighting vehicle, the fifty-odd men and women stood in slick ponchos with their rifles slung over their shoulders, muzzles down. A crewman pointed out the ball-mounted weapons in the new-model vehicle, which none of the troops had ever seen before. The camouflage-painted personnel carrier, which bristled with all-threat missiles, was just off the production line.

Stephie wasn't interested in the lecture. The time when they might use such a vehicle—when they might go on the offensive—seemed so distant as to be irrelevant. Stephie barely listened to the nerdy lecturer, whose thick glasses would have been so fogged as to be unusable were it not for the rivulets of rainwater washing down them. Instead, she watched her troops like a hawk, punishing any drooping eyelids with loud blows to the helmet. Threatening with menacing glares any straying attention.

"The temperature on the ceramic armor," the crewman continued after one of Stephie's outbursts, "is equalized to within one-half of a degree with the ambient air temperature. That reduces its infrared signature on Chinese night vision devices so much that it's almost invisible."

One of the women was coughing. She slumped under the weight of her fighting load. Stephie maneuvered for a closer look. Every time the woman swallowed, she coughed. She kept opening her eyes wide as if she couldn't see otherwise. Water dripped from wisps of hair that ringed her face beneath her helmet. Her head wobbled, then she saw Stephie. She straightened her back and fixed her gaze on the lecturer.

Stephie called the woman over and pulled her aside. The new recruit was petrified. "Head on over to the battalion aid station," Stephie said quietly. The private wasn't about to argue and seemed greatly relieved that Stephie cared so much. The cherry gave in, finally, to the fever and slumped from rigid attention to barely standing. "I don't want you getting everybody else sick, too," Stephie added. The woman seemed to take offense and smirked before leaving. She looked back over her shoulder—twice—at Stephie as she slogged down the muddy shoulder. Stephie made sure the woman didn't see that she noticed.

"Staff Sergeant Roberts!" the lecturer called out with his hand on the vehicle's armored hide. Stephie nodded. "You wanta take her for a spin?"

Her troops looked at her with grins on their faces. "Not really," she replied, and everyone laughed.

"Well, orders are to give all the officers and noncoms a turn at the wheel," the guy said, "in case the crew is taken out."

When Stephie shrugged and hesitated, there was more laughter. She turned and pointed out the people who found the situation most amusing and said, "All of you, mount up."

"That's not really necessary," their lecturer advised.

Stephie ignored the man. "I said mount up," she repeated, and the ten designated riflemen scrambled through the open doors at the vehicle's rear. Stephie handed her rifle to one of her people, climbed atop the sloping armored glacis at the front, and dropped her feet through the open hatch into the rain-soaked cockpit. From standing on her seat, she sank into the contours of the high-tech compartment, sliding her feet forward and searching for the pedals. But her boots found no controls.

The driver leaned inside from above, temporarily blotting out the sky and sheltering her from the rain. "Try not to get mud everywhere," he cautioned, wiping the glowing screens arrayed in a semicircle before her with a rag.

All the controls were wet. "I'm not going to get electrocuted by this shit, am I?" she asked.

"No," he replied. "It's waterproof. I just don't want it gettin' muddy, that's all."

He walked her through the simple controls. Two levers— one for each hand—rose from the armrests on either side. One five-inch-high and thirty-inch-wide screen ran across the front of the cockpit at eye level. "Push forward on both levers the same amount and you go straight. Pull back the same amount and you go straight in reverse. Push forward or back different amounts and you turn. Push one lever forward and pull the other back and you turn in place."

"Got it," Stephie said.

He leaned in and pressed a button that Stephie never would have found amid the others on the form-fitting console before her, and the engine rumbled to life. "All right," he said, pointing at two buttons just above her right shoulder. "Hatch open. Hatch closed. Have at it."

He withdrew, and the rain poured in. Stephie hit the button above her shoulder with the red down arrow, and the hatch closed and squeaked with its tight fit. The heater automatically turned on, and she felt the warm, wonderful gust. There were no ports from which she could peer, but the thin, wide screen was a televised approximation. The driver's position was totally encased in armor except to the rear, where if she had wanted to she could just barely squeeze through to the troop compartment from which came her troops' excited chatter.

"You ready back there?" Stephie called out.

"Are we there yet?" someone replied to peels of juvenile laughter.

"I gotta go potty!" a woman complained jokingly to still more amusement.

The screen before Stephie was empty. The open road was clear. She pushed forward on the levers till they hit the stops. Her helmet slammed back into the armored bulkhead. There were screams from behind her. She could feel the acceleration in her stomach. At first, the forty-ton giant swerved from one side of the two-lane, east-bound highway to the other. By the time she got the two levers equalized and the vehicle straight, they were doing forty-five miles per hour.

The troops behind her were shouting at her to be careful. One woman stuck her face into the small passageway and began to scream at her to slow down. Stephie pulled back on the right lever, throwing the vehicle into a turn. With a gut wrenching drop they descended into the median between the east- and west-bound lanes. More screams erupted from her passengers, and Stephie's jaw was jammed to her chest as they ascended the far shoulder of the interstate.

For a moment, they were airborne. It couldn't have been more than a few inches high, and the suspension cushioned their return to earth with amazing softness, but the moment of free flight in the massive beast was enough to bring pleas of mercy from the rebellious load in back.

She did slow, but not in time to straighten up on the west-bound lane, as she had intended. They descended over the far shoulder at almost thirty miles per hour, and she thought better of trying to turn on the down slope.

Screams of men and women rose above the whining turbine as they plummeted down the far bank. Stephie's heart jumped when she saw the barbed wire fence, but in a flash they were through it. It hadn't even made a sound that was audible to her inside the armored cocoon. Nor did the brush and small trees that she bowled over while trying to avoid the larger, thicker pines.

"Please!" came the cries from the rear.

The armored vehicle began to slow as they reached the foot of a tall, treeless hillock. That pissed Stephie off, so she jammed both levers forward again to the stops. The whine of the turbines kept rising like jet engines for a few seconds after they had received their "full power" command. The number on the speedometer at first held steady at "30," but then it began to fall.

Stephie noticed that all her weight was on her back, but the top of the hill that filled her wide screen seemed attainable. The vehicle's metal tracks began to slip every so often. Each half-second loss of traction brought still more evidence of terror from the helpless lot in back, and raised the first traces of true fright in Stephie. But even more terrifying to her was the speed, which had fallen to "15" despite the shrill tone of the maxed-out engine.

Graphs popped open on incomprehensible screens. Bars rose through green, through amber, and into the red. "Caution!" flashed insistently on several displays. A pleasant female voice like on an aircraft flight deck just before a tragedy began calmly reciting a litany of dangers. "Engine temperature warning. Hydraulic pressure warning. Oil pressure warning. Vehicle attitude warning. Traction warning."

Come on! Stephie urged silently as the speed dropped below "10." The crest of the hill was only a couple of dozen meters away. *Just a few more seconds,* she thought as she felt her weight shift ever higher up her back in time with the falling speed.

"For the love of God!" screamed someone behind her just as they pulled over the lip of the hill going four miles per

hour. Stephie eased off the levers, which returned to the neu-
tral position and brought the vehicle to a stop. The engine
dropped to idle. The screens went from glaring red to soothing
green. The voice of her computer copilot fell silent and satisfied.

Stephie looked back over her shoulder into the troop compartment. Everyone was slowly climbing off the pile of humanity at the closed double doors at the rear. With a grin on
her face, Stephie said, "I guess I forgot the 'Fasten-Seat-Belts'
sign!"

"There aren't any fucking seat belts!" came one woman's
shout.

"Must be an oversight," Stephie noted, returning her eyes
to her screen. There was a farmhouse across a dale a half a
kilometer away, but she wasn't certain about the terrain in
between. They'd been assured that no mines had yet been laid
between the interstate and the surrounding skyline on which
Stephie's vehicle now sat, but she knew nothing about the
defenses further out.

She pushed her left lever forward, and pulled her right lever
rearward. The mere hint of movement and slight rise of engine noise brought instant terror from behind her, although
all Stephie did was pivot the vehicle in its tracks. "Knock it
off!" she commanded as the hilltop paraded across the wide
screen. When Stephie saw the highway below, she released
the levers and the vehicle stopped turning. *Responsive,* Stephie marveled.

Down below, she could see her entire platoon. They had
obviously sprinted after the runaway vehicle. John was climbing over the trampled barbed wire fence, leading the lecturer
and vehicle's driver along a path of churned brown earth that
rose up the soggy green hillside. They were coming to Stephie's rescue.

"Will you let us out, please?" came a reasonable request
through the narrow passageway behind Stephie's seat.

"Would everyone please return to your seats and place your
tray tables in the upright and locked position?" Stephie said
with a broad smile.

She nudged the vehicle forward. Almost immediately the

nose dipped. Shouts rose from her reluctant cargo. A hand reached out to grab her shoulder, offending her greatly. She nudged the vehicle a few feet forward, and they were off to the races.

Although she gave the vehicle no power, the engine whine and speed readout both rose as they went over the edge and began to race down the hill. Ten miles per hour. Twenty. Thirty. Forty. She kept the vehicle straight with tiny adjustments to the levers. John stood upright waving his arms over his head before he and the others scrambled out of the vehicle's path. Thankfully, the vehicle's speed maxed out at forty-five, and the rest of their platoon—standing on the shoulder of the road directly ahead—dashed to either side.

The fence was a blur. The vehicle's undercarriage thudded against the shoulder of the interstate, and Stephie's head and neck were buckled. They landed with a *bang* on the interstate's pavement and Stephie pulled both levers to the rear. The vehicle slipped to the left and right, and there rose a terrible grinding sound from the treads as the bulkheads shuddered violently.

Stephie released the levers, and they came to a stop.

It was so quiet from the troop compartment that Stephie at first worried that she'd somehow killed them all. She turned to look over her shoulder just as someone found the button to open one of the double doors. The cherries poured out through the opening and onto broken highway pavement left in the wake of the metal treads. Like rats from a sinking ship, they clawed their way out and formed yet another pile on the ground outside.

The rest of the platoon gathered around, doubled over at the waist and laughed with wild and total abandon.

Stephie heard a dull thumping on the hatch above. When she turned back to face forward, the middle of her wide viewing screen was covered by a camouflaged trouser knee and wet poncho. She didn't have to see more to be told who it was. "Oh, boy," she mumbled before pushing the up arrow above her right shoulder.

The hatch squeaked and opened with a hiss. Rain poured into her eyes. Gray sky profiled the sight of John Burns, whose jaw jutted out in anger hotter than she'd never seen before. The driver squeezed by him, cursing and stabbing at the button to turn the engine off.

"Jesus Christ!" was all he said to Stephie, shaking his head and looking at her as if she were insane.

Stephie got out without looking John in the eye. The lecturer and the driver knelt beside the front fender inspecting the tiny scratches and bits of tangled barbed wire that protruded from the previously mint condition vehicle. Cheers and raucous applause rose from the vast majority of her platoon that hadn't been along for the ride. Stephie nodded and acknowledged the praise, avoiding John's burning gaze as she climbed down.

The shaken troops from the rear had now risen, but some stood grabbing their knees as if queasy from seasickness. The vehicle's engine emitted rapid popping sounds.

The lecturer got in Stephie's face, wearing a look of disbelief. "It handles pretty good," she said, "but there were some complaints about spilled drinks by the passengers."

The majority of those gathered there—her audience and new fan club—roared with laughter. A smiling Stephie dared look at John. That was all it took. That was all he wanted. He turned and departed immediately without saying a word.

She'd fucked up, she knew it. She'd disappointed him, and therefore she'd disappointed herself. There was a buzz from her troops that was infecting even the victims of her little thrill ride, who stood unsteadily on their feet but with smiles spreading on their faces.

"Who's next?" Stephie asked in a monotone.

Her squad leaders instantly stepped forward to volunteer, but the lecturer—the vehicle commander—said, "No! No more! That's it!"

A groan rose from all quarters, and the complaints began. Stephie quieted them all with a shout. "*All right!* Knock it off!" Her troops again looked at her with wary, puppy-dog eyes. They sensed that her mood had returned to normal. "Grenade throwing practice! Let's head to the range! Everybody throws dummy grenades—fifty throws—then one live grenade at the end! Let's go! Move out!" They all turned and began to trudge through the rain. "On the double!" a pissed-off Stephie commanded, taking her rifle back and passing her troops. The thudding boots and small splashes followed her down the highway. She looked for John, but couldn't find where he'd gone.

BESSEMER, ALABAMA
November 2 // 2030 Local Time

Jimmy and Amanda Lipscomb hung out in the storm cellar with Hart, who had grown comfortable in the ten-by-twelve room dug out of the side of a dirt slope. After over two weeks of immobilizing, elevating, and icing his ankle, it was finally beginning to heal. It obviously wasn't fractured, but the sprain had been bad. His trek of many miles after injuring it must have done the most damage.

"Did you kill a lot of 'em?" the boy asked.

"Jimmy!" his sister snapped. "Dad said not to ask him any questions."

"Listen to your dad," Hart said. "He's trying to protect your family."

"Yeah, well," Jimmy replied dismissively, "there's talk at school about resistance."

"Shut your mouth!" Amanda chastised. "Don't say that word again! Ever!"

"Amanda's right," Hart advised. "It's too dangerous to join any resistance groups. They're probably just a Chinese setup to lure people into a trap."

"But I could join *you*!" Jimmy blurted out. "Word is that you guys stashed guns and ammo in the hills. You *had* to! Stuff's gettin' blown up every *night*! The Chinese are real jumpy. They go around town in tanks, or on foot but scared-like, with the last guy in line walkin', you know, backwards. I wanna help!"

"You want to kill the Chinese who invaded America?" Hart asked. Amanda let the question stand and waited for her younger brother's response. "Could you kill those soldiers?"

Jimmy shrugged in confusion at the obvious answer. "O'

course! I'd kill every last *one* of 'em if I could! I hate 'em. I don't even get what you're askin'."

It all seemed so straightforward to the boy, and maybe at his age it was.

"Then wait till you do understand," Hart advised. "Wait till you meet some Chinese soldiers who treat you nice. Do you a favor. Act like regular guys. Wait a couple of years till you're not quite so sure about whether it's right to kill them for just doing their job. Then you decide what's right and wrong, not before."

"Jimmy! Amanda!" came their father's distant shout.

The well-behaved boy rose immediately, but he hesitated on the steps leading out. "So wait two years?" Jimmy asked urgently. "Till I'm sixteen?"

"Something like that," Hart answered.

Jimmy grinned, nodded, and bolted outside. Amanda followed, but stopped at the door and said, "I'm sixteen."

Hart said nothing in reply.

ARMY HEADQUARTERS, ATLANTA
November 5 // 2245 Local Time

Lieutenant Wu and the other junior officers secured Top Secret files after a meeting of Sheng's general staff. Colonel Li stood by the door casually overseeing the process. Each set of files and notepads—used or not—went into a "DE-STROY" bag. The irreversible plastic ties at the mouths of the bags were pulled tight with audible clicking sounds. The instructions on the side read, "Class One Incineration Required."

Like the other lieutenants and captains, Wu worked his way around the table dropping files and papers into the sacks. He pulled the sacks closed and handed them to fellow officers, who hustled them to a cart. Wu had to wait for someone to return before he could even touch the papers at the next place. That was the rule. Always two people. Never one. It reduced the odds of spying.

Finally, Wu's partner—a captain—returned. Wu bagged more files and briefing books and handed the sack over. The captain left the quiet room. Wu moved down to the head of the table—to General Sheng's place—and waited.

There was, just then, absolutely no one in the room. It was a major breach of security. Colonel Li had disappeared. The other teams disposing of files had finished their work. Wu's partner had not yet returned. There was only one set of files left on the table: the commanding general's.

Wu looked down. That act alone—the cast of his gaze—was suspicious enough for counterintelligence to send a staff officer like Wu to the front. The red, stamped wax seal on Sheng's file was broken. Wu reached down and opened the file: an offense punishable by death.

The file was neatly divided into sections. On the first page of each section was a picture of an American and a caption bearing a name. The first three appeared to be publicity photos. Portraits of subjects neatly framed by the camera. A man wearing glasses in a professional business suit. "Hamilton Asher," read the caption. An American air force general with close-cropped silver hair. "Martin Latham" was his name. "Thomas Leffler," a rotund old man whom Wu recognized to be a senior American politician. But on the last page Wu found not a portrait, but a crude video capture of an attractive American woman putting on sunglasses leaving the White House. Beside it was a picture of the same woman—years younger, maybe in her twenties—at an outdoor restaurant in a Chinese city. "Dr. Clarissa Leffler," Wu read, mouthing but not speaking her name.

Wu let the file fall closed and waited, staring at the far wall as if at attention.

Colonel Li happened by the open door and looked in. "Ah! Lieutenant Wu? Has everyone run off and left you?" He casually strolled into the room.

"Apparently so, Colonel Li."

Li took Wu's sack and held it open. Wu deposited General Sheng's file and briefing book into the bag, which Li closed with a clicking sound. "I'll take this to document security on my way back upstairs," Li said helpfully.

"Yes, sir," replied the ramrod straight lieutenant.

Li smiled.

• • •

When Wu returned to his luxurious quarters in an antebellum southern home, he got undressed in the dark and crawled into his tall four-poster bed. The rocking mattress caused Shen Shen to stir. He lay on his back, and she curled up against him. Her bare skin was warm against his.

"Hi," she said sleepily, in English, before she began kissing her way down his body. *Why would Sheng leak that particular information to me?* Wu tried to decipher before he finally succumbed to the mechanical but effective ministrations of General Sheng's secretary.

7

President Baker tossed newspapers and magazines onto the long conference table one at a time, allowing the slaps of paper to speak for themselves. The *New York Times, Time,* the *Wall Street Journal,* and *Newsweek* all had articles criticizing the army's tactic of choice, which was bunkering.

"I've got a prime-time news conference in an hour and a half," Baker said, "where I'm gonna be asked fifty times by fifty people in fifty different ways why we chose to re-fight World War I in the Twenty-First Century." There were stern looks from the ground pounders, none sterner than on the face of U.S. Army General Adam Cotler, Chairman of the Joint Chiefs of Staff. Baker picked up *Time* magazine. Its cover juxtaposed black-and-white pictures of haggard doughboys in trenches with similar color images from the Savannah River. "It's a legitimate question," the president opined. "One that I'm beginning to ask myself after none of the three successive lines we have prepared have succeeded in stopping the Chinese for even one *week.* Have you read in here, General Cot-

ler, what your now retired predecessor wrote?" Baker
thumbed for the page.

"I've had a long talk with him about it, sir," Cotler replied.
"Yes, sir, I've read it."

Baker read an excerpt nonetheless. " 'The principal strength
of static defenses is their ability to bring intense firepower
across their front from covered positions. Their principal
drawback is that, once breached, the immobile defenders are
unable to reorient themselves to repel attacks against their
flanks. You cannot pick up and move a trench or a concrete
bunker.' " Baker looked up at Cotler. "That sounds like pretty
levelheaded commentary to me. I'm going to be asked by a
rabid White House press corps why, after half a century of
planning for mobile warfare, America has chosen to return to
the trenches of Verdun? What would your answer be, General?"

Cotler squared his jaw either in anger or grim determination, or perhaps both. "Military technology swings the advantage, Mr. President, from the offense to the defense and back
again. We are now squarely in a defensive phase of the technological cycle both on land and in the air. All-threat weapons
give crews attached to infantry squads—both Chinese and
American—the capability of blindly firing a missile into the
air and killing a tank over the horizon up to twelve miles
away, or—by raising the weapon's elevation and spinning a
dial—killing a supersonic jet fighter at sixty thousand feet, all
with the *same* missile. They have virtually cleared the battlefield of armored vehicles and close air support. What's left is
infantry and artillery.

"Modern artillery, Mr. President," Cotler continued, "is
devastating when employed against unprotected infantry. A
single 155 mm self-propelled Howitzer can fire twelve
rounds," he held up his forearm at a 45-degree angle—fingers
extended straight like a gun barrel—steadily lowering its angle to the table in a dozen jerky motions, "depressing the
elevation to time it so that all twelve rounds land on target
simultaneously. That gives every gun the firepower of an entire battery of artillery. If each shell were loaded with cluster

munitions and dropped on a Chinese infantry company maneuvering in the open to attack our positions, all 150 enemy soldiers would die."

"Then why hasn't that been happening?" Vice President Sobo asked.

"It *has*," Cotler replied. "Over, and over, and over."

"Then why hasn't that stopped the Chinese?" she pressed.

"The Chinese have a lot of infantry companies," came the general's terse answer. He turned back to Baker. "Estimates are that we have killed—in five weeks of combat—one *million* Chinese troops. That's twice as many as they lost in the entire six-month Indian Campaign. The wounded probably number another three million. While some of those wounded return to duty after a couple of weeks to a month, they're still losing almost seven hundred thousand troops a week."

"But with the ports of Mobile, Gulfport, and San Diego fully functioning," Elizabeth Sobo read from her briefing book, "they're landing over four hundred thousand troops per *day*. They've landed seven million men in the South, one million on the West Coast, and a half million in Hawaii. And from estimates of troop strength in Cuba and the Canary Islands staging areas, and the number of transports our submarines have spotted in the central Pacific or rounding the Horn of Africa, they can sustain that landing rate for some time to come."

"But not forever," Cotler objected. "That's where our fixed defenses affect the equation. The ratio of our KIAs to the Chinese is one-to-fifteen overall, but at the Savannah and Santee Rivers it was over one-to-*fifty*. And from what Dr. Leffler reports, the Chinese domestic political will to sustain those casualties will break long before their theoretical military limit is reached."

"Is that your plan?" Sobo asked. "For Chinese domestic political dissatisfaction after ten years of war to grow so great that they just give *up*? If that's your plan, General Cotler, you'd better inform the president, because it seemed to me that we have all along been talking about *winning* this thing militarily, not politically!"

Cotler was not in a good mood. He was the senior general

in the United States armed forces being called to task by a former trial lawyer turned Congresswoman. But he knew his place in the democratic system. *Or does he?* Bill wondered as he saw the man's jaw grind. "Madam Vice President," Cotler said, pausing to wring the animosity from his tone, "to kill one million Chinese soldiers in mobile, open-country warfare, we would sustain losses something on the order of one-to-five, one-to-four, or one-to-three. That's *assuming* we can give ground and fight defensively!" His ire was bubbling over again, and he took a deep breath. "Instead of 67,000 dead and 192,000 wounded, we'd have lost two or three *hundred* thousand dead, *three* times that number wounded, and *half* our stocks of armored fighting vehicles. *And* we'd be in exactly the same positions we find ourselves in today. But by forcing the Chinese to breach those defensive lines through Atlanta and along the Savannah and Santee Rivers, we've made the best use of the terrain *and* of the current state of military technology."

"And if making the best use of terrain and current military technology isn't enough?" Elizabeth asked.

"Then we lose," Cotler answered with finality.

A chill descended on the room that left Bill Baker fighting quivers. He steadied his voice before he opened his mouth to speak. "But just like the Chinese have a finite number of troops they're willing to expend, we have a finite amount of territory that we can trade. Mile by mile, they're seizing our land, our resources and our industrial base. About five percent of our population—thirteen million people—got trapped in traffic jams and are now in Chinese hands. Some of those traffic jams, I might remind you, were caused by American MPs blocking roads so that our combat troops could escape the Chinese pincers." But Bill didn't need to tell Cotler. The scenes of fleeing civilians pleading to be let through road blocks had been replayed repeatedly on news networks. Bill yielded the floor to the general to respond in whatever way he chose.

Cotler heaved a deep sigh, looked around him at army staffers, then spoke with hands lying on the table clasped as if in prayer. "Mr. President, to withstand and decisively defeat a frontal assault by the entire Chinese army, we would first have to attrit them substantially, extend their supply lines from the Gulf Coast, and found our defenses on an impregnable line. That line would consist at a minimum of three heavily engineered defensive belts several miles in depth, each supported by preregistered, massed artillery. They would be linked by interconnected communications trenches running from line to line for rapid, covered reinforcement, resupply, and redeployment. There would be lateral defenses prepared along the natural terrain to channel Chinese penetration into killing fields as they advanced from the first line to the second, and the second to the third. The cost in materials and months of labor—the engineering, the concrete, the steel, and the millions of tons of earth to be moved—would require a commitment of resources greater than that ever expended by this nation or any other. And more than that, Mr. President, it would require the commitment—body and soul—to hold that line of every man and woman from the lowliest private to the commander in chief."

Cotler again looked around the table, but this time at the senior officers from the navy, air force, and marines. "It is the recommendation of the Joint Chiefs, Mr. President—with one exception—that we build that line. That we man it. And that we hold it no matter what the cost."

There were no challenges from the vice president. It was the president's turn to speak. "Which one of you disagrees?" Baker asked the senior officers.

"I do," air force General Latham replied.

"And how do you propose to win this war?" Baker asked.

"By the annihilation of Chinese forces with nuclear weapons," Latham answered unflinchingly.

Baker nodded and forced himself to revisit the option he rejected nearly every night as he lay in bed with a soundly sleeping Clarissa. He had seen so many maps and computer simulations of the nuclear campaign that it was easy to play the Wagnerian drama out in fast forward. Red pock marks along the coastline of the United States proliferated within weeks to number in the tens of thousands. The plague dug ever deeper inland as missile defenses were eroded away by nuclear fire. In the end, two or three months into Armageddon, "America" consisted of little more than a federal government redoubt—currently under construction in Omaha, Nebraska—protected by her remaining few thousand surface-to-air missiles. Baker imagined rising to the surface of that bastion to view the nighttime sky from some medieval turret or battlement. In his mind, the horizon would glow red from a hundred artificial dawns. The ring of fire from nuclear-tipped defensive missiles and nuclear-tipped attackers would contract ever nearer by the hour until "America" finally ceased to exist.

The president turned back to Cotler and asked, "Where do we build that defensive line?"

Cotler nodded at a technician, who put a map on the wall screen. "Even with maximum effort, it'll take us two or three months to build," he said. Baker was focused on the triple strand of thin blue lines that ran up the Potomac and Occoquan Rivers through the Civil War battlefields of Manassas. They looped around Dulles Airport before again tracking the Potomac along the Maryland-Virginia border west from Whites Ferry.

"Can we hold the Chinese south of Washington for three months?" Baker asked.

Cotler could only shrug.

"Let's bring III Corps back to the east," Baker proposed.

"But their stores just arrived in Southern California," Secretary Moore pointed out. "The 1st Cav and 1st Armored are two days away from step-off on an offensive designed to pin the Chinese on the coast."

"Bring 'em back," Bill ordered. "I and II Corps will just have to hold. If they need help, take it from X Corps farther up the coast."

Clarissa lay in Baker's bed, watching the press conference on TV and eating popcorn.

"As I said," Baker replied to a reporter's question, "the army's plans for fighting this war from fixed defensive positions are undergoing a thorough, bottoms-up review. I would expect that we will soon shift to a battle plan that places greater emphasis on our forces' superior mobility."

The same reporter had a follow-up question. "I know I'm the one who asked you about our plans—and thank you for answering, Mr. President—but don't you think the Chinese might learn something militarily useful from your reply?"

"Only if they believe I answered your question truthfully," Baker said with a twinkle in his eye.

Clarissa—and the reporters crowding the White House briefing room—laughed.

It was the only light moment in an increasingly dark, accusatory confrontation. "Is it true that you have written off the West Coast to concentrate on saving the Philadelphia Naval Shipyard?" and "Is it true that we have suffered over a quarter million U.S. troops killed?" were two typical questions that Bill flatly denied. He grew less congenial, shorter in his replies, and even began to ignore questions he didn't like by simply pointing at the next reporter. He was angry by the end, and even though he had just said, "I'll take two or three more questions," he stormed out on hearing the first.

"As I'm sure you heard, Mr. President, earlier tonight on CNN your ex-wife suggested that you are keeping your daughter in a combat unit so that you can fade the political heat from American parents whose own children are also in the army. Mrs. Roberts asserted that, so long as your daughter remains in combat—or if, God forbid, she is seriously wounded, killed, or captured—you are immunized against charges that you are insensitive to the plight of . . ."

Bill turned and left the podium mid-sentence to a torrent of shouts of, "Mr. President! Mr. President!"

"That bitch!" Clarissa cried out when Bill entered. He had come straight from the briefing room. His face was still coated with pancake makeup. He tore his jacket off and yanked at his tie. Clarissa tried to massage his shoulders from behind, but he recoiled from her contact. She said, trying to sound soothing, "I don't know how they can ask questions like that."

"Did you know?" Bill asked accusingly. "About Rachel's interview on CNN?"

Clarissa shrugged. "It was all over the news. Do you mean nobody told you?"

"No! And I'm starting to wonder what *other* things people aren't telling me!"

Clarissa was instantly on guard. "Like what?" she asked with growing trepidation.

But it was nothing more than anger, fatigue, and paranoia talking. She wrapped her arms around his neck and kissed him, then led him easily to the bed. There, she was in charge. He followed her gentle commands and forgot, for a moment, the worries and strains that consumed his life.

When Clarissa fell asleep, Bill rose, dressed in jeans, and roamed the halls of the White House. Even in the early hours of the morning, people worked. He stuck his head inside offices just long enough to disrupt everything, then moved on, ending up in the empty Oval Office. A locked drawer in his desk contained unread reports. He hadn't reviewed any of the day's mounting pile, which he laid on his blotter pad, but his computer screen lit when he sat. He always carried the remote in his pocket at the Secret Service's request. They—and only they—knew where he was, and they knew all the time.

He had only one message that his personal computer thought he should read. The computer's program had been written by Dr. Richard Fielding, a brilliant artificial intelligence professor from MIT and now Director of the CIA. It wasn't surprising, therefore, that the program had decided that it was Fielding's message that he should read.

Bill had been so impressed with Fielding's broad-ranging intellect that he had appointed him the head of his intelligence agency. It was only over time that Fielding had become the man Bill trusted most.

The computer screen flashed, "Call Holding." The ID showed that the call was from Fielding. Bill said, "Answer," and Fielding appeared. "Up late again, are we?" the CIA director asked from Bill's computer monitor.

"There's a good movie on," Bill replied.

The smile Fielding flashed faded quickly. "I'd like to talk to you, Mr. President," he said.

Bill shrugged. "I'm all ears."

"I mean in person."

The president arched his brow. "I'll be here," he responded.

"I'm on the way," Fielding said, and the screen went black.

Bill noticed a pile of documents that required action. He initialed, initialed, and initialed, then was asked to sign something. On careful reading he found that his signature would purportedly authorize the quartering of troops in private homes. *Isn't there something in the constitution about that?* he thought. He searched the Constitution on the computer. It was Article III in the Bill of Rights. "No soldier shall, in time of peace, be quartered in any house without the consent of the owner, nor in time of war but in a manner to be prescribed by law."

He was no lawyer, but this was clearly "in time of war," and there was no law passed by Congress of which he was aware. He scrawled across the top of the document, "UNCONSTITUTIONAL."

Bill then began to scan the accumulated reports. They ranged in importance from the trivial to the monumental. Fears of an imminent poultry shortage in one thirty-page memo gave way to a dry, three-line report that Chinese scouts had been checking beach gradients in New Brunswick Province, Canada, just north of the undefended Maine border. Doing paperwork for Bill was like the old adage about flying: hours of boredom interrupted by moments of stark terror.

Distribution of food. Relocation inland of plant and equipment. Protests by Virginians about the demolition of towns and cities when the Chinese were still in South Carolina. Dwindling war stocks in the Atlantic States, bulging depots in untouched Louisiana and Texas, and the key to their efficient redistribution: holding I-40, which split Tennessee west-to-east.

•　•　•

Richard Fielding gently shook the president awake. Bill swung his feet to the floor as if caught sleeping on the job. He looked to the window to confirm that it was still dark. Several times, he had spent the night in his chair.

"You're not getting enough sleep," Fielding advised.

"I was just taking one of those power naps you swear by," Bill replied, still trying to collect his thoughts.

The CIA director pulled a chair around Bill's desk and slumped into it. He bore no files, photos, or papers of any kind. He crossed one leg over the other one and wrapped his hands around his knee.

"Bill," Fielding said paternally, "what I'm about to tell you is going to make you very angry. But you've got to hold that anger in and not let anybody see it, because what I'm about to say you cannot legally know." Bill was already angry in anticipation, but he nodded. Fielding glanced at the door, which he had closed after entering, and cleared his throat. "The FBI has photos of Clarissa Leffler romantically cavorting with a Chinese fellow about a decade ago while she was a graduate student in Beijing."

Bill's anger flared white hot. "They have absolutely *no* . . . !"

"He was a colonel in Chinese army intelligence," Fielding interrupted. "A 'recruiter,' in the parlance. A recruiter of foreign agents."

The news hurt Bill, because it would be used to hurt Clarissa. He felt deflated. "What a crock of shit. The fact that some sleaze seduced a twenty-five-year-old graduate student who was ten thousand miles from home doesn't make her a traitor!"

Fielding shook his head. "No, it doesn't. But the sad fact of life is, in these times, I wouldn't clear her to work at Langley in any job whatsoever. Not in a million years. It would be too risky. And it looks doubly bad because it was Art Dodd who hired her. He's under a cloud of suspicion of his own ever since his meeting in Geneva with the Chinese minister of trade—Han Zhemin's father—two years ago."

"But that fuck Asher is just using all this to try to get at me!" Bill snapped. "He's going to . . . to ruin her." Bill rose and paced behind his chair. "He'll leak it to the press."

"No," Fielding remarked, "he won't. It's been filed under seal with the DC Court of Appeals in support of his National Secrecy Act subpoena granting him surveillance rights inside the White House. It'll probably end up at the Supreme Court."

Bill sank back into his chair. Asher finally had his suspect. A way to stick his big nose under the tent. "That son of a bitch," Bill said, looking up at Fielding. "So how did *you* hear about Asher's report if it's under seal?"

"I never reveal sources who have demanded anonymity, Mr. President. They cease being sources. Besides, the more important question is not who my source is. It's who Hamilton Asher's source was for ten-year-old surveillance photos taken in Beijing."

Bill narrowed his eyes in focused thought, then looked up at his most trusted security advisor. His meaning was clear. The source was Chinese.

Fielding rose and stood facing Bill. "And remember what I said about you not telling anybody any of this?" Fielding asked. "That means Dr. Leffler, in particular. Do not tell Dr. Leffler that she's under suspicion of treason during time of war."

"*What?* And why the hell not?" Bill demanded.

Fielding frowned but didn't shrink from Bill's glare. "Because, sir, I will turn us both in for having violated the National Secrecy Act," he replied. Both men's jaws were firmly set. "I learned long ago never to trust anyone. Anyone. You should get some rest, Mr. President. Good night." He turned and left Bill alone.

Bill returned to his residential quarters and crawled into bed next to Clarissa. She was sleeping on her side facing him. He lay there studying her face, her lips, her soft eyes . . . which opened suddenly, then closed quickly, jarring Bill. It hadn't been the bleary, semiwakeful gaze of a person roused from sleep. She had been awake all along, and after a moment she covered too quickly by pretending to awaken, yawning, seeing him awake, then quickly kissing him passionately—aggressively—soon pinning him to the bed with her body.

FLORENCE, SOUTH CAROLINA
November 11 // 0945 Local Time

The morning was cold, Stephie thought, but not so cold that it froze men to inaction. Plus, after five miles of march, most had unzipped their gear and removed woolen caps. She worked her way back down the ditch from the point man, inspecting each soldier along the way. All lay prone beside a county road with weapons shouldered at pavement level. The veterans seemed ready, but resigned and fatalistic. The cherries, in stark contrast, were petrified.

Three weeks after the mass influx of replacements and a dozen field training exercises on company, battalion and even brigade levels, the commander of the 41st Infantry Division had reported to the Pentagon that his unit was combat ready. Staff Sergeant Stephanie Roberts disagreed.

"You know what to do if we get ambushed?" Stephie asked a frightened female replacement.

She had to lick her chapped lips twice and swallow hard before she could answer. "Go to ground?" she tentatively replied.

"Okay, but where?" Stephie asked in a steady, quiet voice. "In the middle of the road?" The cherry shook her head, and her helmet flopped from side to side. "On the side?" Stephie coached her. The replacement nodded, and her helmet flopped back and forth. "That's right, but which side?" Stephie asked as she took the woman's helmet off to tighten its liner.

The cherry didn't know the answer to the platoon sergeant's question and grew so upset that her eyes watered. She finally shrugged pathetically.

"We're gonna advance in column," Stephie explained in a quiet voice. "If they open fire right on you, go to the side of the road away from the enemy. If they open up on any other part of the platoon, go *toward* the side that the fire's coming from, move off the road, and try to flank the ambushers. Same thing if they fire defilade straight down the road, only try to follow the others to one side or the other. After you clear the road, you've gotta get up and maneuver, understand? There may not be anybody there to organize the attack. You've gotta do it on your own initiative in an ambush. Somebody's pinned down, and it's your job to counterattack the ambushers. Every second counts, so don't freeze up. Your buddies' lives depend on you, just like yours depends on them. Understand?"

The bareheaded cherry nodded, self-consciously placing wayward strands of matted hair behind her ears. "What if the ambushers are on *both* sides of the road?" she asked. "Should I just follow everybody else?"

There probably won't be anybody to follow, Stephie thought, but she said, "Just get off the road and return fire." Stephie replaced the helmet on her head, put her hands on the private's thick, Kevlar-padded shoulders, and gave an approving nod like a mother sending her child off to school. "You'll do fine. Just don't freeze up. You're gonna be scared. That's natural. Everybody's scared. But the thing is you've still gotta maneuver and fire your weapon. Understand? You may feel so sick with fear that you've gotta throw up. That's okay. Go ahead. But you've got to fight. You've got to fire your weapon at the enemy. Understand?"

The woman nodded again. The short, jerking motions didn't shake her helmet loose. Stephie moved on to the next guy. The large African-American machine gunner lay on his side holding a cross made from leather shoelaces to his lips and muttered a prayer with his eyes jammed shut.

A crackle overhead sent Stephie flat to her stomach at the bottom of the roadside ditch. The machine gunner's eyes shot open when the first shell exploded two hundred meters behind the last man in their platoon. The blast wasn't the stunning body blow of heavy 155 or 175 mm guns, but part of the steady rain of light artillery that began bracketing the road behind them. They could, however, still kill a standing man at that range. Stephie raised her head to ensure that everyone was down and saw only one helmet up. It was their platoon leader, Lieutenant John Burns, who nodded at Stephie. She nodded back.

Telephone wires alongside the road behind them danced and fell. Roadside mailboxes in the rural outskirts of the small town were blown into the expansive front lawns of houses set well back from the road. Tree branches on the wooded lots were clipped from trunks and crashed to the ground. All the windows along the front of one ranch-style, one-story house imploded from the concussive force of a near miss.

When the barrage was not adjusted up the road toward their platoon's position, Stephie knew that they hadn't been spotted. The blind, indirect fire was either random "H&I"—harassment and interdiction—or it was blocking the road ahead to screen the flanks of some maneuvering and therefore vulnerable Chinese unit.

A fireball lit the sky behind them as a shell exploded high in a tall pine. One of the prone soldiers at the rear of the platoon's column began to curse in shouts. "Oh, shit! Goddamn! *Aw! God! Ah! Ah!*" John rose. Stephie cringed as she watched him sprint down the ditch. Shrapnel skipped at high speed along the road at Stephie's eye level. The metal pole from a basketball goal directly across the street rang like a bell. John dropped safely beside the wounded man, who clenched his left calf like a cramping runner.

John pulled his combat knife, and the cherry's screams grew to howls. "No-o-o! No! No! No!" A veteran pinned the wounded man to the ground and grabbed his flailing hands while John split his trouser leg from boot to knee. John began to probe the wound with the sharp tip of his black knife. He was hurrying, Stephie knew, to get the white-hot shrapnel out of the guy's leg before it burned deep into the soldier's muscle and bone. The remainder of the brief barrage consisted of steady shrieking by the wounded soldier punctuated by thundering, body-clapping booms.

Both the barrage and the screaming seemed to end at the same time. A medic had administered morphine to the man. Stephie rose and moved down the ditch toward John, stopping at each soldier to ask if he or she were okay. Many of the cherries were too frightened to say anything in response, forcing Stephie to demand a spoken, intelligible reply. That was how she found Third Platoon's most serious casualty.

The woman—a medic—stared blankly at Stephie. At first, Stephie thought the woman was simply frozen in terror. "Are you all *right?*" Stephie repeated testily. The woman looked

Stephie straight in the eye, but said nothing. "*Answer* me!" Stephie demanded. Still, nothing. Stephie dropped to her knees and turned the medic onto her stomach. She flattened the fabric of the unresisting woman's BDUs and searched up and down for punctures.

"What are you doing?" a male cherry asked from the slowly gathering crowd.

Animal answered for Stephie. "She's checking for wounds."

Stephie could feel the medic begin to shake. "You're gonna be okay," she said as she rolled the woman over and searched her front. "It's all right," Stephie assured the replacement. "I don't see anything wrong. You're gonna be fine. Just relax. Take it easy. Can you tell me where it hurts?" The medic's breaths were coming in shallow pants, and her face had grown deathly pale.

"Where is it?" Animal said angrily as he patted up and down the medic's thighs and pelvis and checked his hands for blood, finding none. John appeared and knelt at the woman's head. He removed her helmet. A dozen bobby pins held her dirty blond hair neatly tucked into place. John lifted her head into his lap. Her eyes were now glassy and unfocused. "Where the fuck *is* it?" Animal raged as he searched.

John's raised fingertips smeared with the faintest tinge of pink. The wounded medic began to convulse. She bucked and emitted a horrible gurgling sound. They turned her over. Animal forced her jaws open and inserted the handle of his knife into her mouth to keep it open. With his fingers, he fished the tongue that she had swallowed from her throat. John pulled the medic's hair from the base of her neck. A red welt no bigger than a mosquito bite rose on her smooth, white skin. At the center was a tiny pinprick from which seeped thick, pinkish fluid.

"She's stopped breathing!" one of the cherries shouted. They rolled her onto her back, removed Animal's combat knife, and began mouth-to-mouth resuscitation. One cherry frantically unzipped her flak jacket and began pumping the center of her chest. John cradled her head in both hands and looked at Stephie and Animal. Even as the others continued their lifesaving efforts, John pressed the now still medic's eyelids closed.

The replacements gave up one by one. "What the hell happened, sir?" one asked John. They all waited, but he didn't answer. Stephie watched him closely. He held the lifeless girl's head in his lap with both hands as if it were a priceless treasure, not a corpse.

"Shrapnel splinter," Stephie answered for John. "Caught her right under the helmet. Must've gone straight into her . . ." She cut short her unscientific autopsy report and again looked at John, who sat there unmoving. "All right!" Stephie said loudly as she rose to her feet. "We're bunched up! Get back to your positions and prepare to move out! Let's *go*!" She ordered Dawson to take charge of the casualties. The man wounded in the calf lay limp and exhausted as a medic bandaged his bloody leg. "Take turns with a fireman's carry," she suggested. "Head back to the trucks at the rally point." A male soldier hooked two pistol belts together, which he would drape over his shoulders and in which his wounded comrade would ride piggyback.

"What about her?" a cherry asked, looking down at the dead medic.

Stephie replied, "Body bags have handles in the corners."

The man seemed upset by her answer. The woman wasn't dead to him yet. Stephie dug into the medic's first aid kit and handed the man a compact, tightly folded plastic square. After hesitating a moment, he began unfolding the black bag.

Stephie turned to John and said, "We gotta get moving." John lay the woman's head on the ground with the greatest of care and rose slowly. Soldiers lifted her body by the armpits and ankles and laid her in the long bag. "Recover her ammo and other gear," Stephie ordered. The men hesitated before complying. Reluctantly, they laid her medical kit, magazines, and grenades on the ground beside the bag. "Leave those for graves registration," Stephie instructed as one cherry fished out a sealed letter the medic had addressed and stamped. The replacements would soon learn the drill. When all the usable gear—including canteen—had been salvaged, the pale medic disappeared from toe to head to the tearing

sound of a zipper. In death, her face was peaceful and pretty.
One young soldier who must have known her was crying.

The platoon re-formed in the middle of the road and continued toward town as Dawson's Second Squad trudged off
in the opposite direction. John had kept Dawson's weapons
crews, meaning that the short-handed platoon still numbered
forty-eight troops, most raw and green. Their orders were to
enter the town and probe for contact with the Chinese. If the
enemy cut and ran, they were a patrol trying to fix American
positions. If the Americans were forced back, they reported
having struck something hard. Both sides lost people to glean
intelligence of fleeting tactical value.

Twice in the next half mile, their platoon's point man—a
veteran from Third Squad—went to ground. Every man and
woman was wired tight and scared to their limit. People dove
into the ditch along the right side of the road as if their life
depended on speed, which it did. Stephie watched the road
ahead through the point man's camera. The first time he went
to ground he zoomed in on a hungry dog rummaging through
an overturned trash can. The second time she saw nothing at
all. Both were false alarms. The cherries cursed as they
brushed the dirt from their gear. The tension was released.
Maybe they wouldn't make contact, the cherries thought.

The tension built again with every meter their patrol came
closer to the Chinese. In half a mile, half of the cherries and
an even greater percentage of the veterans were visibly shaking. When an electric frisson of fear charged through Stephie,
she surreptitiously checked her hands. They quivered noticeably. It was a tremor that spread like an Ice Age throughout
her body.

When the point man scampered off the road a third time,
four dozen troops dove into the ditch. There was an annoying
rattle as weapons were seated to shoulders. Their firepower
was such that each soldier—alone—could be critical to the
survival of every other soldier in the platoon, and each understood that fact. Each could be called upon to fire to the
end as the Chinese overran them, or ordered to rise up and
storm the enemy.

"If we all just do our jobs," Stephie prayed they had ab-

sorbed. She had spent time—one on one—in actual conversations with each new soldier, relentlessly pounding them. *"We don't let each other down. We stick together. Everybody together. Nobody lets his buddy down. That's what we expect from you,"* she would say, and then, for the capper, *"and that, whatever your name is, is what we offer you."*

The eyes of about half of the cherries—male and female—teared right up, and their voices thickened as they pledged their lives in trembling, nasally tones.

"I got movement!" came the point man's voice.

Fear shot through Stephie's every nerve ending, assaulting her bodily. Her ears popped. Her head rushed. Her lungs froze. Her throat burned. Her stomach churned. And her limbs shook with full-body fear.

"Did they see us?" John whispered over the MES.

Stephie cringed at every word spoken over the radio, even her own.

"Negative, negative," came point's reply. "We're good. Out."

Stephie's earphones suddenly began emitting a steady beeping. Everybody's did. Enemy radio net operating in area. Probably not more than a few hundred meters. The tiny electronic warfare packs mounted to their shoulder straps didn't know what the Chinese were saying on their own digitally encrypted, wireless local area networks. They could, however, reliably tell you that their LAN was very, very close.

Two hundred meters ahead lay a strip center with a large, empty parking lot. Stephie keyed the platoon talk button. "Dig in. Dig in." She didn't identify herself. They all knew her voice.

John didn't countermand Stephie's order, and fifty shovels were pulled like swords from backpack sheaths. Stephie flipped the blade to ninety degrees and with grunts and all her might gave the earth a few, hard chops. Her example was soon followed by all within sight, as cherries redoubled their efforts.

The strip center had a video rental store, a bike shop, a children's hair salon, and a Chinese restaurant. Stephie's blade hit rocks eight inches below ground level. She didn't try to go deeper, but chopped and scraped to lengthen the scratch in the ground. The shopping center ahead was anchored by a chain grocery store. Stephie kept her eyes on the storefronts but saw nothing.

The first Chinese soldier appeared at the far corner of the strip center.

"Drop!" John snapped.

The Americans dropped. Not all at once, but within a second or two.

A long line of Chinese soldiers followed their point man. One by one, the soldiers in Third Platoon settled in behind weapons. Some were raised so quickly that Stephie worried they would be noticed by the Chinese, or that an idiot would accidentally loose a round. She keyed her mike and reminded them to, "Hold your fire."

The enemy soldiers were tense. But when they saw the Chinese characters on a sign outside the restaurant, they pointed and laughed until an officer started shouting. His voice was loud enough to carry the distance to the Americans as he berated troops, who came to parade-ground attention. They weren't nearly as professional as the Chinese troops Stephie had encountered before. The officer grabbed men, physically spread them out, and delivered a high-pitched scolding before the march finally resumed. It reminded Stephie more of a prewar field training exercise than a serious combat patrol.

So the Chinese have cherries too, she thought, calming.

John began assigning fires to targets over the radio, taking a risk with every word. "First Squad, you take the lead. Third Squad, the center. Fourth, you take the rear. Second Squad's machine gun, take out that officer, then fire at targets of opportunity. Commence firing when I open up. Out."

He gave the squad leaders time to relay more specific targeting down to their fire teams. The Chinese officer stood in the parking lot next to his radioman, watching his men instead of his front. His men were distracted by sights in display windows and were angrily rebuked by NCOs.

They're green, like us, Stephie thought. *Maybe greener.*

A second Chinese platoon fanned out across the open, concrete parking lot. John quickly reallocated the fires to include them. Stephie looked over her shoulder toward their rear.

"Listen up," she said when John was finished. "The rally point is the far side of that stream three-quarters of a mile back. The far side of the downed bridge. Rally there on command if we have to pull back fast."

That done, she turned her attention to the enemy. The hundred or so men had absolutely no cover in the parking lot and couldn't possibly dig in. Their CO was easy to pick out. He shouted unrelentingly at his troops. Stephie didn't speak a word of Chinese, but the order was clearly understood. They were all bunched up. Almost shoulder to shoulder. "*Spacing!*" the officer shouted. In soccer, bad spacing gave up goals. Here, the mistake doomed them.

John Burns fired a three-round burst

Every last man and woman in the platoon fired. Fifty weapons roared simultaneously. Display windows collapsed in avalanches of glass. Chinese soldiers spun, twisted, tossed their weapons in the air, and died. Twice, Stephie had targets blown out of her sights before she finally found one helpless, weaponless man crawling across the pavement.

Her first round struck him near his kidneys. He rolled over and frantically patted his side and waved his hands in air, not knowing what to do. Another Chinese soldier lay facedown on the concrete blindly firing his rifle above his head on full auto. Stephie's first shot knocked the rifle to the pavement. He grabbed his hand and might have lost a finger or two. Maimed and disarmed, he held his helmet to his head with his one good hand. Stephie's next shot glanced off his helmet and struck his shoulder. Her third shot struck his neck and killed him.

All eighty Chinese soldiers at the strip center lay grievously wounded before the first armored vehicles appeared. Five lightly armored, wheeled scouts with sharp-edged, amphibious hulls sped down the street just beyond the parking lot. Tracers from their 25 mm cannon streaked straight toward Stephie. Grenade-sized explosions tore sheets of asphalt from the road at face level, but four American missiles struck the first three vehicles. The fourth and fifth vehicles retreated behind the screen of smoke from their comrades' burning vehicles. Several American infantrymen fired ballistic rockets, but the unguided missiles all missed. The scouts roared away down the county road past a service station on their way toward threatening the Americans' rear.

John shouted orders over the radio. "Chambers! Take Third Squad with your and Dawson's weapons crews through the woods to the road behind us and nail that fucking armor!" Stephie twisted around to confirm that they complied. The dozen soldiers rose and sprinted through the trees toward the rear. The residential street behind them was barely visible through the thin stand of slender pine trees.

Flames sparked from dozens of trunks as the two scout vehicles opened fire into the woods with explosive shells from their turret-mounted automatic cannon.

She could no longer see Third Squad, which had gone to ground.

"I'm goin' to check on Third Squad!" Stephie shouted over the platoon net.

"Stay where you are!" John ordered, but Stephie was already up and running. "Stephie!" he shouted as she headed toward the blistering swath of fire. Pops of flame randomly blasted tree trunks and limbs. She dropped to the ground just ahead of raking fire from a 25 mm cannon, whose glancing blows off trees showered her with stinging splinters. But the *whoosh* of American antitank missiles and solid *thumps* of shaped charges ended the rain of cannon fire.

She scampered forward through the trees, stooped and low until she saw—on either side of the smoking hulks—a dozen assault rifles blazing straight toward her. Bullets snapped through brush, creased bark, and zipped by her head as she flattened herself onto the ground. The Chinese armored cavalrymen had dismounted before their rides had been hit. They were well led—leapfrogging by fire and maneuver—on a headlong charge into the woods.

The two machine guns accompanying Chambers' Third Squad blazed not twenty feet behind Stephie. Their stupendous roar fried her nerves. Their grazing fire streaked directly over her head. They were close enough that she could feel their coughing heat.

"He-e-e-ey!" she screamed into the platoon net. *"I'm in your line of fire!"*

"We got you!" she heard John shout. "Just keep your head down!" came his unnecessary warning.

The two M-60s ate through hundred-round belts of full metal jacket 7.62 mm ammo. The sheets of lead buzzed just inches above Stephie's body. The cutting sounds of high-velocity rounds were ominously audible even over the staccato roar of the two awesome guns.

As she lay on her stomach with the back of her helmet to the machine guns, she saw movement just ahead. A Chinese soldier was crawling forward through the brush. Stephie risked rolling onto her side to slowly raise her rifle. All she could make out behind a tree not fifteen feet away was a bent knee under camouflage trousers. The machine guns behind her had switched to more selective six-round bursts. With her M-16 parallel to the ground, she flicked the selector switch to "semi" and aimed straight at the man's knee. A coiled cord from his radio handset dangled directly in her line of sight. She could hear the man blathering breathlessly—panicked—in Chinese.

Her rifle bucked. Her shot cleaved the man's kneecap and shattered his knee. His head and shoulders came into view as he buckled in pain and screamed at the top of his lungs. She fired again and knocked his helmet off. The dazed man arched his neck to look straight at Stephie's muzzle.

When he closed his eyes, she blew a hole in the center of his face.

The machine guns ceased fire. The sound of thudding footfalls approached. A line of American infantrymen stormed past Stephie toward the killing field ahead. The soldiers from Third Squad charged through the woods and fired point-blank into the semi-living and the dead until they had "swept" the woods by killing all of the surviving Chinese.

Sergeant Chambers helped lift Stephie to her feet. Tiny wood splinters protruded from the camo fabric covering her body armor. She winced at the annoying pain from the tiny splinters embedded in her unarmored arms and legs. She rose and wandered over to the Chinese soldier whom she had shot at close range. His body bore insurance holes from Third Squad's sweep of the woods. From the handset of the man's field radio, which looked like a green plastic telephone, came shouted queries or orders urgently spoken in Chinese. Stephie picked up the handset and keyed the button in the center.

"Hey!" she shouted to the man on the other end. "Get the fuck outa my country!"

Several of the returning men and women from Third Squad laughed in a hyperactive, post-survival agitation. After a long pause, they all heard a tinny voice over the radio shouting in Chinese.

"Come'n get it, motherfucker!" Stephie shouted, her finger on the talk button.

An M-16 fired from just beside Stephie, startling everyone. John Burns had blasted the radio transceiver into pieces. "Everybody outa here! On the double! We're pulling back!"

He glared at Stephie, then took off.

After the others raced past, Stephie caught up with John. "Why are we withdrawing?" she asked. His jaw was set, and he didn't answer. "John! We were supposed to hold till we were pushed off our ground! We haven't been pushed one inch! We're just giving up ground!" She grabbed his arm and yanked him.

"We're pulling back!" he shouted, and he pushed her and began to run. He motioned for soldiers to hurry with vigorous jabs of his finger. When they emerged from the woods, the platoon was in full retreat. Medics hurriedly bandaged flesh wounds. A man hopped out down the road on one good leg with the support of a buddy. Chambers appeared with a body bag slung between four laboring men.

"Who was it?" Stephie asked in the past tense and the impersonal pronoun.

"A new guy," came Chambers's reply.

Stephie nodded.

Despite the losses, some soldiers—having survived their first blooding—gave each other high fives.

Stephie chased after and fell in beside John as they brought up the rear at a trot. Behind them, the shopping center was littered with Chinese dead. Third Platoon had lost only one killed but had wiped out an entire enemy infantry company. No other Chinese units were in sight.

"John, our orders were to hold our ground!" Stephie said.

"I called in the contact," he responded.

"Did they countermand our orders?" she asked.

"I'm the tactical commander," he replied. Like the captain of a ship, there was only one tactical commander, who under army regs was given the final say. When they rounded a bend and could no longer see the smoking battlefield, they followed their platoon onto the better footing of the road. "John, our *orders* were . . . !"

Without warning, the woods from which they had just emerged exploded. Everyone dove back into the ditch as heavy rockets streaked down out of the sky. They plummeted at high speeds and extremely steep angles. Concentric rings of white vapor expanded at high speed from the bursts and popped Stephie's ears. The waves of over-pressure nearly brought tears of pain to John's eyes, whose hands were clamped over his punctured eardrums. A dozen crushing explosions felled trees and torched dry brush.

When the last echoes of the heavy barrage rattled through the trees into the distance, Stephie found John's eyes boring angrily into her. "What did you think that guy was doing on the radio?" John snapped with a fury that Stephie found surprising.

"Well, I didn't think he was calling in fire on his own *position*!" Stephie countered.

"Nobody said that he did!" John shouted. "That scout squadron leader prob'ly just called in his coordinates and told them that he was in contact! Their fire controller decided to waste his own people to get at us! But god*dammit*, Stephie, the point is, do you wanta *live*? Do you want to *survive* this war?"

"I wanta *win* this war, John!" she replied. "I wanta fuckin' *win*!"

CAPITOL HILL, WASHINGTON
November 15 // 0900 Local Time

Bill Baker's entourage cut a campaign-style swath through the crowds of congressmen, staffers, tourists, and media gathered in the high-ceilinged rotunda. The onlookers' applause reverberated nicely for the television microphones as Bill smiled and waved into the bright camera lights. He shook hands, pointed, nodded, and winked, working the crowd before briefing Congress in closed, executive session on his plans for the defense of Washington.

He had chosen to give the briefing to the leadership of the House and Senate in person and by coming to the Hill. In part, it was calculated political symbolism meant to shore up support in an increasingly hostile Congress. But even more importantly, Bill had in recent weeks felt a growing sense of obligation to obey the solemn and now ancient rituals of American democracy. To him, delivering a report—in person—to America's elected representatives on the defense of the capital required a trip to Capitol Hill.

Bill worked the rope line two-handed, shaking hands both low and held high over the shoulders of people in the front row. He could barely make out the faces of the people he greeted against the glare of dozens of television lights held even higher. The unblinking, hard stares of the Secret Service agents, however, seemed untroubled. A half dozen of them surrounded Bill within inches of him but never touched him or obstructed his progress. They carried their heavy coats draped over their forearms on the unseasonably warm day. Their armored coats covered pistols that the agents held drawn, cocked, and pointed at the chests of men, women, and children with whom Baker exchanged pleasantries.

When Bill came to the end of the rope, the faces of the people who greeted him were familiar. "How are you doing, Mr. President?" came the salutation from a Republican senator whose hand Bill shook.

"Well, I'm getting by, Jim," Bill replied before moving on to shake the hands of the junior members of Congress.

"You gutless bastard!" came the shout of a Democratic

congressman from Florida. The noise and commotion in the rotunda quieted noticeably as everyone's head turned to the man, including the watchful gaze of half a dozen Secret Service agents. Bill stepped up to the seething man, whose face was set in a sneer. "You come up here smiling like you're at some goddammed campaign stop and meanwhile my district and a hundred thousand of my constituents are in Chinese hands!"

A new person—Frank Adams, Bill's chief of staff—appeared at his side. "We're late, Mr. President." He grabbed Bill's elbow and tried to lead him away from the ugly scene.

Bill pulled free. "Listen, this is a terrible time for America," Bill reasoned, "and especially for our countrymen who find themselves trapped behind enemy lines. I pledge to you, their elected representative, that I will do everything in my power to aid them and to . . . !"

"Oh, bullshit!" the man interrupted. "You really *'feel their pain'*, don't ya? You goddamned traitor! While my people are bein' worked to death in slave labor camps, *you're* shackin' up with a Chinese-sympathizin' *whore!*"

Baker gave him a hard punch, which landed squarely on the congressman's face. A hundred flashes went off in the harsh glow of the television lights. Cameramen jostled for a better view. The man collapsed into the arms of his colleagues, and the Secret Service took over from there. The coats came off their arms to reveal not pistols but Uzis. A dozen new agents appeared from out of nowhere and roughly parted the shocked and stirring crowd. They expertly whisked Bill into a nearby office. By the time the door was closed behind him, Bill's instant of satisfaction at decking the congressman had given way to sickness and regret over the act.

No one said a word. The office was filled with people, but they were all stone-faced and armed. They didn't look at Bill. They looked at the doors. They listened to their earphones. Some watched video screens worn instead of wristwatches. Outside, there was commotion. Bill could hear loud speeches rife with indignation and condemnation being served up to dozens of cable news networks. Clarissa's name came up several times. Bill winced each time he heard it. Shouts of "Down here!" by journalists and "Halt!" by Secret Service agents descended into fruitless requests by the press for access to their president, all of it caught on camera.

But inside the office—in the eye of the storm—there was total silence.

The agent in charge nodded at one of his men, who unlocked and opened the door. A gush of angry noise poured through the narrow crack. Frank Adams slipped inside and then pressed the door closed with his back.

He heaved a deep sigh, looked at Bill, and arched his brow. "Well, I just spoke to Tom Leffler. He's canceled the briefing." Bill's eyes closed, and his head drooped. He nodded slowly. "Oh, and it gets worse," Adams reported. "I asked the leadership—the *Republican* leadership—to have Capitol Hill police clear the halls and provide a way for you to get out of the Capitol without being molested, but they refused. You're gonna have to do your exit in front of God and everybody."

"We can get you out of here, sir," suggested his special agent in charge.

"I'm not going to exit this building through any tunnels," Bill declared.

"Keep your chin up," Adams advised.

Bill squared his shoulders, set his jaw, and tugged his suit into place. Adams opened the door to a dozen flashes and the blazing lights of television cameras. Bill followed the agent in charge down the hall amid his phalanx of bodyguards.

"Is it true that you're having an affair with the Speaker's daughter?" came the shouts.

"Is Clarissa Leffler a Chinese agent?" drew Bill's angry stare.

But the reporters' questions were nothing compared to the gauntlet that Bill ran next. As he turned a corner, the corridor was lined with congressional staffers and aides, who began to "boo" their president. Bill stared at them and felt a rush of fear—of panic—as the young aides and secretaries practically doubled over with the effort, wearing faces set in angry masks. The change had come over them almost instantly. One waved a sign over his head with a hastily scrawled "Shame!" written on it. All of it was, he knew, being broadcast live to

the people he was supposed to lead in a war for survival of
their nation.

CIVILIAN HEADQUARTERS, ATLANTA
November 15 // 1330 Local Time

Han Zhemin watched the American television coverage of
Bill Baker's punch in slow motion from half a dozen different
camera angles. He felt a mixture of intrigue and bemusement.
No one did scandals as well as the American press. Within
minutes, the networks had come to common agreement on a
name—"Clarissagate"—though each now possessed its own
proprietary title screen. Most of the graphics, which signaled a
return to the coverage following brief commercial interrup-
tions, were variations on the same them: a montage of photos
of the president and his mistress superimposed over the presidential seal or the White House. And every comment by
anyone willing to appear on screen—of which the number
seemed limitless—interrupted regular programming as "breaking news" and led to a rehash by expert commentators, who
summarized what had happened so far in the hours-old scandal.

He changed channels and saw stock footage of the attractive young woman in a strapless evening gown at a fund-
raiser for her father. Coincidentally, Han noted, the
fund-raiser had been held in the same city where Han now
sat. Nice shoulders and slender neck. Pretty face. Han smiled.

When he looked up, he saw Wu. Someone had let him into
Han's office unannounced. He stood beside his father's desk
staring at the television. He wore camouflage battle dress and
webbing that to Han—in the fleeting impression made by his
sudden appearance—made him look like a soldier. His features were still those of a child, unlined by worries or age.
But his back was straight. His shoulders broad. His hair was
shorn. And his face and neck were tanned.

Wu turned his attention to his seated father, who quickly
looked away. On television, an angry Tom Leffler stood before a cluster of microphones, and Han raised his TV's volume. ". . . nothing to say to him. If he has something to say

to me, he knows where to find me." The old man left the podium to a torrent of questions. "Can you still work with the president?" and "Has your daughter confirmed to you that she is now living at the White House?"

"Wu," Han said after muting the television, "we live in interesting times." The pictures switched to a sneering Bill Baker, whose car entered the White House gates with the president staring straight ahead and ignoring the clamoring reporters and flashing cameras. "You magnificent *bastard!*" Han shouted at the screen, laughing. "Fucking the daughter of the Speaker of the House!"

And you were always better than me, Han thought, but didn't say.

He handed Wu a memorandum authored, Wu read, by both Han *and* Wu. It was addressed to the prime minister and marked "TOP SECRET—EYES ONLY."

Han said, "Sign that at the top. If anyone asks if you actually saw or heard all those things, you should of course tell them that you did."

"But *none* of it is true!" Wu objected vehemently. "I didn't hear General Sheng plotting against the defense minister with the commander of the Beijing Military District!"

"That's really beside the point!" Han replied testily.

"You're trying to set Sheng up!" Wu accused. "But General Sheng isn't the one who has committed treason!"

Han glared at his son through squinted eyes. "Just what do you mean by that?" he asked coolly and in tones carefully measured to contain his outrage.

"General Sheng isn't a politician," Wu asserted. "He's a soldier."

"But the defense minister *is* a politician," Han replied. "He'll believe that Sheng is plotting a coup because that is what makes sense in his world. If the army wins the war, Sheng will be a political threat because he will be a national hero. Never mind that several *million* Chinese soldiers died in the process and that Sheng's brutality virtually destroyed the intangible spirit that makes America what it is! You've seen what Sheng is doing in those camps, Wu!"

"There have been partisan attacks," Wu justified half-heartedly.

Han cocked and shook his head. "What would you do," Han asked, "if *your* country were invaded? I know you better than you think. You secretly admire the Americans for every fanatical, suicidal partisan attack, don't you?"

Wu's head rose so quickly that Han's observation was confirmed. Wu's averted gaze merely completed the picture of a boy at war with himself.

"And so," a dejected Wu mumbled, "you plan to falsely accuse General Sheng of treason? To destroy him?"

Han smiled and unlocked a drawer electronically by pressing in a combination on a touchpad. "The facts," Han said, laying the report in front of Wu. "The numbers are summarized in the table at the top." Han waited while Wu read. Number of American civilians taken prisoner by the army. One million. Number of American civilians confirmed in labor battalions. Six hundred thousand. Number of American civilians confirmed killed in captivity. Forty thousand. Number of American civilians *estimated* killed in captivity. Three hundred thousand. "I can take you to the camps," Han offered.

Wu shook his head and in a daze took a pen from his father's desk and signed the top of the memorandum.

Good, Han thought. One less thing—Wu's trustworthiness—to worry about. Complicity made for good allies.

"Now," Han said, "any progress learning the identity of Sheng's spy in the White House?"

Wu stared at the pictures on television. In an old clip from some campaign victory, the president's mistress, then just a girl, stood beside her mother on a stage. "Clarissa Leffler" the caption read beneath the clear oval centered on her image. The rest of the picture was masked in a muted gray.

"Wu?" Han snapped impatiently, noting his son's fixed gaze. "If Sheng has someone highly placed in Baker's administration, she could be of incalculable intelligence value to him. She might just be *the* deciding factor in this war. Have you found out who she might be?" Han asked.

"What about her?" Wu asked, indicating Clarissa Leffler

on the television. "The American press is reporting charges that she is a Chinese sympathizer."

Han sat perfectly still. "The daughter of the Speaker of the House?" he asked. "President Baker's mistress? You think she is an army spy?"

"She's the head of the China Desk at the State Department," Wu ventured. "She has probably spent time in China. Studied there."

Han's mouth curled in a parody of a smile. Wu was guessing. He had nothing.

Han's reaction obviously angered Wu. "Have you had any contact with the Americans since your meeting with Baker in the Bahamas?" Wu asked brusquely.

"What?" Han asked in surprise both at the question and Wu's tone.

"Have you had any direct contact with the American government since your trip to the Bahamas?" Wu repeated.

"We're at war," Han replied. "Such things are difficult to arrange."

"You didn't answer my question," Wu noted.

"Who are you to ask me *anything*?" Han exploded. Wu didn't look away. He stared back, further infuriating Han.

"I am an officer in the Chinese army," Wu answered, heading for the door. He stopped and turned. "And treating with the enemy during time of war is treason."

Wu left Han, his heart pounding, sitting in shocked silence at his desk.

GEORGE WASHINGTON PARKWAY
November 17 // 1015 Local Time

Clarissa had taken the George Washington Parkway from Washington through heavy construction traffic. Military policemen had blocked civilian autos for convoys of cement trucks headed out from the city. The outermost of the concentric rings of defenses were under construction twenty-five miles away. The engineers—working inward—had yet to fell the wine-colored maple trees lining the Potomac River to clear the way for the capital's last-ditch defenses.

She pulled into the stone-rimmed observation park. It offered a vantage that almost brought tears to her eyes. The rocky cliffs overlooked Georgetown. A lone oarsman plied the silky waters of the Potomac. She got out of her car into the crisp air of her home.

"They'll lay guns right on the city," Bill had said to her the night before with tears in his eyes. She looked across the narrow river. "Direct lines of sight to . . . everything. The Washington Monument. The Lincoln Memorial. They'll level the city if they breach our last line in Virginia and make it across the river. It'll be Stalingrad."

Her father sat on a stone wall looking across at Georgetown, both his and her alma mater. She noted that he wore the same coat, gloves, and hat—all black—that he had worn to her mother's funeral. She wondered if he'd even been shopping in the two years since. As she neared, she saw that he was muttering to himself. Arguing with some inner self that somehow, in him, found voice.

"I know, I know," he said.

Tom Leffler didn't look at his daughter, but he quieted. She waited some time for him to speak. "I remember," he finally said without looking her way, "when you were a child. Yesterday. It was only yesterday. Your mother and I brought you here for picnics, do you remember?"

Clarissa curled her lips in imitation of a smile. "Mom would never let us pick up a hamburger on the way."

"She would always make something special," Tom Leffler said distantly. He could no longer remember anything, his appointments secretary had told Clarissa. But he remembered all the details of decades past, both important and trivial. "Always something special," he mumbled.

When did he get so old? Clarissa wondered. Her earliest memories of her father had been speeches. Boring dinners in hotels where she never ate because her mother had fed her long before. Every year, he gave a speech at her school. More and more, he appeared on television. She was twelve when she first had been moved to tears by his fiery oratorical skills at a Republican convention. He was a junior congressman, but he had been mentioned as a future candidate for the presidency after his thrilling keynote speech. To her, he had become not only a national leader, but practically one of the Founding Fathers. His name, in Clarissa's starry-eyed opinion, belonged in the pantheon of great American patriots.

"I'm sorry," she said, "for embarrassing you." Her father said nothing and stared blankly out through bleary eyes. His paper-white skin was wrinkled into ridges and lines.

"Do you love Bill Baker?" he asked, still staring at the city's sights.

"What?"

"He's a good man," Tom Leffler opined. "A good man."

"*What?*"

His eyes rose to hers. "I said he's a good man, and I asked if you love him."

"I . . . No! *No-o-o!* What are you saying?"

He seemed dejected. His chin dropped into the loose folds of skin at his collar. "I want you to find happiness. I want you to know the joy of visits to this park with your child . . . and your husband."

She couldn't believe the turn the conversation had taken. She had come to talk to him about the coup, but he sounded as if he were matchmaking with its target. "Dad, we ate those wonderful lunches in fifteen minutes—sometimes in the car—so you could get back to your office. Half the time, you were on the phone. I remember when you opened the door, stood outside, and said, 'There!' just because Mom had asked you to come see how beautiful the turning colors were."

He was staring at her now. "Those are the favorite memories I have in life."

His pathetic statement hung in the air. Clarissa couldn't believe that she had so defiled his artificially pleasant recollections. The picnics *were* wonderful, but what she remembered most were what seemed like the hours of preparation. She and her mother had carefully spread mayonnaise on sandwiches or cut tiny cheese wedges. What for her busy father had been a few minutes stolen from a hectic schedule had, for Clarissa and her mother, been the centerpiece of their day.

"You're at grave risk," he said to Clarissa. She felt a chill, and turned her collar up against the wintry gusts. "There's a

very nasty story circulating." She swallowed the fear that constricted her throat and threatened to block her air passages.
"Is it true?"

"What?" she croaked. "Is what true?"

"Did you have an affair with a Chinese army colonel—a
recruiter for their intelligence services—when you were
studying in Beijing?"

Clarissa's head spun from the totally unexpected question.
"What? Who?" She had engaged in only one affair during the
three years she had been at Beijing University. He had been
her only Chinese lover. She had met him in class. He had
been fluent in English and had helped her become fluent in
Chinese. They had talked of their shared desires for a free,
democratic world. He had said all the right things until the
last few months, when he had seemed to change and begun
to argue every point. His parting words—delivered with a
smile—had been more political than intimate. "I live in my
world. It can be yours only if you choose it."

"He wasn't," she lied, "a spy. Not really."

"Oh, God, Clarissa," her father said with eyes sinking
closed. "You've seen what the piranha do in this city! How
they tear their opponents apart with attacks on everybody
around them! And something like this? At a time like now!"

"I didn't *know*! I mean, how do we know it's true?"

"These things are always true," her father lamented.

"But it was so *long* ago!" she exclaimed. Her father gave
a defeated shrug. *If only everyone knew the truth,* she thought.
Knew how patriotic she was. *But they* would *know!* she realized. Right after the coup! Everyone would know that she
had risked all to save her country from defeat by the Chinese!
Would a Chinese agent plot with other American patriots to
attack Chinese forces with nuclear weapons?

Her mood brightened, and her panic subsided. "Now is the
time for all good men to come to the aid of their party," she
said.

Her father reacted immediately—shushing her—and took a
paranoid check around. He leaned over and whispered, "God
Almighty, Clissa. Where did you hear that?"

"I'm a member," she explained, "of the coup."

His jaw dropped. She told him about his muttering of the password in the video call and the mysterious E-mail that the phrase had unlocked. "But how would they have known that I told you about . . . ?" he began, then his eyes widened. "The bugs in my house! It was them!" He turned to stare at her. "You're on the inside," he said ominously. "You're in."

She had known that all along. She had knowingly made the decision to join. But something about the way that her father confirmed the fact scared the hell out of her.

"Don't ever speak those words again," he warned sternly, but in whispers. He looked all about the empty scenic overlook. "What we were talking about before—the scandal—that was public ruin. Hell, *they* could be the ones who leaked word of your affair with Baker to damage him politically. But participation in a coup, Clarissa, could get you killed."

She felt physically ill. "Oh-God-oh-God-oh-God!" she moaned. She sat on the stone wall beside him and buried her freezing hands between her knees to stop the trembling.

Her father was shaking his head and mumbling, "I'm sorry, Beth. I'm sorry."

"Dad?" Clarissa snapped loudly in frustration. He refocused on her, but his mouth hung open in a pathetic, almost demented display, like a frightened, weak old man. "Who's behind the coup?" she asked, but he wouldn't tell her, saying that information could also get her killed. "But if the plotters are on the NSC," she reasoned, "then why, I've been wondering, do they need *my* reports about . . . ?"

"I have been contacted," Tom Leffler interrupted dejectedly, "by one organizer. By the man I believe to be the leader. He isn't on the NSC."

"Who?" she asked in a plaintive tone. "Who is it?"

Her father shook his head. "There are some things you shouldn't know. Things that could put you—your life—at risk." He remained adamant in his refusal.

"Is it going to happen?" she asked in a barely audible voice. "Are they going to move against Baker?"

"They're not there yet, I don't think. I was approached, in a very tentative way, to get a reading on my leanings. I was asked a series of hypothetical questions that started with the very general. Things like, 'Do you believe that the fate of our nation hangs in the balance?' and 'Would you rather play by the rules and lose the war, or break every rule and win?' I got the sense that, if I answered every question correctly, the conversation would go on, so I did and it did. I shaded the truth to make it go on. I knew the buttons to push. And the questions grew steadily more pointed. 'Do you believe that America was wrong in dropping atomic bombs on Japan during World War II? Do you believe that the world would be a better place today if India had used nuclear weapons against the Chinese? Is there a moral difference between using nuclear arms against invading troops in the field, and cordoning off a captive city's population and incinerating them?' The questions weren't written down, of course, but they were, very clearly, carefully scripted. Each flowed naturally from the preceding question. The whole interview took over an hour."

"And you passed the test?" she asked. "They told you their plans?"

He shook his head. "They didn't tell me anything. They asked me. But the last two questions were, 'Should America use nuclear weapons if all else fails?' and 'Will Bill Baker take that step?' "

"And what were your answers?"

"Yes and no."

"And that's how the interview ended?" Clarissa asked.

Tom Leffler nodded. "He got up, shook my hand, and left. But there was something in the way that he shook my hand. He held it for a long time."

"You answered all the questions correctly," she observed, and he nodded his head slowly. "Then you're at risk too, Dad."

"But I'm untouchable," he replied. "You're a . . ."

"A pawn," she finished for him, supplying the word he wouldn't use.

"You're too close. There are people," Tom Leffler whispered, "who would do anything to lop off Bill Baker's head. To them, he's America's Nero. You're very close to a very dangerous confrontation. Too close. Far, far too close."

"I'm going to quit," she resolved. "I'm going to E-mail them today and inform them that I won't participate any further in any coup." She was actually greatly relieved to be getting out of a conspiracy that had caused her feelings of unrelenting guilt.

"Whatever you do, Clissa," Tom Leffler said, "don't do that. The moment you cease being useful to them—the moment they question your loyalty even in the least . . ." He couldn't bring himself to speak the words to his only daughter. His "Clissa," a name that had stuck when his darling girl had first tried to pronounce her own name.

"Oh, Beth," he said. "I'm sorry."

"Mom's not here," Clarissa said gently. "She's dead, Dad."

Tom came to and said, "Do you understand exactly what I'm telling you? Don't try to back out of the conspiracy! Do everything they say! Don't change a thing that you're doing, or . . ."

His warning trailed off. She took a deep, steadying breath, nodded, and scanned the treeline, the parked cars, the hills across the Parkway.

A sniper could be anywhere.

8

Just after dark on a clear, cold night, Captain Jim Hart had left the storm cellar and gone to check his personal cache of supplies, which he had found undisturbed. He had gotten four large aerosol cans—each with a pistol grip and a three-fingered trigger—and fence cutters and a gas mask. The three-mile trek through rough hills on his still sore ankle had taken almost two hours.

He had then set out on his first mission in a month. It had been a bad sprain, and his ankle still hurt, but he could get around on it with no problem. He could even jog at a decent clip as he had tried on several evenings behind the Lipscombs' house, mainly just to sweat and get some exercise. But the basic reason that he'd been lying low was that he was comfortable, safe, and warm in the storm shelter, and if he tried to conduct operations from there, he might endanger the Lipscombs.

But Amanda Lipscomb had returned from high school the day before with a valuable report. The Chinese army had begun using the gymnasium as a secure barracks for transiting troops. Hart had reconnoitered the school before the war as part of his inspection of every square meter of his area of operations. Amanda had drawn a layout of the school and of the Chinese deployments there on which Hart would now stake his life. It was time to return to work.

The basketball gym's locker rooms were shared by the football stadium via a passageway that led under the stadium's bleachers. Amanda had been a cheerleader and knew the layout well. The stadium was bounded by a cyclone fence, which Hart counted upon to give the Chinese a false sense of security. Obscuring the base of the fence was a thick hedge that would provide Hart cover for his approach.

That approach had been uneventful. Hart lay flat in the bushes beside the fence watching the stadium and grounds through light-amplification goggles. Listening. Trying to sense the presence of any hidden Chinese sentries. There were thirty trucks parked on the opposite side of the stadium guarded by two, two-man foot patrols. The Chinese were low both on gas and on trucks for transportation, so they didn't risk taking to the roads at night. They instead hunkered down in secure oases like the gym for fear of Hart's Special Forces comrades. In the morning, engineers swept the roads for mines and patrolled them until the sun went down and they again retreated into lager.

Hart's senses told him he was all alone. He carefully cut metal strands—one after the other—with the faintest of *clicks*. He then pulled the fence open toward him to afford himself potentially life-saving egress, but at that moment surviving the night seemed highly unlikely.

He knew he was making a mistake. He'd been inactive for too long, and to make up for lost time he had decided to attack a high-value target. Adding to his haste had been the knowledge that the Chinese would steadily improve their barracks' defenses. If he struck quickly, he had rationalized—on the second night they'd used the gym—there might still be chinks in their armor. But really he was simply satisfying his urge to kill.

His sole chance for survival was stealth. If a single man raised the alarm or fired a shot, Hart would find himself amid a swarm of enemy soldiers. In order to get out alive he would have to penetrate the hive and kill silently from within. He therefore kept his rifle slung over his back.

When the hole in the fence was large enough, Hart crawled through and rolled into an open culvert. The concrete ditch, meant for drainage, provided cover all the way to the stadium. When he reached the stands, Hart lay low and listened but heard only the sound of his beating heart. If there were patrols, they were few and far between. Hart made his way under the bleachers toward the gymnasium. While still some distance away, Hart saw two men smoking cigarettes in the darkness, standing guard at the locker room doors. They spoke softly, laughed quietly, and stood close together. Killing them became Hart's first task.

Moving deliberately, he inched his way closer. An opening through the stands led from the playing field to the gym's locker rooms, but little wind penetrated the high-walled cavern. The hollows underneath the bleachers—like the enclosed gymnasium—would be ideal for the weapon Hart had chosen. He quietly donned his gas mask with night vision goggles worn outside. He rotated the spray can's safety soundlessly to "on," twisted the nozzle to "Max. Range," then proceeded even closer for the kill.

The last few dozen meters took fifteen minutes. At twenty feet, he rested the can on a dusty girder with excruciating care just as a Chinese soldier lit another cigarette. Hart's goggles dramatically exaggerated the sudden blaze of light, and his breath froze in his chest. But the brilliant flame winked out just as quickly as it had flared. Only the tip of the soldier's cigarette glowed brightly as he inhaled.

Hart smelled the pungent odor of marijuana. The sentry passed the joint to his buddy with a giggle that was stifled so as not to waste the smoke that filled his lungs.

Hart relaxed. Not only did the stoned soldiers present easy targets, they obviously weren't expecting any officers or NCOs to drop by. He aimed the can's crude fixed sights. He was at the limit of the weapon's rated range. But the two soldiers did him the favor of standing side by side as they shared the joint with their rifles slung over their shoulders.

The cyanide made a high-pressure squirting sound. Both men's heads recoiled upon being struck by the narrow spit. Hart watched as they frantically wiped their cheeks and mouths, but the liquid had already expanded into a gas. One man fell to the ground sideways like a tall tree. His rifle clattered on the cement. The other clawed at his neck and chest, knelt, sat, curled up, and died.

Hart again inventoried his senses. Again, they told him, he was alone. With the can in hand he rushed to the door. As quickly as he could, he dragged the lifeless lumps into the shadows. The locker room door, he found, was unlocked.

So far, he thought, *so good.*

He proceeded in total darkness through banks of lockers that glowed an eerie green in his goggles. He stopped by the showers and heard the steady breathing of someone sleeping. Down the next aisle of lockers, a soldier—the interior guard— lay sound asleep on a bench. Hart twisted the nozzle counterclockwise to the center—to "spray"—and walked right up to the man. A quick jet of fine mist caused the sleeping man to cough once before descending into eternal slumber.

It was so simple.

Hart listened again. There was now no breathing in the locker room except his. He stopped at the double doors into the gymnasium on which Amanda had thoroughly briefed him. "No, they don't squeak," she had told him. "At least, I don't think." He removed the safeties from his three remaining industrial-sized insecticide cans, and rotated the nozzles fully counterclockwise to "fog."

He carefully opened the doors—which made no noise— and walked headlong into a soldier.

The barefoot man was heading straight for the bathroom. Hart sprayed before the Chinese soldier even raised his drowsy eyes toward the menace. His eyes bulged, and he dropped to his knees with his mouth open wide in a voiceless scream. He watched helplessly in his last second of life as Hart hurried past him.

There were hundreds of cots laid out in rows all across the hardwood basketball court. Hart pulled a can's trigger back until it locked wide open. The huge can belched clouds of cyanide gas. He set it down in the tunnel leading to the locker room and locked open the trigger of a second can. He sprayed from side to side as he ran past cots and set the can down at center court. The first coughing and a few squeaking noises petrified Hart, who pulled and locked the trigger of his third can and jogged down an aisle between the cots spraying the lethal fog left and right. Rarely did anyone even rise half way toward sitting, although a few managed to twist themselves out of bed and fall to the floor. It was there the heavy gas was thickest.

He placed the third can to block an exit at the bend in the stands and locked the nozzle open on his fourth and final can. He ran the length of the court again dispensing death. But by the time he reached the final exit, no one even stirred. He set down the hissing can and took one last look at the barracks turned gas chamber. Several hundred Chinese soldiers now lay dead.

Hart made it back to the storm cellar just before sunup.

"Did you do it?" he heard Amanda ask from the darkness. She flicked on a battery-powered lantern by his bed. Amanda and Jimmy sat there waiting.

"What are you doing here?" Hart demanded as he flicked his rifle's selector switch back to "safe."

Jimmy said, "I saw you leave."

"Did you blow up the gymnasium?" Amanda asked. Hart frowned but said nothing. "Did you even *go* there?" she persisted, and he nodded. "Were there any Chinese soldiers there like I said?" He nodded again. She and her brother grinned at each other. The rumors about Chinese troops bunking down at their school had proven true.

"Did you do *anything*?" Jimmy asked. Hart nodded. "What?"

"Look," Hart snapped, "I don't wanna talk about it! Okay?"

They both looked hurt. In a fit of pique Amanda said, "We'll find out when school starts anyway." Hart imposed upon himself a vow of guilty silence.

"Did you at least kill any of 'em?" an exasperated Jimmy persisted.

Hart nodded but would say nothing more about the inglorious battle he'd just won. He shooed them away. Jimmy climbed out first. Amanda stood before him. "I was afraid the doors would squeak."

"Go," Hart said, and she complied.

FAYETTEVILLE, NORTH CAROLINA
November 23 // 1830 Local Time

"Shit," Stephie said as she stood on a hillside overlooking the narrow draw. "There must be a hundred of 'em." The afternoon sun had raised a sickly sweet smell.

Animal spat on the piles of Chinese bodies. At the base of the hill on which they stood, Third Platoon provided security for engineers who wired vast stores of Chinese supplies for demolition. They used forklifts to evenly distribute pallets of Chinese ammunition among the fuel, food, and new shipments of winter clothing.

John Burns, looking at the bodies filling the small cut between two finger ridges, said, "They were machine gunned."

"We better get some intell guys here," Stephie suggested, "before we pull back."

The steady stream of Animal's urine began to rain on the bodies.

"Zip it up!" John barked.

"God*dam*mit!" Stephie shouted.

Animal looked back at them in surprise. "They're just dead Chinese!" he said.

"Their hands are bound!" John explained, pointing at the dead soldiers. "Tied behind their fucking backs with plastic! They're barefoot, Animal! They were massacred!"

Animal put himself back in his pants and said nothing, but he hung his head in tacit apology for the desecration.

Over the company net, John and Stephie heard Ackerman order them to blow the dump and hit the road. "There's Chinese armor counterattacking from the south."

John reported the details of the slaughter they had discovered to the company commander. Ackerman changed their orders, directing them now to hold their ground until brigade intell arrived.

Their 41st Infantry Division had made a tactical counterattack in the wee hours of the morning and had penetrated over a dozen miles into Chinese lines. Their battalion had seized and were ready to destroy a primary objective: an entire Chinese army group's forward stocks of supplies. But what had been planned as a quick hit and rapid withdrawal had now been extended a bit longer by Third Platoon's discovery.

"I don't get it," Stephie said, still staring at the reeking bodies. "They've been dead for a day or two. You can smell 'em all over that supply depot. They just marched them up here, greased them, and then didn't even bother to bury them! Surely everybody who came through that depot down there for resupply could smell 'em," she said, pointing toward the stacks of supplies in the net-covered supply dump. "All the transportation guys would know all about the slaughter."

Stephie understood finally, and looked up at John. He nodded simply and remained silent.

Animal waited—watching the two of them—then said, "Am I supposed to be picking up some mental, like, signals between you two? 'Cause I'm not."

"They're deserters," Stephie explained. "The Chinese shot them and left them up here so they'd rot. So the truck drivers who visited every battalion in the army group would spread the word. So the clothes they handed out would stink from the bodies of the men they'd shot for desertion."

Animal's jaw drooped open as he made a face. "That's fuckin' *harsh*."

A smile made a brief foray at Stephie's lips as she looked at John, but she banished it. John, however, had to pinch his lips closed and turn away. They both had had the same thought again.

"Okay," Animal said. "Now this is gettin' spooky! Ten seconds ago, you two were tryin' to make me feel like shit about taking a leak on those fuckers. Now you've got some kinda inside joke goin' about the whole thing!"

"Not a joke," John said. "I feel sorry for those guys."

"But they're starting to shoot their deserters," Stephie explained. "In large numbers. They're starting to have mass desertions, Animal. Don't you get it?"

Suddenly, a broad grin lit the big man's face. "Yeah. *Yeah!* Fuckin' *A*, man!" He ran off down the hill shouting, "Hey! Hey, come up here and take a look at this shit!" to other soldiers from third platoon.

Stephie snorted in amusement and turned to John, only to find him standing there with his eyes closed praying. She was stunned. She'd never seen him pray. Or wear a cross, or a Star of David, or whatever. Stephie lowered her own head, but her eyes studied him. She was dying to know what he was praying for.

He looked up at her, and her lips mouthed, "Amen," reflexively.

She turned to him. They stood close and swayed even closer to each other. But neither took that last step to close the gap. John glanced down the hill toward Animal, who like a tour guide was explaining to a gaggle of cherries the significance of what they were about to see.

"And *voilà*," Animal presented, waving his arm through air over the open grave. "What you see there, kiddies, is victory. They're starting to shoot themselves."

One of the female cherries staggered, took a couple of steps, doubled over, and vomited. Stephie attributed the episode to a nervous stomach following hours of tense combat. But then two of the other replacements stumbled off and spilled the contents of their stomachs. It forced Stephie to realize just how much she had changed. How readily she had accepted the sights and smells of death.

"What the fuck?" Animal cursed disapprovingly. "It's just a bunch of dead chinks!"

One of the female Chinese-American cherries stared back at him, then down at the piles of decaying teenagers. She turned and stomped back toward the supply depot.

"Hey, I'm not a racist!" Animal knew enough to shout after her. He then snickered sarcastically and muttered, "Bitch must be on the rag." The other replacements did their best to force themselves to look at the atrocity as if it were one more obstacle along the course to becoming a veteran. "All right!"

Animal shouted, having grown tired of the gawkers. "Show's over! Get back to your posts!"

A fusillade of tank cannon rattled through the hills on the far side of the cleared junction of two state highways where the supply depot had been placed. Out of the overcast sky above swooped inbound American missiles, which paused to circle underneath the layer of clouds. When their cameras pinpointed the attacking Chinese tanks, they streaked to a spot directly overhead and scattered smaller submunitions in the air. The hundreds of tiny antitank missiles shot almost straight down just beyond a ridge a mile away. Their shower of *pops* must've killed dozens of tanks. The hundreds of missiles were designed to cooperate with each other in assigning targets to avoid duplication. The network of tiny computers only survived a few seconds. It was destroyed when the shaped charges burned through the vehicles' thin top armor.

A Humvee skidded to a stop in the dirt at the edge of the depot. The backdrop of heavy fighting in the next valley over sent the brigade intell officers up the hill at a trot. One put on his gas mask and descended into the slight depression to search the bodies. Two others carried cameras and microwave gear, respectively, which they set up at the lip of the draw. The intell people all worked hurriedly—glancing repeatedly at the far ridge and not even greeting John and Stephie—as if they were petrified of being caught at the front.

When one man found the microwave carrier signal, the other began filming. He panned his small, handheld camera across the piles of bodies, zooming in for close-ups. John was called away to a company meeting by Ackerman. Stephie told Animal to round up his squad for a withdrawal back to their lines. When the camera lens swept over Stephie, she waved.

BESSEMER, ALABAMA
November 23 // 2300 Local Time

Amanda knocked on the shelter's door and awakened Jim Hart, summoning him to the house. "What's up?" he asked as he followed her through the cold darkness.

"There's a lot of trouble at school," she said with her head hanging.

"Like what kind of trouble?" Hart asked.

"They're looking for who did it," she explained. "And they're actin' real mean, too. Pissed off. Not like before."

Those words could easily have described Amanda's parents as well. "They're lookin' ever'where fer you!" the drunken father shouted as he paced the kitchen. The rest of the family and Hart sat at the breakfast table. "And I don't blame 'em! Shit! Ya kilt three hun'erd of 'em like they was bugs!"

"That's what he's *s'posed* to do!" Jimmy objected.

"You hush up!" his father snapped. He turned back to Hart. "They got soldiers out beatin' the bushes for you, boy. People been disappearin' from their houses. They hung a man in front of the courthouse for shopliftin' some food for his fam'ly. All on account of you!"

Hart nodded. He had gone on missions on each of the last two nights and had noted the increasing number of patrols. On the second night, he had also taken an inventory of his cache and noted that his supplies had dwindled significantly. At most he could go on half a dozen more missions. "All right," Hart said, "I guess it's time to go."

His announcement created a stir. Jimmy exclaimed, "No!" Amanda looked beseechingly at her mother. The father took a triumphant draw from his flask.

The mother said, "Where to?"

"Back to friendly lines," he replied. "Back to America."

That announcement evoked an even more profound, if silent, response.

"We're goin' with you," the gaunt woman said.

"What?" her husband shouted. "What in the *hell* are you talkin' about?"

"This ain't no place to raise these kids," she said steadfastly.

"So you're gonna take 'em halfway across the country— across the front lines—with a man the Chinese are on the lookout for?"

She nodded at Hart. "If he'll have us."

Her husband didn't await his reply. "Well *I* ain't goin'! I got me a better job now than before the war!"

"That's 'cause you don't gotta do nothin' but show up," his wife shot back. "Nowadays, you even come home from *work* drunk."

"I put food on the table!"

"With Chinese money," Amanda muttered.

Her father backhanded her face with a loud slap.

Hart had his hand around the man's throat and slammed him back into the wall before he even thought about what he was doing. The man's breath stank of alcohol. His eyes bulged wide from Hart's grip. His wife held onto Hart's arm and told him gently but insistently to let go. Amanda cried from her place at the table.

Hart leaned over to whisper in the man's ear. "Touch her again, and I'll kill you." He let go. The man coughed, sagged, and rubbed the red outlines of four fingers imprinted on his unshaven neck. His gaze never returned to Hart as he staggered toward the living room unscrewing the top on his flask.

Amanda's head lay on her crossed arms. Hart bent over and rested his hand lightly on her back. "Are you okay?" he asked.

She surprised him by bolting to her feet. He caught a glimpse of a tear-covered face before she threw both arms around him and sobbed. He patted her back softly and looked at Jimmy, who stared with clenched teeth toward the living room.

"I wish you'd beaten the crap outa him," Jimmy said.

"Jimmy!" his mother corrected instinctively.

"Why not!" Jimmy replied. "He beats the crap outa me and Amanda! And you, too, Mom!"

When she just hung her head, Hart began to pry Amanda's arms from his neck and to head for the living room. Amanda wouldn't let him go. "No!" she begged. Her mother grabbed his arm and they both held him. He allowed himself to be restrained not by their grasps but by their pleas.

"Just get us out of here," Amanda begged in whispers. "Take us with you back to America!"

WHITE HOUSE SITUATION ROOM
November 24 // 0745 Local Time

After the NSC meeting broke up and the room cleared, Bill had the technician replay the end of the video. "Freeze it," he ordered. The uniformed airman hit a button on his console, then rolled a dial back until the frame was filled with the image he knew the president wanted to see: a picture of his daughter.

No comment had been made when the scene had first been shown, although whispers had circled the table when the president's daughter had appeared on the screen. Bill studied the picture, frozen on four wall screens of Stephie standing beside the open mass grave and waving. She had to have known that Bill might see the video. She was waving at her father.

She was filthy and had a bandage covering the entire right side of her neck. Her combat boots were dust-colored. Cargo pockets bulged from baggy camouflage trousers. Although she was slender, she looked stocky under the flak jacket. Equipment hung off her webbing: three canteens, dozens of ammo pouches, pineapple-shaped grenades, stubby, bullet-shaped 40 mm grenades, a knife, a flashlight, and small kits of various sorts with plastic clasps.

Her helmet bore scars from near misses. Bill felt his skin crawl at the harrowing stories those marks told.

Stephie stood there with a half smile—one corner of her lips turned up—and waved her open palm from side to side. The sight struck Bill with almost physical effect. It was the same girl he had seen on the sun-baked front lawn of her beachfront home in Mobile, Alabama, fourteen years before. She had begged him to stay for lunch. Pleaded that she had so much to show him. Rushed across her bedroom and randomly retrieved drawings and dolls and hairbrushes in a desperate attempt to trick him into remaining awhile longer. But Rachel had paced the hall outside and stuck her glaring face into the room more and more frequently. She had agreed to give Bill only half an hour, and she was tapping her watch with her jaw set in anger as he exceeded his allotted time.

When Stephie had said good-bye from her lawn, she had tried to smile, but the effort had obviously been forced. The same girl now stood beside piles of rotting bodies and was similarly unable to muster any joy from her life.

When Frank Adams appeared in the door tapping his watch, the experience that Bill relived seemed complete. He studied his daughter one last time, then waggled his fingers at her image in a halfhearted wave. He glanced across the darkened conference room at the technician, who quickly lowered his gaze to his glowing console. Bill rose slowly and headed for the elevator. He fought the tidal wave of depression that threatened to swamp the embodiment of America's storm-tossed ship of state.

Clarissa and Vice President Sobo chatted stiffly in the corridor as they awaited the arrival of President Baker. The uncomfortable conversation between the president's mistress and constitutional successor ended promptly on seeing him down the corridor, even though Bill was intercepted at some distance by his military aide.

"Mr. President," the navy lieutenant commander whispered, "we've succeeded in establishing intermittent contact with a Marine colonel in Hawaii. He commands remnants of forces from all four services—about twelve hundred men and women—and he's in contact by radio with some of the other units. He's asking for orders, sir." The military aide didn't say, but it was implicit, that the colonel was asking for permission to surrender.

"I'd like to speak to him," Bill responded.

"Well, sir, he's on short-wave radio. The atmospherics are screwy—a weak signal comes and goes—but we expect we'll be able to raise him again in a matter of minutes."

Bill nodded, and he and the aide approached the two waiting women. Clarissa flashed Bill a smile, but he couldn't manage to reciprocate. He was unable to muster any feeling other than sadness.

Elizabeth Sobo said, "The Secret Service won't let us both go on the same helicopter. They won't even let us both go

to Andrews at the same time. My plane is waiting in Baltimore."

When Bill glanced at the South Lawn through two glass-
paned doors, two Marines in dress uniforms crisply opened
them. "You take Marine One," Bill said. "I'm going to order
our remaining troops in Hawaii to surrender. I'll meet you in
Omaha."

Sobo smiled at Clarissa. Frank Adams, Bill's chief of staff,
had advised against taking Clarissa on the trip even though
the exercise on which they were embarking had been kept
totally secret for political reasons. The full-dress rehearsal
would test the command and control systems at America's
alternate national command center in Omaha, and leaking
word of it might damage American morale. Sobo's eyes now
took in the ornate White House hallway: crown moldings,
ancient portraits, niches filled with statuary, lush Oriental runners. "Something tells me," she said wistfully, "that our accommodations in Omaha will be more Spartan."

"And as I recall," Bill replied, "the Spartans all died to a
man at Thermopylae. Maybe that's a bad choice of meta-
phors."

Sobo pondered Bill's remark with a grim expression on her
face, then finally and simply said, "Maybe." She turned and
headed through the open doors. The Marine guards closed
them behind her as the helicopter's engines began to whine.

Bill, Clarissa, and Bill's military aide stood alone in the
corridor. After a moment, the lieutenant commander said,
"I'll, uh, go check on the second helicopter."

"As soon as you raise Hawaii, come get me," Bill directed,
and the man turned, nodded, and left.

The instant they were alone, Clarissa said, "Bill, I got a
target letter. I'm the target of a Justice Department investigation under the National Secrecy Act." She waited, but Bill
did nothing more than arch his brow. "You *knew* about this?"
she asked accusingly.

"No," he replied. "I didn't . . ." He couldn't think of the
words to speak that were both truthful and that didn't violate
the pledge of confidence he'd made to Richard Fielding. But

Clarissa was far too insightful not to notice his dissembling, and she looked instantly stricken. She heaved a deep breath and turned away in shock. "Clarissa, I . . ." he began again, but faltered. She shook her head slowly.

Bill reached out to rest his hand on Clarissa's shoulder. "We'll get you a first-rate lawyer."

"I already *have* a lawyer!" she snapped as she pulled free. "My *father* got me one!"

He wanted so to comfort her. To be outraged and vengeful and fiercely protective of his lover. "This is clearly a purely political ploy," Bill reassured her. "And I *promise* that the White House will fight the stunt tooth and nail."

From her angry glare, he concluded, his pledge of support was obviously lacking in fervor. The sound of Marine One's engines rose to a whine even through the closed doors, momentarily drowning out their conversation as the helicopter labored skyward. But the stunned, hurt gaze that Clarissa fixed on Bill spoke volumes in the silence.

A thundering blast shattered glass and felled the two Marines at the door. In a rush of random observations, Bill saw glass glittering from the folds of his suit jacket as he wrapped his arms around Clarissa. He saw crimson blood on the neck and shaved head of a hatless Marine who struggled to rise to his knees beside the door. And he heard the crash of Marine One onto the South Lawn, followed moments later by its still spinning rotors, which plowed into the grass.

Strong hands ripped Clarissa and Bill apart and hustled them in opposite directions down the corridor. Four, five, ultimately eight Secret Service agents surrounded Bill, all of them laying their hands upon him. Pushing him at nearly a run with a force that he was powerless to resist. Holding bunches of his jacket's fabric in grips firm enough to have supported him even if Bill had gone totally limp.

He craned his neck and shouted, "Clarissa!" repeatedly. Finally at a turn in the hallway he caught sight of her. A single Secret Service agent with his machine pistol drawn waited while Clarissa bent over double and vomited onto the Oriental rug.

ROANOKE RIVER, NORTH CAROLINA
November 25 // 1115 Local Time

The air was cool, but the smoke from the last dawn attack had cleared, and the sun had burned through the haze and was now warm on Stephie's neck, arms, and feet. She sat atop the stinking hulk of a Chinese tank they had destroyed the night before. The river flowed around the treads with a gentle trickle. Her socks were laid out on the armor, which was still warm from the conflagration that had consumed it. Her combat boots, which had been soaked while wading out to inspect the kill, were unlaced and peeled back to dry. She had removed her helmet from her matted hair and itchy scalp.

She was studying a newspaper she'd bummed off a medevac pilot but only had time to scan in the hectic minutes after the fight. When they had hoisted Sergeant Chambers into the chopper's well equipped medical bay, she had seen the picture of Marine One's wreckage lying in a heap on the South Lawn on the folded paper pressed against the Plexiglas canopy. She now read the article under the banner headline that dominated the front page of the *Washington Post*: "Vice President of United States Assassinated." Underneath, the subheadline read, "President Baker Was Assassins' Likely Target."

According to the article, Stephie's father and his lover had been saved by a last second change of plans. A news analysis down the center of the page cautioned not to assume automatically that the murderers were Chinese. Its author remarked that rumors of coups had abounded in Washington for weeks, which was the first that Stephie had heard of it.

She was shocked. *A coup?* she thought in disbelief. A coup!

Stephie looked up from her paper to confirm that their now veteran platoon was busy policing the battlefield. They fished Chinese rifles from the water where they had been dropped. They pried the pistol grips of machine guns from their dead crewmen's hands. They climbed over armored fighting vehicles and unscrewed mounts atop which sat 12.7 mm heavy guns and automatic grenade launchers, stripping vehicles of their weapons. But because they knew they would be falling back, the Americans left the Chinese bodies for the Chinese to bury.

She returned to her newspaper. The FBI was going to lead the investigation.

"You should put your helmet back on," John Burns said.

Stephie looked down at him as he waded through the shallow water from the nearby bank. "Where's Becky?" Stephie asked.

"That's the first time you've ever asked *that* question," John replied. "I don't know where she is. At company HQ, I suppose. Put your helmet on."

Stephie held her hand up to the quiet horizon. "We sent patrols three miles south of here. I don't hear anything." The water trickled around the treads.

"Is that tank clear?" John asked.

"I haven't checked it yet," Stephie replied.

"Don't you think you *should* before you set up camp and take a break from the war?"

Stephie angrily put the newspaper down and rested her rifle atop it like a paperweight. She yanked a flashlight off her webbing and peered inside the hatch. Everything was charred black and thick with ashes. Three shapes generally in the form of humans sat upright around the breach of the main gun. Their features were melted, burned, and carbonized.

"All clear!" Stephie yelled at John as she grabbed her paint can and sprayed a large, white X on its turret. She then settled down to read the newspaper again.

John climbed up onto the tank and sat beside her. "What's gotten into you?" he asked.

"I should ask you the same fucking question," Stephie replied without raising her eyes from the article.

John was silent for a long enough time that Stephie's eyes wandered over at him surreptitiously. He was staring at a box on the lower lefthand corner of the front page. In it were listed the names of the vice president, her aides, the Marine flight crew, and the Secret Service agents who were killed in the assassination. It was the same box that he had scrutinized when she had first looked over the paper, and he fell into the same funk as before.

Their eyes met. Their faces were close. "Don't worry," John said, "your father will be okay."

"Yeah, well, there's talk in here about a coup."

"He's a helluva lot safer than *you* are," John replied, and he put Stephie's helmet on her head.

She kissed him—again surprising him—and began to pull her now dry socks on her feet.

WHITE HOUSE RESIDENTIAL QUARTERS
November 25 // 2330 Local Time

"You've got to be careful, Dad!" Stephie's warning echoed through Bill's head. *"Don't go anywhere!"* she had said urgently from the small window on his computer. *"It's too risky. Stay in the White House. Double your guard. Triple it! And don't trust anybody. Treat everybody like they're out to get you, because somebody sure is."*

Bill knew Clarissa was awake even before he entered his bedroom. He could see light under the door. But he still turned the doorknob carefully, soundlessly.

Clarissa half sat, half lay in bed with both hands clutching the comforter to her chin and her head on an upturned pillow. She looked at Bill with only her eyes, which arched once in a greeting that was joined by a perfunctory wave with the fingers of one hand. Her toes pedaled hyperactively under the covers.

"How are you doing?" Bill asked.

"Fine," she said a little too quickly. She had been waiting up for him and was wide awake.

He began to undress in silence. He lay his cuff links in a small saucer on the dresser and looked into the mirror. She was staring at him.

Bill turned to Clarissa. "Are you all right?"

"Sure!" she said without a trace of sarcasm. Her toes wiggled nonstop. The shadows from the lamp on the nightstand that her body cast moved rhythmically with the blanket, dramatizing the slight evidence of her anxiety.

There were some papers lying on top of a manila envelope on the night stand under the lamp. Bill hadn't noticed them before. Wearing only the trousers from his suit, he wandered over to Clarissa and kissed her on the lips. There was no passion in the formality.

"What are those?" he asked, nodding at the papers as he sat beside her.

"Oh, a subpoena," she said as if at the minor irritant.

Bill snatched up the stapled papers. She was being summoned to appear at the District Court for the District of Columbia to give testimony. At the top was the uninformative style of the case: *In re the United States of America*. The only things that appeared the least bit informative were a passing citation to the National Secrecy Act and a full-blown *Miranda* rights warning on the second page.

"What *is* this?" Bill asked.

"I don't know!" she blurted out, looking stricken.

Bill wrapped his arms around her, and she dissolved into tears. "Don't worry. Don't worry," he repeated in a calm, soothing voice. "Don't worry, Clarissa."

Her sobbing subsided, and she slumped back against her pillow.

He rose and finished undressing. Again, he felt her gaze boring into his back. When he climbed into bed beside her, she still sat in exactly the same position that he'd found her in. And her toes still pedaled up and down. Up and down. He looked at her, and she reacted as if she were forgetting something and quickly reached for and turned off the lamp.

After a brief rustle of fabric as she settled down under the covers, there was no other sound but the toes working up and down. Up and down. She obviously remained wide awake.

He reached out to comfort her, and she immediately rolled on top of him. Kissing his face, and forehead, and eyes. Kissing him with her open mouth and moving—hungrily—against his body.

BESSEMER, ALABAMA
November 29 // 0930 Local Time

They had waited until the moon had dwindled to at least a quarter crescent and the weather seemed reasonably clear.

Hart had wired his weapons cache to blow before striking out for free America. The Green Beret, the unemployed waitress, the teenager with a crush on Hart, and the young boy to whom Hart was a hero left the drunk husband and father standing mute in the doorway. His cursing had ended hours before and given way, by degrees, to pitiful pleas for his family to stay. But the tiny group was resolute and tightly bound in the face of the man's relentless desperation. The man's trump card— his beatings of his wife and children—had been taken by Hart six nights earlier in the kitchen.

For no one had any doubt that Hart would kill the man on the slightest provocation, and in that they had been right. Hart had had to stop Jimmy from rubbing it in. The boy had bravely stood his ground as his father had berated him for being a worthless and no good shit, knowing full well that Hart stood beside him ready to break his father's neck if he so much as raised his hand. And it was during those tense few days of a family rending itself apart that Hart had caught Amanda looking at him. Her mother had noticed the girl's infatuation long before Hart, a fact she'd told him with a knowing and stern glance.

The glance had been so stern, in fact, that Hart had confronted the woman in the kitchen. "Look, about Amanda . . ." he'd begun before faltering.

"She's too young," the woman had said.

"What? *No-no-no!* All I mean is she's just got a crush. Jeeze, I'm thirty-*one!*"

"You don't look it," she'd replied skeptically. "You two ain't done nothin'?"

"*What?* Good god, *no!* *Je*sus!"

It had been an awful conversation, and it had left a lingering and vaguely nauseating aftertaste. Amanda's mother had departed, apparently still dissatisfied with Hart's answer that Amanda's frequent visits to the storm cellar had been to talk, just like Jimmy's. And the woman had kept her eye on her daughter, who had made murderously fierce faces in reply.

The four of them now trudged over the dark hills with two weeks of supplies on their backs.

For days they had debated whether they could pass themselves off as a family, with Hart playing the father and the real mother in her original role. Amanda had bitterly, excessively, and repeatedly mocked the prospect. "Him? Married to *you*!" she had said, hurling more insulting laughs her mother's way. Later, Jimmy had told Hart—in private—that Amanda had suggested to their mother that *Amanda* play the role of wife, and that her mother could be their *grand*mother.

Jimmy had laughed in recounting the shouting match that had ensued, but had then gotten to the real point of his visit. "Since, you know, we're gonna go, like, cross-country. And you'll be wearin' a uniform and carryin' a gun. I mean we won't be tryin' exactly to hide from 'em. Well, ya see, actually I'm a crackerjack shot with a deer rifle! Got a buck at near 350 *yards* last year! And I'd like to take my rifle. I'd like to carry it. Loaded." When Hart had failed to reply, the boy had hung his head in dejection. Hart hadn't been able to see his downcast eyes. When the boy spoke again, he'd been on the verge of tears. "I feel, sorta, *bad*," he had almost whispered with his voice quivering and cracking. "About runnin' away. Leavin' home, ya know," his tear-rimmed eyes had looked up at Hart, "without a fight."

Hart had explained how they weren't spoiling for a fight. How if they were ever spotted, they would probably all die. How he carried a weapon for use only as a last resort or if their sole option required killing a sentry, hopefully silently.

When they reached the dark county road, Hart dropped his gear and rifle and climbed over a barbed wire fence. His fellow travelers handed his gear over after him. Jimmy then passed his pack to Hart and unslung the deer rifle he carried. Hart took the weapon and waited while Jimmy joined him in the ditch beside the road.

The mother came next. Hart took her pack and helped her over as the staples holding the wire to the posts began to give with croaking sounds. He offered the same assistance to Amanda, and the wire gave entirely. She collapsed into him—rocking him back a step—and never turned her face from his.

"Be careful!" her mother chastised from the darkness.

From the look on Amanda's face Hart realized the girl—in her mind—was playing the role her mother had denied her.

FEDERAL DISTRICT COURT, WASHINGTON
December 2 // 0930 Local Time

"Please state your name," the assistant U.S. attorney prompted.

"Clarissa Jane Leffler," Clarissa answered. She sat in a dingy grand jury room facing two dozen silent accusers. Mostly old, mostly women, mostly black, they watched her impassively, their heads filled with . . . what? What evidence had the government put on before her appearance?

The Justice Department lawyer, who had treated Clarissa with apparent politeness on meeting her outside the grand jury room, was now chilly and correct. "And where do you currently reside?"

"Currently?" Clarissa asked. He nodded. "Well, I guess . . . the White House." Most of the grand jurors found her answer cause for significant looks at one another. Was it titillation, or did it prove some significant element in the government's case? She had met with her lawyers for days. They had no idea what facts Hamilton Asher had mustered that might possibly put her in legal jeopardy. But how could they have known? She hadn't told them the truth.

Her reluctant inquisitor—mid-thirties, short hair, glasses, in a conservative suit with jacket buttoned—proceeded with the preliminary phase of her questioning. Date of birth, addresses of prior residence, the particulars of her education and career. He ended with her current job. "As head of the State Department's China desk," he asked, segueing into what could only be phase two, "do you have access to national security secrets?"

"Yes, of course," Clarissa replied, taking time to sip from the government-supplied glass of water. "I have," she cleared her throat, "top secret clearance."

He nodded, conveying the impression that he was on her side. Secretly rooting for her. He turned to walk toward his table as if to get his notes, but surprised her by asking a question with his back turned. "Ms. Leffler, have you ever had an unauthorized discussion of classified military information?"

There it is, she thought. "Excuse me?" she asked, although she'd heard the question clearly. Her examiner repeated his query word for word. She cocked her head in confusion. This was her chance. He was offering her the opportunity to come clean. To bare her breast. To purge herself of the poison that had seeped into every cell of her body until she felt sickened from head to toe.

To ruin her life and her father's life, and to spend the next however many years in prison.

"No!" Clarissa replied. "Do you mean have I ever disclosed military secrets to anyone? I have not. Never."

Her questioner seemed satisfied, and never once forayed back into that territory. In fact, he had no questions of any substance whatsoever thereafter. Her testimony concluded a few minutes later.

TENNESSEE RIVER, ALABAMA
December 4 // 2045 Local Time

After four nights of walking on foot through the dark hills of northern Alabama and five days of lying under Hart's remaining infrared shelters, the three civilians were totally exhausted. It had gone from mild, to brutally cold, and then back to mild again, making survival in the elements a challenge. But they had made relatively good time, and so at sunset Hart had asked whether they wanted to rest the night.

The answer had been unanimous shakes of their heads, and off they had marched.

It hadn't been long until they had reached the Tennessee River, and Hart had consulted a special map. He hated having to rely upon it, because it was shared with other Special Forces operatives in the south. That meant the Chinese would have recovered it from the dead bodies of countless of his comrades. But the map was unlike any others. It showed secrets of the terrain that would have long since been expunged from ordinary maps.

They traced the twisting black river until they found the dark skeleton of the abandoned train trellis. The tracks and right of way for this section of railway had been abandoned in favor of a newer bridge several miles upstream. Amanda had pled in whispers for him not to leave them, but Hart positioned the three Lipscombs behind a cold, rocky ridge and crept forward to watch and listen.

All was still. He used binoculars—switching from light amplification to infrared—to scan the bridge and the banks on either side. This wasn't the first river crossed in their trek, but it was the biggest. Hart's special map of forgotten treasures had yielded this nugget: safe passage across an obstacle that would otherwise have been insurmountable. All the newer crossings—train and road bridges—were heavily guarded by Chinese troops. Their small group took the less traveled way.

Hart extracted a directional emissions monitor. When fully unfolded, it resembled a foot-wide fork of a directional rooftop antenna. He removed the lens caps from the infrared and magnetic detectors and powered the device up. Using the sights, he panned the monitor across the length of the span and its approaches on either side of the river. The tiny LED atop the pistol grip glowed green. The Chinese hadn't installed any electronic monitoring devices on the trellis.

When Hart returned to the rocky outcropping, the Lipscombs were gone. He felt a rush of panic. The darkness around him was alive. Instinct took over and he got away from the spot.

He heard laughter. Male voices. He smelled wood smoke. His heart almost pounded out of his chest.

Hart headed for the sound of laughter. Images blossomed in his mind to explain the sounds. The thoughts left him in a cold, killing rage. They were all dead, the three Lipscombs and Hart. He would provide the symmetry by killing the Chinese.

The guards had made camp in a small hollow protected from the cold wind by steep, rocky walls and tall trees. They had added wood to their campfire until it blazed brightly and popped. A dozen Chinese soldiers sat in a semicircle around the fire laughing and smoking cigarettes. Two men sat on a log and groped Mrs. Lipscomb, who was held half-reclining between them. But most of the attention was on Amanda, who danced in the firelight.

Hart tried to make his mind perform the military calculations. He struggled to work the problem. He counted ten men. Ten. That was a full squad. They were all accounted for unless there were attached weapons crews. Would they give these infantrymen a machine gun or missile crew? Hart couldn't see anything other than rifles that rested on the ground beside the soldiers. Why would they bulk up the infantry squad with crew-served weapons? The bridge was of no military usefulness. They were there to stop civilians from fleeing, not fight American soldiers.

And if there were any attached weapons crews, they would be at the campfire. They wouldn't miss Amanda's show. One soldier jabbed a bayonet mounted to his rifle at Jimmy. The boy's mouth was covered by the hand of a Chinese soldier, who held him pinned on the ground in front of him with the heels of both boots, which were wrapped tightly around him. All eyes were on Amanda, who began to undo her blue jeans in a slow motion, musicless dance. She was sobbing and swaying in the light.

Hart could think no longer. His mind could manage no more logic. He selected his weapon. *Close range,* he thought. He pulled the machine pistol from where it had been tucked snugly on his pack and not used since the war began. He checked to make sure the thirty-round mag was seated, and the two others taped to it were full. He waited until Amanda stepped out of her blue jeans to the cheers of the Chinese soldiers and pulled the bolt back with a loud *clack*. He made his plan. The only trick was to ensure that, if it wasn't going well, he saved his last rounds for Amanda.

He rose and walked upright down the hill straight toward the camp.

They weren't smoking cigarettes, he realized halfway there. They were getting high. The soldier with the bayonet poked Jimmy with its sharp tip, and Amanda began to unbutton her flannel shirt on the freezing night. The two men molesting her mother had her clothes half removed.

When Hart got to the edge of the clearing, several soldiers saw him. Their cheery grins had only a moment to fade.

His 9 mm Heckler & Koch roared as he walked right into

the camp. Some men were mowed off the logs on which they sat. Others threw themselves backward in an attempt to save their lives. With all his might, Hart held the weapon steady and fired from right to left. The men nearest him were riddled with bullets. The man with the bayonet was struck squarely in the back, and the man holding Jimmy was hit in the chest. Hart couldn't tell if he'd hit everyone between Jimmy and Mrs. Lipscomb, but no one reached for the rifles, which lay propped on the log. Just in time, Amanda dashed away from the sheets of Hart's fire, which raked across the two bolt upright men groping her diving mother.

The straight stack magazine was empty. Hart flipped it over and seated a fresh thirty rounds while recording the locations of the moans and the rustling through the brush. Jimmy bolted across the camp toward his mother as Hart killed the easiest first. Men lay twisted and tangled where they had fallen or been pinned just behind the log bench. The smoke curling at the muzzle of his small black weapon was replaced by brief, foot-long jets of fire. One man tried to rise, and Hart flattened him with his boot and fired straight into the back of his head, which came apart. He counted as he went. There were seven lying draped over the log.

He pulled out his flashlight and found two blood trails. One led to a cowering, grimacing man who had dragged himself into a bush. He held his entrails in his belly as his other bloody hand was raised to Hart's flashlight. His palm and fingers did nothing to stop the half dozen 9 mm rounds Hart fired in a fraction-of-a-second burst. The second blood trail led Hart in the direction of a man whom he could hear whimpering in the darkness.

The young Chinese soldier was hit in the shoulder and bleeding profusely. There were no pleas as he squinted into the glare of the light. He lowered his forehead to the ground dejectedly, then rolled his head to look away from Hart. That wasn't good enough. Hart put the light on the ground, grabbed the man's hair, and jerked his head around. The dirt stuck to his tear-covered face as he began to sob.

"Open your fucking eyes!" Hart demanded as he jammed the muzzle into the man's mouth. He yelped in pain as the hot gun sizzled. When his eyes shot open, Hart released the man's hair and pulled the trigger.

Only three rounds came out. His magazine was empty.

He looked around, listened, but heard nothing. He turned the flashlight off, stood upright, and inserted the third magazine. He lowered the night vision goggles onto his eyes and hit the power switch. The world alit in the green, flickering glow from the campfire thirty feet away. Hart turned back to the camp to see the Lipscombs gathering and comforting themselves in a small, traumatized huddle.

That made nine, Hart thought to himself.

No one had made it out of the open end of the hollow from which Hart had come, weapon blazing. The hills around the camp in the other direction formed the walls of a three-sided box. Number Ten was somewhere in that box. Hart unfolded the metal stock of his machine pistol and raised the weapon to his shoulder. Bent forward slightly at the waist, Hart began his slow walk through the artificially lit night. He swept the weapon and his gaze from left to right and back again as he took each methodical step forward.

"Captain Hart?" came Mrs. Lipscomb's tentative call. Hart ignored her, intent on his prey. *"Where are you?"* came Amanda's shaking, ragged voice. He looked around. Jimmy was finishing his study of a Chinese assault rifle and pulling the bolt back.

Hart returned to the hunt. Up ahead were two large, half-buried boulders. A scrubby bush grew from the small deposit of soil that must have collected between them. He could see nothing suspicious, but his intuition made him pause. Having spent so many weeks as prey, his mind made an informed guess.

He switched to infrared, and the contours of a hot body glowed brightly in the bush. Hart could tell that the man had no weapon, for he lay in the fetal position with both hands tucked under his armpits. He didn't seem to be bleeding, which would have left warm phosphorescent splashes and trails on the ground and leaves. As Hart got to within a few feet and stood over the man, the high-resolution screens in his goggles clearly showed the man shaking.

"Captain Hart, are you *alive*?" Amanda yelled in desperation before collapsing into noisy sobs.

Hart kicked the man's boots. The soldier retracted his legs as if he'd stepped on an electric eel and lay curled in a tight fetal ball. "Come on," Hart said. "Get up." It took Hart kicking the man again for the soldier to admit to himself that he'd been found and to rise, reluctantly, to his feet. He was, apparently, unharmed. Hart pressed the machine pistol to the small of his back and pulled the trigger to within a feather's touch of firing. He put the man's hands on his head and patted him down from head to toe, tossing to the side anything that he found clipped to his belts or in his trouser pockets.

He prodded the man forward and walked behind him. "We're coming in!" Hart announced on seeing that Jimmy held the assault rifle to his shoulder.

Hart and his prisoner stepped into the light of the roaring campfire. Jimmy's muzzle joined Hart's on their target: a short, slender teenager, whose chin was buried to his chest and whose eyelids drooped in utter depression. Amanda rushed to Hart and clung to his side, shivering and sobbing.

"Did they get on the radio?" Hart asked. Jimmy didn't answer. He held the rifle to his shoulder with his cheek planted to the stock and his right eye to the rear sights. His jaw was clenched and his cheek was twitching. He clenched and unclenched his cramping right hand, which was wrapped around the pistol grip of the weapon.

Hart turned to their mother, who sat on the bloody log in a daze. "Did they radio anyone after they found you?" She looked up at him with exhausted eyes and shook her head slowly.

"What does it matter?" Amanda said in a voice thickened by tears. "Everybody heard the shooting."

"Maybe," Hart said. He looked up at the high, surrounding hills. "Maybe not." The cold air would carry the sounds, but the hollow would reflect the noise upward. And they could well be ten miles from the nearest Chinese.

"Why didn't you kill *him*?" the anxious Jimmy asked, still taking aim at the face of their captive.

Hart looked around at the large quantity of weapons littering the camp. All were loaded. The downcast eyes of their prisoner had surely noticed. "I don't know," Hart replied, but in truth he did know. The killing rage that had consumed him had waned with his execution of Number Nine. By the time he'd found Number Ten, he had no more killing left in him.

"Well, what're we gonna do with him?" Jimmy asked.

Amanda was calmer now. She still held onto Hart, but she held her head upright and stared at the prisoner, sniffing to dry her nose. "Let's kill him," she answered her brother calmly.

Hart opened his mouth to object, but stopped himself. He had just marched through that camp and dispensed death with total abandon. Bullet-riddled bodies lay cooling all around. Why stop at Number Ten? Especially when it made practical sense.

But the problem was, it didn't seem right to him. Somehow, justice had been served. In the randomness of death, the tenth Chinese soldier had survived the killing long enough to become a prisoner, and you didn't kill prisoners. Or did you?

They all looked at Hart now. Amanda, who had proposed the murder, with doe-eyed innocence. Jimmy, with hyperactive flits of gaze only momentarily distracted from his weapon. Mrs. Lipscomb from behind a lens of numbing shock. And the Chinese soldier, who looked up though his chin was tucked meekly to his chest.

"We cain't let him go," Jimmy said.

Amanda detached herself from Hart's side and picked up a rifle. Hart watched. So did the Chinese soldier. Still sniffing, she turned the rifle over from one side to the other until she found the selector switch. Maybe because she had seen her brother chamber a round, or maybe because she'd grown up in a gun-owning southern family, she knew to yank back on the bolt. It didn't go all the way back, and she put the stock between her knees and pulled again. A round was ejected, and a new cartridge fed cleanly into the chamber.

"Is this on 'safe'?" she asked Hart, holding the receiver up to Hart. He looked and confirmed that the selector switch was on safe. She flicked the switch to "fire" and leveled the weapon.

The Chinese soldier stood beside the fire five feet in front of the girl.

Hart jumped when the weapon roared. The flame shot almost the entire distance to the weapon's target, and the Chinese soldier was hammered backwards to the ground.

In the silence that followed, Hart heard another *click*. Amanda slung the now safed rifle over her shoulder and began to collect bandoliers of ammo. Jimmy did the same. Hart didn't object, and they crossed the river and continued on to the north.

9

A fog hung over the quiet, frigid battlefield. Jim Hart and the Lipscombs carefully picked their way across a charred landscape covered in mist. Jimmy and Amanda held their rifles at the ready, but Hart knew that they would be useless. They were midway between two armies whose arsenals dwarfed their puny weapons.

The little band had reached the front the night before. They had waited anxiously for sunrise to the immediate rear of the Chinese army lines. Twice patrols had passed close. The danger was inherent in Hart's plan. Their survival depended on timing. They would cross in the hour before dawn, pass through enemy lines in total darkness, and reach American lines by the first light of dawn.

So far, Hart knew, they had been lucky. There had been no morning attack in their sector. Fighting had risen with the white glow in the sky until it had raged a few miles to either side of their crossing point. The rattle and crash of battle had masked what little noise the four of them had made as they crawled on hands and knees through no-man's-land along frigid streams that cut deeply into the earth.

"I'm f-f-freezing," a shivering Amanda whispered. Like the rest, she was soaked through from the water trickling through the streambeds. Hart briskly rubbed her arms and legs through soggy clothing. Her breath came in quaking puffs through chattering teeth.

Jimmy was the color of paper. Mrs. Lipscomb's eyes had sunken deeper into their sockets above black bags that made her look ill.

"Okay," Hart said at a normal volume that sounded like a shout. He stood upright.

"What are you *doing*?" Jimmy asked in alarm.

"Everybody get up," Hart ordered as he extracted the white sheet they had made back at the Lipscomb's home. "Come on, get up."

"But they'll see us!" Amanda cried.

"We want them to see us," Hart explained.

"The Chinese?" Amanda asked.

"No, the Americans."

The Lipscombs looked at each other, then slowly rose with a rustling of fabric and a few grunts. They followed Hart and his white flag forward. Northward. Toward America.

Their eyes roamed the hills and trees. With every step Hart grew more tense, but his face remained serene. He even smiled for the benefit of Amanda, whose eyes were wide with terror.

At the top of a slight rise, Hart saw several armored fighting vehicles—both Chinese and American—holed and still. At the far side of the narrow field in which they sat there rose a wooded ridge. He paused and waved the white flag. The Lipscombs looked from him to the empty landscape and back at him again.

When nothing happened, Hart lowered the flag and headed across the open dale. He hadn't taken five steps when a single shot rang out.

The dirt kicked into the air ten feet in front of his boots. The Lipscombs flung themselves onto the ground and Amanda called out to Hart, but he was grinning and waving the flag in figure eights over his head.

Moments later, a squad headed down the opposite ridge single file. Their circuitous route was carefully plotted. They wove their way through the minefield that lay ten feet in front of Jim Hart's boots.

"So . . . what are you saying?" Amanda Lipscomb asked Hart. She sat in the army ambulance with three blankets wrapped around her shoulders. Her face was ruddy from windburn and exposure. Her hair was a rat's nest of tangles, twigs, and pine straw. But she looked at Hart with eyes wide and pleading. "You're saying good-bye? Just like that?"

Hart shrugged and sighed. Amanda's mother and brother— similarly swaddled—looked on.

"But . . . But I thought . . ." she began. She turned to her mother with her plea. Mrs. Lipscomb cast her a sympathetic look. Desperate, Amanda turned back to Hart. "But after the war, right? You've got to go fight, but after the war you'll find us. You'll come find us."

Find me, Hart knew her to be saying. He frowned.

"You *will*," Amanda persisted. "You will. With all we've been through . . . You saved my life! You saved all of us. You'll come and find us. Promise me." Hart said nothing. "Promise me!"

"All right," Hart said. "I'll look you up after the war, if . . ."

"You will," Amanda repeated. "You will." She rose and tried to kiss Hart on the lips. He turned, and she kissed his cheek. He kissed her forehead, shook hands with and then hugged Jimmy, and then hugged Mrs. Lipscomb.

"You will," Amanda said as Hart climbed down from the ambulance with his rifle. "You will."

RALEIGH, NORTH CAROLINA
December 8 // 0845 Local Time

The Filipino nurse pushed the door open. Wu entered the Eleventh Army Group's officer's forward field hospital. The portable beds covered nearly every square meter of the otherwise empty school cafeteria. Wu stopped at Aisle Number Seven. The bandage-covered patients lay head to head. As Wu walked down the narrow aisle, he saw that the rows of beds were pushed together in sets of two with just enough room on one side of each to allow the linens to be changed. Doctors with palmtops strolled slowly from bed to bed and spoke briefly with nurses and patients.

A man on a stretcher—covered head to toe by a blanket— was taken from his bed through doors leading to the daylight outside. Orderlies stripped his bed, dumped the stained sheets into a large, wheeled trash can, and remade the bed with fresh linens in under thirty seconds. Another man on a stretcher— this one living—was being brought in from the kitchen-turned-operating-theater. He took the dead man's place in the newly made bed.

They are efficient, Wu thought. *They have experience with casualties.* A fluttering in his belly left him unsettled at the realization. Further upsetting was the foul smell of bowels and the even fouler scent of antiseptic detergent. But most disturbing of all were the moans made faint by stupefying drugs dripping from overhead bags.

Equipment had been rolled up to beds based on wounds. Inflated oxygen tents entombed burn victims. Other devices inflated or suctioned lungs—Wu couldn't tell which—through tubes disappearing into nostrils and mouths. Still other machines displayed vital signs, processed urine for men with no kidneys, and scanned brains for flickers of life.

Wu searched the large room for Lieutenant Tsui, his best friend from military school. They had shared the same room for fourteen years, from age four to just last summer. Tsui was the closest thing to a brother that Wu ever had.

The faces of the patients were unrecognizable. They were either bandaged or swollen to horrifying proportions from some anatomically distant wound. A touchscreen computer was attached to every bed railing. Doctors and nurses punched beeping buttons. Case histories and vital signs popped into windows. At the top of the small screens were the wounded officers' names.

Bed after bed, Wu checked the names and saw the most

unsurvivable wounds imaginable. Easily a third had lost entire limbs. Arms were severed singly. Legs seemed to be lost in pairs. But even more devastating were the burned and the crushed. The former were semicomplete patchworks of engrafted artificial skin left bare behind plastic sleeves filled with pure oxygen. The latter were reconstructions in progress, as indistinguishable as burn victims with heads and hands swollen to many times human size.

"Wu?" came Tsui's familiar voice.

Wu's lips twitched suddenly—inexplicably—as he almost began to cry. He forced himself to look. Tsui had lost both his legs. "Hi," Wu said in English. Tsui said nothing from behind bandages that covered the right half of his face. Wu slowly approached the bed with its green glowing screen. Tsui's heart beat safely in a window. Wu held his helmet in both hands. He twirled it and looked down at it, then up at Tsui. "I'm really very, very sorry," he whispered in Chinese.

Tsui said nothing, but began to sob. Tears welled in Tsui's eyes and rolled down his cheeks. Tears flowed from Wu's eyes also. He slipped his arms under Tsui and hugged him. "It's not fair," Tsui squeezed from his chest. "It's not *fair!*" he raged in anguish. Wu grabbed Tsui's cotton gown in his hands. Tsui's fists clutched at Wu's thick, camouflage blouse.

"What happened?" Wu asked. Tsui's grip, then his hug, released. His friend lay back onto his bed. The nineteen-year-old lay limp, staring away from Wu. "What *happened*?" Wu repeated.

"What does it matter?" Tsui mumbled.

Wu stole a glance. The sheets on his bed below his hips were pancake flat. "You know, Tsui, this doesn't necessarily mean that this is the absolute end of your career. There are posts you could take. Wounded veterans are showing up in staff positions more and more. I could, maybe, if you want, get you a job on General Sheng's . . ."

"I don't *want* a career in the army!" Tsui snapped with surprising vigor. Doctors and nurses looked. Wounded soldiers raised their heads. "I've changed my mind! I don't want to be a soldier! *I want my legs back!*"

Everyone was staring not at Tsui, but at the outsider: Wu. The healthy one. The staff officer in the clean battle dress.

GREENSBORO, NORTH CAROLINA
December 8 // 1430 Local Time

Shen Shen tried to stop Wu from entering General Sheng's office. "I'll tell him you're here!" she exclaimed. She wrapped her arms around him from behind, but Wu pried himself free and opened Sheng's door.

The old general sat alone at his desk scribbling notes on a map. He laid the pen aside, as if he had been expecting Wu, and patiently waited. The lieutenant came to attention before the commanding general's desk. A worried Shen Shen closed the door.

"I'm sorry about your friend," Sheng said in a disarming voice. Its timbre said instantly that he knew Wu's pain. The small old man sat slumped in his chair. He spoke slowly. "My roommate from military school died in my arms. I held my hand over his mouth for two days after the North Vietnamese ran out of morphine. There was only one lantern in this operating room in a tunnel complex beneath a small village. The air was stale and thick with odors."

Sheng's fading memory flickered out, and he looked up at Wu. "You came here for a reason. To say something to me."

"I am a soldier," Wu said simply. "We are at war. I should be in the field. In combat. I should fight."

Sheng stared back expressionless, then cocked his head and squinted.

"That's all you have to say?" Sheng inquired.

"My father is a traitor," Wu imagined that Sheng wanted to hear. "Yes, sir," was Wu's reply.

The old commander of Eleventh Army Group (North) nodded. "I remember when I was your age. I pulled strings to go to South Vietnam. I saw my first American there. He was even younger than me. He shot me right here," Sheng said, pointing to the scar running across his forehead just above his left eye. "He came over to me thinking I was dead. From the look on his face, he couldn't believe what he'd done. He started crying." Sheng sighed. "It was the hardest thing I ever did in my life, killing that man."

"Harder than killing American civilians?" Wu asked.

Sheng's face hardened. "You do not know what it means to say that you are a soldier," Sheng said to Wu. "You do not know what it takes."

"Do I get a combat command, sir?" Wu asked.

Sheng seemed reluctant to let the subject move on, but he sighed and sat back in his chair. "I got a call from Beijing half an hour ago" Sheng said. Wu dropped his eyes to the floor. He had gone over Sheng's head and called Beijing directly. "You can go to the front," Sheng continued, "but you shouldn't get yourself killed. Great things lie in store for you, Lieutenant Wu."

The prophecy hung in the air. Wu looked down at Sheng, whose eyes had sunk to his desk. Wu saluted and did an about-face.

In the outer office, Shen Shen hugged him. Wu just stood there, absorbed by Sheng's remark. "*Great things lie in store for you.*"

The defense minister had just used the exact same words.

WINCHESTER, VIRGINIA
December 13 // 1615 Local Time

There were pale shadows on the gray winter day, though no sunlight penetrated the haze. Master Sergeant Stephanie Roberts—hunched in a fighting hole, watching her breath form before cracked lips—was wrapped head to toe in cold-soaked gear. But she was on her first ever tactical command. The chill Stephie felt came not from the blustery day, but from the fear of getting all her people killed.

She waggled four fingers in the air and pointed. A fire team burst into a dark building. She waited for the eruption of fire and fountains of death that didn't come. She waved, pointed at the unlucky squad leader whose attention she caught, and made a sideways chopping motion through woods that could be mined or manned by waiting Chinese. Ten crouched and terrified men and women walked straight into what could be the muzzle of a machine gun, but wasn't.

She was the leader of a unit that plied the field, and she was totally responsible for her crew.

They advanced quietly. No radio. No microwave. No laser and no IR. Even their new camos absorbed their body heat. Stephie had made First Lieutenant John Burns—the new Charlie Company CO—give Stephie her old Third Platoon. The previous commander had been shot through ear to ear in intense fighting that had proven the onset of a major attack. Major Ackerman—battalion operations officer—had approved Stephie's promotion. She now commanded a platoon.

Pounding thuds blasted the earth for miles in both directions, but the front line was fractured by every ridge into dozens of individual battlefields. Each valley was a different war. For the past few days, those wars had resulted in American victories, which had taken either perfection or piles of American bodies to attain. Lately, it seemed, it had taken both.

Stephie looked up from the bottom of a steep cut between two hill masses. Third Platoon would stop the Chinese there. The creek bed at the bottom of the cut was dry. The winter run-off had worn a deep furrow through the hills.

Noise and smoke drifted through the trees high above. They were the only intelligence she had. She hadn't been in radio contact since they'd entered the valley, and she'd dispatched two runners who hadn't yet returned.

Stephie felt confident leading the platoon into combat. She had placed the four squads and laid their fields of fire. She would say when to open fire and when to pull back.

"Where's that arty?" came Animal's bitch over the radio.

Stephie was pissed that he broke radio silence. She had placed herself in position to steady the left side of the platoon. Animal—Staff Sergeant Simpson—anchored the right. His flank was filled with jumpy, first-action cherries. Stephie had put them there because it had looked easier to hold. It ascended half way up a gentler right-hand slope strewn with large rocks, logs, and berms. In contrast, Stephie's two squads on the left lay astride the dry creek bed. On their left was a steep, unscalable wall.

It was down that creek bed that any attack would come.

Stephie had led Third Platoon several hundred meters out in front of the twisting, turning, unconsolidated front lines. They had climbed out of trenches with packs on their backs and headed up toward the enemy like infantry. But they weren't patrolling. They wouldn't rush back to friendly lines on contact. Their plan was to ambush the unsuspecting Chinese attackers by being where they weren't supposed to be: out in front of their lines. And after Stephie's platoon plugged the creek bed and fixed the Chinese, the artillery would . . .

But with no radio there would be no artillery. That part of the plan had already gone to shit. John would never have sent her on that mission without artillery on her call, but he would, she felt sure, have sent others. And those others, Stephie concluded, would hold their ground, just as Stephie would now hold hers. Third Platoon would blunt any Chinese attack down that creek bed.

She scanned the row of helmets fifteen meters to her front. Her men and women lay in a line of shallow holes. That line conformed to the V-shaped contour of the deep cut. The V began on her left at a raw stone outcropping ten meters up the ridge. It descended to a point at the bottom of the streambed and climbed the gentler ridge to their right until it reached the last and luckiest cherry. That lone soldier, highest up the hill, was the most likely to survive. He or she was practically out of the fight. He or she could easily crest the lip of the finger ridge and slip back to friendly lines. He or she might at least report where, when, and how they had all died, but that wouldn't answer the all-important, "Why?"

Why?

She shook her head and refocused. The only decent footing for the Chinese, who would be advancing straight downhill, was down the pebble-strewn creek bed. That was where Stephie's two machine guns lay dug into the banks.

She spotted the helmet of the new leader of First Squad— her old squad—who commanded both of the guns. She pressed the Push-to-Talk button. "You okay up there . . . ?"

she began, but stopped because she had almost said "Sergeant Johnson." Stephon Johnson was long, long dead. The realization hit her like a fist in the stomach.

What is *that new guy's name?* she agonized. The replacement's name simply wouldn't come to her, but others came all too easily. Sergeant Kurth. Peter Scott. Tony Massera. Rick Dawson. Patricia Tate. And what was that poor new guy's name? *Oh, yeah,* she remembered. *Shelton fucking Trulock.* Stephie remembered each and every death. The way it had happened. The time of day. How she had felt—tired, stunned, saddened, sickened, indifferent—in the few moments after the tragedies during which her memories were being recorded with utter fidelity and focus.

Through her earbuds, with crystalline digital clarity, she heard, "You talkin' to me, Sarge't Roberts?" It was Smith. The guy's name was Smith. *Smith, of course.* "Cause I'm good. I'm good to go. Ain't nobody comin' past these guns. Like I said, you can count on . . ."

"All *right*!" Stephie commanded. He fell quiet.

Smith's first name was either "Sayed" or "Said." There had been much debate. The newly arrived Arab-American corporal had just been released from the hospital after recovering from wounds received right after the invasion. To Stephie, he was a combat veteran. She'd put him in command of her old First Squad. Only afterwards had Smith confessed his secret to her. He'd been a raw recruit—a private—when he'd ingloriously received his Purple Heart. Possession of the medal, whose owners had proliferated in the grinding, bloody war, had made Smith a PFC. Then, when he'd reported for duty, the 41st Infantry Division had made him a corporal. But the problem tormenting Smith was that his combat experience had consisted of a grand total of six blood-soaked minutes.

She'd listened, then given an army reply. "*Fuck*, Smith! Shit! You're a goddamned seasoned fucking combat *veteran*, man! A lean, mean killing ma*chine*! *Je*sus! Six *minutes*! *Shit!*" She had rocked him with a surprisingly hard blow with the heel of her hand to his body armor. He had smiled. There wasn't much else he could do. "So *you're* my squad leader,"

Stephie had said. She had held her hand out for a high five, and he'd given it up with a wrenching slap. But then he'd frowned. She had worried about that frown ever since.

Squad leaders had to be rock-ribbed. They were linebackers. The rebar in concrete. The spine that held the line. Their most important function was simply to stand their ground, for that resolve would hold eight other men in place. But if a squad leader ran, so would his eight soldiers. Then the only retaining wall against the flood were the platoon sergeant and the platoon leader a dozen meters to the panicked herd's rear.

Stephie had introduced Smith by calling the platoon together. Ever since the days of Ackerman, Third Platoon had been formal. Stephie had said, "Corporal Smith is the new leader of First Squad. He's returning to the Forty-first after recuperating from wounds suffered in the battle for Birmingham, Alabama." Her tone had clearly been respectful. *Birmingham*, the cherries would've thought. *Those were bad, bad times.*

Throughout the introduction, Smith had just stood there, unsmiling. He had said nothing. Acknowledged no one. Betrayed no hint of an expression, all of which was read by the troops to be surliness.

Shortly after the meeting, rumors had begun to spread. Smith was a stone cold warrior man, they whispered. The son of a bitch was *fierce*. Not just mean. A motherfuckin' killer. Kinda quiet on R&R, ya know. But really, deep down, he was ruthless. Merciless. Dark. Dangerous. Brooding. His soul was calloused by the chaffing of his memories of the rivers of blood that he had shed. He was, they all finally admitted, a terrifying slayer of all things living.

Smith had been hit early on in the war. They had discussed that fact. Charlie Company had been patrolling the hills and clashing with Chinese patrols for two weeks, and they had lost only eight, two dead. That was nothing like the casualty rates in the early major attacks, although everyone knew that the Chinese were gathering themselves.

Just like Smith, everybody got hit in a major attack. But the key fact was that Smith hadn't been killed. Nobody even knew where his wound was until a recruit from the shower

tent reported that Smith had been hit in the ass. And in his
lower back. And in the backs of both thighs and in the left
calf. It looked like buckshot, the recruit had reported. "Shrapnel," Stephie had explained.

Combat, the uninitiated all thought, was natural selection.
The fittest, the strongest, the baddest survived. And the baddest of the bad came back for more. It was total bullshit, but
Stephie didn't correct them. It had been she who had started
the rumors.

Don't fuck with Corporal "S." Fucking Smith. Don't ask
him shit about anything. Try to get outa having to wake him
up. Don't bug him. Don't tell him anything about yourself.
Don't think that you deserve to know any fucking thing at *all*
about him. Just do *what* the fuck he says, *when* he says it,
and keep your distance as much as you can.

But. But. But. When the shit gets real deep, stick to him
like a second skin. Dig in close by. Sleep close to him. Go
on patrols with him. *Don't* go on patrols with*out* him. And if
you're going to be overrun, fold back onto him. Rise up from
your position, risk death or court-martial, and rally to his side.
But whatever you do—no matter how confused the situation—
never, *ever* lose sight of Smith. Your squad leader is your air
supply. Your way home.

So Master Sergeant Stephanie Baker had explained in casual one-on-one talks. She wasn't, just then, the president's
daughter shooting the shit. She was Charlie Company's first
sergeant, the senior NCO. She made the rounds to steady the
troops and reminisced about the war. About the legendary
battles of the past. Her combat patrol on the beaches of Mobile. The first clashes with Chinese MainFor at Atlanta. The
stoic stand at the bloody Savannah River. She told stories of
infantry warfare to impressionable young infantrymen. To
kids fresh from the heartland via ten weeks of accelerated
boot camp.

Third Platoon was green. Greener, even, Stephie thought,
than the original Third Platoon on its patrol of her hometown.
Of the forty-two troops under Stephie command, twenty-six
had been with them less than two weeks. Fully half of those

had yet to see any combat at all, having been left intentionally behind on combat patrols.

Oftentimes, the replacements' arrival had been macabre. The cherries climbed down from trucks to see the men and women they were replacing get loaded into the vehicles that had brought them. Some were on bloody litters. Others were in bodybags. Raw recruits thus got the opportunity to see the fate that awaited the guys who stood in line next to them.

But now they were all needed, veteran and cherry alike. Any day would mark the beginning of the Battle of Washington.

Animal sighed over the radio. "That fucking artillery has been diverted."

Stephie pushed the PTT button and replied with, "Shut the fuck up!"

"We ain't gettin' no support!" came Animal's retort. "They've forgotten about our asses. Or they're up to their *own* asses in the shit! The plan's been changed, only those little fucks forgot to tell us!"

"That's bullshit!" she replied. "They'd tell us."

"When was the last time you heard anything from anybody?" Animal asked. "What's your signal strength? Mine is shit!"

Stephie raised the small stick that dangled from her helmet and read its tiny color LCD display. The cellular radio signal strength was a barely visible nub. She arched her neck to curse the high ridges between which they lay and cranked up the gain.

A squeal climbed in strength in her right ear, lighting up her command channel with unintelligible electronic noise. After a few seconds of steadily rising squall Stephie could make out a human voice from the howling. A few seconds later, she realized it was a man, and that the man, whoever he was, was shouting. Then the tone—desperation—became clear. Finally, she recognized the words. ". . . outa there! Pu-u-l-l ba . . . !" Then the voice.

It was the voice John Burns.

A helicopter's rotors beat at the air to their rear. John's voice grew ever clearer. John wasn't on the helicopter, as much as Stephie knew he'd want to be. The helicopter's radio was simply relaying his urgent orders.

"Pull outa that valley right now 'cause they're comin' through and not stopping!"

Artillery crackled overhead.

"Say again!" Stephie shouted in anticipation of the roar that was soon to follow. She burrowed deep into her hole, and the earth and air shook. Rock chips peppered the boulders. Twigs and branches scratched off her helmet.

"Stephie . . . !" she heard over her earbuds. But the excited shout was drowned out by the deafening barrage. Dozens of heavy shells slammed into the ground to Third Platoon's front. The concussive waves reverberated across Stephie's position.

"We're taking fire!" Stephie screamed over the company net.

"Those are *our* guns!" John shouted back. "Pull back! Do it now! *Right* now!"

Stephie understood the situation from the tone of John's voice. Something bad was coming. "Animal, you heard him!"

"We're outa here!" he replied. Just then, the Chinese guns opened fire.

"All squads, withdraw to the rally point!" Stephie commanded when the first American rose.

"Smith!" Stephie shouted. "Covering fire!"

Smith's two machine guns both roared instantaneously. But as Stephie watched, two of Animal's retreating cherries fell in the hail of Chinese fire. Their buddies retrieved the writhing soldiers and dragged them toward the rear, heedless of their wounds. The troops on Stephie's left flank fared slightly worse. By the time they passed Stephie's position, most were clutching at spurting wounds or holding gaping rends, eyes wide with shock and fear.

"Smith!" Stephie shouted. American artillery lit the rocks ahead with concentrated fire. Smith stuck hard by his two machine gun crews. John shouted in Stephie's ear, but she ignored him. In the fires from the artillery barrage, Stephie could see thousands of Chinese soldiers pouring down the narrow ravine toward the guns.

"Smi-i-ith!" Stephie shouted, but to no avail. Some men sprinted by weaponless. Without leadership, they would arrive at the rally point and keep running. "Smith!" she screeched. "Get back here! We're pulling back!"

Bullets smacked into the hard earth and snapped through the branches. The zipping sounds forced Stephie's head down. When she raised her head, she raised her rifle and felled two enemy soldiers, who climbed up the steep slope on their left for better shots. "Smith! God-*dammit!*"

Smith rode the two big guns like a trick rider. He lay hunched over on the bank almost leaning against one. The other gun fired a continuous stream of lead from directly across the streambed up the hill past Smith's outstretched finger.

Smith pointed, and the guns laid waste to dozens of on-rushing Chinese, just as Stephie had planned.

"Stephie, for God's sake, answer me!" John called pitifully.

It was her last chance to escape. Smith and the four men in the machine gun crews—fifteen meters closer to the enemy—had already let their last chance pass.

"*Smith!*" Stephie screamed one last time as she pushed herself out of her hole. She half expected the guns to fall silent as the five men tried to disengage too late. But it wasn't her nerves that held them in place. It was Corporal "S." Fucking Smith—the rock—whose radio was obviously shot through.

A couple of minutes later, when the two guns finally died, almost in unison, Stephie finally paused from her flight to the rear. Breathing hard, Stephie called over the radio, "Last position is clear! Adjust fire to last position! Fire for effect! Fire for effect!"

"Stephie?" John interrupted over the company net.

"Adjust fire to last position!" she repeated.

"But Stephie . . . ?" he questioned.

"The valley is clear! Fire for effect! *On my fucking authority!*" She resumed her personal retreat with her back lit by flame.

Major Ackerman arrived with an old-fashioned pad and pen. "Casualties?" he asked at the front bumper of his armored car. John Burns looked at Stephie. "Four dead," she answered woodenly. "Eleven wounded. Six missing, presumed KIA."

Ackerman wrote. That pissed Stephie off. She heaved a sigh, rubbed her eyes, and dabbed her runny nose on her sleeve.

"How about enemy casualties?" John asked.

Stephie licked her chapped lips and shrugged. "I dunno." She looked away, exhausted. The panicked hour that it had taken to round up her stray platoon and to treat dying men and women in the dirt behind cold rocks had sapped hours of strength from her reserve. That reserve was dipping dangerously low. She cared very little about anything. When the well went dry, she wouldn't care at all.

"Take a guess," Ackerman prompted.

She had to think. *Enemy casualties?* "From the artillery? And the two guns?" Again she shrugged. "A hundred. Two hundred. Three hundred. I dunno."

Ackerman wrote something.

"Are you writing down a number, or are you writing down something about me?" Stephie asked. Ackerman and John both looked up.

"How many days have you been in combat?" Ackerman asked.

"It's been over two weeks since we had a break," she replied.

"He means you," John said gently.

"How long?" Ackerman repeated, pen in hand.

"You want me to count all the way back to Alabama?" Stephie asked.

"I mean continuous combat?" Ackerman said. "How long?"

Stephie sneered and turned from Ackerman to John. "As if you don't know."

Ackerman put his pad and pen into his blouse pocket.

"Thirty-five days, Stephie," John supplied.

"That's too long," Ackerman concluded.

"Oh, well no fucking *shit*!" Stephie snapped. Ackerman's driver and commo at the rear bumper overheard. Ackerman headed for the passenger door. "I'm pulling Third Platoon off the line."

"I did *not* fuck up!" Stephie heedlessly blurted out. "Is that what *you* think?"

"*No*, Stephie," John insisted.

Stephie glared at Ackerman. From his clenched jaw, she saw, he would yield not an inch. Knots bulged from his cheeks as he contained his anger. "Everyone has a limit," said a man who was clearly within sight of his. He turned to John Burns. "I'm giving Third Platoon to brigade HQ for local security." He slammed the door and was gone in seconds. Dirt laid for traction on an icy road shot from his car's six oversized, knobby tires.

"That's not what he meant," John assured Stephie in the silence that followed.

He tried to take her arm but she tore it from his grip and stormed off. She fled to hide not her anger but her reaction to it. Her eyes flooded with tears, and her mouth quivered and twitched. One shot at combat command was all she got.

WHITE HOUSE OVAL OFFICE
December 13 // 1845 Local Time

Bill closed the thousand-page report. He had blocked out the entire afternoon to read it behind closed doors. The hastily assembled blue ribbon investigative committee had worked around the clock in the weeks since the murder of Elizabeth Sobo and the half dozen aides and Marine One crew members. They had left hundreds of loose ends dangling, but one conclusion had ample support.

The bomb had been meant for Bill.

He called his secretary. "Is Fielding still out there waiting?"

"He's in the Situation Room, sir," she replied.

"Get him up here."

Bill reread the committee's conclusion. They had not yet determined whether the assassins were foreign or domestic. The report, however, was exhaustive and thoroughly researched. Bill turned to one particularly irksome page. The committee had noted Clarissa's nausea immediately after the bombing and attributed it to understandable shock. After all, she had been prepared to board the doomed flight, which ruled her out as a potential suspect. But a footnote reported that the FBI disagreed. Clarissa remained on Hamilton Asher's list of suspects.

Richard Fielding entered the Oval Office.

Bill dropped the report on his desk with a thud. "That fucking asshole Asher is willing to frame *Clarissa*—and let the *real* murderers go *free*—just to take a cheap political shot at me!"

Bill telephoned the chief justice of the United States in Omaha, which was the emergency relocation site for most of the rest of the federal government. "It's despicable!" Bill said as they waited.

The chief justice appeared on the video screen. "Good evening, Mr. President."

"When will you be ready to hand down your decision about the National Secrecy Act?" Bill asked angrily and abruptly. The astonished chief justice replied that he couldn't discuss matters before the Court. "I'm not arguing the goddamned case, but that Act is unconstitutional and you damn well know it! I need your decision, and I need it now! I'm fighting *two* wars: one against the Chinese and the other against Hamilton Asher. He's subpoenaing, following, and probably bugging half my staff, who are working on highly classified war plans! How the hell do you keep a military secret when the FBI is bugging you? It's *outrageous*, and our young men and women's lives are at stake! Our nation's survival is at stake! All of Asher's activity—all of it—is being conducted under the authority of an Act that I'm confident you've already voted to rule unconstitutional! Now all I'm asking is that you get whatever clerk you've got drafting that opinion off his *ass* and get that ruling out! There's a war on!"

"I can assure you, Mr. President, that we understand the urgency of the situation," the chief justice calmly replied.

A calmer Baker thanked him and hung up. He had vented some of his anger, but the lid still rattled. "The instant that decision comes down," he said to Fielding, "I'm telling Treasury to cut Asher's budget by 80 percent, and I'm telling Defense to revoke the draft exemption for his agents. He's got almost 12,000 able-bodied men and women prying though the trash cans of my staff. We could form a *division* out of his people."

Fielding delicately cleared his throat. "Uhm, Mr. President," he nonchalantly inquired, "who will perform domestic counterintelligence after you cut the FBI?"

Bill smiled at Fielding's guileless attempt to restore his agency's former stature and budget at the expense of Fielding's old nemesis at the FBI.

"Oh, I dunno," Bill replied. "Do you think the CIA is up to it?"

Fielding shrugged and said, "It's against the law for the CIA to operate domestically."

Baker stated, dictatorially, "Until we win this war, *I* am the fucking law."

Outside Fredericksburg, Virginia
December 16 // 0230 Local Time

It felt to Hart as if his face were cut by blades of ice blown on the wind. Part snow, part frozen knife, the breeze sliced sideways across the crackling brush in which he lay.

He was at home.

Hart had spent only one week behind friendly lines. Most of it had been spent sleeping. Sleeping while waiting on a ride. Sleeping while waiting for new papers to be typed up. Sleeping on trucks, and planes, and helicopters. He had found it hard to break from the newfound body rhythm. He had had to shake himself awake as he crept through friendly lines and returned to occupied America.

But now, Hart had no such problems. He was wide awake. For beneath his vantage lay one hundred thousand Chinese soldiers. At least, that was what the infrared looked like as he panned the camera across the dark valley.

He was perched atop a microwave tower almost two hundred feet above the earth well inside the Chinese defensive perimeter. To the naked eye—in total darkness—there were only black treetops. But on the screen before him were a hundred thousand bright spots. A hundred thousand faint emitters of heat. Bright and fatter were the running engines

or electric generators. Shining conduits—heating ducts—
snaking from tent to glowing tent. But mainly there was an
army of dim glow worms. Hart could see them clearly—snug
and warm in their slumber—through the unshielded canvas
of their shelters.

The microwave tower was an obvious choice for Hart's
remote recon. From the antennae and cabling nothing would
have appeared amiss to the brave Chinese engineer who had
scaled to the height from which Hart now clung. But inside
the metal post—impervious to X-ray inspection—was the
transmitter into which Hart's camera was now plugged.

"Pan the camera left thirty degrees," directed his mission
briefer, who was controlling him from Washington fifty miles
away. Hart swung the camera—and the picture on his and the
briefer's screens—thirty degrees to the left. He was a human
pan-and-tilt camera mount in a gusting winter wind high
above the frozen earth.

The cold was perfect for this mission, which had to be done
at night. The digital infrared video camera saw only heat.
During the day, the earth's warm background glowed brightly
and obscured all but hot engines or open fires. At night, the
cold-soaked black canvas was filled with red dots, some moving, some still. He panned slowly on distant cue from one
end of the valley to the other. The four-inch screen displayed
stick figures everywhere. Everywhere. Everywhere.

"That's about it," his briefer said over the microwave. The
stereo sound was clear over the two small ear buds. "Is the
security still good?"

Hart glanced down toward the trees, whose tops danced
between his dangling feet. He was tethered to the antennae
mounts and being blown with each solid gust. The pictures
would have been useless but for the camera's built-in stabi-
lizer.

"Security's fine," he replied into the boom mike.

"Then reacquire and track that convoy," came the terse
command.

Hart leveled the lens on the dozen-vehicle convoy and
zoomed in. The searing engines contrasted sharply with the
black night earth. They halted midway down the valley. Over

a hundred glowing stick figures climbed out. Hart held the camera steady and waited. The mission was nearing its end.

He felt as if there were something more that he should say to his briefer. He hadn't known the man from Fifth Special Forces Group. He had said they needed an experienced hand for this mission—like Hart—not one of the six-month wonders who'd just been handed his green beret. There had been scattered reports, he had informed Hart, of a Chinese troop buildup. The planners had pinpointed this valley as an ideal staging area. The briefer and the other tense officers with whom Hart had met showed keen, almost edge-of-the-seat interest.

"Why that valley?" Hart had asked them immediately.

"It runs north-south straddling a highway straight to DC," his briefer had answered. The colonel had only one eye. From shooting the shit, Hart had dated the wounds of the Special Forces officer to the Caribbean campaign when the war was still in its infancy. Only now had the grievously wounded man hobbled back to duty for perhaps the war's final hours.

The engines of the dozen vehicles in the convoy were noticeably dimming. Cooling after having been shut off. They were parked, possibly for the night.

"All right, mission complete," came the colonel's call. "Execute your egress."

Hart would be leaving the immediate danger of the tower, but he would remain behind enemy lines. He wasn't headed home. Or maybe he was already there. After only a week of vacation in a foreign land still free from war, he was back behind enemy lines.

"Do you copy?" asked the one-eyed colonel. "Execute egress. Mission accomplished."

Hart realized that the camera still recorded the cooling vehicle engines.

"Copy," Hart replied into the mike. He reached for the power switch, but he hesitated. "There's a whole lot of 'em down here," Hart said, stating the perfectly obvious. In his mind he saw Chinese troops parading down Pennsylvania Avenue in Washington, DC. Climbing atop famous statues for photographs like all conquering armies. "If they come your way," Hart said, "kill 'em all. Don't let 'em take the capital."

After a pause, the colonel replied, "Roger that."

Hart clicked the camera off, unplugged the three jacks, and climbed down the narrow ladder to the dark, still earth below.

When he'd made it out through the fence surrounding the tower, his gut had told him he was safe. He'd gotten several miles away before he'd stumbled into a patrol carrying flashlights, automatic weapons, and the most dangerous tool of all: field radios.

Hart lay in a drainpipe under an asphalt county road stuffing foam plugs deep into his ears. He couldn't run away. There was no cover. It was wide open terrain. He'd be seen and shot to death instantly. And yet it was routine for a patrol to check places like pipes!

He'd fucked the puppy, and he knew it. It was over. He was finished. He was dead.

Jesus Christ! he raged through gritted teeth.

Out of nowhere, his eyes teared up. He couldn't fucking believe it! *Shit!* He gasped as his lungs seized up and his breathing grew labored. He raised his infrared lenses and rubbed his eyes with gloved thumb and index finger. He sniffed to clear his nose and dropped his lenses.

"Fuck it," he mumbled on hearing the approach of the patrol. From the sound of their voices the Chinese soldiers were loose. At ease. They thought that they were safe.

Hart raised his fearsome weapon to his cheek and wrapped his left forearm in its sling.

But survival behind enemy lines depended on stealth. You lived only if there was one hundred percent silence. If no one outside your killing zone heard the bedlam of death that lay inside that zone. Hart's only luck came in the form of the high ridges and thick pines that rose all around the pipe and the asphalt road. Sound wouldn't carry far through all the acoustic reflectors. It would be measured in feet, not in miles. If he got another break and the patrol outside was a squad, not a platoon, Hart could manufacture the life-saving silence. He would kill every living thing within earshot of that pipe before they got a radio call off, or he would die in a ten-second blaze.

That was where his weapon came in. He'd chosen well at the Fifth Special Forces Group's supply depot in Maryland. In place of polished wood stock there were slender black tubes clutching a thick box magazine. It was short and inelegant, but it had the highest cyclic rate of fire in the arsenal: twenty-five rounds per second.

Instead of a bayonet it was tipped with a fat, foot-long silencer. But that name—"silencer"—was bullshit. The people you were shooting at knew you were there. You couldn't "silence" the visceral feeling of armor-piercing rounds coming at you at just under the speed of sound from a range of thirty feet. You didn't miss the heat and the jetting flame from the sawed-off implement of close-in death. If you lived long enough, you'd remember the stench of its breath.

A faint red glow leaked into the slender drainpipe. The goggles that wrapped around his eyes registered the ambient heat that flowed into the cold concrete tube. The raised front sight of the carbine-sized machine pistol that loomed before him emitted a signal that Hart couldn't see. The signal informed his goggles where the weapon was aimed. His goggles put a green dot on his retina that displayed the aimpoint. That brilliant dot now wobbled slightly in the round end of his tomb.

His cheek hurt from the press of the cool stock. He was both pissed at himself and sick with self-pity. It was a stupid, *stupid* fuck-up to get trapped! And now he would die because of it.

Voices drifted nearer. He instinctively wrapped his sling once more around his left forearm. Tighter. The strap encircled his left elbow. The machine pistol was too light and would ride its box magazine into the sky. The sling—and Hart's concentration and nerve—would hold it down.

Without taking his cheek from the stock, he unzipped a flap at his hip. Three fragmentation and three stun grenades peeked from individual sleeves. They were his last resorts.

A shaking beam flashed into the ditch beyond the far end of the pipe. With the brief burst of light, his goggles switched to the visible spectrum. The reds were replaced with a haze of cobwebs that he hadn't seen until then.

Smoke. The excited, almost random thought ricocheted through his mind upon seeing the cobwebs. The Chinese used light amplification. They'd be blinded by smoke. But infrared would see right through it!

He held his machine pistol left-handed and swept his helmet and goggles from his head. Squatting, he cradled them in his lap and unfurled a tightly rolled gas mask from its home on Hart's belt. Since the gymnasium he hadn't been without it. He hadn't used it since then either, until now.

The seals sucked tight on Hart's face when he inhaled. On went his helmet and goggles, and within seconds up came his weapon.

They were close. He could hear numbers of them on the road. They were the ones fate had sent to kill him.

He opened the pouch covering his four smoke grenades with a plastic *tick,* and he grimaced. But they were still a dozen meters away and he was underground.

With one last nod—to himself—he straightened his tense, cramping back and scampered down the length of pipe toward the enemy.

He plowed through spiderwebs, banged his helmet on the ceiling, scuffed his rubber cleats, and splashed through puddles, each noise threatening to end his life. But he had to get to the far end of the pipe before the Chinese. If he got caught inside, he was dead. A grenade explosion would be channeled out two ends of the pipe's barrel, and he would be caught in the channeled blast's path.

When the opening to the red night loomed large—six feet away—the patrol arrived outside. Hart could hear every word, but he understood none. It could be five men. Or ten. Somewhere in between lay the bright line between life and death. Somewhere between five and ten men was a number of enemy soldiers one beyond his ability to kill. Or, at least, beyond his ability to kill without also dying.

But that was what was going to happen anyway, he knew. All he was left with was, *How many can I kill before they kill me?* His attention was drawn more and more to the tragedy of it all. His life would end then and there.

A powerful beam of light arced into the sewer where Hart would die. The rivulet of water shimmered like ocean caps on a bright summer day. It was a digital artifact created as his goggles toggled from infrared back to visible light. It was artificial, but it was the last beauty that Hart would ever see.

The tears returned to contort Hart's face behind his mask, but this time he ignored them. He pulled a smoke grenade from its pouch with his right hand.

The flashlight was extinguished. Hart raised his right arm like a quarterback.

A lazy order was issued from the road paralleling the ditch.

Hart's thumb popped the safety on the thin, cylindrical smoke grenade. His left hand held his automatic weapon steady. They were trained to fire weapons with either hand in case of wounds. The imaginary aim point projected into his eye rested on a distant bend in the ditch and displayed its range: "11" meters. The bend appeared to be a bulging concrete access to a manhole around which the ditch had been dug. In infrared, its armored hide was black. Cold, hard cement. Hart's refuge. His hope. His only chance.

Eleven meters, Hart thought. Ten or twelve steps on the dead run.

The number dropped suddenly to "5" as the dot refocused on bent, springy knees. Fatigue trousers bloused into combat boots. Hart's last breath turned solid in his lungs as a dozen pairs of legs skidded down the dirt sides of the ditch or splashed into its sloppy center.

Hart hurled the smoke grenade out of the red opening, barely missing his executioners' legs. Its handle flew off mid-air and tumbled out of the pipe. He switched the weapon back to his right hand as it skittered through the dirt and into the water.

There was a startled call in high-pitched Chinese—more a frightened squeal. Then laughter. A joke. They teased the guy for being scared of what they must have assumed was a scampering rat.

The red dot steadied on the stooping torso of the poor bastard in front. He fumbled with a bulky, high-powered flash-light.

The squeal of the smoke grenade was twice the volume of a man's shrill scream. The Chinese spun and shrunk in terror. Smoke spewed out of the fiercely whistling grenade, filling the ditch, the road, and the trees from two brilliant torches: one at either end of the glowing red cylinder.

Hart pulled the trigger, and his weapon jerked wildly in his hands. He fought to keep its muzzle down as it hammered his shoulder. Flame jetted from its short barrel and long suppressor. Hands, thighs, knees, shins, and pelvises were snapped like twigs. The Chinese soldiers at the other end of its muzzle were splintered by dozens of devastating blows.

Hart charged toward the opening still killing. Twenty, thirty, forty rounds were fired before he burst from the pipe. Subhuman shrieks were loosed. Hart charged down the trench—stopping at nothing—with his trigger pinned to the pistol grip.

Long jets of flame from his weapon silenced screams from left and right. He swept the bucking barrel from side to side, leapt over falling bodies, hurdled the smoke grenade, and ran out of ammo just as he collided with the cold, hard concrete. He smashed his cheek, his gear, and both his knees with stunning force into the immovable, manmade fixture. He bounced back onto his butt, landing with a grunt.

He had lived.

It was a total fucking miracle.

But only a momentary advantage existed. When the confusion ended, he would be hunted and killed by the survivors who had remained on the road. With one hand, he straightened his goggles. With the other, he felt his way to the opposite side of the manhole. Hart reloaded and climbed up the ditch wall onto the hard, half-buried concrete bulb. Through the all-enveloping smoke he could clearly see six glowing Chinese soldiers dead in the ditch. Amazingly, the six glowing Chinese soldiers on the road were frantically donning protective gear. Masks, suits, gloves, the whole works.

The Chinese thought that the smoke was gas.

They knelt on the road as if in prayer—weapons and gear

strewn all about—mistakenly believing they had just been doused with human insecticide. Some ghastly fucking chemical mine left behind by American fanatics. They abandoned all reason in their pursuit of speed.

None had taken the time yet to use the radio.

Hart jammed his rifle to his soldier and began connecting the dots. He switched to three-round bursts, zoomed his goggles to "2X," and put a green dot on a glowing red head. The rifle shook and burped. The man was gone. No one heard Hart's weapon. No one saw the man fall. The whistling smoke grenade obscured sight and drowned out sound. As soon as the dot settled on the next man Hart squeezed the trigger. A spray of warm red blood cooled to black in midair.

It was marksmanship practice from fifty feet. Hart chopped men down one by one. All would have been done in seconds had not one fallen in death upon another. In the moment's forewarning, the last man alive dove into the ditch and crawled into the pipe that had been Hart's refuge. Hart stitched the ditch with nine rounds, but missed.

"Shit," Hart mumbled before movement from the road— from the wounded—drew quick, certain bursts. One. Two. Three. Hart put an insurance round into each of the glowing forms on the road. All dead, except for the one in the pipe.

He climbed back down into the ditch, took a deep breath, nodded to himself, and pressed his helmet to his head.

He headed back for the pipe. It loomed dark and cold ahead. It was suspended at its end above the washed out ditch. The grenade emitted dying jets of flame and—unseen to Hart's IR goggles—billowing, thick smoke. He passed the still warm bodies littering his path and stood to the side of the black pipe. Only this time, *he* was on the outside and his enemy was within. Trapped. Hopeless. Dead.

The man in the pipe shouted through ragged tears into a radio. He called, and called, and called in Chinese, pausing only to suck in panicked gulps of air. His voice shook, trying to whisper, but gave in to the beast and shouted into the unresponsive device.

Hart nosed the muzzle of his machine pistol into the pipe and pulled the trigger as tearful pleas came in Chinese.

Hart pulled the trigger. The machine pistol shook hard for two seconds. The burp echoed from the far end of the pipe, then there was total silence save for the hissing static over the Chinese man's radio. The radio waves didn't penetrate concrete pipe and the earth on top of it.

The flashlight with its stocky battery lay at Hart's feet. He picked it up and turned it on. Smoke swirled in the pipe. The light drew no fire, so he tentatively peered inside. He could see nothing but clouds of smoke.

He clicked off the powerful light, and the white clouds were replaced by the red and the black of Hart's hot and cold world. The goggles switched back to infrared. The only exception to the cold blackness were the white-hot weapon that Hart held, the cooling red cartridges scattered about the bottom of the pipe, and the faint glow of a cross-legged dead man, flung over backwards by fifty rounds.

Hart stood amid the glowing dead he'd strewn about the ditch and the road. He felt invincible for a moment, but the adrenaline wore off a mile or two away. From there on he just felt sick.

10

The gyrating helicopter bucked beneath Wu as he ducked beside a ball-mounted, six-barreled aircraft cannon. The Gatlin gun–style weapon aimed down through clear armored glass, pivoting with digital quickness. His thumbs were jammed hard into his ears, but still he jumped when the fearsome 30 mm loosed a one-second, one-hundred-round buzz. The vibrations penetrated him to the core.

The Virginia countryside streaked beneath Wu's boot heels, which were braced semisuccessfully against the slippery, see-through deck, which was composed of translucent laminate. A rubberized, half-meter-wide strip down the center of the nearly invisible fuselage looked like a catwalk on a daredevil aircraft.

Six hollow-eyed soldiers sat opposite Wu on the other side of the rubber air bridge. They eyed him with sullen curiosity. Some had gingerly boarded the helicopter at the division staging area still limping from wounds so recent that Wu thought they might not yet have healed properly. When they had all crowded into the side of the compartment away from Wu, he had thought that it was because they didn't care for him. He wore crisply laundered battle dress and unscuffed webbing. The black assault rifle he had checked out of the armory bore no nicks, dents, or scratches. Wu knew that his appearance was described by the common soldiers—derogatorily—as that "new-in-box look."

But now he realized that the half dozen young veterans knew better than to sit next to the infernal, remotely operated gun. Another hundred-round burst of explosive rounds gave Wu an unpleasant rush of adrenaline like at an unexpectedly slammed door. He followed the streaking tracer rounds to the forest below. Fire rose from a stream's bank a kilometer away, and white splashed from the water as the gun buzzed again.

Wu shied away from the warming barrels. The pilot flew extremely low in a pitching circle round and round the smoking target. A crewman appeared from the flight deck up front, duckwalking his way rearward toward Wu. Treetops flashed just meters beneath the crewman, who negotiated his way from one hand strap to the next. When he arrived beside Wu, he pulled a jack from the bulkhead and plugged it into Wu's helmet. Wu reached up and inserted the earbuds dangling from the Kevlar.

"We'll be done in a minute!" shouted the crewman over the intercom. "We got diverted by a ground controller! They've got the gun!" he said, nodding at the pivoting machine cannon. A television camera mounted on the fuselage outside matched the gun's pivots and sweeps. "It's a forward observer team!" the crewman said, cupping one hand in another as if grasping and directing an imaginary joystick. "You know, they have a screen and control our fire direction system! We just fly over the target area till they release us! There's just one hold-out! We shouldn't be long!"

Wu raised the stubby boom mike on his chin strap. "You say there's just one man down there?" Wu asked.

The crewman shook his head. "It's a woman, apparently!" he shouted. "One woman with a rifle in the woods!" He made a face and shrugged as if to say, *"Who could imagine such a thing?"* then duckwalked back to the cockpit.

As he'd predicted, the wild flight steadied suddenly. The gun returned to a lower, stowed position. The aircraft left the smoking target area. *Mission accomplished,* Wu thought. *Woman dead.* He had the rest of the flight to celebrate the victory in silence. His mood matched that of the six soldiers staring at him

The helicopter landed in the parking lot of a gutted suburban mall, and Wu exited into the chill. The downdraft from the rotors intensified, forcing Wu and the others to their knees until silence reigned in the absence of the powerful aircraft.

Wu rose and looked around. The wares of various stores and their packaging were strewn like debris blasted from smashed doors and broken windows across the pavement. But there had been no explosions other than social disorder, Wu thought. The stores had clearly been looted.

Several of the soldiers with whom he'd flown in headed for the mall, but Wu's attention was fixed on the wooded hills to the north. It had taken ten days and three more visits to General Sheng before Wu's reassignment had been approved. *Personally* approved, in fact, by the defense minister. Shen Shen had used the time to lavish Wu with sex in her desperate attempt to talk him out of going.

He shouted at the would-be scavengers and pointed toward the front. Toward the rumble of artillery and the ominous curtain of black smoke that marked the American defenses surrounding the great naval base at Norfolk, Virginia. The near constant crackle of massed small-arms fire formed a wall of noise that seemed to come from all points of the northern horizon. Against that patter played the percussion of light artillery. Drumrolls of dozens of rounds timed onto their targets. The even deeper pounding base of heavy rockets promised a finale, but there was no end to the symphony. No final movement, just the staccato melody of infantry weapons that always carried the tune.

The morning air was chilly. They crossed abandoned fields on the rural outskirts of the small southern town. Climbed over a barbed wire fence. Ascended a wooded hill.

Patches of snow clung to the shades under the brush. Despite the fury from the front, the woods seemed almost quiet. The young soldiers Wu led—veterans at age nineteen or twenty—all held their rifles at the ready. He had no idea what they expected to encounter, but he unslung his rifle, confirmed that the magazine was full and seated, and held it at port arms.

They crested the hill and descended toward another open pasture. An inflated green dome sat in the center of the field surrounded by thousands of brown slashes in green grass. It was as if treasure hunters had systematically excavated the rolling landscape in search of some mislaid plunder.

But they were graves, Wu realized. Failures buried all around the besieged, portable field hospital. The desperate facility they approached was overcrowded. Men lay on litters on the ground under the open sky just outside. Nurses and doctors tended to soldiers, whose arms were raised to shield their eyes from the sun.

Wu led his small group in a wide semicircle around the moans of pain, which easily carried the distance. Their pitiful voices turned the symphony of weapons into a tragedy. The faint wails drowned out the sound of fighting that would surely add to the hospital's load.

A young Chinese nurse wearing an apron that flapped with trotting knees intercepted Wu's small party. "We need blood!" she demanded. "It won't take ten minutes!"

Wu never stopped walking. He shook his head and waved her off like a beggar. "*Please,* sir!" she squealed. "The medical staff can't give any more! Men are dying for lack of a transfusion!"

Wu halted his march, turned, and followed the nurse. The soldiers followed him.

Lieutenant Wu eventually reported to his company commander with drill-field precision. The grimy captain rose to his feet in a bullet-riddled house that smelled of fire and stared wide-eyed at Wu. "Why are you here?" he asked in a high-pitched voice. It was obvious the man had been told who Wu was.

Wu took a seat, and the captain did the same. The senior officer leaned forward—hands on his knees and attentive—

while the junior officer lounged in his chair and casually removed his gloves. "I need combat experience," Wu answered honestly. "Preferably, command of an infantry platoon."

"You must be *insane*!" the captain practically shouted. "Do you realize what you're asking? How short the life expectancy of an infantry platoon leader is? In six weeks, my four platoons have been through *seven* platoon leaders!" He leaned closer and lowered his voice. "Your family would *hang* me if you die!"

"Almost all of my classmates became platoon leaders," Wu insisted. "*They're* my family."

Thoroughly dissatisfied with the answer, the captain nevertheless had no choice but to relent. He had already received his orders. He stood, shook Wu's hand and dismissed the lieutenant. When Wu left, a colonel entered from the next room. Headphones dangled from his neck as he retrieved and packed his hidden microphone and camera.

"Did you get what you needed?" the captain asked.

The senior officer only smiled as he finished up, and the captain didn't press him for an anwer. It was best not to ask too many questions of a man who had come straight from the defense ministry in Beijing.

Wu joined his new troops in the middle of a patrol. It was an awkward, "Here's-your-new-platoon-leader" introduction whispered by the captain to groups of two and three soldiers at a time as they huddled behind cover. As the company commander departed, Wu noted, he stopped and whispered to the platoon's noncommissioned officers, informing them, Wu suspected, just who the hell Wu was. Each time the captain made such a stop, the sergeants' eyes darted to Wu.

Wu didn't lead his men, he followed them toward a metal-sided auto garage on the outskirts of a besieged American town. Their mission seemed simple and low-risk. "Sweep a three-hundred-meter front from the highway to the power lines," the platoon sergeant had explained to him, watching Wu for any reaction. Wu had just nodded.

As far as Wu could tell from the map, the small community they entered had no name. It had formed, however, one of the links in the outer defenses of the Norfolk Naval Shipyard. There were bodies—American and Chinese, mainly Chinese— lying in twisted heaps all across the landscape. *The random litter of human remains on a battlefield,* Wu thought, noting the sights and smells with interest. He tried to make out from the pattern of strewn corpses and bloodstains what exactly had happened in the fight. In the end, however, he concluded that it made no sense. Chinese. American. American. Chinese. The bodies were mixed. Draped, in some places, atop fighting holes whose original owner could have been soldiers from either army.

But Wu knew what had happened without direct, empirical study. The big picture told the story of the small. Repeated Chinese attacks had finally broken the enemy. They had over- whelmed them, Wu thought as he stared at the embankment of a small, nearly empty artificial pond. The berm of mud and grass had offered attacking Chinese temporary shelter, Wu guessed, until some unseen American gun had opened fire from a supporting position. Thirty men lay dead in a nearly perfect row. A picket fence of corpses inclined at forty-five degrees with their feet in six inches of water.

The company commander had his choice of platoons for Wu to command. All had lost their lone officer. The unit he had chosen was the one platoon not joining the main attack against the local militiamen—middle-aged retirees from mil- itary service who now worked at the port—who were tena- ciously defending the city. The job of Wu's platoon was to kick in the doors on outbuildings and kill ill-equipped parti- sans and desperate stragglers cut off from friendly lines.

Wu knelt behind the bumper of a car whose hulk sat atop concrete blocks. His soldiers, he noticed, had grown wary and lay prone in hollows and behind cover. Four of his men, led by Wu's platoon sergeant, pried open metal doors just wide enough to toss grenades into the darkness. Wu thought that he heard the sliver of a shout from inside just before the explosions lit the windows, shattering them. The metal siding was riddled with shrapnel and smoke belched out.

Wu rose and headed for the entrance, but his platoon ser- geant—who saw him approaching—quickly issued orders.

Before Wu could cross the yard to the entrance, two soldiers stepped into the doorway.

Both died instantly in a rip of gunfire that sent Wu to his belly. Without receiving any orders to open fire, Wu's platoon began the total destruction of the building. They were arrayed in a semicircle around the front of the garage. It was a free-fire zone right over Wu's head. The platoon sergeant and the two survivors at the door tossed more grenades inside. By the time Wu had crawled back to his former cover, his platoon sergeant had ordered a cease-fire. After sixty seconds of automatic weapons fire and two dozen hand-thrown and tube-launched grenades, every square foot of the garage walls bore ragged, smoking holes.

Again the platoon sergeant sent men inside, and again there was firing, but this time the intermittent reports came only from Chinese guns. Wu strode up to the dark, smokey garage—rifle in hand and safety off—just behind several additional soldiers, who had obviously been tasked by the platoon sergeant to act as Wu's human shield.

Once inside, it was obvious to Wu that the garage was a primitive American field hospital. The nearly dead lay moaning amid the dead. There were male and female soldiers, doctors and nurses, and civilian men, women, and children. All had been ripped to bloody shreds. A young girl, maybe ten, held her hand up and outstretched toward Wu. Blood covered her face and chest. She didn't point at him. Her palm was down as if she sought out Wu's hand to help her rise to her feet. But she might as well have pointed. Her high-pitched moan might as well have been an accusation. A curse that would stain his soul for all his days.

Wu's men busily put the survivors out of their misery with single, jarring shots. The Americans were all so badly mangled it was clear that none would survive. It was the only humane thing to do. But still there were tears and whimpers from the Americans. Not pleas for their lives. All were far too grievously wounded. Their sounds were instead mostly nonsensical laments at their horrifying and sickening ends. Wu watched one American nurse hold her hand over the eyes of a legless soldier as a smoking muzzle touched the side of the man's head.

Wu jumped when the shot was fired.

The nurse began coughing up and drowning on blood. A single red hole in her green hospital scrubs was the only sign of her fatal chest wound. Another shot blew her head open while she was busy coughing.

The young girl at Wu's boots lay wide-eyed, but her arm had sunk to the ground. A sergeant held his muzzle over the girl, but looked at Wu.

Wu fled the gore, the cries, and the reek of the slaughter for the crisp sunny afternoon outside. The shot that rang out at his back might as well have struck Wu. He fell to his knees, wrapped his arms around his belly, and shook uncontrollably.

This wasn't the way he'd thought it would be.

NORTHERN VIRGINIA
December 19 // 1830 Local Time

The weather was mild, and Stephie's Third Platoon lounged in their fighting holes dug in a ring around the camouflaged, net-covered inflatable tents of brigade headquarters. Men lay with their heads on their packs and held bellies swollen with hot food. A cook in an apron walked from hole to hole and poured steaming hot coffee into aluminum mugs.

"Care for some coffee," came a deep voice from behind Stephie. She turned and then scrambled to attention before the brigade commander. The one-star general made the fifty-meter walk from his tent to her hole to check on her almost every day. He held out a steaming ceramic mug that bore the West Point logo. She took it out of politeness and stood at ease.

The general looked at the darkening sky and said, "Word is that this weather will hold overnight but that a cold front is passing through tomorrow. You and your people have enough blankets and heaters out here?"

"Yes, sir. We'll be fine. Thank you, sir."

"I got something for you," the man said, reaching into the large field jacket pocket that draped over his thigh. It was a closed, folded palmtop that he opened and powered up. After a couple of beeps he handed it to her.

The frozen image of Stephie's father filled the small plasma display. "Just bring it back when you get through," he said, turning to leave her alone. She sank onto the lip of her fighting hole and put her coffee mug onto a flat sandbag. She hit "Play" and her father came to life.

"Hi there, sweetheart," he said with a smile. "I've heard about your new assignment. I have to admit that I've been sleeping a lot better since you got it, although there is no place that's really safe anymore. Your mother has been calling me almost every other day since she found out that you and I E-mail each other. She's pretty perturbed that I don't give her your address."

Stephie laughed.

"Your stepfather got a job working for a defense plant in Michigan. They've settled in Dearborn, and I told them I'd pass along their new address." Stephie got a pad and pen and wrote down their address and phone number. "She was relieved when I told her that your platoon had been pulled back off the line." Stephie clenched her jaw and frowned and wondered once again just how Third Platoon had managed to draw such light duty.

Her troops, however, clearly didn't mind at all. Quite the contrary—all they cared about was that their short-term lease on life had been extended. But Stephie had grown to hate the easy job. She had begun taking an ATV up to the line to look for John and the rest of Charlie Company. Sometimes, they were in their positions. Other times, they were in the shit. Each time, she found them, however, they were fewer in number. John had received a battlefield promotion to captain by Lieutenant Colonel Ackerman, now battalion commander.

There was no such opportunity for upward mobility at brigade HQ. No career advancement due to the death in combat of your immediate superior. Up to the rank of lieutenant colonel—battalion commanders—casualty rates were high. Battalions were sometimes overrun, but not so the brigades commanded by full colonels or brigadier generals.

"Anyway, you'll be happy to know I followed your security

advice," her father said. "In fact, I'd guess they quadrupled or even quintupled the White House guards. The place is crawling with Secret Service agents who look more like infantrymen than bodyguards. So I'm okay, honey. I just hope you stay that way too. I'm thinking about you. Praying for you. I can't wait to see you in person again. Maybe I'll take a trip soon to visit the troops, you never know."

He grinned, but it was a sad expression.

After he signed off, Stephie said, "Good-bye, Dad." She kissed her fingertips and pressed them against the display.

With a sigh, Stephie drained the last coffee and rose to return the mug and computer to the brigadier general who resided at the center of their defensive positions. The brigade staff's night shift was arriving through the barbed wire gate fresh from sleeping bags, and were being met by a dozen drowsy office workers heading off to bed. The men and women stood under the camo netting just outside the polyurethane tent getting updates about the jobs being handing off.

Stephie frowned at the sight. Her platoon was on duty twenty-four hours per day. Lying in the rain. In the snow. In the open.

Out of the twilight came a howling that sounded like death itself. A ferocious popping noise erupted from the direction of the brigade radio transmitters 700 meters away. The staffers ducked and began shouting. Some ran in stooped sprints for ballistic shelters holding their helmets clamped to their heads. Others dropped where they lay and crawled aimlessly or curled into fetal positions.

Stephie walked up to them as the distant rocket barrage fell silent. It was a hit and run, quick strike against pinpointed radio emissions. The rumbling echoes were replaced by the laughter of Stephie's third platoon. Her infantrymen sat heads-up in their fighting holes drinking coffee and pointing at their favorite panicked staffer.

"Would you mind returning these to the brigade commander," Stephie said to a woman who lay prone at her boots. The captain arched her neck to peer up under the brim of her helmet, then rose and brushed the dirt from her uniform.

"Thanks," Stephie said as she handed the palmtop and mug to the captain.

The general emerged from the tent and took a look at the tower of smoke that rose above the trees across a pasture. "All right," he shouted to his staff and to Stephie, "let's pack it up and relocate!"

Shit! Stephie thought as she headed out to the perimeter. Instead of relaxing that evening, they'd have to dig new fighting holes, string wire, lay mines, run fiber optic for the Intranet, and then pick it all back up again by first light, maybe sooner.

When she gave the order, one of her men said, "Shit!"

"Shut the fuck up and get moving!" Stephie snapped. "And quit teasing brigade staff, goddamit!"

PETERSBURG, VIRGINIA
December 21 // 0630 Local Time

Lieutenant Wu was awakened by a gentle shaking of his shoulder. He had been so deep in sleep that it took several moments for him to claw his way back to the surface. In his nightmare, he had been lying in a mass grave filled with Chinese and American soldiers and civilians. He gasped for air and sat upright as the dirt rained down on his face.

After a few blinks of his eyes and arches of his brows, he found himself in filthy battle dress and boots on a bare mattress in the bedroom of the modest home. He had been so tired when he crashed there that he didn't recognize anything.

General Sheng's aide, Colonel Li, stood over Wu, whose head ached instantly. A dry cough in the frigid air sent daggers through his skull. His mouth tasted of the fear and nausea from the slaughter the day before.

"We have to talk," Colonel Li said.

Wu rolled his boots to the floor and paused to take a painkiller. The aid stations dispensed them freely to lines of troops who formed every morning for sick call. Most just took the pills and returned to their units without further attention to their variety of ailments, which ranged from an accumulation of minor scrapes and bruises to gaping emotional wounds.

Wu knew why Li was there, and Wu would fight not to be recalled from combat. But part of him longed to be ordered back to Sheng's headquarters. Ordered back to Beijing. Ordered to go anywhere away from the carnage, which left him sick, and demoralized, and desperate for air.

The two officers walked through the house past exhausted soldiers, who had scrambled to slouching attention. Li, dressed in crisp and clean battle dress, seemed uncomfortable under their sullen stares, and they marched out the front door into the dawn of a new day.

The bracing blast of cold air caused Wu to zip closed his jacket and sleeves. He briefly removed his helmet to don a wool cap. The rolling lawns and street were dotted with craters two meters in diameter dug by heavy 155 mm or 175 mm artillery. The trees around the holes were stripped bare of bark. The houses were windowless. A single American armored fighting vehicle was being dragged off the street by a Chinese tank recovery vehicle, which beeped like a garbage truck as it slowly backed up.

"Let's walk," Colonel Li said. The two headed down the sidewalk, marching in step. Wu fully expected Li to explain that his time at the front was over. That the defense minister had changed his mind. Or that Wu had seen enough combat already, which was true. Or that Wu's grandfather or great uncle had intervened.

"General Sheng is making a terrible mistake," Colonel Li whispered. Wu was shocked. He stopped and turned to Li, who spoke to Wu in seeming earnest. "The troop buildup here, south of Washington, is just a diversion," Li explained in low, worried tones. "Sheng has ordered a third invasion of America without informing Beijing."

"An invasion of what?" Wu asked. "Where?"

"A direct invasion of Philadelphia. The navy will overwhelm and sink America's last two carriers at sea, then land troops at the Philadelphia Naval Shipyard and seize their two arsenal ships, which are only a month away from launch. But it's a terrible mistake. Our sources have reason to believe that the missile launchers on the arsenal ships are already operational. If they are, they would devastate the invasion fleet and massacre hundreds of thousands of soldiers and sailors."

Wu's eyes drifted to a large crater half-filled with water from a broken main. A blood trail ran half way across the street and ended—unsuccessfully—in a large dried stain. It was impossible to tell whether the blood was Chinese or American. Not that it mattered.

"We've lost over two million dead," Li whispered. "That number could double if Sheng goes forward with his plan to invade Philadelphia. We could lose this war, and if we do heads will roll."

"Why are you telling me this?" Wu asked.

Li waited until Wu's eyes rose to his. "You can stop the invasion."

PETERSBURG, VIRGINIA
December 21 // 1345 Local Time

Han Zhemin was so impatient that he rolled the window on his limousine down to monitor his driver's query. It was maddening that the military policeman could only generally direct them down the highway toward Wu's corps or division.

"Just go!" Wu shouted out the window to the driver.

The car proceeded down the road. Han raised the window against the chilly gust. *How could he be so foolish!* he raged in clench-teethed silence. The prime minister had railed at Han for not safeguarding Wu's life. For the entire way he was treating his son! "He's just a boy!" Han's father had chimed in. "We trusted that you would keep an eye on him!"

"You're driving him into the arms of the military!" the prime minister had chided.

Han loosed a sigh of exasperation so loud that it came out as half grunt, half growl.

"His unit is not far from here, sir," Han's aide announced over the car's intercom.

Han sealed his frustrations more tightly to hide them from the prying view of his solicitous aide. In so doing, the pressure mounted. He had gotten a message from Wu to meet him at the front. At "my unit," the printed E-mail had pointedly remarked. A quick phone call to General Sheng had confirmed the fact that young Wu had decided to take part in the war.

Han had exploded at the news. "How could you *dare* let him risk it?" he had challenged.

General Sheng had cut his tirade short. "The defense minister ordered me to comply with Lieutenant Wu's request."

Han's limousine slowed and was directed off the Interstate. The two short bridges that had spanned a narrow stream had been dropped. The noise level rose as the big black car crunched onto the makeshift, gravel-covered detour. It slowed to a crawl as it crept down a steep grade toward the water. Engineers were pouring rocks and dirt from a dump truck into the water in what appeared to be a constant battle to maintain the temporary crossing. The earthen construct had been laid across a series of enormous concrete pipes through which the calm stream flowed unimpeded. At first thaw, however, Han thought, the waters would rise and sweep the puny bridge from their way. That should make things more difficult for Sheng.

As the car inched onto the bridge, Han peered up at the broken spans forty meters to his right. Welding torches blazed as the two sides of the bridge arched toward each other anew.

Despite the fact that Han's limo was heavy with ceramic armor and bullet-proof glass, the six-hundred horsepower engine and four-wheel drive train easily scampered up the opposite bank.

There, the highway turned into a continuous mass encampment. The car accelerated along the Interstate, which seemed extraordinarily smooth in contrast to the detour. But Han's attention was fixed on the sides of the road. Amid the trees, under netting, were tanks, self-propelled artillery, armored fighting vehicles, assault bridges, and thousands upon thousands of tents. Colorless smoke rose from chimneys built into the canvass. Entire companies of men exercised in formation in the earthen streets amid the organized rows. Other companies lined up outside huge mess tents. The occasional roadside house bore the look of brigade or division headquarters with armored command cars sporting tall aerials just outside.

Han counted only the headquarters units until they rose into the dozens. By his rough estimate there were over a million men staging south of Washington, DC.

At the banks of the Potomac, Han went on foot in search of Wu. He was thankful that the ground was frozen solid. Otherwise, his dress shoes would have sunk into mud up to his ankles.

The hollow-eyed draftees whom his aide asked for directions also looked frozen solid. Boys of twenty struggled to their feet like old men. Their faces were raw and chapped. Their lips were cracked and bleeding. Their replies were spoken in flat, lifeless voices.

And the disrespect in their manners, their slouches, their sneers was palpable.

"Do you know where the unit is, or don't you?" Han's incensed aide repeated.

The private shrugged. Han stepped closer, drawing the soldier's attention and noticeably elevating his level of anxiety. He reeked of marijuana. His eyes were bloodshot. His gear was grimy and in disarray. His comrades eyed the encounter with bemusement from all around. All were armed and, Han presumed, dangerous.

"What's going on here?" Han asked.

"Whatta ya mean?" the disrespectful private replied. There was muted laughter, which pleased the insolent bastard.

"I mean why are these troops massed here?" Han asked, holding his arm out to the teeming woods. "What have you been told?"

The man laughed. He no longer needed encouragement from his friends. His motivation clearly came from within. "What have I been *told*?" he repeated mockingly. "Well, hm, let's see. They said the war would be over by last month, which is true, I guess, for most of the guys we came ashore with who're buried all along this fucking highway."

The anger of the men was raw. Han felt comfortable challenging Sheng, but not men such as these. They had so little to lose. He looked around but saw no officers or NCOs, though even they held little prospect of discipline. It had been a decade since most senior NCOs last had returned to China, and if the war in America lasted much longer, few would ever make it home.

"They said the Americans would be out of artillery after the first few weeks," the soldier continued, not threatening, but angry. "Instead, we get pounded all the way up to the line of departure, then pounded all the way to first contact! They said there'd be no partisan activity because our enemy is soft, but we get shot in the back with hunting rifles when we're taking a crap, or standing in line for food."

"When they bother to feed us!" another commented.

Han's aide was so shocked by their mutinous demeanor that his jaw drooped in wide-eyed outrage. Han, however, had to stifle the beginnings of a grin. "My question was," Han continued reasonably, "why are troops massed here? Did they tell you your purpose?"

The man snorted, then sniffed through a congested nose. "They said we could go home," the private replied in a defeated voice. The comment held no vigor. It was as if broaching the subject led to an avalanche of depression. "They said we could all go home if Washington fell." He glanced up at Han as if seeking confirmation or denial. "Is it true?" the private asked. The one-time cynic had irrationally turned optimist.

"What do you think?" Han asked, smiling wryly.

The man's eyes sunk closed as if his worst fears were confirmed, and he slid to the ground down the slender tree against which he leaned. Han departed lost in thought, but saw that his aide kicked the private's legs. The sitting boy didn't give any indication that he'd even noticed.

"Why are you being so *stupid*?" Han raged at his son. Wu's troops stood in a cluster behind him. They glared at Han, but he ignored them. "How could you *dare* risk your life in combat?"

"I'm a soldier," Wu replied in an almost inaudible voice.

"You're not a soldier!" Han snapped. "You're my *son*!"

"You've never *acknowledged* me," Wu answered rapidly, as if he were prepared for the opportunity.

Han was rocked by Wu's unprecedented insolence. "Everyone knows," Han muttered dismissively, "*exactly* who you are."

"No one knows who I am," came Wu's baffling but confident reply. Before Han could respond—before he could even begin to decipher the meaning of his son's comment—Wu said, "We've got to talk." Wu's remark assumed the tenor of an order when Wu marched away. Han's astonished aide cast Han a look of outrage.

Han Zhemin followed a silent Lieutenant Wu back to Han's limousine. Seated inside and alone, Wu told his father of the secret plan revealed by Sheng's aide-de-camp. "But I think that what Colonel Li told me is a lie," Wu commented.

"Of *course* it's a lie!" Han burst out, disparaging Wu's sophomoric observation with his tone. "Look at the forces Sheng has massed for a ground assault on Washington!"

"But why would Sheng send Li to lie to me like that?" Wu asked.

"To catch you and me committing treason," Han answered, rolling his eyes at the child's naive question.

"What treason?" Wu objected vehemently, with his brow furrowed deeply in confusion and alarm.

"The treason that I will commit when I pass Colonel Li's intelligence on to the Americans," Han explained as if to an imbecile. Wu ignored the slight and asked what his father was going to do. "I'm going to pass the intelligence on to the Americans! Why is it that you're too dense to understand these things, Wu?"

"But you know that the plans are false," Wu noted.

"Good God!" Han said in English, shaking his head before continuing in Chinese. "Of *course*! I wouldn't tell them our *real* plans!" Han snorted in amusement at his hopeless, lost son. "We have to seize the arsenal ships, Wu. If Baker diverts men from the defenses around Washington to repel an invasion from the sea, Sheng will break through and take Philadelphia by land. So, you see, I'm going to help Sheng win the Battle of Washington by doing what he suspects I've been doing all along, which is passing military secrets to the Americans."

"Have you been passing secrets to the Americans?" Wu asked.

Han smirked. "No, but I would if it were the right thing to do."

"Meaning," Wu translated, "that if Sheng's victories were coming too easily—if the price he paid in soldiers' lives was too low—you would try to even up the scales and extract a higher price."

"Sheng has passed secrets to the Americans," Han replied.

"That's changing the subject, and I don't believe you," Wu said. "It's a simple question. Would you aid the American war effort for domestic political gain?"

Han smiled and rocked back in his seat. "Some questions cannot be answered yes or no. And besides, your question is hypothetical. Sheng's casualties have been staggering, and when he strikes at Washington, they're going to double or triple. Did you know, Wu, that the defense ministry has 'slowed down' the process of notifying families of the deaths of their soldier sons? And any mention of a casualty in a letter or E-mail home gets you sent straight to the front."

Han laughed at Sheng's stupid plan. "They actually plan, you see, to dribble out these notices. You know. Ten or twenty thousand killed per month. They're apparently sitting on almost a million killed, and the family doesn't even know it yet." He roared with laughter.

"I don't believe you," Wu said.

"I think they've planned a big gush of the notices around January 15th," Han said, looking for the correct piece of paper on his desk. "No," he said, finding it. "The 16th. After they win the Battle of Washington. They will explain the sacrifices as necessary to attain the glorious victory over the United States of America. But the flaw in their otherwise competent plan is that in the numbers." Han tried to hold in the cackles. "Because you see, by then they will have lost more killed than they had committed to the battle! Some investigative news program is going to have a *field* day with that obvious lie. I'll see to it. And thus, the army's victory at Washington will become China's national tragedy."

"What if the Americans win the Battle of Washington?" Wu asked.

Han laughed, but without as much gusto as before. "You don't know the Americans very well, Wu. They can't take what Sheng has in store for them. He's relentless. He won't stop. He will break their backs with his human sledgehammers, and in the process he'll break his own back as well. The Americans will lose, and Sheng will lose, on the banks of the Potomac River."

Wu avoided his gaze. The silence grew more strained the longer it lasted. "Well," Wu finally said, "I guess," he shrugged, "I should get back to my platoon." When Han said nothing, Wu looked at him. "Unless, maybe, the prime minister would be offended."

Han snorted again and smirked. This time he understood the boy. He'd had enough of a taste of war. Wu looked down at his boots and at the rifle that he held between his knees. A smug, self-satisfied Han pressed the intercom button. "Driver, take us back to Richmond."

CIVILIAN HEADQUARTERS, RICHMOND
December 21 // 1530 Local Time

Han Zhemin's limousine pulled up to his headquarters. Han's aide got out and waited on the street for Han's nod before opening his door.

Father and son had said nothing to each other on the long drive back. Both had stared out at the sea of humanity and their impressive stockpiles of equipment. Wu remained firmly planted in his seat, but finally broke the silence. "I should return to Sheng's headquarters," Wu mumbled.

"What*ever* you do," his father said, "steer clear of Sheng's headquarters. And any ports, and staging areas, and airfields. Position yourself upwind of any strategic targets, not downwind. And I absolutely forbid you to go anywhere near the front. That's a direct order. Do you understand, Wu?"

Wu now understood his father's plan perfectly. "You're going to convince your old friend President Baker to defend Philadelphia against invasion," Wu said in an accusatory tone, "by diverting troops from his defenses around Washington. When Washington falls, Chinese troops will press on toward Philadelphia by land, and President Baker will have no choice but to use nuclear weapons . . . *just* as the Chinese civilian leadership had warned would happen. We're not going to seize the shipyard in Philadelphia. We're going to destroy it in nuclear retaliation! You are going to ensure that the prime minister's warnings come true! You're going to ensure that the Americans go nuclear! And the prime minister will then use the horrendous casualties to attack the defense minister politically!"

"You *see*!" Han said, particularly animated. "And you thought you weren't suited for the family business."

The silence again fell upon them. The good humor of the father contrasted sharply with the mood of the son. "What if President Baker still refuses to go nuclear?" Wu asked through gritted teeth.

"There are always contingency plans," Han replied with no suggestion that he was willing to say more.

Han nodded at his aide. The door was opened. "Remember," Han said, "stay away from and upwind of high-value targets." His aide slammed the door behind him.

Wu sat in the silence for a moment. The driver's hands gripped the wheel as he glanced into the rear view mirror. Wu pressed the "Talk" button on the intercom. "Take me to army headquarters."

WASHINGTON, DC
December 22 // 1000 Local Time

President Bill Baker and Speaker of the House Tom Leffler inspected pockmarked landmarks in the nation's desolate, evacuated capital. At the foot of the Washington Monument, they shook hands with the lone tourists to be found: a family visiting from Wisconsin.

"What brings you to town?" Baker asked the parents.

"We wanted to see everything," the mother replied. "To show our kids, you know, while we still can." The two sullen grade schoolers looked up mute and expressionless. They hurried off to take in the sights before Washington fell. The encounter cast a pall over the two elected custodians of America, who strolled on under the watchful eye of 300 Secret Service agents. The serious men and women of Baker's protective detail wore dark sunglasses and carried infantry weapons. Their business suits bulged with ammunition. The tight sphere of bodyguards stifled the conversations of the two politicians.

When Baker noticed the pace of the aging Leffler slow, he steered them to a bench, and they sat. Agents positioned themselves phalanx-like around their charges. The engines of several black-painted armored vehicles in the distance revved to life as they moved a few meters to be better prepared to react should the need arise.

Leffler's mouth constantly drooped open. His jowls hung loose just beneath. He'd aged ten years, Baker thought, in the last two. It wasn't the war that had done him in, but the loss of his strength and light: Beth Leffler.

"Tom," Bill said gently, "the Supreme Court just held your National Secrecy Act unconstitutional." Bill handed Leffler a faxed copy of the opinion, but the Speaker didn't look at it. "Listen, Tom, we're the leaders of this country, you and I. If you've got a problem with something—with anything—let's talk. But I've been hearing things." Leffler's bloodshot eyes focused on Baker, who looked off at the Washington skyline.

"There are people," Baker said in a faraway voice, "who think the monuments we've erected in this town are America. They think, therefore, that we've got to use every weapon in our arsenal to stop the Chinese from taking them, or we lose the war right here. They don't think that our men and women in those bunkers along the Potomac can do the job, so they want to use nuclear, chemical, even biological weapons all across Northern Virginia." Baker's voice was breaking. "But I will never do that." He tapped his clenched fist against his thigh. "Never! I will fight to the last man on the last peak of the Rockies because, Tom, there will always be someone on that peak. With a rifle. Fighting. That's America, Tom! *That's* America."

Tears welled up in Baker's eyes. Unexpectedly, Leffler put

his arm around the younger man—his daughter's lover—and finally spoke. "I'm worried about Clarissa."

"Tom," Baker said in earnest, "I care for her deeply. I have no intention of hurting her." But Leffler was shaking his head. He was talking about something else. "Do you mean," Baker asked, "you're worried about her *safety*?" Leffler drew a deep breath—suddenly agitated—but wouldn't look Baker in the eye. "Tom," Baker continued, "do you know something about the vice president's assassination?"

Leffler's eyes grew unfocused as he shook his head. "I swear to God," he mumbled, "that I knew nothing about it."

Leffler had used the word "knew," not "know." Baker believed him, but wondered at the choice of words. "Are you worried, Tom, about the FBI?" he asked. Leffler immediately turned to face him. Baker whispered to his newfound confidante. "Because I'm getting ready to cut Asher off at the knees. That ruling you're holding is the end of his Gestapo tactics."

Leffler said, "You know that they're after Clarissa. They say they're going to arrest her . . . as a Chinese spy."

Bill's anger flared. "Has Asher been putting the squeeze on you, Tom? *Threatening* you?" *An enfeebled old man!* Baker thought in outrage, but obviously didn't say. "That son of a *bitch*!"

Bill was still uttering curses when the head of the secret service detail apologetically interrupted. "It's the secretary of state, Mr. President."

Bill took the secure cell phone the man proffered, and with residual anger snapped, "*What is it?*"

The undaunted secretary of state immediately reported, "Han Zhemin is requesting another meeting."

NORTHERN VIRGINIA
December 23 // 2310 Local Time

Major Jim Hart tossed and turned inside his sleeping bag. He lay buried under a pile of leaves at the foot of a tree. It was a cold night, but at least it was dry. He snorted in frustration at life. Clouds billowed from his parched sinuses.

Since his last close scrape a week earlier, his controller—the one-eyed colonel—had ordered him to lie low and do nothing. Hart had chaffed at the order ever since.

He knew he had done enough for one war, but as the week wore on, the inactivity filled his veins with toxins. The only cure for the malady was to act. Like an athlete who needed to sweat, Hart needed to fight.

He knew that a major battle loomed. He was behind Chinese lines exactly twelve miles from the front. He clung close to those lines in case he got the order to come home. There, he remained hidden from the Chinese helicopters, which sprinted low through the valleys on training runs. He stayed clear of the Chinese trucks and armored vehicles, which rumbled ceaselessly down the country roads. And he avoided the Chinese artillery, which filled the flats under camouflage netting. Any day now, Hart knew, the long guns would begin raining death on young Americans who defended their nation's capital . . . and his.

How do they do it? he thought for the hundredth time. Angrily. Trying to imagine the hell of riding it out in a bunker. Waiting to die like rats on a good tank shot, or the inevitable Chinese overrun.

Hart's teeth snapped. He started. The sound was loud, and the pain sharp. He was in a helluva place to break a fucking tooth, but his tongue discovered no sharp edges. The pain went away, but the anger didn't. Hart decided, resolutely, that he should fight. Even if they called him back to friendly lines, he should fight before he went.

What if they don't call me back? he thought. *What if they just keep me here, fighting, till I'm killed?* His stomach knotted into a pit and turned. The gassy pain and taste of bile in his mouth made him want to sit up and take a swig from his canteen. But he was too tired, and he didn't want to go through the effort of covering his fucking bag with leaves again.

The war for Hart was now against the cold and the longing for a shower and a warm bed. At least, he thought, the air was clean and fresh. Not like, he imagined, life in a bunker. *Even the word,* he thought. *"Bunker."* It sounded like "tomb," or "mausoleum." *Or what was that word?* he thought. *"Sepulcher,"* said the other voice in his head. The voice that kept him company.

Hart had conversations with himself more and more frequently. It hadn't been like that when he'd stayed with the Lipscombs. A melancholy overcame Hart when he thought back to that time. He'd had daily contact with people. He would talk to Jimmy and Amanda after school, and their mother and father after dinner.

Now I'm just lying here talking to myself, he said to himself. *I need to get back into the fight. Blow a fuckin' bridge. Snipe at a convoy. Plant a mine, for Christ's sake!*

But his controller had ordered him not to do anything that might risk discovery. *"Go to ground,"* he'd said. Why, Hart had asked? The Special Forces colonel, somewhere in an underground command center in Maryland, had said something about "national strategic assets." His first words had been cut off by a drifting microwave carrier wave. He'd said something like America was conserving all its national strategic assets.

That was Hart, he had finally realized. Hart had become too valuable to be put at risk.

Back in Maryland, Hart had been told what had happened to their unit. He wasn't supposed to know in case he got captured, but a sympathetic staffer had told him anyway. Before the start of the war, the 5th Special Forces Group had scattered 4,600 Green Berets throughout Alabama and Mississippi. Of that number, 4,100 were missing and presumed killed or captured. Another 300 were known to be killed in action, usually by public execution. The final 200 had appeared on lists as prisoners of war.

"Those numbers," Hart had noted, "add up to 4,600." The staff officer had nodded. "What about me? I survived," Hart said with agitated vigor.

"You're part of the rounding error," the staffer had said.

The words had lingered with Hart. In a war in which millions die, what does one more death matter?

Maybe I'll make it back, he thought as he looked up through bare limbs at bright stars on a frigid, clear night.

Maybe I won't, said the other voice in his head. *It doesn't really matter,* both agreed.

CIVILIAN HEADQUARTERS, RICHMOND
December 24 // 1600 Local Time

Han sat at his desk on the third floor of an ordinary American office building. The plan had been for his headquarters to be located in the state governor's mansion, but it had been destroyed by retreating national guardsmen. The dingy insurance company office that now housed his headquarters was the best they could do for the time being. They would finish refurbishing the fortieth floor any day. Maybe then, he thought, in the more comfortable surroundings he would feel more like himself.

An explosion shook the windows and doors, and rattled Han's nerves. There had been no air raid siren. The blast had come from just outside. Rips of machine gun fire followed.

Han's heart froze in his chest. *This is it,* he realized. He tapped his flush video display, which rose from the desktop and offered a view of his waiting area. Soldiers in dress uniform—his security detail, or imposters—rushed into his waiting area.

The door burst open. Han jumped. Soldiers with rifles poured through. He braced himself. But instead of delivering executioners' bullets, they rounded his desk from both sides.

"Down, Administrator Han!" one shouted.

Han was seized by both arms and levered to the floor. His rib cage crashed painfully onto a leg of his chair. Han was roughly pressed up under his desk, which was armored.

The soldiers were there not to kill him, but to protect him. Han's lungs thawed. He took the first breath of his new life. And the second. And the third.

The rattling gunfire on the floor beneath them was not enough to disturb Han's euphoria over the reprieve. Han elbowed a soldier and twisted into a more comfortable position amid his fortress desk and half a dozen bodyguards. One soldier's radio tracked the progress of the partisan attack on Han's civilian headquarters.

"They're in the staircase! They're in the staircase!" leaked from the nearest soldier's earbuds. Automatic weapons blazed in concrete hollows outside his door. "Get down that hall! They're setting a charge! Use grenades! Use *grenades*!"

A dozen grenades exploded like miniature artillery on an indoor range, shaking the building.

There followed rips of automatic weapons fire.

Nothing.

Silence.

"Building secure."

The protective screen made way for a chipper Han, who rose and dusted himself off. "I want a full report on how those partisans got into this building," Han said, dismissing soldiers who were quite happy being dismissed.

On a sofa in the waiting room sat a grimy soldier. His rifle rested across his thighs. He appeared unconcerned by the recent, nearby fighting. He wore dusty full battle dress. Held his helmet in both hands. His hair shorn to a tanned scalp and neck which bore a long red scratch.

He looked straight into Han's eyes.

"Who is that?" Han asked as his aide closed the door from outside Han's office.

His aide—who was acting quite shaken by the attack and obviously wanting to get away—stuck his head through the door. "He, he arrived unannounced, sir. Not on the . . ." He coughed. "The agenda, which is full. But he refused to leave, sir. I've already called security, but obviously they have been occupied."

"What does he want?" Han asked, sniffing the air. "And find out if there is a fire in this building. I smell something."

"There *is* smoke. Yes, sir. I smell it myself. And to speak to you, sir. He wants to speak to you."

Han was incensed. "You should *tell* me these things!" He pressed his flush video display, and it popped from the desk. With two presses of a button, the camera found the soldier.

His aide stepped inside. "We didn't know if we could trust him."

"How did he get up here with a weapon?" Han asked. "And

of *course* you can trust him! He's sitting in a waiting room *waiting*! Ask him to come in!"

The man nodded as if that had been his plan all along. "Yes, sir!"

The combat officer—a major—was ushered into Han's office. Han watched carefully as he leaned the rifle against a chair by the door. As he did, Han heard the *click* as he engaged the rifle's safety.

The soldier, despite being a major, couldn't have been a year older than thirty. That was the way it was during wartime. Five or six years after commissioning, the surviving twenty-somethings commanded companies. Surviving thirty-year-olds commanded battalions of six hundred eighteen-year-olds.

The officer stood at attention before Han's desk and saluted.

"What can I do for you, Major?" Han asked graciously.

The soldier eased and then said, "The army is going to massacre my men, sir. They're getting ready to execute all of my men. Four hundred of them."

"For what?"

"Desertion, sir. They're holding them in pens at a high school on the northern edge of town."

The gears in Han's mind were now thrown in motion, grinding through the possibilities. Was this man part of some trap being set by Sheng? Or perhaps were his men truly guilty of some properly documented act of treason? Would Han's intrusion constitute civilian interference with the military's good order and discipline? That would surely be intolerable to the defense minister and indefensible by the prime minister.

Or was this just what it seemed—a plea from a soldier with a conscience—and therefore just the opportunity for which Han had been looking to escape the straightjacket of his official "agenda"?

"Why was your unit charged with desertion, Major?" Han asked.

The man grew suddenly animated. "It's total bullshit!" He leaned over Han's desk and moved to rest both hands atop it, but when Han recoiled in his chair, he restrained himself and stood stock-still. "My engineering battalion was ordered to move our bridge sections forward to a grid square that, when we *got* there, was still occupied by entrenched American troops!"

"Is the ultimate objective of your bridging operation the Potomac River?" Han asked abruptly.

The major was thrown for a moment and didn't answer. He looked around Han's office. Its official decor included limp flags in stands and pictures of Han shaking hands with the prime minister. Han waited. The major swallowed, then nodded. "I radioed that we couldn't proceed any further because we were taking fire. The regimental commander said if there were enemy troops in our position, we should dismount and take it. But they were in concrete bunkers with interlocked fields of fire that had been cleared out to a thousand meters! They had minefields that would have to be swept! Tank traps and obstacles that would have to be blown! All the while under intense direct fire! I knew there must have been some mistake, so I went straight to division headquarters."

Your first insurrection, Han thought approvingly, and nodded. So far, the story hung together. The man had broken the chain of command in bypassing his obdurate regimental commander. If that was his nature, then his ultimate mutiny would be to come to Han, the civilian governor and titular head of the military body.

"While I was gone," the young officer continued, "my men came under heavy indirect fire from American artillery. My second in command ordered a tactical retreat out of the *impact* area and ran headlong into the regimental commander, who was coming forward to bully me into an attack. I don't know what really happened next, but the regimental commander threw a fit, screamed out orders that my staff ignored, and summarily executed six of my officers, right on that road, with his pistol!"

Han nodded again. It was a highly plausible story. To cover his ass, the hotheaded regimental commander had to arrest everybody and see to it they were executed.

"The next thing I know, my entire battalion is being held

at this camp. When I went by there, I was turned away and told that it was too late. That a court-martial had sentenced all four hundred of my men to death!"

"Aren't you also subject to arrest and court-martial?" Han challenged. "This regimental commander of yours doesn't exactly sound like the forgiving sort."

"He's dead. As the military police were disarming my men, one of them killed him."

Han nodded slowly, letting the pieces settle into place. There were no rough edges. They all fit. "And so what do you want me to do?" Han asked.

"I just want you to do what you think is right," the man said simply, "Administrator Han Zhemin." His eyes were lowered to the floor.

Was his evasive answer deferential, or was it legal entrapment? He was asking Han to take a fateful criminal step, to cross the line by openly interfering with the military justice system, the army's most vital organ.

"How did you get here?" Han asked, but his visitor didn't seem to understand. "Did you drive? Do you have a vehicle?"

"I have an ATV. It's parked outside." The raised a finger to the window.

Han rose and looked down at the street. A beat-up, camouflaged all-terrain vehicle sat alone on the street many stories below. "Let's go save your men, Major," Han said. "But first I've got to change clothes."

Han rode alone in his armored limousine behind the major's ATV. Both were surrounded by Han's usual entourage of armored fighting vehicles filled with security troops.

When they arrived at the suburban high school, they were waved through by the sentries at the gates. The first things Han noticed were the stadium lights, which lit the darkening sky. The second things were the long, brown ditches that had been scraped out of the earth by bulldozers. He ordered the convoy to halt just beside the stadium's entrance. There, Han got out.

The late afternoon air was frigid. Han's aide joined him—shivering and stamping his feet—and said, "You were right to change into your ski jacket, sir." The man still wore his pinstriped suit and wool overcoat. Han had made a quick stop by his quarters and donned thermal underwear, boots, black jeans, and a three-thousand-dollar black ski jacket. He pulled his black ski cap onto his head and tugged at his black gloves.

The army major joined them, and they headed into the stadium. Thousands of young soldiers knelt on the American football field with their hands on their heads. A ring of machine guns hemmed them in the unfenced area.

Han's arrival under the lights with the major created quite a stir. They proceeded to a small raised stage. A long desk covered with a green cloth formed what he imagined was the courtroom, where the trial by the three-judge military tribunal had been conducted. The hearing had presumably been short. It was so cold outside.

The camp commander was organizing platoons of men to begin the process of sectioning the captives and mowing them down. To the uninitiated, the process seemed straightforward. But Han knew from long experience that the operation—to be conducted safely—required planning and attention to detail. The common tactic employed by the army was to pardon the best-behaved among the forty-odd men per execution section as they stood with their boot heels to the open pit. That way all could be led like sheep to slaughter, each vying to outdo the others when complying with their captors' orders.

The dirty little secret, Han knew, was that there would be no pardons, just as there would be no survivors to spread the cruel truth about the army's tactic. For the sole reward, in the end, each of the men pulled from the ranks was to become the final section of the day to be executed.

The surprised camp commander met Han before he got to the raised, open-air courtroom. Han was flanked by his aide and the army major and backed by a small army of his own. His army-provided bodyguards—two dozen armed soldiers incongruously wearing dress uniform—looked uncertain of their role. The camp commander—a colonel—and his staff all saluted Han.

Han made a show of paying no attention to the salutes.

Instead, he cast a stern gaze across the sea of the prisoners' faces. All were fixed on him. After hours of facing near certain death, something unexpected was happening.

Even the guards' eyes were on Han, he noticed. The men who ringed the captives and held rifles and machine guns on their comrades looked at the civilian Administrator and waited. *For what?* Han wondered. *What's in the hearts of the men that would do the killing?*

Like the major, Han ignored the chain of command. Unlike the major, however, Han didn't go over the camp commander's head. He went under it directly to the colonel's troops.

Han ascended the raised platform and removed the microphone from the table, where it sat before the empty seat of the center of the three judges. When Han clicked the microphone on, he heard a snap over the stadium's PA system.

He turned to face not the four hundred attentive faces of the deserters, but the several dozen armed guards who surrounded them. The camp commander and his staff exchanged thoroughly confused glances.

"Stop this crime!" Han's voice boomed over the loudspeakers. "Stop this! Immediately!" he commanded. The prisoners' elbows began to turn from side to side as they looked at each other and at the guards, but their jailers' faces remained fixed on Han. "You're not butchers!" echoed Han's words through the empty stadium's stands. "These men before you are helpless human beings! They're soldiers—like you—caught up in this horrible war!"

Now, the guards looked around at each other. Nothing outwardly changed. The guards still held guns pointed at their captives. The prisoners still held hands pinned to their heads. But subtly—invisibly—the ground was shifting beneath their feet. The rationalizations upon which the executioners' obedience to orders were founded began, slowly, to give way.

"You men all witnessed this supposed 'court-martial'!" Han shouted in an accusatory tone. "Was it fair? Was each of the men before you proved to be a traitor to his country whose punishment should fairly be *death*?" Han hurled the words from his chest even though the volume on the PA system had obviously been set to maximum. The presiding military judge had presumably been trying to bolster his suspect authority. Now, the sheer volume of the speakers made Han's exhortations impossible to tune out. In a divine voice, Han continued his novel appeal to the humanity long suppressed within the camp guards.

Weapons held in the hands of doubting troops began to sag. Animated conversations sprung up between men previously silent in their shared guilt. Han discontinued his speech when it became totally unnecessary. The prisoners sensed his victory too. The muzzles of machine guns that protruded from above bipods in canvas-covered trucks disappeared into the recesses of their vehicles. Guards—now completely oblivious to the prisoners—congregated and argued with their rifles slung over their shoulders.

Thousands of prisoners' elbows began to descend to their sides. There were tears. Hugs. Men who collapsed to the grass in utter emotional and physical exhaustion.

All of it stopped when the wild-eyed camp commandant appeared at Han's side. He was both outraged and terrified. He looked from prisoners, to guards, to Han. All three returned his gaze. All three were arrayed against the man.

Of the three, the most menacing by far were the colonel's own guards. From the sneers on the faces of the men nearest the stage—and from their clutch of their ready weapons—Han sensed that the camp commander faced imminent mutiny. His men were ready to allocate moral culpability to the officer who had ordered all the executions past.

The camp commandant sensed the danger too. With mouth misshapen in anger he glared at Han and seized the microphone held in Han's gloved hand. Han released the mike, but the loud rattling over the PA system sounded like a scuffle. The colonel's fierce snort was clearly heard by all. He was incensed. Fuming. Bug-eyed.

The army, Han had always felt, was a metaphor for prison, and the draftees were its prisoners. And nothing, he knew from long experience, reflected more poorly on a Chinese army officer's record than losing control of his troops.

The colonel nervously eyed his wavering men one last time.

Despite his full boil, he chose the rational course: order over chaos. He chose to lead the men in the direction that they were already headed, which was the least perilous course from among a variety of even less appealing options.

"Release the prisoners!" the colonel abruptly ordered.

A cheer instantly went up. Men rose to their feet, and despite their cold-stiffened limbs many leapt into air. They hugged each other and even began hugging their would-be executioners. In the rising commotion, Han headed for the major, who was already being besieged by his elated troops. Those same men also lunged for Han. Han's army bodyguards raised weapons to fire, but Han held out a hand like a traffic cop as the freed captives fell to their knees before him. They grabbed the hems of his jeans and gushed their sobbing, eternal thanks. Han motioned the beaming major over as still more of the man's battalion arrived to share in the joy.

"Thank you, Administrator Han!" the major shouted over the noise.

Han could barely see his bodyguards, who were being jostled and hugged by the smelly throng. "I want to ask you for a favor!" Han yelled to the major.

"Anything!" the beaming man replied.

Han parked the major's beat-up ATV on an empty roadside in northern Virginia. The night was dark and still and cold. The sky glittered with stars.

He zipped his jacket closed at the sleeves and neck, and pulled his wool cap over his head. If his bearings were true, the place where the Americans said he should cross the front was less than a mile away. He headed over a low, wooded hill.

Wood smoke wafted pleasantly through the frigid air. At the crest of the ridge, he saw its source. A small country road wound its way through a cluster of dark homes. Han headed through the widely dispersed rural community.

He should have kept his distance from the houses. There could be a dog or an owner with a gun. But his curiosity was piqued. On passing, he looked in through the windows. Most of the homes appeared to be empty. The few whose chimneys contributed to the cheery, ski chalet smell of the valley were dimly lit by candles.

In one such home he saw an old lady. The frail-looking, white-headed woman sat in a chair wearing a jacket. A thick blanket covered her knees. That she stayed behind as everyone else fled advancing Chinese troops made sense to Han. She was old and rooted firmly in her home. What Han didn't understand was how she thought that she could possibly survive the winter.

He dropped to the ground when he saw movement from inside the room with the old woman. Two young children wearing pajamas—a boy and a girl—appeared at the woman's side. One carefully held a mug so as not to spill it. The other held a small plate. The old woman smiled, rubbed the backs of their heads, and relieved them of the treats. The kids disappeared, and Han maneuvered to a different vantage. The children shook presents under a Christmas tree, which was decorated with everything but lights. Their parents settled onto the floor beside them in the glow from the flickering fire. They all laughed at something their little boy said as he held a package with an earnest look.

Han moved on toward the front lines. It seemed a misnomer on such a peaceful night. No rifles cracked, or machine guns burped, or bombs or shells burst. All was quiet on the eve of the titanic battle for America's capital.

"Front lines" was a misnomer in another sense as well. As Han had been advised, he ran into no Chinese troops. Sheng's army didn't fear imminent American attack. It didn't cling to the front in hardened bunkers like its enemy. And it couldn't mass for attack while manning a continuous line. Instead, it pulled back to have room to maneuver—to stage for its offensive operations—free from the prying eyes of the enemy's tactical intelligence. Its electronic sensors were set to detect groups of a half dozen or more seeking to infiltrate south through the porous edge of occupied territory. Rear area security troops at the numerous roadblocks Han had passed would take care of the smaller incursions.

The going got tougher in the thick woods that lay beyond the sleepy rural community. Twigs and branches reached out of the darkness to scratch at Han's jacket, gloves, and face. The footing grew uneven on his climb up a ridge. Several times Han stopped, thinking that he'd heard a noise. At the crest, he saw what he was looking for: a streambed that marked the formal edge of Chinese territory.

The stream, Han was sure, stood out on the map. It looked like a good line of demarcation for Sheng's cartographers. A convenient boundary to delineate friendly from enemy territory. A handy natural feature to prevent tactical commanders from straying beyond approved limits of advance. It cut through the hills and, if flowing, would have to be bridged. But at this time of year, the stream was a mere trickle.

The gentle breeze died momentarily, and Han heard the noise again. Voices. Singing. He strained to discern anything more, but he couldn't glean either their direction or their language, so he proceeded down the hill. By the time he reached the trickling water, the mystery of the singing was solved. It was in English, and it came from the opposite side of the stream. It came from American bunkers on the hill just above. Han stopped to catch his breath and to listen.

He couldn't make out all the words, but he understood that they sang something about a drummer boy. The mixed male and female chorus softly repeated the strange reprise. ". . . a rum-puh-pum-pum. Me and my drum." It was a pleasant, almost stirring Christmas carol sung by hundreds of soldiers in low, peaceful voices.

The stream was so low that he had no problem finding an unbroken bridge of stepping-stones to cross. When he reached the far bank, the singing had stopped. There was a distant rustling noise, then nothing. He proceeded not five steps before again pausing to listen and to peer up the hill into the darkness.

The bushes on both sides of Han shook. Dark forms lunged at him, tackling him to the ground. There they held him, arms pinned behind his back and face pressed into the dirt. The cold barrel of a pistol kissed his cheek.

"Don't say a word," a man whispered in English.

Han sighed in relief. He was safe.

PART THREE

I have seen war. I have seen war on land and sea. I have seen blood running from the wounded. I have seen men coughing out their gassed lungs. I have seen the dead in the mud. I have seen cities destroyed. I have seen two hundred limping, exhausted men come out of the line—the survivors of a regiment of a thousand that went forward 48 hours before. I have seen children starving. I have seen the agony of mothers and wives. I hate war.

Franklin Delano Roosevelt, Speech at Chautauqua, New York (1936)

11

Han stood close to the crackling fire in the cozy room complete with rock hearth, plush rug, and roughhewn wood walls. He was rubbing his hands together when Bill Baker entered.

"This is Dr. Clarissa Leffler," Baker said, introducing the woman who trailed him.

Han was surprised. He arched his brow and gently held Clarissa's proffered hand in his while shaking it slowly. Intimately. He did not offer his hand for a shake.

Baker said, "Clarissa is the head of the China Desk at the State Department. Given her obvious interest in Chinese political matters, she requested the opportunity to meet with you."

"I'm quite pleased for Dr. Leffler to join us," Han said graciously.

"Oh, no," Clarissa said, shaking her head. "I just wanted to . . ." But Han took Clarissa's elbow, ushered her to a sofa by the fireplace, and sat down beside her. Baker stood for a moment glaring at Han, then sat in a chair across from the two.

Han exchanged pleasantries with Clarissa in Chinese. When she replied fluently—as intelligence reports had disclosed that she could—he complimented her. Baker waited stoically for Han to return his attention to him and the language of their conversation to English. After the ever gracious Han finally turned to Baker, Han said, "I certainly hope that you maintained strict secrecy about this meeting. I am, you must understand, somewhat personally exposed."

"I am officially up here for Christmas," Baker replied tersely.

Han nodded, smiled, and winked at Clarissa, which seemed to infuriate Bill. *The unofficial story,* Han was saying that he understood, *was that the president and his mistress were having a holiday tryst.* Clarissa sat on the edge of her seat and looked at Baker, not Han. "Excellent," was Han's only comment.

Clarissa rose. "I'd really better be . . ."

Han rose also and said, "That's quite all right. Please stay. I'm sure you have the necessary security clearance."

Baker kept his eyes on Han. He looked angry and suspicious.

But Clarissa was insistent. "I really should leave you two . . ."

"The Chinese army plans to invade Philadelphia by sea," Han said quickly. Bill bolted to his feet. "The buildup south of Washington is just a diversion," Han continued. "Most of the troops whose unit locations you now place in northern Virginia are, in fact, aboard troop transports headed for the Philadelphia Naval Shipyard." Han smiled and looked back and forth between the stunned Clarissa Leffler and Bill Baker. "General Sheng plans to capture your two arsenal ships intact."

"Why are you telling me this?" Baker asked.

Han looked Bill straight in the eye and said, "I owe you one."

"Bullshit!" Bill shot back.

Han smiled. "Let's just say, then, that we have a coincidence of interest. You want the Chinese army defeated, and so do I."

"What do you want in return?" Baker asked.

Han shrugged and made a face. "Nothing. I come bearing this gift for you."

The two men stood facing each other, and Clarissa looked back and forth between them.

"And you want me to defeat your invasion?" Baker asked. "Slaughter your troops? Why?"

"Ask the head of your China Desk," Han said pleasantly, smiling at Clarissa.

WHITE HOUSE SITUATION ROOM
December 25 // 0230 Local Time

The people packed into the underground Situation Room sat in silence around Bill and Clarissa under the oppressive burden of deciding what to do. Each man and woman there—heads of powerful national security agencies—felt the weight bearing down upon them. To save America, they had to discern truth from lie. They had to trust or distrust, that was the choice.

All watched a video of Han Zhemin's revelations over and over, taken from a dozen different angles by as many hidden cameras. There were snorts and heads shaken in disbelief. But all sat on the edges of their seats, and no one ventured an opinion until the last video had been shown.

Secretary of Defense Bob Moore was the first to speak. "Either he's telling the truth and they *are* going to leapfrog our lines, or the son of a bitch is lying and they're plowing head and shoulders into our lines at DC. If we guess wrong, we lose the war."

"But he *is* telling the truth!" Clarissa blurted out. Gazes from around the room ringed the low-level functionary, who had leapt into a dialogue between the president and his secretary of defense. Bill watched and listened intently as she spoke quickly and gesticulated wildly. "The battle between the Chinese civilian and military leadership is entering a critical phase! You all saw the report from Beijing! The defense minister wouldn't arrest the commander of the Beijing Military District for anything less than plotting against him! He must have been planning a coup! And who could possibly be in a better position to oust the defense minister than the man who commands the troops in and around the capital? And that second-tier general would never plot a coup alone, but there have been no other arrests!"

"Which means what?" her superior—Secretary of State Dodd—asked in a chilly voice.

"Meaning the civilians had to be behind it!" There was a general commotion at Clarissa's leap to that conclusion. "It's do-or-die time!" she persisted over the disturbance. "Han Zhemin is trying to ensure that we—America—win this war! He's offering us victory, because only a bloody military defeat would restore the balance of power in Beijing that has tipped in favor of the army with every mile of America they've taken from us!"

Heads turned and eyes flitted in furtive, silent counsels, but no one ventured a critique of Clarissa's analysis. Everyone checked and rechecked their neighbors, then everyone decided that now was not the time to speak.

Almost everyone, that is. "There are over three million Chinese troops massed in northern Virginia," Richard Fielding noted. He was addressing not Clarissa, but President Baker. "They're real. We've got good, on-the-ground intell. But where is this mythical invasion fleet?"

Bill turned to Admiral Thornton, chief of naval operations. "Any sign of Chinese naval activity that might indicate staging for a seaborne invasion?"

"No, sir," Thornton replied, shaking his head. "Nothing. But . . ."

Baker waited, then had to ask, "But what?"

The balding admiral pressed his lips together and frowned out of one corner of his mouth as if he were smiling. "But we wouldn't necessarily know." His chin dropped as he avoided eye contact. "We missed the invasion fleet that hit the west coast. Missed it entirely. We had submarine pickets out. Search planes. Surface patrols. And they slipped right through all of it. They've destroyed our line of listening devices on the outer continental shelf using remotely piloted, deep-dive submarines. We'll double, triple the patrols, but what I'm trying to tell you, Mr. President . . ."

"I understand," Bill said. "Your point is taken."

"I'm sorry, sir," Thornton said. "I'm sorry."

Now was not the time for pride. Now was the time for straight answers. Bill nodded.

"Then what Han said *could* be true!" Clarissa exclaimed, seizing on the point. Thornton shrugged. "Why would Han lie?" she asked the room, growing confident that she was persuading them. "Why would he want the Chinese army to win?"

"Because he's Chinese," Richard Fielding quietly suggested.

Again, no one else ventured into the debate. The Situation Room fell quiet.

"We can only defend one, sir," commented General Cotler, the chairman of the Joint Chiefs of Staff. "Washington or Philadelphia?"

Everyone turned to Bill for his decision, but he ignored them all. He had been staring the entire time at Clarissa and felt intense guilt for allowing his suspicions to creep in. *It's just paranoia,* he assured himself. But it had become a way of life. Of self-preservation. Of survival. And it nagged at him. It forced him to doubt. It forced him to scrutinize Clarissa.

"Do you trust Han Zhemin?" Fielding prodded.

Something in the way that he had framed the question made clear the choice that Bill was going to make. He turned from Fielding, to Moore, to Clarissa.

"We defend Philadelphia," Bill said simply. She smiled.

"Will I see you upstairs?" Clarissa asked Bill at the door of the now hectic Situation Room.

Aides rushed in and out carrying chin-high stacks of black binders. Generals and colonels buzzed in a beehive of activity all set in motion by Bill's wrenching change in strategy.

"I've got a lot to do," Bill mumbled. He half turned to the room.

Clarissa made a sympathetic face, but she was beaming. "It's gonna be okay," she whispered. "This is the break we were waiting for!" Despite the late hour, she was alert, almost giddy. Bill couldn't even reciprocate with a smile. She took a step foward but controlled her impulse to kiss him, then laughed at herself, touched her forehead, and covered her grin with her hand. Her sole expressions of intimacy were to grab and squeeze his hand, and to lean even closer and whisper. "I'm going to take a quick check of my office, but then we can rendezvous upstairs, *if* you know what I mean."

Bill nodded and watched her walk away. He was still standing there—long after she was gone—when Richard Fielding stepped up to his side.

"Clear the Situation Room," Bill said softly. "Everyone out but the principals."

When the doors were closed and the room was still, it seemed nearly empty. Bill Baker stood before the principals of the NSC. He gripped the back of his chair and looked out over the room. He didn't doubt his decision. He lamented it.

"Han Zhemin is lying," he said. "We will defend Washington, DC, against a ground attack with every available soldier, Marine, sailor, and airman. But we will make them think that we're defending Philadelphia. Those are your orders."

The perspectives on Baker's plan by those in the room were numerous and varied. No one was quite so intrigued, however, as the director of the CIA. Bill turned to Richard Fielding and said, "Come with me," as he headed toward the door.

THE STATE DEPARTMENT, WASHINGTON
December 25 // 0315 Local Time

Clarissa's mood had changed for the worse with every word of the E-mail she read. Her throat constricted. Her mouth dried. The subtle shakes of her head became involuntary, repeated utterings. "No. No-no-no!" she muttered. Her mouth hung open as she carefully reread the E-mail.

> *Now is the time for all good men to come to the aid of their party. The nation stands at the brink of defeat and extinction. There are no new plans for winning the war. No new hope that anything waits at the end of this*

ordeal other than subjugation—state by state—by the
Chinese. The current leadership is bereft of visionary,
war-winning plans. There is only one option left to us.
We will not go quietly into the night. Now is the time
to act. Be prepared.

Prepared? *Prepared?* Be prepared for what? Clarissa was
desperate. What to do? What to do?

She ground her teeth as she deleted the E-mail with the
Department-of-Defense-provided shredder. Her eyes then flit
about her desk as if in search of an answer. She felt sick with
worry. Sick with fear. She covered her face with her hands,
pressed her fingertips to her closed eyelids, and shook her
head slowly from side to side. "Oh God," she said through
her hands.

Clarissa looked around abruptly at her door, which was
shut. She knew what had to be done. She opened a window
on her computer monitor to compose a message, which she
would send, via the anonymous router, to the equally anonymous coup plotters.

> *Listen, I don't know who you are, but don't do any-*
> *thing yet!!!! President Baker has just issued orders that*
> *might win the war! He has received critical, high-level*
> *intelligence from Han Zhemin that the Chinese are*
> *planning to invade Philadelphia! We will redeploy to*
> *defend the shipyard and crush the Chinese landing. It*
> *will be a huge military victory that will reverse the*
> *fortunes of the war! We won't have to take any other*
> *action. So whatever you do, don't take action now!!!!*

With Clarissa's heart pounding and finger shaking, she hit
the mouse button and sent the message. She quickly shredded
the copy of the message in her sent mail folder, rocked back
in her chair, and let out a large sigh of exhaustion.

Was it too late to stop the coup? Would her message be
enough? Simple pleas to wait for Baker's plan without spe-
cifics about that plan, she had realized, wouldn't have done

the trick. So she had given the plotters details that carried weight. Facts that should give them pause.

Her father! Maybe *he* could ensure that the coup was called off. She would have to meet with him.

Clarissa nodded off, not once, but three times. First, she needed some sleep. Bill would be expecting her to be waiting in his bed.

After one last check to ensure that the incriminating E-mails had been deleted, she turned off the computer, rose to her feet, she turned off the lights, and headed out.

Moments later, the door to the darkened office opened. Men wearing suits and latex gloves entered but didn't turn on the lights. With penlights on earphones and whining electric screwdrivers they opened a bay in her computer. Within seconds, they plugged a cable into a hidden jack, powered up the internal disk drive in Clarissa's computer, then unplugged their portable computer. With a few short whines of electric screw drivers, they were done.

Thirty seconds after they entered the office, they departed leaving no trace of their intrusion.

WHITE HOUSE OVAL OFFICE
December 25 // 0445 Local Time

Bill Baker could see nothing through the newly installed metal shrapnel screens that covered the windows and walls of the White House. But he could hear the commands shouted from the lawns outside. They were routine for that hour of the morning. The number of troops dug into slit trenches just inside the White House fence was doubled in the hours before the sun rose. Although they were miles behind friendly lines, the predawn reinforcement was standard procedure for all U.S. Army troops in the field. Dawn attacks by the Chinese were a daily ritual.

Bill peered out the window through a crack between two reactive armor screens. He could see a flickering fire in a barrel on the lawn and tried to make sense of the scene. The only way he could bring it into focus was to close one eye. At first he assumed the fire that rose from the large drum was to warm the throng of guards. But a steady procession of men in suits—Secret Service agents—hurrying back and forth between the White House and the fire betrayed its true purpose.

The agents dumped files and papers into the outdoor incinerator under the watchful gaze of agents with assault rifles on their hips.

A deep rumbling in the distance announced the coming of day. Bill sank into the chair behind his desk to listen. He was exhausted by the late hour, the lack of sleep, the strain of the momentous decision that he had made and all the other decisions—most wrong—before it.

The drumroll of artillery at the front almost thirty miles away inspired not awe but sickening dread. Its individual beats were swallowed by the distance, but the earth quaked beneath the blows. A thousand guns. Ten thousand. Stephie.

Bill covered his face, and tears filled his eyes. His chest bucked with each silent sob. Behind the shield of his hands, he let himself go. His face contorted. All semblance of control was abandoned. He allowed himself what he fought to keep from everyone in the world. He jammed his eyes shut and clenched his teeth to try to ride out the wave of agony.

The emotional storm ended abruptly, and he let his hands drop to the desk. His face was wet, but he felt strangely calm. He sniffed and dried his tears.

Deep blasts sounded from the southern fringes of Washington, DC, on the Virginia side of the Potomac. The long-range Chinese guns reached out for the capital and fell in Alexandria. The Pentagon was a gutted shell. National Airport's runways were pitted, and birds flew through its open terminal. Bill could hear the jarring explosions of individual heavy shells landing singly. Deliberately. Their sole purpose, in Bill's mind, was to warn all who still remained in the juggernaut's path that the end was nigh.

Boom.

The windows of the Oval Office rattled.

One million American soldiers dead, wounded, or captured.

Bill heard the familiar shriek of an antiaircraft missile propelled by compressed gas from its launch tube in Lafayette Park and rising like a reverse bolt of lightning—from the ground into the sky—when its solid-fuel booster ignited and left white embers of burnt air in its wake.

Boom.

A car alarm on the drive below sounded.

From Mississippi to Virginia and half of California firmly under Chinese control.

Richard Fielding entered the Oval Office to find Bill staring into empty space. He crossed the room, unlocking and unzipping his valise, and extracted a single sheet of paper with a single paragraph printed on it.

Bill sat at his desk and read Clarissa's E-mail.

"It's not exactly what we thought," Fielding said. "But she's spying for some group of coup plotters."

"I don't believe it," Bill replied.

Fielding saw through Bill's lie, though he didn't say so. Instead, he remarked, "At least she *thinks* that they are coup plotters. The people on the other end of that E-mail could just as easily be the Chinese military. On the *other* hand, somebody planted that bomb on Marine One. And our people are convinced that it was an inside job, Mr. President."

"But who?" Bill asked feebly, but thought, *Why, Clarissa, why?*

Fielding shrugged. "Apparently, Dr. Leffler doesn't know who it is," he replied. "But I'd bet that her father does." Bill opened his mouth to rebuke the man, but Fielding detailed the suspicious behavior of old Tom Leffler, Bill's mentor. Asking his secretary how to shred E-mails sent and received. Asking the deputy national security advisor over lunch who had attended particular NSC meetings. Buying a pistol at a Reston, Virginia, pawnshop. Incessantly having his house swept for bugs. Meeting Clarissa at a scenic overlook just off the George Washington Parkway.

Several times, Bill had considered interrupting with an angry demand to know just who had authorized the surveillance of the Speaker of the House, but each fact—however obtained—deflected his objections. The picture was sketchy. The dots could be formed into any pattern the viewer chose. In Bill's fertile mind, fears sprouting spontaneously from depression and paranoia. Only breathing seemed difficult.

"We've got to know..." Bill began before clearing his throat. "We've got to get to the bottom of this."

"Are you giving me the authority to investigate?" Fielding inquired. Bill, slack-jawed, held Clarissa's E-mail and nodded. "Will you tell Justice that you granted me that authority?" Fielding asked. "I need their support."

Bill nodded.

Fielding looked at him for a long while before he spoke. "Sir, until we know for sure whether there is a coup in the offing, it would be best if you weren't in the White House. Obviously, they can penetrate the security here."

Bill replied that Vice President Simon was orbiting Omaha aboard the emergency command aircraft.

"I'm talking about you, sir," Fielding said. "Your safety. It would be better if you evacuated Washington."

"I'm staying in the White House," Bill mumbled, sounding more like lethargic than heroic.

After a moment's hesitation, Fielding nodded, accepting the decision as final. "Sir, as far as this whole matter with Dr. Leffler goes, I'm willing to testify," Fielding said, carefully choosing his words, "that you have been using Clarissa all along to pass disinformation on to the Chinese." When Bill focused on Fielding, the CIA director said, "It'll give you cover—political *and* legal—when we arrest Dr. Leffler."

Arrest, Bill thought. *"When we arrest Dr. Leffler."* Although he had not fully digested that fate for Clarissa, his thoughts skipped ahead. *What will her punishment be?* High treason during time of desperate war for national survival. What penalty did societies like America mete out for such crimes? The obvious answer pressed itself down upon him. His eyes sunk closed. The justice would be swift. Harsh. Unforgiving.

"We've got to use her," Fielding continued. His eyes sunk closed. Bill opened his eyes. "We've got to mislead the coup plotters, or the Chinese, or whoever it is that she's talking to in order to find out who they are. Who killed Vice President Sobo. We've got to use her father, too. As we sit here right now, we know nothing. They could be moving against you even as we speak. They could be moments away from ripping the Constitution to shreds and killing you, Mr. President. Now is not the time for compassion or half measures."

Bill stared out across the Oval Office with an unfocused gaze. " 'Now is the time for all good men to come to the aid of their party,' " he mumbled before wincing. With his eyes still pinched closed, he said, "I'm setting her up to commit a crime—while under government observation—for which the punishment would be death."

"Her crime has already been committed, Mr. President. But if you want, I can get with Justice and maybe avoid the death penalty. But there are political considerations to taking that step. There are other traitors—collaborators in occupied territory—with whom we'll one day have to deal. If you give special treatment to Dr. Leffler, it's bound to come back at you in the political arena. But I think, maybe, there's a way to handle that, too."

Bill was too drained to ask the ever-capable Fielding how. He silently assented with yet another nod. Fielding went on and on about operational details and plans. Security. Staffing. Procedures. He extracted a legal document from his valise, and Bill signed the authorization for the CIA to conduct surveillance inside the White House. It was the same authorization that he had so angrily denied Hamilton Asher's FBI. Through it all, only one thought echoed through Bill's mind. *All the women that I love betray me.*

"Mr. President?" Fielding asked softly, but insistently.

"Hm?" Bill replied, confused momentarily before looking up at the man.

"I was saying, sir, that she mustn't suspect a thing. There must be no change that would alert Dr. Leffler to the fact that she's under suspicion. There should be no change in your routine whatsoever. Do you understand? Do you understand how important that is, Mr. President?"

Bill's gaze had sunk to the man's tie as Bill drifted with the current of Fielding's words. Bill blinked, drew a deep breath, and looked Fielding in the eye. Bill nodded his agreement to the plan.

WHITE HOUSE RESIDENTIAL QUARTERS
December 25 // 0515 Local Time

The lights were out when Bill entered his bedroom. He threw his clothes on the back of a chair and climbed into bed wearing his underwear. The bed was warm.

Clarissa rolled against his side. She was naked. Her skin was smooth and warm against him. She smelled of some fragrance. Not perfume, but skin and hair.

She climbed on top of him and began to move against him.

"Merry Christmas," she whispered.

It took her diligent efforts before their lovemaking could begin. They each ended in shattering ecstasy. In their guilt there was illicit excitement.

INTERSTATE 66, NORTHERN VIRGINIA
December 25 // 0940 Local Time

Stephie watched trees streak by the truck through the tailgate and through a flapping tear in the canvas at the front. Everybody was on the move. The highways were jammed. The entire army was heading in one direction.

"Washington, DC," announced the green road sign on an overpass, "32 miles."

The good life at brigade headquarters had ended hours before. Trucks had arrived unexpectedly. Stephie had assumed that brigade HQ was moving again. But Animal had snapped from where he stood peering inside the back of a truck, "Everybody pack yer shit!"

The trucks hadn't been empty. Haggard, grimy troops had climbed down from the tailgates. An exhausted John Burns stood staring at Stephie from a distance. Neither said a word as Stephie's Third Platoon began to gather their gear just ahead of a rippling chain reaction of sergeants' barks, but Stephie never took her eyes off John.

His silence was how she learned that what was coming was bad.

• • •

Everyone but Stephie was sound asleep as their truck rolled
through northern Virginia. Stephie could never fall asleep on
the road. It took a sense of security she had never possessed.

Suddenly, the truck's brakes began a long, low moan that
rose to a high-pitched whine as the convoy pulled to a stop.
In the silence, the roused soldiers jammed into the back heard
the steady crackle of rifle fire.

For an instant Stephie was back in Alabama in the early
days of the war, fleeing the ever-closing Chinese noose. She
turned on her radio and instantly heard Animal's voice.

". . . hell's goin' on?" he demanded, angry and agitated.
"Did they cut the fuckin' *road*?"

John Burns pulled open the canvas at the tailgate. Stephie
smiled reflexively.

Then the president of the United States stepped up to John's
side.

He was surrounded by a tight cluster of Secret Service
agents. Soldiers from nearby trucks peered out at the sight.
The half of Stephie's platoon crammed into the truck with
her wore stunned looks. Stephie climbed down and stood before her father, peering up at him without saying anything
until they hugged. He wrapped his arms around her body
armor and pulled her tight. She held her rifle by the front grip
and hugged him back. She felt the rifle sway slightly in her
hand behind her father's back as a Secret Service agent en-
sured that the safety was on.

"Let's go sit somewhere," Bill Baker said, "so we can talk."

She followed him up a hill that rose from the highway and
quickly spotted the source of the steady small-arms fire. A
farmer's field on the opposite side of the highway had been
turned into a noisy, impromptu rifle range. Soldiers lay prone
behind rifles and machine guns laying waste to stationary paper targets at the absurdly close range of 100 meters. An NCO
passed out single magazines to men and women who waited
in line for spots at the range. A civilian woman followed the
NCO with Styrofoam cups of coffee and small biscuits. Some
of the waiting soldiers wore fatigues covered in the grease of
some vehicle on which they had been working. Others wore
aprons still stained with the contents of huge vats in which

they had cooked first mess. Still others wore scrubs bloodied in some overworked surgical unit. All of the rear-area troops, however, wore helmets and combat webbing.

This is it, Stephie thought, feeling a frisson of fear shoot through her veins.

Her father put his arm around her shoulder. She looked up and found him watching her intently. He squeezed her to his side, and, it appeared, he almost began to cry before he turned away and they headed on.

Agents fanned out through the trees ahead of them. Stephie carried her rifle, as always, but it was unneeded inside the thick cordon of security. They sat beneath a tree on the hill-side above the highway. The rest of the 41st Infantry Division gawked as they passed Charlie Company's small section of vehicles that had halted on the side of the road beside Marine One.

They crested the hill and stopped beside a rock outcropping in the relative quiet of the opposite slope. She rested her weapon against the mossy stone. Agents formed a 360-degree cordon but kept their distance. The rifle reports from the road-side—like the fighting they portended—seemed both comfortably far and dangerously near. Her father didn't take his eyes off Stephie, who removed her helmet and combed her bangs with her fingertips. He laughed when she looked up cross-eyed at the thin locks on her forehead. She gave up and returned her helmet to her head with a frown.

He smiled at her, still staring.

"What?" she asked, rubbing the grime from her cheeks with a firm swipe of both hands that stretched her skin tight.

His reply was unexpected.

"I'm more proud of you, Stephie, than of anything or any-one in the world." She winced, and her gaze fell to the hard dirt beneath her boots. "You're a hero" he said, "and you give me the strength that I need to carry on."

Stephie turned away and worked her teeth against each other.

"What?" Bill asked defensively. "Did I say something wrong?" She shrugged, frowning. "What?" he demanded.

Stephie wheeled on him and snapped, "I'm not a hero! I'm

just a regular soldier! I'm just doing my job like everyone else!"

"And to me that makes you a hero," Bill explained in a whisper at which his brittle emotions tugged. Tears filled his eyes and thickened his voice. "All of you. We owe you a great debt, Stephie. Don't you realize that? You think you're just doing your duty. There's a war. You're eighteen. You go. It's that simple. But it's *not* that simple! You're only a child! How do you *do* it? And *why*? Five years ago, you were just, just . . . !" He choked on the words.

His face was contorted in agony. His jaw quivered.

She went to him and again removed her helmet. Her hair hung in strings, but she sat beside him and laid her head on his shoulder. A dam seemed to break inside him. His hands shot to his face—covering his mouth, nose, and eyes—but they failed to contain the raging flood of tears underneath. She wrapped her arms around him and felt him shake. Uncontrolled whimpers escaped.

She squeezed and held him tight until the quaking subsided. "We do it for you," Stephie said in answer to the question that had seemed to trouble her father so. Her smile grew into a grin. "We do it so that you'll be proud of us."

He gently broke free of her embrace and stood.

"Is something the matter?" Stephie asked. Her father seemed distracted. "Did I say something wrong?"

He retrieved a linen napkin, which he unfolded. In it lay a plastic bar—black against its bed of white—so small and yet so significant.

"Is that," Stephie asked, heart pounding, "for *me*?"

"Congratulations," her father said weakly and in a scratchy voice. He cleared his throat. "Congratulations, Lieutenant Roberts."

Stephie leapt to her feet, mouth agape. "I can't be*lieve* it!" she exclaimed, closely inspecting the priceless piece of plastic jewelry from all angles. Laughing, she rose onto her tiptoes and kissed her father's cheek. He held onto her again, and for a moment she thought he would resume his crying jag. But he released her, and she saw that his face was a pale blank that contrasted sharply with the good cheer that she felt on the huge accomplishment.

"But I'm not a lieutenant, yet," she said coyly. Her eyes darted to her collar once, and then once again when her father failed to understand. Her master sergeant's impressive array of chevrons and rockers still occupied the place where the black bar should be.

Bill replaced the old insignia with the new one.

"No-o-w," she said, "swear me in."

"What?" Bill asked.

"Swear me *in*!" she demanded, grinning. "I wanta take the oath."

"Oh. Well, I'm afraid—I'm sorry—but I don't know the oath."

"*I* do," she shot back, beaming. "I, sort of, learned it. Word for word."

She laughed. He looked as if he were ill. Stephie straightened her face, stiffened her back, and raised her right hand, but then giggled with joy and apologized. "Sorry. Okay. Okay." Standing there, hand raised skyward, she began with mock seriousness, but ended in total earnest.

"I, state-your-name," she laughed. "No, start over." She wiped her mouth, as if to manually rid her face of its inappropriate expression, and then cleared her throat. She straightened her back again and she grew an inch taller.

"I, Stephanie Amanda Roberts, do solemnly swear that I will support and defend the Constitution of the United States against all enemies, foreign and domestic; that I will bear true faith and allegiance to the same; and that I will obey the orders of you," she smiled, "the president of the United States and the orders of the officers appointed over me, according to the regulations and the Uniform Code of Military Justice. So help me God."

Her hand remained in air until she felt self-conscious and lowered it, extending it to her father for a shake. Instead, he hugged her tightly, and she hugged him back. "I'm so proud of you, Stephie," he repeated.

"And I'm incredibly proud of *you*, Dad," she replied.

When he pulled away, she saw the dark look on his face again. "Hey!" she prodded in high humor, shaking him with hands on his biceps. "What's the matter with you, Dad? Are you worried or something? About me?" She shook him again, this time more gently. "It's okay! I've *made* my peace with God. I've lived through more in this war than I *possibly* could have hoped for. And this is such a beautiful day!" she said, breaking free and gesturing toward the late afternoon sky. "I've had plenty of time to get ready, you know, for whatever happens."

He winced with each point that she made until, in the end, his eyes were near shut as if he were falling asleep. He tried but couldn't speak, and turned away, drawing oxygen into his chest pant by pant.

"Dad?" she asked, then asked again. "Dad?"

He faced her and handed her a velvet-covered jewelry box. Inside, Stephie found a silver cross studded with diamonds. Her jaw dropped again as she extracted the necklace. "It's a," Bill managed to say with obvious difficulty, "a Christmas present." He sounded like he was in a fog. Dazed. "Merry Christmas."

With dirt blackened fingers she slipped the silver necklace over her neck. "Wearing jewelry is against those regulations I just swore to obey," she said. Her father stared at the cross, which glistened in the thin morning sun. "It's beautiful," she said with her chin tucked to her chest before dropping it under her body armor but holding her hand pressed flat above it.

She rose onto her toes and kissed his cheek. He grabbed his chest and turned his back to her. She thought he might be having a heart attack. She held her hand up to touch his shoulder, but her fingers hovered above his suit jacket. He seemed so close to breaking down again.

They returned to the highway holding hands. Both were oblivious—for different reasons—to the entourage of bodyguards that fanned out a hundred yards in every direction. Stephie chattered, telling him tales of everyday life. Her father remained mute and pasty in color. Several times she stopped talking midsentence and looked down at her hand, which he crushed tightly in his clammy grip.

A truck pulling a flatbed trailer with a huge, low-slung main battle tank atop it belched dark clouds as its old engine tried to resume highway speed after slowing to pass the parked convoy. *"Vic-to-ry!"* shouted a young soldier who hung out of the open window of the cab. He held two fingers in a "V" to the president. In the traffic jam behind the slowed tank carrier came trucks filled with young men and women, all Stephie's age. They peered at the spectacle on the sides of the road—at Marine One, the well-dressed Secret Service agents, the president—from around canvas, from cabs with windows lowered, from machine gun mounts atop armored cars, and they began to hoop and shout. Bill acknowledged each vehicle with a wave, but then the next truck applauded and cheered.

"Give-'em-hell, Mr. President!" the soldiers shouted to their commander in chief, who smiled and nodded awkwardly. "We're gonna kick their butts back to Beijing!" came another cry from another truck. Stephie was thrilled to see the adoration of the troops for the man whom she also adored, but her father seemed disconcerted by the raucous greetings and shouts. Scrawled in white paint on one of the old green trucks were the words, "Going home to Miami!" with the same words repeated beneath it in Spanish. The driver—with the truck still moving slowly—climbed out onto his window and caught the attention of the president with thickly accented shouts hurled over the roof of his cab. "Hey! Hey! Mr. President! We gonna fuck they asses up, man!"

The two soldiers riding in the cab pulled the crazy driver back to the wheel and then rained shouts and blows onto him. The driver responded with combative, shouted defenses, but returned the straying vehicle to the road.

"Sir," the head of his Secret Service detail said, nervously eyeing the southern hills, "we ought to get going."

Stephie took a step back and saluted her father just like all her other comrades in arms.

"Don't you worry, Mr. President!" shouted one of the passing soldiers. "This is the Fightin' 41st! Nobody's gettin' into Washington, sir! Just ain't gonna happen!"

A fountain of cheers rose from all around, but especially from Charlie Company, which was gathered about their parked trucks. Stephie still stood ramrod straight with her fingertips held steady to the brim of her helmet. She was filthy. Small, iron-on patches of shiny fabric patched rips and tears in her uniform and still further randomized the mottled woodlands camouflage pattern. Her once black combat boots were so scuffed and scraped as to look ready for the trash heap, but their heels were locked tightly together in good military form. She had never been more proud. Proud of Charlie Company. Proud of the Fightin' 41st!

And proud of her father, who finally returned her salute. When they embraced a final time, she heard over the continuing jubilation from the procession of vehicles the ragged breathing from her father's chest. She understood then how near he was to breaking down again, so she pulled herself from his arms, which were reluctant to free her.

"Good-bye, Dad," she said simply.

He tried to reply, but couldn't. His lips contorted, and he dashed off through the gap in traffic created by the outstretched arms of a Secret Service agent. At first he just walked quickly. Then, he began to jog before finally disappearing with head bowed into Marine One.

ALEXANDRIA, VIRGINIA
December 26 // 1015 Local Time

Wu looked out of the armored command car as he was driven along the pleasant residential streets of the suburban Washington town. The cold wind whistled through the open hatch in the roof as a soldier in the rear stood behind a machine gun. Wu's hopes sank as he saw no sign of life in neighborhood after neighborhood. No smoke from chimneys. No cars. No trash at the curb spirited out of houses in the middle of the night by frightened homeowners.

The residents of Alexandria had had the time to evacuate,

and they had taken that opportunity. Perhaps some day soon, Wu thought, the people of America would have nowhere to run. The thought—of victory—was strangely upsetting.

Every so often, they passed blackened armored fighting vehicles. Some were American. Their sides bore the Chinese character for "safe" drawn in thick white paint. But most of the dead vehicles were Chinese. Fifteen-, twenty-, thirty-to-one had been the lopsided Chinese losses as they jockeyed for position on the outskirts of the American capital. As Wu's armored command car wove past the obstacles, he grew ever more upset.

One of the soldiers in the back leaned forward in his seat with his head bent over a map.

"Left, left!" he shouted too late.

The driver slammed on the brakes, cursed, threw the vehicle into reverse, and backed up. He gunned the engine and made the left turn with knobby tires squealing. The driver liked high speeds, Wu had noted. He seemed to hate stopping and hated backtracking even more. Wu now scrutinized the dark, mirrored windows with a new degree of alertness. He joined the other jumpy soldiers in the command car in their search for a life-saving, split-second warning of an ambush. They weren't worried about American Special Forces teams despite the fact that all knew their rear to be crawling with the highly accomplished killers. Those professionals would never attack during the day. They worried instead, Wu knew, about partisans. Patriots. Suicidal fanatics who cared not between night and day. Between life and death.

The navigator in the rear made the driver slow at the next intersection. The machine gun's ring mount atop the roof squeaked as the gunner swivelled the weapon left and right. "Hurry *up*!" the driver urged.

"Ma-puh," the navigator tried to read off the street sign that lay—uncollected—beside the curb.

"Maple," Wu read for him, translating it into Chinese. "This is it. 'Maple Street.' "

"Turn here!" the navigator prompted, and the vehicle's turbine engine whined to life.

The navigator counted off the houses in Chinese by the street numbers stenciled on the curb. "6707. 6709. 6713. 6715! There! There it is!"

Wu's eyes were already fixed on the one-story redbrick home. It looked old, but at one time it must have been respectable. The white paint was peeling off the eaves. Straw and leaves obscured the yellowing grass. A decrepit car of indeterminate color sat parked under a blanket of half-melted snow.

Wu opened the front passenger-side door. The five soldiers began to pour out.

"No!" Wu ordered. "Stay in the vehicle."

The men looked at each other. None wanted to get out of the armored car. None had wanted to go there all alone, without even informing the local commander of their whereabouts. But they were, Wu could tell, almost equally concerned about his safety. About their own fates were Wu to meet with any harm.

"I won't be long," Wu said to pacify them. He stepped out into the fresh winter air.

The adhesive letters affixed to the metal mailbox were half missing, but the name was clearly "Fisher." Wu headed up the front walk. His boots crunched through the unswept leaves. He climbed the three concrete steps to the front door and raised his gloved hand to knock. He hesitated, then took his gloves and helmet off. He put both under his arms and knocked.

There was no answer.

He knocked again. And then again, more loudly. And then a last time. He heard no noise from inside. She wasn't home. She was gone. She had fled like the rest of them.

Wu's heart plummeted. He bowed his head and sighed. Of course she would want to escape the dangers of the fighting, Wu thought, but that rationalization did nothing to cushion the disappointment.

He glanced back at the armored car. The faces of the soldiers were fixed expectantly on Wu. He returned his gaze to the front door. *This is, still, her home,* Wu thought. He re-

corded the sights, sounds, and smells of the home, but found
the effort unsatisfying.

He abruptly unslung his rifle, stepped away from the door,
and fired at the knob. The soldiers at the street were half out
of the command car before Wu motioned them back inside.
On Wu's third shot, the hardware popped off the door and
fell to the front steps with a metal jangle heard as the echoes
from the rifle's report died down.

When Wu pushed hard on the door, however, it didn't
budge. It was bolted shut from the inside. He cursed, pulled
a grenade from his webbing, and walked down the few steps
to the sidewalk. He warned the anxious soldiers inside the
vehicle by showing them the hand grenade. The machine gunner protruding through the roof sank inside, and the bullet-
proof windows ascended with a hurried electric hum.

Wu pulled the pin and gently tossed the grenade under-
handed onto the porch. It landed at the threshold beneath the
front door. Wu turned and jogged a few steps along the front
wall of the house. The grenade burst with a stunning blast of
noise and heat. The explosion echoed with a crackle up and
down the street. Wu headed back, waving the smoke from his
face as he climbed the three debris-strewn steps.

The door frame was now hollow. Shattered shards of the
wood no bigger than his arm lay scattered about the carpet in
the foyer.

Wu entered the home.

To the right was a living room with worn chairs that had
once been nice. The upholstery was covered with poorly
matched covers on the arms. Framed photos, rocked off their
perch atop the mantel, lay amid broken glass in front of the
fireplace.

Wu stooped to pick up the frames. Behind the jagged glass
he found old pictures. Two attractive young women on a ski
slope with their arms around each other wearing dark sunglasses and bright, white smiles. Han pulled the photo from
the frame and turned it over. At the bottom corner, written in
blue ink, he read, "Rachel and Cynthia, Spring Break, 1996."

There were other photographs as well. Prom pictures. Aging but handsome parents. Wu lingered. Studying the images.

But there were no pictures of the life that interested Wu most. The secret life, long forgotten.

"What do you want?" came the quivering question in broken, accented Chinese.

Wu turned to stare at the middle-aged woman, who wore layers of sweaters under arms crossed in a hug.

"My God in heaven!" she whispered in English before gasping in shock and grabbing a chair to keep from falling. Wu took a step toward her, but she stumbled—supporting herself hand over hand along the chair back—and collapsed into the seat. There, she stared at Wu in disbelief. Through the onset of tears, she spluttered, "How did you . . . ? You found me. You found me."

"Why did you give me away?" Wu asked in English.

"I *didn't*!" she screamed, doubling over with the effort and the obvious anguish. Her incipient tears seemed to be aborted by memories that flashed behind a faraway look. In a drained monotone, she began to explain. During her pregnancy in Beijing, she said, they had treated her like royalty. But the moment Wu was born, they had taken her straight to the airport! She protested her blamelessness throughout. Her tone rose from wooden to shrill.

"You could have written me," Wu responded. His depression leveled his voice to what sounded like calm.

She had been *scared*, she replied. They had warned her. Terrified her! The secret of her affair with Han Zhemin and of the birth of Wu that resulted from it had been the biggest secret of her entire life. The change in her treatment at the hands of Wu's family—especially Wu's father—had been so abrupt. So menacing.

"My entire *world* came crashing down!" she shouted. "My parents were dead! Rachel was my only family! But do you think, when Han sent me home, that my sister greeted me with open *arms*? After what *I* had done? Her life was in shambles because of me! At least that's what she told herself! Her life was pretty much always messed up. She went from flying around with your father in wide-body jets outfitted like Air Force One, to being married to a redneck engineer in

Mobile-Goddamn-Ala*bama*! She hasn't spoken to me—not one word—since your father . . ." She didn't finish.

"Since he what?" Wu asked through squinted eyes.

"You don't know?" she asked in delicate tones.

"I know you never once tried to get in touch with me!" Wu blurted out. "I know that I have spent the last fourteen years of my life in military schools! No family. No-no-no . . . !"

"No mother," she completed for him, stricken. Out of the corner of his eye he saw her approach. She held her hand out, hesitantly, but resisted the impulse to lay it on his shoulder. "Wu, there's so much that you don't know."

"Then *tell* me!"

She jumped. Frightened of him. He lowered his head, sighed, and wished what he'd said had come out differently. But she riveted him with her story—*his* story—the sordid history of their branch of the family.

"My sister—Rachel—you know who she is?" Wu nodded. "And you know who her first husband is, right?" Wu nodded again. He knew about the odd lines that strung him together with Stephanie Roberts and the president of the United States. "Your father had an affair with my sister," Wu's mother explained. "She left Bill Baker to run off to Hong Kong with Han."

"Your father broke up their marriage by seducing her."

"Why?" Wu asked. "They were best friends."

She shrugged. "Because he could," she said.

Wu was shocked, but there was more.

"Less than a month after Han set Rachel up in a house over there—a *palace* is really a better description—I get this call from Rachel. I've got to come visit. Right now! She sent me a ticket. First class. I got there and," she shook her head, "I couldn't believe it. The cars. The boats. The helicopters and jets. The *house*! The money, it was, unbelievable."

Wu nodded to hurry her on.

"Rachel was pregnant," Wu's mother said simply. "With Bill's child. With Stephanie. You've got to understand, my sister was desperate. We tried to figure out how to get her an abortion, but we were in Hong Kong. We went to a doctor, we thought anonymously, but it got back to Han that night. He was furious. We didn't even know why! He left and went to Beijing. Servants started packing up Rachel's things! She begged me to go to Beijing and talk to Han. She *begged* me!"

"So you went there and fucked him," Wu said.

Cynthia was shocked. "How *dare* you! You're just a child! You don't know anything!"

"But it's true, isn't it?" Wu said.

She hung her head. She was far away, lost in thought. "He was so . . ."

Wu waited, then finished her sentence for her. "Powerful? Wealthy? Handsome? Which was it?"

"It was *all* of those things, and *more*," she replied. "He was frightening, Wu. I was scared! And he *always* gets what he wants, doesn't he? Don't you understand? He always gets what he wants."

"So he got you, and then he got you pregnant. And then you had me, and then he dumped you."

Again, she was far away, but she shook her head. "No. After I got pregnant, he never laid a hand on me. He treated me nice. Great! The gifts! The luxury! I was the *queen* of Hong Kong, for nine months. He was always away on some important diplomatic mission in Asia! Signing nonaggression pacts with all those countries that China was about to conquer. But, every once in a while, a photo in the newspapers or on TV would show your father in the background at some reception, or at an official gathering, or at *whatever*. That's how I would know that he was in Beijing, never in Hong Kong. *I* was in Hong Kong."

"So my father," Han summarized, chuckling bitterly, "broke up the marriage of Bill Baker and your sister. Then *you* took your sister's place as my father's mistress!"

The slap came unexpectedly, and it stung. Wu resisted the urge to touch his smarting mouth.

"I'm sorry," his mother said, drawing her offending hand back to cover her mouth. "Oh, I'm sorry! Please forgive me!"

"I have nothing to forgive," Wu said as he brushed by her for the door.

She caught him from behind and wrapped her arms around him. She kissed his neck and pecked her way around to his cheek. He stood there like a statue until she stopped.

"My God," she said breathlessly, "what have they done to you?"

Wu pulled free and crunched through the debris for the empty front doorway.

"Wu!" she called out. Her plaintive tone made him stop. Made him turn. She stood there, arms wrapped around her layers of sweaters, peering at him in desperation. "Your father's checks stopped coming when the war started. It's been nine months since I got the last one. They weren't much, but they were all that I had, so I stayed here—in my house— when everybody else left. In case, you know, they start coming again now that, I mean, this is Chinese territory. I mean, the mail works. The checks can get through now."

Wu turned and left.

"I love you!" she called after him.

When Wu climbed into the command car, they all looked at him. Wu's mood was surly, so they said nothing. His mother stood in the broken doorway of her home, her arms wrapped even more tightly around herself. The soldiers in the car glanced back and forth between the two—curious, quizzical, prying.

"Do you want to go to army headquarters, sir?" his driver asked.

"No," Wu replied. "I want to go to the front lines. I want to find my platoon."

The soldiers again looked at each other. The driver—stuttering in fear—said he had orders to take Wu to HQ. A seething Wu bored his gaze into the man. "And now you have *new* orders!" The driver was petrified. "And after you've dropped me off, return to this house, have that door repaired, and leave that woman with enough provisions to last the winter."

The shaken man started the engine and, with great temerity, asked who the woman was.

"She's nobody," Wu replied truthfully.

CIVILIAN HEADQUARTERS, RICHMOND
December 27 // 0515 Local Time

Han Zhemin was sitting at his desk when the door opened without warning. It was General Sheng. Han tensed. But the military television cameras that trailed the old man thawed the fear gripping his chest. On seeing the news media, he knew that he would not be executed summarily. That sort of thing was never done on television.

"You're up early today, General," Han said pleasantly.

"Administrator Han Zhemin," Sheng replied formally, "you are under arrest."

Han rose, smiling for the cameras. His aide helped him don his jacket. "What are the charges?" he asked as his arms went in their sleeves.

"Inciting treason," Sheng replied, "among guards at a prisoner camp."

Han grinned broadly and cocked his head. *That's all?* his demeanor asked. Sheng's lip curled and twitched before he turned away. Both knew he could beat those charges in the all-important court of Chinese public opinion. Han Zhemin, noble Administrator, fighting a one-man battle to put a stop to the Chinese army's atrocities. It had been the plan that all thought would win. The prime minister, himself, had taken credit for it. The proof of what Sheng's troops had done in America, when uncovered by friendly civilian newsmen, would damn senior defense officials. The army would never press that case.

They might, however, try to prosecute Han's true treason. But Sheng made no mention of his trip to Camp David. Not yet, at least. Not yet. Perhaps their evidence was insufficient. More likely, they would not press any more serious charges until the political battle with the civilians in Beijing was won. His execution would not mark the beginning of any victory by the military over the civilians. It would signify the beginning of the end of it.

All now depended, therefore, on America's losing the Battle of Washington and going nuclear to stop a runaway Chinese victory. Han knew Bill Baker as well as he knew anyone on Earth. He had been Han's only true friend at a time when having friends had seemed so important. In the decades since, Han had read every article about the rising politician and watched video of Baker's every speech and interview. He was certain—absolutely certain—that Bill would resort to nuclear weapons before he would let Philadelphia fall. He had pinned all his hopes for winning the war on his two precious remaining arsenal ships.

Han stood before Sheng—before the whirring television cameras and baking lights—composed and confident. He led his arresting entourage out. The fact, though subtle, would undoubtedly register with the always attentive viewers back home.

On the street outside, the cameras were turned off. Sheng and his sniveling aide, Colonel Li, walked Han silently to the armored fighting vehicle that would take him to military prison. There had to be at least a battalion in full combat gear surrounding Han's headquarters.

"All this?" he asked Sheng in amusement. "Just for me?"

Colonel Li looked smug. General Sheng was less sure of himself.

All of the sudden, a rumbling sound poured down the streets. The low frequency noise gave no hint as to its direction. No point of origin for the sonorous sound. But everyone—civilian and soldier alike—looked toward the north. Toward the front. Toward the Battle of Washington.

The metal doors of the armored fighting vehicle stood open before Han, who turned to General Sheng. "I wish you the best of luck in your battle," he said. Colonel Li snorted at Han's snide remark. But Han said, "No, really, I do. Win the Battle of Washington. Storm Philadelphia. Seize the arsenal ships before it's too late."

"And then what?" Sheng unexpectedly asked Han.

Han smiled. "Drive inland to victory! Fight on, and on, and on, and on." All the soldiers, who were there to arrest Han, instead stared at Sheng. "You should always have a plan, General Sheng. Yours should be to take the rest of America."

He climbed into the vehicle, and the doors closed behind him. The soldiers around Han seemed appropriately stunned by the conversation they'd just overheard.

NORTHERN VIRGINIA
December 27 // 0630 Local Time

Major Jim Hart awoke with a start to the end of the world.
Ten thousand guns opened fire all at once. The surrounding
hills belched thousands of rockets, which shrieked from rails
on long white tails of fire. He noted the time on a watch dial
lit by the sky's brilliant strobes. All hell had broken loose at
0600 sharp

This was it. The attack.

Don't break, he prayed, but not to God, whom Hart had
lost somewhere in the war. *Don't break,* he prayed to the
soldiers in the bunkers. *Hold the line. Just this once. You can
do it!*

He rolled over and checked his microwave transceiver. The
antenna had a lock on the controller's signal. But the one
earbud he kept in his ear as he slept, which monitored the
microwave, was deathly silent as if they had all fled to shelters.

"Echo Foxtrot Two One Nine calling India Zulu Four Four,
do you read me, over?"

He was about to repeat the call when he heard, "This is
India Zulu Four Four. Chop Block. Chop Block. Chop Block.
Acknowledge."

Hart frowned in frustration and keyed the mike. "Acknowledge. Chop Block. Out."

"Chop Block," Hart thought. Go to ground. Avoid contact
with the enemy. Await further orders.

The first explosions began splashing violence around Hart.
Counterbattery fire from American guns. Their fire controllers
pinpointed Chinese batteries, using radar that tracked Chinese
artillery shells' trajectories. Bursts from American return fire
lit the flats all around the now fleeing Chinese self-propelled
artillery. The fin-guided American rounds sought out the infrared shapes of the racing vehicles. Their trajectories bent in
midair to follow them down a road. Half of the guns and
launchers never made it clear of the killing radius formed by
the extreme limit of the shell's ability to turn.

The long-range battle moved to another valley and blended

into the constant sound of distant fighting. Intense fighting.
Desperate fighting. Fighting everywhere around him.

I'm too valuable for them to use, Hart mocked in anger.
Or I'm too useless, came another voice with a different point
of view. The war had reached a critical phase and would now
be won or lost by draftees. Infantry fillers. Clerks and
programmers were handed rifles and sent into concrete
trenches and bunkers to fight to the bloody fucking death.

It infuriated him. Flu-like chills rippled down his body. He
was of half a mind to grab his rifle, march to the nearest
Chinese sentry, and blow him away. The little voice in his
head took the half-baked plan and began to reel off improb-
able projections of the enemy body count. Ten to one casualties. Fifteen to one. Twenty to one.

Always something or other to one, Hart thought. *Always I
would die.* The tempting voice fell strangely silent. There was
no voice counseling him to choose life, which one day might
yet hold beauty. Amid the thunder of war both near and far,
it was that silence that saved Hart's life.

He lowered his head to the rock hard towel and listened to
the war. He heard Chinese volley fire degenerate into individual shots. He could feel the impacts of exploding American
shells through the ground.

After a few minutes, he drifted off to sleep.

MCLEAN, VIRGINIA
December 27 // 0730 Local Time

A handheld television camera recorded every move made
by Junior Lieutenant Wu. The graying, bushy-haired civilian
cameraman transmitted unprecedented live images of war to
a prime time audience of one billion Chinese. Two dozen
channels of popular programming had been interrupted for the
prime minister's brief, jarring introduction. "My grandson,
Han Wushi," the old man intoned, "is an eighteen-year-old
officer in the war our military is fighting. He, like all the other
flowers of our youth, has reached this moment of truth on the
outskirts of the American capital. Please watch this live, un-

edited broadcast from the Battle of Washington, and pray for Lieutenant Han Wushi with me."

All were then transfixed by the first ever uncensored glimpses of hell.

Wu's face filled the screen as he flinched and hunched his shoulders under a murderous artillery barrage. Dirt pelted his cheeks and rolled off his helmet after each near miss. The audio and video drama was relayed via a tall microwave mast several hundred meters away to a van several miles to the rear. From there, it passed through a high bandwith network backbone to subsea cables crossing the Gulf of Mexico. The fiber optic bundle popped above ground in Nicaragua for an instant, then plunged deep into the cold waters of the Pacific.

It rose again—a fraction of a second later—in China. Nothing distinguished the single, hair-width tube carrying Wu's picture and voice from the multitude of others in the thick package of cabling. Until, that is, network control room monitors lit with flashes and loudspeakers sounded thundering booms.

And when the signal arrived, at long last, a half second later in the living rooms of China, the sights and sounds of China's war in America assumed the face of Han Wushi.

Rocking bursts unsteadied even the electronically stabilized camera and maxed out the six LED columns of multichannel audio just as European television networks switched to the feed. Weekend soccer and basketball games were interrupted. The audience swelled by another five hundred million people, who like their Asian counterparts were as shocked and appalled as they were enthralled.

For it wasn't heroism that all saw in Wu's grimaces. It was a desperation at the bleeding edge of life. He lay in the bottom of the ditch beside a suburban street whose pavement was being blown skyward in huge, jarring sheets. The scene was compelling. Universal. Wu was The Everyman. He was Chinese. He was American. He was German, British, and French. Each powerful blast sent Wu's face careening off-screen momentarily, and all waited and watched with one question on their minds. *Is he alive, or is he dead?* Each time, the camera returned to Wu. Each time, against mounting odds, Wu lived.

During the trauma shared with billions, Wu became an icon for the horrors of war visited upon young, fresh-faced innocents. He also became an instant worldwide celebrity. The brief connection established between the boy and the aged prime minister—explained to European viewers by anchormen's voiceovers—afforded Wu the identity that he never had before possessed. From nonperson he had become the young heir to a reigning dynastic power.

But the sketchy introductions of the star of the real-time docudrama left gaps in Wu's personal story to be filled by the imaginations of billions. His, all presumed, had been a life of high Chinese post–Communist nobility, all of which was now at risk just like the lives of the commoners. "Why would he do it?" rang out across millions of living rooms in a dozen different languages. What would motivate a young prince to jeopardize everything when he surely could so easily have avoided the danger? Or was it that he could not escape his obligations? Was his family making him fight? But why would civilian, vaguely antiwar politicians ask so much of such a young boy?

There were a myriad of questions and answers with endless permutations, but the billion viewers each had one thing in common. It now mattered urgently, to each and every one of them, whether this boy survived the lethal festival of real-time, televised violence.

The American barrage suddenly lifted. The camera stilled, focused, and framed Wu expertly in high-quality, high definition. The latest and the best equipment in the hands of the best combat photographer to have survived ten years of war. No expense had been spared for this unparalleled extravaganza. In the background, all could hear the thunder of intense bombardment, but around the hero there was a momentary respite from the violence.

Wu rose. Clumps of earth rolled off his battle dress like the premature fill of his grave. In the background, some soldiers rose. Others would never move again. There were repeated shouts of, "Are you okay?" In Europe, blazing computers translated the Chinese and simultaneously displayed subtitles. In the foreground came Wu's commands.

"Everybody up!" he shouted. "Advance toward the bunkers!"

The grim survivors—three dozen strong—trotted up an ordinary suburban American street toward the wooded crest of a hill ahead, from which rose towering sprays of fire. It was now the Americans' turn to seek shelter from the ballistic storm. The cameraman followed.

Wu skirted smoldering craters in pavement and lawn alike. The houses lining the street were alternately in pristine, pre-war condition, and blazing hulks victimized by errant rounds. After a long, camera-jolting sprint, the cameraman caught up with and walked alongside Wu, filming him in heroic profile, and then pulled ahead to get a shot of Wu leading his men up the hill.

But the photographer wasn't foolhardy. He knelt, and a ten-foot-tall Wu jogged past, stooped at the waist, rifle in hand. The camera panned to follow, but fell progressively further behind and took longer and longer shots at higher and higher magnification. Despite the covering bombardment, half a dozen of Wu's men were blasted off their feet by the deep rattle of heavy machine guns. Each could just as well have been Wu, which brought home the reality of the drama.

A one-second screech preceded a stupendous, unexpected mass Chinese rocket barrage. The ground was knocked from beneath the cameraman. On large-screen televisions all around the world, the fall and bounce of the camera sent people clutching for their seats or averting their gaze from the dizzying and soon-to-be-horrifying video. But the veteran journalist raised the camera with half a dozen grunts. The screens in cafes, living rooms, and offices steadied on grey geysers of earth rising from the ridge-top skyline. The eruptions of soil slowed and then fell back to the ground in long arcs. Large clumps of debris plummeted earthward trailing black tails of smoke like evil comets.

Without pausing to take in the scene, the combat photographer grunted again and abruptly sprinted forward. His expert, zigzagging dash transmitted dizzying slurs of pixilated video, but the digital audio that it captured was even more disconcerting. Noise was slung around rooms when surround sound processors faithfully decoded the ever-changing direction of the screams of pain and the cries for help recorded by the bouncing camera.

"Everybody up!" suddenly came the steady voice of Lieutenant Han Wushi, which grew louder with each long stride the racing cameraman took. "Keep moving! Advance! Knock out those bunkers! Get on top of them now! Everybody go! Go! Go! Go!" To Chinese viewers the shouts evoked tingling skin. Bravery in the face of the enemy. To nonChinese, however, the determined, foreign commands evoked the terror of being confronting by an unstoppable force. *"Take* the hill! *Take* the hill! *Take* the hill!" Wu shouted in raspy growls. *"Charge for the guns!"*

When the picture steadied on Wu—outstretched arm dramatically sweeping toward the hill—all saw that his men did indeed rise to attack. A crackling roar rose in intensity and volume from the surviving Americans straight ahead, who fired blindly out of the smoke that billowed from craters bracketing their bunkers. Wu's men, however, were fully exposed to the random fire of the heavy machine guns, which raked from side to side in well-planned sheets of death. Strings of fist-sized divots rose from pavement and cut the slow and the unlucky in half or sheared heads from bodies in anything but clean fashion. The camera searched for Wu. A Chinese soldier lay behind a tree picking out of his arm the long splinters of wood blasted from the trunk of his slim cover. Soldiers made suicidal dashes through supersonic scythes. Some made it. Others died horribly. Slender trees were shaken and felled. Cedar fences exploded with huge holes. Rubber trash cans were blown across yards and shredded by repeated blows. Parked cars were rocked and flattened by angry machine cannon spewing exploding rounds.

The camera found Lieutenant Wu alive. Far ahead. Shouting commands heard only by frozen, cowering soldiers.

The cameraman rose but remained low to the earth as he sprinted after Wu. In the sky above, a black thunderhead of smoke from the Chinese rocket bombardment blotted out the sun. Through the thickening veil of haze at ground level from the multitude of fires and explosions, Wu disappeared and reappeared frequently, seldom little more than a dim profile that flashed past the camera. Twice, Wu rousted soldiers hunkering low against death. Twice, the cowering men had charged up the hill and disappeared into the smoke until they were illuminated by brief, fatal blasts. Heads in living rooms all across the world swivelled to the peripheries of their ultrawidescreens as men tumbled from all manner of blows. Viewers shouted in fright until family members pointed at the peripatetic young officer on another part of the screen and shouted, "There! There he is! He's alive!" The cameraman rose again to follow Wu, passing one bloody remnant of a human being just as he was dying, but before he had figured out what had happened.

The camera caught glimpses of Wu only episodically, but the pattern was clear. When a soldier's nerves flagged, Wu appeared at his side. The lens zoomed in for close-ups of Wu lying beside men under the eaves of houses, in shrubs, behind cars. He never kicked or berated them. He never brandished his rifle or threatened them in any way. Instead, he got into the faces of the petrified boys, looked them in the eye, and spoke to them calmly until he got a nod, then Wu got to his feet and led.

His men followed. All of them. Every time.

The closer the attacking platoon came to the American bunkers, the more frequently the camera lost them in the thickening smoke. It always found Wu again, but fewer and fewer of his men reappeared.

The camera swung around to point back down the hill toward their line of departure. Through the drifting smoke, it recorded a landscape of the dead and the writhing near-dead. Water poured from a main broken by a shell crater. The river turned pinkish as it washed down the street over the corpses. But the pools that collected beneath the bodies sprawled across sidewalk and lawn remained an undiluted crimson. Debris large and small—some with licks of flame still rising— was scattered everywhere. Clutter amid the carnage.

The camera ended on a close-up of Wu, who had reappeared at the cameraman's side out of the haze. "Advance toward the guns!" he shouted. Again, he swept his arm forward, toward the enemy, in a pose suited to a heroic war monument. But Wu wasn't made of marble.

The flesh-and-blood statue rose and advanced on the enemy. The camera's lens and then the camera followed. The only thing you could see through the smoke ahead were continuous bursts of orange fire jetting from machine guns that protruded from bunker firing slits. At first, the only people advancing were Wu and the cameraman. Wu didn't even bother to fire at the concrete facades of the bunkers, he just advanced. And somehow, impossibly, he lived. Slowly, one by one, men joined him. Not eagerly, or even willingly, but because they had to; for Wu disappeared into the smoke, attacking the enemy alone.

A dozen reluctant warriors were stooped low but advancing under the withering American fire. Suddenly, the bunker that dominated the street was lit by a devastating ripple of explosions. The images of the young soldiers twenty meters ahead of the camera were framed by fire. Half were blown to the ground, and half dove as a second salvo of a hundred heavy mortars struck the bunker and surrounding trenches simultaneously. Their blast toppled trees, broke every window on the street, and stunned all living things into total inaction except for the veteran combat cameraman. The camera shook as he sprinted up the hill after Wu.

The young lieutenant sat helmetless in the middle of the street facing up the hill. Like a monk on the verge of self-immolation, his back was straight and his legs were crossed at the ankle. The camera drew even with him. The lower half of his face—the half below the long fissure creasing his cheek—was pouring blood. His face had been rent by a near fatal bullet.

A medic, miraculously, arrived from the rear wearing a strikingly clean and fresh uniform. He dragged a now roused and struggling Wu off the street and collapsed underneath his patient behind a stone retaining wall. The camera followed and watched the rendering of expert medical aid. The medic's boots were locked around Wu as if in a wrestling hold. From beneath Wu, the medic cleaned the wound and then closed it with a combination of staples and epoxy.

Only then did Wu's men finally rally to their leader. They gathered around him behind the wall and sheltered against the storm of metal. With his face freshly bandaged, Wu struggled to his knees. Then, onto all fours. Finally, squatting, he got to his feet. Swirls of smoke—alternating black and white—drifted across the sunless, gray scene. The right hemisphere of Wu's face was covered by white gauze and stripes of tape that crossed skin and scalp in utilitarian medical fashion.

Wu looked at the nine souls left under his command. They slumped against the rough, white rocks seemingly content to survive the war. Dirt from flower beds overhead—churned by steady steel rain—splashed in the air and rained onto heads.

Wu unexpectedly dashed past the camera out into the open. He didn't head up the street, but across it, where he retrieved his helmet and rifle. When he returned, he shouted in a raspy voice words that were, by now, familiar to all. "Everybody *up*! Advance toward the bunkers!" he yelled. But the words that magically drew everyone to their feet were, "Follow me!"

Nine soldiers, a medic, and a cameraman rounded the retaining wall. Six soldiers and the cameraman rejoined Wu amid the rubble just beneath the dominating bunker. The behemoth's concrete hide—now charred and gashed—had been poured into the ruins of a demolished house, which had been built at a tactically commanding bend in the street at the top of the hill. Wu stacked grenades in piles while lying low beneath remnants of the brick and stone house. A steady rain of bullets chipped at his cover. His men did the same, and on Wu's signal each hurled a grenade toward the firing slit. Six grenades missed. One went in.

After the seven grenades went off, the high-pitched scream of a woman caused all to hesitate until exhorted anew by Wu. The remaining defenders of the bunker fired furiously into the rubble, spraying chips onto the attackers. The American machine guns in the bunkers to either side of Wu's target couldn't slew their weapons enough to give their comrades supporting fire. The Chinese attackers were in a gap between interlocking fields of fire. That gap was filled by riflemen in open trenches. But open trenches had been a poor place to weather the barrages, and the fire of the few defenders was sparse.

Two of the next seven grenades made it into the firing slit, although one was hurled back out. Flames shot from the bunker. Screams followed close behind. On the third salvo, one of Wu's men lost his life along with most of his head. After three more barrages of spinning hand-hurled explosives, the smoking bunker fell deathly still.

On Wu's hand signals, the five soldiers followed him straight up to the bunker's hard wall. The last man in line flew to pieces when he stumbled and tripped a mine. Some of the pieces of him landed in the path of the trailing cameraman, who caught up with Wu at the rear of the bunker where it opened into the trench. The journalist and camera slid down the sloping walls of a crater that had once been the vertical walls of a trench.

Wu's platoon, now a squad, pumped rounds into the bunker's concrete hollows. A ricochet struck one man in the hand. He dropped his rifle and shook his hand as if he'd been stung by a bee. His palm had been holed straight through.

A swarm of Chinese gunships buzzed low overhead. Their rockets blazed at the next line of defenses. One of the follow-on troops joined Wu's men and pulled a small cannister out of his pack. Everyone fled to the safety of a deep crater as the man fused the fuel-air explosive and tossed it inside the bunker, then scampered away. The cameraman slid in just behind. The camera spun toward the sky, which exploded in flame as the bunker and all within it were fried.

The cameraman panned across the half dozen survivors from Wu's original platoon of forty. They lay beside Wu at the bottom of a huge crater blasted out of the soft, streaked earth. In the background, water gushed down the hill from a hundred ragged punctures—large and small—in a green water tank.

A new line of Chinese troops rushed past the crater. American heavy machine guns opened fire as the first men crested the hill. Soldiers tumbled backwards from the ridge as the second echelon carried the battle on to the second line of American bunkers. Medics fought desperately and mostly unsuccessfully to staunch the fountains of blood. The scene was a repeat of the hell Wu's lucky few had just survived.

And there were still three lines of bunkers left to go.

ALEXANDRIA, VIRGINIA
December 27 // 1515 Local Time

General Sheng—followed by Colonel Li—strode into his forward headquarters with a scowl on his face. The middle school basement was filled with broken, dusty desks and scattered high-tech accouterments of command. General Sheng's gaze was drawn not to the glowing computer displays but to an ancient fallout shelter sign on the wall. He shuddered involuntarily.

Despite the enormity of the Battle of Washington—on which, General Sheng felt, the fate of the war surely hung—he was transfixed by the scenes on a small television monitor. He ignored the glowing field maps, whose unit markers seemed stuck in cement. A group of officers was gathered before the television, on which the roar of battle could clearly be heard. The officers parted as General Sheng approached the screen. That's when he saw Lieutenant Wu. The boy slumped—exhausted—in a crater. He was breathing heavily and was visibly drained, both emotionally and physically. A massive bandage covered the right side of his face.

Colonel Li demanded to know who had authorized the civilian telecast to be broadcast from the front. "Where is their goddamned control van?" he railed. "Do you mean it's being microwaved out *live*? Find out where it's being recorded and . . . ! What the hell do you mean it's being fed straight to the subsea cables! Who approved that?"

"The defense minister," General Sheng answered from behind. Colonel Li turned to look at Sheng in shock. "The defense minister authorized the broadcast," Sheng repeated in a lifeless, defeated tone.

All of the officers turned to the screen and waited to see what Wu would do next. The legs and boots of the second wave up at ground level were clearly visible as they sprinted past Wu's crater. The camera expertly panned across the dis-

mally few survivors, always returning—adoringly—to the
star. To the bandaged face of the brave young lieutenant.

Colonel Li was back on a different phone. He cupped the
receiver and whispered to Sheng. "The national networks
have all interrupted regular programming. They're broadcasting completely uncensored!" Sheng's aide again listened to
the phone, then reported, "They're all 'Wu-this' and 'Wu-
that'! His history! His *family* history! Who his *father* is!"

An annoyed Sheng just waved Li to silence.

"Sir," came the new voice of Sheng's general in charge of
operations. "The attack has bogged down on our left. The
412th and 526th divisions are not going to reach their objectives. They've been badly mauled by the first belt of the
American defenses."

"Send the 131st and the 1107th," Sheng ordered, still watching Wu on TV. Wounded men were being dragged back over
the ridge on which Wu took cover. Others—unwounded—
were returning as well. The second echelon's attack was losing its momentum.

"The 131st has already been committed in the middle,"
Sheng's operations officer reminded.

"Then send the 305th," Sheng ordered.

"But they're not yet up to full strength," began the two-
star general.

"Send them anyway!" Sheng snapped. The officer nodded
before departing.

Over the television's speaker, Wu's radio was alive with
orders from some officer far down the chain of command
from Sheng, but far above the lowly lieutenant. Everyone's
attention was riveted to those shouts over the radio.

MCLEAN, VIRGINIA
December 27 // 1520 Local Time

"Attack! Attack! Attack!" came the tinny shouts over Wu's
field radio. The orders were plainly heard by the half dozen
men in the crater.

The combat photographer climbed up the loose walls for a
view of the carnage ahead. The viewfinder and screens of the

world's television sets filled with the second system of inter-locked American bunkers. They were clearly thicker and stronger than the first. Explosions churned the smokey, shat-tered landscape around the bunkers in a scene straight out of hell, but still flames dotted the firing slits. The paltry few Chinese attackers crawled forward under withering fire.

The cameraman slid back down the crater wall to the fire-blackened bottom and turned the lens again to Wu.

"All units! All units!" cried the officer over the radio. "At-tack the second line of defenses immediately! Repeat! Attack the second line of defenses immediately!"

"What are we going to do?" asked Wu's lone, surviving NCO, a squad leader. Seeing Wu's silent stare, he prodded, "Sir?"

Men screamed from their wounds outside the shell crater. Inside it, all eyes were on Wu. The camera lens zoomed, Wu guessed, for a close-up of his face.

"Sir?" the sergeant repeated. "What are our orders?" Men now streamed back over the ridge, sprinting helmetless and weaponless, with blind panic on their wide-eyed faces. "Lieu-tenant Wu, what are our orders, sir?" pestered the persistent squad leader.

"Attack! Attack! Attack!" shouted his superior officer.

"Withdraw to the rally point," Wu ordered woodenly.

The sergeant and men stared now not at Wu, but at the radio. Wu repeated authoritatively, "We will withdraw to the rally point. Those are my orders." When he had their full attention, he said, "You did all you could—you did your jobs—but this battle is over for us."

"Attack! Attack! Atta . . . !"

Wu shut the radio off with a click.

ALEXANDRIA, VIRGINIA
December 27 // 1525 Local Time

General Sheng shut his eyes as Wu led his men out of the crater. They followed, as always, only this time toward the rear. He even collected the disorganized, fleeing men from the second echelon, whose attack had been routed by the unbending American defenses. When Sheng opened his eyes, Wu had retraced his steps all the way to the line of departure, and had collected a unit that numbered over twice as many men as the platoon with which Wu had begun the day. The hundred-odd soldiers didn't know who Wu was, but they followed the calm officer who commanded without threats or bluster and with an ease with which one could only be born.

"I want a copy of that broadcast," Colonel Li ordered. The technician who sat beside the monitor nodded.

Another staffer pointed to the television screen. "They're keeping count," said the excited major, "of how many soldiers are following Lieutenant Han Wushi!"

Sheng looked. The counter read "105" in the corner of the screen. "One hundred and seven, now!" reported the reporter. The counter clicked to "107." And so it went.

Colonel Li finally approached Sheng one hour and fifteen minutes later. He had been avoiding Sheng. Distancing himself. *You pathetic, gutless coward,* Sheng thought, and then he smiled at Li.

"I'll convene a court-martial before sunset," Li tentatively suggested, "if that is your order, General Sheng."

"Colonel Li," Sheng said. "What is your combat record?"

Li's eyes widened. "Sir?"

"Oh, yes," Sheng said. "You have one week of duty on your combat record in the final days of our glorious rout in the Indian War. You are correct. It is not enough for an officer of your rank. I will consider your request."

"My *request*?" Li blurted out in confusion.

"But for the time being," Sheng said, "I need your full assistance here." Colonel Li lowered his eyes. He understood the threat. "Commit the reserves," Sheng ordered. "Commit all army group and army reserves to the attack. I want to reach the Potomac before dark, and I want to be across in strength by midnight."

Li nodded. His eyes never rose to Sheng's, remaining on the floor as they should. The bastard ran back to his bank of radios and maps and screamed orders to scrambling staffers like a son of a bitch, which was how Sheng had used him and why Sheng still needed him.

What a fool you are, Sheng thought with venomous hatred for the spineless sycophant, who survived by sheer brutality. *Can't you see?* Sheng thought as Li cursed at the chief medical officer. The counter on the Han Wushi show read "1,239," and was rising. *It's all over but for the end.*

12

"Stand your ground!" Stephie shouted into the radio as the Battle of Washington began. Artillery rolled through the hills toward their line. The bursts rose above the ridges and toppled trees. What finally came into view were straight rows of salvos being walked by computer toward their bunkers. It was World War III fought World War I-style on a crystalline Virginia day.

The Forty-first Infantry Division was compacted into a one-mile front on Washington's last line of defense. The icy Potomac River flowed at their backs. Stephie's platoon held onto the last six hundred meters of northern Virginia. They had no room to maneuver or withdraw. Every last man and woman knew that they made their stand here.

Curtains of brown earth rose skyward in ever-approaching rows of death. Trees were severed near the base like twigs and spun sideways through the air. Clouds of mist formed on the edges of rapidly expanding bubbles of shock. Each line of bursts leapfrogged the prior one. Each shook Stephie's insides with greater and more terrifying violence. At four hundred meters, shrapnel began pelting the bunker's concrete, and Stephie hit the deck. In the flashes of approaching hell, she took one last check of her bunker. Fifteen men and women lay curled along the walls preparing for prenuclear high explosives, which to them might as well have been nukes. Both were the destroyers of worlds.

Although Stephie and Animal had tried to prepare the cherries for what was coming, none had ever been through the body rocks at the Savannah River. Their thumbs were jammed hard onto the high-tech baffles in their ears. Their skin was greased with flash cream to prevent the sunburn that lay on the fringes of the real, bad burn. Their biochemical protective outer gear—camouflage, one-piece suits with clear plastic faceplates—was also fire resistant. Their Kevlar helmets and body armor covering them neck to thigh prevented penetration of thick slugs of shrapnel. But there was nothing to protect the young men and women from the fear that raged against their rickety defenses.

The world began to buck up into Stephie as the barrage neared. To the concrete's thump was added the quake delivered by the air. She jammed her eyelids shut. Both radio nets—up and down the chain of command—turned to spikes of static in both ears. A tidal wave of violence washed over them at an inexorable, horrible pace. Her body ached worse with each and every blast. Each blow shook the unitary bunkers, which had been poured as one unit around plastic forms. They shook and nauseated their contents, but they didn't crack. At least that was the theory.

When the rows reached the bunker, one 175 mm shell struck the roof of the bunker. Stephie was bounced three feet into the air.

Stephie's ears popped, and she couldn't breathe. Not because the air outside had been sucked from the bunker, which it had, but because the wind had been knocked from her chest. Her diaphragm had been paralyzed by the blow. Flames had obviously shot through the bunker, because smoke swirled thickly. Her helmet filled with the voice-activated screams of the wounded over the radio.

Stephie tore at the zipper to her suit faceplate. She ended

up ripping the entire hood from her head and tearing the helmet and the shouts from her ears. She coughed and sucked the air through balky lungs.

"Oh, God, moth-*e-er*!" came a boy's scream from across the smokey enclosure. "Mother! Ah! Please! God!" The wails rebounded off walls at double their volume.

We've gotta fight, Stephie suddenly realized. She drew a deep, faltering breath and tried to shout. "Every . . . !" she began before she coughed over and over. Then, to her great surprise, she vomited.

The heaves lasted several seconds.

"Oh-h-h! Jesus! God!" shouted a grievously wounded cherry.

"Everybody," Stephie shouted, spewing strings of spittle, "up to the firing slit!"

She struggled to rise to the firing slit, and saw their killing field filled with attacking Chinese soldiers. Her head dipped, involuntarily, in momentary disappointment. There was no way that they could hold. This was the end of everything.

She raised her head and then her rifle, and turned to her shell-shocked troops. "Get up here God-*dammit*!" she shouted.

She shouldered her assault rifle and spewed thirty rounds down the hill in a burst that spanned thirty meters of front. Half a dozen Chinese had fallen, maybe more. She reloaded and raked back to the left, then reloaded again and laid it on to the right. As Chinese fire increased, she dipped beneath the concrete wall to reload her smoking weapon.

A woman, Stephie's age, clutched at Stephie's calf. She was blown half to fucking pieces. She had dragged herself, leaving a trail of blood, over to Stephie. To the LT. To her one last chance at life.

Stephie looked the girl in the eye and shook her head. The girl laid her head down, and Stephie started to cry. *"Fight!"* she screamed at everyone. *"Fight!"* she shouted at the harried medic. She jammed the box magazine into the assault rifle and tore her bloused trousers from the dead girl's grip. She resumed killing, through flowing tears, with evangelical passion in a state of pure hate.

"Angel Three, Angel Three, do you read me!" came John Burns's shout over the company commander's net. His bunker was consumed with the sound of explosions. The sound of hand grenades!

". . . getting overrun! Repeat! CP overrun!"

Stephie began moving on hearing the word "overrun."

"You! You! You! You! And you!" she shouted as she clapped her hand painfully on helmets and shoulders. The three men and two women all looked at her. "Follow me!" Stephie shouted before heading for the exit.

Five infantrymen followed.

Chinese infantry poured into the bright trench line on the sunny hillside just to the north. "They're in," she advised her troops before leading them in an attack on the breach, and toward John's bunker.

Stephie in front dropped prone and fired on seeing the first Chinese soldiers. Two of her soldiers just behind her fired over her head. A half dozen Chinese died instantly. They had looked lost in the mazelike fortifications.

"Come on!" Stephie said, grunting and rising and running toward the enemy. They found only bits and pieces of Second Squad, First Platoon, strewn about a crater. White streaks rose from the inverted point of the conical hole, which split the middle of the trench. She and her team climbed onto the collapsing remains of firing posts and sprayed Chinese troops thirty meters beneath them, surprising them and hitting a dozen as they labored up the slope.

"Come on!" Stephie shouted, leading toward the opening of John's bunker. When she finally found it, she saw no one. Black smoke drifted out. "Can you hear me?" she whispered into the radio. They heard nothing in reply.

It could be the concrete, she thought, leading five people blindly forward. Slowly. So slowly that the two soldiers behind her—anxious not to get left behind—stepped on Stephie's boot heels.

"John," she whispered into the microphone, edging her way toward the bunker, "can you hear me?"

"Stay away!" John screamed from inside.

"Let's go!" Stephie hissed to her army of five. They rushed

forward toward the sound of his voice. Entered the bunker. Zigged and zagged through the entrance.

A rifle butt clanged off Stephie's helmet like a sledgehammer. A fusillade of fire exploded above her. She drifted. Drifted. Drifted.

Stephie awoke to ragged pleas in a familiar voice.

"Ple-e-ease!" Becky Marsh wailed. "Please! Oh, God, ple-e-ease! Pluh-ea-ea-ea . . . !" Her sobs trailed off into spasmodic gulps of air.

Stephie opened her eyes. Her head was propped up. She saw Becky kneeling in front of a half dozen rifle muzzles. Two of Stephie's five soldiers lay dead in spreading pools of blood. Outside the bunker, the sound of fighting was intense.

Inside, the half dozen Americans were lined up along one wall of John's command bunker. The tense, frightened Chinese held them at gunpoint with their backs to the opposite wall. From the looks on the faces of the Chinese soldiers, their tight grips on their rifles, and their fingers pulled hard against their triggers, it would be over in seconds. They were awaiting a one-word command.

Stephie looked up at the man who cradled her head in his lap. His face was swollen to half again its normal size. Both eyes were nearly shut. His lower lip was cracked open and misaligned. "John?" Stephie tried to say. The left side of her head pounded in pain.

"She! There! Her!" Becky shouted on seeing Stephie stir. Becky slid on her knees to Stephie's boots, which Becky slapped. "She's the president's daughter! The *president*! Do you understand? Of the United States! President *Baker*! She's President Baker's *daughter*!"

Stephie kicked at Becky's hands, but it was too late. Several Chinese soldiers turned their heads to each other in surprise. Several of them obviously knew enough English to understand. Most of the guns were lowered or swung away. Two men went to Stephie. John tried to fend them off with his hands, but the Chinese raised the butts of their rifles. Stephie yelled, "No!"

A sergeant came over and pushed one of his men to the concrete. He bowed his head to Stephie, as if in acknowledgment of her station in life, and helped her sit straight up. With gentle tugs of her arm and nods of his head, he was pulling her away from the others.

"No!" Stephie said to the sergeant, who instantly released her arm. She grabbed onto John's shoulders and waved her hand across the half dozen mostly wounded Americans. "Together! We all go together!" She knit her fingers into one and clasped her hands tightly.

Becky repeated, "Together! Together. We're all together."

The sergeant issued an order, and they were all herded outside. Stephie felt naked without a helmet when the cold air touched the blood, which dried slowly on her face below the wound under her hairline. But one young Chinese soldier found her helmet, ripped the ear buds out, and put it on her head. The were marched onto the forward slope and away from the capital they defended. As they crested the ridge, Stephie looked back over her shoulder. From where she stood, she could see the Washington Monument. Down below, great geysers of white water rose all around Chinese engineers, who were building a pontoon bridge. Burning bits of the bridge spun lazily downstream. Engineers lay dead—by the hundreds—on the beach. The Potomac was filled with the bodies of Chinese soldiers, which flowed slowly to the sea.

In that glimpse, she knew that the Chinese were losing the Battle of Washington.

Stephie marched away from the river and into Chinese territory with a smile on her face.

John, Becky and Stephie were separated from the other, mostly wounded soldiers amid a pen holding over two hundred POWs. A Chinese nurse had treated Stephie's wound with stinging alcohol and steri-strips. At Stephie's insistence, she had taken a look at John, but the nurse had quickly frowned and made a pained face at the condition that he was in. Hours had then passed during which the cold had settled into the idle soldiers in the open-air camp. Bright lights shone on the prisoners from beside dark profiles holding rifles. Few slept despite the early morning hour.

"I saved your *lives*," Becky whispered, tired of being ostracized. "I saved *all* our lives."

Stephie had to agree, but still she loathed Becky. John moaned from his fetal curl. The blows from the butts of Chinese rifles had viciously targeted the American officer. His skull felt soft beneath his scalp from swelling that Stephie was sure meant a fracture. Cracked ribs made his breathing difficult. And he wouldn't let her look at his bleeding groin, where he kept both hands sandwiched between his thighs.

"Look," Becky said, "if we all stick together, we'll get through this thing okay. They're not going to do anything to you! You're the president's *daughter*!"

"So I keep hearing," came Stephie's bitter retort.

Becky finally shut up. Stephie knew that Becky had used her tactical acumen to choose—incorrectly—to ride out the battle with Charlie Company. She had confided to Stephie that Ackerman's placement of the battalion HQ was at what she'd overheard was a vulnerable stretch of the line. Her old Charlie Company had been in a better position, or so Becky had thought.

John awoke from his semicoma to grab Stephie's hand. She asked in an upbeat voice as if to an ailing child, "How are you *feeling*?" He squeezed her hand with surprising strength before the grip faded and John's hand returned to his groin. Stephie stared at the blood smeared across her palm.

Chinese soldiers created a stir as they marched straight up to Stephie and pulled her to her feet. John feebly grabbed a soldier's ankle before the man shook his boot free. Other soldiers then raised a groaning John to his feet. Becky bolted upright, unprompted. The three were led down a narrow aisle through exhausted American POWs. The sullen prisoners stared in silence as the procession passed until one man, on recognizing Stephie, finally shouted, "Keep the faith!"

Stephie found the wounded first sergeant in the crowd and nodded in reply. Other prisoners had heard the call as well.

"Fuck 'em!" another man shouted, drawing menacing chatter in Chinese from one of Stephie's guards. But it didn't stop the growing torrent. "Ar-*my*!" one woman called out. "Give 'em hell!" came another cry. "God bless America!" "Tell 'em to go fuck themselves!" "Long live the United States!" But the shouts that attracted the growing chorus consisted of one, simple word, which was chanted in unison by hundreds.

"Vic-to-ry! Vic-to-ry! Vic-to-ry! Vic-to-ry!"

By the time the small procession reached the wire, Stephie's jaw was set. Her muscles and fists were clenched. Her lower lip quivered on the verge of tears. She was ready. She was committed. Nothing would break her.

ARMY HEADQUARTERS, RICHMOND
December 28 // 0845 Local Time

Lieutenant Wu created a stir as he passed through the halls of Sheng's army headquarters. All had seen him and had known who he was when he was on staff, but now something had changed. Many of the file clerks and secretaries who now lined the doorways had earlier gotten video calls from home. "Of *course* I know him!" they had replied excitedly. "I used to sit next to him in the cafeteria every day!" Many now sought his autograph on passing, but Wu was too determined to be slowed by the respectfully proffered pads and pens.

Shen Shen intercepted him at the top of the staircase. "Wu!" she exclaimed, throwing her arms around his neck. She pointedly kissed him—for all to see—openmouthed on the lips, her first ever public display of intimacy. "Your *face*!" she squealed, touching the bandage on his cheek and curiously smiling as her fingertips caressed the gauze. The dueling scar beneath, she clearly thought, would now permanently prove his valor. His manhood. Shen Shen's gaze shifted to the wave of whispers that rippled up the corridor. Her kiss had ignited a buzz of excited chatter. Shen Shen beamed up at her prize.

Wu pried her arms from his neck and proceeded down the staircase.

"No!" she cried out, grabbing him from behind. "I have a message for you!" she shouted as he fought her slender, vine-like arms. "The prime minister asked that you telephone him immediately!"

Wu ignored her and descended into the bowels of the building. In the basement, bayonets at the ends of rifles were crossed in front of Wu's filthy body armor, but when Wu's eyes rose from the black blades to the guards' faces, the rifles quickly parted.

"Where *is* she?" Wu asked.

The guards looked at each other, then back at Wu. One confided in a lowered, conspiratorial tone, "Colonel Li said no admittance."

"Where is she?" Wu repeated with a menacing edge. The junior sergeant immediately wilted and led Wu to the cell door. The second set of guards saw Wu and came to rigid attention. Wu nodded, and the door was opened.

A woman screamed to the smacking sound of a wet cane. The metal door clanged shut behind Wu. "Roberts!" came a spasmodic, shouted reply. "Stephanie! *Second* lieutenant! Seven-five-nine, two-nine . . . !" The smack of another lash cut short her scripted reply.

Wu headed toward the bright, stagelike lights. General Sheng and Colonel Li stood beside a television camera just outside of its field of view. Two American POWs—one a battered man wearing black captain's bars, the other a whimpering woman—stood off to the side.

And there, under the lights, was Stephanie Roberts, who sat bound to a wooden chair, bent over forward with her T-shirt in tatters. Her camouflage blouse lay on the floor beside her. She was half naked from the waist up. Her back was red with welts. Her face was buried in her knees. Her breasts were pressed flat to her trousers.

Sheng and Li stared at Wu. He walked up to the two senior officers, who never took their eyes from his. The eighteen-year-old junior lieutenant stood toe to toe with the seventy-year-old commander of Eleventh Army Group (North). Wu had received no invitation to join them there, but neither Sheng nor Li questioned his presence. No one in the room said a word until Colonel Li nodded at the captain, who expertly wielded the cane.

"You will read the statement on the TelePrompTer," the captain commanded in English. He leaned closer to her ear and whispered barely loud enough for Wu to hear. "These lashes aren't meant to break you. They're meant to break your friend, the captain. Brace yourself, and watch how he flinches."

Stephanie turned her red, tear-covered face toward the two standing POWs. The lash came down with a jarring snap. Wu flinched with a start, and the American captain took a half step forward. A guard held a rifle to the prisoner's head. The guard's finger was on the trigger, but his eyes were on Sheng and Li.

"It doesn't hurt!" Stephanie shouted to her fellow prisoner, then she dissolved into sobs. The captain milked the tears from her by whispering into her ear. She turned her head, but he found her other ear. Then her other, and her other, in succession. Wu couldn't hear anything but the hisses of the torturer's siren calls. But he was promising her, Wu felt sure, some easy way out.

A gurgling sound came from the American captain. He had walked as far as he could, hands bound, with a rifle muzzle pressed into the soft underside of his jaw. The cane *smacked* again with startling force. Wu jumped.

"You don't have to be here for this," Sheng commented in a low tone meant to be private.

"General," Wu replied without looking at Sheng, "I trust that you do not intend to harm this prisoner."

"President Baker's daughter?" Colonel Li replied exultantly. "No. We won't harm her."

Li pulled his automatic from its holster. With the weapon pointed toward the ceiling, he strode up to the American captain and the quaking female private.

Stephanie Roberts's bare arms—tied tightly behind the chair—were taut. Tensed. Rigid. Her face and wide-eyed gaze were fixed on her comrades and on Colonel Li. The captain holding the wet cane awaited Li's cue, then struck Stephanie's back with a loud *smack*.

"Stop it!" gurgled the American army captain through a mangled jaw and bloated, black lips. Li put his pistol to the man's head. Wu expected a fatal shot right then and there, and opened his mouth to call Li's name, but with Li's aim held steady on the man's forehead Li turned to Stephanie Roberts and said, in English, "Perhaps you'll reconsider."

"Don't do it!" the slurring army captain shouted.

"No!-No!-No!" came Stephie's rapid-fire pleas. They saved the American captain's life, Wu knew. The man was obviously too valuable alive.

But the female private became hysterical. She screamed and sobbed and fought the restraints while squealing like a wounded, trapped animal.

A shot rang out. It caught the Chinese soldiers holding the woman's restraints off guard. It took them a moment to realize that they were covered in gore from the shot to the woman's head. They let her slumped body collapse to the concrete floor. On Sheng's nod, they dragged her from the room. Both Stephanie Roberts and the American captain stared at the blood trail. The girl had been about Wu's age, he guessed.

Wu turned to Sheng, but the old general wouldn't look Wu in the eye.

Li returned the pistol to the American captain's head. The guards holding the man shied away from the impending splatter. With his jaw set and his fists clenched, Wu glared at Li, but Wu could do nothing more. It wasn't time. Those were his orders. But this only served to make it easier for Wu. To rid him of paralyzing conflicts.

"I'll read it! I'll read it!" Stephanie screamed through spasms of tears.

"Don't! No don't!" the American captain shouted.

But it doesn't matter! Wu wanted to say to them both. *Read it. Don't read it. It's not in the least bit important!*

Stephanie's hands were unbound, and she slipped them into her army blouse. A female makeup technician tried to fix Stephanie's face, but Stephanie snarled as if she would bite the woman's hand. The technician recoiled, then retreated, and Wu stifled a smile. Stephanie sat there, defiant, staring unblinking into bright lights. Her hair was pinned into clumps of strays and tangles. Her face was red and wind burned and shining. Another effort to apply makeup met with a shout of, "Leave me alone!" that brought rifle muzzles hard to Stephanie's ribs. But they did leave her alone.

She read woodenly, without emotion or inflection in her voice.

"My name is Stephanie Roberts. I am a second lieutenant in the United States Army. My father is president of the United States, and I was captured while fighting your army." She licked her lips and swallowed before continuing in a voice that cracked and broke repeatedly. "I have personally witnessed atrocities by American troops against defenseless Chinese prisoners. My government has gassed and shot hundreds of thousands of Chinese POWs in violation of the Geneva accords. Illegal chemical and biological weapons have been deployed repeatedly and illegally on order of . . . of . . . of my father, the president. I . . . I regret this horrible sin against humanity and against China, and I deplore all such criminal acts by my government. I beg the Chinese peoples' forgiveness," she finished, speaking rapidly, "for the horrible loss of life by so many honorable Chinese soldiers."

There. It was done. The army television producer smiled and nodded at Li. Stephie bent over and resumed her sobbing. Sheng's aide twirled his finger in the air to keep the camera rolling. The Chinese public would be treated to a dramatic departure from Stephanie Roberts's previous stiff manner. The moment the lights went out, she covered her face with her hands, but remained doubled over. Her hands were pried from her face and again bound behind her. Her face, however, remained planted between her knees. Her back heaved repeatedly in anguished but silent cries.

The only thing that drew her attention was the American captain. She watched him being taken away, then again buried her face. The camera, TelePrompTer and lights were removed.

Wu glared at Sheng. "You don't seriously expect," he said icily, "that confession to be of any value whatsoever with the American people."

"Its intended audience is not the American people," a smiling Li replied on behalf of his boss.

Wu ignored him and asked Sheng, "Is that how you're going to explain all the casualty notices that we've been holding? By claiming that they were captured and then massacred by the Americans?"

General Sheng wouldn't return Wu's iron stare. He and Li

departed, leaving Wu with the guards and with Stephanie.
"Out!" Wu ordered in Chinese. "All of you! Out! At once!"
His tone drew a glance from Stephanie. The guards filed past
Wu for the door, which was quickly closed behind them.

Wu was now alone with Stephanie.

She stared up at him. At his half-Caucasian features. They
had always been apparent to Chinese on first sight. Wu hadn't
thought that they would be so obvious to foreigners.

Wu drew his combat knife. Her eyes went straight to the
serrated black blade. He came toward her, and she averted
her gaze but said nothing.

"I'm not going to hurt you," Wu assured her in English,
but she obviously remained unconvinced. He rounded the
chair, and she turned away from him as if to avoid watching
her horrible end. She winced in agony as he cut the plastic
cuffs that cut into her wrists. She brought her hands to her
chin and her elbows to her sides but remained doubled over
and resumed crying.

On the floor beside the chair lay a diamond-studded cross
at the end of a broken silver necklace. Wu stooped, picked it
up, and held it out to her. She didn't notice, so Wu pried open
one of her clenched fists and lay the necklace and cross in
her hand.

Her head rose. Her face was newly soaked. Wu reached
into the cargo pocket of his trousers for a handkerchief, but
he felt something else. He handed the cheap plastic ring that
he'd found in the Savannah River bunker to her.

She took it, looking back and forth between it and Wu.
With brow knit and face contorted in confusion, she asked,
"Who *are* you?"

"A friend," he said.

Stephanie Roberts stared straight into Wu's eyes for what
seemed like forever, then said, "*Fuck* you," and lowered her
face.

Wu hovered there. This wasn't the way their meeting was
supposed to go. But this was the way it was, Wu resolved.
He leaned close to Stephie and said, "I'm sorry." He kissed
the part in her hair and left.

•   •   •

Han Zhemin sat in his cold cell living on tiny bits and pieces of intelligence. He had no windows, so he had waited for, but not felt, the nuclear rumble. He had listened for the excited chatter of the guards that had not come. Both should've happened by now. According to the prime minister, the army's plan was to swiftly exploit the breakout after sweeping over Washington. Unlike the large distances that separated objectives in the American South, Midwest, and West, the dominos were close together in the compact Northeast. If all had gone as per the plan—if the army had overrun the capital by midnight—Philadelphia would've been under attack by dawn.

And the deep rumbling of nuclear war would've penetrated the depths of Han's cell.

The single gunshot from down the basement corridor had riveted Han. It had left him tense; every nerve ending alert. From that moment forward, Han had heard every sound. The squeaking of metal. The clang of a closing door. The clicks— metal taps—common on staff officers' boots. The tapping sounds came ever closer to Han's cell.

Keys jangled in the door. Han was instantly petrified. His hands were freezing, but cold rivulets of sweat ran down his sides. Breathing became a difficult, voluntary act. He would now learn whether he was going to live or die.

General Sheng and his aide entered. Both wore sidearms. No television cameras followed them.

"I apologize," General Sheng said in a beaten tone. His eyes never rose from the concrete floor. "The charges against you have been dropped."

Han smiled. The terror and the agonizing, paralyzing fear were both gone in a flash. He rose, stretched as if after a night in uncomfortable accommodations, and put his jacket on. "So, how goes the war, General Sheng?" Sheng's face hardened into a sneer when he saw Han's amusement. "Not so well, I gather," Han commented, smiling. The pieces all fell into place. The army must have lost the Battle of Washington. The plans would now all have to be reworked.

"I thought," Sheng said, "that you might like to know that Lieutenant Wu fought with distinction, and that he survived the battle with only a minor wound. You should be very proud."

Han ground his teeth. Wu had disobeyed Han's direct orders. It was too much! Han had done all that he could for the boy, but this last act of defiance by Wu had truly gone too far. He would call the prime minister and decide upon Wu's punishment. To Sheng and Colonel Li, however, he said, "But you're wrong, General Sheng. Lieutenant Wu's service record in this war is of no consequence to me whatsoever."

As Han spoke the words, Wu silently entered the room on rubber soles not adorned with taps.

"Oh," Sheng said, smiling at Wu, who in turn glared at his father. "Administrator Han," Sheng continued, "I trust that you enjoyed your trip to Camp David." The remark registered on Wu's face as a deeper furrowing of his brow, but Colonel Li broke into a grin. Sheng clearly believed that his proof of the treasonous trip would grant him perpetual sway over Han.

But Han, as always, was steps ahead of the plodding soldiers. Han straightened his lapels, buttoned the collar of his dress shirt, and tightened the knot of his tie. Han smiled at Wu, but the boy wore a grim mask. "Unfortunately, General Sheng," Han said in a breezy tone, "it appears that my deception plan, undertaken at great personal risk, wasn't enough to ensure your army's victory in the Battle of Washington. I passed along your false plans for an invasion of Philadelphia to President Baker just as you had intended, General Sheng."

"The Americans obviously didn't believe your disinformation," Sheng noted, "if that's, in fact, what you passed." His accusation—that Han might have aided Baker by communicating the truth about their plans to attack Washington—told Han that Sheng's intelligence in Washington was incomplete. "Their entire army was waiting for us in prepared defenses along the Potomac," Sheng commented.

Wu waited for Han's reply.

"General Sheng," Han said smugly, smiling at his son, "I would've thought that your plan might have anticipated that possibility."

Sheng immediately turned and left. Li followed close behind. The cell door remained wide open.

"Let's go," Han said to Wu.

Wu followed his father.

Soldiers escorted them up stairs and into an ordinary office corridor. A uniformed, female clerical worker emerged from an office and her eyes shot wide. She immediately rushed back inside chattering, "It's him! It's him!" She caused quite a stir. Han pressed the "Up" button on the elevator panel.

Camera lights began to bathe their backs. Han resisted the temptation to turn and face the network television camera crews, who had appeared out of nowhere. He wanted to seem nonchalant. His victorious exit from military prison was about to become part of his legend. Han snuck a peak. The glare came not from network camera crews, but from an ordinary soldier's handheld videocamera. A pimple-faced boy was recording the scene on his private camcorder. A secretary arrived with her eyes on her own camera's screen, adding another glowing light to the glare at the elevator. Others followed to record the moment. The hallway filled with lights.

They all want to record history! Han realized. He smiled, straightened his back and squared his jaw. He held the pose until the old-fashioned elevator sounded a *bing*.

Han waved before entering the elevator. Wu followed him in. The closing of the doors ended the artificial blaze. Han smiled at Wu, who slumped—uncharacteristically—in the corner of the compartment.

Those were ordinary rank-and-file soldiers, Han thought in amazement. *Even* they *could sense my power.* Han had been like a *hero* to them! Han had always thought that the subtleties of power were understood only in the rarified air of Beijing. But perhaps—after a decade of civilian domination of the news media—politics had finally reached the masses. Han was flattered, ecstatic, and dutifully impressed. *It's a sign of the common man's development,* he concluded, *to recognize my destiny of greatness.*

The elevator announced their arrival at the ground floor. The door opened onto a warm bath of lights from dozens of camcorders. It was an other unbelievable outpouring of populism! Han strode out of the elevator to present his fans with the picture that they coveted.

But he suddenly found himself totally in the dark. The glare
of the lights that had temporarily blinded him had passed. No
one jostled Han, but their behavior dealt him body blows.
Their cameras were held above him, to the sides of him, peering around him.

Everyone struggled to get their shot of Wu.

Wu stared at Han from the brilliant glow of the young
soldiers' adoration. They avidly wished Wu their best with
eager, vibrant smiles. Han grew furious, turned, and began
dodging Wu's onrushing fans, who surged in as Han stormed
out.

"There he is!" a woman shouted, and Han looked on instinct. But she was pointing over a sea of heads at his son.

Han pushed outside through a revolving door and stood on
the front steps alone, ignored, irrelevant. The chill washed
over him. He filled his lungs with the cold air. It was quiet
on the street, so unlike the commotion inside. Han searched
the street at the bottom of the steps. There was no press. No
waiting car. No motorcade. No entourage. The only vehicle
other than four guard tanks was a camouflaged ATV around
which lounged a few, smoking soldiers.

"Let me give you a ride," Wu said from behind. The revolving door continued to turn as the sea of people surged
out of the building, bringing with them noise and brightly
glowing camera lights. They spilled down the steps and
formed a tunnel of well wishers all the way to the camouflaged military vehicle. When Wu headed down, applause
broke out. The throng turned toward Wu with clapping hands
like sunflowers to a passing star.

Han followed his son.

BANKS OF THE POTOMAC RIVER, VIRGINIA
December 28 // 0900 Local Time

The American soldiers that Bill Baker passed were exhausted but jubilant. They were grimy. Many nursed wounds.
But all were unbowed. On the DC side of the riverbank, Bill
gave a lounging gaggle of bandage-covered soldiers the "V"
sign for victory. A surprisingly loud cheer from the hundred

bedraggled men and women rose up in reply. Victory, even for the wounded, was sweet.

Bill crossed the rickety pontoon bridge to the Virginia side of the river within sight of Georgetown University. There, he made the rounds shaking hands and slapping backs. Dust rose from body armor with the latter form of greeting. "How far have you pushed out the lines, Colonel Ackerman?" Bill heartily asked the officer.

"About seven miles to the south from here," he replied in a monotone that struck fear in Bill's heart. From the look on the battalion commander's face, Bill suddenly feared the worst. "Let's go inside," Ackerman said, holding a hand out to the dark, sandbagged bunker. His grease-painted face was drawn and gaunt. Black bags hung beneath hollow eyes.

Bill felt sick to his stomach as he entered the bunker just behind his edgy Secret Service agents. Once inside the empty chamber, Bill turned to the man. "Just give it to me straight, Colonel Ackerman. Where is she?"

"She's missing in action, Mr. President," Ackerman replied. "Gone without a trace. The Chinese broke through our lines in four places. She took a detachment from her bunker to try to plug a hole at her company command post. We found her weapon, and two of her troops—dead—in the command bunker that was overrun, but your daughter, her company commander, and several others are missing."

"John Burns was among the missing?" Bill asked, and Ackerman nodded. "She went to save him?" Bill asked, and Ackerman nodded again.

Bill closed his eyes and rubbed his eyelids. "And there's no trace of either of them?" he asked.

"No, sir," Ackerman said softly. "I . . . I want to apologize, Mr. President. I . . ."

Bill shook his head and held out his hand to silence Ackerman. "I want to be alone," Bill said.

Everyone cleared out of the bunker. Bill sank onto a stool. His eyes drifted closed again. His breathing grew labored. *What am I going to tell Rachel?* was his first, crushing thought.

CIVILIAN HEADQUARTERS, RICHMOND
December 28 // 1150 Local Time

Han sat alone in his dimly lit office before piles of ignored reports. His mind reeled at the enormity of the change that had occurred during the short time that he had been in the army prison. *Why?* Han agonized. It couldn't have been by chance.

Han's aide had recounted the bizarre sequence of events that had led to Wu's sudden stardom. He had shown Han the videotape of his valiant attack on Washington followed by his humane decision to end it. The result was obviously a combination of stupefying luck by Wu, and magnificent orchestration, but by whom? No one on Han's staff could answer that question. In between breakfast, a shower, and dressing, Han had consulted by telephone a dozen ambassadors, administrators, and other functionaries in China's vast, transcontinental officialdom. None knew who was behind it. Some thought that it must be the army. Others, had left unstated the obvious.

Han's father and uncle must have been behind Wu's launch into official greatness.

The knock on Han's office door startled him. He saw that, on entering, his aide's eyes were furtive and downcast. *Agitated,* Han thought. Dispirited. "Lieutenant Wu to see you, sir," the man said.

Wu entered wearing fresh camouflaged battle dress. He found his father—hands pressed to his desk—leaning forward in his seat. The doctor had given Wu painkillers. Shen Shen had made him take them. She had been all over him, kissing, caressing, desperate. He hadn't told her of his plans to return to the front. She had watched him on television just like everyone else. But her desperation seemed, to Wu, to peak only after he had survived and returned to instant celebrity. She now urgently wanted to seal the deal. *"I love you,"* she had passionately exhaled in between rapid, smothering kisses.

Han simply sat at his desk, Wu noticed, wearing a dress shirt and tightly knotted tie. Strangely, he wore no jacket, and he was mute and incommunicative. *Vertigo,* Wu thought. Han

Zhemin—Administrator of Occupied America and expert fencer at the great heights of the pinnacle of world power—has realized just how far down the ground is.

"I'm here," Wu tested carefully, "for the teleconference."

Han's eyes arched wide. "Teleconference?" Wu nodded. Han consulted his printed schedule. "What—what teleconference?" His mouth was so dry that his words stuck together.

Wu felt a numbing pang of sadness. A dull ache seized his heart. He didn't like seeing his father like that. "I was told to be here at noon for a teleconference," Wu explained in low tones.

"By whom?" Han snapped quickly. "Who told you to be here?"

"Shen Shen," Wu answered.

"The teleconference was called by the prime *minister*?" Han asked, seemingly in sudden alarm.

"*I love you,*" Shen Shen had said to Wu. That was all he could think, at first. He had to look away from his father, who was totally self-absorbed. Han buzzed his valet and paced the room mumbling to himself. He was oblivious to the devastated Wu.

Shen Shen, Wu thought. *Shen Shen.*

"*You swear you're not a spy?*" Wu had asked her a dozen different ways. "*Nobody sent you? You're not a plant?*" She had lied to him each and every time, sometimes with unequivocal words of denial, other times with ardent shakes of her head and grunts of "No!" as her hips ground against him and her tongue searched for his.

But in an insignificant slip, Han had betrayed her. "Shen Shen works for the prime minister?" Wu asked in a voice that he fought to keep from croaking.

A valet brought Han's jacket held open in his two hands. "Hm?" Han responded. "Oh, yes. She spies on Sheng for us," Han said, his eyes faraway as he slipped into his jacket.

"And she spies on me too," Wu mumbled in a footnote that passed unnoticed. Han was too involved with his teeth, baring them into a well-lit mirror held aloft by his pinch-lipped manservant. Han missed Wu's tone, his anguished facial expres-

sion, his rounded shoulders that were usually square. He had
no idea how much Wu now hurt.

Wu waited until the valet had left them alone, then asked,
"Were you her conduit to Beijing?"

Han was bracing himself against the window. Looking out
at the gray day. "What?" he replied over his shoulder.

"Did you," Wu repeated, "*personally*, pass Shen Shen's
intelligence back to Beijing?"

For the first time, Han turned fully to Wu. He cocked his
head, studying his son. "What are you getting at?" Han asked.
"Does this girl interest you?"

"You slept with her," Wu said. "How many times?"

Han's aide knocked on the door and stuck his head in.
"Pardon me, but you're both wanted in the teleconference
center."

Han and Wu strode through the now luxuriously appointed
civilian nerve center that managed occupied America. The
seat of power was called simply "the fortieth floor." Every
well-dressed civilian lieutenant and foot soldier—officials and
support staff alike—was hand chosen for service at the business edge of Chinese bureaucracy. All manned an outpost at
the frontier of a faraway war.

The ancients in Beijing never ventured far from the Asian
continent. Beachhead America had been stormed instead by
thousands of young, elite corporate warriors. Sharp suits worn
by sharp professionals. All groomed. All fluent in English.
They were the best of the very best. All possessed superlative
skills at both corporate governance of conquered territory and
life-or-death combat against hostile allies in the Chinese military.

Wu was the only person wearing a uniform in the inner
sanctum, and every corporate warrior that he passed clearly
knew exactly who he was. The corridors seemed unusually
filled with loitering staffers who cast stealthy glances Wu's
way. The bolder thirty-somethings in buttoned suits nodded
and smiled at Wu. Information techs and personal assistants
ten years their junior couldn't help the shock of seeing the

white bandage on Wu's face. For them—like Wu—this was their first war.

When Wu glanced at his father, he saw that Han was shocked. His bastion had been breached by Wu's surging popularity. Han's mouth hung open slightly as he watched his people watch Wu. He dabbed at dry lips with his tongue but said nothing. He checked repeatedly to see that his jacket was buttoned, though he was immaculate and groomed after a shower and close shave. His hands fidgeted about his tie, collar, and hair, though none were out of place.

It hurt Wu to see his father like that. He felt awful for a man who felt nothing for him.

His father had always been power incarnate. The living representation of the concept in human form. All of Wu's life Han's mere existence had propelled him forward. A million courtesies had been extended to the young Wu. Privilege granted the boy not for money, but to curry favor with Wu's powerful family. Credits banked with perhaps what might become the greatest dynasty in China's history.

Han Zhemin—the manifestation of Wu's security and Wu's only link to that dynasty—was crumbling right before Wu's eyes.

The windowless core of the fortieth floor was tightly guarded by at least a platoon of civilian bodyguards. The new, thick-necked imports were everywhere, and they were armed to the teeth. They wore Kevlar fashioned into attractive black business suits. Their ear buds would've been invisible had it not been for the stubby mike protruding from one lobe. As Han and Wu passed, the stone-faced killers whispered into their radios, and doors just ahead of them opened on cue.

But the most noticeable feature of the menacing, silent brutes was the black, full-size assault rifle that each carried at port arms. Their trim waists bulged with magazines of ammo inside loose-hanging but well-tailored body armor. Their only gesture to office decorum was to hang their black form fitting helmets on the backs of their necks where—with the proper choreography—they might remain just out of sight of television cameras.

Their scalps bore only black bristles, Wu noticed, except for the women. They had hair cut fashionably short. A style, Wu thought, that wouldn't get flattened under a helmet's webbing. The black-clad, well-armed females who were sprinkled among the men carried box-fed automatic weapons. They wore differently cut black suits, but the dead-eyed women were obviously made of the same material as the men.

They're security ministry special ops, Wu realized. Probably arrived straight from the elite divisions in and around Beijing. Wu was fascinated. He'd never seen the cutting edge of civilian steel. The men and women who preserved the lives day to day of the prime minister and his government. Surely, this must signal that the conflict with the military was reaching a climactic finale.

Han led Wu past a receptionist into the communications center. An older, stockier man stood at a desk issuing orders into thin air. The directional microphone, barely visible at his earlobe, picked up his low murmurs. He wore the black uniform of security ministry troops. He had the look and tone of voice of an officer.

Wu stopped beside the officer and casually asked, "How many of your men have arrived from Beijing?" It was Wu's first informal test of his new power. Would the graying security ministry officer give the young army officer such vital intelligence?

"In Richmond?" the older man replied. "A division." He seemed to take pleasure from Wu's surprise at how large the security ministry force was. A smile from one soldier to another soldier, of a sort. "The prime minister is waiting, Lieutenant Han Wushi," Wu's new comrade in arms intoned.

A division? Wu thought. Ten thousand troops? Civilian soldiers from Beijing deployed in strength outside China for the first time in a decade of war.

Wu followed his father through the final door into a darkened circular conference room. The only light came from the epicenter where a four-seat teleconference station glowed. As he had done the last time they had spoken to the civilian leadership, Wu took a seat opposite Han before a console with a camera, speakers, and a wide, solid blue screen. His father—

whose face was well lit—stared at Wu from a distance of five feet. Han's face was expressionless. They couldn't yet see Beijing, but Beijing was probably already watching them.

Pictures nearly simultaneously sprung into three of the four windows on Wu's console. The prime minister's suddenly beaming face was flanked by the trade and security ministers. The fourth pane remained dark. "Han *Wu*shi!" the prime minister exclaimed. The three old men grinned and almost cheered Wu's name. Wu's glowering father was now just a glum witness to events.

"Can I take this opportunity," the beaming prime minster said, "to say just how *honored* we are to have you in our family." As Wu looked across the consoles at Han, he couldn't help but be struck by the contrasting impact of the praise on father and son. The prime minister's words meant so much to Wu's devastated father, and so precious little to an unmoved Wu. "Your name is on the lips of Chinese everywhere, Han Wushi," continued the prime minister. "Your bravery is unsurpassed."

Wu looked away from the screens in disgust. "Don't be so modest!" the minister of trade—Wu's grandfather—teased Wu. The two brothers—the prime minister and minister of trade—both laughed.

The security minister smiled, but said nothing. Wu focused on the man, a fact noted by all.

"I have a question," Wu said to the aged security minister in the dishwater gray suit. His skin hung loose, and his lips were thin, but his black eyes sparkled in the camera light. He nodded for Wu to proceed. "Why did you send security troops to America?" The prime minister and minister of trade looked at each other then waited.

The internal security general in civilian's clothes simply shrugged. "Security," he answered, "over Chinese territory."

"And General Sheng invited you here?" Wu pressed. He looked up at his father. Han ever so noticeably shook his head, cautioning Wu.

"We do not need to ask General Sheng for permission," the prime minister reminded Wu.

"Then," Wu said slowly and carefully, "there will be war between security troops and the army."

Everyone fell silent. Wu had asked a question that should not have been asked. "Not necessarily," the prime minister said. "The army defends the borders. The security ministry defends what's inside those borders."

"Every*one* who is inside those borders," the security minister clarified.

Wu nodded at each of the faces of the decrepit old men. He understood the security minister's thinly veiled, evil threat. The civilians' trump card was the families of the military's officer corps. "I have another question," Wu said. "A request, actually." The minister of trade in his window looked at the prime minister in his. It was then that Wu realized all three men were together in the same room. They were in the same type of teleconference apparatus as Wu and Han.

That must be rare, Wu reasoned, *for all three to be together.* But they were approaching a culmination, he knew, of the political war. It would end—soon—one way or the other. The four men awaited Wu's request. "I would like President Baker's daughter released and returned safely, immediately."

The three men in Beijing faced each other in turn.

"I want," Wu repeated, simply, calmly, "the safe return of Stephanie Roberts."

The minister of trade apologized and asked Han and Wu to wait. Their screens went blue and their speakers silent. Wu found Han gazing across space at Wu with a pasty-faced look of astonishment. Han's world, Wu understood, was changing with dizzying rapidity. His constant, forced reassessment of Wu's place in that world had left Han looking pale and sick. What new power had been bestowed upon the boy for him to make such presumptuous demands?

But even as Han remapped the topography of power, Wu knew that his father wouldn't remain adrift forever. Han Zhemin was too skillful and had worked too hard on his life-long ascent of the summit. Once his cartography was complete, Wu knew, Han would set a new and again confident course.

The images of the elderly civilian triumvirate reappeared on Wu's and Han's screens. Wu knew instantly from their grim faces that they could not promise what he wanted. The prime minister's face bore a look of deep concern. "We all empathize," he began, "both with President Baker and his daughter. She should never have been in combat to begin with. We will make private demands—and we will publicly criticize as heartless any unseemly plans the army makes for the girl—but direct action on the matter is simply impossible."

Wu rose from the teleconference center consoles.

"Wu!" Han snapped in horror.

But the prime minister raised his hand and shook his head. "Lieutenant Han Wushi," he said, using—for the first time—Wu's army rank, "I ask only that you not irreversibly choose your allegiances without long and fully considered thought. We," he said, nodding at his brother, "are your family. Many things change in life, but blood always binds. It binds us together, and it binds us to our duty. The family supports and protects, and it must itself be supported and protected."

"I *am* protecting my family," Wu said before leaving his wide-eyed, speechless father.

Just outside the door, Han grabbed Wu's arm and yanked him around. Han's eyes were wide, and his grip painfully tight. He angrily propelled Wu down the hallway, opened a door, and motioned for a startled woman—who sat at her computer workstation putting on lipstick—to get out of her office. She closed the door behind her, and Han swept the room with his handheld monitor and found it free of bugs.

Han faced Wu. "That video of your attack on the American bunkers," Han began, scrutinizing his son, "was it faked?" Wu didn't understand and cocked his head. *"Were there Chinese troops in those bunkers?"* Han demanded, seizing Wu by both arms and shaking him.

"Are you asking," Wu replied slowly, "whether the attack was staged? Whether Chinese soldiers killed Chinese soldiers?"

"But no one killed you," Han noted in explanation of his suspicion. "Defense minister Liu did it in Tokyo—reenacted the seizure of the Imperial Palace—just because they didn't have good video for the evening *news*! They've become *experts* at the deception!"

"You're insane," Wu said.

"They didn't tell the attacking soldiers in Tokyo," Han responded. "The defending soldiers were convicts with a death penalty hanging over their heads."

"That's ridiculous!" Wu exclaimed, breaking free of Han's grip.

"But it happened," Han commented calmly. "Did you see the bodies in that bunker?"

"They were burned."

"By whom?"

"By a soldier," an increasingly troubled Wu replied, "in the follow-on forces. He had fuel-air munitions."

"Had you ever seen that soldier before?" Han persisted. "Did you order him to burn the contents of that bunker? Did you ever see him again?"

Wu shook his head and turned away. "This is totally absurd!" He spun on his father. "Too many years of plotting and conspiring with those old bastards in Beijing have left you suffering from certifiable paranoia!"

Han didn't exactly smile, but his eyes softened. "Perhaps you're right. I mean, what kind of men would do such a thing? But one more question," Wu's father asked. "How were you wounded, do you remember? You couldn't tell in the video. There was so much smoke. How did you get that wound on your face?"

Wu couldn't remember. He raised his hand to the bruise on his forehead that had been red but was now turning yellow and brown with a tinge of purple. He had never figured out precisely what manner of projectile had struck him soundly just underneath his helmet but had not even broken his skin. He had been dazed and only semiconscious when the searing pain had creased his cheek.

Han watched his son. Watched his hand rub the bruise on his forehead. "Have you ever seen the effects of a rubber bullet?" he asked. Wu lowered his hand. His eyes remained on the blank wall before him, but he was listening. "I have," Han continued. "In our shipyards in South Korea. We couldn't kill the workers, who were rioting because we had decreed that they had to eat their meals at the yard, rather than take the food home. They were sharing the food that we gave them with their families, you see, and weren't getting enough calories to be efficient on the job. Anyway, the troops fired rubber bullets at them. They're really, sort of, these little bags filled with rubber beans, and they deliver knock-out blows without causing too much damage."

"This is all a product of your twisted, sick political game-playing," Wu snarled.

"But what I'm saying is true," Han said. "I saw it with my own two eyes. I didn't see the first time that the riots were broken up. I was in Hong Kong when I got the call to go to Seoul. But I arrived in time to see a reenactment of the riots being shot by the military. By the officer in command of naval construction, General Liu. You see, their first thought was to cover up the riots. On reflection, however, the disinformation specialists persuaded Liu that word of rioting shipworkers might lull the West into thinking that their naval construction program, which was proceeding apace, was instead experiencing delays. So I got to watch what Liu assured me was a faithful reproduction of the riots while standing beside military camera crews. They rounded up the shipworkers, set a few vehicles ablaze, and even destroyed a rusty old crane for a backdrop, then opened fire with these little beanbags."

"I don't believe you," Wu persisted, but with flagging self-assurance.

"Have you inspected that laceration on your face closely?" Han asked. "A bullet goes straight. The wound would be shallow at the fringes and deeper at the rounded center of your cheek. Any bones in the way would be shattered. A knife, on the other hand, would follow the contours of your face, and the width of the laceration would be much narrower than a 5.56 mm round."

Wu's eyes now peered through the empty wall and stared at some imaginary point a thousand meters away. Or even farther than that. At the battlefield that had felt so real.

"Do you want to save that girl's life?" Han asked softly. Wu turned to him and nodded. "But you understand, don't you, that those old men back in Beijing want her to die. They can get more political traction with the story of her mistreatment by the army if she's killed, preferably by torture. They could then harness public outrage. Do you understand? They want her dead."

Wu nodded.

"If you really want her returned home safely," Han persisted, "if that's your 'thing,' then I can help, but you've got to trust me." Han's pitch hung in midair. Wu stared back at him. "I'm your *father*. You should *trust* me," Han said, breaking into a calculated, self-confident smile.

But the smile faded when Wu abruptly brushed past Han for the door, which Wu slammed in his father's face.

WASHINGTON, DC
December 28 // 1200 Local Time

Clarissa found her father sitting alone in a park where she had played as a child. He didn't notice her approach as he mumbled aloud to himself. His conversation was animated. The public display of his rapidly advancing senility pained her greatly.

When the old man realized that his daughter was close, he was startled. She smiled at him as she would at an infirm. It was a smile meant to ease his passage through this difficult period of his life, but it appeared to do him no good. He was pale. His bleary eyes were bloodshot. His back under thick clothing was rounded and permanently humped.

Clarissa, by contrast, was young, slim and straight. She drew a deep breath and said, "Do you remember when we used to come here?" She sat on the strap seat of a child's swing opposite her father. She began to sway, propelled gently by her toes. "You met Mom and me here once, do you remember?"

From the faraway look on his face, she assumed that he hadn't heard her, but then he nodded. Far from easing his worries, her remark seemed to have agitated and upset him. His face looked stricken. "You were wearing a . . ." he began, but the words were choked off. He swallowed. ". . . a yellow dress. It tied in the back. It was one of those things. Those . . . What do you call them?"

"A sundress, Dad," she supplied in a soft voice.

"You were eight," he said. She thought he would start crying. He was in far worse condition than she had realized. The war must be taking a toll. *Or is it something else?* she wondered.

Clarissa crunched across the smooth gravel to join her father and put a hand on his shoulder. "Has the coup been called off?" Clarissa asked in a low voice. Tom Leffler's face shot up as he looked at her in sudden alarm. His eyes went from riveted focus to darting and shifting evasion. As he became overwrought, she became defensive. "When you asked me to meet you here," she said, gushing words, "I thought, surely now, after we won the Battle of Washington, there's no need for a nuclear strike!"

The old man acted as if he were nodding off to sleep. His eyes sank nearly closed. His lips moved, but no sound came out. She realized that he was praying.

"Dad," she said quietly, but with urgency, "*talk* to me." She sat beside him and took his gloved hands in hers. "Concentrate," she exhorted. He opened his eyes and looked at her, and his lips still moved, but said nothing intelligible. "If you're telling me," she continued, filling the silence, "that they're still going forward with the coup, then we've got to stop it. *I'll* stop it if I have to!"

"Gotta go," her father said, rising abruptly.

The child sensed the extreme danger from the behavior of her parent. Clarissa felt a prickly, unpleasant sensation as she rose from the bench. She tried to act normal, but her eyes were drawn to the long rows of dark windows at the nearby elementary school, to the ice-covered cars and vans parked along the sleepy residential street. Something was wrong. She could feel it.

"Okay," Clarissa whispered, her eyes darting about in search of the threat. She turned to leave, but her father surprised her by reaching out and grabbing her face in both hands. He pressed his lips against her forehead and held her. Awkwardly, Clarissa hugged his rounded back. As the kiss turned into a father's hug, she could've sworn she heard him mumble, "Forgive me, Beth."

Clarissa jammed her eyes shut and squeezed him tight. The closer Tom Leffler came to death's door, the closer he drew to his wife.

She broke the clench. "Let's talk tonight," Clarissa said, and then marched toward her car. There was no one anywhere. No movement. Nothing. Maybe it was just an old man's frail nerves. In her father's current condition, she couldn't really tell. Maybe he was imagining things. Remembering things from long ago. Maybe the coup had already been called off. Of *course* it had! We had stopped the Chinese! For the very first time! Somehow, Bill had managed both to defend Philadelphia from invasion and Washington from attack. He was a genius. A savior. Everyone must see that now. History certainly would.

By the time she started her car and pulled away, she was elated. Her last sight of her father, however, elicited sickening pity again. He still stood where she had left him. Head bowed. Baffled. Clueless. Unable even to make the simplest decisions or take the most basic acts.

After Clarissa drove away, Tom Leffler stumbled toward the unmarked van at the service entrance of the elementary school. He raised his gloved fist to knock, and the doors burst open. Agents sprang outside, grabbed the old man under each arm, and roughly pulled him inside. The thin daylight was extinguished with the slamming doors.

"No death penalty!" Tom yelled at the top of his lungs as they stripped the wires from the lining of his overcoat. They were rough with him. Tom was shocked. He stared up at the banks of cameras focused intently upon his park bench. "I'll tell you everything," he bellowed, "but Clarissa gets a plea!" Handcuffs were slapped on his wrists. He repeated his mantra in a loud voice, each word clear and forceful. "No-death-penalty-for-*Clarissa*!"

"That's the deal," confirmed Richard Fielding, director of the CIA.

WHITE HOUSE OVAL OFFICE
December 28 // 1400 Local Time

Bill's head lay on arms crossed on the historic desktop. He heard the door open, and he debated lifting the heavy weight to see who it was.

"Mr. President?" came the familiar voice of Richard Fielding.

Oh, he thought, *that.* With the greatest of effort, Bill looked up at the director, who again unzipped a locked valise. The door behind Fielding, Bill confirmed, was closed. "Is it true?" Bill asked. "Is Clarissa . . . ?"

He couldn't speak the words, but Fielding clearly could. "Yes, sir. She's part of the ongoing coup attempt." He extracted a single sheet of paper that he held suspended in air. Bill glanced at the short paragraph printed on it. "But that's not why I'm here, Mr. President."

Bill screwed up his face in confusion. The printout, now extended to him, obviously held the explanation.

Bill reached for it, but couldn't take it into his hands. He saw Stephanie's name in the body of the paragraph. His fingers, just inches away, couldn't find the edge of the paper. Fielding guided the sheet into Bill's hand. The page shook like a leaf in the wind. Bill seized it with both hands, but still it shook as if he were palsied.

Arching his eyes wide and blinking to clear them, he took a deep breath and read what he expected to be the report that he had long feared. *"Roberts, Stephanie, Lieutenant, U.S. Army, was confirmed killed in action . . ."*

To: The President of the United States of America.
From: General Sheng, Commander, Eleventh Army Group (North).
Subject: Prisoner Exchange.
Under the provisions of the Geneva Convention, I propose an exchange of prisoners at the Highway 301 bridge across the Potomac River at noon on December 31. The Chinese army will deliver into U.S. custody ten thousand American prisoners of war, including Second

Lieutenant Stephanie Roberts. In exchange, we demand that the president of the United States surrender himself into Chinese custody for trial on charges of crimes against humanity. If this offer is not accepted by 1700 hours today, you will be tried in absentia *and Second Lieutenant Stephanie Roberts will suffer your punishment.*

Stephie was alive. A smile bloomed on Bill's face. He raised his gaze to Fielding's severe visage. The perceptive professor's eyes dropped to the floor. "Before you make your mind up about this offer, Mr. President, would you give me the opportunity to make a few points."

"You're too late, Dr. Fielding," the elated commander in chief replied. He felt as if a great weight had been lifted from him. As if in a world of compromises he had finally been afforded one perfect, clean fix.

"Then one point, only, sir, if I might," the CIA director insisted. "Exchanges are tricky. Physically. Mechanically. Logistically. I'm talking just the pure nuts and bolts of the handover."

"What's so tricky?" Bill asked. "They hand over the ten thousand prisoners first, then Stephie and I just walk out onto the bridge and . . ." He stopped himself. They would both be there exposed on a half destroyed bridge. The Chinese could pour fire onto them. There would be no chance of escape. "But they want me alive, not dead," Bill countered, rebutting the obvious point to which he had leapt after catching up with Fielding. "They want a show trial with me as its star defendant. We'll cross the bridge. I'll walk more slowly than Stephie. She'll make it to the friendly bank before I make it to the Chinese side."

"What if the whole thing is a trick?" Fielding asked, ruthlessly shredding Bill's perfect fix.

"They want me alive!" Bill insisted. Fielding yielded that point with a nod. Still, Bill knew that he had cut short Fielding's long list of reasons why he shouldn't turn himself over to the Chinese. First and foremost, Bill presumed, was his constitutional duty. He felt compelled to defend his decision.

"This country will go on without me. The war will be prosecuted. The nation led. Glen Simon is a good man. That's why we have vice presidents. I'll transfer my authority before I walk out onto that bridge. I'm not king, I'm president. The succession will be seamless." Fielding opened his mouth to speak, but Bill said, "And as for the propaganda value to the Chinese, how do you think our fighting men and women will respond when they learn what the Chinese have done? Hell, Richard, I'll be a fucking martyr, and their anger will be worth two new divisions!"

Still, the CIA director obviously had points to make, so Bill cut to the chase. "Look, we don't know what they'll do when I walk out onto that bridge, but we do know what will they do if I don't. I intend to accept that offer by five o'clock this afternoon."

Fielding lowered and nodded his head.

"So, there you have it," Bill said. "That's your answer. Take every precaution you can think of. Do anything you can to counter any Chinese dirty tricks. Get Vice President Simon back here to the White House before the 31st. But make the arrangements, and whatever you do, Richard, make absolutely certain that by five o'clock this afternoon you have communicated my unequivocal acceptance of the Chinese army's offer."

Fielding nodded with his lips pinched shut and his objections cut short.

"Now," Bill said, the decision made, "tell me about Clarissa."

RICHMOND, VIRGINIA
December 28 // 1445 Local Time

The line of sick American civilians stretched from the door of the clinic down the sidewalk to the intersection fifty meters away. They were pale and gaunt. Women holding babies. The elderly maintaining their place in line while sitting slumped on the pavement. Shivering, sweating people with blankets draped over them.

Wu climbed out of the command car at the entrance. The

bleary eyes of the Americans regarded him with terror. One, a tall man with a blanket covering his head, turned away. The civilians closed ranks around him, hiding him. Drops of blood dried on the white concrete beneath him. *American Green Beret,* Wu thought. *Probably armed.*

"You cover the front," he said to the soldiers who piled out of the command car. "Stay here."

Wu climbed the steps to the clinic alone. Inside, the sights of the crowded waiting room were pathetic, and the smells were sickening. The air was thick with vomit. Bowels. Foul breath coughed from diseased lungs. A nurse—an elderly African-American woman wearing a strangely fresh white uniform—walked among the patients with an old-fashioned clipboard, not one of the newer penboards. She didn't need real-time access to insurance data. She simply catalogued their ailments, giving each a number. She was up to number 879.

"Where is the doctor?" Wu asked the woman.

Her hatred of Wu shone from her burning eyes. She seemed on the verge of spitting in his face, but she led him down a hallway filled with people and into an examining room. An old woman lay on the table. Her jaw quivered, and she stared at the ceiling. Her middle-aged daughter held her hand.

The doctor turned to Wu. He had a three-day growth of gray stubble, bloodshot, bleary eyes, and an apron stained with ugly yellows and browns.

"I want to ask your opinion," Wu said.

"*My* opinion?" the man replied, his eyes glancing across Wu's bandage. "Your hospitals are well-stocked with equipment and medicine. I'm down to a few samples that I've been hoarding for the seriously ill."

"I want to ask your opinion," Wu repeated.

After a moment, the man crossed the hallway into his office. Wu shut the door behind him. "Drop your pants," the doctor said.

"What?"

"I can identify which venereal disease you have," the American physician replied, "but if you need penicillin, you're going to have to get it from Chinese army stocks. I've been out for a month."

"It's this," Wu said, peeling the bandage from his face with a painful tearing sound.

The doctor eyed the wound from a distance, then turned on the lamp atop his desk and twisted it so that it shown up, not down. "Come here," he said, motioning Wu forward. He donned reading glasses, grabbed Wu's chin somewhat roughly, Wu thought, and turned his head to the side. With his free hand, he prodded Wu's face, stretching his skin and causing Wu to wince. "No infection. They used adhesive glue instead of stitches to close it up. I didn't know the Chinese army had plastic surgeons on staff."

He turned off the light.

"Was it a woman, or a card game?" the American doctor asked.

"What do you mean?"

"Who cut you?"

"I was wounded," Wu replied, shaken. "In combat."

"Don't tell me our guys are using sabers," the doctor said.

"I was hit by a bullet. Nearly hit, I mean. It grazed my face."

The doctor turned the lamp on again, and again took control of Wu's head, turning it this way and that. He extinguished the lamp.

"Whatever you say," was his response.

"What do *you* say?" Wu asked.

"About that cut on your face?" the physician replied. Wu nodded. "I say you were cut with a knife. Maybe even a scalpel, the incision is so narrow. You'll have a scar, but not like the one you'd have if you'd been grazed by a bullet." He reached up and pressed on Wu's cheekbone. Wu's head rocked back, and his cut stung. "That bone would be gone—fractured in a half dozen places—if a bullet had entered here," he said, prodding the lower corner of the cut, "and exited here." Wu withdrew his face before the man could hurt him again.

The American snorted in amusement or disgust, Wu couldn't tell which. "I've heard of men shooting their little toe off to get out of combat, but I've never heard of them slashing themselves across the face. It must be gettin' pretty bad on you guys." The beginnings of a smile lit his face and a twinkle his eye. "I heard things didn't go so well up at DC." He couldn't hide the smile any longer.

"Thank you," a devastated Wu said. The doctor was ill prepared for that response, and his smile faded. He taped the bandage back over Wu's face. Wu, lost in thought, turned to leave.

"Why don't you just give up?" the doctor Wu asked from behind. "You're never gonna win this war," he said to Wu's back. "I've never been more convinced of that fact than right now. Before the invasion, I had my doubts. My fears. But now, I'm certain we're gonna win this thing. And when we do, well, you'd better get the hell out our way young man. You'd better start shootin' off major pieces of yourself 'cause we're in a bad fuckin' mood and there's gonna be hell to pay."

Wu never turned back toward the man. He marched past the halls of the sick and out into the fresh air. The line hadn't moved an inch. In fact, it now wrapped around the block and disappeared out of sight.

When Wu got into the command car, he turned to his driver and said, "Radio for a medical team to come down here and assist at this clinic."

The sergeant seemed hesitant. "Lieutenant Wu, sir," he stumbled, "the field hospitals are overflowing with casualties from the battle."

Wu jerked his head to the man. *"Do you know who I am?"* he shouted. The eyes of the driver and the men in back widened. The driver nodded. "Then get on that radio and relay that order. Now."

ARMY HEADQUARTERS, RICHMOND
December 28 // 1915 Local Time

The keys jangled outside Stephie's cell door. She rose from where she had lain on her stomach to sit on her bed. Her back stung as if she'd been branded, but a young female nurse—empathetic and consoling—had applied a balm that had helped.

A young Chinese guard in starched garrison uniform brought Stephie her dinner on a silver tray.

The door remained open. A second guard peered inside until he saw her looking at him, and then he receded from sight. Her waiter—with an automatic in a white leather holster—removed linen napkins from her steaming bowl of rice and chicken. The tall, muscled twenty-year-old—groomed and shorn of hair like a headquarters show horse—kept stealing glances at Stephie as he arranged her silverware.

They were alone.

Stephie whispered, "Do you know what's happened to the American captain who was brought in with me?" The soldier focused his eyes on his job of arranging the salt and pepper. She could read nothing in his face. It was a blemishless mask. The lacquered brim and chin strap of his hat gave him the look of a toy soldier in the *Nutcracker*. "Come on," she whispered urgently, "I *know* you speak English! Is he *alive*?"

The Chinese soldier—bent over at the waist before her just inches away—gave her a millimeter bob of his chin. It was the most infinitesimal of movements, but it *was* a nod. It was, most definiately, a nod.

A great weight was lifted from her. Her font of information finished and marched off toward the door. He was her lone contact with the outside world. She had to think of another question quickly. The only thing that came to mind was, "Why are you in my country?"

It stopped the guard in his tracks.

The Chinese soldier turned to her with the most pathetic of faces. He squinted, and his mouth parted slightly, which for the mannequin-turned-man was clearly a look of anguish. He glanced up at the far wall of Stephie's cell, then abruptly turned and marched out the door. He had turned the wrong way, away from the door. He'd spun 270 degrees to the left instead of 90 degrees to the right, and in the process he had glanced up at the wall. It wasn't much, but Stephie understood what he was telling her. She knew every inch of her cell. She hadn't needed to follow his eyes to her cell's lone vent. She didn't want to get the guy into trouble. There was a camera and a microphone in the air vent, he had told her. It was just as she had suspected since she had first prowled the cell.

She ate her meal in silence and dissected their exchange. At first she concluded that the guard was simply saying *"I can't talk because we're being watched."* But the more she thought about it, the more stunning became her realization of what the soldier was actually trying to say. *Could it possibly be true?* she wondered. The guard had been handpicked to provide security at what looked like a major army headquarters. He was surely the most loyal of the loyal, and he looked the part. Stephie's skin tingled with what his reply might have meant.

When she'd blurted out, "Why are you here in my country?" the man had looked straight at the camera. He had looked at the security that watched the security. At the officers who manned the monitors. At the authority that they represented, which rose above the lowly enlisted man all the way back up to Beijing where they might even be watching the video feed live.

It hadn't been much. A little glance. Some carefully controlled shock at her question. A not quite so innocent look at the camera. But what had just happened was that an ordinary soldier had just risked his life simply to tell Stephie that he didn't want to be there. That he was only in America because of "them." They had ordered him to come, he had apologized with a look. Her skin tingled with excitement at the import of the soldier's unspoken remark.

We've won, she realized. *It's over.*

13

"Echo Foxtrot two one nine, do you read, over?" came the words in Hart's dream. "Attack Beijing. Repeat. Attack Beijing." Suddenly, Hart wasn't in the rolling hills of northern Virginia, but looking down on the Chinese capital, which looked—strangely—like Birmingham, Alabama. He marched into the Chinese city laying waste to buildings and cars with weapons that blasted entire blocks into rubble, but couldn't seem to kill the Chinese soldiers scurrying underfoot. Point-blank fire inexplicably missed them. He was Godzilla with a full-auto grenade launcher.

"Echo Foxtrot two one nine, do you read, over?" Hart opened his eyes. It was night. Time to go to work. "Echo Foxtrot two one nine, do you read me, over?" It was no dream. All was quiet in the dark woods save the sound in his ear.

He cleared his throat, pushed the "Talk" button, and said, "This is Echo Foxtrot, I read you, over."

"Echo Foxtrot," came the familiar controller's voice, "this

is India Zulu four four. Able mind. Able mind. Do you copy? Over."

Hart panicked at the total blank that the encoded challenge drew. He had memorized dozens of sign-countersign combinations, all of them chosen because they had no natural associations. But that security protocol also made them hard to remember. "Echo Foxtrot," the impatient controller repeated, "I say again. Able Mind. Able Mind. Over."

It was his last chance. A failure to reply—correctly—within the next few seconds would mean the end of his war. There would be no further use in communicating with the one-eyed colonel. No words—no explanation—would rebut the presumption that the Chinese held a gun to Hart's head. Hart would be on his own to make it back to friendly lines. A little voice in his head said, *Quiet. Say nothing. Go home.*

"Home game!" another voice shouted. That was the correct reply.

Home. Home. *Where is that?*

With his heart pounding, he keyed the mike. "India Zulu four four, this is Echo Foxtrot two one nine." What? What? He keyed the mike not knowing what he would say. "Home game," came his reply to himself. "I say again home game. Home game. Over."

The Green Beret colonel responded quickly with orders. The first mission in a long, long time. "Proceed to map coordinates Echo Golf six three seven four, Kilo Alpha two niner seven three. Over." Hart pulled the sleeping bag over his head, turned on his flashlight, and fumbled with his map. He found the grid coordinates, which were unique to his map for security reasons. The point on the map to which they directed Hart was on the Chinese-held Virginia bank of the Potomac River. There, the grounds of the captured U.S. Naval Weapons Laboratory sat astride a state highway. The most prominent geographic feature was the Highway 301 bridge, which, while damaged and unusable to vehicular traffic, still stood. "Use caution," the controller advised, "but use all possible haste. It is imperative that you be in position by 0400 hours the day after tomorrow."

Hart was close, relatively speaking, to his objective. But fifteen miles of cross-country terrain should take two or three nights of forced march. He would have to do it in one.

"Roger, copy," Hart replied. His skin tingled. This was it. Something big was up. He could feel it. "What are my orders upon arrival, over?"

He swallowed.

"You are to go to ground, reestablish communications, and await further instructions, over." All of the excitement—and fear—drained out of Hart. *Fuck that!* came the chorus of insubordinate voices in his head. "Do you copy, Echo Foxtrot?" asked the Green Beret colonel.

With the greatest effort, Hart replied through teeth clenched in anger, "Copy."

"Echo Foxtrot, this is India Zulu. One additional instruction. Take your long gun. Do you read, over?"

So that was it, Hart thought. *Assassination. The long gun. A scope job. He might just possibly get away. Live.*

"I read you five by five," Hart replied. "Echo Foxtrot, out."

WHITE HOUSE RESIDENTIAL QUARTERS
December 28 // 2300 Local Time

"Bill!" Clarissa exclaimed. "You can't do it!" Bill didn't reply. "You're the *president*! There's a *war* on!"

"It's done," he muttered as he untied his shoes and prepared for bed.

"You can't! You just . . . ! You can't! *Please.* Please."

"Vice President Simon has a lot of good people to back him up. Loyal people." He didn't look at Clarissa as he climbed into bed.

She fell quiet. Her chin was tucked, and her loose hair curtained her face. "I love you," she faintly whispered as if to keep her voice below microphone detection.

I love you too, Bill thought. *I think.*

He rolled to her and turned her to him. He took her face in both of his hands. With his lips three inches from hers, he stared into her eyes. "Say that again."

She never blinked or turned. On her way to his lips, she said clearly, but softly, "I love you."

He grabbed her face and held her lips almost touching his. "Then I love you too."

NORTHERN VIRGINIA
December 29 // 0530 Local Time

Captain Jim Hart reached his objective just before daybreak, drenched in sweat, legs and back aching. The predawn darkness around him was alive with noise but no light. Earthmovers growled in forward and then chirped in reverse. Trucks driven by IR-goggled troops rolled down the roads with headlights extinguished.

At the end of a fifteen-mile march, Hart had to do dash-and-drop maneuvering to get closer. His lungs were on fire with the frigid air. He heard hammering. Nails into wood. Like the Chinese were building gallows.

He was close. He needed to cough and cough and spit, but he got the tones in his ear buds. Enemy tactical net—a low emission radio system as good as the Americans'—was inside of a few hundred meters.

He had to assess the situation. He had to climb a hill. *Climb this one,* suggested an exhausted voice in his head. *This one right here.* Hart made his legs take him up. Everything began cramping at once, and all across the tops of both quadriceps, fire erupted from his thighs.

Hart had to stop halfway up and stretch. Everything hurt. He rolled on the ground, counting to thirty as his knotted muscles were smoothed. He was running on empty. He needed to eat, he decided. Despite the close proximity to the enemy, he washed down three bites of an iron-tasting power bar, touched his toes one last time to loosen his piano-wire hamstrings, and then hauled the long gun the final one hundred meters uphill.

At the crest, he saw nothing on the overcast night with light amplification other than the bright river. He switched to IR, and the cold water went dark. Hundreds of Chinese soldiers swarmed the near base of the bridge.

They were 400—maybe 500—meters away. Hart wasn't the best shot, but he could do 500. He crested the ridge onto the forward slope so as not to present the enemy with a profile along the skyline. He moved fifty meters to his right where the reverse slope at his back was unscalable. He wanted no surprises from behind. Hart settled in among the rocks and brush and set up the microwave receiver.

The brief burst of static through his earbud alerted Hart that he had carrier. The microwave beam instantly tightened to Hart's exact location and changed encoding systems. A *beep* instantly alerted Hart.

I've got mail, he thought, waiting expectantly.

"Echo Foxtrot two one nine, do you read, over?" came a voice that Hart didn't recognize. Hart acknowledged. "Stand by for orders," someone said to Hart from the other end of the transmission. It was to the north. Hart could eyeball it and see that it came from across the Potomac. From the American side. There was no possibility of a Chinese ruse.

For the next half hour, Hart received incredible, detailed orders from unrecognized voices. He requested for clarification of practically every aspect of his mission. *This is un-fucking-believable!* all the voices sung in harmony. Hart demanded time and again that they repeat the astounding instructions. But he never asked that they explain them. He asked what, when, how, where and who—especially who—but never why? That would have been improper.

The orders consisted of a dizzying series of, *"If this happens, then do that, but if that happens, instead do this."* At each major juncture in the decision tree—at each moment in time at which Hart would have to make a critical, life-or-death choice in a fraction of a second—he was asked to repeat the orders. The series of conditional actions required of him to take. The half dozen voices scripted Hart's orders wielding logic with mathematical precision. There was never any doubt as to what Hart should do. If A, then fire, otherwise do X. If B, then fire, otherwise do Y. The orders followed each branch to a certain and usually fatal conclusion.

But sometimes the result was otherwise. "Do nothing." Sometimes, the unknown controllers went back to the trunk and followed another, radically different branch. It was up to Hart—the national strategic asset—to keep it all straight.

He repeated instructions, but Hart wasn't yet satisfied. His mind reeled from it all.

Hart nearly forgot about the swirl of enemy activity around him and almost missed a patrol that passed within sixty meters of his well camouflaged position. Nearby movement occasionally interrupted his replies, and his controllers waited patiently without needing explanation.

At the end, a controller—somebody Hart didn't know at all—asked, "Echo Foxtrot, two one nine, do you acknowledge the orders?"

"Echo Foxtrot," Hart replied, beaten down into a daze, "acknowledged."

"Do you have any questions?" the guy asked.

Hart's mind spun. *"What the hell is going on?"* he wanted to shout. "And where's the one-eyed colonel? Who are you? Shit!" But he was expected to ask only about practical details. They wouldn't tell him anything more. He was behind enemy lines.

But there was one practical detail that his briefers had omitted. "What about my egress?" Hart demanded.

There was a long silence. "Use the best available means," came the anonymous reply. A new, deeper, more sympathetic sounding voice said, "After this, you can bring it all the way home, Echo Foxtrot."

There would be little chance of that, Hart knew. "Copy," he whispered through a hoarse throat. He wasn't used to that much talking. "Two one nine, out."

WHITE HOUSE OVAL OFFICE
December 29 // 1000 Local Time

Bill didn't want to transfer his powers in the Situation Room. He didn't want a presidential succession taking place in a bunker. The throng had gathered, therefore, in the sunny Oval Office. The biggest change was that the rocket screens had been removed from the windows. Bright daylight again streamed in. The United States had won the Battle of Washington and pushed the Chinese back from the city. It was that scene—one of victory—that Bill wanted history to record.

An ashen Clarissa stood just inside the doorway together with Bill's appointments secretary, steward, and others from his personal staff. The cabinet was gathered around the desk at which Bill sat. The military brass—returned to wool uniforms of greens and blues—stood in a ring just outside. Two large, flat-screen monitors had been wheeled in beside Bill's desk. One bore the image of the vice president, who was on the airborne command post over Baltimore. He would land and make his way to the White House as Bill headed for the prisoner exchange site. The other screen bore the chief justice of the Supreme Court, who was in a deep underground bunker in Omaha. The president pro tempore of the Senate, and Tom Leffler—Speaker of the House—sat in chairs on the opposite side of the president's desk.

Upon her arrival, Clarissa had tried to whisper to her father, but he had halted her with a quick shake of his head. After a sick-looking smile at Bill, she had receded to the doorway. She looked fresh and beautiful. "*I love you,*" she said to Bill with slight movements of her lips.

The young widow, Bill thought. *Straight out of central casting.* Wearing a proper dress. Clutching a handbag to her thighs. Trying to hold up. To get by. To make it through.

Her father slumped—a shell of his former presence—and glared through greasy eyes at Bill.

"Sorry to keep you up there so long," Bill said to the vice president on the monitor as they got started. The Republican congressman and former secretary of defense had been on a military command and control airplane the entire month since he had been confirmed as vice president.

"That's all right, Mr. President," Glen Simon replied. Bill had informed him of his decision to hand himself over in a quick audiophone call the day before, but this was the first time the two had faced each other. It was made doubly awkward by the presence of so many people. "I can't tell you, Bill, how much my heart goes out to you," the vice president said. "What you're doing, it's . . . Well, you're a remarkable man, Mr. President. And this office is yours. You go get your daughter. We'll get you back here—some way—even if we have to fight all the way to China to do it. I pledge that to you."

"That's exactly what we've got to do," Bill said to the man soon to occupy his chair. And to his cabinet. And his military. And to all the rest of posterity via the cameras, which discretely recorded the ceremony. "We were fools. We fell asleep. We made the mistake of allowing ourselves the luxury of thinking that national survival isn't solely and completely dependent—ultimately—upon brute force. Our nation is still rising up from that slumber. In two years, we'll have put twenty arsenal ships to sea. Let's see how the Chinese deal with that." There were nods from the Joint Chiefs and many in the cabinet. A couple said, "Here-here." "But we can't stop until we win this war. Until the Chinese military is demolished and all the world is liberated. You cannot shrink from the fight once it's conveniently far away. It is your duty to press on—press *on*—to total victory so that our children's children can know total peace."

The room was silent. There was no tumultuous applause. Sobriety reigned. Somber heads were bowed, as Bill looked down at his script. "Mr. Chief Justice," he read into the monitor beside the vice president's, "whereas tomorrow morning, at zero six hundred hours Washington time, I will cross the Potomac River and deliver myself into the hands of this nation's enemy; and whereas immediately prior thereto, I desire and intend to transfer, automatically and without further process, the powers and duties of the office of president of the United States to Mr. Glen Simon, Vice President of the United States, who will thereupon become the acting president of the United States."

Bill cleared his throat, which constricted with fear.

"Whereas I have further been advised by White House counsel and the National Security Council that a temporary transfer of power pursuant to Section Three, Article Twenty-Five of the Constitution of the United States would entitle me to reclaim the office of president while still in the hands of the enemy by transmittal of a written declaration to the President Pro Tempore of the Senate and to the Speaker of the

House of Representatives, which declaration might be obtained by duress; whereas, as a consequence, I, Bill Baker, president of the United States of America, hereby request that the chief justice of the Supreme Court of the United States certify a conditional transfer of the authority and duties of the office of president in accordance with the procedures set forth in Section Four, Article Twenty-Five, of the Constitution of the United States of America."

Bill looked up at his cabinet. Almost all had fought long and hard on a political campaign dedicated solely to getting Bill elected so that he could save the country. Some were bitter over his abandonment of that country. The rest begrudgingly understood. Bill lowered his head from their silent gazes and returned doggedly to his lawyers' script.

"Whereas, in the opinion of White House counsel and the National Security Council, any attempt that I might make while in Chinese captivity to reclaim the office of president could be forestalled by delivery of a written declaration to the President Pro Tempore of the Senate and the Speaker of the House of Representatives that I am unable to discharge the powers and duties of the office of president by the vice president and a majority of the principal officers of the executive branch of the government of the United States."

Bill sat back. It was the chief justice's turn.

Clarissa—standing in the doorway—caught his eye and shook her head. Anguish crimped her lips. The young widow could hold up no longer. She turned to hide her face, then had to walk away.

"I have in my possession," the chief justice said from a bunker deep under Omaha, "a written declaration by Vice President Glen Simon and by a majority of the principal officers of the executive department of the government of the United States." The white-haired man held up a legal document. "In it, there is a conditional finding that you will be unable to discharge the powers and duties of the office of president from the moment you ascend the Highway 301 bridge across the Potomac, until the moment that you return to territory in the possession and control of the United States."

Baker nodded. "I agree with that finding," he said, deviating from the script. He wanted no rumors among historians that this transfer of power was in any way a coup.

The chief justice stayed on track. "Have the President Pro Tempore of the Senate and the Speaker of the House of Representatives each received an original copy of this declaration?"

The President Pro Tempore stated, "I have, Mr. Chief Justice."

Tom Leffler's jowls sagged as did the rest of Tom. An aide whispered feverishly into the man's ear. "I do!" he said suddenly. "I have a copy."

"Now, therefore," the chief justice proclaimed, "Mr. President, Mr. Vice President, officers of the executive department, members of Congress, I do hereby certify the transfer of the power of the president of the United States of America from Mr. William Baker to Mr. Glen Simon effective as and when provided pursuant to Section Four, Article Twenty-Five, of the Constitution of the United States of America. And may God have mercy upon us all."

ARMY HEADQUARTERS, RICHMOND
December 29 // 1300 Local Time

Stephie's cell door opened. The guards all wore heavy wool coats. One put a long overcoat on Stephie's shoulder. They escorted her outside. She thought at first it was for exercise. The only other possibility was a firing squad. But they'd probably do that in the basement.

Stephie passed cell after cell of solid metal doors.

At the end of the corridor they waited for an elevator.

"Stephie?" John asked from behind.

She turned to see guards holding each elbow. He was battered and swollen, but she threw her arms around him. He grunted. She pulled away. "They haven't treated your wounds, John! *Jesus!*" He was bent and shuffling. Stephie looked from guard to guard. "He needs a doctor! You've got to get him help!" They ignored her by feigning incomprehension. "You speak English!" Stephie shouted. "*All* of you!"

The elevator made a *binging* sound. They were ushered

aboard. John leaned heavily on Stephie. That fact alone frightened her. They were taken to a limousine in an underground garage.

Inside waited the Chinese lieutenant from the torture room where Becky had been killed and Stephie had been forced to denounce her nation and father. The guy, who sported the same large bandage on his cheek, helped buckle John into his seat. John slumped against the restraints and exhaled as if through the pain of walking to the car he had been holding his breath. The car pulled away and he drifted off into semi-consciousness.

That left Stephie and the Chinese officer. *Or Chinese-and-something officer,* Stephie thought as she studied his features. His eyes were rounded and features vaguely Caucasian.

"He needs a doctor," Stephie said.

"You're going home," the lieutenant replied.

Stephie felt a jolt of excitement chill her body. *Could it be true?* she wondered. *Is it possible?* "We're just getting handed over?" she asked.

The enemy soldier's gaze dropped. Bare winter trees flashed by outside. "No," he finally answered. "You and ten thousand other prisoners of war are being exchanged for your father."

"Wha-a-at?" Stephie exclaimed. John's head rose. "He can't . . . ! He . . . ! He . . . !" She ended by jamming her eyes shut, covering her face and clawing at her hairline. Of course he would! It was all her fault! She felt sickened by the guilt.

She heard a *beep*. The lieutenant was sweeping a black electronic device across the car. The tiny LEDs remained green.

The officer, who spoke with only a slight accent, said, "I wish that I could tell you that your father is in no danger, but the exchange will take place on a bridge over the Potomac River. After the other prisoners have crossed, you and this captain on one side, and your father on the other, will head out onto the river. You will meet at the middle. Please tell your father to be ready to drop to the ground."

"What?" Stephie asked. "What do you mean?"

"You're a soldier," the bandaged Chinese officer answered.

"He should drop to the ground, take cover, if anything happens. And if he has any means of taking his own life, he shouldn't be too quick to use it. Wait."

"So you can torture him," Stephie said, her upper lip twitching in outrage at the bastard's obvious ploy.

"I cannot promise you that he will live," came the lieutenant's straightforward reply. "If it is not *right* that he lives," he said, choosing difficult words carefully, "I will do my best to end it quickly for him. And you. And the captain. But the situation right now—on this side of the front—is extremely," he searched for the word, "*fluid*. All that I can say is that I have a plan—orders, to be more accurate—that might allow me to save all of your lives. I promise you, Lieutenant Roberts, that I will do all that I can."

"Why?" Stephie asked. "Who are you?" She looked around the limousine, wondering why a young lieutenant rode in it. Where were the colonels, the generals, who would accompany the president's daughter?

"I am the son of Han Zhemin," the Chinese officer replied, "Administrator of Occupied America. I am the grandson of the minister of trade, and the great-nephew of the prime minister. My name is Han Wushi, and I am your cousin, Stephanie Roberts."

"My *cousin*?" Stephie replied. The man nodded. She laughed at the ridiculous remark. "How can you possibly be related to me?"

"Your aunt," Wu replied, "Cynthia Fisher, is my mother."

"Aunt *Cynthia*?" Stephie burst out, then laughed derisively, shaking her head. "I'm, uh, listen, I appreciate any help you can give us, but you're mistaken." The Chinese officer's features, Stephie now realized, were somewhat vaguely western. He simply stared back at her. "My *aunt*?" Stephie said. "And your father, the head *administrator*?" Wu nodded. "The guy who was," Stephie paused, "my father's," she paused again, "*roommate*?" Wu nodded again. "How?" she asked. "When?" But Stephie immediately knew the answers. She put it all together in a flash, connecting the dots of history from newspaper and magazine articles. "Your father and my aunt . . . ?" Wu nodded a third time. That explained why Stephie's mother never spoke to her sister. Rachel Roberts was a dyed-in-the-wool prude and bigot, who must have gagged at the thought of her sister having sex with a Chinese man. But one thing didn't make sense. "Why have I never heard about you?" she asked.

"As you should know," Wu replied, "important men often have secrets. They are simply better at keeping them in my country."

Stephie nodded slowly, in shock. "How did you end up in the Chinese army?"

"I am Chinese," Wu replied.

"Born and raised there?" Stephie asked. He nodded. *Aunt Cynthia went to China to give birth?* Stephie thought, trying quietly to decipher the stunning series of revelations. His rich family must have paid for the trip, the doctors, everything. Her mother's family hadn't been wealthy.

She turned to the attentive Chinese officer, who didn't avert his eyes. The bandage covered his right cheek. "You were wounded?" she asked. "In the battle at the Potomac?"

He nodded once, but his eyes left hers.

"If your family is so rich and powerful," she asked, "why are you fighting?"

Wu said. "That's a very strange question coming from you."

"But things are different," Stephie replied, "in my country."

"What do you mean?" he asked, suddenly keenly interested.

"Well, in America, there's politics. My father can't, you know, pull strings to get me out of the draft."

"So," Wu summarized, "you are saying that how things appear to the masses is important. The fact that they see you—the president's daughter—at the front has meaning. Political importance." Now it was Stephie's turn to nod. "Have you ever considered," Wu asked, "going into politics yourself?"

Stephie snorted. "Me? God no!"

Wu stared down at the floor, seeming lost in thought, while Stephie scrutinized him. She studied the strange new entrant into her family circle until he raised his gaze to meet hers.

"Things are not so different," he said, "in my country. At least when it comes to politics."

She shook her head and rushed to explain. "I'm not saying that the only reason that I fought was because of politics! I fought because, because I *love* my country! Because fighting for it is right! Because I couldn't live with myself if everyone else . . . !"

Before she could finish, Wu was nodding. "Me too," he said softly.

The road leading down to the bridge was bumpy. It had been pitted with craters and refilled with soft earth that was already deeply rutted. The limousine squeezed past truck after truck returning empty up the hill from the riverbank.

The last few hundred of the ten thousand American POWs waited impatiently to join the single file that extended from the Chinese side of the river to the American. The chain of men—many wounded and leaning on comrades—carefully skirted the large holes in the bridge that looked melted straight through the pavement. In places the bridge tilted precariously. But the antlike procession crossed the perilous span heedless of the danger that lay ahead. The American soon-to-be-former prisoners of war knew too well the dangers that lay behind.

Stephanie, John, and Wu emerged from the limousine into a blaze of camera lights so bright that Stephie had to shield her eyes. From behind—in a whisper—a Chinese military officer in dress uniform politely asked her to lower her arm. When she did, the throng of cameras pressed close, leaving only a tight corridor that led to a raised wooden platform.

Wu and Stephie each took one of John's arms and helped him ascend the few steps onto the open-air stage. There they joined waiting Chinese dignitaries above the sea of journalists.

The Chinese general and the colonel who had murdered Becky smiled at their approach, but a well groomed man in a dark civilian business suit stepped forward. Cameras flashed as he grinned and clapped his hand on an unsmiling Wu's shoulder. Stephie saw the Chinese civilian wink. Wu did not reciprocate.

That's his father, Stephie realized. The handsome man

turned his attention to Stephie, ignoring John. "Ms. Roberts," he said, "I am Han Zhemin." He reached out and deftly grabbed Stephie's hand for a shake. But when he raised it to his lips for a kiss, she snatched her hand out of his.

There was laughter from the gathering on the stage and from the larger crowd around it. A rapid-fire series of flashes meant to record the kiss had instead recorded her insult. Han's smile faded briefly before it lit anew with disingenuous humor that he feigned to share with the throng. Stephie watched him boldly present his amusement at her rejection to the gathered corps of Chinese reporters.

His son—Lieutenant Wu—watched also. He was not in the least amused. In fact, he seemed nervous. Fidgety.

Ringing the podium were dozens—perhaps hundreds—of cameras. Large round lenses of high-def TV cameras held by civilian and military film crews. Digital still cameras with long lenses trained on them by Chinese photographers in uniform and in blue jeans. And dozens of small cameras and camcorders held not by professionals, but by individual soldiers, mostly officers. All expectantly recorded the historic moment by focusing on the star attraction: the daughter of the president of the United States.

The last in the long line of American prisoners was now on the bridge. Stephie imagined their joy at returning home, but it was an emotion that she couldn't share. For somewhere at the far end of the bombed-out bridge was her father, who was about to make the ultimate sacrifice. Stephie was sickened by the thought and almost lost her balance.

Wu's hand shot out to grab her arm, a fact recorded by a hundred flashing cameras.

HIGHWAY 301 BRIDGE, MARYLAND
December 29 // 1400 Local Time

The sun glinted off the Potomac, whose gray water flowed into a finger of the Chesapeake a few miles to the east. Hart could see that the carpenters had built not gallows, but a raised wooden stage surrounded by platforms now filled with cameras and lights. All lay on the shoulder of the road at the foot of the Highway 301 bridge five hundred meters from Hart's vantage. He risked raising his head a few inches above the ground. The brown plastic leaves that hung from the mesh covering his helmet, which matched the fall foliage that littered the Virginia woods, tickled his cheeks and jaw.

From his position on the forward slope of a hill facing the bridge, platform, and river, a swale descended to his left toward a dry stream that ran through a saddle between the hills. Both would afford him his only hope of survival. His eyes traced the swale and then the bed until it disappeared into a concrete pipe running under the tracks of a rail line.

The only problem was that he couldn't see where the pipe came out.

Bill's limousine door opened, and he jumped with a start. But it wasn't quite time yet. Outside, Baker caught a glimpse of the river and bridge beside which they were parked. Richard Fielding got in and closed the door behind him.

"Are you about ready, Mr. President?" Fielding asked. The question left Bill petrified, but he nodded. The doctor, who had given Bill a final check-up, had advised him to eat well. They had made him a sumptuous lunch before leaving the White House. Bill and Clarissa had sat silently across the dining room table. Neither had touched their meals.

Bill hadn't managed to choke any food past the lump in his throat. It was probably a good thing, he thought, as his unsettled stomach now churned. As if reading his mind, Director Fielding produced a pill that Bill assumed was an antacid or a sedative. The small capsule lay in his dry, meaty palm. Bill looked up at him before reaching for it.

"It's not water soluble," Fielding said, hand extended. "Just put it in your mouth between your cheek and lower gum. If you accidentally swallow it, you'll be okay. Just wait for it to come out—intact—and you can use it then."

Bill nodded. He understood now. He took the small, hard capsule. "What do I . . . ?" he began, but quieted when he heard the quaver in his voice. "How do I do it?"

"You bite it," Fielding answered. "Just bite it. That's it.

You'll have to bite hard, but once it pops, well, that's all you have to do."

"Ho-okay," Bill said with a sigh meant to mask the quakes in his lungs. He tried slipping the pill into his jacket pocket, but found that the pockets on the strange, heavy suit were there only for display.

Fielding tried to make light of his unsuccessful efforts. "The Chinese do a remarkably good job on these Kevlar suits," he said, holding it open so that Bill could slip the pill into the breast pocket of his dress shirt.

"They're heavy," Bill said.

"Do you want something else?" Fielding asked. "A Valium?"

Bill shook his head in jerks. He felt silly. For months, his daughter and millions like her had fought a war of immense and intense brutality. What Bill now had to do required not a tenth of their bravery, but he was petrified. He looked up at Fielding.

"What if it's a trick?" Bill asked for the hundredth time. It wasn't a question that called for a reply. That question had been answered—none too satisfactorily—in the quiet, early morning hours. Bill had asked the question only to get reassurance, but that was one thing that the skeptical Fielding was ill-suited to provide.

"We've provided for that contingency, Mr. President," Fielding said. "If for some reason the pill doesn't work, just stand as still as you can. You understand?" Bill nodded. "Without you, they'll find your daughter of limited use. There'll be no reason for them to harm her. We'll trade for her. Get her back quickly. It'll work out, Mr. President."

There was a knock on the window, and Bill shivered suddenly. He wanted to change his mind and ask for the Valium so that he wouldn't throw up from fear, but the door opened, and he got out into the freezing day. The shivering got worse. An army officer ushered Bill and Fielding to a semicircle of sandbags in which stood a massive set of periscoping binoculars on a tripod. Bill looked through the lenses and saw a crowd of people at the far side of the river. At their highest power, he could clearly make out Stephie standing next to a slumping American prisoner amid Chinese soldiers and a lone civilian. They stood atop a small platform ringed by hordes of the press mixed in with a curious, pressing audience of soldiers who numbered into the hundreds.

Bill suddenly felt calm. He stood straight and nodded. He was ready. They climbed the grassy bank to the roadway. The thick suit pants made it difficult for Bill to bend his knees for the effort. Several times solicitous soldiers helped. At the top of the American side, there were no cameras or press, only main battle tanks and a stream of former prisoners of war, who descended from the bridge and hugged each other and waiting comrades.

When they saw Bill and his small entourage heading down the road toward the bridge, the sobs and jubilation ended. Bill didn't acknowledge them—he was too lost in thought—but they acknowledged him.

"Long live the United States!" a man covered in black, caked blood shouted on the quiet winter afternoon.

"Stay on the right side of the bridge," an officer from the Army Corps of Engineers said to Bill. "It's more stable there." He tried to say more, but he was drowned out.

"Long live the United States!" rose the cheer from the newly released POWs, who lined the cratered road leading up to the bridge. *"Long live the United States!"* came a dozen, then a hundred, then a thousand rising voices until the riverbank was filled with their roar.

Bill shivered again, not from fear, but from pride.

He slipped cyanide tablet into his mouth and ascended the bridge.

HIGHWAY 301 BRIDGE, VIRGINIA
December 29 // 1415 Local Time

Han Zhemin and the others on the platform could clearly hear the Americans' cheers. Han looked at Bill Baker's daughter. Her eyes—shiny with tears—were fixed on the distant riverbank. Wu's eyes were fixed on her.

General Sheng stepped up to Stephanie Roberts, but he didn't repeat the mistake of trying to shake her hand. He wore a self-satisfied smile, which forced Han to hide his own amusement. "You are now free to go," Sheng said to Stephanie Roberts in strained English.

"Burn in hell, cocksucker," she replied.

Han laughed out loud and waited as Sheng got a whispered translation from Colonel Li. Stephanie Roberts waited also. General Sheng was not in the least amused. That was what the girl had waited to see.

Han walked over to Stephanie grinning broadly and said, "You're just like your mother."

"What?" she shot back. "My *mother*!"

The battered American captain seized her by the arms and turned her toward the steps. She kept looking back over her shoulder at Han even as she and Wu helped the wounded man descend into the gauntlet of fiery cameras.

Jim Hart alternated the aim of his sniper rifle back and forth between the president at extreme range and his daughter, who was slowed by the limping, sagging soldier. At high power, he could see the grimace on the man's swollen face and Stephanie Roberts encouraging him with words. Those two—still on the Chinese side of the bridge where Hart lay—were easier shots. There was a long, fresh streak of what looked like urine down the man's right pant leg, but in the smear that he left after resting for a moment on the white concrete railing Hart could see that he was bleeding profusely.

The woman, who was practically carrying him, saw it too. She had seen a lot, Hart had read in his one week back in the world. *Time* magazine had done a long piece on her experiences in the war. When he had begun reading the article, he had expected her exploits to be minor brushes exaggerated for dramatic effect, but they weren't. She was the real deal. A soldier. A combat infantryman.

Hart's aim returned to the president. He flicked the scope to full power. Bill Baker had arrived at the center of the bridge and waited next to the electrical house, as agreed with the Chinese. He watched his daughter slowly weave her way past giant holes in the sturdy bridge. Chinese commanders, Hart had been briefed, had seized the bridge before U.S. engineers had destroyed it. Half a dozen aircraft had been lost bombing the bridge.

The president's daughter helped pull the sagging captain over the upturned lip of a penetrating splash of pavement. Somehow, the concrete and steel structure hadn't been dropped by the pounding from dozens of thousand-pound bombs. No vehicles could make it across, but humans could. The bridge was bent and twisted, but some engineer long ago had done his or her job.

"It's just a little farther, John," Stephie urged. She tried to talk him into rising from the knee that he had taken when he had said that he felt light-headed. The blood that he had vomited trickled down the listing pavement. "There's an ambulance waiting for you. Come on, John. Now!"

She squatted, slipped her forearms under his armpits, and lifted him to his feet with her legs. He groaned and whimpered. His head flopped as though his neck were broken. "Come on!" she said, panting from the effort of holding him upright. "We're almost there." She could see her father straining toward her. He had already taken several steps past where he was supposed to wait. *"No! Stop!"* she called out, waving him back. John saw what was happening and, with her arms around his waist, began to shuffle forward on knees that threatened to buckle with every step.

Stephie kept an anxious eye on her father. When she came near enough, her plan was to talk him into making a run for it. *But what about John?* she thought. Her mind was in a race against her feet. She had to decide what to do before she reached her father, who waited twenty meters away.

John groaned something.

"It'll just be a minute more!" Stephie promised.

"There's something wrong!" he forced with extreme effort and pain through a broken jaw. She thought he was dying right then and there, but he held up his arm and pointed toward her father. "It's a trick," John said with crushing disappointment. "Oh, God, it's a trick."

She saw now what he saw. The door to the concrete electrical house at the center of the bridge was cracked open. She could see a rifle muzzle.

"Dad, go back!" she shouted, waving her arm. "Run!"

The door burst open, and out rushed Chinese troops. They tackled her father at the dead run with their shoulders. He hit the pavement with the weight of the two men. One cupped the back of her father's head with gloved hands.

The men who followed the Chinese out of the electrical house were shot to pieces. Cored pillars of gore shot from rib cages. Heads burst. Arms flew from sleeves. Boots bicycle-kicked high as their legs pinwheeled away. All before the roars of American machine guns arrived.

Ching-ching-ching-ching-ching! sounded heavy bullets off girders as the burping roars rose half a mile away. John pulled Stephie to the ground just as a Chinese soldier jammed an acrylic chock in one side of her father's mouth. The man's latex fingers rooted in the other side of her father's mouth as he thrashed but was pinned and being frisked by the other soldier. The man searching his mouth found what he was looking for and threw it through a bomb hole in the bridge.

The American heavy machine guns shooting at the bridge fell silent, but Chinese tanks opened fire. Cracks and nearly simultaneous booms dueled for sonic primacy from opposite riverbanks. Towers of smoke rose from American lines, but no fire came in return. Discipline held among nervous American gunners, whose earphones were certainly filled with panicked, frenzied shouts to "Cease-fire!" With their president exposed in the middle of a bridge, the Americans took the blows and died by the dozens while holding their fire.

"Cease firing *now*!" an enraged Wu ordered General Sheng, shouting over the roar. All but the two cowered on knees, all fours, or bellies. Sheng and Wu stood upright. "Give the order to cease-fire!" Wu demanded again.

Wu had never been this angry in his life, and that was good. He needed that anger and the adrenaline rush that he got from the jarring blasts of massed artillery. Sheng looked at Wu's face and snapped the order to a communications officer lying prone at his feet. "Cease-fire," Sheng said. The officer relayed the command. Ten long seconds passed. Thirty rounds rocked the air. Wu and Sheng stared at each other.

With one final, laggard *boom*, a quiet descended upon the river. Wu said to Sheng, with no menace or ill will, "There is an honorable way."

Sheng's eyes arched wide. His mouth gaped. Colonel Li rose to his feet, but not beside Sheng. He kept his distance. His reaction reflected a highly evolved political instinct. Massively parallel calculations led to neutrality over loyalty in a single, cold beat of Li's heart. Sheng's face closed up tight. His eyes and lips were pinched slits. It was a hard look.

All right, Wu thought.

Hart's crosshairs danced across the helmets of the men lying atop the president. Only the two were left alive on the bridge. Seven others lay sprawled in widening pools of blood. But the two who pinned the president clung close to their quarry.

The technical dilemma was gruesome. His .50 caliber could splash high velocity bone splinters onto the president. It would spew Kevlar shrapnel. And if Hart's scope had the wind, humidity, or air pressure off, the half-inch-thick shell could go through the top of the president's head and out the bottom of his heel. Plus, Hart would get only one shot before the remaining soldier hugged the president tight. Even if Hart could cleave off the side of the man's head, the Chinese would kill Hart then simply hose down the bridge with fire and kill everyone on it.

At the far end of the bridge, Hart saw just now, an American infantry company was on the move. They double-timed it up the bridge with slings snapping and weapons at the ready. An almost identical scene was being played out on the near side of the bridge, only this one by the Chinese. The two companies of infantry converged on the center of the span.

The situation was hopeless. "*Shit,*" Hart cursed under his breath. In about five minutes, there would be a firefight. The five people pinned down in the middle—including the president and his daughter—would certainly die along with a couple of hundred dismounted infantry.

Hart changed his aim a fraction of an arc second. The crosshairs moved from the helmets of the Chinese soldiers onto the bare skull of the president of the United States. *"If it's a trap,"* Hart had acknowledged three times, *"I'll do the president! All right? Over!"* But his finger didn't pull. He hesitated.

They hadn't said that he had to take his first shot.

The Chinese soldier's breath stank as he held Bill's hair in a painful grip and spoke to him from two inches away. "Your daughter will die," he said, "if we don't get off this bridge now." Bill was so close he could hear the man's orders stream over the radio from his earphones. "Your choice, Mr. President."

Bill nodded.

The two men stuck to his sides, shielding him like bodyguards, Bill decided. He stood straight up to offer a better target, but one of his protectors punched him in the gut to double him over, almost knocking his breath out. They then ran him—one of his hands pinned behind his back—toward Stephie and the wounded soldier.

"Dad!" Stephie said, sobbing as they hugged each other. The Chinese soldiers hugged them both but pressed hard, short-barreled weapons to Bill's ribs and Stephie's chin. Bill finally recognized the swollen face of John Burns, who stared up through glassy eyes with a pool of blood at his crotch and a Chinese soldier's knee to his unresisting chest.

"Let's go!" one of the soldiers ordered, forcing Bill to his feet. Stephie stood. The other Chinese soldier grunted as if he had trouble rising, then rolled over onto the pavement, reaching in vain for his knife, which was sticking out of the small of his back from just under his body armor.

John had drawn it from the now empty scabbard on the man's boot.

The strap on a machine pistol slapped as the lone remaining Chinese soldier whipped the weapon toward John Burns. Stephie growled, "No!" and lunged.

Burns grabbed the muzzle.

It roared into John's hands and blazed into his face.

Stephie tackled the Chinese soldier onto his side.

The smoking machine pistol remained clutched in the hands of the bloody pulp that had once been John Burns.

"*Grrr!*" Stephie gurgled as she clawed at the eyes of the shrieking soldier. "*Yi-ah-h-h!*" he screamed as he unsuccessfully fought her two hands with one of his and tried to crush her throat with his other. Stephie bulled out her slim neck, and her face went red. She was sobbing as she jabbed her sharp chin down against his grip and tried to kill him with five fingernails. She finally found his eyes. The Chinese soldier screeched and thrashed his head from side to side as he defended now with both hands. She gasped for air. He arched his back, but she held her position on top of him with the toes of her boots spread to either side, killing him in slow motion. "Die, you motherfucker, die!" she grunted. He screamed and tried to bite her hand.

Bill pulled the machine pistol from John Burns's bloody fingers and held it against the soldier's head. "Die now," Stephie said as she suddenly sat back on her haunches and completely ceased her attack.

Bill blew the top of the man's head off with a shocking, sickening burst. Stephie sat atop the gory sight, however, wiping her hands on the man's chest. She had gouged out one of his eyes.

Stephie grabbed the machine pistol from Bill. He just watched her. Astonished by her callousness. She dropped the magazine and reloaded a new one from the dead Chinese soldier's pouch. Her victim might as well never have existed. Nothing existed for her except for the approaching Chinese. Bill followed her gaze. He could already see the bobbing helmets.

"Stephie, no," he said.

"They're coming," she said without looking at her father. "Run for it!"

"No!"

"Get going!" she shouted, looking around the listing bridge for cover.

"We both go!" Bill said.

"You're going! I'm staying!"

"No!" Bill shouted.

"You're the president of the fucking United States and I'm a soldier!" she screamed, beginning to cry. The Chinese troops were close. Soldiers with rifles were climbing onto girders to take aim directly at the exposed pair. Bill grabbed the warm barrel of the machine pistol and pressed it to the concrete. It fell from Stephie's hands. She dissolved into his arms, sobbing.

"John!" she kept saying as she heaved sobs into Bill's chest. "Jo-o-ohn!"

"He was a Secret Service agent, Stephie," Bill told her, rubbing her back as the Chinese neared. "He was assigned to your unit to protect you. He was just doing his job."

"*I* know all that!" she blurted out, sobbing like a child. "I've known from the very beginning! It was so obvious! But I love him! And he loves . . . ! He loved . . . ! Oh God! Oh God why? Why? Why? *Why?*" she screamed, flailing her arms. She could say nothing more. Her back heaved in Bill's arms. He stroked her head and neck, telling her that everything would be all right.

Chinese troops—breathing heavily, sweating, scared—assumed positions all around Bill and Stephie. Over the crest of the bridge's center, Bill could see the helmets and muzzles of American soldiers, who had barely lost the footrace. The Chinese escorted Bill and Stephie toward the Virginia bank. The Americans held their fire.

Hart had a piss poor shot amid the cluster of escorts who ringed President Baker. They surrounded him with a human shield and kept him stooped low. It was so useless that Hart found himself raising his eye from the scope and glancing toward his lone escape route.

He would never make it to the round black hole in the earth. Every Chinese soldier for a mile would hear his booming .50 caliber rifle. He would drop the weapon and sprint. Fire would fill the woods, rising in caliber to main tank guns maneuvering along the roadside below.

If by some chance he made it over the skyline, down the reverse slope, and into the dark pipe, then what? There could

be a metal grate on the opposite end. He'd be trapped. He'd
die. The end.

The president and his daughter stepped off the bridge.
Hart's crosshairs danced across the president's head. He
couldn't get off a kill shot. A single round perfectly placed
in the center of his skull. Suddenly, the president popped into
the open. The soldiers parted. Lights bathed the man and his
daughter.

Hart was so astonished at the easy shot that he again slowed
down and thought about the situation. *"Under no circumstances,"* the briefers had pressed, *"are you to allow him to
live."* Hart watched the president through a high-powered
scope as he climbed onto the platform. His orders didn't seem
adequate all of the sudden. Hart couldn't execute his commander in chief just yet. *Assassinate*, he thought for the first
time. The word didn't sit well with Hart. Having disobeyed
express orders after the Chinese had sprung their trap, he
couldn't decide what to do or when to do it. Hart simply
joined the president in the last few precious moments of a life
that was less than full.

Where is *he?* Bill Baker wondered as he scanned the high
hills. He tried to keep his distance from Stephie, but she kept
pressing close to his side. Her head drooped. Bill held his
high. Waiting.

"Don't worry," whispered a young Chinese officer to Stephie.

"Fuck you," Stephie replied, her nose thick with congestion
from crying.

Bill stared at the young Chinese soldier, whose cheek was
covered with a bandage. He was half-Asian, half-Caucasian,
and he returned Bill's quizzical look.

"Bill," Han Zhemin said, "I'd like you to meet my son.
Han Wushi." Han appeared beside Bill, blocking Bill's line
of sight to the hills.

Do it now, Bill thought with his teeth grinding. He watched
Han, waiting for his head to explode but knowing it wouldn't
register in the milliseconds left in his life before the bullet
struck him. Below, cameramen swayed as they jostled for

position. Bill was quite familiar with media frenzies. Perhaps it was the actor in him, or perhaps the politician, but he could see in his mind's eye what the cameras saw. They would swing toward him and Stephie—passing over Han—focus, then return to Han's son. Always to Han's son.

The boy—a young army officer—was the star of the show. Bill and Stephie were co-stars. Han Zhemin was an extra.

"President Baker," came a reedy and frail, heavily accented voice. Han stepped aside to reveal a short general with a broad smile. His aide stood a half step behind and to the side. All fouled the aim of any sniper in the wooded hills behind them. "I am General Sheng. You are under arrest for . . ."

"No," interrupted Han's son, the young, bandaged officer. His pistol rose from its holster and fired. Bill jumped. Han jumped. Stephie clutched her father as if to throw him to the ground.

The old general fell dead with a disgusting red hole in his forehead. An instant pool of thick blood gathered beneath him.

Another shot. Bill jumped. Stephie pulled him backwards and stood in front of him.

The general's aide lay dead beside the old man.

The lieutenant's smoking pistol pointed stiff-armed into thin air.

Han Zhemin stared wide-eyed at his son and at the smoking muzzle. He was terrified, Bill thought, of his son, who stood there prepared to kill him. No one made a move to interfere.

Bill shoved Stephie aside.

"Wu," Han whispered, bowing in supplication.

All Bill heard was the whisper of electric motors in two hundred video cameras.

Wu lowered the pistol. None of the thousand people surrounding the platform said a word.

Wu didn't reholster the gun, Bill noticed. He gripped it repeatedly. Maniacally or angrily or agitated.

"Wu," Stephie suddenly said, her eyes on the pistol. "Don't. Life's not over, yet. Don't, *Wu*, don't." She never took her eyes off the pistol, which Bill now understood the boy was considering using on himself.

Bill put his arms around his daughter. She hugged him, and lay her head against his chest. The young lieutenant—eyes wet—stared at their embrace.

Someone from the mass all around the platform shouted something in Chinese. It was almost instantly repeated. It unleashed a torrent of cries from dozens, and then hundreds of soldiers near and far. All shouted with abandon that became totally synchronized passion. Rhythmic. Chanted. Adoring. Bill didn't speak a word of Chinese, but their three joyous words told Bill everything.

"Han!"

"Wu!"

"Shi!"

The soldiers shouted over and over and over.

Hart's bare finger rested hard on the cold trigger. His crosshairs were on Bill Baker's head. There were no orders expressly covering this situation. No "if-a-Chinese-lieutenant-shoots-a-Chinese-general-then . . ." contingency plan. Hart had nothing to fall back on but his standing orders. *"If he's taken, I do the president!"* Hart had repeated four times to his insistent, persistent, unknown briefers.

There were no exceptions. No uncertainty. No qualifiers. No modifiers. Just total, crystalline clarity on that single point.

Hart half expected his high-powered rifle to explode in his hand as it unleashed a round ending Baker's life and his own. Hart's trigger pull suddenly seemed too firm. Hart eased the dry skin of his trigger finger off the rigid, grooved metal.

When the Chinese lieutenant led the president and his daughter off the podium, turned for the bridge, and passed the waiting row of limousines on a path toward the river, Hart rested his finger on the outside of the trigger guard and used the scope for observation. By the time they began to ascend the bridge, Hart had begun stealing glances at the round drainpipe down the hill to his left.

He felt a sudden, growing void. A need to populate his future with details. *I make it back, then what?* he thought with growing alarm. It was a question that he couldn't answer. He lost track of time. Checked less and less frequently on the bridge. The need to plan consumed him.

He needed a life. Quickly. A life.

Wu turned to warn President Baker and Stephanie Roberts, who followed him in silence. They edged past a huge black pit melted straight through the center of the bridge's pavement. The white line ended at thin air then reappeared undisturbed down the middle of the listing highway.

Wu turned again. The two walked hip to hip in a supportive, loving embrace. But the daughter leaned noticeably upon the father, whose eyes remained peeled on Wu.

Wu knew he ought to be thinking about what lay just ahead. It was a whirlwind—a grueling pace—choreographed by the finest staffs to the very last, fragmentary detail. He breathed deeply of the cool wind on the bridge. That place, there, was freedom. Maybe the last he'd get to feel for a while.

When they neared the three dead soldiers at the center of the bridge, Wu saw that the faces of the American captain and a Chinese soldier were gruesome and mutilated. A second Chinese soldier had a look of shock on his face and a knife sticking out of his back.

Stephanie Roberts stared from inside her father's arms with eyes dry and a blank face.

Wu turned and led them on toward the center of the creaking, rusty bridge. They passed the seven dead Chinese soldiers that lay scattered about the electrical house.

"Halt!" all heard shouted in English from behind twisted rebar up ahead.

President Baker raised his hand and motioned toward the American soldiers. They lowered their aims from Wu's chest and face.

"May I have a word with you?" Wu asked President Baker. "I'm sorry," he said, turning to Stephanie Roberts. "In private, if you don't mind."

Stephie shrugged and headed up the bridge toward the waiting American soldiers. Two riflemen and a medic rushed out to meet her. "I'm all right," she said, warding off their solicitous, grasping hands. "But there's a dead American captain down the bridge a few dozen meters. I'd appreciate it if you'd . . ."

She didn't have to finish her sentence. The first lieutenant motioned for a squad to jog down the bridge. Stephie's gaze followed them, and she saw the animated conversation that her father and Wu were having. At least her father was animated. Lieutenant Wu was calm and composed. When her father queried, Wu nodded. When her father shook his head in angry disbelief, Wu assaulted him relentlessly with words. Wu remained expressionless. Her father grew distraught.

"What the hell's he doing?" a senior noncom asked the first lieutenant.

"He's taking too long," the officer said to Stephie.

Stephie proceeded back down the bridge to rejoin the two men.

"I don't trust you," she heard her father saying.

"Yes, you do," the Chinese lieutenant replied.

Both turned to Stephie as she approached and interrupted their private discussion. Her father, however, kept shaking his head, and finally he said, "But why are you telling me this?"

Wu's lips turned up in what was almost a smile. "Now is the time for all good men to come to the aid of their party."

The words seemed to bring the exchange to an end. Stephie's father stared at Wu with mouth agape, scrutinizing him. "Uhm, Dad," Stephie said, "we've gotta go." His eyes were fixed on Wu, and his brow was knit with concern, but he nodded. Stephie turned to Wu. "Why don't you come with us?" she suggested. She took both of Wu's hands in hers. He stared down at her grip. "Come to our side! Walk over this bridge with us! If you go back, they'll hang you for sure!"

Wu said nothing. Her father spoke for him.

"No," he said, staring at Wu. "They won't harm you, will they?" he asked. "It's exactly the opposite, isn't it?"

Wu looked at him, betraying nothing, then back at Stephie's hands.

"Come with us anyway!" Stephanie said, squeezing.

"I cannot," Wu replied, "come with you."

"Why *not*?" she demanded, squeezing his hands again. Stephie was distracted by the passing of the detail of American soldiers, who double-timed, carrying a black body bag by the handles built into the bag's four corners.

Wu pulled his hands back. "I am Chinese!" he blurted out, suddenly exhibiting emotion. He composed himself and repeated, more slowly and with emphasis, "I-am-Chi*nese!*"

"Execute your orders!" shouted Hart's controller via microwave. Hart didn't risk replying. There was some chance that his whispers might be overheard, as he lay—without moving a muscle—awaiting darkness. There was some chance also that they might convince him to fire at the president, so he lay there, without moving a muscle, listening to the frantic and desperate voices. "Open fire!" screamed one. "Fire, goddammit!" came another voice. "*Do him now!*" came a third. Nowhere did he hear the voice of the one-eyed colonel. He planned to look the man up and figure out just who the fuck the assholes on the other end of the microwave beam were.

The moment that the president and his daughter sprinted into the cordon of American soldiers who had never left the bridge, Hart's earbuds fell deathly silent. There wasn't a voice to be heard.

Cameras swarmed the Chinese lieutenant with a white bandage on his cheek. A large contingent of troops—wearing black, not army green—arrived in black armored fighting vehicles. The black-clad troops surrounded the young lieutenant, but he wasn't under arrest. They took his orders, and the soldiers in camouflage gave the phalanx wide berth.

A limousine door was slammed in the face of the startled Chinese civilian in a black business suit, who recoiled from the spraying gravel of the spinning tires. Then, it was all over but the cleanup. A few macabre shots by the press of the bloody officers on the platform, then everyone called it a day. Surely an eventful day, Hart thought. He wondered if it might even be historic.

He was a witness, but to what he had no idea. He couldn't for the life of him figure out what had just happened even though he had a lot of time to think it over as he waited for night to fall. Down below, the valley emptied. Nobody was interested in patrols anymore. The bodies of the general and his aide were tossed—Hart thought disrespectfully—into the back of an open truck.

When the western sky grew dark, Hart decided that he had to try to check in, but the microwave link to Maryland was dead. There was no one on the other end of the line. It was, he concluded, his last official duty.

After a night of hard movement and a tense day spent lying still, the simple act of moving hurt him terribly. As his muscles limbered, however, he felt better and better. By the time he reached the railroad tracks he was practically jogging.

He dropped flat to the ground, thinking he had heard a sound, then resumed at a much slower pace. When he heard it again—a clicking sound—he dropped again. Far ahead, where the fallen railroad bridge that paralleled the Highway 301 bridge descended into the water, a pinprick of red flared in his infrared goggles. Hart got the range—150 meters—when he raised his rifle scope to his eye.

The cold tide of air carried the same clicking sound to him again. He was downwind. The noise surfed the breeze in his face. In his crosshairs, there appeared the glowing face of a Chinese soldier. He used a balky cigarette lighter to try to light a long pipe. Two buddies who had joined him in the one-man fighting hole used their gloves to shield the flame.

Hart rose and trotted into and down the dry streambed. When he got to the pipe, he lowered his goggles and peered inside. He could see—unobstructed—the glowing red circle at the far end. The pipe looked clear. There was laughter from the three upwind Chinese soldiers. They were all alone or they wouldn't be getting high. Shit duty in the middle of nowhere.

Hart considered killing them before he left. He could do it—quietly—but when they laughed again, he headed into the pipe. There was no grate at the opposite end.

HYATT REGENCY, RICHMOND, VIRGINIA
December 29 // 1630 Local Time

Wu entered his hotel suite like a burglar. Shen Shen was humming a popular American tune from the bedroom. Her matching, five-piece designer set of luggage lay on the made, king-sized bed beside his green duffle bag.

She appeared through the doors wearing panties but no bra, fresh from the shower. She folded and packed a sheer white camisole and zipped her bag up. When she turned, she saw Wu and came running, breasts bouncing, into his arms. She threw her arms around his neck and kissed his face and mouth while pressing herself flat against him.

Wu pried her arms loose, and she was alert to the danger.

"I'm glad you killed that old bastard!" she blurted out. "And Li! I've dreamt of doing the same thing! I can't count how many times that filthy bastard . . . !" Wu couldn't look her in the eye. "It was brilliant!" she said, trying to flash her smile. "You're a hero! You should see the press! I talked to my mother! They're replaying what happened this afternoon at the bridge and then broadcasting footage of Sheng's atrocities! It's all falling into place!"

Wu headed for his bag. He could feel her standing there, watching him. "Wu?" she called out. He threw the thick strap over his shoulder. "Wu?" she repeated, the rest of her question implicit in her frightened tone and wide eyes. She covered her breasts with her arm, the first hint of modesty Wu had ever seen her exhibit.

"I've got to go," he said.

"What is it?" Shen Shen asked, not budging from the doorway.

"I know who you work for," Wu replied.

Shen Shen bounded toward Wu, but restrained herself, pulling up just short. She placed her palms on his chest to hold him there. "Did your father tell you that I work for the prime minister? But it's not *true*!" she said as if the clarification made everything all right. "He only *thinks* that! But the truth is," she looked around and whispered, "I *really* work for the defense minister!" Her breath was warm against his neck.

"I know," Wu replied coolly.

Shen Shen was shocked. She took a step back. *"How?"*

"The defense minister told me," Wu answered.

She now seemed totally disoriented. Her eyes darted about so rapidly that she appeared to experience motion sickness.

"You . . . ? You talked to him? To the defense minister?"

"I've got to go," Wu said, trying to get around her.

She stepped in front of him and grabbed his arms. "Wu? Are you going back? To Beijing?" He didn't answer. "Tell me! What's going to happen?"

The left corner of his upper lip curled. "Tell the defense minister that I said, 'Yes.' "

She waited for more, but that was it. " 'Yes' what?" she asked. Wu pushed past her. " 'Yes' *what*, Wu? 'Yes' what?" she cried.

"Tell him!" was all that Wu said.

His last sight of her was as she lay crumpled on her knees on the carpet. He closed the door. His armada of black-suited security troops filled the hallway.

Wu nodded, and the commander of his security detail gave the orders. They headed for the elevator with a purposeful stride.

CIVILIAN HEADQUARTERS, RICHMOND
December 29 // 1900 Local Time

Han's top aides were clueless. No one had known in advance about Wu's murderous, mutinous plans, and no one now knew anything more. They sat around a conference table in what had been the seat of power but was now just a dilapidated office building. "The rumor is," his female head of intelligence suggested, "that Sheng was organizing a coup attempt against the defense minister."

Han rolled his eyes. "There *is* no coup!" he snapped. "That was planted disinformation!"

His outburst did little to foster a more open discussion, which remained muted until one of his bolder aides said, "We need to do something. We're just sitting here! We've got to exercise power, if only to prove that it still exists. If we can display strength, people will rally to it. The people aren't behind the military. They will back us if we exercise power. They will defer to it. Acknowledge it."

And thereby make it reappear, Han thought. *They're almost there.*

"Administrator Han, sir, have you tried the prime minister?" Han had gotten no answer from his uncle, so he ignored the aide's question. "The minister of trade? The security minister?"

No one in Beijing would take Han's calls, not even his father and uncle. He could feel the power draining away by the hour. The general commanding the division of security ministry troops newly arrived in Richmond didn't return any of Han's numerous telephone calls. Wu had checked out of his hotel, Shen Shen had tearfully reported. Some of Han's senior staffers had even abruptly disappeared. They had returned home on previously unscheduled leaves at this critical moment, surely understanding there would be no place for them upon their return. *If they return,* Han thought in despair.

"What are we going to do?" a female aide finally asked in defeat.

Still, Han thought in frustration, they're missing the obvious. He sighed and shook his head. There was silence as all stared at him. Waiting for him to speak.

He finally gave up on them. "All right," he informed the group, "here's what we're going to do. We are going to launch a coup." There were stunned looks on faces. "Not in *Beijing!*" he shouted. "In Washington! Send out the code." There was inaction. "The code! The *code!* Send out the code!" He switched to English. " 'Now is the time for all good men to come to the aid of their party!' "

WHITE HOUSE RESIDENTIAL QUARTERS
December 29 // 2300 Local Time

Bill waited outside Stephie's bedroom in a wood-backed armchair. His only company in the ornate hallway were silent, stone-faced Secret Service agents wearing black body armor and carrying long rifles. When the door opened, Bill rose. Rachel Roberts and her husband exited Stephie's room. Rachel came up to Bill but kept her eyes on the Oriental runner that spanned the length of the corridor. "The doctor said she needed her rest," as if to suggest that he couldn't see his daughter. She then brushed past him and headed into the bedroom next door, where she and her husband were spending the night.

Hank Roberts—Stephie's stepfather—held out his hand, which Bill shook. "Thank you," Hank said, before he began to cry. Bill put his arms around the man and felt his own eyes water.

When they parted, Bill went to Stephie's door and knocked lightly.

"Come *in*," she said in a high-pitched voice.

Bill found her lying in the four-poster bed wearing a night shirt with a frilly trim. Her head was propped up on two thick pillows, but her body lay flat except for her toes. Stephie held the top edge of the sheet up to her shoulders with both hands. Bill sat on the bed beside her.

She looked down at the lace trim of her bedclothes. "Mom bought this for me," she said. Stephie was scrubbed and fresh. The doctor had said her wounds were relatively minor. At least those that you could see. Stephie sniffed. Her eyes were red, and black bags formed half moons beneath them. Still looking at the girlish trim of her matronly nightshirt, she said, "I think it makes me look like a freak."

First Bill, then Stephie laughed, but Stephie's laughter turned to tears. She sat up, and they embraced each other. Again, Bill tried to calm her while being careful not to touch her back. He had seen a photo taken by the doctor of the red welts criss-crossing her skin. He had to fend off the cold tide of anger to continue his tender care.

Stephie sank back down to her pillow and told Bill stories about John Burns. There was some laughter, but mostly it was tears. Bill told her about how he had known John, who was one of the youngest members on the presidential detail. When he had volunteered and been selected to guard Stephie, John had met with him in the Oval Office. He didn't repeat to Stephie the vows that John had made—unsolicited—but he had promised the president that he would give his life to save her. It was the pledge that Bill had wanted to hear, and he had stamped his seal of approval on the young agent's mission with a single nod of his head. John's death warrant.

"There's something else," Stephie said out of the blue,

"that's been bothering me. Lieutenant Wu—that Chinese officer who saved us—he said, well, that he and I are cousins." She studied Bill's carefully masked face then went on. "He said that his mother is my aunt Cynthia. My mom's sister." She waited.

Bill said, "Did you ask your mother?"

Stephie snorted. "She wouldn't tell me shit." She stared up at Bill. "Will you?"

"This really should come from your mother," Bill tried.

Stephie scoffed at the suggestion with a roll of her eyes and wave of her hand, then pleaded with him. "Don't I have the right to know things like this? I'm not a child anymore!"

Bill tried to placate her with vague apologies for her mother, but in the end all that would do was the truth. The whole story. "Han Zhemin seduced your mother and broke up our marriage," Bill began. An explosive puff of air escaped from the incredulous, scoffing girl. That wasn't the mother that she knew. Bill struggled to explain. Rachel was young. Han was rich and glamorous. Han was what she had thought she'd married in wedding Bill. It was as much his fault as hers. He hadn't told her that he planned on leaving Hollywood for a dreary life at graduate school. Han offered her everything that she'd wanted. Luxurious private jets carrying her to exciting world capitals. Extraordinary wealth in the hands of a man who had been born and bred to spend it.

Stephie was incensed. "So she *wasn't* a small-town, church-going *saint* like she always made out! She was just a gold-digging *whore*!"

"Stephie!" Bill chastised. "She was young! *I* was young! We were *all* young, and young people make mistakes!"

"So when Han Zhemin—on that stage by the bridge—said I was like my mom . . ." She choked on indignation, then let out a grunt of anger. "That *bastard*!"

"He is a bastard," Bill agreed. "About a month after they ran off to Hong Kong, your mother found out she was pregnant with you. She called her sister—your aunt—who flew to Hong Kong. Rachel asked Cynthia to go to Beijing and explain to Han that she was expecting. To explain that it was my child."

"Mom was in Hong Kong," Stephie commented, "and Han was in Beijing? Why?"

"He'd probably already tired of her," Bill replied.

"So Aunt Cynthia flew to Beijing, and he boned her too?"

"Stephie!" Bill said, grimacing. "That's really, sort of, crude."

"Well, *Jesus*!" she said. "That's what *happened*, isn't it? He *'seduced'* her, or whatever you wanta call it. He knocked her up, and out pops Lieutenant Wu!"

"You'd better get some rest," Bill said.

"*Talk* to me!" Stephie demanded. "Don't leave! *Please*!" He took her demands that he not leave her as something more than they were. Bill's eyes filled with tears. "I'm sorry," Stephie said, putting her arms around him. "I'm sorry. I love you. I love you, Dad. What I mean is, we haven't talked about *you*. Tell me. About you." Bill pulled away and shrugged, dabbing at the tears that pooled in her long eyelashes. "I wanta know," Stephie insisted, "about you." Bill nodded and smiled. "So who's this woman I keep reading about. Clarissa Leffler? Do you love her?"

The question shot through Bill like an arrow. He felt its shaft with each throb of his heart. "It's complicated," he mumbled, struggling with the words.

"So you love her," she deciphered, "but something's wrong." Bill snorted bitterly but couldn't form his lips into a smile. "But what could be wrong? I think you two would make a great couple! You're the president. She's the daughter of the Speaker of the House. She's beautiful," Stephie said, reaching for her own, unkempt hair as if to make the point by exhibiting beauty's opposite. She slapped the bed with red, chapped hands. "And she's so well-*educated*!"

"You will be too, Stephie," Bill interrupted. "I know how high your grades and college board scores were. You can get into any college that you want."

"And I'm the president's daughter," she said, grinning broadly. Instead of chaffing at the presumed advantage of her birth, she seemed to relish her title—"First Daughter"—because it seemed so new to her.

"And, you're a war veteran," Bill added, smiling with his daughter.

"So-o-o," Stephie said in a girlish, teasing voice, "what's so wrong with my new mom, *Clarissa*?"

"She's a spy for the Chinese," Bill said almost without thinking. Stephie laughed. The smile drained from his face first, then from hers.

"*What?*" Stephie exclaimed when she realized that he wasn't kidding. She sat bolt upright.

There was a volume and an edge to her reply that convinced Bill, once and for all, that Clarissa's crimes would never be forgiven by the American people. Maybe he could forgive her—rationalize massively—but practically no one else would. And Bill's defense of Clarissa could not keep her from jail. Only a pardon would do that. But if he pardoned her, it would bring him down with her. He could never again lead the nation in war against China.

"You mean all those ugly attacks in the press," Stephie asked, "at the beginning . . . ?"

"Were true, as it turns out," Bill answered. "The sad thing is, Clarissa doesn't *know* she's a Chinese spy. She thinks she's part of a group of ultrapatriotic Americans, like she is."

"What kind of group?" Stephie asked suspiciously. "What are they after?"

Bill shrugged. "They want to kill me, actually."

"Oh!" Stephie expelled sarcastically. "*That* explains it!" She needed her sleep, but he was agitating her. He had wanted to calm her down before bedtime, but instead she had grown livid. "You should fucking *arrest* her! Is her *father* in on it?" Bill nodded. "Then arrest *his* ass *too*!"

"It's all under control," Bill assured her. "And Stephie," he suggested with an awkward laugh, "you really ought to start watching your language."

"You sound like Mom," Stephie said, sinking back to her pillow and grimacing upon her back's contact with the mattress.

"Well, I mean, it's all right for the army, but it sounds a little out of place in the civilian world."

Stephie studied him now through narrowed eyelids. "What's

that supposed to mean?" she asked with budding outrage. "Are you suggesting that I'm not in the army anymore? Is that what you meant by that 'veteran' remark?"

Bill opened his mouth but ran out of words before he'd even begun. He was totally unprepared for her question. "Well, after all that's happened . . . What I mean is, Stephie, that your mother and I just *assumed*, I guess, that you would've felt that maybe you'd done enough fighting, you know, for one war. I don't mean to suggest that you should resign your commission," Bill lied, "but maybe you'd consider a reassignment."

"I'm an infantryman," Stephie said reasonably enough, again sitting up. But again she began to grow agitated. "And I'm a damn fucking *good* one! We're at war, and, and, and the Chinese army occupies *half* our fucking country! And . . ." Bill was motioning for her to stop. Nodding his head. "I'm going back to my unit tomorrow!" she blurted out defiantly.

"But," Bill objected, "your wounds."

"They're nothing!" she cried. "I'm not quitting! I'm *not*!" He tried to get her to lie down in a more restful pose. "I'll tell you the *same* thing I told Mom! Over my dead fucking body!"

In spite of himself, Bill burst out laughing, just as Stephie did an instant later. "You *said* that?" Bill asked. "To Rachel?"

"Yeah," his daughter replied, again the little girl, arching her eyebrows and waggling her head. "I did."

"Okay, then," Bill said. "Okay." He kissed Stephie's smooth and soft forehead.

She wrapped her arms around him and kissed his cheek three times. It was the same hug and the same kiss from the same girl whom he'd first met when she was an equally serious four year old.

"I love you, Dad," she said.

"I love you too," he replied before rising and turning out the lights.

Bill found Clarissa sitting propped up on pillows kneading the sheets with both hands. The fabric was wrinkled from the tight, repetitive clutching. It was at least half an hour's worth of work. The gripped fists gave her a hunted look Bill thought as he undressed. Or maybe he was just projecting. She said nothing, and neither did he.

She'd returned to the bedroom from her office saying nothing to anyone even in reply to casual greetings. Bill and Fielding had scrutinized her demeanor close-up on ultraslow, ultra-HD digital video recordings. Bill had gone from feeling sickening guilt over spying on her, to a love for her that lay crushed under the weight of what he saw.

For when Clarissa had entered the elevator alone, she had broken down completely. It wasn't that she had taken the chance that there was a gap in the security. She had to know that she was being watched. She was rising three floors to the personal residence of the president of the United States, but even so she couldn't control her sobs. It was as if a blow had knocked the air from her, and Bill felt exactly the same blow. He had watched Clarissa turn into the corner of the elevator and heave soundless cries. Her hand gagged her mouth to prevent her outburst, but still she muttered stifled, pitiful pleas. Lonely cries to which Bill deeply yearned to reach.

Thus had he joined her in the only place where Bill had said, "No cameras," to the Secret Service. His personal residence was free of all bugs, friendly and not.

"I thought," Bill said without thinking, but luckily with his back to the bed, "that you were going to your office."

"I *did* go to my office," Clarissa replied defensively. As if she was covering up for her infidelity, which she was, though not sexual. She was faithful to him in every arena except the political, where she plotted with his enemies to kill him and to rip the Constitution to shreds. "I just got back! An hour ago. I did some paperwork. Sent some E-mails."

"You didn't stay long," Bill noted, hanging his pants over a chair. "Is anything up?"

"*Why* don't you turn around and *face* me when we talk?" she demanded in a shrill tone and at an urgent pace.

Bill turned and smiled as he had always done for the cameras. It was too easy. "Is something wrong?" he asked innocently. "Something, maybe, at your office?"

"My father . . ." Clarissa began before her eyes began to

dart and search the far corners of her mind for an exit. "He wasn't at his office. I spoke to his chief of staff and secretary. He wasn't at home. Or the club. Or any other place that I checked."

Bill knew that Tom Leffler was holed up with lawyers under arrest for high treason during time of war. "He'll turn up," Bill said lamely as he climbed into bed next to Clarissa, feeling as heartless as he actually was.

"Something's happened to him," she said calmly. Since Clarissa hadn't exclaimed her conclusion, Bill had missed the great leap she'd made. She turned to Bill, and he looked into her eyes. She was panicked. Trapped like the cloth in her white-knuckled fist.

"But *you've* seen him," Bill said, disgusting himself. *"Lull her into a false sense of security,"* Fielding had advised. He looked away and turned off the light. "Your father was in the Oval Office," he said, then sat there in the dark thinking, *You also saw him in the park.* "This morning," he continued guiltily, "when I handed over power to Simon. And he accepted my written declaration this evening when I returned and the chief justice certified me to be president again."

"Why wasn't I there?" Clarissa asked from the black pit of the lightless dungeon.

The rustle of her hair against the pillow signaled a turn of her head. He was taking too long. "Well," Bill ventured in a measured tone meant to put her at ease and to give him the time to swallow the clot in his throat, "there wasn't much of a ceremony. It was just a repeat of what you saw this morning. We just went ahead and did it."

"My father was in the White House? Tonight? And he didn't come to see me?"

"No, he was patched into a videoconference call," Bill explained.

The room was still. "Patched in by whom?" Clarissa asked.

"White House operators, I guess. You know he's tracked by NCA locators. He's in the chain of presidential succession. High up in the chain, as a matter of fact. Third behind me and the vice president."

That had been stupid. Clumsy. He waited. She said nothing

for several long, excruciating seconds during which he braced himself, but nothing happened.

"He's an old man," she murmured. "I worry about him. Since Mom's gone."

He's on suicide watch, Bill thought. The man who'd been Bill's mentor. Who'd handed him the baton of leadership of their party when Bill had won the presidential nomination. He had trapped that man—the Speaker of the House—in an act of treason.

"If, if," Bill faltered, "if you want to talk to him, I can arrange a videoconference." He hadn't talked such a thing over with the attorney general, but he assumed that it was his decision. Fielding would record the whole thing. It would certainly be the smoking gun. "If, you know, you want privacy—if you need to talk about something only with him, something that's too personal to talk over with someone, you know, else . . ." *Like me,* he thought. *The assassin's target.* "Your line would be totally secure," he pledged, lying with a suddenly steely conscience.

"No," she finally muttered. "If you say he's all right, that's good enough for me."

Bill had misplayed his role. Perhaps he had overplayed it. He rolled his back to her. She made no move to lie in a more comfortable repose. His sheet, in fact, disappeared millimeter by millimeter into her clenching hands.

"Do you . . . want to?" she asked tentatively. Wide awake. Terrified and alone.

"I'm tired," Bill answered.

She almost instantly rolled onto her side facing away from him. Fielding had warned him—daily—*"No changes in routine . . . especially intimate routine. She'll be sensitive to any backing away."*

Bill desperately wanted to end the charade there. That's what any decent man would've done for the woman he loved. And he *did* love her! Or maybe he couldn't love anybody. He had done nothing to get Rachel back. Not even return her desperate calls from Hong Kong. Why didn't he just shout out, *"Now is the time for all good men to come to the aid of their party!"* Or better yet whisper it. *"Don't say or do any-*

thing, Clarissa. Everybody knows. You're in huge trouble, but you've got my undying support!"

And the hell with every American who thinks otherwise. He would resign. Abandon the throne for the woman he loves during time of war for national survival. It would be, he knew, a quixotic suicide dive into the history books. And what in God's name would Stephie think about it as she returned to the front line?

"Beginning at 0800 hours tomorrow morning," the E-mail sent anonymously to Clarissa had read *"monitor the subject closely and report immediately—immediately—any changes in security or any unscheduled movements that the subject makes."*

"Subject," was the way the plotters referred to him. "Target," was what Fielding had said that word meant. Clarissa had read the same E-mail.

She sighed, just then, from somewhere behind his back.

Bill rolled over and put his arms around her, which she instantly seized and pulled tighter. He kissed her thick hair, which smelled as always, of the same fragrance. Some scent, Bill thought as he inhaled greedily for the last time, whose origin he would never know. She turned to him. She felt warm against him. His desire for her rose. "Is there something you want to tell me?" he asked.

She froze for a moment, then rolled away again. *She isn't going to tell me,* Bill thought. Amazed. Shocked. She knew they were going to kill me and hurl America into nuclear war, and she wasn't going to say anything at all.

He rolled away from her.

14

The Oval Office was brimming with staffers. The White House press officers' explanation to journalists about the activity was that, "This is a get-back-to-work day for the president."

Bill sat at his desk ignoring the energy secretary's report as Hamilton Asher entered the room. The FBI Director grinned and shook hands with Bill's inner staff, working his way to the president.

"Hamilton?" Bill said, not extending his hand.

"Mr. President," Asher replied, smiling. "I appreciate you inviting me to the NSC meeting."

"It's about time the FBI returned to the table," Bill offered in a flat, unconvincing tone. He felt no charity toward Hamilton Asher. He intended to attend the man's execution.

"And here are the disks," Asher said, putting the slim envelope on Bill's desk. "They contain the video files that you requested." Asher lifted his fingers off the slim package and took a step away. He looked at his watch and said, "The meeting's about to start." He departed within seconds. Within seconds more, the Oval Office was empty.

WHITE HOUSE SITUATION ROOM
December 30 // 0805 Local Time

Clarissa sat next to her father, but could get nothing out of him. Bill had asked her to attend the NSC meeting, mumbling something about important developments. It was her first time in the Situation Room since just after their Christmas Eve meeting with Han Zhemin at Camp David. Clarissa bit her nails thinking, *Han Wushi! They'll want a report about Han Wushi's rise to popularity and power.*

Her father stared at her. He was pale, crinkled, and sagging, and his eyes were bloodshot, but he peered at her with pity. "You look sick!" she whispered, mainly in anger. He sat there, slack-jawed, and said nothing. "What's *wrong*?" He just shook his head. "Why are you here?" she asked. He shrugged. "*Talk* to me!" she exclaimed, raising her pitch but not her volume, which remained inaudible to the others gathered around the long table.

"I love you," was all he said.

They're going to kill Bill! she realized instantly. *They're going to assassinate him right now.* She rose and . . .

Her father's suddenly strong grip hurt her wrist as he pulled her back to her seat. He held her hand under the table. Despite her twisting he wouldn't let go. Her father had gripped her wrist roughly the way he had when she had misbehaved—a means of brutish control. It was his only form of abuse or corporal punishment. "Let *go*!" she hissed through clenched teeth.

"It's too late," he said.

She ceased her struggles immediately. "No-o-o. No, *no!*"

Hamilton Asher entered the briefing room, causing a stir.

A muffled thud from above sounded as though someone had dropped a heavy book on the floor above. Only there was no floor above. The Situation Room was a hundred feet beneath ground level. Every general, cabinet officer, and aide looked at the ceiling in unison. For a single, awful moment, time stood still for everyone in the conference room.

The phone rang. General Cotler, chairman of the Joint Chiefs, stabbed a button on the speakerphone. Sounds of shouting and confusion filled the background as a shocked, female aide shouted. "The president! There was an explosion! In the Oval Office!"

Cotler boomed, "Has the president been harmed?"

"He's *dead*!" she screeched.

Clarissa's world shattered to pieces. She rose halfway but was pulled back to her seat by her father's grip. "I've-got-to-go. I've-got-to-go. I've-got-to . . ." She started to cry. Her father put his arm around her.

"They're *all* dead!" the aide continued. "That whole side of the building is gone! Aw, God . . . !"

"Get the vice president," Secretary of Defense Moore ordered. A communications officer went to work.

"We're at risk here," General Cotler noted. "We're all bunched up."

"You go," said Secretary of State Art Dodd to Bob Moore. "Get somewhere safe. Quickly."

"I'll stay in touch," Moore replied, grabbing his jacket and briefcase. Cotler pointed to colonels and navy captains like a squad leader. "You, you, you. Go with the SecDef." Moore and his troop of uniformed and civilian aides headed for the elevator to brave the dangers above.

"Oh-God! Oh-God! Oh-God!" Clarissa hiccuped with three unsuccessful gulps of air. She shook her head so hard that her hair lashed at her eyes. Her father dug his fingernails into her wrists. Clarissa pulled away from the son of a bitch, then slapped at his shoulders and face. *Fucking murderer! Murderer! Murderer!* she thought.

"Would everyone listen up!" came a shout. A bark. A command from Air Force General Latham. The graying, standing officer lowered the telephone from his ear. "The vice president's alternate national command post was shot down by three long-range fighter-interceptors!"

"Over Kansas?" shouted Secretary Moore.

"Impossible!" General Cotler challenged.

"It happened," Latham responded. "They made a low-level, hypersonic ingress."

Cotler didn't deal any longer with the air force chief of staff. "Find out," he ordered an army colonel, "in the next five minutes, whether there is a 1,000-mile trail of physical damage on the ground in the wake of those 'hypersonic fighter-interceptors.' And get search and rescue aircraft and an investigative team in there *now*."

"I've got pilots on CAP over the crash site," Latham announced. "There are no survivors."

Art Dodd pointed at a dark plasma display. "Put pictures up there. I want to see it. Right now."

"I'm working on it," the air force general replied.

Everything was moving so fast. Consequences hurtled by unnoticed at first. It took people time to catch up.

Clarissa was the quickest of them all. "You're the president," she said out loud to her father. The old Speaker contemplated his lap, humbled, Clarissa thought, by the office that lay at his feet. *Or he's just old,* she amended. He would need all the help he could get.

"We should swear Mr. Leffler in," all heard from the opposite end of the room. It was Hamilton Asher. Hamilton Asher. *Hamilton Fucking Asher!* Clarissa raged. He was a dead man. She could get back at him. Avenge Bill's death. She could use her father's power to destroy the monster. The killer of innocent people.

Color test bars and then a picture filled the screen behind Art Dodd. A blackened smear with licks of flame here and there blotted out orderly rows of wheat. The flat field was adorned with twisted, unidentifiable scraps of metal and with lesser debris of nonmetallic origin.

The swearing in was organized quickly. Surprisingly quickly, Clarissa thought as she gnawed on two nails, looking around to see if anyone else seemed suspicious by the rapidity with which the transfer of power was arranged. It would have been better to have built some disorganization into the process. The chief justice appeared on a screen. The words they used, Clarissa thought, all came from the constitution, but this succession, for the first time in American history, was *extra*-constitutional.

She put the thought from her mind. There was too much work to do. Her feeble father had to build a new administration during a desperate war. As her father raised his hand and slurred his solemn oath of office, Clarissa's planning raced ahead. *Trust*, she thought. *Trust. We've got to get somebody we can trust.* Of all of Bill's senior advisors, Clarissa decided, Richard Fielding was probably the most trustworthy.

"Mr. President?" General Latham intoned the instant the ceremony ended. Directly beside him stood Hamilton Asher. "You have now assumed command of the armed forces of the United States of America. The Chinese are undoubtedly behind these assassinations," the air force chief of staff began, "or they're gonna learn about them very soon. Either way, they might just see a vulnerability. A moment of opportunity."

"To strike us?" Cotler asked. "With nuclear arms? We have absolutely *no* indication that . . ."

"This situation is highly unstable!" Latham argued both to Cotler and to Clarissa's father. "President Leffler hasn't had his transition briefing. I'd like to lay out a few options. Give him his nuclear command and control briefing. Transfer the codes."

Latham! Clarissa knew instantly. *And Asher.* They'd come to collect on her father's lone "campaign promise." The sole precondition to her father's succession to Bill's office, and, she realized for the first time, to her father's continued survival. If he refused, they would query the next man in line. Perhaps, they already had.

Cotler nodded reluctantly for Latham to proceed with the briefing, but Clarissa wondered whether Latham would have stopped even if General Cotler had refused. Three or four sentences into Latham's nearly whispered lecture to Clarissa's father, however, Cotler barged in and shouted in anger.

"You're giving him *specific* first strike options!" Cotler raged. "What *is* this, Martin?"

"If they attack us without attrition of their forces, Adam," Latham replied, apparently from the heart, "we're dead. As a country. It's over!"

"But there *is* no attack under way!" Cotler objected. "For Christ's sake, General Latham, our defenses will give us plenty of time to . . . !"

"Mr. President?" Latham asked suddenly. "What are your orders?"

"*What?*" was shouted from both Cotler and Admiral Thornton, Chief of Naval Operations, who were on their feet.

"We attack," Clarissa's father croaked, "as planned."

"As *who* planned?" Art Dodd demanded.

"He meant as General Latham advised!" Clarissa cried out, rising to lean out over the table and defend her otherwise defenseless father. Hamilton Asher, a far better armed protector, stood at her father's other side.

"General Latham . . . !" began Cotler before turning to the other end of the table and seeing that his air force counterpart was on the phone.

"Two-niner-echo-gold," he was finishing into the mouthpiece. A cadre of air force officers stood at the back and sides of his seat. "Hello?" Latham said into the handset. "Does anybody read me? Hello? Hello! *Hello!*"

The image of the vice president's wreckage on the screens froze like a video recording.

For a moment, Clarissa thought that maybe the Chinese truly had launched a sneak attack.

The double doors burst open, and Clarissa jumped and then gasped. Bill Baker and Richard Fielding entered on the crest of a wave of Secret Service agents, whose weapons were drawn and raised. "You're alive," Clarissa whispered to Bill, who looked her hard in the eyes. The agents fanned out in both directions and circled the table, swarming everywhere and yet focused on discrete targets. The first to be handcuffed—roughly and quickly—was air force General Latham. Some of his uniformed aides were singled out and arrested. Others were asked to step aside.

The swarm appeared behind Clarissa, who'd sunk into her chair beside her father. She felt the agents keenly at her back. Her skin tingled as if waiting for their sting. Asher grunted loudly as his arms were yanked around to the rear. Handcuffs descended upon her father's unresisting wrists.

"Dr. Leffler," some faceless reaper politely called out from behind. She stood and faced the agent, maintaining her composure. Maybe this was something else entirely.

Both her wrists were gently seized. The cuffs fit them tight together. Clarissa's jaw hung wide in shock. They led Asher past stern-faced generals and cabinet secretaries. Tom Leffler followed—head bowed—in abject shame. Agents escorted Clarissa by the elbow down the gauntlet of silent stares. Men and women. Soldiers and civilians. Aides she'd never before met. All glared at her with a look of intense and personal loathing. Hated. Her usually rapid facility for comprehension totally failed her at that moment. She couldn't understand why they hated her.

"You're going to be shot," Richard Fielding audibly assured General Latham.

"I've always been ready to give my life for my country!" Latham replied, drawing rafts of shouts and angry calls from dozens of military officers. The spontaneous outburst came from all ranks and all services. It came from those most deeply offended by Latham's blasphemous profession of patriotism: his fellow officers. And the only person more shocked by it than General Latham was Clarissa.

For she shared the officers' enmity toward Latham and Asher. She felt it, firsthand, just as they did. The only difference between them and her was that she shared Latham and Asher's guilt.

Bill stood directly in front of Clarissa, blocking her way. "I'm *innocent*!" Clarissa pled. "Bill, I didn't . . . !"

"Now is the time," he interrupted, "for all good men to come to the aid of their party."

OUTSIDE RICHMOND, VIRGINIA
December 31 // 0840 Local Time

The American assault had bogged down.

On the eve of the attack, Lieutenant Colonel Ackerman, commander of Third Battalion, had given Stephanie Roberts a provisional field promotion to First Lieutenant, whereupon she had become executive officer of Charlie Company. When the company commander—straight from a war spent at a desk with a bad back—was blown to bits by a mine ten minutes into the fight, Stephie had become commanding officer, C Company, Third Battalion, 519th Infantry.

Charlie Company had been decimated in the defense of the Potomac River, even though several of its leaders had, like Stephie, been repatriated in the prisoner exchange. The company—typically reinforced and fielding up to 150 soldiers—was down to only 80 men and women. They had reorganized from four platoons into two.

Second Platoon now waited on First Platoon's covering fire.

Stephie and her commo crawled through a parking garage toward the hesitant First Platoon under a thick sheet of Chinese fire. First Platoon was heads down behind a concrete wall that periodically burst into flame. Men and women lay in blood—shrieking in agony—being tended to by frantic medics. One of the wounded, Stephie had learned over the radio, was their platoon leader.

"I need fire!" Animal shouted from behind the Thai restaurant just outside. The unit he commanded—Second Platoon—was pinned under heavy fire.

"Hang on!" Stephie shouted back.

Eighteen-year-olds lay under the lip of the ground-floor, concrete wall. Most still wore their packs. All were terrified. They'd spent their short army careers in bunkers and trenches. Their war had been different from this. Though fighting from fixed positions had been horrifying, this, apparently, was worse. It was worse, Stephie knew, because it was different.

"This shit's too thick!" Animal cried out over the radio. "We can't make it across that street, Steph! Shit! I got four machine guns on my front! No way! No how!"

"Copy!" Stephie replied curtly. A long row of frightened eyes hunkered beneath the chipping, flaming wall and stared at their new CO. Squad leaders were either dead or tending to the numerous wounded. Second Platoon was, for all intents and purposes, leaderless.

"All right, listen up!" Stephie yelled at the ragged top of her lungs. Even the medics momentarily stopped amid the

spurts of blood and thrashing limbs of pinned comrades. The clock ticked. The Chinese could be maneuvering against them. Stephie made it as short as she could. "Plan's changed! New plan! *This* platoon takes the objective! Second platoon lays fire! This is an attack! Each and every one of you attack! Nobody is going to stop! The faster and harder we do this," she shouted, pounding her clenched fist into her palm, "the more *violently* we do this, the more fire we lay down on the enemy *as* we do this, the more of us that come through!"

She was catching eyes in turn, belting equal doses of courage into each section of the long line of suddenly petrified soldiers.

"We attack! *Attack, attack, attack!* We're infantry! This is *our* country!" Men and women around squared their quivering jaws and gripped their weapons with bloodless knuckles. "Drop your packs! Combat loads only! *Squad* leaders, over here for a meeting!"

Stephie got on the radio and relayed the orders to an appreciative Animal. From the noise in the background, it was clear that Animal's platoon was enduring withering fire. Stephie turned to the new maneuver unit, reorganized them from four squads into three, and gave each missions. She went from soldier to soldier, slapping legs, squeezing arms, tapping body armor and helmets. She made physical contact with all thirty men and women and waited for each one to give her a nod. To make a personal, tacit pledge to her—a solid, binding commitment through eye contact alone—that they would follow her in the attack.

The thin metal roof and poles of the breezeway connecting the garage to the gutted office building emitted "chinging" sounds from steady Chinese fire. They headed out of the garage and lost their first soldier—a woman—in the tiny gap between the garage and the bombed-out building ten meters away. Half of the platoon had already made it through safely. The half that followed continued unmolested. The woman in the middle was hit in the face and killed instantly.

Stephie led the platoon through the charred, gutted office building, whose walls and exposed girders sang with randomly fired enemy rounds. The two armies were separated by a suburban street across which Stephie's First Platoon would have to attack. Animal's Second Platoon was holding their fire from an adjacent Thai restaurant in which Animal had positioned them. Its front wall, Stephie could see through the empty window frames, puffed and flamed from the impact of Chinese rounds.

Stephie's boots crunched through the ash on the totaled ground floor. Although the fires had obviously died out hours earlier, smoke still filled the gutted remains of the building. The stench was so great that Stephie's eyes watered. The taste fouled her mouth. To its credit, the structure still stood.

As they neared the row of offices along the street-side wall—the front line—explosions erupted at close range. Everybody dove into the soot as random chunks of shrapnel crashed into walls, but Stephie realized that it was American covering fire. "Where are you?" Animal screamed over the sound of the barrage.

"We're almost there!" Stephie replied. "We're going on my order! Sixty seconds!"

She turned to the prostrate attackers. "Everybody up! That's our support!" she said, pointing toward the hellish blaze from which they cowered. "We go in forty-five seconds. In line! Let's go! *Move! Move! Move!*"

She led them through an office that had been turned into a crater. They climbed down the ledges of broken foundation into the glassless atrium created by a thousand-pound missile warhead. Then they crawled up the dirt to ground level and emerged from the building into open air.

There lay the principal advantage of the avenue of attack Stephie had chosen: an intact, three-foot-high brick wall. Stephie lay amid cigarette butts in the outdoor smokers' haven and directed First Platoon's three squads in either direction from the crater. She didn't have to tell them to keep below the wall. The hot flame and roar of the barrage and the smacks of shrapnel against the building's hide above them did that for her. She did, however, have to tell them to crawl faster by shouting, "On all fours! Go! Go! Go!"

It was a race against the clock. Artillery barrages couldn't last long. Chinese missiles would be airborne in a minute, at most. The armored, self-propelled American guns had to be five hundred meters down the road before they struck.

Just as First Platoon made it into position—a long line of human beings facing the road and the enemy guns on the opposite side of it—and Stephie reported, "We're there!" to Animal, the barrage lifted. "Lay it down!" Even before the echos from the artillery died down, she shouted over her platoon's net, "First Platoon! *Advance and fire at will!*"

They climbed over the wall and brushed aside the crisp and blasted hedge on the other side and began their run across the open street.

"A-h-h-h!" Stephie yelled—deep and guttural from the back of her throat—as she crossed singed grass and cracked sidewalk. The noise she made was half a voluntary growl to steel her nerves and will her body toward the guns that lay, unseen, ahead. The sound was also half an involuntary wail of anticipatory agony. The same shouts rose from the other soldiers in First Platoon as the line made it onto the street's pavement. Surviving Chinese gunners who raised their heads were met by fire from Animal's Second Platoon. Every rifle, machine gun, and missile launcher from their sister platoon loosed a volley that streaked past parking meters and mailboxes and smacked broadsides into the blazing walls and windows of the strip shopping center on the other side of the paved dividing line, forcing the Chinese defenders to drop or die.

Only three of Stephie's soldiers fell on crossing the road. They were dragged to cover writhing and trailing blood across concrete. It was a remarkable feat. Stephie remained with First Squad to stay roughly in the center of the platoon. On their left, Third Squad's objective was a small, free-standing dry cleaner. Although it appeared empty, they hosed it down with fire before entering it and informing Stephie over the tactical net that it was clear.

On Stephie's right, the men and women of Third Squad tossed grenade after grenade into the blazing, two-story furniture store, which was attached to the long U-shaped shopping center that was their objective. First Squad—led by

Stephie—would launch the whole point of the battle: a sweeping action.

They received fire from the rear door across a small, park-like sitting area. There were no windows facing the grassy side lot, only the one door, and it exploded with grenades fired from launchers mounted underneath assault rifles. "They'll be waiting for us behind that door!" Stephie shouted to one of the two engineers she'd scrounged up on her way back to her unit from Washington. The other one had been hit crossing the road. "We need to blow that wall open!"

Under covering fire, the combat engineer and two riflemen dashed to the brick side wall of the shopping center a dozen feet from the lone and now empty doorway. Seconds later, they scrambled away from the smoking satchel—sitting wedged against the wall atop a water meter two feet off the ground—with even greater haste. The last man in line was blown from his feet, but he was lucky. The smoke quickly cleared in the light breeze and water spouted from the broken pipes. A limbless Chinese corpse lay draped through the ragged hole in the wall.

Stephie lead the attack through the hole, opening fire into the black, smoke-filled hollows even as she approached the building. On Stephie's command, she and the eight surviving soldiers of First Squad hurriedly tossed hand grenades in rapid succession past the jagged rows of broken bricks, and then dove to the ground beside the wall. The last woman barely escaped the nine firecracker blasts.

Stephie immediately climbed into the choking smoke. More bodies—soldiers cowering in the store's back office—littered the floor. Stephie led the two squads inside, wading blindly through the swirling haze in a stoop, ramming the shinguards and kneepads sewn into her trousers into an overturned filing cabinet. Twisting her ankle on a shattered half brick. All the while worrying about the jumpy soldiers behind her as much as the Chinese to her front.

"Another charge," she whispered to the engineer, pointing through the office doorway into the still hallway just beyond. He looked at her as if she were crazy. Using high explosives in such near proximity in the enclosed space. "Give it a good hurl," Stephie suggested.

He swallowed hard and crawled forward under cover of First Squad's weapons, which were trained on the doorway. He fumbled with the fuse, then pulled it, arched his back, and heaved the heavy canvas satchel through the doorway and out of sight down the corridor. Chinese fire peppered the door frame above him as he scampered on elbows and knees toward Stephie as fast as he could.

She lowered her helmet to the floor and plugged her ears with her thumbs.

The explosion hit her hardest through the floor. It bucked up into her cheekbone like a punch. All around her debris bounced into air or tumbled from shelves. One of her women screamed when a filing cabinet was toppled onto her. Choking smoke and dust fouled the air.

"Let's *go!*" Stephie shouted before coughing.

She rose quickly but was the third person through the doorway. Her soldiers were learning—or relearning—an important lesson of infantry warfare. If you want to live, you follow hard behind your fire support. You kill the enemy in the seconds before his mind clears and his senses and nerves steady. The corridor erupted in brief pulses of full-auto flashes from the two soldiers' weapons. Stephie followed, but found nothing living to kill.

They used four more satchel charges as they blew holes in walls and cleared their path of reeling defenders. It was easier than it should have been because the Chinese were done. Fought out. Finished. They fired on first sight of an attacker, but then either ran away or curled into a tuck under the hail of return fire. Either way they died without making a stand.

Stephie led her infantrymen in a crawl across a showroom from washers to dryers, which did a piss poor job of stopping Chinese rounds. She lost two people—a man and a woman—who sat upright behind the appliances to reload their weapons.

Third Squad covered their rear. Second Squad joined the remnants of Stephie's First Squad in the attack. Stephie led them through the next hole in the wall, and they sprinted across the flaming showroom floor of a carpet outlet, which the Chinese had set on fire before they abandoned the store. The fumes from the burning merchandise were choking. Three Americans fell, one dead. By the time they made it through the blaze, the Chinese were in full retreat.

That retreat became a slaughter when Animal's Second Platoon crossed the road, flanking and routing the flanked defenders left behind to cover the withdrawal. Easily a hundred fleeing Chinese were mowed down in a field behind the shopping center, all shot in the back.

Fire and maneuver was new to the former American bunker troops, but it was what they had all been taught in basic training, and what they had witnessed the Chinese do. It was infantry combat. It was victory. They exulted in it.

There were high fives from the surviving attackers. Hearty handshakes and hand slaps between the two, reunited platoons. Some men hugged in mutual celebration of life.

But Animal and Stephie didn't celebrate. "How many?" she asked in a quiet voice on greeting Animal in the shelter of the smoldering ruins of a house behind the shopping center. Chinese lay sprawled—twisted and contorted—all around. Some, Stephie noted in satisfaction, hadn't bothered to bring their weapons with them in their flight.

"Seven," he replied, "three dead. I got two medics staying with 'em."

"I lost more," she said. "Twelve, I think. About half dead. *Sh-shit!* We gotta do better next time."

"We will," Animal said confidently. "Fuckin' A."

Ackerman's voice over the radio called for the casualty count, and Stephie reported. "We could use an hour or two," she requested. "We need some time."

"Negative," Ackerman replied. "We got 'em on the run. We got tracks on the highway moving up on the right." Stephie could hear the cracking bolts of main battle tank fire. It had been a long time since she'd seen American armor not buried—hull defilade—into defensive works. The army had been marshaling their mobile strike forces over all the long months of the war. On the road up to the line of departure, she had seen miles of the beasts parked bumper to bumper. "We gotta keep going," Ackerman continued, "or this war will leave us behind. It should be open-field running up ahead. Our armor is threatening to break through on both flanks. The Chinese are running," he said with what Stephie thought must be a smile on his face.

She and Animal rounded up her two platoons, made contact with neighboring companies, who were also advancing, broke through a wooden fence, and entered a peaceful neighborhood. The quiet street was an odd pocket of tranquility on the raging battlefield. Although explosions and towering smoke and flame rose from surrounding firefights, the pleasant street of one-story houses lay seemingly undisturbed by war. Still, Stephie proceeded cautiously. It was Mason Street in Atlanta all over again, only this time in reverse. It was the Americans—now combat-hardened veterans—in the attack against newly arrived Chinese cherries. They advanced from house to house ready to fire on sight of movement.

A white flag suddenly protruded from a window. Stephie assumed that it was surrendering Chinese. Charlie Company's day had begun in reserve. By the time they were taken up to the step-off line—riding aboard armored fighting vehicles, not canvas trucks like before—small pockets of surrounded Chinese were being mopped up by survivors of the first echelon to plow into their lines. The American victors were rough with their bedraggled captives—dragging them by their hair across pavement on knees with hands and ankles bound—but none, as far as Stephie could see, returned the treatment received at Chinese hands by Becky Marsh and John Burns.

"If you see a weapon," Stephie said into her voice-activated mike as she approached the window with her teeth clenched and her rifle butt to her shoulder, "kill 'em all." She kept the open window above the flag in the raised front sight of her M-16. Surrendering was always a tricky maneuver. Things could go wrong. A lone Chinese holdout could doom their already disarmed comrades with a single, futile shot. Stephie was ready to do the killing. There was no sense in taking unnecessary risks on the eve of a battle's victory.

"*Hello* out there!" shouted an old woman in a thin, frail voice. "Hell*o-o-o-o*!"

Stephie's first thought was that there were hostages. "Come

out with your hands up!" she ordered in a shout. She then saw to it with hand signals that she had two machine guns on the front door. But out came a white-haired lady in a house-coat. From behind her came agitated shouts of family members. "Mother!" a grown man barked in what sounded like frustration. But the old lady waved the white flag until she saw the American soldiers, then threw it on the steps. In its place, she pulled from her housecoat a long wooden spoon to which she had mounted a small American flag. She waved the limp stars and stripes in figure eights above her head. "Hoo*ray*!" she shouted. "Hooray! Hooray for our boys and girls! Hooray for America! Hooray for America! Hooray!"

Tears flooded Stephie's eyes, but not from anger. In a rush of unexpected emotion, her jaw dropped, her skin tingled, and she cried. The jubilant old woman danced and turned to the front door as Stephie and the others lowered their weapons. "It's all right! They're ours! They're our troops! Our troops! They're *ours*! They've come back!"

The tears that rolled down Stephie's face had come out of nowhere. She wasn't mad. She wasn't sad. But she cried.

Out of the recesses of the house came an extended family. Middle-aged father, first, then mother and two teenage children, a boy and a girl. Their dog bounded out, and the boy chased it. The golden Labrador ran straight to Animal and licked his face. "Good boy," Animal said, scratching its matted coat. "Thatta boy."

Other front doors opened as people tentatively emerged from hiding. Nearly half the houses, it appeared, were occupied. "They went that way!" some civilians called out to the nearest American soldiers. "Come on, I'll show you," a young girl of about ten—wearing her soccer team's warm-ups—said, tearing off toward the enemy before being grabbed by her mother. The girl stood there on toothpick legs and held out her thin arm out, pointing.

Animal dispatched a squad to check, but Stephie could tell that the war had already passed this small, middle-class neighborhood. She could tell by the receding sound of American main tank guns that the battle was being carried away by vehicles faster than foot sloggers could travel. She could tell by the scenes of neighbors greeting neighbors in what looked like a spontaneous block party, but was more of a reunion among the isolated holdouts.

A small gathering of civilians had been directed by soldiers to Stephie, the commanding officer. All stood behind the outstretched offering held aloft by the old woman with the flag. In her hands was a sheaf of papers. Another family brought up their small bundle of green forms and added it to the woman's stack.

"What?" Stephie asked. "What is that?"

"We wanted you to see this," the old woman said. She had large, sad eyes behind thick glasses. She looked like she hadn't showered or eaten properly for a long time.

"What is it?" Stephie asked, taking the forms in her hands. At the top was printed the heading, "Declaration of Loyalty." Small Chinese characters and numbers in the margins gave the form number.

"None of us signed that thing," a man said from the crowd. "Not a single person on this block."

The old woman in the housecoat in front of Stephie explained. "If we signed it, the Chinese said we'd get food and medicine. That all we had to do was just sign. None of us did. Not a single one!" More of the forms were added to Stephie's stack.

Stephie nodded and read the pledge of loyalty to China, renouncing their citizenship of the "former United States." She reached into her pocket and pulled out a cigarette lighter. The civilians and soldiers broke into smiles and laughter when she lit and dropped the declarations onto a front lawn. The dry, crinkled paper flamed brightly and was quickly consumed. The old woman, the other adults, and then the children stomped the smoking ashes into the yellowed grass. Stephie's soldiers took their turns in the ritual with twisting boots long after the forms had ceased being anything more than a symbol.

"I wish all the others could be here to see this," Animal said softly to Stephie.

Their names, their faces, their smiles all came rushing back. They were victorious, but John Burns was still dead. "Let's move out," Stephie said, seeking escape from the memories and the silent stares.

BEIJING, CHINA
December 31 // 2130 Local Time

Han sat on the raised dais at the sumptuous Beijing banquet far from the no-man's-land at the table's center. He felt disoriented after the long flight from America, which had taken a circuitous route through South America and the South Pacific after Hawaiian airports had come under attack by stray bands of roving American Marines, who were all supposed to be dead by now.

The huge room was abuzz with dinner conversations among the thousand or so dignitaries in attendance. The tables filling the large hall were all round. Their animated talk was jovial and excited. The people at the long, straight table on the dais faced not each other, but the gathering. The arrangement allowed for little conversation, especially, it seemed, in the immediate vicinity of Han. The lead table's configuration was also symbolic of public life, Han thought. Family relations existed solely for display to the masses. Behind the facade, passion was reserved for mistresses. There was no such thing as love. It had, through the generations, been bred out of the ruling class.

Han leaned forward over his uneaten dinner to peer down the long table toward the center at his left. The table's occupants were divided—in equal, negotiated numbers—between civilians on the right as they faced the ballroom, and military officers and their wives on the left. Han was buried—exiled to oblivion—off to the far right of the long, linen-draped table amid minor uncles and distant cousins. People whose names he'd never even bothered to learn. To his left, in the distance, lay the tense border between the civilian and military leadership.

Han's father and mother sat near the center. Nearer still were the prime minister's wife and the prime minister. And on the very brink of the great divide sat Wu—deal maker *extraordinaire*—who wore not a uniform, but a dark business suit. It was the first time that Han had ever seen the boy in civilian attire of any kind. Throughout the long dinner, Wu's place at the center of the political world had been bathed in television camera light and immortalized in bright flashes for the stills.

Han leaned further out over the table. Next to Wu—on the far side of the dividing line—sat Liu Yi, the beautiful, favorite granddaughter of the defense minister. The match that had—until Wu's conniving—been intended for Han. The old general, Liu Changxing, and his wholly unpresentable wife were at Yi's elbow. Then came Yi's father, also a general, her mother, and all the other officers and wives descending in rank and importance until they reached the dregs of political power toward the far end of the table: junior officers invited to the dais by virtue not of their rank, but for propriety's sake because they were relations. They were, in order of importance, Han's military counterparts.

How dizzying had been Han's fall from power. He had done all that he was supposed to do, followed every order, but still that had not been enough. He had made no major miscalculations—no missteps for which he was being punished—but he had returned to Beijing in the wee hours of the morning to find only a dark car on an even darker tarmac.

Han had spent the day trying to meet with Wu, but his son had been busy with meetings and meals. Everyone in Beijing was beating a path to his feet. A crush of onlookers and spontaneous cheers awaited Wu's every stop on his whirlwind debut in the capital of the world. National television programming had been interrupted by breaking news stories at Wu's every sighting. Emerging from the security ministry. Arriving at the ministry of trade. Lunch with the council of ministers, then an afternoon visiting various military commands. The public adoration that awaited him at each stop wasn't orchestrated by the government, which was what had made it such a phenomenon. China had never seen anything like Han Wushi: prodigal son, military hero, and idol and savior to a television audience numbering in the billions.

For Han Wushi had become the symbol of hope. He was, Han thought, like a gigantic movie screen on which was pro-

jected the hopes of viewers all across the Chinese empire. To
some, Wu's dogged determination in combat held out the
promise of winning the war. To others, his refusal to continue
a suicidal attack meant that the end of the senseless blood-
letting was near. To all, Wu meant change, and change was
what everyone wanted. A new face. A fresh wind in the stale
corridors of aging Beijing power. Wu was perfect in his role
as all things to all people, because to the wider world, Wu
was a blank. Tabula rasa. Unsullied by years of political in-
fighting.

And he was also, at the same time, both a member of the
civilian royal family, and a soldier with a long red wound on
his face from a grazing American bullet.

Wu hadn't done this alone, Han knew. And it hadn't been
done quickly. It was a plan hatched at the very top, months
earlier, perhaps even before the invasion. Whose plan it had
been—civilian or military—Han didn't know, but in the end
both had endorsed it. Wu had been used by both the prime
minister and the defense minister, but he had also done his
share of manipulating. The murder of Sheng and Li, Han was
certain, had been ordered jointly by the prime minister and
General Liu. The former because Sheng had always been a
threat. The latter because Sheng might become one. But the
return of Bill Baker and his daughter to American hands had
been all Wu's idea, and he hadn't told anyone about it. It was
a measure of Wu's newfound political power that neither the
civilians nor the military challenged him for it, which was
wise. Wu's conciliatory gesture toward the enemy had been,
like everything else Wu had done, wildly popular.

Wu, beholden to no one, was now a force unto himself.
The old fools on both sides of the bitter political divide
thought they could contain that power and use it to their advantage.

The others seated around Han were staring at him just as
Han stared at his son. Han sat back and picked at his food.
Still jet-lagged, he had arrived at the banquet hall that evening
and been ushered to the rear of the receiving line. The queue
was long and led, he saw, to the brave, bandaged young Wu
and the beautiful, exquisite, beaming young Yi, whom Wu

had met for the first time on arrival at the banquet hall. The wait in line gave Han the time to compose his greeting. To Wu, it would be somber pride. A firm handshake. A pinched smile. A nod. To the vivacious Yi, it would be an upbeat, "Perhaps I can show you Disney*land* the next time you visit America." After all, just before his departure from the soon to be renamed "Han Wushi Airport" in Atlanta, Han had been handed power for administering conquered territory in the west as well as in the east of Occupied America.

But everyone had been called to their tables for dinner before Han had reached the guests of honor. Now, he probably wouldn't have the chance to speak to either of the newlyweds, whose hurried wedding ceremony was sealed in private at the banquet hall before the deal could come undone. Han had cursed on hearing the news. It had fouled all the plans on which Han had spent the day working. The two halves of the political world at the center of the table had been joined before he could get organized.

The buzz in the great hall fell silent like a field of crickets on the approach of a predator. Defense Minister Liu stood behind his seat. A boom mike held by a soldier hovered just out of the cameras' fields of view. Before him—sitting mute and expectant—was everybody who was anybody in Chinese politics. Ministers. Generals. Agency heads and CEOs. Ambassadors and governors returned on short notice from the far-flung empire. And each was accompanied by their all-important and rabidly political wives, who had been invited to the supposedly social occasion.

All rose—Han among them—as the defense minister lifted his glass. The sound of a thousand scraping chairs fell silent in seconds. "I would now like to toast," the general boomed over the PA system and over the speakers of a billion television sets, "a young man who stands for all that we hold dear. A member of one of China's greatest families. The bearer of the legendary name of 'Han.' A decorated war hero who led his men valiantly in the victorious Battle of Washington! And the newest member of my proud family! *To Han Wushi!*"

There was an instantaneous response.

"To Han Wushi!" the thousand dignitaries roared in unison amid the blazing flashes and humming television cameras. The shouts of Wu's name were an oath of loyalty to the new regime. A pledge by civilian leaders and military officers alike that they were united in the spirit of young Wu for the greater good of China. A testament to the shared, secret fear, Han thought, of the wakened giant across the seas, whom China's army had failed to strike dead in its sleep. Han mouthed the words as a lone cameraman snapped a picture of him before scurrying toward the center of the world: Han's son and daughter-in-law.

All stood—some on tiptoes—to watch as Wu and Yi took to the parquet dance floor. Bathed in the brilliant glow from a dozen television cameras, the young couple—China's prince and princess—waltzed amid a forming ring of smiling generals and cabinet ministers. Old men in uniforms mixed and conversed jovially with old men in suits in a way that they hadn't done for the last decade. An even thicker ring of flashing still cameras sent the unmistakable message to all of China and the rest of the world.

Unbeknownst to Han, the civilian leadership had ridden two horses into the final confrontation with the military. At the last moment, the prime minister had chosen compromise instead of the confrontation that Han had been chosen to lead. The change in policy had led to the change in personnel. Young Wu—the perfect hybrid of the military and the civilian—would steer China away from its destructive political collision.

Out with the old, Han thought bitterly. *In with the new. The king is dead. Long live the king!*

Han rose from the table and slipped—unnoticed—out of the ballroom. The political animals who'd once bowed down to Han now ignored him completely. He was the bitter past. Wu was the shining future.

Han returned immediately to his apartment. There, Shen Shen waited before the television set in her short negligee. Her eyes were red from crying, but her jaw was set in anger. She had returned to Beijing with Han on his private jet, scheming and plotting the entire way.

"Did you talk to him?" she asked Han.

"No," he replied, "but Wu is making the rounds at corporate headquarters in Hong Kong tomorrow. He'll be staying at the family's home. I can get you in there."

"Will he be alone?" she asked.

Han nodded and smiled. "Yi is staying in Beijing."

"What about tonight?" Shen Shen asked. "Do they have separate beds?"

"I doubt it," Han said, laughing cruelly.

Shen Shen ground her teeth. "But still, he goes off and leaves her the day after their wedding." She turned back to the television. Young Wu laughed gaily as he spilled the champagne that he was attempting to pour into Yi's mouth. Yi was older than Wu—twenty-one—but she giggled like a girl half her age. All the ancients who were clustered around them—whom Han had never in his life even seen smile—laughed with the two frolicking young people. The broadcast symbol of the happy lives that lay ahead—some day—for all of China's returning soldiers.

"Bitch!" Shen Shen cursed, crushing a satin pillow in her hands.

"I'll take care of her," Han said, "you do your thing to Wu, whatever that is." He smiled, turned off the lights, and found her body in the glow from the flickering television, at which the two lovers stared until both reached orgasm.

PHILADELPHIA NAVAL SHIPYARD
January 15 // 1330 Local Time

Captain Stephanie Roberts, United States Army, stood atop the platform overlooking the sparkling blue water. A dozen surface warships dotted Philadelphia's harbor, but Admiral Thornton, her escort, was telling her that the arsenal ships' most important escorts were invisible. "Our New London shipyard in Connecticut has been turning out attack submarines at a fast clip," said the chief of naval operations, wearing dress blues with gold epaulettes. "Those subs will keep the seas around the battle group clear of Chinese submarines." The admiral looked exceedingly pleased, Stephie thought, to begin playing—at long last—a starring role in the war. "The exact number is classified, of course," he leaned closer to Stephie and whispered, "but it's more than the Chinese think we're capable of producing. Way more." He winked at Stephie, and she smiled.

Down below, bands played to crowds of sailors in navy blue and civilians waving flags and holding aloft banners printed with patriotic slogans. Stephie guessed that the civilians were workers and families. "Are you on leave?" Admiral Thornton asked Stephie.

"Yes, sir," she replied curtly.

"Where is your unit now?" another senior naval officer asked.

"Southern Virginia," Stephie replied.

"God bless 'em," the jubilant Thornton commented to the smiles of officers and their wives in the two rows of seats behind Stephie. "Well, we oughta start making things a little easier for you. Right, boys?" Thornton asked the all-male senior naval officer corps around him. There followed a chorus of, "Yes, sir!" from the men in blue.

Stephie turned away and thought disparagingly, *Navy kissasses!* Thornton waited for her to say something. "When will the arsenal ships actually put to sea?" she asked. "I mean, with crews and ready to fight."

"Well," Thornton replied, "that's actually classified also." He leaned over to her. "Next week," he whispered. The captains and rear admirals who surrounded them all suppressed knowing grins with contortions of their faces. They clearly couldn't wait.

The bands stopped playing, and Stephie's father's voice boomed over the loudspeakers. Stephie watched her father on a television monitor. He stood at the bow of a massive arsenal ship five hundred meters away. His speech to the crowds was short but was punctuated by a dozen outbursts of applause, cheers, and shouts from the adoring crowd. No cheers were louder, however, than after the last words that he spoke.

"I commission this vessel," he boomed triumphantly, "the U.S.S. *Ronald Reagan*!"

The roar rose up as he smashed a bottle against the hull of

the half-million-ton behemoth. Stephie looked out from her own, distant platform at its long, flat deck, which resembled a supertanker's. But instead of oil it contained eight thousand vertical, auto-reloading silos. And in its bowels, 100,000 special-purpose missiles of ingenious variety filled its magazines.

"Men and women of the United States Navy," Bill Baker shouted, "man this vessel and bring her to life!"

The bands played again. Sailors in dress uniform sprinted up the gangplank. A dozen fighter aircraft did a flyby, followed—appropriately—by a flight of sixty missiles, which performed orchestrated aerobatics overhead. When they burst in a perfectly timed unison, it was Stephie's turn in the limelight.

She was petrified. Her hands were so cold she tried not to touch her own skin. Television cameras turned to her. Her father, on his identical platform, smiled as he watched her on his monitor.

Admiral Thornton handed her a huge magnum of champagne in a mesh net at the end of a long rope. Stephie stepped up to the huge cluster of microphones, squinting as camera flashes nearly blinded her. She cleared her throat.

"Go ahead," Admiral Thornton whispered.

With all her might Stephie swung the bottle through thirty feet of open air. The buzz from the crowd below rose even before it smashed against the mammoth black bow.

There was a smattering of laughter from the crowd. She winced. She was supposed to do that at the end, not the beginning.

"I fucked up," Stephie whispered to Admiral Thornton. She was too close to the microphones. Laughter erupted, this time, at great volume, from the thousands of people gathered below and from her father on the platform's television monitor. Stephie felt the blood rush to her face.

"Go on," a grinning Thornton directed.

Stephie cleared her throat again and stepped up to the microphone, following the script that she had memorized the night before. "I commission this vessel," she said in a voice that resounded over the PA system across the docks, "the

U.S.S. *Bill Baker*! Men and women of the United States Navy, man this vessel and bring her to life!"

The crowd cheered wildly, far louder than before. The band struck up the national anthem. America returned to the sea.

PENGUIN PUTNAM INC.
Online

Your Internet gateway to a virtual environment with
hundreds of entertaining and enlightening books
from Penguin Putnam Inc.

*While you're there, get the latest buzz on
the best authors and books around—*

Tom Clancy, Patricia Cornwell, W.E.B. Griffin,
Nora Roberts, William Gibson, Robin Cook,
Brian Jacques, Catherine Coulter, Stephen King,
Jacquelyn Mitchard, and many more!

**Penguin Putnam Online is located at
http://www.penguinputnam.com**

PENGUIN PUTNAM NEWS

Every month you'll get an inside look at our upcom-
ing books and new features on our site. This is an
ongoing effort to provide you with the most
up-to-date information about
our books and authors.

**Subscribe to Penguin Putnam News at
http://www.penguinputnam.com/ClubPPI**